THE BORROWED WIFE PART I

YOYO OPOKU

COPYRIGHTS

This book is a work of fiction. References to real people, events, establishments, organizations, or locations are intended only to provide a sense of authencity and are used factiously. All other characters, and all incidents and dialogue are drawn from the author's imagination and are not to be contruced as real.

Any resemblance to actual persons, living or dead, business establishments, events or locales is entirely coincidental.

All rights reserved. No part of this book may be reproduced, scanned or distributed in any printed or electronic form without prior written permission of boh the copyright owner and the above publisher of this book.

Please do not participate in encouraging piracy or copyrighted materials in violation with the author's rights.

ISBN: 978-0-692-94140-9

Cover design by Advancedfrequency.com

Editing by Greeninkproofreading.com

U.S. Congress Copyright 2016 by Yoyo Opoku
Printed and bound in USA

Published by Stilcray Publications
P.O. Box 188
Mt. Vernon, NY 10551

THE BORROWED WIFE PART I

DEDICATION

To the Ghanaian woman who came to America with a burning desire to become a star but instead gave me life and the desire to continue her journey. Mommy, I was always listening.

Part I: Vida

I can't tell anyone yet. The only way to know for sure is to try it again tonight. Finally, no more name calling, jokes or stupid songs to hurt me. Tina Williams will beg to be my friend tomorrow.

*

The bathroom has a hospital smell; a mixture of Dettol and Irish Spring. The summery gold batik dress falls to the floor and I adjust my underwear with the white lace trim band over my waistbeads. My light pink towel capes around my shoulders. Stiffness of the towel makes it difficult to tie a knot so it hangs around my neck like a shawl. The slightest tug will unravel it. I climb over the white toilet seat and notice the ashiness of my legs. I stretch to open the window. Fear and the cool breeze immediately hit me, but I still contort my body to break free out the window. *Don't be afraid now, Vida.* The distance to the ground is scary. This is the furthest I've come. The sun is setting and the sky is turning an orange haze. Ahhhh, the smell of jollof rice and a warm bath beckons me back inside, but determination and curiosity push me forward.

"Yaa, don't forget to wash all yur yesses and noes and in between yur toes."

I turn my head inside making sure she doesn't discover my secret. "Yes, Mommy." The breeze brings the scent of Mrs. Chin's curried goat. My heels press against the cold brick.

I hear Mr. Brooks and friends playing dominos again in his garage. *Wait. I haven't thought this through. This is no way to leap out and fly.* The tree in front of me presents another idea. I jump down from the window and recover quickly from the pain when my knees crash onto blades of grass. My plan forges forward. I climb the tree swiftly and suspend myself on one sturdy branch.

This will be a much better launching point. I position my cape once more. I lift my arms above my head, and make sure my fingers are extended. With all my strength, I jump off the branch.

In a nanosecond, the possibility is real.

Then defeat.

My body descends quickly and I hit the ground like mincemeat. There's ringing in my ears and my head feels like it's way too big to carry. A red Honda Accord slows down and then stops.

"Hey little girl, are you okay?" The driver calls out the window.

"Yep." I immediately wave the man away and limp to the front door. My lightning bulb idea didn't take in consideration my reentry in case I failed. I ring the doorbell and the man in the Honda creeps slowly forward, perhaps ensuring someone will come to attend to me.

Nobody but my mother would come. When she opens the door she doesn't know what to make of me. Her eyes shift in confusion and disappointment. I look down in shame while her voice rattles me.

"Yaa...oooooh my goodness...How?...On earth...?"

"I...I..." I'm half naked. I cling to the towel as though it holds sentimental value. She removes the towel and evidence of broken skin in various places mimics a fight with a dog. The newness of my panties gone.

"Yaa...waz goin' on?" she screams anxiously. The man in the Honda Accord gives a slight honk and drives off. *What unicorn story can I tell her?*

"...And don't give me unicorn stories." *She's discovered me once again. Okay, this will have to be the truth. She has to know who I really am.*

"Mommy, I'm Superman," I say and lift my arms above my head. Grass and dirt stains decorate my Alexander's panties.

"Waat? Ehhhhhh...heh...heh...heh," she says in her deep Ghanaian accent. Her eyes shift, continuing the conversation without words. Then she adds a touch of sound that begins from the back of her throat, a result of years of conversing in tribal dialects. She clasps her hands together.

"Oh my goodness...dear Lord wat iz happenin' to you? Do you want me to send you to Ghana to live with Auntie Awo and yur sista?" *I've heard this threat before.* "If dis iz wat watchin' TV iz doin' to you, I'm goin' to unplug the TV from now on."

I hang my head in shame and she moves aside so I can enter.

"Do you hear me?" She tugs at my ear, which lets me know she means what she says.

"Yes, Mommy."

"Go and haf yur baf. I will check on you soon."

That night as I reminisce over my failed attempt, I realize I overlooked a necessary device. As lovely as lace trim white cotton panties from Alexander's are, they are not the ones Superman wears. I will have to convince Mommy to buy me red underwear.

Chapter 1

It's a jam tonight. Celebrating my boo boo birthday.
Don't forget your FMPs or dungarees. Richards place Apt 8-C
9 pm until…the cops come banging on our door. LMAO.

Abla throwing a party for a new boyfriend? She's never dated anyone this long since Kwesi. Things must be getting serious. Could it be possible that my sister is in love?

Part of me just wants to go home and lay underneath the covers. The woman in me convinces me to come and try to have a good time. *How many nights can I sit by the phone waiting for Mensah to call? No. He will not consume my thoughts again.*

Tonight sets a new record for me, on time and the first guest to arrive. My eyes lazily scan Richard's condominium. Three bulky black leather chairs, a coffee table and a wall unit huge enough to prevent me from extending my legs. The dining table is covered in ivory linen with matching napkins. Fresh cut flowers and candles are fixed as centerpieces. Pictures of half-naked, full-figured African women occupy the wall opposite the table. Abla's photos grace several spaces on the wall, but my eyes stay fixated on the wall above the television. A simple frame with the words: "To anyone who is homeless, I say find a home."

Where did I hear that before? It has all the earmarks of an Ablaism, but no, it's not. I recall—a quote by Ben Okri that I found on Pinterest.

"Hello, dear. Thank you for coming," Richard says as he emerges from the kitchen. We embrace each other warmly.

"Thank you guys for inviting me. What's the magic number?"

"Guess." He is dressed casually, wearing jeans and a red polo shirt. He has an athletic build. Grey hairs sprinkle his head and beard. He is definitely older than Abla. *Maybe late forties.* I rest a hand on my chin before blurting something flattering.

"Thirty!"

"Wow, I may have to keep you to myself." He embraces me again. "I passed that age more than a decade ago. A proud forty-six," he says.

"You should be proud. You look great."

"And you are looking lovely, as usual. What can I get you to drink?"

"Baileys with ice is fine."

"Okay, my dear. I will be back." He vanishes back into the kitchen.

A familiar voice emerges from the bathroom. "Yes, you are looking lovely tonight, Vida." It's Felix.

"Thank you, Felix." *Has he been in the bathroom all this time?* He gives me a light hug and a gentle kiss on the cheek. Well, that makes two guests so far. He sits across from me and picks up a Guinness from the table beside him. He holds the Guinness in his left hand and thumbs through Richard's CD collection with his right.

"Here you go," Richard hands me the glass with ice buoyantly occupying the surface of the cream liqueur.

"I believe you two know one another," Richard says.

"We've met on several occasions at the park." My words jump over Felix before he gets a chance to reply.

"Yes. I used to watch the Sassi Strikers games at Memorial Field on the weekends," Felix says. Felix came to the games regularly from what I remember. The girls would often make jokes about the friendly stalker. He liked me, but I never considered him as anything other than an admirer. Even while I dated Mensah, I imagined he thought I may entertain him beyond the park. He hasn't changed much. Still tall and slim and still a bit shy. Abla told me that he got married and had three daughters.

Abla doubles as the local TMZ in Ghanaian social circles. She keeps me informed daily of all the scandalous comings and goings in the community, including Felix's separation from his wife.

"Oh, look at that, small world. Felix and I began by driving yellow cabs when we first came to this country. Look at us now," Richard says.

"We didn't do too badly," Felix says.

"Honey," Abla's voice breaks our amusement.

"Looks like I have been summoned. Please excuse me." Richard dashes back into the kitchen.

It's just the two of us again. Felix is dressed casually. His brown boots remind me of long narrow canoes. The black blazer hangs on him like a big, bulky blanket. He glances at me and a warm smile greets him.

My examination continues. His black slacks, three sizes too big, look like he is wearing parachute pants. He looks rather uncomfortable sitting in the sofa trying to maneuver the beer bottle and the CD collection. Sweat falls down the sides of his face like a leaky faucet. Two cellphones are clipped to his belt. *How important must you be to carry two cellphones to a party?*

"Do you like Hilife music?" Felix asks.

"Yes."

"What about Hiplife?"

"Yes. I like that too."

The concentration of my gaze causes him to look up briefly and then cast his eyes down.

"You know the younger generation has forgotten about the roots of Hilife," he says. He shifts his eyes away every time our gazes meet.

"So where are you staying now?" *Vida, why did you ask that?* He looks surprised and impressed. *Censor your information. Great, now he will think that I've been checking on him, especially now that I know he is a bachelor.* The hardest thing about gossip is knowing what to keep to yourself and what to ask the person involved.

"I'm still in the Bronx and I've been staying with Richard on occasions." He smiles as though we are making a connection. "It's been a while…are you still playing with the team?"

"No, just taking a long break. I have other things taking precedence," I say. It's been three years since I played a match with the girls. Now that Memorial Field is under renovation, I learned the Sassi Strikers have been practicing in Van Cortlandt Park. Family and work make it harder and harder to practice and attend games. There is so much going on with my life. My life with and without Mensah. *Vida, you need to start playing again. Too many distractions.*

"Family time can be very demanding," he says. "How are your boys?"

"Great. Thank you for asking."

"You may have heard that my wife and I are separated. Right now, I just want to make the transition as easy as possible for the girls."

There are several stories as to why Felix and his wife separated. One story is centered on the fact that his wife didn't want to work and expected Felix to handle all the expenses of raising a family. Another story is Felix suffered from what some men suffer from when driving taxis for long hours daily: the inability to "do their homework" according to Abla, or what the medical profession calls impotence. And the most recent and hard to believe story is about him cheating. He doesn't fit the bill. He certainly doesn't have the words to convince me to drop my panties for him.

"I'm sorry to hear that. Just try to take it one day at a time."

"Thank you. So, where do you work?"

"Right now, I am a patient advocate for Prestigious Nursing Agency."

"Oh, okay. I thought you worked at Jacobi Hospital?" *Well, look who is keeping tabs on who.* "Do you like it there?"

Great question, Vida. Tell him that you couldn't stand the sight of the blood, shit, vomit, urine and death on a constant basis. "It's good. I'm glad that I am helping people in other ways. I prefer the administrative track more so than bedside care. So now, I make routine visits to patients and make sure they are applying for services and getting the proper medical care. I work four days out of the week, so it allows me more time with the boys."

He shifts his eyes away from me again. "Interesting quote," he says pointing to the plaque above the television. "It's rather assuming. Who wants to be homeless? I'm sure the people on the streets don't want to stay on the street. They are looking for a home. But sometimes, whatever the reason, it's not that simple to find a home."

"I believe 'home' means a number of things to different people. Like for me, it means happiness, security, love, my children. So, I believe if you are lacking something then you better get it."

"Hmmm," he says. "You make an excellent point, but I believe Okri is just making a statement. You do know he was homeless at one point in his life."

"Hmmm. No, I didn't know that."

He smiles brightly. Probably giving himself a mental pat on the back. The music occupies the silence between us. It's been about twenty minutes since Richard disappeared into the kitchen. And Abla hasn't left the kitchen since I arrived. This is not the type of party I envisioned this evening. I examine the settings again, lazily taking in the décor and then my eyes rest on the dining table. Four place settings on the dining table. *Just four?* No other guests have arrived. It's just me and Felix debating quotes and interpretation…*Just me and Felix. Shit! This is a set up.* As lady like as possible, I slide out of the deep leather coach. The harsh leather emits unpleasant sounds. Felix rushes to his feet.

"Please excuse me," I say.

"Is there something I can get for you?"

"No, I just need to see my sister."

"Okay, I'll be here waiting for you." *Yes, I bet you will.*

In the kitchen, Richard and Abla are sitting by the windowsill in a tight embrace.

"Hey, Yaa. Deer goes my sexy lil sista." Abla moves away from Richard quickly.

"Oh, you are Yaa? So you are Thursday born," Richard says. My family members are the only people who call me by my Ghanaian name. Richard grabs Abla closer to him again. "You call your sister by her Ghanaian name. Why won't you allow me to call you by yours?" He wraps his arms around Abla.

"Because I want different. Somedin' just for you and me." Abla presses her lips against his.

"Okay, my lady. I will definitely put some thought into it." He looks in my direction once again. "Yaa, can I get you something?" Richard says. *He must be part of the family now.*

"No, I'm fine. Can I have a word with Abla?" I say.

Richard walks toward me. "Sure. Let me make sure Felix doesn't hijack any of my CDs." He chuckles and walks out of the kitchen. I turn to Abla with a 'you-should-know-better' look.

"Get my jacket. I have to go."

"Yur leavin'? We didn't cut da cake." Abla looks shocked.

"It is already after eleven and I promised Auntie Cece that I would be home early. This is a really nice birthday party." My speech doesn't change the expression on her face. She's upset.

"You need a backup babysitta. Anyway, Felix will be upset to see you leave," Abla says.

"Felix, huh? I should have known better. You're trying to hook us up. Just throwing a 'birthday party' for your boyfriend, huh?"

"Yur alwayz tryin' to psychodrama things." She means psychoanalyze. It's taken all my life to get used to Abla's way of talking. Sometimes I correct her and other times I go with the flow. "Watz wrong if a sista tries to connect two people togeta? It just so happened dat Felix and Richard are old friends. Now he doesn't look so creepy."

Fried chicken is resting next to the stove and I put one in a paper napkin.

"Richard says he really, really likes you. 'Member how he uze to camp out every weekend to see you play? Anywayz, watz wrong wit connectin' two people who know each otha?"

"Oh, is that what you call it? A connection? Looks more like match making. I told you, Abla, I'm not ready to start dating. I'm still married."

"Hey, hey…don't start dat. Mensah iz leadin' hiz own life and you haf to start leadin' yurs. You can't keep waitin' until he shows up. Datz not marriage." She is right, but this is a topic we have exhausted a hundred times before.

The chicken is still hot and it dances in my mouth before I can fully enjoy it. "Please, I need to go. Where is my jacket and umbrella?" She reluctantly opens the closet and hands me my belongings. Felix approaches us.

"Hey, there you are," he says. "Are you leaving? The party hasn't even started yet."

"Yes, I know. I have to get home a bit early because of the kids."

"Ooooh, pleazzzzze," Abla says. "*Aaaagyei!*" she yells when I discreetly pinch her.

"Let me walk you to your car." Before I can decline his offer he reaches into the closet and takes his coat.

Abla and I make eye contact and my teeth are clenched but my lips are moving. "Tell him to stay. I don't need him following me."

Abla follows my lead. "Why? He really, really likes you." We probably look like crazy animated cartoons as we try to communicate through clenched teeth. She finally pulls me further into the kitchen, away from Felix. "Lissen, you betta stop dis cry-cry song. You need to get out deer. You wasted enough of yur youf on dat sonna bitch. Who knows wat hez doin' on da West Coast. And wif—"

"And nothing. We are still married in the eyes of our family," I say.

"Yur da only person who sees it dat way. Do you know where he iz? Didn't you say dis waz goin' to last six months? Haven't you noticed dat ever since da kidz loaded dat video wif him in da park, he doesn't even call as much? My sista, wat more proof do you need? Hez livin' a double life. 'Member da story I told you about Mary Gagkwa and her husband? Da man had another family in Ghana. Not one but tree children." She holds up her fingers to emphasize her point. "Right underneath her nose for almost twenty years. Come to find out dat deer waz multiple wives and children. Dey all came out durin' hiz funeral. Hey! Hey! Hey! Come and see. Mary never said a word. Mary! Trust me. Da woman truly lives up to her name because if it waz me, Rosemary Abla Frimpong, everyone in Ghana will know me by now." She takes out disposable bowls and scoops jollof rice, chofi and fried chicken inside. "Da writin' iz on da wall, my dear sista." Her voice lowers. "I'm tellin' you, dis iz like Mary Gagkwa's story. Yaa, yur smart, but sometimes you can be foolish when it comes to dis." She pokes my chest. Not exactly where my heart is, but the message is correctly stated.

Richard stands behind me and I turn to give him a hug. "I'm sorry. I will have to make it up to you, dear." He gives me a kiss on the cheek. I turn to face Abla again. "And I guess I will see you tomorrow. Thanks for the invite." She squeezes my hand and I know that is her way of showing me she is concerned.

"Ready?" Felix asks.

Felix walks behind me. He is still humming the song playing in Richard's apartment. "Do you like Daddy Lumba?" he asks. He doesn't give me a chance to answer before asking me another question. "So where in the Bronx are you?"

"The northeast part. Off of Baychester Avenue."

"Some nice houses up there. I'm thinking about getting a place in Tracey Towers." Oh my goodness, if New York is Ghana then Tracey Towers is Accra. They should really think about renaming the building Makola Market.

"That's nice," I say.

"When Abla told me that she wanted to have this get together for Richard's birthday, I knew you would be here."

"You were hoping to see me here?"

"Yes, of course. I'm a big fan of yours."

"Really, a fan of mine?" We walk in the direction of my car and I hit the remote starter. It's September but unseasonably cold. Hard rain is falling on us like pins.

"Yes, you're really good. If I recall, your movements were fast and skillful," he continues.

"Thanks. Sometimes my son and I play a couple of games to keep me active, but nothing compared to my heyday."

He stops walking beside me. "You look great. Especiallyforawomanwiththreekids." He stumbles over his words. "I mean you look great." He returns my smile shyly. "I don't remember the weatherman saying it was going to rain this evening. Do you?"

"There was a light shower before I left the house." Lately, the weather has been just as unpredictable as my marriage. *Shit. I almost bust my ass.* I take little baby steps toward the car. I chose today to wear these Brian Atwood ankle boots.

Felix notices my extra cautiousness. "Why don't you wait here and I bring the car to you?"

"Oh, that's not necessary. Plus, I'm almost there." I point to the car with the engine running.

"Are you okay to drive? It's starting to rain very heavy now," he says. "If you don't mind, let me drive you home and I'll take a cab back. Trust me, Vida, it's no trouble at all."

"Thank you very much for walking me to the car. Enjoy the rest of the evening." *He should take the hint by now.*

"Weshouldarrangeforaplaydate. Maybeiceskating or something?" he says. Again, his words are rushed. Heavy rain beats against us. The combined sweat and rain beating on his face make it hard to distinguish which is which. "I think we have a lot in common and a lot to talk about."

"We do?" I say.

"For starters, we both like soccer. We both went to school in Ghana."

"No. I was born here and went to school here. Abla was born and raised in Ghana," I say firmly.

"That explains it."

"What?"

"The way you speak."

"And what does that sound like?"

"You definitely sound American. I mean…you don't speak with an accent."

"And neither do you." He chuckles.

"I've been here a long time. We have a lot to talk about. Maybe we could have dinner this weekend?" he says. His confidence level rose from the timid man sitting across from me in Richard's living room.

"I'm not sure what my sister has told you. But I am going through a separation right now and I am not looking for anything in terms of a relationship. I just have a lot going on."

"Trust me, I know. And I am not putting any pressure on you. I just really would love to spend some time with you. We can talk on the phone. Just like friends," he says.

Damn. He's persistent. Maybe I need a little distraction from what is going on in my life with Mensah. Some amusement will help me get through this. It's warm inside the driver's seat. He assists me with the seatbelt across my shoulder. *He's nice, but I can't envision him in the role of Mensah. He doesn't have the swagger that Mensah has. His walk is fast and a bit stiff.* My mind is drifting again and I allow it. *What kind of lover could he be? A generous take-command lover? Or a student who needed constant reinstruction? Would he eat my Ginger cookie better than Mensah? Can he leave me trembling the way Mensah does? Could my skin feel like fresh baked sugar bread when Mensah trails his tongue from my breast to my navel? Could he make me come over and over again just by stroking his fingers over my pussy? NO! NO! NO! He can't.* His lips, thin and dark, disturb me. Images of me easily crushing him in between my thighs. And another image of him pounding on me like an exhausted track runner on pavement. My face hardens thinking about the disappointing possibilities. This is tragic. Mensah has spoiled me for everyone else.

"Vida, did you hear me?"

No, I didn't. I'm having a sexual breakdown. "I'm sorry, what did you say?"

"Would you give me your number?" He is drenched in cold rain.

"You really should go. You'll catch a cold."

"Not until you give me your number." *I'm surprised Abla didn't give it to him already.* "Or I can give you my number and you can call me at your convenience?" he says.

Mensah will be hard to duplicate, but I need to start moving forward. "Okay," I say quietly, handing him my phone.

He keys his number into my cellphone. "I saved it under Felix Dobere. Give me a call and let me know that you reached home safely."

"Sure," I say.

He leans forward into the window of the car and plants a cold wet kiss on my cheek. "I will be waiting for your call." I try to fix my face to a more appealing smile.

*

My GPS tells me it's only seven minutes to Memorial Field from Richard's condo. I should go home, but I'm still thinking of Mensah and I don't want to go home to a lonely bed. *Well, it won't be too lonely. MJ should be making his way into my room after midnight with his own unicorn story of monsters underneath his bed.* The heavy rainfall subsides. I step out of the car and walk toward the gated fence. The cold air turns puddles on the ground into thin sheets of ice. This is unusual weather for September.

Thoughts of Mensah fill me. *Damn, I miss him. But I hate him right now. How can I want him and hate him at the same time?* I pull on the chain link fence. This was the place we first met, Memorial Field. My second home. The field where the Sassi Strikers practiced and held games over the course of ten years. Demands of family life consume most of my time now. *No, that is an excuse. Worrying over Mensah took me away from the field.* My last match here was against the Trinity Squad. We lost miserably. My heart wasn't in the game. Mensah and I fought the night before. Stupid allegations with no basis, he would say.

The field is not like it used to be ten years ago. Overgrown weeds and graffiti change the landscape. *Maybe one day if I make it as a successful writer, I can come back and fix it up. Writer? Vida, when was the last time you wrote anything?* Too many thoughts tonight. *Anyway, when I do become a successful writer, I will restore this field again.* God knows Mount Vernon needs this recreation.

I check my watch. It's getting late, I have to call Auntie Cece. I get back inside the car and search my bag for my cellphone. Great, only one percent charge left. *Why didn't I charge it at Richard's place? No, a better question, why haven't I bought a car charger by now? Always putting things off until it's crucial.*

YOYO OPOKU

    Her phone rings once and then goes straight to voicemail. "Hi Auntie, making a stop before getting home. Will be home in less than—" My phone powers down before my message is complete. At least she knows that I am on my way home. The weather warms up a bit and the night sky looks heavy. The thin sheets of ice appear to be cracking. I devour the chofi before setting off.

Chapter 2

"Sometimes it feels like yur watchin' a movie." Abla's words are the first thing that comes to mind as the white lights advance toward my car. *Fuck! This is really happening.* My nails cut through the leather of the steering wheel and my neck jerks back. There is pain on the left side of my face and ringing in my ears, perhaps from hitting the steering wheel. Repetitive blinking confirms eyesight is still functioning. My chest rises and falls and I temper my breathing. Toes and legs are moving. Another deep exhale and I push the side airbag inside the doorframe. The gear is not moving and then a final shove moves it to P for park. The view is clear and a white Lamborghini faces me.

Blood laces my fingers from my bruised knuckles. I feel moisture on the side of my face. A trickle of blood cascades down. The rearview mirror provides the image of a small gash over my eyebrow. There is another ringing sound, but this one is coming from the four-wheel horsepower in front of me. There is extensive damage to the front and right side of the vehicle. Smoke rises from its hood. Deep breaths confirm the smell that has suddenly encroached me. *Gas.* A quick release of my seatbelt and I stagger one leg at a time onto the wet asphalt. *Baby steps, Vida.* I move toward the other car.

The door of the Lamborghini falls open. *Someone is coming out. Okay, that is a good sign. Life.* I walk as quickly as possible back to my car, slipping and sliding in my Atwood ankle boots.

I've never been in a car accident before, but Abla has been in several.

"You know it iz about to happen, but you can't react quickly enough. Den deer times when it catches you off guard."

Although her license is suspended, she offered me her fail proof survival guide of what to do when involved in an accident:

"You haf to be smart, Yaa. Deer are so many scam artists out deer and iz alwayz da innocent who gets fucked. Take my advice, if you get into an accident where you don't wind up dead or badly injured, alwayz get da make of da car and license plate right away in case dey run. Never get out of da car—unless it catches fire. Da one dat gets out first cause da accident. Don't talk; moan like yur havin' sex. Don't admit to anydin'.

In fact, don't talk until da ambulance gets deer. And make sure you get taken to da hospital even if da only ding dat happens iz yur wig falls off."

Okay, so I fucked up on one point so far: I'm already out of the car. And I can't make out the license plate on the other car. Legs and sandaled feet finally emerge from the vehicle and step slowly in my direction.

I slide my body down the side of my car and sit on the ground. "Ooohhh…Ohhhh…" I moan softly. "My head…the ringing in my head." Peeking slightly through my lashes, I see the person stumble in my direction. I try to make out the features of a man's face.

He is a white man with shoulder length inky black hair. Blood is streaming from either side of his face. The white T-shirt he wears is stained like red graffiti. He drags his sandals across the ground balancing himself against the mashed up vehicle. Though it is September and unseasonably cold, he is wearing only a T-shirt and khaki shorts. He approaches me and rests his body along the hood of my car. Then he skates his hands across it until he reaches where I'm groveling next to the rear car door.

"Ooooooooo…my head…the ringing." My Oscar-…okay, Emmy-winning performance continues. "I can't feel my fingers."

He wipes his hands on the already soiled shirt and stands above me. "Hello, are you all right?" he says. Tilting my head upward, my eyes blink trying to take focus of the man holding onto the roof of the car. Blood continues to stream across his face, making it hard to distinguish where the bleeding is coming from. This alarms me.

"Oh my goodness. You're hurt," I say.

"Ma'am, ma'am," he says and then falls to the ground like a bag of cement. I spring up.

"Oh my God. Sir, are you okay?… Sir…please say something." I prop him up against the car. There is more blood and this time it is coming from the corner of his left eye.

"I'm all right. I hit my head against the steering wheel," he says. A British accent. His voice is clearer kneeling beside him.

"Okay, I need to call 911. Let me get my phone." The ringing in my ears causes me to shout. *Shit, I forgot, my phone is dead.*

"No! No police. I will be fine. I just need to get back to the hotel," he says.

"Why not? You—*we* need an ambulance," I say. He struggles to get up and he leans his back against the car. The chill is back and a few flakes descend from the sky. "Great. Flurries in September," I say.

"Is everyone okay? I saw everything." A man's voice emerges from the darkness. His feet barely touch the pedals of an overly worn bicycle. He examines the Lamborghini and then languidly slides in our direction. The stench of beer hits me before my eyes register his disposition. His eyes are droopy and red. An old man and with several layers of clothing, which explains the inability to pedal the bike. The black baseball cap barely covers his head. He is wearing open toed sandals like the mystery man bleeding to death here. He continues sparking the air with his drinking habit.

"Hey, hombre, I saw everything. Don't worry, I will be your witness. This girl came out of nowhere and ran the red light," the old wino says.

"What red light?" I'm on the defense. "There's no red light here. There used to be a stop sign over there, which this man apparently didn't see." I point to the curvy intersection where a bent stop sign and shrubs have been pummeled by his vehicle. We are not far from the Hutchinson River Parkway. This is the industrial area between Mount Vernon and the Bronx. There are no businesses opened this late. I recall a diner and gas station up the block. I look around and see no cars approaching in any direction. The old man eyes me suspiciously. "And what do you mean witness? What exactly did you see?" I say.

"Hija, no denying it. You ran the stop sign and then ran into this man's car." He has a Spanish accent and speaks coherently even though he looks and smells like cheap beer. The scent of alcohol hypnotizes me into nausea. "Yo, hombre, let's call the police. Oh shit! You bleeding and shit. Yo, Hija, it don't look good for you. I hope you got good insurance. Blanco is going to sue you for everything you got."

"Please, no police!" the British man says again.

"No police?" The wino looks shocked. But he mirrors my exact sentiments. *Why doesn't he want police called?* "Okay, Hija, I think he wants you to pay up. Yo, Blanco, look at the car she is driving. A Honda CRV. It's not even new. We should just let the insurance take care of it. Don't worry, now they quick to cut a check." The old wino takes it upon himself to represent a man we both know nothing about.

The British man posts himself against my vehicle. Despite his injuries, he looks well built. Tall, muscular, but not over bearing. Nails trimmed, goatee groomed, hair disheveled from the accident. But overall, a man who takes good care of himself despite his bad choice in clothing.

If Abla were here, my neck would be in a brace and I would be on my way to Montefiore Hospital. But curiosity presses me to continue the interrogation. "Is this car stolen?" I ask.

"Please, no police…it's not stolen. I don't have a driver's license and this car is not registered," the British man says lowly.

The wino interjects again. "What! What you say, Blanco? Oh no, this is no good for you." The wino moves closer to me. "Hija, call the police."

Yes, I should, but I don't want either of them to know that I don't have a working cellphone. Plus, who does this wino think he is? Why is he calling all the shots? He switches alliances quicker than a New York Knicks fan.

He continues, "This changes everything, hombre!" He leans closer to me and whispers, "Listen, Hija. Look at the way he's dressed. Like he's going to sleep or something. He's no car thief, wearing sandals and shit. Look. It's colder than my mother-in-law's bed out here, let's not waste time. I've seen this type of situation before. He is probably some spoiled rich white boy high on drugs, that is why he doesn't want the police." *For a wino, his observation is making sense.* "No disrespect. You're a fine woman, but your ride could use an upgrade. This is a win-win situation for you. Get him to repair this Honda, get some more money for pain and suffering and then we out."

The stench from his breath is unbearable, but my intuition tells me to align myself with this wino who is looking out for himself rather than this stranger who doesn't want the police notified. *I mean, somebody might have heard something. It's only a matter of time before the police come anyway. I hope.*

"Are you listening, Hija?"

"Will you stop calling me Hija? I am not your daughter."

"Oooh, shit. You know Spanish?"

"Pocito," I say lowly.

"I knew there was something special about you. I got your back. Okay, Hija, check it out—"

"Oh, now you have my back!" *Despite his flippant loyalty, my odds are stacked better with him than against him.*

"Look here. He's in the Bronx."

"Technically we are still in Mount Vernon."

The old man rolls his eyes. "Okay, whatever. Check it out. What's a British dude in jacked up sandals doing in the Bronx-slash-Mount Vernon driving this sort of car? It don't look good for him, that's why he don't want the cops. We can use this to our advantage. Tell him we gonna call the cops if he don't give us one thousand dollars each."

"What? First of all, you came here half-assed siding with Blanco with the fancy car before hearing what actually happened. Now you think you deserve a thousand dollars? For what?"

"Listen, Hija, don't make this a race issue. I'm trying to help you out and shit. We are in this together. We don't know this cat. He could be dangerous. Maybe he's running away from something. We get a couple hundred. Your car don't look too bad. His shit is fucked up." He points to the other car. "But we don't give a shit about him."

Okay, now what, Vida? There are lights up the block and I know I'm not too far away from the diner. *I could leave and call the police or Daniel. Will this mystery man actually fix my car? But if I leave, he may run away too. And then I'm assed out. Fuck. Why me? Decisions.*

I move farther away from the British stranger. The wino follows behind me with his bike. "Do you have a phone?" I ask the wino.

"Are you calling the cops?"

"No, I am not calling the cops. I need to check on my kids." *Auntie Cece has to know what is going on. A generic message will have to do right now. No sense in worrying her.* He hands me his phone. It's beat up and looks like he uses it as a coaster for his beer. I cautiously press several buttons, but nothing happens. "How do you make a call?"

"It don't work."

"So why did you give it to me then? You're talking all this shit and your phone doesn't even work."

"I just remembered. Hija, be patient. I'm an old man." He shrugs his shoulders indifferently. "I don't have kids I need to call so it don't botha me. I just keep it for the time."

I have no choice. I am going to have to ask the British stranger for assistance. "Sir, do you have a cellphone?" I say.

"No, not with me," he says.

"Great. It's snowing. None of us has a cellphone that can call anyone." Blood continues to stain his T-shirt. "Sir, you are badly injured, you need medical attention. I need to call 911." God forbid this man dies out here. Sudden recollections of Mr. August in Jacobi Hospital flood me. He was the first patient that I saw die and I spent several months in therapy sessions beating myself up for it.

"I know I am injured, but I prefer you didn't. I know it is an unusual request. You don't know me and I can't verify who I am, but I really don't need this to become bigger than what it is. I would rather you call someone who works for me. He will see to our injuries and compensate you for the damages to your car. You have my word. But please, no police or EMS."

"Your word don't mean shit out here. You're not even American. You know how many IDs I can show you right now?"

"Quiet down, wino, this is Mount Vernon, not the wild wild west."

"Wino?" He turns up his nose.

"Sorry. What's your name?"

"Just call me Colt."

"Really? Like Colt forty-five?"

"Listen, shit happens." He takes heed and lowers his voice. "Okay, how we know you ain't gonna run away or stiff us or something? We don't even know who you are or who owns this car." Colt surprises me with the comeback. It's the forceful male presence I need backing me.

"Do you have something in the car with your name or address? We need some kind of assurance as to who you are," I say.

"My name is Julius Gallo. I arrived in New York this evening, so that is why I don't have the car registered yet. I can pay you for the damages, but unfortunately I don't have money on me. I can get it to you when I get back to the hotel."

"Adios, Hija." Colt mounts his bicycle and motions to leave.

"Wait." My body is a roadblock in his path. He gets off his bike.

"This is not looking good for you either. This sounds like some loony tune case escaped from Bellevue or something," Colt says.

"I give you my word that I will repair your car. I will give you an additional ten thousand dollars for the inconvenience I've caused you. We just need to get a phone and call the hotel," the British man says.

It's cold and there is a part of me that believes he is telling the truth. Nonetheless, I need to stop his bleeding. I search my car for some sort of first aid. MJ's training pants will have to serve as a bandage. "Here, let's clean you up at least and see if we can stop the bleeding." He allows me to clean his face with a napkin. "Hold this over your eye," I say. He places his hand over the training pants and presses them firmly against his face.

"Yo, Hija…ven aqui."

Maybe I am multilingual after all. My mind decodes Spanish into English and we reconvene in our prior meeting place.

"You think he is telling the truth?"

"I'm not sure if he is, but at this point we need to help him."

"Yeah, you right, Hija. If he dies here then we are screwed," he says, agreeing and nodding with his selfish logic.

"Colt, you have to go up the block where the lights are on. Maybe there's a phone you can use. There's the diner a couple of blocks up. They're open twenty-four hours."

"First, that diner is under construction, but I think the McDonald's on Conner Street is open, and second, Hija, how come you calling all the shots? I don't work for you."

"Okay, you can stay with him and I'll use your bike to go."

"Wait, wait, we just met. I can't trust you with my bike."

"First of all, it would make sense for you to make the call. What happens if the police do show up? You don't want the police here asking a lot of questions. Which one of your IDs has the cleanest record? An injured white man in Westchester with an old man smelling like Colt forty-five by his side with multiple IDs. That sounds like trouble to me."

"Okay, okay Hija, I will go, but what am I getting out of it?"

"Don't worry. Make the call; when you get back I will take care of you." I rest a comforting hand on his shoulder.

"Nah, Hija. You got a nice fat ass, but I am getting too old for that shit now. I don't even think it will wake up. I need money."

I step closer to his nauseating breath. "What the hell do you think I'm talking about? I will give you twenty dollars when you get back, and if the man's story pans out, I will give you another five hundred."

"Oh, my bad. You said you were gonna take care of me and put your hand on me and all…you know…all soft and shit…got me thinking. Anyway, I got it, Hija."

"See if you can get a tow truck and then call the hotel and ask for—"

"Vincent," the British man interjects. "Just mention the name Vincent in the Summit penthouse suite. I don't have the number. They will connect you."

There is no need to whisper anymore since the British stranger clearly hears everything we are plotting. "Okay, got that? Vincent at the Summit Hotel penthouse suite." My disposition turns to the British man. "I'm sorry, what was your name again?"

He answers through jittering teeth, "Julius Gallo."

Colt mounts the bicycle and half pedals up the block until darkness grabs him out of view.

I start the engine of my CRV and turn the heat to full blast. "Get into the back seat. You need to warm up. It's getting cold out here." I assist the British man into the back seat and place my infinity scarf around his neck. The training pants are caked with blood. The glove compartment has an under stocked first aid kit with a few alcohol wipes and two finger bandages in it. I use the last three alcohol wipes to clean the caked blood and I rip open the last one of MJ's training pants. "I don't think it's that deep. The bleeding looks like it has stopped a bit." He grabs both of my hands. "Sorry, did that hurt? My hands are a bit cold."

"It's fine," he says.

"Does anywhere hurt?"

"No." His eyes are closed and his hair feels like frost.

Kakra's gym bag is in the backseat. A couple of T-shirts, a hoodie and socks are inside. "Take off your shirt. You can wear my son's hoodie." He does as he is instructed. Kakra's hoodie is extra tight, but it serves the purpose. "How do you feel? Any pain?"

"Thank you. I'm fine under the circumstances." It's cold and the car engine emits strange sounds.

"Turn it off. You're going to destroy the belt on your transmission and you may be leaking gas," he says. The car is quiet again and the view in front of me haunts me. Just ten minutes away from home and look where I am.

Adjusting the rearview mirror to see the stranger behind me, the image of his head tilted back and eyes closed worries me. *Keep him talking, Vida.*

"So, is this your first time in New York?"

"No."

"Where are you coming from?"

"London."

"Are you here on business?" He doesn't answer. After a brief silence, my interrogation continues. "I think you can get an international driver's license or something like that in New York. How long are you staying here?"

"Don't worry, I will try not to die in your car," he says. He is making light of the situation, but his facial expression and tone doesn't change. The thought of him dying from this accident makes me feel ill. My days will be filled with countless therapy sessions. And all the fucking Mensah and I used to do in the backseat would be overshadowed by death.

Mr. August invades my thoughts again.

I went in to take his vitals and he mentioned that he had a terrible headache. I told him that I would return with some pain medicine. We laughed about the breakfast served that morning. He said he enjoyed it immensely and that it was the best breakfast he had in a long time. Just bland oatmeal and hot tea with milk. When I returned, he looked like he was sleeping and then the monitors started blinking and alarms sounded throughout the unit. A team rushed in and I couldn't move. I held the pain medicine in my hand while men and women in scrubs attended to him. The first week on the job and my patient died.

"Are you hurt?" he says after another brief silence.

"I'm fine. It's just a flesh wound on my forehead I think." There are still traces of blood on my fingers. It doesn't look too bad.

"How old is your child?" he asks. *How does he know I have children? Oh, that's right, the training pants and Kakra's gym bag.*

"The youngest one is four."

"How many children do you have?"

"I have three boys."

"Wow. Wow. Three boys," he says. His tone makes it sound like a herd of cattle. "Without a doubt, you have your hands full."

"Yes. They are quite an energetic bunch." His temperament seems more inviting.

"Do you live around here?"

"Yes, not far. Less than ten minutes from here." *Shit, maybe that is too much information about myself. I don't even know who this guy is.*

"I see," he says. "I'm sorry, I didn't even get your name."

Should I lie? After all, is Julius Gallo his real name? The woman in me says he is telling the truth. *You have enough going on, Vida, to try to keep up with another unicorn story.* "Vida." My name lingers in the air after debating the consequences.

"Do you have a last name, or are you an entertainer like Madonna?"

This time without a debate, a response. "Vida Frimpong." It seems right saying my maiden name out loud, especially considering the state of my marriage. It will take a while to start getting used to saying it again.

"Vida Frimpong," he says it correctly. "That's a very unique name, Vida Frimpong."

"I'm sure in Ghana it is as common as John Smith is in America."

Silence cuts through the car again. He readjusts himself in the seat. "But there is only one Vida Frimpong that drives a Honda CRV and lives less than ten minutes from here and unfortunately at two o'clock today has gotten into an accident with Julius Gallo. So you see, you are very unique after all."

"Yes, now that you have given me that perspective." He is quiet again. "Are you here on holiday?" My inquisition is back on him.

"No."

"Business?"

"Something like that."

"Are you familiar with this area?"

"Yes…I mean no!" he says. "I got lost when I got off the exit."

"Where were you trying to go?"

"I just wanted to take a drive and I went farther than I thought."

"Bad weather for a drive and you certainly weren't dressed for it," I say.

"Yes, I know. Like I said, I traveled farther than I expected to."

Ten minutes go by and no word from him. His eyes remain closed. Fearing the worst, I initiate another topic of discussion. "Do you think he got lost?"

"Who?" he says lowly.

"Our rescuer," I laugh. "The old man. Colt," I clarify further.

As far as my eyes can see there is no figure in the darkness. The snowfall is getting heavy and it's nearly impossible to see anyone coming or going. Snow covers the car windows and it's been a half an hour since Colt left. The blood has stopped streaming, but bloodstains are tattooed around his face. I clean it with the last alcohol wipes.

"How do you feel?" I ask.

"Vida, Vida," he says my name over and over again like I'm a long lost friend.

"Are you okay?" My fingers caress his shoulders, awakening him from his half unconsciousness.

"Vida," he says in haste and grabs both of my hands. "Sorry, did I nod off?"

"I guess you did," I say gently. "I don't see the old man. I'm gonna have to get some help."

"I don't think it's safe for you to be out here alone. Let me go."

"You are in no condition to even walk."

"Ms. Frimpong, I can manage."

"It's snowing very heavily and all you have is this hoodie and shorts. You'll freeze and collapse within a few steps from here," I say. *Why is he so adamant about not calling the police or even EMT?* "I don't think my conscience could bear sending an injured, bleeding man out in the cold. If Colt doesn't come soon, I'll have to call the police. We could be doing more harm than good by you sitting here waiting."

"I understand. Let's wait a couple more minutes. My apologies. I realize that I have put you under a lot of undue stress."

"Is Vincent a doctor?" I ask.

"No, but he will take care of things for me."

A faint honking approaches us. The snow stops falling and what remains on the ground quickly dissolves. Yellow and red flashing lights break through the darkness. Jumping up and down while waving my arms finally gets the attention of the tow truck driver. "Over here!" The driver notices me and picks up speed in our direction.

"Oh, thank goodness, the tow truck is here. It's really cold; let's adjust this scarf." I toss my jacket around his shoulders.

"Ms. Frimpong, no, please don't…"

"Stop it. You are cold and bleeding. I'm okay. I can bear the cold a bit. Plus, I am a wearing a sweater."

"No, I don't need your jacket. Please put it back on."

"Mr. Gallo, this is not a discussion. Wear the jacket. Once you warm up, I'll take it back. Please." My tone is firm and nonnegotiable. The arm length of the jacket is short and snug. After several pulls and jerks, the zipper rises to the top of the jacket adding a layer of warmth.

"Hi folks, nasty weather to get stuck," says an old white man with white hair and a white beard as he gets out of the truck. He bears a resemblance to Santa Claus minus the belly.

"Hi, thanks for coming."

"I'm Jake. Hey, I hear you guys need a tow. Looks like a nasty accident," he says.

"Well, no…aahhh, yes…but we have already made arrangements for repair, so no need to call the police."

"Okay, so what are we doing now? Do you have a repair shop that you want to tow it to?"

"We are towing the vehicles to the Summit Hotel," Mr. Gallo says.

"Both cars?" Jake asks.

"Yes, both cars," Mr. Gallo says.

"That's going to cost you. It's about a hundred and fifty dollars each mile."

"That's fine," Mr. Gallo interjects. Jake looks as surprised as I am. He definitely exaggerated the price. But in this type of weather at this hour it would be stupid to start haggling.

"You got a nasty cut over there. Don't you want to go to the hospital?" Jake asks.

"No, just to the Summit Hotel. Please."

"Are both of you going?"

"Yes," Mr. Gallo replies before I have a chance to think about it. *Why should I follow a complete stranger to another location? What if he is a serial killer or some cannibal or a sex trafficker?* Mr. Gallo turns to me. "Ms. Frimpong, I know it's an odd request, but I will not harm you any more than what I've already done."

I hesitate. Abla or Auntie Cece should know what is happening. Yet his injuries look severe enough for immediate medical attention.

"Ma'am, are we going to the Summit Hotel?" Jake notices my apprehension. *I mean, we are going to the city. It's not like he can kill me and stuff me in a body bag and toss me into the Hudson River. No, stop it, Vida. It will be okay. I'll just make sure I get the money to fix the car and then leave.* I nod in agreement. "Okay, hop in the front seat and I'll load the vehicles," Jake says happily.

Julius unzips the jacket and takes it off. "Thank you, Ms. Frimpong," he says.

"Take it easy," I say.

He sits down and I slide in beside him. It's warm inside the truck, but smells like I suspected. An old bar. Evidence of beer caps decorate the carpet mats. A cellphone lays on a bunch of papers and clothing. "Can I use your phone?" Jake sees his phone in my hand and looks at me skeptically. "It's a local call. I just need to call my kids and let them know I'm okay."

Mr. Gallo leans closer to me. "Tell him I will cover the bill."

"We'll cover the charges," I yell.

He gives me the thumbs up. *Geez, everyone is out to make a buck.* The phone looks like shit and I press the buttons with the tips of my fingernails. I select the speaker icon and hold it away from my face. No answer again. Bronx Tow is clearly written on the truck and I make sure I include it in my message.

"Hello, Auntie. Sorry for the inconvenience. I got in a little bit of car trouble, but I am fine. Bronx Tow truck is here helping me out and I am using the driver's cellphone because my cellphone died. I should be home within the hour. Good night. I love you." *I can't tell her that I am leaving with a strange man to get money for the damages to my car because just thinking about it sounds irresponsible.*

"Sorry to have inconvenienced your evening," Mr. Gallo says.

"Some things are beyond our control and happen for a reason. Thank goodness we are alive. That is what matters now. I hope Colt is okay. If he doesn't come soon, we will have to leave him." I stick my head out the window looking for any trace of Colt and his worn bike. "Okay, let's call the hotel."

The phone directory connects us with the Summit Hotel. Okay, it's an actual hotel. That is good to know. A pleasant man connects us to Vincent in the penthouse.

"Hello."

"Hi good evening. Well, good morning. I'm here with one of your…your…friends, Mr. Gallo, and he wants to talk to you."

He picks his head up and I hold the phone the same distance away from his face to speak.

"*Buonasera!*"

Vincent's tone doesn't seem pleasant or maybe it's a cultural thing. They rumble off briefly and then add some words in English. "Within the hour," Mr. Gallo says. He leans his head back. "You can hang up. Thank you."

Okey, so he does know someone named Vincent. I make mental check marks to rule out insanities. "Is all well? Vincent doesn't seem happy."

"Vincent is rarely happy. He is waiting for us."

"Okay, that's good," I say. *I hope.* "Mr. Gallo, so, you speak Italian?" I ask.

"Please call me Julius, and yes, I do. Do you?"

"No, not quite. My neighbor's mother next door was Italian and she didn't speak English that well. She used to watch the boys for me when they were younger. I picked up a few words here and there. I understand a great deal of Spanish, though. Well, I believe some words are similar in pronunciation. Like I heard you say '*Buonsara.*'"

"*Buonasera,*" Mr. Gallo corrects me.

I repeat it again. "In Spanish, it's buenos noches."

"Yes, you are correct, Ms. Frimpong."

Jake loads my vehicle last and then hops in. Julius closes his eyes and leans back.

"Is he going to be okay? I can drop you folks at the hospital and then take the cars wherever you want."

"To the Summit Hotel." Julius lifts his head and opens his eyes. "Please." His voice is stern.

Jake gives me a head nod. "Okay, to the Summit."

Chapter 3

We arrive at the hotel and I help Julius out of the truck. I hold onto him as we walk toward the gate underneath the hotel. He punches a code on the security pad and the gate swings open. A large silver-grey haired man and a slim young man rush in our direction. "Oh my goodness, what happened?" the young man in uniform says. The image of sunrays above the word "Summit" is printed on his uniform. *I can't believe I'm here. I just need to hurry up and get the money and leave.*

"I got into a car accident with this young lady," Julius replies. He is still holding the training pants over his left eye.

The young man examines him and starts dialing into his cellphone. "I will get the doctor, Mr. Gallo," he says.

"Don't bother. I've already called one. He is on his way," the large man says.

"Ms. Frimpong, this is Vincent," Julius says in a low, demurring tone. "Vincent, this is Ms…" He pauses and clears his throat. "…Excuse me, Vida Frimpong."

Vincent's eyes grow larger and he gives me a slow glance over.

"Hello," I say as cheerfully as I can under the circumstances. I extend my hand and he is reluctant to give me a handshake. He looks at Julius, who doesn't look in his direction. Fear stirs in me. *What did he tell him over the phone? Maybe it's like he said, Vincent is rarely happy.* I don't know anyone here, but I am glad that Jake is still in our company.

Jake unloads the damaged Lamborghini into an empty parking space and hands me my keys. "Hi, I'm Jake." Jake grabs Vincent's hand and shakes it like a gear shift. Vincent doesn't look enthused.

"Where are the keys?" Vincent says.

"Oh, here you go." Jakes tosses the keys in the air and Vincent grabs them.

"Ms. Frimpong, may I?" It takes me a second to decode what he wants. I remove the car keys from the bunch of keys on my chain and hand them to him. He moves closer to examine Julius. "Little gash, my ass. You need at least ten stitches." His husky Italian accent suits his demeanor. "Let's go upstairs."

We follow Vincent and Julius to an elevator with two security guards standing side by side.

"Call Dr. Jesup again and tell him we need him immediately," Vincent instructs one of the men.

We ascend in the elevator. It is aesthetically appealing with marble and light blue glass tiles. There are six buttons in the elevator: lobby, garage, penthouse, open and close symbols, fire alarm and a speaker button. The penthouse button lights up and a computerized voice announces that we have arrived. The doors open up to a massive hallway. The floors are tiled black and white marble. Jake gives a loud whistle.

"This must cost a lot of money for one night," he leans over to confide in me. "He must be really loaded." Vincent leads us through another door. A tall, slender white woman rushes into Julius's arms.

"Babe, where did you go? I was so worried about you. You left your phone and everything. You didn't tell anyone where you were going. Oh my, what happened?" She studies his injuries and then looks at me and then Jake. "What are you holding over your eye?" she says. English is not her first language, but I can't pinpoint where she is from. *Perhaps she is Italian too.* Her long thin blonde hair hangs by her waist. She runs her hands through her hair trying to give it volume at the crown. No makeup except for a bright red lip stain. She looks richly spoiled. Her long silk gown is barely tied at the waist—revealing more of her than we need to see.

"I'm fine," Julius says. Vincent scrutinizes him more closely. He mutters something again in Italian and walks away.

"No, you're not," the woman insists.

Jake gives another whistle. "She's hot," he confides in me again. "And he's loaded," he reminds me.

My eyes scan the large floor-to-ceiling windows, a grand piano on the far side of the room. Minimalist furniture. A winding staircase on the right side of a massive kitchen.

"Penny, this is Ms. Frimpong and Jake. They assisted me tremendously this evening. If it had not been for Ms. Frimpong, I don't think I would be here this evening," Julius says.

Penny's face hangs ghostly with her hands clamped against her mouth. "Oh my goodness…that is terrible. Nice to meet you," she says and extends her hand for a handshake. She examines me a bit too long and the cattiness showdown begins. Her hard gaze is on me.

Don't worry, dear, I'm married. At least on paper, I still am. My thoughts once again focus on Mensah.

Penny embraces Julius again. This time she wraps her long arms around his shoulders and drenches him with kisses.

Yes, we get it, that's your man. I roll my eyes.

"I'm fine," he says again, trying to fend off the excessive affection.

Vincent enters the room again. He addresses Jake. "This should handle the towing and your time this evening. I am sure that we can keep this matter quiet." Jake counts the cash and his face beams. His eyes grow larger with every hundred dollar bill.

"Not a problem…mum's the word. I have the paperwork. Need a signature so that my boss doesn't think I goofed off all night." Vincent gives him a stern look and hands him another stack of hundreds. "You know what, let's forget about the paperwork tonight. I'll just tell him that I wasn't feeling well again. Don't worry, it's like we never met." He shakes Vincent's hand. He leans into me. "Hey, good luck. This is our lucky night."

"Security will see you out," Vincent says.

"Thank you very much and I hope you get better, mister…anyway, have a good night." He waves ecstatically while exiting the room.

"Young lady, can I get you a drink?" Vincent addresses me. Penny cuddles Julius up the stairs.

"No, I'm fine," I answer. It's just him and me now. Something about his presence stirs fear within me.

"May I use the restroom?"

"Certainly." Vincent leads me to a door by the front entrance. Inside, I immediately lock the door behind me. *Vida, what are you doing here? I should have just called the police and then gone home. Me…that's my problem. Always thinking about other people and that car. And so what? It's just like my marriage. Damaged.*

I sit on the toilet and let the faucet run. I'm suddenly aware of my surroundings. The bathroom is lavishly decorated. There is a big bouquet on the bathroom sink with a card nestled beside it.

YOYO OPOKU

Mr. Gallo,
It is with great honor that the Summit staff welcomes you to your hotel. We know that we will exceed the standards you set out for us. Your personal assistant is available every day and at any hour you so desire. We are here to make your stay with us as enjoyable as possible.
With best regards,
Mr. Hollanderman and the Summit Hotel Staff

Shit! This is his hotel. At least his story is panning out. Well, that doesn't say much. He didn't even know the number or where it was located. He is probably so wealthy that he doesn't keep up with details like that. My hands stroke up and down the faucet. It looks like gold. *So this is how the rich live.* After washing my hands, I examine my cut in the mirror. *Not bad.* I use the terry cloth towel next to the sink to clean up the dried blood. As I exit the bathroom, Vincent's presence startles me.

"I hope everything is okay," he says.

"Yes," I say. I try to keep a certain distance away from him. "May I use the phone?"

"Certainly." He pulls a cellphone out of his pocket. I reach for it but then he pulls it back. "We are looking for as much discretion as possible, Ms. Frimpong. Please remember that."

"Sure. I understand." *Fuck, what could I say with him standing right next to me? All this secrecy. What is he, some kind of diplomat or royalty? I will have to Google him when I get home.* I move a few steps away, but Vincent doesn't lose sight of me.

Auntie Cece's voicemail again. No message this time. I dial Abla's number, but it also goes to voicemail. I leave a message. "Hey...um...maybe you're sleeping by now. Had a bit of car trouble. But I'm fine. Had it towed, but I'll be home soon. Not far away. In the city at a hotel. My cellphone died, so that's why I'm using this number. I'm making arrangements, but will be home shortly." *This should be enough clues for Abla in case...stop it, Vida...good thoughts.*

It is times like these I wish I could speak Twi. If I spoke Twi, I could tell her exactly what was going on without alerting Vincent. I understand Twi and I know a lot of vocabulary, but not enough to communicate a message effectively. My speaking in Twi is like asking

Abla to talk in Shakespearean English. A poor way of communicating and nothing would be understood.

After leaving the message, I hand the phone back to Vincent. There is a knock at the door. The security guard opens it. A casually dressed, average sized white man carrying a black satchel enters the room.

Julius carefully descends the staircase. He has on clean clothes and his hair is combed back. The cut is visible. Penny hovers over him like he's an injured child.

"Good evening, where is Dr. Braun?" Julius asks.

"Um, I am Dr. Jesup. Dr. Braun left this morning, he had a family emergency. I am well aware of your condition, Mr. Gallo. I work for Dr. Braun in his New York office. I've been assisting him on several of his patients' surgeries. Well, enough about me. How are you feeling?"

"Okay, considering the circumstances. Can you please examine Ms. Frimpong first? She was also involved in the car accident."

"Of course," he says.

"Just a little cut and whiplash. Nothing that Motrin can't handle," I say. The ringing in my ears has stopped.

"Please, Ms. Frimpong, may I? It will only take a moment." He approaches me with his black satchel. The benefits of the rich. A doctor a phone call away, right away. He takes the flashlight and moves it back and forth across my face. He examines my head and shoulders. The pain is in my shoulders. He notices me squirming.

"There are some bruises here, I am sure from the seatbelt. On the scale from one through ten, how bad is the pain?"

"Four," I say.

"I have some ibuprofen to help you with the pain. I can take care of the cut on your forehead tonight. It doesn't look like you will need stiches. If you come first thing in the morning, we can run some more tests. Here is my card." He extends a card toward me.

"Oh, that won't be necessary. I'll see my physician tomorrow. I don't want to take up too much of your time. Right now I just need to get home to my kids," I say.

"Ms. Frimpong, I am sure Dr. Jesup can forward any test results to your physician. Why don't you let me handle your care now?" Julius says.

"Thank you for the gesture. But I feel more comfortable with my doctor."

"Okay, I understand. Where is your physician?" Julius asks.

"In Westchester," I say. *Really, more information, Vida?*

"Okay. Just give me the name and phone number and I will take care of your bill," Julius says.

"Thank you. That is kind, but I have health insurance, so I'm covered," I say as Dr. Jesup cleans and dresses my wound. He then moves over to the black stool Julius is perched on and begins his examination.

"Ms. Frimpong, Vincent will escort you home," Julius says.

"No worries. It's awful late. I can just catch a cab."

"Please, Ms. Frimpong. I don't think it would be appropriate putting you in a cab by yourself after such an accident, especially at this hour. I assure you that Vincent's driving is much better than mine."

Dr. Jesup gives a brief chuckle. "I wanted to ask, but I decided to reserve my comments. Now I understand how you got into this predicament," Dr. Jesup says.

Julius frowns his face. "I was fine. I made it to the Bronx. The change in weather interfered with the lasers on the dashboard. It is something that I will have to pay close attention to now that I am here," Julius says.

"This could have ended very badly," Vincent chimes in. He crosses his arms over his chest.

"Well, thank goodness it was Ms. Frimpong who discovered me, right? Which reminds me, there is a man in the area named Colt to whom we also owe a debt of gratitude. Please be sure you find him and compensate him, Vincent," Julius says.

Vincent raises his eyebrow as if he has more questions, but only says, "Of course."

"Can you detect the light?" Dr. Jesup says. He flashes the light in his eyes just as he did to me. Julius moves his left eye in the direction of the light. Dr. Jesup then moves his fingers across Julius's face. His eyes don't move.

"Let's try it again," Dr. Jesup says. "Hmmm. This time I saw a little movement in your left pupil," Dr. Jesup says.

Everyone's attention is on Julius as Dr. Jesup continues his examination. "This cut can use a few stiches. I can start working on that now. But I want to run more tests on your left eye."

"Is there something else I need to be concerned with?" Julius says.

"No, not really. I need to run more tests. Tomorrow…well, I should say eleven a.m. today."

"Fine," Julius says.

"This time leave the driving to Vincent. The last thing you want in the headlines is 'Julius Gallo, blind billionaire, attempts driving in New York City.'"

"Blind?" The lethargic feeling disappears. "Holy shit!" I thought I used my inner voice, but all eyes dart to me.

"Didn't you know?" Vincent says.

"No," I say.

"Thank you, Dr. Jesup. I will see you later in your office," Julius says.

"Yes, I suppose." Dr. Jesup examines his watch. "Until then." Vincent escorts Dr. Jesup to the door.

Penny has been eyeing me suspiciously since I entered the room. Now Julius stands up and whispers something in Penny's ear. She blushes. She gives him another deep kiss and then looks in my direction. *This is so not necessary.* "Good night. I hope you feel better," she says to me. *She didn't mean that shit with her cattiness, accent and all.*

"Shall we?" Julius says. He follows behind me as we walk out of the suite. There is a single table and mirror placed opposite the elevator. On the table is another huge assortment of flowers and a hotel card. The same handwriting and signature. Two security guards and a gentleman in a grey suit are waiting outside.

"Hello, Mr. Gallo, my name is Mr. Marshall. Mr. Hollanderman requested that I attend to your needs. Let me first state, it is an absolute pleasure to be at your service. I was told by Mr. Francis of the mishap this evening. You don't have to worry. We will exercise complete discretion in this matter."

"Thank you," Julius says.

"Staff is available at your service twenty-four hours a day."

"Yes, I am aware."

"Please, Mr. Gallo, if you should need anything any time of the day or night, I am at your service. Your collection of cars with the exception of the one damaged this evening is located in the garage. I've already spoken to Mr. Vincent and we are arranging the repairs on both vehicles," Mr. Marshall says.

"Thank you. I am making my way to the garage now." I just met Julius, but his frigid face and sighs show that he is annoyed.

"Please allow me." Mr. Marshall presses the only button for the elevator. The door chimes and immediately opens. Julius doesn't move and neither do I.

"Mr. Marshall, thank you for your assistance. I will contact you if I should need anything else," Julius says.

"It would be my pleasure to escort you downstairs," Mr. Marshall says.

"Mr. Marshall, I am not sure what you've heard or what you have been told. But I like my independence. I don't pay people to follow me around to push my buttons. I can move back and forth quite independently. There are only six buttons in this elevator, correct?" Julius asks.

He nods and then answers. "Yes, sir."

"Good. Hardly rocket science to move from the garage to the penthouse. But in case, by sheer amusement, I should get lost, I know how to ask for assistance."

"Oh, Mr. Gallo, I hope I haven't offended you. I was instructed to be at your service twenty-four hours. We are all very eager to offer any assistance to you," Mr. Marshall says.

"Ms. Frimpong." Julius motions me to get into the elevator and follows behind me. "Well, you can tell Mr. Hollanderman thank you for the outstanding service, but this is my hotel and I will notify him when I need my diapers changed." He raises his hand in a gesture to stop the security guards from following. They stand back while the door closes. He is familiar with the layout in the elevator. He coasts his hand to the garage button. He stands facing me with his hands on either side of his waist and gives a deep sigh. "What a night."

Stop staring, Vida. I can't help it. *It never occurred to me he is blind. You nearly killed a blind man, Vida.* Not only would I have to deal with therapy sessions, but my place in heaven would be questionable. "I am sorry about this evening. It never occurred to me you couldn't see." *Shit...is that the politically way to say it?* "I mean visually disappear..." He raises his head and his eyes stare me down. "Fuck!" *Keep talking, Vida, you're on a roll.* "I meant to say visually impaired," I say, this time speaking slowly and pronouncing every syllable.

He smiles. "You don't have to worry about correct verbiage. I knew what you meant the first time. It's not every night a blind man drives into your car."

There, he said it. It was his fault. My smile is a bit wider from his admission. "Yes, so true."

He smiles again. "I guess I've just incriminated myself."

"True again."

"Here we are..." The door opens and I follow behind him. It's the same hallway we walked through less than an hour ago. This time, with no assistance from Vincent, he walks casually down the hallway. He stops and then makes clicking sounds. He touches the wall. He kneels down and touches the floor. We continue walking until we reach a large metal door. There is a keypad to the left of the door. He punches a series of numbers in and the door opens. Inside is a collection of cars. Vincent is standing next to a large SUV.

"Thank you for your cooperation. Vincent will take care of the necessary details. I will be in touch. Good night," Julius says.

"Good night, Julius." I extend my hand, forgetful of his condition. I lower it quickly so I don't look foolish in front of Vincent. Julius extends his hand toward me and I shake it.

As Vincent speeds along the I-95, countless thoughts joggle in my mind. Every bump we hit brings me back to my current state. *How could a blind man get from Manhattan all the way to Mount Vernon? He guards his independence, but how does he get around without a service animal or cane?*

I'm surprised that Vincent gets me home within twenty minutes with just my address and no visible GPS. "Are you familiar with the Bronx?" I say.

He hands me a bag over the seat. "I emptied your car and packed all your belongings into this bag. I have your car keys and your registration. Here is my number in case you need anything in the interim." He hands me another bag and I can tell it's cash without opening it. He steps out of the driver's seat and opens the rear door for me.

"Thank you," I say.

"We will contact you when your vehicle is repaired. Thank you again for your discretion," Vincent says. He is wearing an all-black suit, tailored just right for his large frame. He is impeccably dressed for a driver/bodyguard, especially at 4:00 a.m. He watches me open the front door and then disappears down the block as the sun begins to rise over the hill.

Chapter 4

A soft scent awakens me. The smell of nutmeg and Egyptian musk. I know who is lying beside me even before I open my eyes. "Hmmm...eeeehhhh, Yaa. And dey say I'm da sneaky one." Abla's snickering voice forces my eyes open. My body feels as though someone used it to pound fufu. "So, you weren't wit Felix las' night becuz he blew up my phone askin' if you made it home okay. I saw yur mist call at tree a.m., den I waz worried. God forbid if somedin' happen to my one and only sista. I heard yur message about stayin' at a hotel." She moves closer to me. "Hmmmm...wit who? Car trouble or you just wanted to sneak out and get somedin' to put you to bed?" She chuckles loudly and my head begins to throb. "And here you are, dank goodness, lyin' in bed, but...alone."

I bury my head back into the pillow. Moving anything besides my neck is not an option. The alarm clock on my right side is blinking 10:15. Not even five hours of sleep. To my left my sister is perched up on her elbows smirking.

"What?" I say. She's fishing for something and there is nothing to tell. *Well, maybe not right now.* She nudges me and memories of early this morning come to mind. "Oh, Abla, this is not a good time for your theatrics. I'm in pain."

"Eeiiiii, dat big? You haf to tell me everytin'. Don't leave any freaky nasty detail out."

"What are you talking about?" Everything always revolves around sex with Abla. There isn't a conversation she has that she doesn't wind up talking about *kotodendens,* penises; *etwes,* pussies; or *ahhh-ahhh-agyei* moments, orgasms.

"Don't do dat. Don't pretend wit me, yur only sista. You know, yur all I have. Yur my everytin'. We come from one motha and one fatha." *Here we go.* This is her way of shaming me into a confession. And it always works. She's been singing her one mother and one father song for all my life. It's supposed to mean we are of the same blood and people of the same blood should always protect one another. No secrets and no lies. Love wholeheartedly. She continues even though I try to block her voice from my thoughts.

"If I should die today, itz you dat will take care of everytin' for me. I haf no huzzband and no friends. Yur my one and only." The pillows can't muffle out her cries. Even though she hasn't shed a tear, her whimpering adds to the performance. I pat her gently on the knee. This always comforts her. She sobers up and continues her inquisition. "Well, when were you gonna tell me about Vincent?"

"Vincent?" Both eyes pop open and my arms pull my body upright. *Shit…the pain.*

"Oooh, yur secret iz out now. I told you. You can never hide anydin' from big sista. Dat iz why you were in such a hurry las' night to leave? I didn't dink you liked olda men, but hez very handsome in a Pierce Brosnan kinda way. And olda men take good care of young girlfriends." She leans over me. "So tell me, does he eat da cookie or does he just nibble and go for da main course?"

"Is your mind always focused on sex?"

She ignores me and continues. "Iz it big like dis?" She extends her forearm in front of my face. "Or iz it like dis?" She holds her thumb up. "Does he have moves? How many *aaaaaahhh-agyeis* did you have? He haz a deep voice, so I know for sure hiz *kote* iz big…" She rambles on, preventing me from answering any of her silly notions. "But he's olda, so he loses inches from shrinkage. How doez hiz balls look? Are dey touchin' da ground? Did you do anal? Don't do anal unless you guys are goin' to be serious, but den again don't do it. You know big dick and anal…no good. But hez olda. Anywayz, tell me, iz it big?"

"Abla! Stop it." My voice cracks. The pain continues from the back of my neck to back of my thighs. It never occurs to her that I was in an actual car accident.

"Lissen, I need you to answer my qweshons. Don't start yur reverse tontology on me."

"You mean reverse psychology."

"Wateva. Stop wastin' time. Talk. He has a thick accent. Watz he, Spanish? No. Italian… no…maybe Greek?"

"I believe he is Italian."

Her smile and eyes grow wider. "Testin' da otha side of da fence. Hmmmm…well, notin' wrong wit dat. As long as he respects you." Her words are laced with hidden meaning. Pancake's father, Jesus comes to mind.

"I am married, Abla."

"Seriously, we singin' dis ol' broken record again?"

"You still haven't told me how you know Vincent."

"If I tell you, will you tell me everytin' about las' night?" She sits up and looks at me squarely.

"Yes, okay. I will tell you everything."

She's like a kid who just found out she is going to Disneyland. "'Member, you promised everytin'. In DETAIL."

"Agreed," I say, knowing full well that she is not going to be happy with the truth.

She sits Indian style on the bed and continues. "Well, he stopt by dis mornin' and said you lef yur cellphone in da car. I askz him who waz he and he said dat you met las' night and he gave you a lift home. I askz him if I should wake you and he said no, dat it waz a long night and dat he will contact you real soon. Den he lef."

"Is that it?"

"Yezzz, now iz yur turn."

"And that's it. He gave me a ride after the car accident. We didn't have sex. You know I could never do that." As much as Abla would like me to move on with my life, I don't see having sex with someone else any time in the near future. I can only imagine Mensah lying beside me. Her childish excitement turns sour with my confession.

"Really, Yaa," Abla's tone sounds just like Mommy. "So you really were in a car accident?"

I pull my hair back exposing the cut from earlier today.

"Oh...shit!" she says. "Whoz fault waz it?"

"The other driver."

"Vincent."

"No. Julius."

"Where iz he? We haf to sue him for everytin'. Wat did da cops say? Where iz da car? Why didn't you call from da hospital? You did follow my advice, right?"

I can't even look at her to admit what I did. All her lessons come to mind, but I didn't even execute one correctly. "Everything is being taken care of," I say, uttering the same sentiments Gallo communicated to me earlier. Her eyes still search my face for more information. Vincent's words also come to mind. *"I am counting on your discretion."* Abla and I hardly keep secrets and it is hard not to confide in her about all the goings and comings in my life. Her loyalty means more to me than some rich stranger.

I spend the next twenty minutes recounting the events including my encounter with Colt and the events at the hotel.

"Shit! You blinded him. Hez goin' to sue us for everytin' we got. Da judge will take away our house. Dey may even lock you up. I can't raise tree kids and a college student by myself." She gets up and paces the room. "Dis iz why you need to lissen to yur big sista. If you went to da hospital we could have used mental block as part of our defense. Now…eeeiii, Yaa…I don't know." Abla is addicted to Court TV and some of her so-called legal counsel comes from watching Judge Judy and the rest comes from growing up in the streets of Accra.

"Were you listening to the whole story or did you zone out?" I ask.

"Okay, it waz kind of borin' after da wino left. Start again when you got to da hotel. Wat happened?" After my detailed explanation the second time, she crosses her arms over her chest trying to comprehend what she heard.

"So, letz see. He waz already blind but hez drivin'? Howz dat possible? A blind man drove from Manhattan to da Bronx. Wat judge iz goin' to believe dat?"

"Why do you keep mentioning judge? I am not going to court. I haven't done anything wrong." She doesn't get it and no amount of energy will make me repeat it for the third time.

"So who iz goin' to fix the damages and pay for the medical billz?"

"He said he would take care of it."

"Why would he do dat? Why not call da police or go to da hospital?"

"Because it was his fault and because he is blind and rich he doesn't want anyone to know."

Abla crosses her arms again and lets out a deep sigh. "Didn't I teach you betta dan dis? Dis sounds like four-one-nine to me. Watz hiz full name? Who iz dis Vincent man? Deer are a lot of four-one-nine boys out deer from every country. You can be too trustin', Yaa. Dat iz yur problem. You haf a good heart and people will take advantage. So, do you have a way of contactin' him?"

"Yes, of course. He owns the Summit Hotel."

"Den we should get a lawyer and start legal actionz immediately." I roll my eyes because she has dollar signs in hers.

"Okay, Abla, I understand. Let me go and see my doctor first. My body feels like an overused sponge. Are the kids up?"

"Yes. I had to push Panin out of yur room. Auntie Cece askz me if we noticed anydin' funny with Panin lately."

"Funny how?" I ask. Suddenly the pain is not my focus. Anything involving Panin acting differently worries me. I wait for Abla to respond.

"Sometimez when he comes from school, he starez out da window for an hour or two before startin' hiz homework." My heart breaks to hear that. He used to do that when he was younger. He would wait by the door for Mensah to come home. But lately I've noticed a series of different behaviors, like walking around the house and turning off all the lights and then walking into the back yard and sitting in the grass staring at nothing.

"He misses his father," I say.

"Don't dey do dat video chat dingy?"

"Sometimes, but lately it's been few and far between. I will have a talk with him."

"Auntie Cece left right after I came. Shez another sneaky lady. Shez alwayz runnin' errands, but do you see her wit any bags when she comes back? I dink she got some Mista hidin' somewhere." Abla chuckles. "I am sure of it. She just wants to look so pious. I know she iz starvin' down deer. We all have da same blood runnin' drew our veins. Even if herz iz haf blood. She has da lustful side."

"Leave Auntie Cece alone. She doesn't want a man. She wants to retire in the comfort of her home and live in peace and quiet."

"Hey, don't be fooled. Everyone needs someone no matta how old you are."

"Is that another Ablaism?" Abla has these sayings that she believes should be etched in stone because they hold truths. I refer to them as Ablaisms.

"It should be. Some people don't want to admit it, but lonelinez iz a silent killa."

Chapter 5

"Mommy! Mommy, guess what?"

MJ plunges toward me as soon as I enter the front door. Abla's peanut butter soup perfumes the house. "Can I get a kiss first?" He steps on his tippy toes to meet me half way. "Okay, sweetie, what is it?"

"You got a new car."

"What?"

"Yeah, Mommy, didn't you notice the car in the driveway?" Kakra says.

"No, I didn't." The three ibuprofen pills the doctor gave me relaxed me completely on the cab ride home.

"Talk about service. Whoz dis guy? Some rich sheik or somedin'?" Abla says. "I'm cookin' when some guy ringz da doorbell and sayz you haf a delivery. I dought some flowers from you-know-who." She rarely mentions Mensah's name because she says it's not worth mentioning.

I peer through the window. A white Range Rover is parked further along the driveway. "Anywayz, I signed for it and told him to park it in da driveway. Deezs are da keyz and registration." Abla nudges me to take the package in her hand.

"Mommy, let's go for a drive." Kakra jumps up and down mimicking MJ's excitement. We step outside. It's as if I am approaching a rare bird. My strides are short and quiet. The children zoom past me, envying the vehicle. It looks new from the outside. No dirt marks on the tires and new factory paint on the exterior.

"Mommy, Mommy, open…open…" MJ pulls on the door handle. Abla and Panin stand in the yard watching me. They hear the sound of the door unlocking and Kakra jumps inside and MJ follows his lead. There is an automatic car start on the vehicle and I press it before sliding into the seat. Lights, indicators and sound come alive inside the vehicle. The new car scent overtakes the fragrant peanut butter soup. Navigation console in front and entertainment screens mounted in the second and third row seats.

"Oh Mommy, we can watch all the movies we want back here," MJ says. Kakra tests the features on several buttons. The mileage on the dashboard reads six. Yep, brand new. The dark grey leather seats complement the vehicle beautifully. *Where is my Honda CRV? The Honda that Mensah bought for me on our fifth anniversary. I need that car back. This doesn't impress me, nor is this what we agreed upon.*

Abla joins us inside the vehicle. Her eyes dance around excitedly. "He also lef some money in an envelope for you." She hands me the envelope. *More money!* A lot more than he promised. Panin stands at a distance on the porch.

"Let's go inside," I say. The lights and sounds turn off with a click of a button.

"I'm going to call Daddy and tell him that we like our new car," Kakra says.

"Ha! Daddy didn't—"

"Abla!" My eyes squint to a slight blink and then a subtle roll of the eye. It's an old habit that we inherited from Mommy; she always said that Africans talk with their eyes and the African stare-down was an effective disciplinary action. Once Mommy locked her eyes on us, we knew we had to behave ourselves or face a severe tongue-lashing. Judging by Abla's immediate silence, it still works.

"Honey, Daddy didn't buy this car. Our car is getting fixed while we use this car," I say.

"Mommy, you sending the new car back?" Kakra asks.

"Yes."

"Why?" MJ asks.

"Because we don't need two cars," I say.

"So why can't we keep the new one and let them keep the old car?"

"Makez sense to me," Abla chimes in and I unleash another stare-down. She retreats into the house.

There is pain in my right knee as I kneel down to MJ's height. He hugs me warmly. "There is nothing wrong with the old car. Just some minor repairs and it's going to run like brand new again. You'll see."

*

We sit around the dinner table and there is an unusual silence until finally MJ speaks. "I don't want the old car. I want the new one."

"We are keeping the Honda." My tone is slightly higher and my words firm. Kakra and MJ pout. "In twelve years you will be driving and you can get any car you like."

"You gonna have to wait your turn, little bro. I'm gonna get a car before you. Right, Mommy?" Kakra asks.

"Provided your grades are good," I say. His face brightens up.

"Then I can drive Auntie to the stores," MJ says.

"Yes, you know yur auntie likes to shop. You can drive me to stores," Abla says.

Panin never approached the new car. His recent calmness is not unusual, but it is out of his routine. Usually he is drumming or playing music right before dinner. But this new behavior concerns me.

"I can't believe we are not keepin' it." Abla talks low through clenched teeth, but loud enough for me to hear her banter.

"No, we are not." *How much money did he send today? Vincent already gave me ten thousand the night of the accident.* I open the envelope. Crisp one hundred dollar bills in bundles of hundreds.

"Itz twenty thousand dollarz," Abla says.

"You opened it?"

"It waz not sealed when dey delivered it. I smelled money as soon as he gave it to me. I had to make sure da amount before da delivery guy lef."

"Wow, Mommy, we're rich—twenty thousand dollars!" MJ says.

"That's not a lot of money," Kakra says. Abla and I look at Kakra like he has three heads. "I mean…who gave us that money?" he continues.

"Guys, this is adult conversation. Eat your dinner," I say. My attention turns toward Abla again. "I'm going to see him tomorrow to straighten this all out." Abla gives several deep sighs. "I know what you're thinking. I just need our car fixed. We don't need a new car. The car that Mensah bought us is perfectly fine." She won't understand even if I try to explain it to her. A new car, a life without Mensah…*No. I can't imagine a life without him. Not now.* Abla gives me a dose of my own medicine by cutting her eyes at me. The air is heavy and neither of us wants to argue. We barely say anything through dinner. It's just the sounds MJ makes blowing on his fufu before he gulps it down.

*

It's ten o'clock and my skin begins to wrinkle like dried apricots soaking in the tub. Abla enters the bathroom.

"Watz wrong wit you?" Abla says. She moves to sit at the edge of the bathtub. "Do you always qweshon when someone doez somedin' nice for you? You can't send dat car back. Iz an insult if you do."

"To who?" I finally step out of the tub and Abla hands me the towel.

"To him."

"How do you figure?"

"If wat you say about dis man iz true, den buyin' a car doezn't mean anydin' to him. He spendz dat kinda money every day. You got a new car and you didn't haf to fall on yur knees or drop yur panties."

"I just want my old car fixed. I am not asking for anything more." I turn away from her and examine the woman in the mirror.

"Dat iz yur problem. Yaa, you deserve so much more and you always dink you deserve just da basics. Yur big sista iz tellin' you, don't return dat car. Enjoy it. End of discussion." We rarely argue, but this car issue will spark the foundation for one. And arguing with Abla is like arguing with a judge. She has to have the last word. "Wat did da doctor say?"

"Whiplash and some sore tissue from the car accident. He gave me some ibuprofen for the pain." There is a faint line across my right shoulder where the seatbelt snatched against my skin.

"No inside bleedin' or broken bones?" Abla asks.

"No. He ran some x-rays. Still got my manufacturer's warranty in good order."

We laugh. "Good. You need to rub some of da shea butta over here and deer." She notes the discoloration on my shoulder and some redness on my back. "Get some rest." She kisses me on my forehead and exits the bathroom.

Sometimes I listen to Abla, but today my gut tells me to find out about my Honda CRV. It's stupid, this debate. I have a brand new car in the driveway and all I can think about how proud Mensah was when he bought me this car. Not a used car or a leased car. Paid for it with all the money he saved. *If I get rid of it that means in fact my marriage is over. It sounds stupid to even make the comparison, but I have to get it back.* The more I think about it, the less it makes sense. My reasons are weaker than a teenaged girl in Forever 21. But I am still debating it. It's a larger vehicle with more amenities, but it isn't the car that Mensah and I made love in. It isn't the vehicle that he proudly drove home and covered with tulips to show to me. My cheeks lift and my face warms up with happy memories. It feels like so long ago when I was happy with Mensah. So much has changed.

 I lay on the bed naked and I am thinking about him again. *Don't cry, Vida. Why did I agree to this arrangement? Because I wanted him to be happy. And it would make us all happy.* Six months, he told me, and then he would be back. He even urged me and the children to move out there with him. But my life in New York is comfortable, predictable and fun. Moving to California without my family would be a drastic change for me. He said he would make it work. Nothing would separate him from his family. *"We will Skype every weekend and talk every night. I won't miss a birthday or Christmas,"* his words echo in my head. Once his contract was over, he would establish a name for his contracting company and be back here in New York. Everything would work out for the best. It's nearly two years now. Our discussions consist of monthly text messages. He broke his promise and everything he placed in my heart. Everything that I am trying to hold onto is slipping away from me. My skin is dried. I look at my feet. I'm overdue for a pedicure. *Gosh, it's been over a month since I shaved Ginger.* I stand up and look at myself in the mirror behind the bathroom door. My hips are a bit wider and my thighs still have muscular tone. I still admire the woman I see. She's been through so much. I sit back on the bed again. I rub my hand in between my legs but don't have the urge to please myself tonight. *What am I going to do with this new car? No. I need the Honda back. This can't be the end of us. It means so much to us...well, to me.*

Chapter 6

"Hi, do you remember me?" Mr. Marshall is standing at the reception desk.

He looks up from the computer screen and studies me. He removes a pair of glasses from his blazer pocket and rests them on the tip of his nose. "Ah, yes. Ms. Frimpong. How can I help you?"

"Is Mr. Gallo or Vincent here?"

"Are they expecting you this afternoon?"

"No. I think there is a big misunderstanding. Can you notify them that I am here?"

"Please have a seat and I will check if he is available."

The plush brown leather chair is welcoming. It's four o'clock and there is heavy foot traffic coming in and out of the hotel. Guests move through the lobby in various attire, some dressed in suits, some in sporting outfits and others dressed for a formal evening in the city.

Mr. Marshall approaches me. "Ms. Frimpong, Mr. Gallo is not in. Perhaps you can leave a note. I will see to it that Mr. Gallo gets it." He hands me a pad and pen.

Disappointed that this isn't going to be a face-to-face conversation, I agree to leave the note. Mr. Marshall is greeted by a female guest. They toss air kisses and he returns to the desk. I break my distraction and think about how to phrase the note without offending him.

Dear Mr. Gallo,

This is a very kind gesture, but I am afraid that the children are attached to the old car. It has fond memories for us all. Please fix my Honda and return it back to its original condition.

Thanks,

V. Frimpong

Yeah, use the children as the reason without appearing as a lovesick fool. Think again, Vida.

Hi Mr. Gallo,

I'm afraid, I can't drive this big SUV. I feel intimidated by its size. I am very comfortable driving the Honda CRV. Please make the necessary repairs and return it to me as soon as possible.

Thank you for your kind gesture,
Vida Frimpong

That sounds silly. Intimidated by its size. I used to drive Mensah's pickup truck. Of course he doesn't know that, but I need to try again.

Dear Mr. Gallo,

My husband is a jealous man and needless to say that it bothers him that another man has purchased another vehicle for me (it's an ego thing—if you get my drift). I'm afraid that I will need to return it. Thank you for the generous gesture. Please kindly return the Honda CRV to its original condition.

Thanks,
Ms. Frimpong

Gosh, it sounds like Mensah chains me to the house. Another page is crumbled beside me. Mr. Marshall eyes me from his workstation. The excuses collect around me like breadcrumbs. My eyes remain fixed on the Summit logo centered at the top of the notepad. And the sunrays spread across the top like arrows. It hits me.

Dear Mr. Gallo,

Thank you for the vehicle, but it is not what I was expecting. Please kindly return my Honda CRV to its normal functionality. I parked the vehicle in the hotel garage and will leave the keys with Mr. Marshall.

Thank you again for your kind gesture,
Vida Frimpong

That sounds better. Simple and to the point. Don't change your mind, Vida. "Do you have an envelope I can put this in?" I ask Mr. Marshall.

"Certainly." Mr. Marshall walks to another desk and returns with an envelope in his hand.

The note fits perfectly in the monogramed envelope. I place the keys in Mr. Marshall's hand. "Please make sure Mr. Gallo gets the keys to his vehicle. I parked it in his garage. Thank you."

I leave the Summit Hotel confident I did the right thing.

*

Music is blaring from the living room speakers when I enter the house. Kakra sings to a song and Panin drums on the dining room table. MJ and Trudy dance off beat. "Where is Auntie Cece?" I say.

No response. They are all in their element. The music quiets down when the children notice my presence.

"Hey Mommy, you're home," Kakra says. MJ leaps into my arms. Panin continues to drum. A quick stare and he places the drumsticks on his lap.

"Where is Auntie Cece?" I ask again.

"She's upstairs doing the laundry," Kakra says.

"Did you guys finish your homework?"

"Yep, I did," Kakra quickly answers, which tells me to look through his book bag for any hidden assignments. There is no doubt that Panin finished his. His homework is always on point with little guidance.

"Hi, Ms. Asare. I finished my homework too," Trudy says. She's grown up to be a fine young lady. Smart, well mannered and respectful. Trudy at the age of eleven seems far more responsible than her mother, Chin.

"Hello, dear...where is Mommy?" I thumb through a heap of mail in front of the hallway table. Solicitors and bills.

"She said she had to run an errand and told me to wait here," Trudy says.

Chin's life as a single mother has its challenges. Errands, moving kids from school to home and then cooking and cleaning. Tasks that must be juggled with the everyday life of raising children and maintaining a household. Unlike me, she has to rely on Trudy to help her raise her other four children. Chin's baby daddy/boyfriend is in prison for the next four years, yet that hasn't stopped Chin from her conjugal visits. Perhaps that is where she went.

"Where are your brothers and sisters?"

"Grandma came to visit, so they're with her," Trudy answers.

"Hey Mommy, we need a name for the baby," Kakra says.

"Baby! What baby?" *My heart, where is it? It's not beating.* Eager eyes search Trudy's and Kakra's faces. It's hard to tell what these preteenagers are up to, what with their social media pages and constant texting. I've noticed the closeness of Kakra's and Trudy's relationship lately. They fought often when they were younger but now they seem closer…too close.

"Mommy is having another baby," Trudy says.

"Really?" I say, relaxing my gaze on them.

"Yes." Trudy sulks into her chest. How on earth is Chin going to raise six children on her own? Poor Trudy already has her plate full.

"How about Nana?" Kakra says.

"And what about if it's a boy?" Trudy says.

"In Ghana, Nana is a title like king or queen, so it can be given to a boy or girl." There are times when the children surprise me. Listening to Kakra explain to Trudy the naming ritual in Akan will definitely count toward proud moments. It's one of the things Mensah can pat himself on the back for.

"So we could name the baby also depending on the day it will be born?" Trudy says.

"Yep. Depending on the day of the week and the sex. But me and Panin are twins, so that is why we are named Kakra and Panin. Kakra, meaning the younger of the twins and Panin is the older twin."

"So why don't you use your African names in school?"

"I don't know. Anyway, I like that I have this other identity—one in school and one at home."

"Yeah, that is neat. But I like your African names better than your English names. Tell me, what is my African name again?" Trudy asks. I'm curious to see if Kakra remembers the names, the lessons his father taught them every Sunday.

"Hmmmmm…a female born on Wednesday is called…" He pauses. "Akua." He looks to me for validation. I give him a wide smile and then a head nod. He smiles. "Yes," he says jubilantly.

"Akua," Trudy says. "From now on, call me Akua. I like that."

"Okay, you guys get ready for dinner." We can spend the whole night discussing Akan naming rituals, but it won't be much of a lesson without the teacher.

Auntie Cece is preparing dinner and I reminisce over the blessings of having strong women to help me on a daily basis. When Mensah moved to California, it was hard to manage the kids and work full-time. Both Auntie Cece and Abla stepped in, playing an extra parent role. Abla stays over on the weekends and Auntie Cece comes by daily. After Uncle Isaac passed away, Auntie Cece made sure she didn't spend a single day not engaged in activity, whether it was picking up the kids for me after school, or driving Kakra to soccer practice, or volunteering at the Ghana Presbyterian Church. Her days are probably busier than an Uber driver. Auntie Cece says that this is Mensah's home and he should still feel as though there is room for him, so she never moved in. I know that isn't the real reason.

Abla and Auntie Cece come together like palm oil and vinegar. They clash on just about everything, especially on the roles of husband and wife. Auntie Cece believes that wives should serve their husbands unconditionally and Abla believes that submission is ultimately the wife's choice.

"*Wo ho etense,*" Auntie Cece says. She promises me that I will be speaking Twi before she retires to Ghana.

"*Me ho ye, meda ase,*" I say. *How are you? I'm fine. Thank you.* These are basic pleasantries that I've said a thousand times. After that, my communication in Twi unravels like a braid in silky hair.

"*Wo be deedee?*" she continues with Twi 101.

"I will eat whatever is ready." My memory forgets the response in Twi, but she smiles forgivingly.

It's not like I don't want to speak Twi. It is a work in progress. I've done well to understand some of the language, cook the food, remember customs and practices, but speaking would require a dedicated tongue. The instruction began with my father, but when Mommy and Daddy divorced, learning Twi wasn't a priority anymore. Mensah began the process again when we were dating, but after marriage, work and family took precedence, and English became a more convenient way of communicating between us.

YOYO OPOKU

I love these moments sitting together like a family having dinner. I look at the seat that Mensah used to occupy and Auntie Cece always reminds me to keep empty. Her words resonate with me. *"That is Mensah's chair and no one else should sit in it."* It's almost two years since I've seen him at the end of this table.

Chapter 7

Not having a car proves to be a real pain in the ass. *Why do I have to feel so sentimental?* I hate public transportation during rush hours. It's always crowded and I have the sad opportunity to be cramped in a train car with inappropriate conversations or entertainment. This is just the third day and at this point maybe I should rent a car if I don't hear back from Julius. I called the hotel yesterday and Mr. Marshall said he delivered my message. *Maybe Abla was right. I did offend him.* I can't focus on the rich man's ego right now. My thoughts are still occupied by Mensah's message.

The car accident was four days ago and he decided to leave me a message last night. The more I think about it, the more upset I become. I replay the message while teenagers discuss girls' anatomy and who has the nicest rap lyrics, Drake or Future.

"Vida, I just got into town and heard your message. How are you feeling? I wish I could hear your voice. How are my boys doing? Kakra says we don't have a car anymore. What did the insurance company say? Anyway, I will try you later when you get home from work."

That's it. Not even one minute long. *He didn't sound concerned. And just got into town? He never told me he was traveling again.* I can't keep up with him anymore. Sadness overcomes me.

"Smile, pretty lady... It's too early in the morning to look so stressed out," a man standing over me says. It is pretty obvious that my feelings show on my face. *Try to think of something other than Mensah.* It doesn't work. The stranger notices my fake smile immediately. "Well, sometimes you gotta fake it till you make it, sista," he says smiling. I smirk when I see the stranger is missing four front teeth.

Thank goodness my clients today are within a mile radius. Going door-to-door is easier than I expect.

My last client for the day, Mr. Jenkins, greets me at his front door. "Still no car, huh?"

"Yeah, still riding on the iron horse, but it won't be long." I think again about Abla's words. *He can't possibly be offended. After all, I'm saving him money by returning the car.* "How is your leg, Mr. Jenkins? Are you still limping?"

"It comes and goes. I'm fine."

"Nurse Mills tells a different story. You haven't been taking your medicine."

"Ahh…dat gurl don' know nothang. I take dem medicine whens I needs it. Seventy-eight years ol' and don't need no babysitta." Mr. Jenkins can be difficult at times and other times a bit amusing to be around. An old southerner from South Carolina, he raised two daughters by himself when his wife passed early in life. The neighborhood in Long Island City has become a hot commodity. On a daily basis real estate agents leave business cards and flyers indicating interest in buying his home. Mr. Jenkins says he will never sell to those sharks, but his recent health issues have me concerned.

"I contacted your daughter about the list of nursing homes. She's coming this weekend to take you to some of them." He huffs at me and I know he doesn't even want to hear the words nursing home. But it's the only choice. His movement is restricted to a few steps to the main door and then back to the couch that doubles as his bed. He will need a wheelchair within the month. "We only want the best for you, Mr. Jenkins. You need more help and it's not safe for you to be here alone."

He gives a big exhale. "I'll check dem, but no promises." Our eyes meet and a reassuring smile tells me he will actually go this time. "So when dat man plannin' fix da car? Miz Asare, don't let no one run no game on ya." Mr. Jenkins only knows about my car accident and Julius's commitment to fix it. The less the better. "Always folks out here takin a'vantage of good folks."

"Yes, unfortunately that's how the world works, but don't worry, not this African girl." My examination is quicker than normal. Nurse Mills has taken a lot of the vitals already. "Mr. Jenkins, do you need anything before I go?"

"No, ma'am. Get home to dem boyz."

*

It's six o'clock by the time I head uptown. Not bad timing, considering that I only picked up MJ and Panin from after school. Coach Richardson agreed to drop off Kakra after practice today. Inside the gate sitting on the front porch is a heavy-set white man. My Honda is back and so is the Range Rover.

"Hi," I say.

"Good evening, Ms. Are you Ms. Fenmong?"

"You mean Frimpong," I correct him.

"Sorry, Ms. I tried my best to pronounce it. Need you to sign here that we delivered the vehicles."

"Vehicles? Just the Honda is mine."

"I was given instructions to deliver the Honda and Range Rover to this address."

"There's a mistake. I don't need two cars. The Honda is mine. You can take the Range Rover back to Mr. Gallo."

"I'm sorry, Ms. Just doing my job. Here are the keys to both cars. The paperwork's in the vehicles. Have a good evening."

He leaves. MJ is excited once again but Panin moves farther away. I move closer to inspect my car. Inside the Honda are new leather seats. A navigation system and a Bose radio replaces a nonexistent entertainment system. The interior smells new and there are new tires as well. Under the hood, everything is in pristine order. I rev up the engine and the only thing that reminds me of the old Honda is the 80,000 miles on the odometer. MJ's booster seat is replaced with a luxurious and more compact booster seat. In the glove department is a note.

Thank you, Ms. Frimpong, for your time. It should ride just like new. JG.

Coach Richardson and Kakra are here. Practice must have drained all the energy out of him because he waves at me gently and walks right into the house.

"Okay, rest up. Big game tomorrow," Coach Richardson says.

"Thanks, Coach." He waves me a goodbye. I usher MJ and Panin into the house.

"Hi honey, how was practice?" He slumps into the couch.

"I'm beat," he says.

"Why don't you wash up for dinner?" He languidly walks up the stairs and Auntie Cece walks through the door.

"Whose car is that in the driveway?" I'm surprised she didn't ask me in Twi.

"Oh Auntie, it's just a rental. I'm sending it back tomorrow." The last thing I need from her is a lecture. I didn't disclose all the events of the crash and this wouldn't be the time to do so.

"The rental is more expensive than the car you use," she says and enters the kitchen.

Thank goodness the cars didn't arrive over the weekend. I would have a hard time explaining to Abla the reason for sending the car back again. Julius is starting to get on my nerves. No phone call or message since my note at the hotel. Now I have a pimped out vehicle and a spare SUV.

Auntie Cece returns to the hallway. She catches me in deep thought. "Is everything okay? How are you feeling? Are you still sore?"

"No, Auntie. I'm fine. Just going over some cases for tomorrow."

She continues, "I nearly forgot to tell you. Yur doctor's office called and wanted to know if you dropped your insurance carrier. They've received payment on yur behalf from Julius Gallo. Is that the man who crashed into you?"

"Yes, Auntie. There must be some confusion. I'll straighten things out first thing tomorrow morning."

"Well, as long as you don't have to pay out of pocket, you shouldn't bother. He should be paying yur medical expenses. After all, it's his fault."

"Yes, of course, Auntie."

I definitely need to speak to Julius face-to-face tomorrow.

*

Driving on the FDR during rush hour traffic is worse than enduring public transportation. *Did the population increase like Gremlins over two years? Does everyone in New York City have to drive?* Hopefully this won't take long. In and out in ten minutes. The garage attendant remembers me from the last time I was here and welcomes me into the elevator.

"Lobby, right?"

"Yes." I give him a polite smile. In the lobby at the reception desk are several unrecognizable faces. I look for Mr. Marshall. An older gentleman greets me in the reception area.

"Good morning," he says. His nametag reads Mr. Hollanderman.

"Good morning. I am here to see Mr. Gallo."

"Yes, please have a seat there." He points to a more secluded spot in the lobby. *Odd. No inquiry as to who I am.* I move to the area as I am instructed to. Paranoid thoughts consume me. *Perhaps he warned the hotel staffers about me. Maybe he is going to come down himself to address me.* It's almost 10:30 a.m. and I haven't seen my first patient yet. *Oh goodness, maybe I should come back tomorrow. No. I'm already here. This should be a quick in and out.*

I have to call Mrs. Shaw and let her know I'm running late. The call goes to voicemail. Thank goodness. She can become overly anxious if I'm even a minute late. It will take me twenty minutes from here to cross the Queensboro Bridge.

"Excuse me, is anyone sitting here?" A young woman joins me in the hideaway area. She is tall, blonde and perhaps a size zero. *Maybe she models.*

"No, I don't believe so," I say. We make eye contact and she smiles momentarily. Her teeth are paper white. She adjusts herself in the chair, her legs maneuvering into a number of elegant poses.

It's 10:35. I should just leave a note like the last time. No. The proper thing to do since I'm here is to thank him. And give him the keys back to the Range Rover. Then tell him I don't need the vehicle. Okay, I will wait five minutes more.

"Excuse me, Madam," Mr. Hollanderman says. "Please follow this gentleman upstairs."

I follow behind a man in the burgundy Summit uniform while reexamining the environment. This is not the same secret elevator we used before. We walk through a long hallway until we reach a large metal door. He knocks on the door and a tall white man opens it. His is stylishly dressed in a deep purple suit.

"That will be all. You will hear back from us shortly," the man in the purple suit says to an older gentleman dressed like a college professor.

"Thank you again for your time," says the college professor. They shake hands. The gentleman in the Summit hotel uniform escorts the college professor out. The man in the purple suit gestures me in.

"Good morning, have a seat Ms.—"

"Ms. Frimpong," I say. This is a large hall with floor-to-ceiling windows. There are two tables and four chairs situated in the room. An oversized couch takes center stage. The man in the purple suit advises me to sit in a chair across from him.

"I don't seem to have you on my list."

"List? What list? Is Mr. Gallo here?" I ask.

"No, he is not. We will be conducting the interviews today."

"Interviews?"

"I'm already exhausted. How many of these do we have today?" Penny says as she emerges from a door on the far end of the room. She looks quite different from what I remember, maybe because she has more clothes on. "I know you." She stops her regal stride and scans me like a copy machine.

"I am looking for Mr. Gallo."

"What are you doing here?" Penny asks.

"I came to speak with Mr. Gallo. Well, actually to thank him."

"What is your name?" the man in the purple suit asks.

"My name is Vida Frimpong. Is Mr. Gallo here?" I ask for the third time.

"No," Penny answers. "Max, this is the woman Julius was talking about." Max paces the room taking quick glances at me. "Call the next person on your list. I want to go to bed. This is so exhausting."

"I bet you do," Max quips at her. "Can we relay a message for you to Mr. Gallo?" Max says.

"No, I just want to thank him for the repairs and his generosity and…" Max and Penny review papers on one of the tables, uninterested in my presence. I continue anyway. "…and to tell him that I don't need the Range Rover. It's parked downstairs in the garage. Here are the keys." My arm hangs in limbo like an unpaired sock, the keys dangling in my hand and Penny's eyes piercing my skin.

"You brought the Range Rover back?" Penny's voice is high and loud.

"Again?" Max chimes in.

Don't start stuttering now, Vida. "Well, yeah. My car is back, so I don't need two cars." I chuckle. Their looks are priceless, as though I said I eat dogs daily. Max adjusts the double knot on the black tie closely pinned to his neck.

"Amuse me, please." He invades my personal space. "You prefer the Honda CRV with the fruit punch, soda and other high fructose corn syrup stains all over the backseats. In addition to…" He gives a long pause and continues, "…unrecognizable gunk on the floor mats and the back seat upholstery of your car. Your precious Honda CRV has over eighty thousand miles, two dents on the back passenger's side door, no navigation, no Bose speakers, no sunroof, no leather seating, no automatic seat warmers, no multi CD disc changer, no entertainment system in the headrest…" He pauses to exhale. "I know all this because I had to bring your car back from Honda CRV purgatory and get it in the condition it is today with the aforementioned amenities. Now it can sit amongst other vehicles on the road and be worthy enough to be called a vehicle." He circles me like he's going in for a kill. "And not only did your Honda get 'upgraded'"—he uses air quotes—"but you got a bonus...and we all love bonuses. A new, straight from the factory, custom-made Range Rover based on specifications any mother would love. But...but, Ms. Frimpong, you decide—for whatever reason that makes sense to you—to return the Range Rover because now you have your precious Honda CRV. And may I add, you would definitely need an upgrade in a couple of years with three growing children."

I know when someone is being a smart ass and clearly Max is doing a fine job of making me look stupid. He is not going to have the last word and I recall what Mensah told me when he brought it home. 'It's really good on gas." Max moves farther away from me, but keeps my gaze as though he is deciding if I am of the human race. "Well, anyway, it looks like he is not here. Can I leave the keys with you?" I turn to Penny for help.

"Oooooh no, you wait. I'll call him." Penny disappears into the same room she emerged from.

"Hmmm, this should be interesting," Max says. He returns to the table and picks up his phone. The oversized sofa is a good distance away from him. I sit on it, either waiting for Julius or perhaps death by stoning.

Told-you-sos are filling my thoughts. This will certainly go down as one of my fuckups. A knock at the door causes Max to rise and glide across the room. His long gait makes walking look effortless. It is the tall blonde model from the lobby. She looks noble walking into the suite. Max looks impressed. The large security guard closes the door behind her as she continues to make her presence known in the room.

"Hello, Ms. Natalie Gruere?"

"Yes, you pronounced it correctly. Parlez-vous francais?" she says.

Max blushes. "Not fluently. But I make it a priority to pronounce names properly. Please have a seat, Ms. Guere." They head toward the large table in the middle of the room. I move from the sofa and pretend as though I am preoccupied with the view outside the window.

"Ms. Guere, how many languages do you speak?" Max asks.

"Seven fluently, but I understand about twelve," she replies.

Before she sits, I take a quick inventory of her. Two things in my opinion separate classes of women. High heels are nice, but a pair of F-M-Ps accompanied with a nice round behind sets you apart.

If it wasn't for Abla, I would never have owned a pair of fuck-me-pumps, F-M-Ps, a title that Abla heard from an Amy Winehouse album. Not all pumps are the same, she tells me. An FMP is a stiletto that carries certain imagery and connotation. There is something about a stiletto that exudes sex appeal, confidence and, well, of course…rich, hot, sweaty, orgasmic fucking. These pumps are always four inches or higher and you don't want to take them off before or during the rapture. If lingerie is chocolate covered strawberries then F-M-Ps are the champagne. They are the cream cheese icing to the red velvet cake. Louboutin, Brian Atwood, Manolo Blahnik, Viktor & Rolf, Chanel, Jimmy Choo, Sophia Webster and Monika Chiang have become household names.

Ms. Guere's low booty fits her thin frame just right with the modest Kate Spade-like black F-M-Ps. She looks quite natural except for the ultra-blonde highlights. She seems sophisticated and worldly. A far cry from Penny. She walks gracefully to the armchair and sits without the slightest noise from the leather. Her long legs reveal flawless soft pale skin. She gently pulls her blonde locks over her shoulder.

"Well, as you know, we are looking for someone who is also fluent in Italian and Portuguese. This is a highly classified assignment with sensitive information, which means we are looking for someone with total discretion," Max says.

"I completely comprehend the magnitude of the assignment. You will be pleased to know that I have written for illustrious and notorious figures. I am sure Mr. Peterson has affirmed my work. Mr. Gallo will not be disappointed." Her last sentence rolls off her lips, hinting to more than what she affirms. Penny enters the room just in time. She frowns at the sight of such European elegance.

"Let me state again that this is not a traditional assignment. It will require a lot of your time and perhaps working conditions that you are not used to. Do you have an issue with this?"

"Not at all. I am very flexible. Mr. Gallo can count on me in every way possible," she says.

"Maxxxx!" Penny shouts and walks briskly toward him.

"Hello, Penny. I told you Mr. Peterson will come through. This is Ms. Guere, the ghost writer." Penny doesn't take her eyes off Ms. Guere as she inches closer for a better view.

"Good morning," Penny says. Ms. Guere responds in Russian, which causes Penny's eyes to grow wider.

"You speak Russian," Penny replies in English.

"Don't you?" Ms. Guere asks Penny. *Perhaps that is the accent that I detected.*

"Oh, yes. Ms. Guere knows seven languages including Italian and Portuguese," Max says.

"Well, that is wonderful," Penny says slowly. Her eyes scan the room and then catch my eyes. I quickly turn to focus on the view outside. Ms. Guere continues to speak in Russian. I turn my attention to them again. "May I?" Penny talks through clenched teeth while scanning Max's tablet. The room feels heavy. Penny, to say the least, does not look pleased. She scrolls her fingers up and down the screen. "Ms. Guere…ummm …thank you so much for coming. Indeed, I see your credentials are impressive. We will be in contact."

"Penny, we haven't finished," Max tries to interject.

"Oh Max, do we really need to ask Ms. Guere any more questions? She is more than qualified. Please excuse Mr. Wilson…he can be overly cautious." Ms. Guere rises and she is a couple of inches taller than Penny, but that is not the only clear difference. Ms. Guere is a newly minted half dollar coin and she makes Penny look like a rusted coin found on a subway platform.

"Right. You have all my contact information, Mr. Wilson. I will be in New York for three more days before flying back to France. So do get in touch."

"Certainly," Penny interjects.

"Okay, Ms. Guere. I guess we will be in touch," Max says.

Max escorts her to the door and there is a security guard and Summit staff waiting outside. Her presence, like just-baked cookies, awakens the people who come into contact with her. Their heads turn to admire her silhouette. "Thank you again, Ms. Guere," Max says. Penny appears to be bubbling with words but she waits for Max to close the door.

"Are you fuckin' mad?" Penny yells.

"Are you?" Max retorts. "She is exceptionally qualified."

"In what? Sucking his balls?"

"Oh come now, Penny. Not everyone has ulterior motives. You asked me to find the most qualified candidate and then you chase her away like an annoying bee—"

"Yes, because that bee is interested in serving him her honey," Penny says through clenched teeth.

"Stop it. You are exaggerating. She is a professional and comes highly recommended."

"Yes Like some prostitutes I know. It doesn't mean it is a good idea," Penny says. "Ms. Freemon." It doesn't sound anything like my name, but I look in her direction anyway. "Ms. Freemon…" she says again.

"Are you talking to me?"

She rolls her eyes. "Yes, isn't that your name?"

"Vida is fine," I snap back.

"Kay…Vida, do you have any more of that mommy perfume?"

"Mommy perfume?" I ask.

"Yes, the stuff you are wearing."

"What makes it mommy perfume?" I ask, not sure if I should feel offended.

"You are a mommy and it's perfume…no? You get it from a pharmacy, no?"

"No, I don't have any mommy perfume," I say rolling my eyes. I don't want to admit that I know exactly what she is inferring. I used to purchase the designer imposter perfumes in all different scents until Mensah spoiled me.

"Max, check the bathroom for air freshener."

"Oh heavens, what for?"

"The last thing I need is for Julius to get a whiff of that blonde slut," Penny says. Although the trail of her scent is dissipating, the room has an air of sophistication. I wonder if Julius has that keen a sense of smell.

"Oooh, jealousy doesn't look good on you at all," Max jokes.

"Prevention is better than cure!" she shouts.

I sit back down in the armchair and watch Penny scamper through the room. *What kind of assignment are they interviewing for? What is so secretive?*

The sound of the door opening brings everyone to a standstill. Vincent walks in; a few feet behind him is Julius.

"Good morning, Mr. Gallo." Max eagerly rushes to greet them.

Penny scans the room, perhaps looking for anything that would alarm Julius. "Hello babe, how was your run? Did you get my message?"

I stand up just as he approaches Penny and me.

"Fine. And no, I didn't get your message," he says shortly. He looks left and right. "Good morning, Ms. Frimpong." *How does he know I'm here?*

"Good morning, Mr. Gallo." *Maybe he can recognize my so-called mommy scent.* The woman in me tells me this is not going to end well, but I press on. "I won't take too much of your time, Mr. Gallo. Julius. First, let me say thank you for repairing and returning my car. I appreciate the upgrade—it was more than I needed, but the boys will surely enjoy it."

"You are welcome. But no thank you needed. It's the very least I could do." Max, Penny and Vincent eye me suspiciously. The room feels like the sun is sitting inside. Heat overtakes my body and I'm sweating in places no one can see.

"Is there something else I can do for you?" His voice is confident and strong.

Just say it and leave, Vida. "Well, the reason for me coming is also to return your Range Rover. The gentleman dropped my vehicle, but made a mistake and didn't take back the loaner you gave me. So it's parked in the garage and here are the keys." I drop the keys on the same table that Max sat across from. "Thank you again," I say quickly and try to rush to the door. His voice emerges, large and stern, filling the room.

"Ms. Frimpong." I turn to look at him.

"Yes?" *Fuck.*

"Pick up the keys." There is silence. I can count each person's breaths. Feeling intimidated, I chuckle, but no one else is amused. I pause for a moment then walk back to the desk.

He continues. "The car is not a loaner. I bought the car for you because you obviously need it for your daily activities. It is your car, Ms. Frimpong. It is not a gift. Just a new replacement for the car that I damaged. As requested, we made the repairs to your vehicle and customized it for a better ride. Again, just common courtesy for the inconvenience I have caused you." He breathes deeply. "It is just common courtesy."

"That is very nice of you, but now that I have my car back, I don't need two cars. I just think it would be a waste of your money to buy me something I don't need."

The expressions on Max's and Penny's faces are indescribable, yet it appears my words are about to unleash the flying dragons. Vincent, Penny and Max stand behind Julius on one side of the room while I and my sentimental heart begin to melt into the floor.

"Ms. Frimpong, do you know how much money I make in a day?"

My first reaction is another chuckle, but everyone else's face is frozen. I sober up. "No, I don't."

"How about how much money I make in a week or a month or a year?" No answer from me, but then again he is not waiting for a response. "What I can and cannot afford is none of your concern."

Okay, this is the cue, Vida. Bow out gracefully. But noooo. The woman in me champions me on.

"I just think you shouldn't waste—"

"Ms. Frimpong. I know we just met under peculiar circumstances, but you should know I will not have anyone telling me what I can and cannot do. The car is yours. If you choose, you can drive it off a bridge or donate it to an orphanage. Or here's an even crazier idea: use it for the purpose it was purchased for. Whatever you choose to do with it, know that you will leave here with that vehicle."

"And if I don't?" *I know…this stubborn Ashanti side in me is urging this silly debate. But neither will I allow some rich dude to dictate to me what I can and cannot do.*

His laughter fills the room, but it's not a 'hahaha' laugh; it's more of a 'you're-fucking-with-me-and-you-don't-know-who-you-are-dealing-with' kind of laughter. He continues. "If you decide to leave this vehicle here because your conscience dictates that you should, then I will have no choice but to show you what I can afford. Call it arrogance or madness, but you will not tell me how to spend my money. Therefore, I will purchase more than enough Range Rovers to fill every parking space within a mile radius of your home and, Ms. Frimpong, that will only be the beginning for me…I will start in your neighborhood and perhaps by the end of the week cover the entire state of New York. And the longer the vehicle stays here, the more I will buy and I will make sure that your neighbors and community know that these are your vehicles occupying the streets of New York. Because no one likes a show off and I'm sure you really wouldn't want the unnecessary attention."

Max and Penny move away from Julius and huddle in a corner by the window. *Fuck, is this that serious? This is clearly not going the way I rehearsed it this morning.*

"I have an idea," Penny says. She steps forward and crosses the invisible line toward my side of the room. Her right arm capes over my shoulder drawing me closer to her. "Ms. Freemong—"

"Vida is fine," I interject.

She continues. "Vida is a writer and she can help you with your project."

"What? No!" This time it is Vincent's large voice that fills the room.

She ignores Vincent and continues. "Well, Max and I discovered she has written for several publications." I knew Max was up to something. He carried his tablet close to his chest and took side-glances at me. He probably Googled me and found the articles I wrote for Face2Face Africa and of course my abandoned blog. "We can use the car as part of the advance for writing the book, and I'm sure we can come up with something that will make all of us happy."

Vincent's face looks unchanged and Julius turns to speak to him in Italian.

"Are you a writer, Ms. Frimpong?" Julius asks me.

"Yes," I say with certainty. My blog and online magazine contributions were a collection of the sexiest F-M-Ps and latest Ankara fashions. But my untitled novel, which I hope to publish one day, is still stored on my desktop computer.

"What happened to Ms. Guere?" Vincent asks.

Penny's face drops. I think she is surprised by Vincent's question. "She is good, but I think that Ms.—I mean Vida—has helped us so much. A new car is not enough to thank her. Don't you think, babe?" She crosses the invisible line again and aligns herself underneath Julius's chin. She pets him gently, soothing the roar that he unleashed moments ago. She continues her feminine draw by placing locks of hair behind his ear. "…And we can trust her discretion. She could have gone to the police or even the media, but look: she's returning the car…" She pauses and looks at me. "…again. Well, she can be trusted, can't she?"

Penny continues gentle strokes across his hair. Julius appears as though he is contemplating the idea. Max smiles gently in agreement. But Vincent stares me down like a truant toddler.

"I am looking for a ghostwriter, but I will take your experience under consideration," Julius says finally.

"Wait. I don't—" I say until Penny places a finger over her lips. Her look of disdain cues me to shut up.

But I don't know Italian and Portuguese. Those are the words pressing to come out. *Wait, really? He doesn't think this is absurd.* A few articles about shoes and clothes don't qualify me as a ghostwriter. *And what exactly am I agreeing to? Could I really do this? Why did Penny drag me into this web? Ah yes, Ms. Guere. Can't fault Penny for keeping her camp THOT-proof. Surely there are more qualified people to do this assignment. Wait! Wait! Vida, why are you tearing yourself down? You* are *a writer. You can do this.* I feel the weight of Abla's words sitting on my shoulders. Everything happens for a reason and maybe this is the catalyst I need to light the fire on my writing career. *But what about the work, the kids? Yes, the kids.* "What about the time?" I ask.

"We can work that out. We are moving from here to Queens. Julius will make it work," Penny says. Julius is quiet, but the fact that he is letting Penny make arrangements tells me that he may be in agreement.

"We will be in touch, Ms. Frimpong. Have a good day," Julius says.

"Okay, well, have a nice day everyone," I say.

Before I exit the room, Julius's voice stops me again. "Ms. Frimpong, are you forgetting something?"

Max gestures to the keys that I dropped on the table a few minutes ago.

I chuckle but still no one is laughing. "Oh yeah. Thanks."

CHAPTER 8

Abla can be persuasive. It was just a week ago that I told her about Julius's offer to be his ghostwriter. And now here we are blocks away from the Summit Hotel for an actual interview.

"I can't believe you convinced me to go through with this," I sigh. Daniel is driving us to the hotel and he decides to take 2nd Avenue downtown instead of the FDR in morning rush hour. I'm not sure which is worse, but thank goodness we are still making good time.

"Do you know how lucky you are? Not because yur my sista. Look at da chances of life you get. Crashin' a billionairez car." Abla fumbles through her bag and rereads the Google search on Julius Gallo, something I never bothered to do. I check my phone for any missed calls.

"Julius Gallo," she reads. "Inventor, businezman and feelanthropist.—Don't include da word disability in dis description. Dis billionaire created several inventions dat has made people wif visual impairments' lives more assessible. But dat iz not hiz claim to hiz fortune. Hiz technology firm Abilities Stimulation Engineering Management haz developed state of da art security systems for government agencies around da world. Under hiz enterportfolio: several luxurious hotels around da world, includin' da flagship Summit Hotel in New York City. Mr. Gallo has teamed up wit German designers to make buyin' and sharin' music possible witin seconds."

As Abla continues to flood my ears with her research on Julius Gallo, my thoughts are still about Mensah. He left me a message early this morning. I check his WhatsApp profile to see the last time he logged on: 6:32 a.m. The profile picture hasn't changed. His business logo of the number three and the words Three Sonz Construction Company. I remember when he told me that he was building a legacy for his sons to follow.

"Dis man has loads of money and here we are. Do you know wat da Ghanaians will say when dey hear dat we are filtee rich now? Dank you, Jesus," Abla says. She raises her head and arms to the roof of the car. I smile in agreement but I'm not focused; Mensah's message replays in my head.

"I know we keep missing each other, but I promise to be home soon. How are you feeling? Did you get the car fixed? Let me know if I should look into buying you another one. Work is hectic, busy and really good. And it's just a matter of time when I can delegate the work to someone else. Kakra sent me the link to the video of the soccer match they won last week. You know how I feel about videos on social media. But I'm proud he is doing well. The scouts will come looking for him soon. He definitely takes after his mother. The boys…all of them are growing up so nicely. I will try to call you before you leave for work tomorrow."

"Are you lissenin' to me?" Abla's voice brings me back to my present situation. "You need presidendation." She means representation, but I allow her to continue her rant without correcting her. "And you need to show you have big people followin' you. If you go deer just by yurself wit dis piece of papa, dey will dink you are some small girl." She waves the contract that Julius's attorney mailed me. I made some amendments including to work weekend nights and maybe during the week when my schedule permits. Under Abla's advisement, I asked for compensation for my 'big people' following me. Really nothing more than family disguised as professionals. "Do you remember da plan?" Her voice is eager and firm.

"I think so…"

She emits a hard snarl. It's more of a long sucking of the teeth, but that sounds takes years of dedicated practice. Abla flexes it readily and naturally. It seems foolish the more I think about it. It is Abla's idea to have 'big people' follow me to this meeting. It looks more professional, she quips. Abla is still influenced by how Africans carry themselves. In Africa, ministers and higher elected officials are accompanied by entourages of security, counselors and secretaries. She says it shows status and level of importance.

"Lissen, letz go over dis again before you embarrass us all. I'm yur PR manaja. Daniel iz yur driver-slash-security and Chin iz yur secretary."

I am not convinced using Daniel is a good idea. He is such a momma's boy. Nearly forty and still lives at home with Auntie Cece. I remember when we were younger and he used to rat me out every time I snuck into my room to read comic books. He couldn't keep a secret even if his lips were sewn together. I can imagine him telling Auntie Cece everything when he gets the chance. *But then again the only family he fears besides his mother is Abla. He may be able to keep this secret a little longer than usual.* "Don't you think it's too much of an entourage?" I say.

"Kwai," she says in her rich Ghanaian accent. This usually means 'Are you joking?' or 'I can't believe you said that.' "You no sabe…because you don't know how to deal wif wealtee people. Iz a good ding dat I saw da contract before you mailed it back. Deer waz so many dings you left out."

"And where did you learn to draft contracts?" I ask.

"Huh, you need to start watchin' Judge Judy. You can learn a lot from her."

"And you know billionaires?" I say with sarcasm.

"Yes. Mr. and Mrs. Lindsey," she says unapologetically. Mr. Lindsey was a retired surgeon and Abla was Mr. Lindsey's personal care attendant for three years. Mrs. Lindsey became wealthy after Mr. Lindsey passed away, which afforded her to hire Abla full-time as a BFF. Abla enjoys an advanced annual salary, paid vacation and European excursions. I am not confident that they qualify as billionaires, but they are as close as we get to wealthy people. "Eeeehhh, trust yur big sista. Leave da talkin' to me."

We finally reach the lounge of the hotel. And we are sitting in the same secluded spot I sat in a week ago. Daniel examines the surrounding decor. Despite the lavish lifestyle Abla has become accustomed to, she is in complete awe sitting in the hotel lobby. "He iz filtee…very filtee rich," she whispers to me.

It's been only ten minutes, but it feels like we've been here for almost an hour. The carpet is heavily worn by my pacing back and forth. A nearby mirror gives me a full body reflection. The navy pinstripe blue suit has some creases around my thighs. I try to smooth some of the creases down. My hair edges look rough and I use the palm of my hands to flatten around the crown and sweep my hair into a tighter bun. My memory brings me back to Ms. Guere in her European sophistication. I loosen another button on my crisp white shirt, revealing the length of my pearl necklace, a gift from Mensah six Christmases ago.

"Yaa!" Abla gives me a quiet shout to grab my attention. While walking back, I take full notice of Abla's ensemble. Bubblegum patent F-M-Ps. They look like Monika Chiangs. Her short hot pink dress reveals toned legs. Gold ankle bracelets embellish each leg.

"I told you to wear da white bustier under dis suit jacket. You need to show some cleavage," Abla says.

"I need to look professional," I quip.

"You look like an immigration offisa," she says coldly. "You need somedin' sexy. You see wat I am wearin'."

"Yes, everyone sees what you are wearing." Her bright dress is a sure contrast from the neutral browns, oranges and cream that decorate the Summit lobby. "You decided to let the 'puppies' out this morning." Her dress is not only short, it leaves nothing to the imagination.

Abla has several theories on male behavior. She believes heterosexual men are more receptive to good-looking, sexy women. The less you wear, the more you get. She has been right many times, but Julius Gallo is going to be the exception.

"Derez notin' wrong wit cleavage," she says.

"You do remember he is blind?" I say.

"Eyez...no eyez...a man knows when a pretty woman iz in hiz presence. It takes more dan looks to get wat you want. Jus' follow my lead."

"Is that another Ablaism?" I say.

Daniel is still taking inventory of every item in the lobby. He does two things with a passion: go to the gym and talk about making money. *Is Daniel's presence really necessary? What writer travels with a security guard? Not to mention, our cousin suffers from diarrhea of the mouth.* "What was the reason for bringing him again?" I whisper to Abla.

"He is the security and body guard," she says with a straight face.

"How many writers walk around with a bodyguard, especially a beginner like me? J.K. Rowling, Stephen King and Chimamadan Ngozi Adichie don't have bodyguards," I say.

"Ahhh, Yaa. Dat iz yur problem. You are not dem and we have to set da tone of wat we expect. And so wat if yur a beginna? Nobody can do wat you can do. So my sista, I beg ooooh, stop sayin' dat."

It's that kind of pep talk that convinced me to take on this project. It's empowering. I nod my head in agreement. "You're right, Abla." She squeezes my hand reassuringly.

My attention is back on Daniel and I observe him in his new role assigned by Abla. He is wearing a suit for once. But on display is a pawn dealer's dream: several layers of necklaces, gold bracelets on both wrists and every finger decorated with various-sized rings.

"*Eh, Vida. Sika wo ha. Eh eh eh*…this must cost thousands of dollars," Daniel says. His eyes are large with excitement as though he discovered the end of the rainbow. He holds the vase above his head for more scrutiny. "This is gold," he says. He stretches his hand to show Abla and accidentally drops the vase but the carpet provides a soft rescue.

"Eh, Daniel, we haven't signed da contract yet. I beg ooooh…we can't cover deezs expenses. Please don't put us in da negative." He places the vase back on the table. "Where iz dis girl now?" Abla says impatiently.

"Who?" I ask Abla.

"Chin."

"What is her role again?" I ask.

"Aaaah…are you lissenin' to me when I talk?" Abla asks.

"On and off, but tell me again. I will get it straight now."

"I told you, I'm yur PR manaja. Daniel handles yur security and Chin iz yur assistant."

"Are you sure this is a good idea?"

"Of course." She walks to the entrance and then back again. "Okay, if Chin doesn't show up, I will tell dem dat she iz busy wit one of yur clients. Don't dink too much. It iz written. You got da job already. Let me talk pricin'," Abla says.

"Ms. Frimpong?" Mr. Hollanderman greets me.

"Yes." I stand up.

"Mr. Gallo is ready to see you now. Please follow me."

We walk down past the lobby elevators into another hallway. Someone is yelling my name. "Vida!…Vida…!" It's Chin. She barely catches her breath.

"Is she with you?" Mr. Hollanderman asks.

No. Her hair looks disheveled and she looks like she's been running for her life. "Yes," I finally say.

"Gurl, you lucky. We were about to leave you. I said ten a.m.…iz now ten dirty. You know deezs rich folks don't play wit deer time," Abla says.

"I'm sorry. I was feeling nauseous coming off the train," Chin says.

Abla draws close and scans her face. "Yur pregnant," Abla says. I knew it already from my conversations with Trudy, but Abla detects it just by giving her a once over. Chin nods her head and opens her jacket to reveal what looks like a five-month pregnancy. "Hmmmm…you see, I told you. You kept sayin' it waz yur fibroids. We'll talk lata. Dey are waitin' for us upstairs," Abla says.

We arrive to his suite. Just as I remembered it. Large tiled floors. A round table in the center of the room with a large floral arrangement. Max and Penny are seated in the sofa. Julius is seated in the single armchair with his back to the huge skyline. Vincent announces our presence. Max and Julius stand to greet us.

"Good morning, Ms. Frimpong. I see you've brought company." *If you really saw, you would see this is a joke.* We look oddly coordinated and a bit over the top for this interview. Julius extends his hand in front of himself.

"Yes," I say and shake his hand. "I came with my PR manager and my assistant and…" I look at Daniel and freeze.

"Daniel iz our security," Abla quickly rescues me.

"Security?" Gallo asks. His eyebrows raise.

"Yes, he travels with us during negotiations. Hello, I'm Rosemary Abla Da'Cruz, Ms. Frimpong's manager." She has disguised her accent with an orchestrated British accent. He extends his hand and Abla holds it with both hands. This is the first time I've heard Abla use Jesus's surname.

"I see," he says again.

"And this is Ms. Jamila Chin, our assistant."

Chin is still scanning the room and taking in the atmosphere. "Wow…lawd, cheese and bread," she says softly.

"Pardon me, I didn't hear what you said," Julius says.

"Oh, nothing. We are admiring de aesthetically beautiful home," Abla says. She is trying too hard to cover her accent.

"I can't take the credit, but I must thank the creative people who work for me. Please, let's sit and talk." He gestures us into the large living space. He looks handsome today without the blood and near-death face. He is dressed in a light tan suit and white shirt. His hair is neatly combed back and the stitches over his eye are barely noticeable.

An elderly lady in a Summit uniform enters the room with beverages, a fruit tray and cheese. "We have some refreshments, please feel free," Max says.

"I might have spoken in haste when I told you that I would think about you working for me," Julius says.

"Oh, are you having second thoughts?" I ask.

"Not second thoughts per se. However, I do feel the need to be acquainted with you a little bit more before I feel confident you can do what is requested. This level of assignment requires a bit of trust and discretion."

"You don't have to worry about a thing, Mr. Gallo. Vida is trustworthy and a fantastic writer. Dat iz all dat she eva wanted to do." Abla tempers her enthusiasm and returns to her orchestrated accent. "She is loyal, hardworking, dedicated and honest. She's also a quick learner. There is nothing that Vida sets her mind to that she doesn't accomplish. Whatever assignment you give her she will be able to do it. To tell you the truth, Mr. Gallo, you will never meet anyone like her."

Wow. Abla's words still me. Our relationship has grown stronger over the years, especially after the birth of Pancake.

Rosemary Abla Frimpong and I are two sisters with different experiences in life. Abla was six years old when my parents left to come to America. They left Abla behind to stay in school. Mommy's older sister Auntie Awo raised Abla. When Abla was still in Ghana, I remember the number of late night calls from Auntie Awo. Auntie cried over the phone one evening and told Mommy they had to bring Abla to America. Whenever the calls from Ghana came, it was primarily about Abla. The conversations consisted of long pauses and sighs. Auntie would say, "Abla hmmmm" or "ehhh…Abla…" or "ehh ehhh…hmmmm Abla," expressions that carried more weight of seriousness than words found in the dictionary. It wasn't until she came to America that I got to know just why Auntie Awo was so anxious to get rid of Abla. Auntie Awo's bar in Community One was a popular location in Tema. Abla tended to the bar on weekends washing dishes and cooking food. But the revenue coming into the bar wasn't just from selling drinks. It turned out Abla rented rooms in the back of Auntie

Awo's bar for men to have sex with the local girls. A big brawl broke out one night uncovering Abla's small entrepreneurial business.

How ironic that my parents named her Rosemary when all she did was give them hell. And I couldn't wait to finally meet her.

"We have some references for you to call also," Abla continues to speak on my behalf.

"I see," Julius says. So far this meeting is making me feel a bit uncomfortable. Now there is silence. Julius speaks after a long pause. "I'm sorry, your name again?"

"Oh. I'm Rosemary Abla Da'Cruz, Ms. Frimpong's PR manager."

"Okay, Ms. Da'Cruz, is your client fluent in Italian or Portuguese?"

"No," I say. I recall telling him the night I met him that I didn't know Italian, but Abla doesn't let that deter her from answering the way she sees fit.

"Yes," Abla says confidently.

"No I'm not." I stare down Abla, but she returns with her own African stare-down.

Julius utters something in Italian and Vincent turns and looks at me. *They are talking about me.*

"It's been a while since she's spoken it. Once she starts hearing it again, it will all come back to her," Abla retorts.

"I see," he says again. *What is it with these two-word responses?*

"What college did you attend, Ms. Frimpong?"

"I graduated from City College with a major in English literature," I say.

"Is that Ivy League, babe?" Penny says. She rises up to sit on the armrest of Julius's chair.

"No, not by any means," Julius says.

"Is that one of those online colleges?" Penny asks.

"It is a four-year college located in Harlem and home to the greatest number of Nobel Prize winners and, just like many colleges, they do offer courses online," I say defensively.

"English literature you say?" Julius asks.

"Yes," I say firmly.

"Are you familiar with Voltaire, Elliot, Adams, Shakespeare, James and so forth?"

"Yes." *Where is this line of questioning going?*

He lets out a grim chuckle. "'Those who can make you believe absurdities can make you commit atrocities…'" The room is silent. "That was Voltaire," he says. Penny chuckles and walks to the bar for a drink.

"Vida knows that. It's an interesting quote," Abla says. Daniel and Chin shift in their seats with the sting in the atmosphere.

"Daniel? Or is it Mr. Daniel?" Julius says.

"You can call me Oteng. My friends call me Oteng." Abla and I cut our eyes at him.

"Mr. Daniel is fine," Abla interjects. She gives Daniel a hard squint that translates to 'You get in line or feel the back of my hand across your cheek.' This ends his jovial disposition.

"How long have you been a security guard?" Julius says.

"About ten years now, but it's kinda on and off. You know, whenever my cousin needs me. I'm there for her. I work nights at JFK airport, so I'm pretty much free during the day.

"Oh, so you don't work full-time as Ms. Frimpong's security guard?"

"Oh, no. Security full-time for what? I mean, she's not as rich as this." He extends his arms to indicate the spaciousness of the room. "But I am there for her if she needs me, you know. You can't give small money chance. This is America and we have to hustle to make it." *Oh, Daniel and his euphemisms.*

"I see," Julius says. I wish he could see my eyes rolling.

"What Mr. Daniel means is that we not using his services as much. You know, Ms. Frimpong's clients work online. Having full-time security may not be needed right away, but once we start your project, this can open up so many opportunities." Abla says.

"I honestly don't see how your client has the time to juggle all these responsibilities with a family and a full-time job," Julius says.

"Well, that is where Ms. Chin comes in. She keeps us organized."

"Yep," Chin says as she swallows another tea biscuit. "Mi gurl knows mi got her. Wat eva she needs." Chin's patois is showing up at the wrong time. Abla gives her the same squinted-eye she gave Daniel. Chin puts the last piece of biscuit in her mouth and slides back in her seat. My neck buckles into my chest. I don't have the power to lift my head up. *Where is a fire drill when you need one?*

"Ms. Chin is very good in organization," Abla says.

"And what are you good at, Ms. Frimpong? Are you good at writing?" Julius says.

"Of course she—"

"I was talking to Ms. Frimpong. I haven't heard much from your writer." Julius's voice is loud and stern. *I don't like it.*

"I believe we discussed my writing capabilities a few days ago before you called this meeting," I say. Penny hands him a drink and sits on the arm of the chair.

"Please refresh my memory, Ms. Frimpong, because what I am hearing so far does not impress me."

"If I may speak, Mr. Gallo. I have the revised contract right here," Max says. He pulls out the contract from a manila folder and stands up to speak.

"To clarify, Ms. Da'Cruz has requested a finder's fee of twenty thousand dollars cash up front before any work commences. And your security team will need a flat rate of one thousand dollars for each social event that Ms. Frimpong would have to attend with you as part of the research. There is some language regarding literary credits, rights protection and insurance that needs to be cleared up. In case there is another accident involved, Ms. Frimpong will need to….you know, beef up her insurance. She has three children that need their mother."

Max smiles. It is not a comforting smile, but something malicious. He continues. "Your total compensation for the assignment is one thousand dollars per day and if weeknights are required, an additional five hundred dollars for night differential."

Fuck, Abla! I hadn't read Abla's revised contract. So busy having Mensah moments consume my life. So busy tracking when he is online, and who he is talking to and where he is. So busy that I can't even do the basic thing for myself and review a contract. Max scans the document and then turns the page. *Shit, two pages. What could she possibly include in two pages?* "Ah, yes. As you so eloquently included in the contract…Extra expenses such as meals, travel, child care and hotel accommodations to be covered by Julius Gallo."

This calls not only for the African stare-down but the shameful ear-tugging. Abla quickly moves to the edge of her seat farther away from my grasp. She doesn't look in my direction but stares blankly around avoiding any eye contact with me. Daniel shakes his head in disgust and Chin drinks more bottled water.

"Is that all, Max...?" Julius says.

"Yes, sir. The other points were a bit ambiguous for me to draw inferences from."

"Do you have anything to add, Ms. Frimpong?" Julius says.

Okay, Vida, don't sink with the ship. "What do you want me to tell you that is different from what we spoke about last week?" I say.

"It appears to me that you may be underqualified to do this assignment. I am looking for someone with more experience and perhaps not such a complicated personal staff. I need discretion in this assignment, not a circus show," he says.

Ouch, that was harsh. Stay focused, Vida. "I may not be widely known or have written bestsellers, but those writers started from somewhere. This opportunity was brought to my attention and I think it would benefit us both greatly."

"A career in writing? Writing a few blog posts and three articles doesn't qualify you as a writer, Ms. Frimpong. As for your entourage, traveling with a concert of people doesn't make you important, no more than me wearing excessive jewelry makes me look rich."

Daniel must feel the comment is aimed at him. He examines the jewelry on his fingers and then waves his hand back and forth in the air toward Julius's direction.

"Don't do that! I am not a dog. If you need my attention...address me," he says brashly. Daniel retreats into the chair. Julius continues. "The fact is the fact. It doesn't change just because you can't face it, Ms. Frimpong." *So what is the point? Did he invite me here just to insult me to my face? These are issues he was aware of.* The air is still stinging with intimidation from the rich blind man in the tan suit who has silenced everyone. *But I won't be bullied by him.*

"Excuse me?" I say.

"Believe me, Ms. Frimpong, you are excused. This is a waste of my valuable time and this arrangement that you've concocted is not in my best interest. And as I stated earlier, don't attempt to bring the car back. You can do with it whatever you like. Have a good day, Ms. Frimpong."

"Mr. Gallo, did we upset you in any way? It wasn't our intention. I know my—" Abla catches herself before blowing her cover "—I know Ms. Frimpong can—"

"Do you know you are an ass?" It isn't how I wanted to address him. But the woman in me champions me on, giving me the needed words.

"Pardon me?" he says. His face looks baffled, but he grins slightly.

"You are a big asshole," I say. *Yeah, go on Vida, give it to him.*

"You can't talk to my babe like that. Who you think you are?" Penny says. She stands up to meet me eye-to-eye. She seems already intoxicated.

"Oh, Ms. Frimpong…I would have thought you would be more original. Tell me something I don't already know," he says. His grin is a bit wider as he sips his drink. My reflection in the window behind him shows my lips curled up and my brows furrowing.

"Yaa," Abla calls from behind me. Maybe it's PMS kicking in, but I feel a rush of adrenaline. I move closer to Julius. He tilts his head upwards and that smile appears again. He rubs his fingers on his lips.

"Thank you for this rather entertaining visit. I think we are done here," he says.

"Okay. I think it's time for us to go," Abla says. Daniel and Chin stand up. "Yaa," Abla calls me again, but I don't want to turn and look at her. I really have more to tell him. He had no intention of giving me this assignment. He just wants what he wants—for me to take the car and shut up. And now he wants to laugh at my capabilities. The fact that I've only written a few articles and blogs. The fact that I didn't go to an Ivy League school like him. And, yes, I have a group of misfits for family and friends, but their hearts are in a good place. The fact that they all came here to support a crazy lie is one thing, but it's entirely another to be shamed and ridiculed.

Penny doesn't move. Vincent walks closer, but Julius raises his hand and Vincent stops.

"Forget about your fancy clothes, your cars, your looks, your British accent, your entourage, your manners and your arrogant personality. At the end of the day, it is obvious, Mr. Gallo, that there is something that money can't buy you. Asshole!" *He messed with the wrong African chick.* His face, once luminous, is now salmon in color. His lips curl downward and press hard against each other. I struck a nerve with him. *Good. He can stew on that in his billion-dollar head.*

"Now I'm ready," I say. Abla takes hold of my hand and squeezes it. We follow behind Daniel and Chin.

Chapter 9

No new messages, but I press the button anyway. I just want to hear his voice again, especially the way he says my name. "Yaaaaa." I stop and play it again. "Yaaaaa." If he only knew that I replay his messages over and over again like an Adele CD. His throaty voice rolls my name off his tongue. *Dinner needs to be prepared and I'm here like a lovesick teenager.* I spot a box of spaghetti on the shelf and on another shelf a bottle of Prego spaghetti sauce. There's leftover hamburger meat in the freezer.

Panin is tapping on the table again. *Is that Kakra's voice I hear singing? They know better.* I yell out from the kitchen. "Your homework must be done for there to be singing and drumming." Now silence. The meat sautés in the pot and I fill another pot with cold water and a pinch of salt. *There it is again.* Faint tapping on the table. *These boys are really testing me.* I march out of the kitchen and enter the dining room. Panin has arranged a makeshift drum set with his schoolbooks and dinner plates on the table. He is using his ruler and pencils to drum, making music with this unusual arrangement. He stands up and hits the ruler harder against the books. He moves toward the wall cabinet and taps the pencil. Kakra looks at me and shrugs his shoulders.

"He just started, Mommy," he says. Kakra rests his hands on my shoulder. "Mommy, he is in his zone again. We might as well just join him." Kakra begins to sing. Both of them could make a nice duo. I signal Kakra to stop, but Panin continues.

"Panin, honey, have you finished your homework?" No response. Panin doesn't speak. His usual yes or no response consists of a head nod or pivoting his neck side to side. When he is in his zone, he is in total obliviousness to his surroundings. It has taken me all his life to decode his behavior. Something is prompting this performance and he has to express it through his drumming.

Panin stopped talking at three and music has been our saving grace. I've come to associate different types of drumming to mean different things. If he starts drumming out of the clear blue, it is because something is bothering him. If he taps lightly on furniture, it is because he is studying a particular song or beat. If he wakes up in the middle of the night restless, something out of his routine is happening.

The first time I saw the word autism, I thought the doctor misspelled the word Austin. "He has Austin like Austin, Texas?" I asked Dr. Lock when we came for our follow-up visit.

"No, Mrs. Asare, it's autism with an 'sm' at the end."

"Why does he have it? What do I do to get rid of it?"

"I've been reading the reports from the psychologist and I am sure she has disclosed her findings. In many cases, parents start to notice something different about their child around eighteen months."

"But he's three and he was fine a couple of months ago. He was laughing and talking. Now he doesn't want to talk or even look at me. That doesn't make any sense."

"I know your worries, Mrs. Asare. There is a lot of literature out there now and early intervention is the key. We know his condition and he will need therapy."

"Will it go away?"

"It's a condition and it won't go away, but he will be able to live an independent life with early intervention. There have been case studies where children grow to finish college and live successful lives. But every case is different. The key is to start him in early intervention now."

I couldn't believe it. And neither could Mensah.

"This is total bullshit. There is nothing wrong with my son," he said.

"Mr. Asare, I know this may be difficult to accept. But again, the key is to get him the resources as soon as possible," Dr. Lock said.

"We don't have this in Ghana. I have twin sons. So one has it and one doesn't. How is that possible?"

"Well, that is the interesting part, Mr. Asare. Most studies have pointed to it beginning before birth. There are a few that have made claims that autism occurs after birth and some claim it is a reaction to vaccination. It is very hard to tell the source, but like I've said, we need to take proactive measures now."

"There is nothing wrong with my son. He doesn't have that aw-ism or aw-whatever. My son is fine. Every child grows up differently. No one will tell him he can or cannot do anything," Mensah said.

Over the course of that year, we had three pediatricians and the diagnoses were all the same. It wasn't until he was six years old that Mensah accepted the fact that Panin was not growing up the same way as Kakra. He tried everything, including asking an herbalist in Ghana to make a tonic for Panin to drink. Every day he prayed over him and massaged anointing oil over his head.

I witnessed many nights of Mensah crying over him. I heard him whispering, "...Just talk. I know you can."

This is our fate. I have to make the best of it. Panin communicates nonverbally, usually pointing to objects he wants or scribbling notes. He becomes frustrated at times when he can't express himself, bursting into a deluge of tears and severe tantrums.

School was my biggest challenge—trying to convince teachers and staff that he should attend the same school as Kakra. They wanted a specialized school for him, but when I forced the administration to test him before making a decision, they concluded what Mensah and I knew. He is more than capable of doing the work. He even excels. So communication is limited to a handheld tablet that he writes his responses on. It is expensive, the school administrators say, and a tiresome fight so that he can sit amongst a class that is considered normal.

At first, when communication was tough for him, it resulted in tantrums and sudden outbursts. We soon discovered that music soothes him. So drumming on cans of vegetables and tabletops brings instant joy and relief.

When Panin is happy, he smiles and maybe offers a chuckle. Sadness brings about a squeezed face, fear and frustration. Routine is paramount. Organization and meticulous detail show in everything he does. Panin doesn't share a love for clothes like his brother, but everything he owns is color-coordinated and neatly in place inside his closet. I've used this organization skill to my advantage. He loves to organize my shoe closet. I must admit, it's been so much easier being able to select a pair of shoes instead of rummaging through the floor of my closet. His bed would make any army sergeant proud. But when

Panin doesn't want to do something, there is nothing you can do to convince him otherwise. That isn't autism, that is the stubbornness he inherited from Mensah and maybe a little bit from me.

He sits still and I finally grab the pencils and move the plates away. "Panin, you know the rules. No music until all homework is done." He rarely gives me eye contact, but now he is intentionally ignoring me. He takes another pencil from his book bag and recommences drumming. "If you continue, you will go straight to your room." I've discovered that this is really no punishment at all. Panin can easily entertain himself alone in his room for hours. I give him the African stare-down and he tries to make himself small by sinking his head into his chest. He doesn't like when I am upset with him. When I am mad, he will sit in the corner and watch me, looking for a sign to tell him that I'm okay. Usually a smile or laughter will comfort him.

"I'm going to count to three, and if I don't see homework on this table…" He pulls papers out from his book bag. Math homework complete. I glance at it quickly. He is doing exceptionally well in math. I haven't seen less than ninety percent on a quiz or test yet. He hands me another sheet of paper. His spelling and vocabulary homework is also complete. Nothing needs correction.

"You still have to read for a half an hour and include it in your reading journal." He opens his reading journal and shows me *The Diary of a Wimpy Kid* on the log for today. *I have nothing to fuel the fire.* "Alright, just fifteen minutes more and then dinner time." Kakra is excited and starts dancing. "Slow down, happy feet. What about your homework?"

"Can't I just copy his assignment and hand it in?" Kakra says.

"And why do you think that would be okay?"

"Well, we're twins and we think alike. So it's just a waste of time for me to do the same assignment."

"You really should be ashamed to even argue that out loud."

"Whaaat?"

If there was a campaign of bare minimum homework, Kakra would be the poster child. Kakra loves soccer, music and clothing. Traits he acquired from Mensah. He is an okay student. But with added pressure from a temperamental mother, he could be an excellent student. Just like Panin, Kakra has musical inclinations. I remember the first time I saw the twins in total unison. Panin was watching television and the Fresh Beat Band song came on. Kakra began to sing and without hesitation Panin walked into the kitchen and dragged out one of my cooking pots. I watched him as he placed it on floor and he beat the pot with his hands. They were happy and I cheered them on.

I can see five years from now that I will have to build a wire fence around the house to keep the girls away. He definitely acquired his father's friendliness and mannerisms. Always giving compliments to me and Abla. He always praises me when I coordinate my clothes to his liking and is observant when I wear my hair in different styles. If there is anything that he acquired from me, it would be the love for soccer. Just like me at his age, he is gaining recognition as a star athlete. I've told him stories of my heyday with the Sassi Strikers. But I want him to be better than me. I want him to continue. When Kakra asked me why I never made it to the pros, I told him that God wanted me to bring him and his brothers into the world. That made him happy to hear. *I wonder what would have happened to my life if I had never met Mensah, but I could never imagine a life without these boys.*

"Mommy, doorbell!" Kakra yells out. *It's 7:30.* "Mommy!" he yells again.

Looking through the partial glass door, the figure outside is blurry. "Who is it?" I ask.

"Good evening, Ms. Frimpong. It's Julius Gallo."

"Julius Gallo?" I say softly. *What does he want?* I stand back. *Maybe he's here to curse me out for insulting him. That was four days ago. He can't still be mad.*

He reads my mind. "I assure you that I am not here for any confrontation. I just really need a moment of your time."

"Kakra, go and check on MJ for me," I say. My eyes search around the hallway and staircase. The house looks decent. MJ's shoes are on the step and I grab them quickly and throw them in the hallway cubby. I open the door. Julius is dressed in a long black wool coat and a hat. He is wearing tinted glasses. He looks exceptionally handsome, for an asshole.

"Mr. Gallo." My body blocks the doorway, waiting for an explanation for his visit.

"Excuse the intrusion. I think face-to-face communication is always best. May I come in?" he says. My body turns sideways allowing him entry to pass me.

"Okay, come in," I say.

"I smell dinner." He exhales deeply.

"Spaghetti. You are welcome to join us." *No, not really. Just trying to be courteous in front of Panin.*

"No, thank you. I don't want to monopolize too much of your time. My apologies for not calling before—"

Kakra's footsteps pound the staircase in urgency. "Mommy, Mommy. It's bad up there. MJ did number two. But he didn't make it to the toilet." His alarmed voice breaks our uncomfortable dialogue.

"Please give me a second," I say. Two steps at a time, I move swiftly upstairs. MJ is rolled into a ball on the bathroom floor. "What happened, MJ?"

"It was coming too fast and…and…and…I couldn't do the buckle…" He points to the buckle on his jeans. I take off his clothes and wipe him down with baby wipes and order him to lie down on the bed until I can return and give him a bath.

"Mommy, who is the man downstairs?" Kakra says.

"Oh, shit." *That asshole downstairs.*

"Oooh, Mommy, you said a bad word," Kakra says. I shrug indifferently and wash my hands. "Watch your brother, Kakra. I will be back."

I jog to the bottom of the stairs and Julius is standing right where I left him.

"Sorry, my son had a bit of an emergency."

"Understandable. You have your hands full with three boys."

Panin is drumming again and Julius turns his head in the direction of the sound. "That's my son Panin sitting in the dining room." I point to the dining room forgetting his limitation.

"He must be the quiet one."

"Can I get you a glass of water, juice or tea?"

"No, that is quite all right. I have imposed on your time as is. I just want to give this to you." He pulls out the contract.

"The contract?"

"Well, this brings me back to the reason I am here. I signed the contract. I've included some stipulations of my own. But everything you have asked for, I've conceded to. I believe weekend nights work best for you and that is also fine with me. I emailed you my house address in Queens and the passcodes. Alice will be there to assist you. I travel quite frequently, so you can reach me by phone or email, but no worries, you can count on Alice for everything. Do you have any questions for me now?"

"Wait a minute...what made you change your mind? I didn't think a City College degree was good enough for you."

"I never said that, Ms. Frimpong..." He sighs. "Please accept my apology. At times...well...I can be..."

"An ass."

"Yes, and on some days a real jackass. It wasn't my intention to degrade you or question your experience as a writer. I don't like people taking advantage of me, that's all. But I do appreciate your discretion. Two weeks ago, you had every right to call the police or showcase the events on social media. You didn't. That says a lot. I value that."

"You never fully disclosed the writing assignment. Is it a memoir, autobiography, scientific notes or what?" I ask.

"I guess you can say a little bit of everything. But the end result would be a finished memoir."

"So you want me to write your memoir?"

"Ms. Frimpong, I have over sixty journals in my library. I am not just looking for a writer to transcribe pages of thoughts. It will probably take a couple of months before you can really know where to begin with me. The hardest part for anyone I suppose is seeing who they truly are."

"Does it matter how the world sees you? I mean, what if you don't like what I write?"

"Quite simple. I won't print it. I see you as someone who likes to be true to herself. You tell it the way you see it and not many people can do that."

Four days ago I swear he didn't think I was good enough to write directions, now he thinks I'm Maya Angelou. "Fair enough," I say.

"Do we have a deal?" He extends his hand. *Hmmm, should you do this, Vida?* The woman in me champions me on. *You need this. Take your mind off of Mensah.. Plus, this will spark the fuel you need to write again.*

"Do you want my hand to fall off?" He has a spot-on imitation of Billy Dee Williams' voice in *Lady Sings the Blues*, a classic movie that I've watched several times with Abla.

"Do you watch…I mean listen…to a lot of movies?"

"Yes…I watch and listen to a lot of movies," he says a matter-of-factly.

I take his hand. "Deal, Mr. Gallo. I can start tomorrow evening."

"Great. I have a benefit concert in the evening. Alice can direct you to everything you need."

"So wait, I'm going to be there by myself? You trust me alone in your house?"

"Well, shouldn't I? Are you planning to redecorate or slide down stair banisters?" He smiles and turns to walk back in the direction of the front door. "Oh, I nearly forgot." He hands me a blue leather satchel.

"What's this?" Inside the satchel are several hundred-dollar bills neatly wrapped. "I thought we agreed the car was a deposit."

"Your PR manager's finder's fee and your entourage's first down payment," he says smiling.

Damn it. I can't continue this unicorn story. It sounds totally outrageous, not to mention taking advantage of a blind man will surely land me a place in hell. Abla and her crazy ideas. I'm surprised that I listen to her so frequently.

"Wait, Julius, I have a confession. I—" He stops me before I can continue.

"Ms. Frimpong. I don't go into business with people that I don't fully research. This is an important assignment and it involves a level of trust and confidentiality. Tell your sister if her client is as good as she says she is, then there may be a brighter future for the both of you."

"You know and you're still going to pay?" *Well, I'm not surprised. He has enough money to trace back my ancestors back to the Gold Coast period.* He smiles again.

"It was a pleasure, Ms. Frimpong. Have a good evening." He descends my stairs effortlessly. Vincent opens the car door for him and he gently glides inside. I stand in the doorway watching as they drive off. *So, I'm going to write a book.*

Chapter 10

"Mommy, if I had to spend the same time you spent creaming my body, I would never make it to class." Pancake's voice grows louder as she approaches my bedroom. I'm still lying in bed engulfed in my new Bed Bath and Beyond duvet. *Please God, no drama this morning.* A gentle knock turns my attention to the door.

"Wat do you mean? Do you know da first impression iz wat lures men to you?" Abla's pitch is higher than normal.

"Auntie, are you asleep?" Pancake says. There's no use, I feel as though I am going to be dragged into a mommy-daughter debate. It's been less than six hours since Pancake arrived home from Syracuse University and Abla is already on her heels. I struggle to sit up. The alarm clock next to the bed blinks 6:15 a.m. MJ was up all night with an upset stomach. Four hours of sleep just won't cut it. *Please go away.* They enter without hearing my response.

Pancake, also known as Akosua Da'Cruz, is extraordinarily smart, strikingly beautiful and resilient. We gave her the nickname not because of her glowing Cuban-Ghanaian complexion but because when she was a toddler she devoured pancakes like a runner drinking water. Abla worried when she didn't eat household diet staples like banku and kenkey. Eventually the indulgence of sweet stacks of flour went away and she began experimenting with a variety of foods, but the name stuck.

"You can be smart, but every successful man wants somedin' nice to hook on hiz arms." That definitely is another Ablaism. "I'm goin' to mix anotha cream for you to take back to school. Look at yur skin. Are you farmin' at school?" I chuckle. Abla's angry eyes focus on me. *Okay, she's not playing this morning.* She exhales intensely and continues. "Let me see yur shoulders."

"Please, Auntie, tell her to stop. Can't I catch a break? I just want to go back to bed," Pancake says.

Abla will often quip, "People who don't care about deer looks make awful lovas." That's an Ablaism.

Abla is as meticulous about appearances as a scientist is with her experiments. And when it comes to her daughter's looks, she is a drill sergeant. Abla's daily ritual consists of baths that last forty minutes followed by application of various creams and butters. There are special cleansers and masks for her face and a jambalaya of soaps for her body. Her daily moisturizer consists of her own special blend of shea butter mixed with fragrant oils and vitamins to keep her youthful appearance. There are special creams for the summer and special creams for the winter. Cream that she applies only to her feet and hands. Other creams for her belly and thighs. Eye cream for the day and eye cream for bedtime. A moisturizer for her lips and neck. An SPF 45 gel for her face and hands. Finally, a detailed application of makeup that lasts twenty minutes. All this is done before a piece of clothing touches her body.

It is a blessing and most times a curse to be under Abla's scrutiny. Whenever she notices my daily beauty regimen lacking she will casually sit on the edge of my bed as though she is making small talk, but really she's gathering information. Her eyes dance around the room in a slight rhumba, quickly examining my bedside table, dresser and then the vanity beside the closet. Whatever appears lacking—shea butter, razors, scented oils, nail polish and pumice stones—will magically appear when I am not present.

There was that incident when Mensah and I went for dinner at a local diner. I was dressed in a pair of jeans and one of my Sassi Strikers jerseys. Later in the evening, Abla pulled me into bathroom for her sisterly talk.

"Yur married now. You must alwayz look yur best. You went to dinner wit yur husband. You must always look sexy. When you feel sexy you feel beautiful. Wat husband doesn't want a young sexy wife? Otha men will wish you were deer wife. And Mensah will feel proud. You must alwayz look good even when you don't want to. When you look good it changes how you dink and behave. You don't want someone to say Mensah married a hopeless lookin' woman. People talk, especially Ghanaians. You must alwayz show a receivin' face."

"What is a receiving face?" She sighed under her breath and looked at me as though I was raised by bush animals.

"When you receive money or gifts, aren't you happy? Yur face shows happiness. A smile. Always maintain a receivin' face around strangers. Don't squeeze yur face like you smell shit. Men run away from deer wives becuz dey alwayz squeeze deer faces. Not receivin' face but deceivin' face. A receivin' face and sexy body alwayz attract good dings."

Abla's scrutiny of Pancake continues and I thank God this is not about me.

"Why are you wearing these pants?" She tugs at Pancake's sweatpants. Her eyes carefully take inventory of Pancake's ensemble: a red hoodie, black sweatpants and black sneakers. *At least she's matching.* "God made us so dat men can worship us. Not to be hidden unda Nike or Adidas sweatpants. If you don't wear heels, yur feet will start to look like beef patties. Dey will be too flat and wide for F-M-Ps. You must train yur feet so you can walk in heels. Men like F-M-Ps." Abla invades Pancake's personal space, scrutinizing everything she sees. Her lips curl and finally she stands beside her staring at the mirror hanging over the bathroom door. "I'm teachin' you dis for yur own good. When I walk down da street, people believe dat I'm twenty-tree. Do you know why?" Even though Pancake replies yes, Abla continues. "Dey dink I'm young becuz da choices I make." Abla stretches her arms up and removes her nightgown. Her breasts stand at attention. She is wearing a black lace thong and four white and gold waist beads in various sizes contour her hips. She parades around the room admiring herself from every angle.

"It's too early for this shit…" I say lowly. She shoots me the eye and I retreat.

"Look at me. Most women wish dey had skin dis soft and supple. I drink one gallon of water a day. I don't use suga and I sleep seven hours a day. Do you know wat I do relijessly no matta where I am?" Pancake doesn't answer. "Yaa, give me da jar." I hand her the jar of shea butter from my nightstand. *This is a new one. She must have placed one by my bed last night.* She holds the jar in front of Pancake's face. "I cream my body day and night. It goes whereva I go."

I used to believe it was just good genes, but Auntie Cece is Mommy's sister…well, half-sister—same mother different father—and her skin never glowed like Mommy's or Abla's. Abla's skin is the color of a tropical mango. A nice mixture of browns, golds and reds. There's not a blemish on her. Abla exhales profoundly again. "Take off yur clothes."

"Ma, I beg oooh. Can't I just go to sleep and we can talk later?"

"Each second yur disopeedent…look at yur eyebrows." Pancake and I both examine each other's eyebrows in the mirror. "You just added anotha wrinkle," Abla says.

"For heaven's sake, Auntie, please help me." I know once Abla takes off her clothes this is going to be an all-day debate about something.

"The quicker you do this, the sooner we can all go back to sleep," I say. She cocks her head back in surrender. Pancake pulls the sweatshirt over her head and removes the sweatpants and sneakers. The reveal shows a different Pancake. Her bra is too small for her double D breasts and her underwear look painfully tight and they barely cover her buttocks. Her waistbeads are strangled above her protruding stomach.

"Ooooh my goodness…LOOK…AT…YOU…" Abla meanders toward her like she is examining a rare sculpture, contorting her face in different poses. "Did we send you to college, or are you grazin' in da fields?" I bite down on my lips hard to prevent myself from laughing. "Yaa…Yaa…look at her…LOOK…LOOK at our daughta." Abla spins Pancake around like a Lazy Susan. She raises her left arm and then the right. "Look…Look…" Then the right leg and left leg. I am not sure what is so alarming besides that she has gained a little weight and her skin looks painfully ashy. Abla makes a sound that only a woman who has spoken years of tribal Ghanaian dialect can make. *That's never a good sign.* "Hmmmm…Hmmmm…Yaa…look…" Abla gasps in disgust. "Look…Look…" She points to Pancake's shoulders and then clasps her hands together in a half clap. *Yep, this is serious enough.* A sound of point of no return.

"What…Ma?…What is it?" Pancake asks.

"I didn't know I gave birth to a zebra." I bow my head down trying to contain my amusement. The weight of Pancake's bra causes the area around her shoulders and back to appear bruised and darkened. "Look at yur knees. Are you crawling to class? Dey are as dark as my *shito*. Nuns spend deer whole life on deer knees, but dey don't have knees as dark as dis."

"What? Ma, you are exaggerating," Pancake says, trying to examine herself in the mirror.

"Oooooh, now you want to look in da mirror?…So you mean to tell me, dey don't have mirrors at school? You just wake up and go. You don't care wat you look like sittin' amongst yur colleagues. Hmmmmmmmmm..." Abla says.

"Pancake, we need to go shopping. We need to get you fitted for a bigger cup," I say.

"Auntie, I know. I promised myself that I would do some clothes shopping. I've just been busy trying to put my parents' money in my education to good use," Pancake says sarcastically.

"Stop da noise...Yes, I send you to school to get an education, but you must keep yur eyez open for yur future huzzband. Dis iz da time to start grabbin' huzzband material." They are both standing in front of me partially naked and all I want to do is snuggle underneath my duvet. *Can't they move this debate outside my room?* "You are not usin' da cream dat I gave you."

"Ma, I don't want to bleach my skin."

"Heyyyy....dis iz not bleachin', dis iz tonin'. A big difference." Not really, but there are ingredients in her cream that will take away any discoloration within several days.

"What's the difference?"

Abla continues through gritted teeth. "Da difference, Mizz Pinstripes, iz dat you won't be mistaken for a leopard wit spots. Look at yur ashy legs and feet. If you lissen to yur motha it will alwayz help you in life." *Yep, that's two Ablaisms so far.*

Pancake's body examination is perhaps as thorough as an ob-gyn examination. Abla asks about her last menstrual cycle and did she feel any pains anywhere on her body. "Remember to always feel yur breast dis way." She demonstrates to Pancake, which reminds me to do my own when I get into the shower. "Now squeeze da nipple...anydin'?" Pancake shakes her head no. "Let me see yur nails. Remember, short and clean. Wat kind of panties are deezs? I didn't buy doze," Abla says. Pancake looks down at them and then me.

"Oh, it must have been Auntie." I haven't shopped for Pancake for quite some time. But I don't interject.

Abla shoots me a look. "Stop buyin' deezs panties. Iz okay once in a while for show, but not every day. Dis material iz not good for yur pussy. Yur pussy iz goin' to sweat and smell like smoked fish..."

Yes, we never have a problem in our household using words like pussy or *etwe* and dick or *kote*. Mommy taught us those are the words we would hear our friends call our anatomy, so we shouldn't shy away from them. As we grew older and more experienced, Abla and I created pet names for our precious female parts. Come to think about it Pancake never confided in me if she created a name for hers.

Abla continues. "Yur pussy needz to breathe around natural elements. Drow it away. We will go shoppin' for some new onez. I know you have a lot of engineerin' courses, but you need to wake up early to cream yur body."

"Really, Ma, sacrifice the three or four hours of sleep that I survive on just to wake up a little earlier to cream my body?"

"Look at me…you see yur auntie…look at her body…Yaa, take off yur clothes."

"Wait…wait…how did this wind up about me now?" I say defensively.

"Yes, Auntie, take off your clothes. Let's get this over with so we can all go back to sleep." Pancake appreciates the diverted attention. It is odd, me being the only one in the room fully clothed.

Abla's eyes narrow onto me. She crosses her arms on her chest and shifts her weight on her left leg. *She's so serious this morning. She could forcefully remove my nightgown.* I stand up grunting and moaning. "Why am I part of this shit? I just want to sleep." I slip the straps off and my nightgown falls to the ground. I stand there next to Pancake examining the curves of my body in the mirror and smile. *Damn, Vida, not bad…not bad at all.* My breasts are big and full. But not as big as Pancake's. She takes after Abla with her big boobs. I apparently inherited all the ass.

"You see…" Abla continues. "Do you see any tiger stripes on yur auntie's body? Look at her knees…does it look like she raises goats?"

"Auntie, you look good for a woman with three children," Pancake says.

"No, she looks good, period." She tugs at Pancake's waistbeads. "Yur waistbeads are goin' to turn to a necklace if you don't start workin' dis stomach out. Look at yur auntie and me. She has tree children, but could still wear a bikini. Don't let dis get out of control," Abla says. She taps Pancake's belly. Thank goodness my waistbeads haven't crept up, which tells me that I am managing my weight well.

I was five years old when I began wearing waistbeads. Mommy made sure we grew up wearing several beads at a time. I started with two and then gradually increased it to six. Now I'm down to three. Every time I feel the beads creeping up my waist and getting too tight, I know it is time to close my mouth—a slimdown methodology that has helped me keep my weight under control.

Mommy would say no one should see your beads except your husband. Make sure they are hidden underneath your clothes. She used to recite the history, reminding me they were adornments women wore during the festivals in Ghana. Over time, the fashion came and went. Now they have become more popular with people from many cultures.

"Mommy, I have something to tell you." We both focus on Pancake and she is smiling. "I lost my virginity." Abla and I stare at each other and then at Pancake. We laugh and embrace her.

Oh my goodness, my little niece has lost her virginity. The same age as me when I was in college. I only hope that the experience was a bit more pleasant than mine. Pancake and Abla sit on my king sized bed as Pancake relays details of her first sexual experience.

"How do you feel?" I ask.

Abla leans closer to Pancake and pulls her into her embrace. She is fixated on this woman in front of us. It is a look so sincere that my eyes begin to water while witnessing mother and daughter give deeper meaning to their relationship.

"It's been about two months now," Pancake says.

"Why didn't you call me?" Abla says, still examining her daughter's face.

"I wanted to wait until I came down this weekend."

"Ehh...my baby..." Abla coddles her again. But she is no longer a baby. She has been a woman for quite some time now. She's joined the ranks of women who have succumbed to the *kote*.

MJ enters the room. He rubs his eyes and yawns widely. He climbs into the bed with me.

"Don't you see me, small stack?" Pancake reaches over to tickle his feet. They tussle and turn onto the bed as MJ squeals out of laughter.

"Do you feel better, dear?" I ask.

"Yes, I'm good. You guys all slept on Mommy's bed?" MJ says.

"How could we? We knew you would climb into bed with your big sweaty feet and take up all the space." Pancake flips MJ onto the bed again and he screams out in laughter.

"I have to keep Mommy company so she doesn't get scared," he says. We all shoot him an 'oh, really' glance.

"Let's get breakfast." She puts the hoodie back on and props MJ on her shoulder.

"She seems so mature. Doesn't she?" Abla asks me. We knew she would come to one of us when she lost her virginity. We always had an open dialogue when it came to sex. My mother made it that way. Some mothers talked about sex in abstract ways, but not Mommy. *"If you can't talk about it, then you can't do it."* Abla and I intend to raise our kids the same way.

"We need to give her the talk...you know. About men and everytin'." Abla's eyes are heavy with tears. The talk is nothing more than Ablaism. The way she believes every woman should conduct herself when it comes to the matters of the heart. The root of her Ablaisms are basic to some degree. *"You can't love anyone till you love all of you. Even da dingz you hate...you haf to learn to love it."*

"Oh Abla, don't start crying...you're gonna get me started."

She smiles and holds my hand. "We didn't do bad. I mean even dough Jesus waz in da Air Force. We did...I mean...She turned out...everytin' I hoped she would."

"We did a great job," I say.

I hear the sounds of Panin tapping against the wall. I'm sure he has already eaten and is waiting for the rest of the house to get up. Kakra is always the last one to wake up.

"Good morning, Panin." He peeks his head into the door. We make eye contact and then he walks away.

"Good mornin', honey," Abla yells to him as he walks away.

"Have you noticed dat hez doin' somedin' new? Auntie Cece asked me, when did he start becomin' so obsessed with TV?"

"TV?" I ask.

"Well, da other day he waz fightin' wit Kakra over some movie. Kakra said he kept playin' da same movie over and over again. But I dought it waz strange becuz he hardly watches TV and now fightin' wit Kakra over TV."

"No, she never mentioned it to me." Interesting that I am learning new things every day about Panin. I've come to accept his quirkiness and uniqueness. "Yeah, it's probably a new thing for him." A week ago Panin spent nearly an hour staring out the window counting cars. Then he logged in his notebook the date, time and number of cars that went by. I remember sitting in front of the house counting cars when Chin and I were kids. We took turns wishing which cars were our cars. I shrugged it off as his form of entertainment. I remind Abla of another incident.

"It's no different from when he used to line up the canned vegetables and count them on the kitchen counter. Remember?"

"It must be an American ding." Abla shrugs her shoulders.

"I'm sure it's nothing. You know it's been a while since they've seen their father. Maybe he just misses him."

"Haf you heard from Da Landlord?" It's Abla's new nickname for Mensah. Her level of affection has changed over the years toward him. I am partly to blame. Crying on my sister's shoulder of the woes of my marriage was never a good thing. When she first met him, she referred to him as "Hershey Kisses," then after we got married it was "Mr. Asare" and when we started having problems, it was just "Mister." Now she refers to him as "The Landlord" because he pays the mortgage on the house.

"We've been missing each other; playing phone tag. The kids spoke with him. He said he is coming to Kakra's game next month."

"Men."

"Yes, men."

"Speakin' of which, howz da RBD?"

"RBD?"

She rolls her eyes. "…Rich. Blind. Dick." We laugh. "You told me he came by yesterday. So, when do you start?" Oh, I nearly forgot. I pull out the drawer and give her the leather satchel and contract. She opens the satchel and her eyes widen as she counts the hundred-dollar bills one at a time.

"Yes! Yes!" She jumps off the bed and nearly falls to the ground. "I told you. Trust big sis. When do you start?"

"I'm planning to go over there tonight."

"Tonight? Dat soon?"

"Well, yeah. I really can't commit to every weekend, but since Kakra has no practice or games this weekend, I can start tonight. Plus Pancake is here, so she can watch the boys."

"I'm workin' dis weekend, if not I would tag along. Are you sure goin' by yurself?"

"Abla, you can't babysit me wherever I go."

"I know, but we don't know dis guy and we can't believe everytin' on da Internet. Where ya gonna meet?"

"His house in Queens. Here's the address." I show her the email on my phone.

"Dis iz Long Island City. Deer are a lot of yellow cab bases and auto shops. Itz really notin' down deer. Nobody lives in dat area."

"Stop being suspicious; you're starting to freak me out. It's not too far away from some of my clients on Jackson Avenue. The neighborhood isn't bad. It's changing. There're a lot of hotels springing up there. It's become the new downtown Brooklyn."

"Huh...You know wat you haf to do when you get deer?" Her tone becomes more stern and serious. "Take a picture of da house when you get deer and send it to me. You still haf da peppa spray?"

"Yes." I nod and I'm already thinking negative thoughts.

Abla continues. "Check da fridge and kitchen cabinets. Don't go to da basement and carry yur cellphone in yur hand any time you move. Carry yur own food and wata." She gets up and paces my bedroom. "Or maybe he hangs bodies in da clozets." Her eyes look wild with fright.

"Will you stop it? Do you think a blind rich man invites people over to kill them?"

"Why do humans eat humans? Crazy iz crazy."

A bit of trepidation courses through my body, but I convince myself it isn't possible for Julius Gallo to be a rich, insane serial killer.

Chapter 11

Could this be the right address? What the hell. Is this a prank? The large building, dull grey and industrialized, stands in the middle of darkness. *Maybe he gave me the wrong address, but Google Maps tells me otherwise.* Not how I pictured it from Mr. Money Bags. The Queensboro Bridge is just three blocks away and the streets are wide enough that they resemble highways. One could easily get mugged, assaulted or killed in the wide-open streets with nothing surrounding it. *Alright, Vida, pull yourself together. Stop thinking crazy.* It looks more like an office building. Three dim streetlights provide the only illumination on the block. I park the car and walk toward an intercom. Rain pours down on me, making it hard to use the swipe feature of my phone. I finally retrieve the email and follow the steps.

"Vida Frimpong," I say my name into the electronic device outside the gate. Even though I have an umbrella, the downpour is beating against my clothes and what is left of the brown paper bag I am holding. My jeans cling to me like paste. The mini monitor searches for some kind of authorization.

"Voice recognized…please enter your passcode."

I try to balance the soaked brown bag, a crappy five-dollar umbrella and my iPhone in one hand.

The automated security announces again, **"Please enter your passcode within ten seconds."**

Crap. Where is the passcode? I know I read it somewhere earlier. A few strokes down I see it clearly in his email.

Passcode is Dim9ight. I quickly type it into the device and await its approval.

"Welcome, Ms. Frimpong," the automated device welcomes me inside the gates. I walk to the door feeling the weight of my soaked jeans. The grand metal door has another intercom fixed to the left. It speaks again.

"Please enter the passcode in the next ten seconds."

I enter the same passcode and a loud buzzer sounds.

"Incorrect passcode. Please enter the passcode in the next ten seconds."

I try again, this time entering the letters and number with pressured fingers into the keypad.

"Incorrect passcode...Please enter the passcode in the next ten seconds."

I quickly search the email on my phone and see that he has indicated the second passcode. *You would have to be high to think you could burglarize this place. These security measures are more severe than nurseries at hospitals.*

"Welcome, Ms. Frimpong, you are the first visitor of the day. Please enter."

The first visitor. So nobody's here, I guess...I hope. The large metal door opens to a lighted hall and five steps. There is another door at the top of the stairs and I quickly scan the email looking to see if there are special instructions. The door opens as I reach the top step. The computerized voice continues.

"The study is located down the hall, second door to your right. Should you need further assistance, you will find me in every room. Welcome again, Ms. Frimpong. I am Alice."

"You're Alice," I say, annoyed. I pictured an older woman resembling Mary Poppins greeting me at the door. Who would equate a name like Alice with a computerized security system? This feels like a 007 movie.

I search the grandness of the space. Never could I imagine that something so beautiful was hidden behind these doors.

"Would you like me to turn on the lights?"

"Yes, please." In an instant, light gives me new eyes to see the grandeur of the foyer. There are marble tiles on the floor and several paintings of beaches and water on the walls. Just before the staircase is a huge male statue on bended knee holding a circular glass table. On the table is an enormous assortment of fresh flowers. I walk over to the stair banister and touch it. I recall Julius's comment and laugh. It is decorative steel with ornamental details along the railings. As I continue to walk through the hallway, my wet jeans create watery footprints on the floor.

I open the second door. It is the library. There are a few ceiling lights on. Alice announces her presence again.

"Ms. Frimpong, would you like me to turn on all the lights?"

For the second time, I answer into the ceiling. "Yes, please." I see the same electronic device by the doorway. This must be the portal to communicate with Alice. The room is decorated in hues of gold and red and purple. A brown leather sectional faces the bookcase. Books line the wall from waist-height to the ceiling. There is a television on the lengthier part of the wall. On the opposite wall are sizeable windows with a huge wooden desk in front of them. It has to be five feet long. A laptop is the only item on the desk.

The warmness of the study alerts me to the fireplace. I feel the warmth coming from that direction, but there is no fire. I move closer to a heat source: a vent on the floor. I quickly take off my jeans and socks and rest them on the vent to dry. There is another vent farther down and I rest my jacket on it. Although my T-shirt is damp, I decide to leave it on to dry on its own. There is a ringing sound and I look around the room for its source. It's coming from my bag. It is 10:30 and I am sure it's Abla.

"Hi."

"Are you okay?" I explain to Abla the extreme details of just trying to enter the building. This doesn't console her and in fact I feel a bit intimidated myself.

"Okay, just checkin' on you. Did you do wat I told you to do? Wherez da picture?" she says.

"It's been raining like sheeps and cows. I couldn't take the photo, but you have the address."

"Yeah. Okay. Anydin' strange?" I would usually roll my eyes, but the big empty house screams scary movie and I'm aware of my delicate situation.

"Well, it was nice having such a lovely sister like you. I will always love you. Take care of my boys."

"Hmmmm. You don't be eazy. Yur makin' jokes and here I am worried for you." I laugh at her seriousness. "Snoop around a bit. Make sure deerz no bodies in da freeza or cabinets."

"Okay, okay," I say quickly, trying to rush her off the phone. She is feeding into my fears.

Positive thoughts, Vida. Positive thoughts, girl. I hang up the cellphone and sit in the leather chair by the desk. I turn the laptop on and open the drawers. There is nothing but a few pens and pads. The desktop screen is on and the word "passcode" appears again.

*Another passcode…cheese and bread…*Alice's voice startles me. **"Are you ready to enter the passcode, Ms. Frimpong?"**

"Yes," I say into the air.

"One moment please."

The camera on the laptop opens and my reflection is on the screen. The screen goes blank. The computer turns back on and the word "passcode" appears.

"I entered the passcode. You are authenticated in my system. Ms. Frimpong, I detect an iPhone in your possession. If you choose, I can communicate with you through various media. Should I send you my contact via your iPhone?"

"I can call or email you?" I ask.

"Yes, you can. Please unlock your device and I will do the rest."

I am a bit hesitant giving Alice carte blanche to my phone. I do have some nudie pics and maybe one or two videos that have me in compromising positions. All of this I sent to Mensah to show him how much I miss him. *What if she downloads all the contents to her cloud?*

"If you prefer, I can email you my contact information." Alice detects my skepticism. **"Here it is,"** she says. The laptop awakens from sleep mode and Alice's contact information is on the screen. A new message window pops up. I type my email address and hit send. **"One moment please."**

I check my phone and an email has arrived from Aliceisalwaysright@asem.com. *Amusing.* "I got your email."

"Good news. You have another mode to communicate with me."

The screen displays motions of water. There are several applications and Microsoft Office programs already loaded. I look around the room for his journals. I open the drawers and see nothing. Maybe he already has them stored in the computer.

"Alice, did Mr. Gallo tell you where he stored his journals?"

"Are you referring to Lord Gallo?"

"Lord who?"

"Lord Gallo, Ms. Frimpong," Alice says.

Just what I thought. *Arrogant as fuck*. "Yes, Lord Gallo." I roll my eyes.

"Yes."

"Yes what?"

"I do know where Lord Gallo stores his journals."

I wait for further response, but Alice doesn't alert me to anything else. "Are you going to tell me?"

"Yes."

What am I missing? I move to the middle of his study wearing only my T-shirt and panties. *Okay, Alice. Do I have to say 'Mother, may I?* "Alice, where are the journals?" My voice is a bit more elevated than normal.

"That is a properly formatted question. Lord Gallo's journals are located along the wall. One moment please."

I'm too curious to be offended by her comment. My eyes scan the room. It must be on one of the shelves on the bookcase. The wall opposite the bookcase splits horizontally and behind it is an enormous glass cabinet.

"Please enter your passcode into the keypad." *Fuck, again with these passwords…passcode BS.*

"What passcode? Mr. Gallo never told me about a safe in the study."

"The passcode is included in the email Lord Gallo sent you."

Again, I scan the email like a Regents ELA exam. "Is it D-I-M-nine-I-G-H-T?" I say, eager to get the safe open.

"I cannot confirm or deny any of your responses, Ms. Frimpong. Please enter the passcode."

Again, I scan the email line by line.

"Should I send the email to you again?"

I'm getting frustrated with Ms. Know-It-All. "No, I have it," I say dryly. "But why am I going through this again? You know who I am and what I'm doing here. Do you know the passcode or not?"

"Yes, I do know it, but do you?"

"Alice. Please give me the damn passcode," I yell into the ceiling. *Control yourself, Vida. You are letting a computerized device get you all worked up.* I'm restless and hungry.

"One moment please."

A brief pause and Alice continues.

"Please store the passcode for future reference." I swipe the screensaver off my phone and switch it to the alphanumeric pad to jot down the passcode. She begins announcing the letters slowly.

"Uppercase 'D'. Lowercase 'i'. Lowercase 'm.' Are you keeping up so far, Ms. Frimpong?"

"Yep."

Alice continues. "The number nine. Lowercase 'i.' Lowercase 'g.' Lowercase 'h.' and…" She pauses. *Is that it?* "Lowercase 't.'"

I repeat what I typed into my phone for confirmation.

"Correct, Ms. Frimpong."

For the love of God. Alice has jokes. "It's the same passcode."

"Ms. Frimpong, you were instructed to enter the passcode. I cannot confirm or deny your response. You should have more conviction in your answers."

"You are not funny, Missy. Were you programmed to have a sense of humor?" *Alice would get the evil eye if only I could see her.*

"My name is Alice. Yes, I do have a sense of humor. It is good to see you have one as well."

I walk over to the monitor and enter the passcode again. The vault opens and in it are several shelves of journals. I count fourteen metal shelves. Each shelf has six journals evenly spaced. I take one off the shelf and it becomes buoyant with absence of the journal.

"The shelves are weighed according to the weight of each journal. Any removal of documentation or insertion can be detected within a hundredth of an ounce. You cannot remove all the journals at once. If an attempt is made to remove any pages from the journals or add any item into the journal, then yellow protocol will follow."

The vault is huge and there is a thermostat within the doorway. Twenty degrees Celsius is registered on the thermostat. *Wow.* This gives new meaning to padlocked journal. They look antiquated but well preserved. Alice continues to talk as I admire the intricacies of the journals. The one in my hands has detailed unique bindings. I admire the design and scent. It smells like old leather. In the binding of the journal are metallic strips mimicking barcodes. I open the pages and note the contrast between the antiquated vanilla paper and heavy black lines. It reminds me of MJ's composition notebook but with thick Sharpie-like raised lines. Scripted handwriting in black-purplish ink decorates one side of each page. I thumb through the pages not taking particular notice of any sentence, but several pages are labeled with a date and a heading that reads "My God." Some pages are dog-eared and others are folded in half. *Maybe a place marker?* I take a step back and admire the vault. Heavy doors and temperature control to preserve the memories. *These journals have a story to tell. A story I'm responsible for writing.*

I place the journal back and reach for another one. The same metallic strip etched in the binding of the journal. Same handwriting. Date in the upper right corner with heading and same salutation. It's been a while since anyone has opened this journal. It creaks open and some of the pages are stuck together. With extra caution, I separate the pages. An audible tearing sound emits in the room. *Shit, did I rip it?* I examine it closely for any damage. *Nothing. Thank goodness.*

"What is yellow protocol?" I finally ask Alice.

"Yellow protocol goes into effect in the case of any damage, removal or destruction of any part of the journals."

"And what happens if there are damages or removal?" I ask suspiciously. I look closely again at the journal.

"It would be wise not to test those limits, Ms. Frimpong."

I think this heifer just threatened me.

Okay. I need food and music to set the writing mood. I place the journal back in the vault and search for my portable speakers to connect to my iPhone.

"Ms. Frimpong, do I detect another device in your possession?"

"Yes, Alice. It's my portable speakers. I need some music."

"Is that necessary for the task you were hired to do?" she says.

"Listen, Alice. I need music to relax me to get the writing juices flowing. I am not about to be questioned about what I need or don't need."

"Huh. One moment please."

She responds this time much more slowly. *Did I piss her off? Is she going to start yellow protocol?* I look around the room to see if anything out of the ordinary is transpiring. Beside the TV, another set of wood panels open. I swallow hard. *This heifer better not be starting yellow protocol.* My hands begin to sweat and I count my breaths. Small black speakers appear from behind the wood panel.

"Should I sync the music from your iPhone to the speakers?"

I pause then answer. "Yes."

"You have quite the music selection. Shall I select it from your recently added folder or your favorites?"

"Favorites." I am still astonished with her capabilities.

"One moment please."

Beyoncé's voice fills the room. "How did you get access to the music on my phone without my password?"

"You should try a more challenging password. Birthdays and names are very easily decoded."

A little bit of remorse sets in. I might have been a bit harsh on her a few minutes ago. I'm moody and have severe cravings for sweets. *Apologize, Vida. She is only doing what she is instructed to do.* "Alice…" I pause and think how I am going to phrase my words.

"You are welcome, Ms. Frimpong." She relieves me from my awkwardness.

Okay, now that music is taken care of, I make my way out the library in search of a bowl and spoon. "Alice, where can I find the kitchen?"

"The kitchen is the first door on the left, but I don't think you can procure food at this hour."

"That's alright, I came with my own treats to keep me going tonight."

"Yes. I detected the barcode on the Haagen Dazs ice cream. Butter pecan. Shall I set the speakers to follow source?" I have no idea what she means, but just to be entertained I say yes. **"One moment please."**

I grab the ice cream and head in the direction of the kitchen. Music fills the hallway and foyer. I reach the kitchen and the lights are already on and Beyoncé is bellowing through the speakers in the ceiling.

Wow, so this is how the wealthy live. I am not surprised by the magnitude of the kitchen. Tall cream cabinets with oiled bronze hardware. A huge floral arrangements sits on the large granite island. There are two stoves and four wall ovens. Two large glass and stainless steel refrigerators.

Suddenly, I remember Abla's rant. My demeanor becomes more constricted. I check the freezer and fridge. I go through all the cabinets searching like an alcoholic after three days of sobriety. Nothing out of the ordinary. Silverware, bakeware and cookware in lower cabinets. China, glasses and pitchers aligned neatly in the upper cabinets. The kitchen appears pristine with new appliances. I bet no one has even boiled an egg in this kitchen. *Alice was right.* No beer, Pellegrino water or even a cracker to procure from this kitchen. The kitchen sink could double as a bathtub, large and deep enough to fit a human body. *Stop it, Vida, good thoughts.*

I walk from one end of the kitchen to the other, taking notice of the oddly warm marble floor. The music sounds awesome in the kitchen and I find myself dancing. I imagine myself having parties here. *Wow, what the Ghanaians would say about the Frimpong sisters.*

I take a bowl from one of the cabinets and scoop the ice cream in. I devour several spoons of ice cream within seconds and then scoop a few more into the bowl. *Okay, that should get me started.* I walk to the other end of the kitchen and place the remaining ice cream in the freezer and examine the make and model of the refrigerator. Viking. Its huge stainless steel frame makes me believe that it must be a special order. Enough to store bodies—my paranoia screams at me again. *Stop it, Vida. No negative thoughts!*

"Well, I see that you've made yourself at home."

"AAAHHH!" My voice overtakes the music. The bowl of ice cream clashes to the floor. Julius takes a few steps back. "Shit. You scared the crap out of me."

"My apologizes. I didn't mean to startle you. I did say hello when I walked in, but you probably didn't hear me because of the music," Julius says.

No, it's because I'm busy searching for dead bodies. My hands grip my chest and my heart pumps at a runner's pace. The music stops and heavy breathing fills the void.

"I wasn't expecting you to be here."

"I live here, Ms. Frimpong."

"I just assumed when you sent the email that you would be out of town."

"I have a habit of changing my mind. Hardly a crime," Julius says.

"No, that is not a crime," I say suspiciously. *Why did he mention crime? What does he mean by that?* I examine him closely and he looks strikingly handsome in a well-tailored black suit, which makes me suddenly aware of my present condition. *Thank goodness he can't see me in my Pink underwear and damp T-shirt.* Shyness overtakes me and I slide gracefully behind the kitchen island. The puddle of ice cream is melting from the warm tiles. He stands inches away from it. *Leave so I can clean up my clumsiness.*

"I see you have gotten acquainted with Alice."

"Oh yes, Alice," I say as I recollect our earlier conversations. "She's no Siri, that's for sure."

"Oh heavens, no. She's light years away in comparison," he says.

He walks over toward the sink and grabs a dishrag from underneath the tub-sized basin and walks over to the exact spot where the ice cream is melting. He bends down and touches the tile until he finds what he is looking for.

"Oh no, don't worry, I'll take care of that." I rush from behind the island to stop him from wiping the mess on the floor, but he holds his hands to gesture me to stop. He skillfully cleans the mess and picks up the bowl of ice cream. His hands grace the island until he meets the edges of the sink. He places the bowl in the sink and opens the faucet to allow the water to fill the bowl.

"Do you have the spoon?" he asks.

"Yes." I release the spoon from my grip and place it in the bowl of water. He rinses it and then moves his hands along the edges of the counter. There is a dishwasher blended well into the cabinets. He places the bowl and spoon inside.

"Is everything all right so far?" he asks.

Well, besides getting caught in the rain and taking a bit longer to access the passcode, being scrutinized by Alice and now standing here in my underwear hoping that you don't notice. I nod and say, "Yes, everything is okay so far."

"Honey, what is taking you so long?" Penny enters the kitchen. "Well, well, well. What is going on in here?" She sees my ass in full view. Our last encounter was less than favorable, and I am mad at myself for standing here in my underwear. I stretch my T-shirt over my Pink underwear, but it is a battle of which-would-you-rather-see, more ass or more boobs. It is times like this I wish I had the ability to be invisible. "Nice panties," Penny says.

Julius turns his head in my direction. My secret is out and I begin to ramble quickly.

"I-got-caught-in-the-rain-and-my-clothes-were-so-wet-and-I-noticed-the-heating-vents-in-the-study-so-I-took-my-clothes-off-and-of-course-I-had-no-other-clothes-and-I-thought-no-one-else-would-be-here-so-I-needed-to-get-a-bowl-of-ice-cream-because-I-didn't-want-to-eat-the-whole-ice-cream-and-then-I-got-startled-when-I-heard-your-voice-and-dropped-some-of-the-ice-cream-and-then-I-was-trying-to-get-back-to-the-study-so-that-I-can-put-my-clothes-on-so-that-you-wouldn't-notice-that-I-am-actually-standing-here-in-my-T-shirt-and-panties-talking-to-you-but-now-Penny-came-in-and-saw-me-and-she-knows-and-you-know-now-so-that-is-why-I'm-standing-here-in-my-underwear."

"What? You Americans talk too fast," Penny says. Julius stands squarely on the opposite side of the island.

"Well, excuse me, I have dry clothes to put on. Have a good night," I say. I feel Penny's eyes watching me as I turn to leave quickly.

"Wow, your calves are huge," Penny shouts. "I work out all day at the gym and my calves never look like that."

I stop and turn around again. "It's part genetics and I guess part soccer games," I say.

Penny laughs. "You? Play soccer? For real?"

"A little bit for recreation now and then keeps me in shape," I say.

Her eyes are fixed on me. Julius is standing beside her absorbing the conversation. *I assume.* The atmosphere is quite uncomfortable and I try to excuse myself by walking backward toward the kitchen door. Julius's voice breaks my movement. "There is a dryer as well as a washing machine in this closet here." He points in the direction of a hallway just off the kitchen. I look. There is another door just to the left of the kitchen.

"Thank you. I will remember that in case there is a next time."

"There is also a guest bedroom with a bath across the hall from the library. You can find a robe in the bathroom," Julius says.

"Thank you again." I tiptoe out of the kitchen and jog down the hall into the library. *That was so fucking embarrassing.* "Thanks a lot, Alice,"

I speak into the air. *She could have at least warned me that the lord of the house is home.*

"Ms. Frimpong, how may I be of assistance?"

I roll my eyes. "No, nothing," I say.

"If you choose, you can say the command 'Good night, Alice' and I will not respond to commands until you say the command 'Welcome, Alice.' Please note, the security protocols will remain in place during the auto response shut off."

"Okay. Good night, Alice."

"Good night, Ms. Frimpong."

A little bell chimes. I pick up my jeans from the floor radiator and they are still damp. I decide to wait a little while before making my way to the dryer next to the kitchen. It is almost midnight and I haven't even started. I take one of the journals from the shelf and sit by the computer. The ringtone sounds again and I rush to my bag to pick it up. It's Mensah. I immediately answer the call.

"Hi."

"Hi, how are you doing?" I can barely hear his voice with the music in the background.

"Okay."

"Are the boys asleep?"

"Yes."

"I'm just calling to check on you guys."

I'm upset his voice doesn't sound the least bit worried. *I was in a car accident for Christ sake and I haven't spoken to him until now. You'd think he would rush back to New York to check on his wife, the mother of his children.* His nonchalance stirs up anger, disappointment and sadness. I won't give him the satisfaction to hear me upset or sad. I respond. "Good."

"Great... I'm sorry we've been playing phone tag. I meant to call yesterday, but things have been so hectic. It's a process out here. I was hoping to speak to the boys before they went to bed." A beep on his phone alerts me that he has an incoming call. He pauses then continues. "I will have more time in the coming weekend so I will call back and speak with them. What time is it there?"

"Approaching midnight," I say with no affection in my voice.

"And you're still up. Are you writing again?"

"Yes." I decide not to give him any information regarding this new writing assignment until we meet.

"You need to get some rest. I'll talk to you later. Good night."

He doesn't wait to hear my response. The silence on the other end tells me he has already left the conversation. Forty-four seconds; it is probably the longest conversation we've had all year. I rest my cellphone on the desk and stare at it. Maybe he will call back. Maybe he didn't mean to end the conversation without hearing my response. I wait and stare. Should I be surprised that this would end any differently? It was just an 'are-you-okay-and-the-boys-must-be-fine' conversation. A neutral conversation without any indication of the present or future condition of our marriage.

There is silence before the next music track begins. *Why am I here? I can't focus. I shouldn't have taken on this assignment. All I think about is him.* This is supposed to help spark my writing again, but right now my mind and body crave him. I remember the last time we made love almost two years ago now. Martha Munizzi's voice breaks the memory. The track "God is Here" rips through my heart. Sadness fills my soul and big uncontrollable tears rush out. The more I wipe my face the faster they fall. My chest heaves up and down, uncontrollable at first then receding to a slow tremble. As the song ends, my burst of melancholy stops and I rest my head on the desk.

*

"Shit." It is almost 2:00 a.m. *I dozed off.* The computer is still on and the journal is on the desk. *Type something, Vida.* I set a timer on my phone for one hour and decide to remain focused for at least that time. Before I begin, I need a refill to spark the writing juices. Julius and Penny must be asleep by now.

"Welcome, Alice."

"Good morning, Ms. Frimpong."

"Can you lower the music?"

"Yes. I can." The music volume remains the same and it occurs to me to rephrase my request.

"Alice, please lower the music."

"As you wish, Ms. Frimpong. Please say 'stop' when you are satisfied with the level." The music automatically lowers.

"Stop. Thanks."

The upper part of my jeans is still damp and so is my jacket. I pick them up and head toward the dryer. In the foyer, I hear faint noises upstairs. *Music?* I place my clothes in the dryer and head toward the kitchen for ice cream. The strange noises appear again. I draw nearer to the staircase. The music stops.

"Oh fuck…Babe, I'm coming again…Oooh, babe, just like that…Oh, babe…Yes! Yes!" The music comes on again and the sounds are drowned out.

Oh my God. He's fucking Penny. Shit! I shouldn't be here. I ditch the quest for ice cream and run back into the library.

I think of an exit plan even though I haven't even typed a pronoun. My phone shows fifty minutes left on my timer. *You need to really type something, Vida. If he comes down tomorrow with nothing to show, you will look like a slacker.* I immediately thumb through the journal and start typing a few random pages without focusing on the words.

"Ms. Frimpong."

"Yes, Alice?"

"Your clothes are dried."

I look at my timer and I have only ten minutes left. In the foyer, music is still playing upstairs. *They must be asleep now.*

The music stops again. The house is quiet. I approach the stairs again.

"*Oh, fuck!*" Shrieks of ecstasy enter the foyer. Various languages mix with the rapid pounding of furniture. "I'm coming again. Fuck me harder, babe!"

"Get the fuck outta here," I say out loud and shake my head. There is no way they are still fucking. A loud thump startles me. And now bursts of laughter. Just how many orgasms did Penny have tonight? A bit of jealousy stirs in me. *I may have some energy tonight. I have to pick up batteries on my way home. Wait, I don't have Billy anymore. I threw it away. Why again? Yeah, that's right, I was afraid of dildo addiction.* Music drowns them out again.

I hear footsteps coming from behind the steps and I rush into the library. *Who can that be at this time?* I didn't even make it to the dryer to get my clothes. The footsteps walk past the library and it sounds as though they are making their way to the kitchen. I stand by the door and decide to wait until I hear the footsteps again.

The alarm from my phone blares out. *3:00 a.m.* I save the work on the laptop and place the journal back into the safe. I look around the library for anything out of place. It is still dark in the foyer and the music is still playing upstairs. This time I don't stop to listen for what sounds will come from upstairs. I run to the dryer get my jeans and jacket.

"Oh! Excuse me." *Who is this?*

"No problem, babe."

She picks up my jeans and hands them to me. She is a tall black woman wearing a mid-length trench coat and bright red F-M-Ps. *Definitely not Penny.*

"Hmmmm, where were you about two hours ago? We really could have a good time. And you have a fat ass. I love fat asses. I bet you taste as good as you smell," she says. She slaps my butt.

"Excuse me?" I say a bit timidly.

"Ms. Jane, your car is waiting." Vincent is standing by the door.

"Oh babe, don't be shy. You're a real cutie pie. Papi really worked us today. We really could have some fun next time. I know he would really enjoy you." She walks closer to me and I move a step back.

"Ms. Jane." Vincent is insistent.

"Papi?" I say out loud. *Shit. Was she the voice shrieking upstairs?* It's obvious that Julius enjoys his independence in more ways than one.

"Good night, sweet chocolate." She stares at me a bit longer than I appreciate. Vincent escorts her outside. Silence again. I rush into the library, shut down the computer and try to leave as quickly as possible in fear of who else may emerge from upstairs.

"Hard at work, I see." Julius struts into the room. His hair is wet and slicked back. He is wearing loose fitting pajama pants. Barefooted. No top. Muscles from his shoulders to his abs look well oiled. His entrance brings in the smell of mint.

"Actually, just wrapping up," I say shyly.

He finds the chair next to the desk. "Did you have a hard time reading the journals?"

He lifts the laptop from the desk and glides his hands over the keys. *Stop staring, Vida.* No, more like gawking. Not that he would notice, but my long hesitation breaks his concentration from the laptop. He is talking, but I can't comprehend the words coming from his mouth. My thoughts are sexual. I imagine him naked. Fucking. And not one woman, but two. And not just two women; the black woman in the trench and Penny. Silly thoughts run through my mind. I look at the outline of his pajamas. *All that fucking. Maybe he has a big dick. I can't tell.* The pants are a size bigger than he is. *How on earth does he manage two women? Is this what happens here at night?* I scan his face and nothing alerts me that he is freaky. He looks like a regular guy. The lady in trench's voice comes to mind. *"I have to tell Papi about you." Was this a habitual thing?*

Yeah, he is Papi all right. He licks his bottom lip and holds it in his mouth briefly. He sits opposite me by the desk. *Stop gawking, Vida.* I can't help it. Fine brown hairs start around his navel and cascade lower down. He smells shower fresh.

"Ms. Frimpong? Vida?"

"Oh, sorry. What did you say?"

"The journals, did you have a hard time reading them?" He looks in my direction.

"No…No…I just kinda skipped through this one or two this evening. I actually didn't have problems at all."

"Good. I'm glad you could read my handwriting."

His handwriting. I didn't even take notice of what I was typing. When did he write this? Was this one of his journals from his childhood?

"May I?" His fingers are on the computer's keyboard, but he looks to me for permission.

"Oh, sure." He types on the laptop while I resume my mental seduction. *He looks like a pussy eater.*

"Ms. Frimpong…?" I continue my analysis. *I wonder if he has ever seen a pussy before. Can he tell the difference. How? Are they all the same to him? I mean, yeah, he is blind but maybe he doesn't have to see it to enjoy it. Or maybe he's like Mensah who likes to talk in between my legs while he devours me. Oh, I'm so ruined…Mensah in my thoughts again. Mensah's spoiled me for life.*

"Vida. Vida?" Julius says my name.

"Yep." His voice brings me back to the now.

"Sorry, you must be tired. I don't want to keep you longer than you planned to stay. Alice is uploading the file."

"Oh, of course. No problem."

He punches a few more keys and the laptop announces it is switching to audio files. I'm still mesmerized by his cool nonchalance. Now he is sitting across from me as though he never busted a nut with two women.

"**One moment please.**" Alice coordinates the transfer. "**Lord Gallo, I have the file. Shall I begin?**"

"Yes," he answers.

"**In the course of a lifetime we encounter obstacles that define who we are and test our limits. My story doesn't begin from the time I remember to walk, but much later when I was an adolescent still trying to make sense of my purpose in life.**" Alice continues to read the document out loud and corrects my grammar. I'm impressed that Julius designed her to suit his needs. He paces up and down in the room until he reaches the bookshelf. He opens one of the drawers and pulls out a cigar.

"Do you mind if I smoke?"

"No, go right ahead."

He lights the cigar and takes long slow puffs. The room smells like vanilla and musk. He doesn't come close, but stands against the bookcase while listening to Alice.

"**Lord Gallo, that is the end of the document.**"

"Size?"

"**Nine pages, Lord Gallo. Shall I provide you with more specs?**"

"No. You've done quite a bit of work this evening," he says to me.

I wasn't the only person working hard this evening. I bite down on my tongue and look away. "I really work best at this time of night. I suppose I'm a bit of a night owl," I say.

"So do I. A lot of my inspiration comes from working late, Ms. Frimpong."

"I bet you do…" *Shit. I said that out loud.*

"Pardon me? I didn't hear you." He moves closer to me and I try to change the topic.

"Oh, nothing. I was just saying that it is rather late. But if this time is not good for you, then I can try to come earlier on Saturday or Sunday mornings."

"Ms. Frimpong, I am in no hurry, so whatever works for you. I don't have an issue if you stay here all night. You are more than welcome to stay in the room across from here. In fact, I would feel more comfortable if you stayed in the guest room down the hall rather than driving home at three in the morning."

"Thank you, that is a very kind gesture, Julius. I don't think that will be necessary; plus I don't want to impose on you any further."

"Stop it…you are not doing anything of the sort. Occasionally I may have a guest or two, but we will try to stay out of your way." *You mean the woman who smacked my ass this evening?* If I don't leave soon, I may say something out loud that I will regret.

"I will have someone escort you home just to ensure your safety. We wouldn't want another blind guy running into you." *He makes jokes with his freshly fucked face.* "You probably have a long day ahead of you. I will leave you to get some rest, Ms. Frimpong."

"Yes, thanks. You should get some rest too. I am sure you must be tired from…I mean…you had a long night…I mean…you should try to rest up so you can function at your optimal level." *I really need to control this fucking mouth.*

"Yes, Ms. Frimpong. I get your meaning," he answers firmly.

Chapter 12

"Eheheh…No fuckin' way." Abla clasps her hand over her mouth again. "You see. Doze rich people haf dat freaky kinky side."

"Just rich people?" I say. But she ignores my commentary.

"And do you dink dey were fuckin' all dat time? Well, den again, it makes sense. Two women…you gotta please dem both." She digresses into different scenarios and I chuckle. Listening to Abla break down her version about early this morning is just as entertaining as what I experienced. "Den you ran into dat girl. Wat else did you say to her?"

"What else could I say? I was so startled and then the way she slapped my butt and looked me straight in the eye as though she was going to eat me alive right there."

"Wat did she look like again? Are we talkin' I-G DOTz or Hunts Point hoes?"

"I think they got rid of the hoes around Hunts Point. From what I remember, she looked attractive, but after she slapped my butt everything was a blur."

"Doez he know?" I give her a bewildered look. "You didn't tell him you ran into hiz plus one downstairs?"

"Nooo! I mean, it's his house. I'm the guest. He sat down next to me reviewing what I typed like nothing happened upstairs."

"So iz dat like a special room? You know, wit chains and whips."

"I don't know. I never made it upstairs."

Her eyes grow wild with interest. "So, he has a *kotedenden* room?"

"What?" My mind begins the translation from Twi to English. "A stiff dick room?" We laugh and she nods her head confirming my answer.

"Eheheheh…hmmmm…if he iz entertainin' two women, den hez walkin' wit a big *kote*. You see God knows wat hez doin'. He can't see but hez blest in otha ways." My sister and her crazy epiphanies. I know where this conversation is going but I've already lost interest in Julius Gallo. My attention is on a missed call from Mensah this morning. No message. I scroll through my phone and check the time. 7:14 a.m. Abla notices my changed disposition.

"Have you spoken to Da Landlord?"

"Yes. Last night." When I got home, I cried myself to sleep again. She used to probe for more information, but lately she refrains from saying anything that will rile me up with sadness.

Chapter 13

"Yaa, I know you are mad at me. But trust me, I'm trying to make a better life for us. I hope you and the kids are fine. I will call back later."

That's it. Not even five seconds. This is the latest message. I've listened to it three times already. Each time I have a different reaction. Right now it's anger.

"Alice."

"Yes, Ms. Frimpong."

"Can you play the music selection from my iPhone?"

"One moment please."

Chrisette Michelle's voice fills the room and I don't feel it at first until my face tightens and breaks in half. The tears build slowly and fall one by one until the floodgates open. Within a few seconds, the screen looks blurry and I find myself weeping uncontrollably. I don't understand why my marriage is falling apart. I know they say there are good times and bad times, but this...this...I don't even know what this is anymore. I try to imagine a life without Mensah. *Can I raise three kids by myself?* The thought frightens me. Nausea fills my belly. I want to scream. *Why are men such assholes? Why can't they see when they are breaking someone's heart?*

"Oh honey, I've been waiting for you. You know how to stir my appetite." The voice behind the door sounds like Penny. "Let's eat before dessert." She laughs.

Shit, they are home again tonight. The napkin on the table provides needed rescue as I try to pull myself together. I rush to the adjacent bathroom and splash cold water on my face. When I return to the study, he is standing there.

"Good evening, Ms. Frimpong."

"Hi. I didn't realize you were home this evening. It's been really quiet upstairs." My mind recalls the early morning events. "I mean, it's hard to tell that you or Penny are even home."

"I'm here now. Can I be of assistance?"

This is my second day and I don't even know what I am writing. "Everything is good so far." He will have to get a unicorn story for now. His brows furrow and he moves closer to me.

"Do you have a cold?"

"Ummm…no…Why?"

"Your voice…seems different this evening. As if you are speaking through your nose."

"Ooh…ummmm…it's just my allergies again." The beginning of another unicorn story. *Vida, you know you don't have allergies.* But I need something to explain why I'm sitting here crying again.

"What kind of allergies do you have?" Julius asks.

"Ummmm…cats," I say.

"I don't have cats."

"Are you sure?"

"Absolutely."

"Isn't that strange? If you had walked in here about an hour ago you would have found me sneezing and wheezing all over the place. Maybe it's just seasonal. Anyways, it's getting late and I'll be back next weekend."

"Okay," he says uncertainly. He doesn't move from where he is standing. I move quickly to the desk and pack my belongings into my bag. I power down the computer and say good night one last time.

"I will see you next weekend, Ms. Frimpong."

"Ummm. Yeah."

I move swiftly to the front door and find Penny standing by the main entrance.

"Are you leaving now, Vida?"

"Yes. Sorry to intrude on your evening."

"You're not *inchewing*." She tries to mimic my words. "You have beautiful hair."

Okay, what does she want? Her stare bothers me and her hands motion toward my hair. I take a few steps back. I just hate when people feel as though they can invade my personal space, especially when they reach for my hair.

My hair journal has been a long struggle. It has seen different phases from threading when I was a child, to a perm which caused severe split ends, then to a Jheri curl, which only led to horrible acne, then to an assortment of weaves and hair extensions. Now after several years of going natural, this is probably the last stop. First I hated the natural look, then I tolerated it when it grew thick and curly. Now, after using the right products and regular deep conditioners, I love how the thick curly black mane falls onto my shoulders. Abla threatens to perm it when I fall asleep, but I swear I will never go back to relaxers or chemicals again.

"Is it all yours?" she asks. *Yes, heifer. Are those breasts all yours?* I give her a solid yes and she stares at me like a McDonald's menu board. "Oh my, what perfume are you wearing? You smell very good tonight."

"It's called mommy perfume," I chime back, resurrecting her own words. She gives a big hearty laugh.

"You are very funny, Vida. Very funny and very beautiful." *This is getting weird.* "Do you like dancing?" She moves a bit closer to me. "You should join us Thursday evening."

"What's happening Thursday evening?"

"We usually attend some nightly outing. It gives him inspiration, so I tag along. But I would really like your company. It sometimes gets very boring when he starts talking business." She smells like Grey Goose. Her tipsiness and accent makes her tutored English sound like patois. I can see her face more clearly. She is definitely over thirty. The creases around her mouth and eyes give her away. She is wearing a short yellow off-the-shoulder dress. It is hard to tell if it is an outfit meant to wear to bed or out of the house.

Maybe it would be helpful to see him in a different atmosphere among people he doesn't fuck or command around. She draws closer.

"We're going to Transit on West Ninth Avenue." I'm hesitant to inquire more. "Come…Come on…We will have lots of fun."

"Ummm. I'm not sure. The school day usually starts early on Thursday. And I have a lot of commitments when I get home."

"You still in school?" she asks.

"No, but my children are."

"I forget you have children. How many?"

"Three."

She looks at me more suspiciously. "You look good. You have to come. We will have so much fun."

Gosh, can she step back?…It's as if I drank the Grey Goose with her. Her breath makes me feel sleepy. *Should I go or not?* I step back and shift my bag to my left shoulder. *I would probably gain some more insight about him.*

Pretending to read the journals is already exhausting. And maybe I can get Abla to tag along. "Alright, I'll come, but my manager has to come also."

"Good. I'll put you and your manager on guest list."

"Okay." I leave and breathe a sigh of relief of finally being away from her tutelage.

Chapter 14

"Are those new?" I scrutinize Abla's shoes more closely. A dreamy pair of shoes that remind me of vanilla ice cream with rainbow sprinkles.

"Yes," she replies coyly. "Iz Sophia Webster. A present from my boo boo." Abla's face is as bright as a campsite bonfire. Her smile consumes her entire face. Gifts from boyfriends are expected, but this love sick Abla is something I haven't seen in a long time.

"And a cute outfit to match." A metallic pink skintight halter dress. She prances around my bedroom and I admire her sexy strut. "Those F-M-Ps definitely bring out the outfit."

"Yeah, I guez iz da shoes dat makes me look different." She glances at her feet and smiles. *No, no sista. It's not the shoes.*

"What do you think I should wear?" I mentally run through what sort of outfit I have that is still club-worthy. I spread a short leather jacket, white tank bodysuit and black spandex pants on the bed.

"Yeah, dat looks good." I try it on and the white tank top reveals too much cleavage and the spandex is stretched to its limits. My ass sticks out like a nun at a swingers convention. "Damn, gurl. Yur ass doubled. Itz gotten way bigga."

"Let me look for something else." All my worthy partying clothes don't fit the right way. Abla stops my search.

"No. Wear dat. We will get some free drinks tonight."

"This is still part of work. I don't think I should drink."

"I'm drinkin'. You can keep yur heavenly fatha holy image. Yaa, wear da spandex. You gonna fit in wit da rest of doze I-G chicks."

I add the finishing touch to the outfit, black suede Kirkwood thigh-high boots. "Do you think it's too much?"

"Hefa, we are goin' to da club not church. When waz da last time you've been to da club?" I pause to think, but she continues. "Exactly. You need to see deezs pussy trappers. Between da DOTz and da cougars we have to bring our A game. Da market iz tough and we can't roll up deer lookin' like we finished bakin' bread. Wear doze boots."

"But we're not looking for men. This is work…research."

"And how many times do I haf to tell you? We dress to feel good. Don't you feel and look good now?" I study myself in the full-length mirror and admire the curves and firmness of my body in the clothes. Abla is right. I feel electrified. "Yaa, you look great. Lissen to big sis. Don't change."

Chapter 15

We arrive at the club. I walk to the security guard at the gate. "Excuse me, but we are supposed to get guest passes."

"Okay mama, what's your name?" A big burly security man shines his flashlight on a guest list.

"Vida Frimpong," I scream over the music coming from behind the doors.

"I don't see you on the list," the big security man yells back in my ear. Another huge man appears from behind the black steel door. "Yo, Duke, do you have a Vida on your list?"

"Are you Penny's guest?" Duke asks us. Abla shouts yes before I can. "Follow me."

We enter the club and it is flooded with people. We walk behind Duke and say excuse me a dozen times as we push through the crowd. I give up on the pleasantries and walk more closely to Duke while holding Abla's hand. She gives me a little squeeze signaling me to take notice of something. I turn my head and see what Abla alerts me to: two women grinding on each other and making out in full view.

We continue pushing through the crowd until we face a large black elevator. Duke presses the button and we wait. I look around and Abla's attention is elsewhere. She gives my hand another squeeze and I turn. We must have walked up an incline because we are on a second level. For a weekday, I am surprised by the people. An auditorium-sized crowd presses together like refugees on a boat. However, Duke manages to cut through and we enter the elevator. He uses a key and presses a combination of buttons. It's just the three of us riding to the space designated by the lighted VIP button. I'm nervous. *Why?* I fan my jacket open for air. Abla senses my discomfort and reassures me with two short squeezes of my right hand.

We step out of the elevator and see oversized white club chairs crowding the walls. There are several canopies in different seating areas. The floor is oval in shape with a balcony that peers down to the other floors. There is a sprinkling of people on this floor. To my left, a group of people dancing with glasses in their hands. Farther down the room more people are laughing, drinking, dancing and—if my vision is not playing tricks on me—one couple is fucking. We approach a large hutch with sheer curtains on either side. I see Penny. She is dancing with two other women. As we get closer, my heart races. *Maybe this is a bad idea.* My palms are sweating and Abla changes her grip on me. She grabs the back of my jacket like a little schoolgirl. "Ms. Pucilli, your guests have arrived," Duke says.

Ms. Pucilli. As in Penny Pucilli. You can't make this stuff up. Penny turns to greet me. "Vidaaaaa. Good, you're here."

I smile and then I lock eyes onto Julius. *Is he surprised or upset? I can't tell.* He gives a mocking grin and then relaxes himself among the women. "Ms. Frimpong, quite surprising to see you here. I wasn't aware—"

"Sorry, babe. I should have—" Penny tries to interject, but Julius cuts her off.

"I'm not disappointed," he says. Penny breathes a sigh of relief. "What would you like to drink? Our bartender Nicholas can serve you anything." Penny sways off beat to the music. Julius turns his attention to a tall red-haired woman swooning over him.

"I didn't picture you as someone who frequents clubs, Ms. Frimpong." The music is loud, but funny enough I can still hear him clearly. He kisses the redhead and then like a child moves her off his lap.

"Well, hardly now, especially on a Thursday night," I reply. He doesn't look in my direction. And everyone around us continues to enjoy the ambiance.

"Did you make an exception for me?" He grins and one of the women lights up a cigar for him.

"I guess the perfect opportunity presented itself. I've been wanting to come here since Transit opened. Plus it's more research and all for the book."

"Research?"

"Yes. You know, get a feel for who you are out of your business element."

"I see," he says.

Not again. Don't start this crap. He remains silent and Abla signals me to Nicholas's presence. He asks for our choice of drink. Of course I know Abla will request pinot grigio. I settle for seltzer water, still trying to maintain a level of professionalism. Abla rolls her eyes.

"Okay, coming right up," Nicholas says.

Abla stretches her neck to check him walking away. He's big and muscular. His light undershirt reveals chiseled abs. She whispers to me, "Hez not a fan," which translates to 'gay' in our code language. Two women get up and start dancing. I try to remember what I wanted to say before Nicholas came over.

Julius's attention is on me. I can feel it even with his tinted shades on. He finally addresses me. "You don't need to see me at a club to get an idea of who I am, Ms. Frimpong."

"Well, you would be surprised what people reveal about themselves without even knowing it."

"I suppose," he says.

Nicholas returns with the drinks and I take my MasterCard from my purse and hand it to him.

"No need to tip me. Mr. Gallo is an important guest here at Transit."

Abla rolls her eyes again and talks through clenched teeth. "Put da damn card away before he gets offended." The music changes and Gyptian begins to fill the club. The crowd responds accordingly. Women are gyrating their hips and men push their pelvises against big, small, flat and apple-shaped asses. Abla shimmies to the music and provides a showcase for everyone to see. Penny and her entourage watch Abla with hungry eyes.

"Come on, Yaa. Let's go downstairs and dance," Abla says.

"Yes, let's go." Penny springs up and takes Abla by the wrist. "Babe, are you coming?" she says, turning to Julius.

"Not tonight. Enjoy." He ushers the other women beside him to go with Penny and then he takes a long puff of his cigar.

It's just me and him. Nervousness causes me to gulp the seltzer water in one fell swoop. *I need to move. Why am I still nervous?* I place the glass down and move to edge of the balcony. The crowd's chants grow louder and now it is Ciara's melodic voice that has the crowd charged. I move my shoulders side to side without moving my feet. I can see from the corner of my eye a nightwalker. I don't know what he looks like or what he is wearing besides the flashlight on his wrist.

"Hey, shorty." *Really, are we still referring to women as shorties in the club?* I'm clearly taller than him even with my modest heel. "You are too fine to dance by yourself." He comes into full view. Short and attractive, but what distracts me is his watch that can probably been seen in remote villages in Ghana. All those diamonds on his wrist, I'm surprised he doesn't have extra security. His watch creates flashes of light with each hand gesture.

"Damn, you fine. And you smell good." He licks his lips as though they are chapped. He moves closer and I move farther away. He starts gyrating his hips. "Let's dance, shorty," he says, trying to inch his waist closer to me.

"Here you go, dear." Julius is standing behind me. I turn around and he hands me a glass of red wine. *Smart guy.*

The flashlight stops dancing. "My bad, playa. Didn't know she was with you."

I give the true shorty a 'sorry-but-yes-I'm-with-someone' look.

"No problem. Honest mistake," Julius says. He stands squarely with his hands on his waist towering over the flashlight. The man struts his beacon of light to the other side of the club. "I think I came at the right time. A minute later and his watch would probably have alerted the coast guard."

"You noticed."

"Even a blind man could see that."

We both laugh. "Yes, it definitely stands out." I take a little sip of the glass he gave me. "What is this?"

"Cranberry juice."

"Oh, I thought it was red wine."

"Tomorrow is a work and school day. I wouldn't want to be accused of giving you a hangover."

"Thank you," I lean forward to tell him. He is standing close. We both peer down at the crowd. Abla and Penny are strutting together on the dance floor. I wonder if he dances. *Or does he come here with Penny to hook up with other women?* The crowd is charged and inviting. It is a sweatbox downstairs, but I still want to go down. It's been a while since I felt this excited to dance.

"I'm going downstairs for a quick two-step. Are you coming?"

"Please do enjoy yourself. I'm comfortable with the view from here." *Is it safe to leave him by himself here?* I contemplate staying, but then I see Vincent standing in the far corner, his all-black suit blending in with the wall. "Go, Vida," Julius says to me.

I make my way downstairs and Duke follows closely behind me. The crowd separates more quickly after they spot Duke walking toward the dance floor. I finally reach Abla and Penny and they usher me inside their Soul Train circle. Julius is looking down but I wonder what he actually sees. *Just how much eyesight does he have?*

"Yaa, show dem how iz done," Abla shouts in my ear. I feel like I'm in college all over again. I pump my arms above my head and move to the beat of the music.

Chapter 16

"Yaa…! Yaa!" Abla's voice alarms me. After all these years, it's hard to tell what is an actual emergency or just her need to spread gossip.

"I'm upstairs," I yell back and she storms into the bathroom. She sits down on the toilet seat.

"Are you still bathing deese boys?" She addresses her comment to me, but she looks at the boys disapprovingly. I continue scrubbing MJ's feet while the twins begin scrubbing their heads. "MJ I understand, but you guys should know how to wash yur ass by now," Abla says. I shoot her the eye.

Lately I've found soiled underwear in the laundry. It is definitely not MJ, which narrows it down to the twins. And I know which of the two it is, but to be sure and not embarrass anyone, everyone gets a refresher course in how to take a bath and especially how to wipe their ass.

"When waz da las' time someone took care of yur housecleanin'?" It doesn't take long to figure out what she is referring to. With Abla every undertone is about sex or appearances.

"Auntie, please talk to Mommy. We are men now. This is embarrassing. We know how to take a bath. We need our privacy as growing men," Kakra entreats. No one responds. Panin continues scrubbing his chest and back.

"Everyone squat and wash well. From front to back," I say. Everyone bends down except for Kakra. I hand MJ the *sapo* and he holds it to his rear like a feather. I take his hand and navigate it to where it needs to go. "Dig deeper and scrub harder."

"Auntie, I'm bathing myself," MJ says. Panin never misses a beat. From the first time I instructed him, he has maintained the same washing routine. First water and then soap and sponge. Start from the top of the head and finish at the bottom of your soles. However, Kakra is still pouting. *You would have thought I asked him to remove a limb.*

"Auntie, this is not fair," Kakra complains.

Abla scrunches up her face and then turns to me. "Why are you playin' hard to get?"

"Auntie, are we playing a game?" MJ says.

"No. Just yur mommy."

I chime in. "No, baby. No games for anyone." I rinse the soap off of MJ and hand him to Abla to dry off. Her attention moves away from me again and onto Kakra. Her eyebrows stiffen like a caricature.

"Anywayz, back to my point. Felix sayz you haven't returned any of his callz. He doesn't know wat else to do. He really—" I shoot her another stern look.

"Abla. Abla, not now." The last thing I need is for MJ to tell his father that men have been calling Mommy.

"Oh, I forgot about Playback."

MJ is a running tape recorder. He plays back conversations at the most inappropriate times. Like the time he caught Mensah and me fucking on the dining room table one night. Months later, during Thanksgiving, he told all the family around the table that they had to hurry up because Daddy sleeps on top of Mommy on the table. From then on, Abla nicknamed him Playback.

Panin rinses the soap off and gets out of the tub. Kakra is still complaining as he rinses off the excess soap. Abla hands Panin the towel hanging behind the door.

"You know da person who complains da most iz da one not doin' da right ding," Abla says.

"What? I'm not soiling my underwear," Kakra says.

"But who mentioned anything about soiling their underwear?" I say. He hangs his head down while guilt consumes him. He makes an attempt at a unicorn story.

"I'm just saying, I bathe myself all the time. I don't need a reminder." *Huh. Trying to persuade me—the queen of unicorn stories.* Abla hands him a towel as he steps out of the tub.

"You prove dat twins are not da same after all." Abla's eyes moves across Panin and then onto Kakra. "You…" She points to Kakra directly below his waist. "If you don't stop drinkin' all doze sugary drinks…hmmmmm, you won't catch up to yur brotha."

"What?...Auntie," Kakra yells. This is my third evil eye, but she doesn't catch my gaze to stop her verbose mouth.

"Abla," I shout. She doesn't turn to look at me. Kakra and Panin were born identical twins and it is hard to tell them apart physically unless they are naked. Kakra looks at his brother's nakedness and then at himself and it occurs to him what we all see.

"I told you I can bathe myself." He storms out of the bathroom with the towel barely covering his nakedness.

"What's wrong with you?" I snap at Abla.

"Doze sugary drinks shrinks *kotes*. I told you dis and you keep buyin' it for dem. Hmmmm…do you see da amount of fruit drinks and soda he drinks a day? On da weekend he can drink tree cans of Coca Cola and den doze power drinks. He has to stop it now before it affects hiz growth."

"He's only ten years old. Stop it with your old wives' tales. I will manage the drinks, but you didn't have to embarrass him like that. He could develop a complex about his body."

She stands up and walks toward the door. "Okay, sorry. I take it back." Abla is notorious for shooting off at the mouth and then in the same breath apologizing. It is a habit she still hasn't grown out of, knowing when to nurse words for comfort and when to fire words for attack. I'm mad. She grabs my hand and squeezes it gently. "Yur right. Sorry. I'm sure he will end up like his cocky fatha. I will say sorry."

"You better," I say. I try to move past her out of the bathroom. But she takes hold of me and sways me back and forth forcing me into a smile. "Alright. Enough."

"'Member growin' up, Daniel waz like dis…" She holds up her pinky finger. "And now, I hear women line up like Ash Wednesday lookin' for hiz ass."

I yell into the hallway. "Okay guys, make sure you grease yourself from head to toe and everything—and I mean everything—in between before you put on your pajamas." I turn my attention back toward Abla. "And who told you that?"

"Please, da women he screws all haf moufs like leaky faucets. 'Member he uze to shit in hiz pants? Now look, hez da hottest ding since powdered fufu."

"I think I need to start having the big talk with the twins," I digress. "They are turning into men right before my eyes. Kakra's voice is changing. And they are both growing so tall. I need to reach Mensah and see what he thinks we should do."

Abla rolls her eyes. "He should be here. Yaa, enuf about him. We can do it ourselvz, like we did wit Pancake."

"Yeah, but it's different for boys. They still need a man's presence. I'll wait until MJ's birthday. If I don't hear from him, then I will ask Daniel to talk to him."

"Oh, noooo. Solve one problem and create anotha. Huh, Daniel will haf dem chasin' women before dey get out of middle school. I will ask Richard."

"Really, Richard?"

"Yeah, watz da big deal?" It is a big deal and we both know it. I am afraid to ask how things are going because I really don't want to jinx it.

"Now, dat iz settled. Should I call Felix to do housecleanin'?"

"No."

"I didn't want to say it in front of da boys, but I heard dat if you don't haf sex after a couple of years, yur *etwe* seals back up." Now she is pointing to me below the waist.

"Bullshit."

"Okay, if you want to try it and see, den go ahead. You will need scissors to cut Ginger open." She tells horrible unicorn stories; in fact her stories are like B-rated movies.

"And who did you hear that from?"

She tilts her head upwards like the answer is waiting to fall from the ceiling before giving a response. "Dr. So-and-so." We both laugh. She sobers up and takes me by the hand. "Look at you. Young and sexy. Are you goin' to waste yur youf waitin' for him to show up? Itz not fair, Yaa."

"I don't need sex…" Her eyes nearly pop out of her head as she claps her hand over her mouth. I can read her thoughts and quickly interject, "…now."

"O-M-G. Shhh…" She puts her index finger over my mouth. "You see now. Look at wat yur sayin'. Deer are spirits in dis world lissenin'. Da Bible sayz power of da tongue. So you want to lay in bed wif yur double A battery plastic *kote* for da rest of yur life?"

She knows about Billy? Now I definitely know she snoops through my things when I am not home. "That is not my priority. It hardly crosses my mind." I look her straight in her face. *That is how you tell a unicorn story.* The truth is that I crave Mensah's lips on me and the scent of his sweat as it drips from his forehead onto my face. The way his ass moves like the second hand on a clock when we make love. I miss my legs wrapped around his waist like a pretzel knot. *Why am I thinking about this? Stop it, Vida.* I continue with my unicorn story. "I have the kids to keep me busy and now I'm writing for Julius."

She moves back and places one hand on her hip. "Cocoa farmers are busy, yur in denial. No one is ever too busy for sex. If possible, people would create anotha hour in a day for good sex. No foolin' me. We're sistas, and da same blood dat flows drew my body flows drew yurs. Not a day dat goes by dat I don't dink about sex. All dis work and no play iz goin' to turn yur *etwe* to a stale root." We both laugh. She places my hand into hers again. "Please, I beg. Give Felix a call. Yur huzzband iz off doin' God-knows-wat while you lay here at night and play with yurself."

"What!"

She shoots me a quick look. "Like I said, we're sistas. Dis separation iz too much for you. Just look at you. Yur young, beautiful and smart. When you dress up and put on doze F-M-Ps, women and men can't take deer eyez off you."

I smooth the shirt over my stomach to reveal two pack abs, but with a couple of weeks of hard workouts, I can get my six pack back.

"You look good, Yaa, but you need to step out of dis house. Art can't be appreciated if itz not seen." I shoot her another glance and wonder if she read that somewhere. "Marriage iz a state of being. If you don't haf a huzzband to call a marriage, den guess wat? You don't haf one." That's definitely an Ablaism. "Sista, yur too fine and Mensah needs a reminder dat if he doesn't handle hiz business, someone will. You haf every right to live yur life."

Her words pierce my soul and she is right about waiting around for Mensah to acknowledge me. I need to do it for myself.

"You see, God knowz wat he iz doin'. He didn't give me yur ass. If he did, I would haf a country named after me by now."

"So, are you and Richard officially together?" I ask her, trying to take the heat off of me. "He really likes you, Abla, and I know you feel the same way."

"Yeah, we are enjoyin' each otha, but I'm not ready to give up my career and become a housewife."

"What are you talking about? You hardly work now. Six months out of the year to be exact."

*

I open the bathroom door to let the steam out, literally. I peek my head into the boys' bedroom. Panin is already nestled in his bed. We both chuckle at how neatly his bedspread is tucked in underneath him. The empty bed that Kakra used to sleep in is still neatly dressed.

"Good night, honey," I say. I never get a response, but occasionally I will get a smile before I leave the room. We check in on Kakra and MJ. Kakra is reading a book to MJ while they lie in bed together.

Abla moves inside the room and then kisses Kakra on the forehead. "Don't pay attention to yur auntie. You know I'm kooky sometimes. I'm just jealous dat I don't have yur super powers," she says.

"Super powers?" Kakra says. "Like Panin?"

"Yes. Did you forget? Yurs iz different from Panin. Don't worry, you will see," Abla says.

"Mommy, is that for real?"

"Of course it is. You do know you are special?" I say.

"Yes. H-E-C-I—handsome, entertaining, charming and intelligent," Kakra says brightly.

"All of that and with a scoop of chocolate syrup on top." It is the best pep talk we can give on the spot, but it works. His face lights up.

"What about me, Mommy? What do I have?" MJ asks.

"Well, you know if we all are special, then of course you are. You can't tell the world. Keep it and protect yourself with it always. God put you on this earth for a reason and soon he is going to tell you what it is. So you have to be ready. Be strong, be humble and be smart."

"But don't forget, too much sugar and you loze yur powers," Abla says.

"Yes, Auntie," they both say in unison.

"Good night, Hercules." Kakra's face turns into a cheesy grin.

"Good night, my queen," Kakra says. I kiss them and leave the door cracked open.

Abla follows me to my bedroom and closes the door. "Did you hear about Kwabena's wife, Fatima?" Abla says. She relaxes herself on my bed.

"No, what happened to her?" I lie beside her on my stomach. I'm sure this will be a juicy story that only Abla can tell with three-D animation.

"She caught him at dat hotel by da highway."

"Which highway?"

She snaps her fingers trying to recall the name. "Da one by McDonald's."

"Oh, by the I-ninety-five."

"Yes, datz it. He called hiz wife to tell her he waz droppin' somedin' off to a client and she didn't say anydin'." Her eyes grow big and she pokes her finger into my flesh to emphasize a point. "I heard she drove to the hotel and hiz car waz…at…da…hotel…in…da…parkin'…lot." She draws the words out slowly, which creates more intensity to the story. I sit up partially with my head resting on the palm of my hand. "She went to the cashier and askz for her huzzband in hiz name. But he had enuf sense to use a different name. So dey couldn't give any information to her. She pointed to hiz car in da parkin' lot and da worker said she couldn't identify who da owna was."

I stop her. "She couldn't or wouldn't?"

"Hmmmm…just wait, let me land," Abla says. "She went back to da car and waited in da parkin' lot. Do you know how long she was deer? Hmmmm." She cuts her eyes and then makes a sound from the back of her throat that only a woman who has spoken years of tribal dialect can make.

"No, how long?"

"Four good hours." Abla raises her fingers to emphasize the number four and turns her lip up in disgust. "How much fuckin' are you doin'? When will you go home to yur wife after fuckin' for four good hours?"

"Hmmmm. You would be surprised." My thoughts bring me back to the first night at Julius's home.

"Eheheh…No. Not him. He hasn't seen hiz *kote* in years wit dat huge Heineken belly. So anywayz, he came outta da room wit da otha woman." Her nose scrunches up to match the furrowed brows on her face. "And come and see dis *unreceiving*-face-woman. A dog face, classless lookin' woman who can't afford a decent wig." Abla claps her hands together as though she is lathering cream into her palms. Her voice is a bit higher than normal.

"Oh my goodness." I finally sit up and meet Abla at eye level.

Abla shakes her head and makes the sound again. This one is deep, no doubt a sound of disappointment. "So, Fatima runs out of da car and grabs da woman." Abla demonstrates by pulling on my arm as though she witnessed the scene firsthand. "And den pounds into her like fufu. She uze her fist, shoe and beat da woman until she cried onto da floor. 'Hey…hey…Fatima,' she tried dough…Oh…hmmm…And da kidz waz shoutin' for Fatima to stop. But she couldn't. Da rage took over her."

"What? The children were there?"

"Oh, I should haf said it earlier. Da kidz were in da pajamaz sleepin' while dey waited for deer fatha to come. Da fightin' must haf woken dem up. Hmmmm…can you imagine? Two beautiful girlz seein' deer fatha and a mistress at da hotel and Fatima beatin' da woman in da parkin' lot. Wat a disgrace."

"Oh my goodness." I cover my mouth and then rest my hands in my lap. Fatima is a nice lady. I always admire her ladylike demeanor when we meet at parties. On Facebook, she seems to have everything together. Her husband a successful real estate broker, kids in private school and a big house in New Rochelle. What a horrible ordeal to go through. If Abla knows, then I am sure that half of the Ghanaian community in New York knows. "What did Kwabena do?"

"Wat could he do? Shameful man. He got caught. I heard he ran to hiz car and sat inside like a hopeless dog. Fatima waz smart. She blocked hiz car wit herz so da only way to run iz by foot. And you know Fatima. Shez a Northerner; thick and tall."

Every now and then, Abla will make comments as though I grew up alongside her in Ghana. She makes reference to a particular region of people or tribe that has unique attributes. I don't stop to ask questions, but nod my head in agreement as though I know what she is alluding to. "Even me, Abla"—she points her finger into her chest—"would dare not cross her."

"But wait, how did she know he was at that hotel?"

"Men dink dey are so smart. He uze a different name alright, but den he haz been uzin' hiz credit card and chargin' da room. Foolish man. She went online and track da card usage."

"Wow, that's crazy. I'm not sure what I would have done if that was me," I say. *Honestly, I do know. I'm sure my beat down would pale in comparison to Fatima's squabble.* The betrayal. The lying. The other woman... It makes me angry to think if that could ever be me. Fighting over a man who doesn't have any regard for his marriage. I'm mad.

"I heard she beat up da girl very bad. Da police came and everytin'."

"What did Kwabena have to say for himself?"

"Hmmmm," Abla sighs. "I heard now he iz beggin' da mistress not to press charges on da wife. Can you imagine?" she says with total disgust.

As sad as it is, it is comforting to hear that I am not the only one who accuses her husband of infidelity. I've never seen Mensah with another woman, but I have had my suspicious even before he left for California. I'm guilty of tracking his whereabouts, searching through his phone, reviewing credit card charges, checking his pockets for anything that would confirm my suspicion. Unknown phone calls at odd times; trips out of the house with no particular destination; long periods of quietness; no solid proof to substantiate my feelings, but I knew he was keeping something from me. Auntie Cece warned me about looking for something that I shouldn't be looking for. More often than not, I would find something to raise my suspicions. To answer Abla's question, I say sadly to myself, *Yes.*

Chapter 17

"I got your message. Yes, we need to talk. Babe, I gotta call you back. Something came up."

Mensah's voice message exactly two hours and ten minutes ago was hurried, hard and hoarse. I'm waiting to breathe normally again. *I hate him. No, I love him, sickly. Stop crying. Control yourself, Vida.* My mouth is dry and I have an uncomfortable feeling in my throat, like a pill stuck. I listen to the message again and for sure that is a woman's voice I hear giggling. Why hasn't he called me back? Anxiety and mad jealousy take hold of me. *Maybe he is in a public place and it's noise from the background. Or maybe there is a woman with him. What would she be giggling about?* I quickly dial his number. His voicemail again and I can't think of anything to say. He's heard all the empty threats of me leaving. Eventually his words soothe me momentarily with the accompanying bouquet of forgive-me tulips. *He knows I love tulips.* I try again and like the last time no message. *Why am I fighting for a marriage that is not working?*

Again, not a single letter of the alphabet on the screen tonight. It's been habitual these last two months. Several journals lay open on the desk. The computer screen stays on inviting me to type at least a sentence. *Focus, Vida.*

"Good evening." Julius approaches the desk and I quickly use my palms to wipe my face. My eyes feel like quarters are resting on my eyelids, but I manage to meet his eye level.

"Good evening, Julius," I say with false jubilation.

"Are you feeling better? Are your allergies still bothering you?"

He must be getting tired of me saying the same thing.
"Ummm...not really. It's much better than last weekend."

"Huh, I thought the rug might have been the culprit. We removed it last week and Vincent made sure that you could see your reflection on anything in this library. I also replanted the tree in the back to the other side of the building. Sometimes ragweed and other pollens can makes its way in. I asked Max to look around for anything else that may cause an allergic reaction, so please let me know if anything else bothers you," he says.

"Oooh. I'm sorry to have put you through so much trouble."

"No trouble at all, Vida."

Shit, he did all this for me and it's just a stupid unicorn story. I feel guilty. "My allergies are actually getting much better. I've been running around town all day, so something might have triggered it this evening."

"I see," he says.

"Ummm…I just realized I have an appointment early tomorrow morning. The kids have their first swim class, so if you don't mind I'll leaving a bit early." He doesn't say anything but takes a seat opposite the desk. *Shit. Please don't ask to read what I've typed so far.* The blank screen is still staring at me. I walk away from him and unplug my charger from an adjacent wall.

"So, how has your day been so far?" Julius asks. He smirks a bit and opens the carved wood box on the desk, which I hadn't noticed until now. He pulls out a cigar and lights it. It scents the air with a musky vanilla fragrance.

"Okay. Just a lot of paperwork with the clients and all." *This reminds me; I need to check in with Mr. Jenkins' daughter. I hope she took him to see the nursing homes.*

"I see. And how is your pussy holding up?"

I move to my original position facing him. *Focus, Vida. Now you're hearing things.* "Sorry, I'm very tired, I didn't hear you."

"I said, how is your pussy holding up? You know, especially after three kids." My butt nearly misses the chair while my mouth flies wide open like a flycatcher. *Yeah, I heard him right the first time.*

"What did you say?" *Like, really, Vida, do you need to hear it again?*

He takes long puffs of his cigar and begins again. "How…is…your…puss—" The words are drawn out one at a time, but I interject.

"Stop!" He is still sitting there as though he asked me if it's snowing outside or what is my favorite color. "Excuse me?" I say.

"I mean, did you tear much after you gave birth? So, how much thread did they use to stitch you back up? I would think a combined total of a spool full of thread would do." He blows smoke. "Wow, come to think of it, that's really a lot of sewing. Three pregnancies is a lot of work on a pussy, don't you think?" He leans back in the chair and crosses his legs because this must be normal dialogue for him. "But it is truly an amazing testament to the anatomy of a woman and no doubt motherhood. All that physical force: sex, daily excretion of fluids, pregnancies, not to mention medical examinations. And you've persevered with three. I'm no expert, but with so many job functions, I wonder does it ever get tired and say, 'This is it. I've had enough. I'm just going to close up shop and stop working.' Which brings me back to my original question, how is it holding up?"

Would it be a crime to slap a blind man? Arrogance is one thing, but downright disrespect is another. He has the audacity to continue. "I mean, is there still traction on the tires, you know, or do you need a 'tire rotation?'" He uses air quotes. *This asshole used air quotes.* I should leave before I say something unprofessional. *No. You need to open your mouth, Vida.* The woman turned badass in me is championing me on. *Wait. Don't lose control, Vida. Where are my hands? Okay, still beside me. Hitting him would be awful. Temper your emotions. Put your hands on your hips. Now address him.*

"What the heck is wrong with you? No, I'm sorry, a better question is, are you on drugs? What—how is this a topic for discussion?"

"Do you feel offended? Please don't be. I have never had a candid conversation with a mother of three before. You are at liberty to answer or not. But I won't know the answer to my question if I don't ask. Just curious. I know this can be a touchy subject for you, especially with everything your pussy has been through." He looks sincere saying this.

Okay girl, smack the shit out of him right now. No. I can't. Use your words not your hands. "I don't feel offended, but I certainly don't feel the need to entertain this conversation." It's hard containing my anger. "I can't believe the things that you say. I mean, really."

"You shouldn't be surprised. We've been working together for several weeks now. Don't you appreciate my candor? Frankly, I find political correctness a bit boring. Life happens in a flash. Here today and, well, spent tomorrow. I pride myself in not worrying or thinking too much about what others think or feel I should do or say. Be yourself and say what you mean. That's all. Don't you think?"

"Well, Mr. Gallo, I appreciate your candor at times, but as my employer, this conversation is totally inappropriate."

"I see," he says. "Well, technically, you are an independent contractor and it is included in the contract we signed."

"Really, that was in the contract? To have discussions about my female anatomy?" *Okay, keep it professional, Vida.*

"Yes. Well, not in layman terms, but in legal terms definitely. I have the right to speak openly about any topic I choose, especially in my home. So, Ms. Frimpong, you have every right to tell me it's none of my business, but you won't sanction me in what I can or cannot say."

"I see." It is my turn to use his zero-value expression. "Mr. Gallo, you may have every right to discuss whatever topic that runs through your mind, but let's be clear, my anatomy is none of your damn business."

"So, Ms. Frimpong, there is a problem with the ride? I mean, that would be the reason why you choose not to answer the question. I've heard some women need whole new transmissions. It would be a pity if you had a slipping transmission. That's costly and it never really rides the same. Well, then again, I also heard about this whole new line of rejuvenation. I imagine it must save a lot of marriages." His composure shows no sign of humility or absurdity.

"This is sexual harassment."

"Oh, come now, Ms. Frimpong. Sexual in nature, but harassment, no. Consider this constructive criticism."

"Constructive criticism? I've had enough of this tortuous conversation. I'm going home. I will see you next weekend. Maybe. Good night." I shove the rest of my belongings ruggedly into my bucket bag in no particular order. His head follows my movement toward the door. His demeanor is still composed. *What an asshole.*

"Good night, Ms. Frimpong, and sweet dreams."

"Asshole." I hope he heard that.

*

After a hot shower, I lay in bed running down the itinerary for tomorrow. *First, swimming lessons for the boys; soccer practice for Kakra; food shopping. Must remember to buy paper towels; go to the Container Store for new food organizers for Panin and more underwear for MJ.*

"Damn it." *The parking ticket. I'll have to look for it tomorrow and pay it online.* Mensah always took care of things like that; now it's one of the many tasks he's abandoned. *Oh, and the mortgage, I have to remind Mensah to pay it again. He should really sign up for online banking.*

The pillow provides needed comfort, but I'm not sleepy. I rub my hands in between my legs, but I don't have the sexual urge. Julius's words leave an anchor in my head. *How is my pussy holding up after three pregnancies?*

He has the audacity. *First of all, they were C-sections...And secondly, it is none of his damn business.* I sit up and rest my back against the padded headboard while maintaining an argument in my head. *I should have given him a good tongue-lashing. I bet no one has put him in his place before. That's why his tongue is so loose. People probably feel compassion for him because he is blind. But you can be blind and still be an asshole. Well, I'm not intimidated by any of it. Julius Gallo is not exempt from an African tongue-lashing.* I'm pacing the room now. The alarm clock on the bedside table reads 12:03 a.m. and it's much too late to call him and give him a piece of my mind.

No, Julius needs face-to-face combat. Before swimming, we will pay Mr. Gallo a visit. No. The children shouldn't witness this. The kids will wait in the car and I will run in and give him a rude awakening. It's about to be hurricane season on his ass. He may fire me tomorrow. Well, I don't care. There is no way that he is going to talk to me that way. Who the hell does he think he is? 12:17 a.m. Damn, that's it. Nine more hours to go before the boys get up. I lay down and punch my fist into the pillow. "Hmmmm," I murmur in Abla's heavy Ghanaian accent. *Tomorrow be tomorrow.*

Chapter 18

I don't even need an alarm clock. There is a peak of skin rising in the middle of my forehead. I notice it as I brush my teeth. It's still there when I come out of the shower. I'm really going to give him a piece of my mind. I round up the kids and systematically buzz around the house preparing breakfast, ironing clothes, packing gym bags. By eight o'clock, we are heading out the door.

"I thought you said swimming is at ten. Why are we leaving so early?" Kakra has always been a late riser. He moves like a zombie toward the car.

"Trust me, Kakra, you don't want to get me started this morning. Pick up your feet like they belong to your body and get into the car." His eyes pop open and he leaps into the back seat. I'm in rare form this morning. It's about to be Hurricane Sandy at Julius Gallo's residence. I turn to the boys in the backseat. "We have to make a stop before swimming."

The words are bubbling in my mouth like hot pepper soup. Within minutes, I whip onto the Triboro Bridge navigating toward Steinway Avenue like a veteran cab driver. Twenty-five minutes later, I am parked in front of the tall grey industrial building. "Okay, I will be back shortly. Panin is in charge."

"How come he's in charge?" Kakra says.

"Okay, Kakra. You are in charge of you and MJ. Panin is in charge of MJ and you." It basically boils down to the same directive, but Kakra smiles with this arrangement.

My fingers dance over the keypad and the gates open. Boy, is he going to get the African Mojo tongue lashing of a century. Alice announces my presence. Flying two steps at a time, I knock on the *kotedenden* room. I really don't give a shit if he is fucking or hanging upside down. A busty Asian woman opens the door. "Babe, are we playing a new game?" She removes an eye mask and steps back, startled to see me.

"Oh, I thought you were Julius." The tan, tall and top-heavy Asian woman is naked. I'm not surprised. She is more attractive than Penny. Her extra bubble lips, blue eyes and bouncy triple Ds tell me she's manufactured in the USA. "Are you playing too?" She looks happy. "Penny never mentioned you, but I'm not complaining; the more the merrier." Penny must have a harem of women.

"Oh, no. I am far from playing any games," I say. "Julius is not here I guess?" I peer over her shoulder without entering the room.

"No. He wasn't lying next to me when I woke up. I think we are playing a new game." She examines me and then opens the door a little more. "Do you want to come inside and wait for him? I'm really good with massages."

"No, thank you. I'll check his study." *Don't lose momentum, Vida.* Rushing down with a little more speed than when I came up, I push the door open without even so much as a knock. He is wearing more clothes than his play date, dressed in a white T-shirt and cargo pants. He doesn't turn around to look at me.

"Good morning, Ms. Frimpong," he says.

No salutations, Vida, straight to the point. "Mr. Gallo, let me tell you something. I don't know who—"

"I'm so glad you came by this morning. I've been expecting you."

"You've been expecting me!" I'm already disgusted. Did he think I was going to play hide-and-seek with his playmate? "Well, this is not a—" He interrupts me again. "I'm sure you thought about me last night. I suppose you went to bed pissed off. Probably fueled with disgust. I am sure many things went through your mind about me. Names I am sure you will share with me later—"

"You are so full of yourself. Let me tell—"

He stops me again. I'm losing momentum. "But first, let me continue. Before you went to sleep, you probably played our conversation over and over again in your head and concluded that I'm out of my fucking mind. I'm sure you lay in bed kicking yourself mentally about things you should have said to me but maybe were afraid to say. Last night, no matter how you felt about me, you slept a little better." He moves over to his table and his hands search for something. He picks up a screw and maneuvers it into a handheld device.

"And do you know why you slept better?" He doesn't give me a chance to respond. "Because maybe for once…last night…you weren't thinking about *him*."

Him who?…Mensah?…How does he know?…Yes…Mensah. He's raining on my bonfire. Last night I punched my pillow thinking of comebacks for Julius and at times laughed at my insanity, but there were no tears for Mensah. He continues.

"Now, this morning when you woke up, you were thinking about me again and the words…ahhhh, the words you should have said last night filled your thoughts. So you drove here this morning, perhaps with children in tow, to give me a piece of your mind. Because after all, I've crossed the line. I had the audacity to talk about a subject that was none of my concern. But nevertheless, you came here to set your boundaries. On point so far?" He chuckles.

He's stealing my thunder, lighting, hail and hurricane winds. My hands leave my hips and relax by my sides. *This is definitely not going as planned.* "I must admit my tactics are not conventional, but it is the end result that I am concerned with." He bypasses me and sits on a nearby stool. "How long can you keep using allergies as an excuse for your melancholy, Ms. Frimpong? Don't you want to be happy? Don't you deserve to be happy?"

Yes. Yes. I do deserve happiness. Tears build up because he is right. I am sad, angry and…and…hungry. No dinner last night and certainly no breakfast this morning.

"Please, Ms. Frimpong, do share with me your thoughts or a beating. Whichever you prefer," he says.

What can I possibly say after that? He walks over to the other desk in the room that houses his cigars and takes one out. He dangles the cigar in his left hand. *Save face, Vida. Don't look like a sucker.* There is a silence between us that is uncomfortable. I break the air. "My anatomy—including my pussy—is off limits for discussion," I say.

"Okay. Understood." He smiles. Still not as much venom on the verbiage.

"Your guest is waiting for you upstairs."

"I know." He smiles a bit wider.

"I have to go now. The kids are in the car."

"You should have brought them in. I would have given them a tour."

"Maybe next time, when you don't have a plus one or two or three here."

He laughs. "Okay, Ms. Frimpong."

"Oh, and by the way, it was two."

"Two?"

"Two pregnancies. Kakra and Panin are twins."

He chuckles again. "Ah, yes. That is really good for you, right?"

"How quickly you forget. This topic is no longer a conversation."

He raises his hand in surrender. "Of course. Pardon me."

"And just to set the record straight, everything is running in pristine order. Still under original manufacturer warranty."

"I'm sure," he says.

Hardly the tongue-lashing I envisioned this morning, but I try to leave more gracefully than I entered.

Chapter 19

"Pussy, say it…iz not a bad word." I was hesitant. I'd heard her say it so many times, but when Mommy asked me to say it, I would refer to it as 'the place down there.'

"You are not in school. Yur home. Say it. PUSSY!"

"Pussy." I whispered it.

"Why are you afraid? Iz me and you in da bafroom. Do you know why I'm bafing you?"

I was eleven years old and that night she sat on the edge of the bathtub with her feet solid inside the tub. Her eyes fixed on me. I was sure it was the fever and the blood on the sheets. I thought I was dying, but then Abla wouldn't have had that childish grin on her face.

"Yur a woman now. Yur menses started. Do you know wat dat means?" I shook my head quickly; it felt twice its size. I felt cold and warm at the same time. "Dat means one day you will haf children."

"Oh, Mommy, I don't want to." She laughed and dipped her hand once more in the bucket. The hot water was welcoming on my tender skin. She opened the faucet again and scooped hot water out with a plastic bowl then poured it over my head.

"Iz important dat you clean yurself very well. Squat, Yaa."

I did as I was told and she took the *sapo* and started from my head, scrubbing with forceful hands. Years of pounding fufu and banku added strength to her upper body. When she reached between my legs, she applied gentle pressure. She dipped the bowl into the bucket again and poured it below my waist.

"Iz important dat no one sees yur pussy. Don't let boys touch her. She is very precious to you and you haf to guard her. Do you understand me?" I nodded, still fearful and watchful of the sequence of colors the water emptied into the drain. First a reddish-pink hue, then white soapy bubbles and finally clear water. "You haf a long way to go. You must preserve yurself for da right person. If you don't cherish yur pussy, boys will take advantage of you." She guided her hand over mine and showed me what needed extra attention. Her head rose to meet my eyes and then she held my hand between my legs. "Dis iz da gate to yur soul. Be very careful who enters. Love yurself, Yaa. Yur pussy iz beautiful because yur beautiful. Take good care of yur body; iz beautiful. Do you understand me?" Her brown eyes heavily watered as she turned her gaze away.

"Here. Show me wat I taught you." She lathered the *sapo* with soap once more and handed it to me.

I traced the path on my skin making sure to add pressure with the sponge to each stroke.

"Front to back," she insisted. "Now rinse." I continued to bathe with her eyes fixed on my every move. At times she guided my hands to underneath my arms, my butt and feet.

"You haf ten toes. Take time to wash in between dem."

I poured the remaining water over me and she filled the bucket again.

"Now take yur soiled undawear and make sure you wash da seat of yur panties very good. I haf new waist beads for you."

After she toweled me dry and applied shea butter to my skin, she tied new waistbeads to my waist. The white and red beads that I wore since my seventh birthday were high above my navel. My new beads were green and blue. After Mommy tied them to my waist she showed me how to put on an Always pad. It looked like a mini pillow as she positioned it on my underwear. "Now put yur panty on," she said. I slipped them on and felt the obvious difference in between my legs. "Are you okay?" I nodded slightly. "You will bleed and when you go to da bafroom to change it, you must wrap it dis way." She held a new Always in her hand and rolled it into a ball. "Use da old newspaper unda da sink to wrap it in and den put it in da garbage can. Do not chrow it in da garbage wifout wrappin' it. Iz not sanitary and people don't need to see dat in da trashcan. Do you hear me? You must take time to wipe yurself clean before you put anotha pad on." She held toilet tissue in front of me and demonstrated. "Front to back. Den put a new pad on."

I lay in bed that night thinking about the events that occurred. Abla knelt beside me. "Does it hurt?" she asked. "You know, cramps?"

"No. Not really." She hovered over me and placed her palm on my forehead.

"Yur fever iz down. Wata alwayz helps da body when iz goin' drew changes. You know you haf to give yur *etwe* a nickname now."

"A name like a pet?" I said.

"Something besides 'pussy' or '*etwe*.' People uze 'pussy' for everytin' now. If you cry too much dey call you pussy. If yur too shy dey call you pussy. Dink of somedin' dat you like. A nickname. Trust me, when you get olda, you will uze it."

I knew Peach was already taken. I'd heard Abla numerous times on the phone with Jesus referring to her *etwe* as the best tasting Peach there was.

"How long will this last?"

"About a week."

"The bleeding lasts a week?"

"Hmmm…" She giggled. "Deer will come a time when you will look for it like yur house keys." I didn't understand at the time, but the following year we welcomed Pancake into the world.

*

The alarm on my phone brings me back to my present state. I adjust the car seat forward and turn the ignition off. I look in the rearview mirror. My face looks like someone who just woke up from a nap. I smooth the sides of my hair into the ponytail.

MJ runs in my direction. "Mommy, Mommy, Coach said I can join the swim team next year!"

"He was pretty good today," Kakra adds.

"Panin, did you like the practice?" He shakes his head aggressively 'no.'

I wish he would play at least one sport. This is the last chance at anything. I should have insisted on sitting in during the lesson, but Coach Richards said no parents on the first day.

"Maybe he just doesn't like sports, Mommy," Kakra says.

"Every person in our family plays a sport. Your mother is a soccer player. Your father loves soccer and basketball. You can't sit all day drumming on everything. Even your auntie used to be a track star. I don't understand. You need something to keep you active. What about running?" He places his headphones over his head and looks away.

Chapter 20

"Alice, play the next track, please," I yell into the ceiling.

"Ms. Frimpong, to better assist you, you can control the playlist through the laptop."

"Oh, that's simple."

"Yes, Ms. Frimpong. Quite simple."

I follow the commands and Andra Day's voice fills the room. I have another journal in front of me. I open it and admire the special details. It smells like old leather. I thumb through the pages. I read a couple of lines, but the words don't lift from the pages. My mind is not focused.

MJ's birthday is next weekend and my to-do list keeps mounting. *Mensah better show up.* He promised that he wouldn't miss MJ's birthday this year, but I wouldn't be surprised. Lately everything has been a disappointment. It's been a couple of weeks since we actually spoke. Phone tag and cryptic emails have taken precedence over usual communication. I pick up my phone again and see no new voicemail. I check WhatsApp to see when he last logged on. It was 6 a.m. his time, which means that he is up. *Don't call him, Vida. The phone works both ways. I am not an option.*

I thumb through the journal some more. The penmanship is neat. I scan a couple of pages and my eyes rest on a paragraph.

Mama caught me again. She wants me to continue my braille lessons but I've already mastered four languages. And certainly there is no need for me to learn another braille language. I sneak away writing in my journal. I know one day, I will see again. I need to continue practicing my penmanship. I mustn't forget. Julius, you have to remember. J...u...l...i...u...s G...a...l...l...o...Julius...Gallo...Don't forget, Julius... please don't—

Wait...there must be a page missing. The next page begins a new journal entry and I can tell from the binding of the journal that a page was torn out. *Okay, Julius what's up? Why did you tear out a page?* I read the next paragraph.

The bleak weather cannot supersede my happiness. Father will visit us today. Mama runs around our home making it presentable for him. I wonder how long he will stay this time. I must show him that I am a man now. I pull out the suits that were delivered to me a month ago. Mama can tell I am excited. She moves my hand to one of the suits. "Are you sure you want to wear this? It is hotter than usual this time of year." The weather doesn't bother me. He has to know that I am a man now. Mama can't tell. But I know he will. He will know without me uttering a word. He will know.

My God...

The alarm on my phone reminds me of the time. It's noon already. Coming in early on Saturday didn't prove to be any more productive than working overnight.

Shit. I didn't order the cake for the party. I close the journal and pull out my to-do list and scribble the word "cake." I run down the list, checking off what I have completed and surveying what has to be done. I am grateful that Abla is home watching the boys this afternoon. This will give me time to run some errands.

DJ? I didn't get confirmation on Daniel's DJ. I need to call him tomorrow as well. I shut down the laptop and place the journals back into the vault. My phone rings. It's Julius.

"Hi."

"Good afternoon, Vida. You've changed your hours?"

"Well, sort of. I had a lot of running around to do last night and I practically fell asleep in my clothes."

"So you came into work this morning. Wow, such dedication."

"Yes, you know me, hard at work." I wonder if he has cameras watching me.

"How are things progressing?"

"Good. You know, just taking my time to read through a lot of the journals before I continue transcribing."

"Okay, whichever method you feel comfortable with. I have a few business meetings, so you can reach me by phone today. I should be back to New York by next weekend."

"Okay, cool."

Should I invite him to MJ's birthday party? I mean, it is a kids' party-slash-adult party. He might feel uncomfortable. Africans party well into the early dawn. *Okay, extend the invite to be polite.*

"Are you free next Friday?"

"Next Friday?" he asks. "Maybe. What do you have in mind?" *Watch what you say around him.*

"Well, my youngest, MJ, is turning five and Abla is turning the big four-oh again, so we are having a combined birthday celebration."

"I see," he says.

"Well, it's at my house. The kids' celebration starts at five and the adults' will more than likely start after nine. So please feel free to come by."

"Okay, thank you for the invitation. Did you get a chance to read the journals on the desk?"

"Ummm…hmmmm…Yeah…I'm half way through." A little unicorn story. *It's not really lying. I read two paragraphs. I should ask him about the torn page, but then I would probably be exposing myself. I don't need him asking me more questions. Play it safe. Don't ask, Vida.*

"Okay, no hurry. Just wanted to get your thoughts."

"Yeah, really thought-provoking stuff. Anyway, we definitely have a lot to talk about when you get back."

"Good. Well then, you enjoy the rest of your day."

"Thank you. You too. Bye-bye." I quickly hang up the phone. *That wasn't too bad. Anyway, after the party, I promise to be more focused. I also need to block Abla's calls when I am here.* I spend so much time gossiping about Julius and his nightly activities in the *kotedenden* room. "Alice, stop the music." I pack the rest of my belongings.

"Are you leaving, Ms. Frimpong?"

"Yes. I mean no." *I need to watch out for her too. I don't need her reporting back to Julius.* I continue with my unicorn story. "I will be back. Just need to run an errand."

"Will you return this evening?"

I pause and then answer. "Yeah." *That didn't sound convincing.* "If not tonight, then tomorrow night."

"Very well. I will take note."

Great, now she's my time clock. Alice seems to know a lot about Julius. Maybe he programmed some of the journal entries into her memory.

"Alice, do you know what is written in these journals?"

"Are you referring to the journals that Lord Gallo hired you to transcribe and write?" *She can be such a bitch sometimes.* I roll my eyes into the ceiling.

"Yes. Those journals, hefa."

"What is a hefa?"

There is heifer, an insult if Abla refers to you in that way, and then there is hefa, which we emphasize with the letter 'a' at the end because it is a term of endearment. We occasionally use it with Chin, but she never likes it. Now here I am trying to explain it to Alice. The word flew out naturally.

"It's sort of flattery," I finally say. "Like honey, sweetie or friend."

"Should I refer to you as hefa?" *Alice is funny. But I need to maintain some professionalism. Especially after the showdown I had with Julius the other morning.*

"No, Ms. Frimpong is fine."

"Okay, Ms. Frimpong. Please refer to me as Alice."

Alice has got a little sass to her. "Okay, Alice, what about the journals?"

"I'm sorry, I cannot provide you with any assistance. I have no information on the contents of the journal."

Damn it. "Thanks, hefa," I say beneath my breath. I push the journals to one side of the desk. *Great, I gotta come back here and read these before I see him on Friday.*

CHAPTER 21

"Let me hear you say it."

"Oh, Mommy." MJ sighs as though he has been repeating himself continuously.

"'Oh, Mommy' nothing. I need to hear you say it."

MJ gives another long sigh before he speaks. "Don't touch anything, don't move anything, don't write on anything inside or outside the house. Read your books and finish your homework. If we have to use the bathroom, we have to come and tell you."

"And…" I say, waiting for the final commandment.

"And what else, Mommy?" Kakra says.

"Oh, yeah…Don't go upstairs," MJ adds.

"Panin, nod if you understand the rules." I look at him in my rearview mirror. He is biting his fingernails and making note of the buildings we pass. He is nervous. One of the things I have been trying to break him out of. It is not our normal routine after school. *Sometimes expect the unexpected.* "Panin, I'm waiting." After a few seconds, he gives me a brief nod of acceptance. "Stop biting your fingernails." He grunts and turns his attention outside the window. "Okay. I am not going to stay long. Just three hours and then we'll leave. Okay?"

I told Julius that I would stop by two days ago, but I had so many things to take care of. I use the children's half-day as a great day to call out and finish some work on the journals. This may not be too bad; I know he is away this week, so the children won't run into any of his sexcapades upstairs.

"Does he have an Xbox, Mommy?" MJ asks.

"I don't think so, and remember what I said: don't touch anything."

I pull up to the building and park within the gate. It is surprisingly quieter than usual. Many days on my way to the Queensboro Bridge, construction on the railroad adds to the sounds that fill up Long Island City.

"Mommy, is this where you work now?" MJ says.

"No, Mommy works here part-time."

"It's a big place, Mommy."

"Yes, it is a big place."

"This place is far," Kakra says.

"Not really. The traffic on the bridge delayed us."

I enter my passcode and usher the children in. Alice welcomes me. *I forgot about her. She will surely inform Julius that I am here with my children.*

"Good afternoon, Ms. Frimpong."

"Hi, Alice."

"Have you changed your working hours?"

Here she goes. "No, just need to catch up on some work and I have a little free time this afternoon."

"Have your guests been approved by Lord Gallo?"

"Approved? They're my children."

"Hi, my name is MJ." He searches the hallway for the voice.

"Good afternoon, MJ."

"Hi, I'm Kakra. Are you a robot?"

"Good afternoon, Kakra. No, I am not a robot. I am Alice. May I ask, who is the third visitor?"

"That's our brother Panin. He doesn't talk. So we will say hi for him," Kakra says.

"Good afternoon, Panin."

Panin hasn't been happy since we set off and now worry consumes him as his eyes search for the source of the voice addressing him. He stands like the other pillars in the front entrance, firm and immobile.

"I will be in contact with Julius later," I add.

"Very well. Is there anything you need from me, Ms. Frimpong?"

"No, not now, Alice. Thank you."

"Oh, Mommy, can Alice make a puppy for me? Like they do in the movies?" MJ holds my hand pleading.

"Are you referring to a toy puppy?"

"No, a real live puppy."

"I'm afraid I cannot."

MJ hangs his head down disappointedly but then, like lighting, a thought occurs to him. "What about a chocolate milkshake?"

"Yes. Possible. One moment please."

"Yes! She's making it for me," MJ says. I move into the study and the room is already lit.

"Ms. Frimpong…I have the menu of several local restaurants in the area that serve chocolate milkshakes. Will you be needing anything else before I place the order?"

Well, I guess I might as well order something for the boys to keep them occupied. "A cheeseburger deluxe for Kakra. Chocolate milkshake and French fries for MJ and Panin…" I think hard. I know how delicate Panin can be with food. "French fries but not shoestring fries, well done, and cheeseburger with just meat and cheese, toasted bun but no ketchup, lettuce or pickles. And I will just take a large tea with lemon no sugar."

"One moment please."

I arrange the kids in the hallway away from anything that is breakable or fragile. Alice alerts me that the delivery will be here in twenty minutes.

"When we leave here are we still going to BBQs?" Kakra asks. "You promised, Mommy."

"But I'm ordering food for you now. How much food are you going to eat in one day? Didn't you have lunch in school?"

"I'm becoming a man now, so I need food to maintain my muscles."

"Yes, you are." I give him a cautionary look. "But not in one day."

MJ is being entertained by his coloring book. I get settled into the seat and open the laptop. The screen welcomes me. The gold and black leather journal sits beside the laptop. This must be the journal that Julius was referring to. I scan the first three pages.

Jamaica seems to be much cooler than Taiwan. Mama made sure she applied mosquito repellant before I left the compound.

I skim two pages and focus on a paragraph.

Stacey Ann was here. Her scent was intoxicating. My palms sweat and I breathe harder than usual when I'm in her presence.

Stacey Ann? *I need to ask Julius about her.* I type her name with a question mark on the laptop. I go back two pages and continue to read.

I didn't want to leave, but Mama said we must go back to the church. She assured me that we would return in the fall. Mama wants me to travel as much as I can. Experience new cultures. She would say, you are not a tree, Diego, you can move freely in this world. Nothing should stop you. Her words, a constant reminder to always take chances in life.

Diego? I type "Does Diego=Julius" with a question mark.

A few more pages are missing again. *What the heck is going on? Why write in a journal and then rip the pages out?* I skip a few more pages, not happy with my discovery or how I am supposed to piece events together. My eyes land on another paragraph.

I could feel Vincent's presence quietly walking behind me. I never alerted him to this knowledge. It was consistent. As I approached the tree in front of the Old Presbyterian Church, he would disappear. I washed my feet and hands as usual. I took out my towel from my backpack and washed my face. I rubbed the damp towel over my hair. I brushed my hair back and continued with my cane in hand, feeling my way toward the tree. Vincent's scent was gone.

"Ms. Frimpong, your order has arrived."

"Thank you, Alice." I grab my wallet from my purse. MJ is already asleep on the sofa. I open the front door to find a plump, short man on the other side.

"Hi, you called for a delivery?"

"Yes, are you from—?"

"The diner on the boulevard. " The short man peers over my shoulder. "Wow, I never knew anyone lived here. It looks like crap from outside." I look up at him. "Sorry. No offense. I mean, it looks like an old factory." I ignore his commentary and rip off the receipt attached to the brown paper bag.

"How much do I owe you?"

"Oh, it's paid for already—and thanks for the tip."

"Really?" *I should shut up and consider this rare mistake as a blessing since I only have twenty bucks on me. But then again, he will be back once he notices the error.* "There must be a mistake. I didn't pay for it. Call the deli."

"No, we good, Ms. You see." A handwritten word "paid" is on top of the receipt. "That's the first time anyone's given me a twenty-dollar tip. Thank you again." He smiles and then rushes to his motorbike.

"Thank you." He probably can't hear me with the traffic building onto the Queensboro Bridge. Looks like everything I ordered is in the bag. I close the door and walk toward the kitchen. "Alice, can you provide me with the number to the deli?"

"Is everything all right with your order?"

"Yes, just a little mistake."

"One moment please."

I sort out the food and then call out to the boys. "Alright guys, grub is here. Kakra. Panin." Only Kakra appears in the kitchen. "Where is your brother?"

He looks around and then shrugs his shoulders indifferently. I give him the eye. He quickly offers a response. "Oh, he's in the bathroom."

"Ms. Frimpong, I have the number. Shall I dial it for you now?"

I walk past the kitchen to check. No sign of Panin. *Maybe the library?* I press Kakra for more information. He is already standing over the food putting a handful of fries in his mouth. "He's not there. Did you see him wander off? Did he…"

He swallows and then speaks. "Maybe he's upstairs?"

"No, not upstairs." The *kotedenden* room. My heart skips beats as I fly over the steps two at a time. The door is slightly open. "Panin, are you here? Panin?"

"Is something the matter?"

It's quiet. No sound of movement. The room is not how I arranged it in my head. I'm surprised that there are no sex-induced apparatus on the walls or swings hanging from the ceiling. Instead, a simple king sized bed with several huge white pillows. Beige drapes hang from the floor-to-ceiling windows. Two huge wooden chests line one wall. They're locked. *Good.* Well, he's not hiding inside. No sign of him underneath the bed. Inside the closet are several shelves with white bedding.

"I assure you, whatever you are looking for is not in this room."

"I am looking for my son, Alice, can you help me?"

"Which son should I locate for you?"

"Panin, please."

"He is downstairs in the extended suite."

"Where is the extended suite?"

"Downstairs behind the staircase. Next to the elevator."

"Elevator?" I nearly trip over my feet running down the stairs in a panicked state. Kakra is devouring the cheeseburger without the least bit of concern for my meltdown.

"You find him, Mommy?" he says with a mouthful of food.

Behind the staircase is a huge mirrored wall. How do I open it? I wait for Alice for further instruction.

"**One moment please.**" The sliding mirror opens and I freeze.

"He's in there?" I have been here for several weeks and never knew that this even existed and Panin hasn't been here an hour and has already located secret chambers. "Panin!" Still no sight of him.

"**You are free to enter, Ms. Frimpong.**"

The hell I will. This is what horror movies are made of. Abla was right. Paranoid cuckoo craziness is occupying space in my head. The dark hallway is lit with several spotlights along the floor. *What will I find? Ghosts? Bodies hanging on meat cleavers? Stop it, Vida. Get those crazy thoughts out of your head. Julius may be an asshole at times, but he's not a serial killer. Or is he?* "Panin!"

"**Ms. Frimpong, it may be easier to get him yourself.**"

Damn it. Simple instructions, and he sat there and nodded, and now look where I am. "Panin!" *Please God, I can't handle ghosts or dead bodies right now. I'm barely making it with the load I'm carrying. Please. No surprises.* I'm a few feet in and I turn around and warn Alice. "Don't close the doors, I need to listen for Kakra and MJ."

Wait until I get my hands on this boy. He is going to wish God is here. What's that? I stop and listen for the sound again. *Sorry, God, I didn't mean that. You know I'm not wrapped too tight. Empty threats, that's all.* There is a bright light behind a door. I push it open and inside is a museum of instruments. Many are enclosed in glass cases and some occupy pedestals in the middle of the floor. Panin is sitting by a drum set.

"Panin!" He looks up briefly and continues to arrange his chair behind the drum set. "What did I say when we got here? And the first thing you do is go off. You shouldn't be here. Let's go."

"It's quite all right, Ms. Frimpong."

"AAAHHH!" *Shit.*

"It's just me, Vida." Julius is seated in a corner with a guitar on his lap.

"Shit. Fuck. You scared the hell out of me!"

"My apologies. I didn't mean to scare you. I assumed you saw me sitting here." Julius looks relaxed in a T-shirt and distressed jeans. Several guitars surround his secluded area.

"What are you doing here?"

"I thought we've been through this already. I live here."

"I mean, I thought you were going to a conference."

"Ah, yes. It's postponed."

"Alice never mentioned you were home."

"Pardon me, Ms. Frimpong, but you never asked if Lord Gallo was home. If I recall you did say you would contact Lord Gallo yourself."

I roll my eyes. *This heifer.*

"Well, here we are. I see it's bring-your-children-to-work day."

"Ha." I laugh slightly to restore my heart rate. "It's a half day and I just thought I could get some work done before heading home."

"Are you not available over the weekend?"

"Ummm, no. But next weekend I'm all yours."

"I see."

"Sorry for the intrusion, I never knew this room existed."

"Well, it's not all stairs and hallways."

"You are a collector of instruments?" The room is filled with several flutes, trombones, guitars, violins, drums, cellos, trumpets and one large harp. "Can you play all these instruments?"

He looks bewildered. *Maybe it's something I should know already. Shit. I need to get out of here before this starts to become an inquisition.*

"Yes. Do you know which one is my favorite?" I survey the room again and don't have the slightest clue which one he prefers. The grand piano is located at the opposite end of the room. He is surrounded by multiple guitars. *Maybe he likes to play the guitar. Fuck. I don't know.* Panin moves away from the drum set and picks up an instrument from a pedestal. I yell.

"No. Put it down, Panin."

"What is he holding?" Julius asks.

"A horn." He smiles.

"You know, Julius, you have such a wonderful collection of instruments here. I would really hate if something happens to them. We'll go. And sorry for the intrusion again," I say. Hopefully I can ward off any more questions.

"If you need to bring the children, it's quite all right. I understand."

"Thank you, but it won't happen again."

"Ms. Frimpong, I'd rather you focus on writing than worry about your children's whereabouts. Please feel free to bring them. It's a big house and I have more than instruments to keep them entertained."

"Thank you, I appreciate that." I turn my attention to Panin. "For the last time, let's go."

"He doesn't talk much, but he knows his instruments. I've been sitting here while he entertains his curiosity. He's not much of a talker."

"Panin doesn't speak. He stopped talking at three. He has autism."

"How does he communicate?"

"He makes sounds, grunts, moans and screams, but no audible words. At school, he uses his tablet to communicate with the teachers and staff. And at home, it's a combination of notes, pointing and just…just the best possible way a mother can communicate with her child."

"I understand." He pauses as though he is in thought and then continues. "He definitely likes the drums."

"Oh yeah." I giggle, recalling the many nights he woke us drumming away at walls, plates, tables, floors and doors. Mensah finally agreed to buy him a drum set to limit the drumming areas.

"Do you play instruments?"

"No, I think the musical people in the family are Abla and the boys. I can't even hum a note on key, let alone play an instrument." His eyes are closed and his face looks relaxed. "Well, again have a good day." I scramble toward the exit.

"Where are my manners? Let me say hello to the children." He follows behind me and we find Kakra in the middle of the floor sleepily satisfied. Julius engages him in conversation. I go into the kitchen and arrange Panin's food, making sure the cheeseburger is separated from the French fries. A thought crosses my mind.

"Alice, did you tell Julius about the food delivery?"

"Of course, Ms. Frimpong." *That explains the payment.*

Chapter 22

Oh my God, it's Thursday. With just one day until MJ's and Abla's birthday party, it feels as though I haven't accomplished anything. I call out from work so I can navigate my way around the busy streets of the Bronx. I know Abla will be tied up all morning at the hairdresser. I have to get all my errands accomplished before the kids get out of school.

My first stop this morning: Second Star Barbershop on White Plains Road. Mensah always prided himself in cutting the boys' hair, especially right before their birthdays. Another task that I used to rely on Mensah for. I texted him three days ago. I didn't leave too much information, just reminded him of a special day in our lives. Still no response from him. Life is easier with him around. I don't need to think about this now. *You won't ruin this for us, Mensah. Vida, don't consume yourself with what is going on with him.*

Once I snap my mind to the present, I push through the barbershop door and look for Spud Mac. "Hey, Mac, can I bring the boys over this evening for a cut?"

"Sure, mama. Low cut with a line?"

"Yes, for the twins. Tomorrow's MJ's birthday and he wants a Mohawk."

"No problem. Mohawk for the little guy. Come by at seven," he says. One task down and a dozen more to go.

An hour later and the vibration in my bag alerts me to my cellphone. Shit, four missed calls. I scroll through the call history. One from Julius. One from Abla and the other two from Westchester Prep Academy. I pull over and play the messages.

First message: "Good morning, Mrs. Asare. Please call me at your convenience, this is Mrs. Anderson from Westchester Prep."

Second message: "Hello, Mrs. Asare. This is Principal Wynns. Don't be alarmed; everything is okay; we just need to talk to you. Give me a call."

A big sigh of relief. *Perhaps they need my firm commitment on volunteering for reading night. Or is it for the bake sale next week at MJ's school?* Bake sales, school trips, book sales and International Student Dinner are events I promised to chair this school year. It starts with an eagerness to volunteer, then life consumes any free time I think I have. *I should really commit to one event this month. Okay, reminder, get cookies from Costco and bring them to the bake sale next week. Or maybe Mrs. Anderson alerted Principal Wynns that I am transferring MJ to the twins' school?* I like Westchester Prep, but now that the twins are graduating, MJ can have his own identity at the school.

Before I drive off, I call Westchester Prep. Another incoming call blocks me. *Julius. Shit.* I haven't been back at the house since I brought the boys with me. I answer the call.

"Hi, good morning."

"Good morning, Ms. Frimpong. How are you and the children?"

"We are all good."

"I should be leaving Denver this evening and be back tomorrow afternoon. How is your progress thus far?"

"Good."

There are unicorn stories and then there are lies. Sometimes too many unicorn stories equals one lie. Content is usually the deciding factor. There is no sense disappointing him when I know I will be back on Sunday to read the journals. The choice is obvious. *Just one unicorn story for today.*

"That's great news. How about the Italian expressions?"

"Yeah, there are a couple of expressions in Italian I need your translation on." *Unicorn story number two is in full swing.* The last thing I remember in the journal was Julius going to the Presbyterian Church. *I don't know why and with whom. Damn it.* My attention got diverted when the caterer called to confirm the menu for the party. *Which journal had the Italian expressions?* I don't remember. Honestly, I wish he would just hang up.

"Oh, which journal?"

"Ummmm....the big one." *That sounds stupid, Vida.* I continue. "There are a lot of expressions in it. I tried to Google the translations, but it's best when we meet." *Unicorn story number three. Well, really a clarification of story number two. No, Vida, you really created a whole new story. Alright, three unicorn stories. Maybe I should slide my finger over the red phone icon and disconnect him.*

"The big one? Are you referring to the black and gold journal on the desk?" he asks.

"Yes, and the other big one on the desk." *Does this count toward unicorn story number three?* I have no idea which journals he is referencing. "It's a lot of information. But we will have every opportunity to talk about it when you get back." *Okay, that's it, Vida. Disconnect him.*

"I see," he says.

Shit, those two words again. *He's probably calling my bluff. I promise, after the party I will take this assignment more seriously.* "It's amazing you were able to tolerate the heat." *Now why did I say that? I need to control this mouth of mine. But I do recall his mother applying mosquito repellant. Was it in the Caribbean? Taiwan? Italy? Fuck.*

My phone beeps. Incoming call from Westchester Prep. Just in time. "Please hold on, Julius."

"Okay," he says. Damn, I want him to take me seriously. Spending nights sobbing over Mensah while listening to my favorite music tracks doesn't help. Nor does gossiping with Abla about Julius's nightly escapades. *Okay, that's it. No more calls from Abla while I'm working.*

"Hi, Principal Wynns, I just heard your message. I was just about to call you. Can you please hold on one second?" *I need to get rid of Julius.* "Hi."

"I'm still trying to figure out which big journal you are referring to."

So am I. "No, don't worry about it. We can go over it when you get back." I exit the car and accidentally drop the phone. "Shit." *I bet the screen is cracked.* I pick it up and to my surprise not even a scratch. "Hello?"

"Should I call you later?" he asks.

"Yes." He sighs disappointedly. "No…No, go ahead." I definitely don't want him calling me later. I have so much to do before MJ's party.

"Wait, can you just hold on for a minute?" I swipe the call-waiting feature. "Hi."

"Vida." It's still Julius. Damn, I disconnected the school. *Alright buddy, wrap it up.*

Another incoming call. Abla is ringing me now. *Bad timing.* I need to get rid of Mr. Money Bags. I place the phone back to my ear and continue to listen to Julius.

"It's best, whenever you come to an Italian expression to just leave a placeholder and we can review it later. I would hate for you to lose momentum. If my memory serves, there shouldn't be many Italian expressions in the journals on the desk. Perhaps you picked up one of my mother's journals?"

"Mother?" This information is new to me. But I can't reveal my ignorance. Did he mention his mother's journals to me? He continues and another beep alerts me to a second call. It's Abla again. *Maybe her hairdresser can't fit her in and she needs the other hairdresser in Mount Vernon.* She doesn't leave a message.

"What do you think?" he asks.

"Excuse me?"

He releases a deep sigh. "What do you think of what I suggested?"

Shit. I'm lost again. Third call from Abla coming through. I swipe so that the call will go directly to voicemail. "Ummmm, well, I think that is very interesting." *That is such a bullshit answer.*

"What part?" Julius asks.

"Ummm. I think the last part." *How many unicorn stories have I told so far?*

A series of beeps chimes through the phone. Several text messages flash on my screen, but the last one grips me. It's from Abla: **"Come to MJ's school ASAP!"** Chill and fear course through my body.

"I'm sorry, Julius. I'll call you back. Emergency…my son's school…Sorry."

I hang up quickly without hearing his response. Abla calls me again.

"Where are you? I've been tryin' to reach you for ova one hour. Come to MJ's school quick before I slap dis heifer." Her tone is serious.

"What? What happened? Is MJ okay?"

"Come now." Loud voices in the background frighten me.

I know that Abla calling anyone a heifer is not a sign of endearment but a sign of combat. The inflection in her tone and her heavy Ghanaian accent emerge without any attempts to camouflage it. She is in fight mode.

A series of horn blasts and foul language converge on me as I run several red lights while honking like a mad woman. I park in front of the school not paying attention to the yellow striped paint marked No Parking. *No ambulance and no police cars. So far so good.* Even though the front office is two doors down from the main entrance, Abla's voice is audible.

"Huh! You don't know who I am? So let me tell you again," Abla's voice sounds from behind the door.

My sweaty palms push the door open. MJ and Abla are on one side of Principal Wynns' desk. On the other side are a Hispanic boy, a short full-figured Hispanic woman and a tall skinny Hispanic woman with multiple tattoos on her neck. Mrs. Anderson stands in the middle of the room with her ponytail disheveled. Principal Wynns' long arms are outstretched like a boxing referee.

"Mrs. Asare, thank goodness you are here." Principal Wynns tilts his head back and breathes a sigh of relief. Abla has one shoe in her hand.

"Hi. What's going on?" I ask, trying to make sense of what I am witnessing.

"Your son threw Voodoo spirits on my son so his penis won't grow no more. Tat's wat's going on." The full-figured Hispanic woman can barely catch her breath yelling at me.

The tattooed neck woman beside her is even more upset. "I'm going to fuck you up, punta!" She is looking straight at Abla.

"You wish you could, mista. No woman who still holds a punta can lay a hand on me," Abla spits. Yep, this has already escalated.

"This shit is wrong. This ain't Africa, negrita. You 'bout to catch a case today," the heavy Hispanic woman says.

"Your son—" the tattooed neck woman continues "—threw this at him and said his penis will shrivel into a pussy." The woman throws a bag onto the principal's desk. "You see why I'm gonna fuck this punta bitch up?" she yells again.

"You don't know who yur messin' wit. Dis negrita iz not scared of you or yur wife. Mi habla español. Su madre esta heifer. Cono." The women spring toward Abla and Principal Wynns barely maintains his forced stance.

"Okay, ladies. Please, please, let's calm down. I don't want to have to call security to remove you," Principal Wynns says.

The bag on the desk looks familiar. I scoop the contents into my hand and know what it is immediately. I laugh, but I am the only one. Memories over twenty years old come flooding back to me. I look at Abla and it makes sense now how the bag of gari ended up in school with MJ. I know why MJ made nonsense threats about things he has no idea of. Abla turns her face away from me. It isn't these women that made her angry.

"You African booty scratcher. You look like medusa. You smell like you come from the jungle."

Tanya Da'Cruz tormented Abla. She hated that her younger brother had fallen in love with a negrita. During lunch recess, Tanya sat with her clique of borinqueas with long, bouncy jet-black hair jabbing jolts of insults at Abla.

Abla pulled out of her pocket a bag of a grainy substance that no one had ever seen before. She blew the powdery substance all over Tanya and recited words that made no sense to Tanya or anyone else. Her final words, which Tanya and her clique of borinqueas heard: "Yur punta is going to seal up like a cave and you will never pee again." Whatever tactics she was going to use to scare Tanya, a fifteen-year-old girl who had just discovered the gazes of boys and kisses, worked. Tanya's parents sent her to Cuba to have family pray over her.

My mother was frustrated and Daddy practically gave up on spanking Abla. She was expelled from school for two weeks. She eventually transferred to a different school, but that didn't stop the bullying from other students. And she never allowed anyone to make fun of her again. Her words always had the proper weight to do the most damage to an insecure teenager.

Abla's words can be venom when she is mad. She doesn't care who it offends as long as you know that you aren't going to hurt her. Standing here looking at Abla, I see a beautiful woman who still carries a scar that none of her body creams can erase.

"You don't scare me. You may have Voodoo, but I have the Santa-Maria," the full-figured Hispanic woman says.

"And where do you dink Santa Maria comes from? You are lookin' at da original. Yur fax copy version won't do notin' to me," Abla says.

"You see. She admits it. She did curse Alejandro," the tattooed woman says.

"Please, ladies," Principal Wynns tries to interject.

MJ's head is still hanging down.

"Excuse me, Ms…" I finally take center stage amongst the circus.

"Ms. Cuerpo," the full-figured woman says.

"Please excuse my sister. We do not practice Voodoo and this is not some kind of spell or spirit. This is food."

"Food." She chuckles, but not in a 'hahaha that-is-a-relief-and-funny' way. Her laugh is full of skepticism.

I take a handful of gari and put it in my mouth. Everyone stares at me in silence. "Yeah, it's gari. I assure you. Gari is dried cassava that has been milled into a grainy powder-like form. Try it for yourself." I extend my hand to the women.

"No. It's evil," the tattooed neck woman says.

Principal Wynns also looks at me suspiciously. "Remember the International Student Dinner last year? I made that bean stew you liked? This is the same powder I sprinkled onto the stew. You said it reminded you of couscous. See?" I pour some in my hand and show him.

"Oh, yes," he says, smiling briefly, though not thoroughly convinced

Mrs. Anderson has been standing here like a peninsula between the band of women. "Mrs. Anderson, please try it. I assure you it's not Voodoo."

The tattooed neck Hispanic woman continues, "Nuhin' gonna happen to her. She already has a pussy."

I turn back to Principal Wynns, the only male in the room who can put these absurdities to rest. "It will help put everyone at ease if you would taste it. I swear that there is nothing evil in this. We don't know or have the capabilities to exercise such craft. Right, Abla?" I shoot her a stern eye and she acquiesces to my statement.

"Yes. Iz just food. But we are not addressin' da problem. Dis boy haz been harassin' my nephew and it haz to stop," Abla says.

Principal Wynns is reluctant but takes a pinch of gari and looks around the room. The room is quiet except for slight sniffles from MJ and heavy breathing. Principal Wynns dabs a little on his tongue and then puts a handful in his mouth. "It's like dry Wheaties without the sugar. It tastes like food to me."

"He's bullying me, Mommy. He says names to me. He says African booty scratcher to me."

I'm surprised that this term is still in existence. I believe every African kid going to school in America has been referenced by this name. It's as generational as chickenpox. I'm sure no one has ever taken the time to research what an African booty scratcher is. It's really stupid. It haunted me just like Tina Williams. Daily name calling only convinced me more that I could be Superman. And once Tina Williams found out about my powers she would be my friend. I just wanted to be a part of her clique.

MJ's voice continues to rip through the room. "And he says we live in huts and show our butts because we don't have underwear…And he says we ride tigers and zebras and we eat with our hands." *Yeah, we eat with our hands most of the time, but that's the only truth I've heard so far.* MJ continues, full of heavy emotions. I've never seen him this way before. The pain in his voice breaks me. *Why didn't I know this was going on?*

"Why didn't you tell me, sweetie?"

"I told Auntie Abla and she says we teach them a lesson. I just want him to stop botha me." MJ grips his arms around my waist. The room is silent again with the exception of tearful cries into my skirt.

"Why does your son call my son names?" I look at both women, not sure who the mother is. Then I address the little boy. "Why are you making fun of him? That is not nice for you to call him names."

Alejandro weeps. "I…I…just want him my friend and he no want talk to me." He cries uncontrollably. "He no invite me to birthday party because he say I can't dance. I just want I no hurt anyone." He embraces the women.

The two women and I stare at each other sharing the same disposition. Nursing crying boys in our arms. It has nothing to do with race, Santa Maria or Voodoo. The desire to fit in and to make a friend is evident.

"Alejandro, you need to apologize to him," Ms. Cuerpo says. Alejandro wipes his face across his mother's thigh and turns to walk in our direction. He hugs MJ from the back. "I sorry. I wan' you my friend like the rest of them."

"MJ, did you hear him?" He nods his head in acknowledgement. "What do you have to say?"

MJ wipes his nose in my skirt and turns to face Alejandro. "I'm sorry. You can come to my birthday party," MJ says. They embrace each other affectionately.

Abla's eyes have a watery pinkish hue. She turns away from everyone as the tears fall. Seeing Abla cry, the image chokes me. We both know the real reason for her tears.

Chapter 23

Sometimes I worry myself for no reason. I look around and see everything perfectly in its place. Balloons are scattered inside and outside the house. Daniel arrives with chofi, wache and goat kabobs for the adults. I strategically separate the food into smaller serving trays and hide one tray away for guests who may arrive throughout the night.

The DJ is still connecting the equipment. Panin and Kakra are dressed in blue jeans and white Ankara shirts. MJ and Abla are color-coordinated in all white outfits. I made sure to have two backup outfits for MJ. Telling a five-year-old boy wearing all white clothing not to dirty himself up is like telling wolves to behave at the dinner table.

A two-tier Spiderman cake sits on the top shelf in the refrigerator. Leisurely footsteps and then hurried running steps begin to emerge from the living room. Pancake is here for the party and sitting in her assigned position preparing games for the children. Chin can barely stand up. She is due any moment now. She fans herself while assembling the rest of the gift bags. Her belly appears as though she is carrying a large cantaloupe. This has to be the boy finally. I check my phone and I've already missed four calls. I listen to each message with the anticipation I will hear *his* voice. A disappointment. All messages are guests confirming the address and time. Just thinking about Mensah puts me in a different mood.

I am expecting Abla's guests any time after nine o'clock. The text message she sent out said to arrive at seven, but I know better. It is the unofficial African time—Ghanaian guests will arrive two to three hours later, followed by the dapper and fashion forward guests—arriving four or more hours late.

A huge white tent with added heat is erected in the back yard. Her guests will appreciate the lavish resort feeling as opposed to their feet being trampled on by high-energy children. The warmth underneath the tent definitely feels like a Caribbean resort. I pull the coolers filled with Guinness and Corona out.

"MJ, please sit in one place. The birthday boy can't greet his friends in dirty clothes," I say.

"Okay, Mommy," he says. As soon as my back is turned, he jets behind me into the dining room where more guests assemble.

"MJ!" The music drowns out my voice.

The air is filled with the scent of grilled tilapia. Daniel stands by the grill applying his special ginger sauce to the fish. "Please, cuzo, not too much pepper for me. You can serve that spicy stuff to your *akpeteshie* friends." I'll never understand why hot pepper balances alcohol, but the spicier the food the better it is for his drinking buddies.

"I got you, cuzo," he says.

"Oh, Daniel, make sure your DJ has that song Abla likes when she enters the tent."

I pause to admire Abla from a distance. She has the skin of a twenty-year-old. Her curly hair cascades down her back. She is wearing a white and gold bustier with white hot pants. African multicolored beaded four-inch F-M-Ps. Nice. *They must be new; I've never seen them before. Louboutins? Brian Atwoods? Sophia Webster?* She sashays out of the kitchen and a glimpse of the red soles gives it away.

"Which song?"

"I told you a dozen times yesterday. Tarrus Riley's 'My Day,'" I shoot back at him.

"Oh yeah. DJ Hollywood is good. He has everything. Hiplife, reggae, R and B, and I know we have to play Madonna for her." I think most Ghanaians over the age of forty have an affinity for eighties pop. Before the end of the night, I am sure Madonna's "Holiday," INXS's "Need You Tonight" and Kool and the Gang's "Celebration" will be played at least once.

Abla's perfume surrounds us. I gently kiss her on the cheek. "You look beautiful, hefa."

She twirls around. "I haf tree more outfits to change into. Dis one covers a lot because of da kids, you know…but lata…" She winks. And I am picturing her wearing an adult onesie with brightly colored F-M-Ps.

"Yes, thank you for sparing the kids." We both laugh.

"Have you heard from him?"

"Him?" I know who she is referring to, but I act naïve. She follows close behind me for a response.

"Yes, *him*." Her tone is low.

"No. But he promised that he'd be here for MJ's birthday party."

She sighs and then forms her mouth as though she wants to say something. She reconsiders. "Lez haf a good time."

The house fills up quickly. Children running around playing, eating, dancing and spilling Capri Suns everywhere. Abla's friends trickle in and the voices of kids are slowly overtaken by adults.

"Vida, big booty gal, you got a visitor." Chin's belly pushes against my side.

Julius is dressed in a casual off white sweater and jeans. His shoulder length black hair is combed back. He is wearing stylish tinted shades. He must have hundred different ones. He could easily be taken for those male models in a Polo ad. He looks arrogantly handsome.

"Hi. You made it."

"Of course I did. I try to make time for what I want to make time for." He leans toward me for a kiss on the cheek. *This is the first time he has done that.*

"Great." I place his hands into mine. "Follow me."

He walks closely behind me while we dodge children sprinting through the house and adults grooving to music. I apologize my way through the warm bodies we bump into. "Don't worry, Vida, it must be a good party. You certainly have a crowd." I feel eyes following our movement. Julius is the only Caucasian in the room, or what the Ghanaians call *obruni*. I already hear the whispers behind me. "Ehh...Who is that?...Where is Vida's husband?"

There is an empty seat next to Auntie Cece. I know how much he guards his independence so I follow his lead without trying to seem motherly. "There is a chair in front of you," I say. He pulls it out without my assistance.

Auntie Cece interrupts her conversation with another guest to show me her displeasure. She squeezes her face as though she is constipated. *Damn, I feel hot.* Maybe I will save the introduction for later. "Good evening," Julius says. Auntie Cece doesn't reply.

"What can I get you to drink? I have wine coolers, beer, juice, soda and water."

"Guinness is fine."

"Okay, coming up." I pray Auntie Cece doesn't say anything inappropriate when I leave.

I return to Julius with a cold bottle of Guinness and a bottle opener. Abla has one arm graciously draped on him. "Here you go." I touch his right hand and he immediately unfolds it to hold the bottle. He fingers the top of the bottle. "Let me open it."

"No need." With the flick of his ring he opens the bottle. He shows me a wide gold band ring on one side and on the other side of the ring are subtle teeth like you would see on an opener. "It's multifunctional," he says.

"Impressive," I say.

"Da Boss said hez pleased wit yur work. You really haf been puttin' in da hours," Abla says.

I'm fixated on her demeanor and pray she hasn't slipped up and alerted Julius to our numerous conversations at his expense. In between the crying fits over Mensah, there were showtime events in the *kotodenden* room that kept me and Abla entertained.

Abla and I could spend close to an hour laughing and jabbing words of sympathy for the poor women who underwent the tireless sexual encounters of Julius and his *kotodenden*. Abla switched the dialect to Twi to make sure he didn't know we were talking about him.

"*Barima, kote ah* say baseball bat?" When Abla combined the Twi with English words it was easier for me to follow.

"How would I know if his dick is the size of a baseball bat?"

"*Ka Twi,*" she hushed me over the phone and reminded me of our subterfuge while discussing Julius's nightly activities. A simple *aane* for 'yes' and *dabe* for 'no' she said. I couldn't respond either way.

Abla is standing quite close to him considering the sweat that is beginning to cascade down her face. I look around and even though the windows are open and the ceiling fan is moving, the extra bodies make the living room a large sauna. Kakra is here.

"Good evening, Kakra." Julius extends his hand.

"You remember me?" Kakra says, surprised.

"How could I forget you? You have a distinguished voice." They shake hands.

"Sweetie, bring us some extra bottles of water. We're sweatin' like pregnant fishes in here," Abla says. Auntie Cece's guests take leave and she turns her attention to Abla and me.

"So, how did you find the last journal?" Julius says.

"The last journal?" I ask. *Please, no questions about work today.*

"Yes. The one I left on the desk." I try to recall our last conversation; a unicorn story. "Well, it's an interesting read."

"I see," Julius says. Kakra returns with the bottled water and Abla and I greedily take sips of it.

"Please keep an eye on the birthday boy for me. I'm sure by now it must be time for his second outfit," I tell Kakra and he disappears. It feels like the sun is resting on my head, especially under Julius's scrutiny and Auntie Cece's motherly eye. This is what coal feels like in a barbecue pit. Julius's questions might just reveal my inadequacies. Abla is usually good at picking up on my discomfort, but right now she is dealing with her own private summer. She fans a paper plate around her head. *I need to change the subject quickly.* I turn my attention to Auntie Cece.

"Auntie Cece, this is Julius Gallo." She eyes him suspiciously. "Remember the weekend writing project that I am working on?" Her gaze is hard on Julius and then she continues the African stare-down on Abla and me. There is one thing we know for sure about Auntie Cece and that is when she is displeased. Abla sometimes tolerates her and other times they go head-to-head in arguments, but one thing Abla can't stand is to be embarrassed amongst her friends. Even as grown women, Auntie Cece has no problem taking off her shoe to give us a good spanking. We sense the tense atmosphere and we both drink the bottled water nervously.

"Auntie Cece, *etesen,*" Julius says.

"Uhhhh…ahhhh…" I can barely speak as water shoots out of my nostrils. Both Abla and I choke on the remaining water barely contained in our mouths.

"*Wo can Twi?*" Auntie Cece says. He rises and then kneels closer to her.

"*Me pa wo kyew, aane,*" Julius says.

"You ladies…ah, what is wrong with you? So you haven't heard of an *obruni* speaking Twi before?" Daniel says. I am not sure when he arrived at the table, but he definitely doesn't create a spectacle like Abla and me. "Look, look you guys just wet the whole place," Daniel continues.

"Shut up," Abla quickly says.

"You speak Twi," I finally say. *Better than me from what I can hear.*

"Yes, of course I do. How can you grow up in Ghana and not speak Twi?" Julius says confidently.

"Since when? You…Ghana? Why didn't you say anything?"

"You don't know?" Auntie Cece says.

"No, how would I have known if he didn't tell me?"

"Oh, Vida, you must have forgotten. Remember, I spent my adolescent years in Ghana with my mother in her mission building churches. Don't you recall, it's in the journal I left for you on the desk that you said you read?" He chuckles. "You're far too young to start having short term memory loss."

Auntie Cece's face is illuminated and Julius continues his conversation in Twi. Abla pulls me away from the table.

"Who iz dis guy? Wat else are in doze journals?"

"I can't remember," I say. The truth is I don't know. I've barely read anything that I can firmly make sense of.

"Wat! Wat have you been deer doin'?" I give her my 'you-really-want-to-go-there' look.

"You've been keeping me busy with your phone calls. How much work do you expect me to get done?" I snap back at her.

"Has he been lissenin' dis whole time to our conversations?" I shrug my shoulders. "So he has been hearin' me talk about his dick and…and…all dat talk about da *kotedenden* room and all." She's terrified and I'm mortified. Most times he is not within earshot when we are talking. I say simple yes and no responses, so that could be about anything. I convince myself that it is not as bad as it looks.

"But we really didn't say anything that bad. I mean, he has a good sex drive…so what if he can screw two or three women at a time? We were really giving him a compliment."

Abla shakes her head not convinced with my reasoning. She leaves me to greet more friends at the door. *Great…how I am going to explain myself now?*

I return to the table and sit beside Auntie Cece while scrutinizing Julius from across the table. *He grew up in Ghana? All this time he must have known what Abla and I were talking about. Fuck.* Auntie Cece and Julius converse like old schoolmates, talking about politics and financial institutions in Ghana. I feel like an outsider listening to them make reference to certain families and chieftain regions in Ghana. Auntie Cece taps me on my knee.

"Yaa, he knows some of our family in Dabala," she says joyfully. Julius continues, reminiscing about the church his mother built—with her own bare hands, he adds. He says something quickly in Twi that I'm unable to translate. Auntie laughs and covers her hands over his. *This woman's still got it. Flirting 101 at its best.*

"Oh, this is quite interesting. I have been trying to get Yaa to speak Twi for so many years. And here you are, you speak better than some children brought up here."

"It's easier to pick up the language when you live in the country. I'm sure once the distractions are gone, Vida will be able to learn." Auntie Cece nods her head in agreement.

"Well, I can't wait to hear yur memoir. It should be an interesting one," Auntie Cece says.

"Your niece won't disappoint me. I believe she will do a fantastic job." He rises. "Ladies, it has been a pleasure, but I'm afraid I have another engagement this evening. Will you please excuse me to leave your presence?" Julius says.

"Oh, certainly. It was nice meeting you again, Mr. Gallo."

"Please call me Julius."

He formally says his goodbyes to Auntie Cece and Daniel. I escort him hand in hand to the front door. "Please take this; it's a little something for MJ." He hands me an envelope with the words "Happy Birthday" written in the neatest penmanship I have ever seen. "And this is for your manager." It is a red box neatly wrapped with a large white ribbon.

Guilt consumes me. *Why hasn't he said anything? He's probably waiting for me.* "Okay, now you know," I blurt the guilty words out.

"Know what? That you lied?" he says.

"Nooooo," I grunt. "It was just a few unicorn stories."

"Unicorn stories?" he says, bewildered.

"Yeah, a unicorn story. It's not like a lie. Lies hurt people, but unicorn stories make people happy." He is not convinced. I try to plead my case. "As a child, I'm sure you heard unicorn stories. Cinderella, Snow White, Sleeping Beauty."

"Those are fairy tales, fables."

"Yes, but as a child you believed them and they made you feel good to hear them. As you got older, you knew that those stories weren't true, but they were still entertaining to listen to. Unicorns don't exist, but does it hurt anyone that someone thinks they exist? Noooo. If I told you that I didn't read the journal because I was busy preparing for the party, you would think I was a slacker. I had every intention of reading the journals before we met at the house. I've…just been so consumed with work and the children and…" I almost say Mensah, but I catch myself.

"I don't get your stance." He mounts his hands on either side of his waist. "Unicorns don't exist, hence making it a fable. And we can deduce fables are false, basically a lie. So you are telling me lies because it is entertaining. Well, I can think of many other things I can be entertained by. Therefore I am back to my original statement, Ms. Frimpong. You lied."

"The word lying seems so harsh. I didn't read that particular journal you left on the desk. Yes, I should have and yes, I should have told you. But I didn't want you to think I wasn't capable of doing the job. I know myself. I can do it. Lately, I lack focus because I allow other things to consume my thoughts."

"That is obvious," he says.

"I'm sorry I lied to you."

"I prefer to believe you are an honest slacker than a unicorn story teller."

"Why didn't you tell me you lived in Ghana?"

"It's all a process, Vida. I told you that we must have trust if this project is going to get along well." He breathes deeply. "Just don't lie to me again."

"No, I won't. I promise."

"Good night, Vida. Enjoy the rest of the evening."

Abla joins me as we watch him effortlessly descend the stairs. "Wat did he say? Waz he mad dat we were talkin' about him?"

"No, he didn't mention that."

"Good. Who is he?" Abla asks.

I am wondering that myself. He enters the backseat of a 5 series Mercedes Benz. For once, my mind is focused on something far more intriguing. *Who is Julius Gallo? What is a young white blind man doing in rural Ghana?* "I need to find out."

"Okay…Now, can we sing happy birthday to MJ so I can change my clothes?"

Chapter 24

It's nine o'clock and no Mensah.

"Daddy! Daddy!" MJ's squeal solidifies my feet. "You're here! I knew it. I told Mommy you wouldn't miss my birthday." MJ sprints as fast as he can into his father's arms.

"Now how can I miss my little guy's birthday?" His presences make me feel small and I try to turn my gaze away from the visiting father.

MJ bows his head as though he is in prayer. "You mist my party."

"No, I didn't. I saw everyone sing 'Happy Birthday to You' and I saw you blow out your candles."

His head rises and he gives a smile that I haven't seen in a while. "You did?" Mensah holds MJ tightly as though he may slip through his arms. "Do you know what I wished for…?"

"No, but you can't tell me or it won't come true."

"No, no. My wish came true, Daddy. You're here." MJ strangles his neck.

"I will always be here for you."

Kakra has a similar reaction seeing his father standing in the hallway. He embraces Mensah and MJ equally. Panin stands by witnessing the affectionate reunion.

"Come here, guy. Look how big you're getting," Mensah says. He reaches for Panin and pulls him into a big bear hug. Panin doesn't push away this time. *He's happy.* The kids tackle Mensah to the ground. "Just look at all of you. Strong and healthy. Mommy is doing a wonderful job looking after you." He glances at me and I quickly turn my gaze away from them. Small thunderous roars are moving in my chest. My body feels warm and my blood is boiling. *There's so much to say, but tonight we are celebrating MJ's birthday.*

He looks a bit leaner than the last time I saw him. His goatee neatly trimmed. His hair low cut. Casual clothing. *Walk away, Vida. No. I really want to run into his arms and tell him how much I miss him. But not tonight. I will not be broken.* My feet are cemented in the same spot. Abla breaks the spell.

"*Etesen*. Welcome home." Her eyes follow me. Abla has the gift of reading people and she can always tell when intervention is needed. I am afraid to show her my fear. She is searching for a sign, anything to tell her that I am not strong enough to face him, to demand what I want. I focus on the crowd under the tent.

"Thank you, sista Abla. You look beautiful, as always. Happy birthday." Mensah gives her a slight peck on the cheek.

"*Medawase*." There is a brief silence between them. "I am unda da tent if you need me." As she walks away, she looks back again for a sign, maybe a red eye, tears, trembling, anxiousness, but instead I display a soft smile. My chest hurts and it feels like someone is sitting on it. My feet once again are cemented. He takes a step in my direction and I can't move back.

"Yaa…Yaa. I'm going home now. " Auntie Cece stops her slow pace to the front door. She claps her hands over her mouth and then raises them toward the ceiling. "Thank you, Jesus. Is that…?" She rushes for my hand and squeezes it tightly. "Oh my goodness…*Akwaaba*…oooo…*Akwaaba*…welcome, my son." She releases my hand and embraces Mensah. "I have been praying for this day. Thank you, Jesus. Eh…look at you. You see now? Look how lean you've become. You need yur wife to take care of you."

"Hello, Auntie. How come you are looking younger and younger every time I see you?"

"Oh my goodness. You and your flowery words." Mensah's charismatic charm works every time. "You look well. I am so glad that I am here to witness you standing right in front of me. Well, we have more time to talk. I am leaving the party to these young folks." She laughs.

"Oh, Yaa, come and see me off. I have to give you the gift for MJ." Her words are powerful. They release the hold on my cinderblock feet.

She puts fifty dollars in my hand and then cradles her hands on top of mine. "He is home, Yaa." I turn my head away in fear of the tears building up. "He is home. Make him feel at home. Are you listening to me?" She repeats herself again and I lose my strength. Tears fall one by one. "Lissen, stop it. Don't let him see you this way. Stop it right now!" She tries to wipe the tears off my cheek. "We will talk tomorrow and please, I beg. No fighting." She looks for reassurance and I nod. I remember her constant mantra and she recites it before she leaves: "Remember, talk less and listen more." She leaves and I return to the kitchen. Abla is sitting on one of the barstools.

"We're movin' da party to Richard's place." There's no music playing and I become aware of the void.

"Why? It's still early."

"You need some time with *him*." She tips her head in the direction of the living room where Mensah is standing. "Plus, I won't have far to travel when da juices start flowin'." She does a body roll and winds her hips. "Or do you need me to stay?" Her voice drops and her composure stills.

"No, I'm good." She searches my face for confirmation. "Really, I am. Go home with Richard." I escort her out of the kitchen and Abla greets Mensah in the hallway. "Mr. Asare, *maadwo*."

"I hope you're not cutting the festivities short because of me," Mensah says. He doesn't move, but he is examining the house as if he is standing in new surroundings. I changed some of the drapes in the hallway and bought a new entry table since he left.

"No. Notin' I do is because of you."

"I don't believe that. You have so much to say in my absence. Now I'm here, say what you need to say to my face." His tone is deep and he knows this will get Abla started. *All she said was good night. Why does he have to stir the pot? Not now.*

"Iz betta I leave now. Prison doesn't suit me."

Mensah chuckles loudly. "Good night, Abla." An entourage of people take the lead and she follows behind them.

In less than an hour, the house is empty again. There is no more trampling of feet across the wood floors. *The boys must be finally asleep.* Mensah carries the last bags of garbage to the side of the house. My last task for the evening is loading the silverware into the dishwasher. I've been standing here nearly forty minutes. I scrub the already washed silverware several times and place them in the dishwasher one at a time. He closes the back door and sits at the barstool by the kitchen island. His eyes are penetrating the back of my head. *Jesus, how am I going to get through tonight?*

"You're doing a great job taking care of the boys." My fingers look like dried fruit. I stop the running water and rearrange items in the fridge like a puzzle. "You look great, Yaa. I mean, you look beautiful, as always." There is no way his charm is going to work on me. I wish music was playing to drown his candy-coated words from my ears. "I really missed you, babe...but...you do know I am making this sacrifice for us?"

Auntie Cece's words echo in my head again. *Talk less and listen more.* No, to hell with that. "Are you joking? Sacrifice? You caused all this. The reason we are where we are is because of those 'sacrifices.'" I slam the fridge door and find my voice.

"And there we are. Silent treatment has never been your style."

"You think you know me, but you don't."

"Oh, I know you very well, Yaa." He moves closer and his hand caresses my cheek. The sound of my hand slapping his surprises him.

"Don't you dare. If you truly knew me, then you wouldn't have done this to us, our marriage, our family."

"We agreed."

"On six months. The most one year. But look at us now—we are in year two of this." I stretch my hands out into the open space between us. "I thought this would finally make you happy and that would make us happy. But now..." I can't describe what we are.

"We've gone through this a dozen times. There is no way to get a business off the ground in six months, build a reputation and make contacts. It takes time. I want a better life for you and the children. Why can't you see that?" His hands rest on either side of his waist and his eyebrows arch as if he is contemplating a chess move.

No. He is not going to win this argument. "When was the last time we spoke? When was the last time you flew home? When was the last time you read to the boys before they went to bed? Or attended Kakra's soccer games?" My voice lowers. "When was the last time we made love?"

"Is this what the whole fuss is about? The last time we made love?"

Of all the things I've said, this is what he rests his sword on. "Is that what I am to you? Fuss? You gave me no choice but to agree to this. We are living separate lives."

"I told you, when things get settled, you and the boys can come and visit."

"Visit? Is that what we are now? Our marriage? Scheduled visits?"

"You could have moved out there with me, but you chose to be close to your family in New York."

"I just can't pick up and follow you everywhere. What about Panin's therapy sessions and schooling? There is so much to consider before we can just get up and leave."

"I know that, Yaa. I know. That's why I needed time."

"Your time ran out a long time ago."

"Don't be that way, babe."

"Ooooh, no you don't. You are not going to get me that easy."

"I'm home. I'm home, babe." He pulls me into his arms.

"Don't you dare. You think you're gonna walk in here after two years and the gates of heaven are going to open for you?"

"So tell me what key to use to open the gates. I'm knocking on the doors of heaven, let me in." His mouth reaches for my lips. I'm mad but my thighs are weak fences. His Armani cologne captivates me. And his warm breath smells like Guinness. "You wanna fight. We can fight afterwards." He leaves deep wet kisses on my neck.

"I mean it. It doesn't work like that." I try to push him away.

"When was the last time we made love in this kitchen?" My mind quickly recounts Valentine's Day before MJ was born. I remember straddling him on the kitchen island. He takes off his sweater and then his shirt.

"Stop it." He unzips his jeans and they fall to the ground. I don't…I can't look away. His boxers hide the big heavy muscle confined underneath. "Don't you see how much I miss you?" He reaches for it and strokes it. *Fuck, this is turning me on right now. Look away, Vida. Don't be a punk. Look away. Be strong.* He steps out of his boxers and there it is standing before me. So many nights I wished he was right here. I feel like I haven't eaten in weeks and a full steak entree is in front of me. He grabs me and his tongue traces the outline of my lips. He tugs on my bottom lip, pushing my pursed lips open.

"Don't be that way, babe. I miss you." Fuck…more slow wet kisses. His hand doesn't have to fight to separate my thighs. Sweat traces from Ginger to my inner thighs.

"Good night, Mensah." I push away and there is a crack in my voice. I'm playing hard to get. And he knows it.

"Ginger needs deep penetrating massages. I'm gonna take really good care of her tonight." He grabs me and I pretend to struggle. His wet lips capture my mouth. It's warm and moist like pie. I chew on his lips fervently. "Oh, babe…just the way I remember it." He lifts me into the air and carries me out of the kitchen.

"I hate you. I hate what you put me through."

"Stop talking." His tongue invades my mouth again. I welcome it. Wet, hot, fast kisses caress my lips and neck. He says my name as though he is making a wish. "Yaa, Yaa…I've missed you." He holds me firm in his embrace. His right hand navigates to my ass and he holds it with such force that I squeal. He squeezes again and lets go. He traces kisses along my cheek to my neck and then my shoulders. My clothes somehow peel off my body. I am standing in the hallway with just my waistbeads on. Fire rages in me and I moan, knowing I want him to fuck me right here.

"Mensah!" I shriek his name. He smiles. He kneels in front of me trailing his tongue down my stomach, then to the little island of hair above Ginger. He lifts my left leg over his shoulder and invades me with long wet strokes. I feel my knees buckling, but he holds me in place. He squeezes my ass and then gives it a firm slap. My beads jiggle on my waist. I cup my breast in the revelry it brings me. "Fuck me." He stands up quickly and lifts me in the air. I wrap my legs around his waist and his hands grab fists full of hair. His dick is neatly upright. "C'mon, babe, put it in. Make Ginger happy." I maneuver my hand and place him inside me. He holds onto me with both hands and his eyes close when he enters.

"Home sweet home."

"Mensah…Mensah," I cry his name and he thrusts faster, then slowly and then fast again. I forgot how strong he is. He holds me tightly as I rock back and forth on his hips.

"Yaa…Yaa," he calls my name and I know within a few seconds his legs will also buckle. He moves quicker and I feel the depth of his dick inside me. The force of my orgasm is surprising. It starts slow then he circles his hips into me and the right move unravels me, leaving my skin tender and sensitive to the touch. He smiles and, as I expected, he holds me firmly as he wobbles on his feet. We collapse to the ground panting like we just finished a Spartan race.

*

I don't know what time I came to bed. The sheets cradle my skin. My legs still feel weak and I try to turn on my side, but Mensah stops me. He grabs both of my legs back onto his shoulders while his head bobs left and right devouring me once again. He moans and sucks on Ginger like candy. His voice arouses me. He rubs his hands over my nipples and I cry out for him to stop, but when his tongue invades a sweet spot, I stretch my legs even wider. He goes deeper and his tongue knows exactly the move to bring me to another epic climax. I hold his head in place. I don't want him to move; I'm close. "Mensaaahhh." My entire body tenses up, but his tongue thrusts deeper. My body still yearns for him. I am weak and I release onto his face. I need him to be inside me. He rises and turns me over to my stomach. My fingers curve around his dick stroking it from behind me. *He…loves…it.* I move to the edge of the bed and kneel in between his legs.

He cries my name out, "Yaa…Yaa…!" Both of my hands grip his dick, sucking, stroking and moaning.

"Do…you…miss…me?" I mouth the words while entertaining the massive muscle in my mouth.

"Yaaaaa…Yesssss." My left hand cups his balls and lifts them to my mouth. I suck hard, applying meticulous attention to each one. I caress the back of his balls and he shudders. His knees begin to collapse.

"Yaaaaaa!" he screams softly and pulls back. "I want you from behind." He yanks me up and tips me over the bed. "Fuck." He enters me. One, two and three hard thrusts. My beads dance on my waist. Again. One, two, three. I moan and he cries out. "Wet and tight, babe." He grips my waist firmly, moving faster and then slowly. "What have you done to me?" I take his hand and guide it to my lips and suck his fingers. I squeeze and release Ginger quickly, sending him over the edge. "Yaaaaa…!" he screams again as he climaxes on top of me. He trails kisses over my back, shoulders and neck. We lay there like corpses one on top of the other.

"Tonight I'm going to sleep like a well-fucked king," he says.

Chapter 25

I jump abruptly and look at my fingers. *Thank God. I still have ten.* I put the knife down.

"You scared the crap out of me." Abla waves a white flag before entering. "Why did you bang on the door like that? I nearly cut my fingers. Where's your key?"

"I wanted to make sure I still live here."

"Of course. It's your house too." Abla navigates to the pots on the stove.

"Hmmm. Kotobre stew and ampesi. Somebody's favorite dish." I pretend not to hear her and continue peeling the yam. "It must have been a very good night to wake up so early and prepare his favorite dish." I rinse the peeled yam and place it in a pot of cold water. "Notin' to say, huh?"

"That was a nice party. I haven't seen Kwesi in years. I can't believe he came." *I need to divert her scrutiny off of me.*

"Well, iz a party wit good music, free food and drinks, even if you are an ex-boyfriend, dat iz still hard to pass up. Don't you see he looks notin' like Richard? He lost hiz sex appeal and hiz six pack. Iz dat crazy wife. She won't give him breadin' space. Hez miserable. Karma iz a bitch. Datz wat happens when you lose somedin' good." She smirks.

"Richard did look nice last night," I say happily, now that she's taking the bait.

"Of course he did. I picked out da suit for him and everytin'. Didn't you see da matchin' outfits?" She gleams. "I waz goin' to introduce Richard to Da Landlord, but…you know he started dat last night? Right?" She eyes me suspiciously. "I waz good even dough he pushed my buttons."

"Mmmmm…hmmm." Her eyes are stern and focused. She examines me. *I am no match for those African eyes.* My soul cowers. There is silence between us and I know she is taking her time to scrutinize my demeanor.

"You…fucked…him, didn't you?" she says slow and low.

"What are you talking about?" I turn my back to her.

Shit. How does she do that? Abla has a sex radar that she swears she inherited from our grandmother. She says our grandmother was able to detect pregnancies and extramarital affairs because the Gods believed she could solve broken relationships. I never believed it, but Abla's revelations always come as a surprise. She tells me that most of the discoveries come to her in dreams. Every now and then she banters about creating an app so that people can pay for her services. Abla is full of gimmicks and campaigns that she never fulfills. She continues.

"I bet you sucked his balls and all." *Guilty as charged. She knows me too well.* I hover over the stew to avoid her.

"Who are you talking about?"

"Eeeediris Elba. Who do you dink I'm talkin' about?"

There is no sense in continuing to deny it. Yes, I talked a lot of shit. Abla is witness to all my rants. Especially this one: *"If Mensah walked through that door, I would tell him to pack his bags and go where he came from."* Or this one: *"I will never lay next to Mensah again. That's it. I'm done."* But here I am, happy beyond belief. Last night wasn't fucking, it was I-hate-you-but-I-love-you-moanful-exhausting-toe-curling-orgasmic-hot-sweaty-makeup-sex and that is always the best kind. I smile like an idiot reminiscing over last night and this morning.

"Oh, Abla…"

"'Oooh, Abla' my ass. Look at you. Yur face nearly broke in haf when I mentioned it. Waz it dat good?"

My smile widens, exposing most of my teeth. That is all the answer she needs. She smiles. "I knew dat waz you screamin' las' night. You always cry like a cat fightin'."

"Liar."

"Don't go deer, sista. If walls could talk…Hmmmm. Do you know how many times I raised da volume on my stereo because all I heard waz 'Eeehhhh…don't stop…Aaaaagyei…hmmm…'" She mimics my voice spot on and I am sure my face has turned strawberry red.

"That's embarrassing. Why didn't you say anything before?"

"Oh, pleaze. Wat should I say? Dat iz wat you guys should be doin'. If it waz quiet den deer iz a problem." She laughs.

"For your information, it wasn't me crying every time."

"Ooooh, I know." We both laugh out loud. "Are you happy?" I nod my head with an overwhelming yes.

"He's finally home. That's all I want."

"Den put da past behind you and move forward. I want you to be happy." She wraps her arms around my shoulders and says, "Alright, I have a lot to do before da outdoorin' tonight. Hair, nails, a new wig and shoes to pick up. Yur comin', right?"

"Oh, shit…I forgot about the outdooring." It seems like Abla gets an invitation every weekend. The customary Ghanaian practice announces to family and friends the birth of a child. Abla says we have moved away from the traditional rites and timeframe and have incorporated American lifestyle in how we conduct outdoorings. She says that Ghanaians living abroad have to customize it to fit everyday life. So instead of celebrating within a week, the acceptable practice is to make sure it is done before the baby's first birthday. "Who is it again?"

"Iz Mike and Lizzie's outdoorin'. Da kid is practically in school now and dey still want to do an outdoorin'. Anywayz, iz a good time to see watz happenin' amongst my people." The primary source of Abla's gossip rests in her attending social events like outdoorings, funerals, parties and weddings. It is a time to meet old friends and make new ones. A time to see who is still together and who has unofficially separated. And a time to showcase the latest fashion. Depending on the crowd of people, it can be like the Met Gala with bespoke clothing and name brand designers.

"You and Mensah haf to come," Abla says. She opens the fridge and then the freezer. "People dink you guys are not togetha. We gonna end doze foolish rumors. Especially Afia and her Sunkist face and Coca Cola hands. Shez so jealous of us, you know. If she even turns her mouf to talk to me, my hand will go rough-rough across her face." Abla's pigeon language and Ghanaian accent can almost be intimidating. Afia is Richard's ex-girlfriend and, needless to say, she had a lot to say when she learned Abla and Richard were the unofficial couple.

Abla continues to cautiously navigate the kitchen.

"What are you looking for?"

"My leftovers from da party. I'm tryin' to remember where I hid dem."

She enters the back yard and then emerges back into the kitchen with three aluminum pan trays. "I thought all the food was finished."

"How long haf we been drowin' parties? You never dish out all da food wiffout securin' some for yurself. You want some?"

"Maybe some chofi," I say, amused.

"Wat was dat about yesterday wif Da Boss?"

"Crazy, right? It never occurred to me that he knew Twi or even grew up in Ghana."

"I dink everyone iz startin' to learn Twi now. Fordham University iz teachin' a course in it too. Hmmmmm…Soon we can't talk about anyone anymore. You need to find out as much information as possible."

"What an odd coincidence this assignment is actually about someone who grew up in Ghana." I reminisce again about the numerous jokes we had at his expense. He understood it all. I can't think about it now, but I will have to make a formal apology.

"Have you told Da Landlord?" Abla asks.

I'm not sure what Mensah will say about my working arrangement with Julius. *Definitely late nights will be out of the question. Perhaps I've gained Julius's trust enough that he will allow me to bring the journals home with me. Yeah, now that Mensah is home, we will need a new contract.*

Chapter 26

It's five hours since Mensah and the kids left for their male bonding. I turn the fire off the kotobre stew and drain the water from the ampesi. In my closet, I look for options for tonight's party. A neatly wrapped shoebox sits in the middle of the floor. Mensah is always spoiling me with shoes. A pair of leopard Brian Atwoods inside. *Definitely F-M-Ps.* There's another box inside the shoebox. I open it eagerly. Waistbeads with colorful tassels and bells. *Hmmm…I may just wear these tonight.* I place the beads back in the box and try on the shoes. They fit like tights. *Hmm…should I wear American attire or Ankara?* A brown and gold Ankara dress catches my eye. A bit too regal for someone else's outdooring, but it has been a while since many of our friends have seen us out together. And it matches my shoes. I hold my breath as I shimmy into the dress. It fits—barely—but I can pull it off just for tonight. Mensah has a shirt with matching embroidery.

Most of his clothes are packed into boxes. It seems foolish for me to have done that now that he's home. I carefully arrange some of his clothes on hangers and take out the shirt and black pants. *Great…clothes are taken care of. Now, what should I do with my hair? Maybe some twist-out waves for tonight.*

The boys' voices travel into the bedroom and I change back to a T-shirt and jeans. Inside the kitchen, they are seated around the kitchen island. They are all wearing soccer jerseys. Panin doesn't even look like he broke a sweat. "Hey, guys. Lunch—well, dinner—is ready."

"We ate at a diner," MJ says.

"But I'm hungry." Mensah taps my butt gently.

"Of course you are—and I also prepared food." He smiles and the boys don't pick up on our flirty dialogue. "Okay guys, go up and have a shower."

"What do I smell? Kotobre stew?" Mensah asks.

"Yes." I hug my arms around his neck and give him a long kiss.

"Wow, I must have done something right last night." A surge of adrenaline rushes in my cheeks as I reminisce over our encounter in the hallway a few hours ago. I kiss him again gently.

"Thank you for the shoes and the waist beads."

"N-T-Y-B-F."

"Best friends forever, right?"

"Of course." Mensah believes that friends never need to say thank you to one another, so in essence saying no-thank-you-between-friends is exactly what he is saying in a glorified way.

Shoot. I nearly forgot to call Julius. It's seven o'clock. I leave Mensah abruptly and rush for my phone in the kitchen. After several rings, it goes to voicemail.

"Good evening, Mr. Gallo. I am sure you are probably consumed with work, but I wanted to take the time to thank you for coming to the party yesterday. We truly appreciate the gifts. Also, thank you for giving me this opportunity to work on your memoir. I am ashamed of myself for lying to you. You are right. This takes a level of trust and I don't want you to think that I am not reliable or dishonest. I just…just…well, it won't happen again. You have my word, if it still means anything to you. Sorry for the long message, but I will stop by tomorrow."

My phone pings, alerting me to a new text.

"In a meeting. Can't talk right now. Do you need me?" *Do I need him? I pause. A thought occurs to me. I wonder how he sends and reads the text message? Maybe he has one of those text to speech devices. Gosh, so much about Julius that I still don't know.* I send my response.

"No. We can talk later. I just left you a message."

A minute passes and he responds: "K."

Well, it looks like you are still in business, Vida. I need to ask Julius about Stacey Ann and the torn pages. Mensah's voice is stern and I can hear him from the kitchen.

"I told you no. Don't put those photos up on social media sites. Let's not go through this again, guys. There are all sorts of crazy people on social media. I don't need anyone having photos of you guys."

"But it's just from the game last week," Kakra says.

"Your mom knows how I feel about your pictures circulating around. I'm surprised she agreed to it." I step out of the kitchen to see Kakra and Mensah struggling with a phone.

"Have you seen this?" Mensah says angrily.

"What is it?"

"Mommy, it's the soccer match we won," Kakra says.

"Babe, it's not on social media. It's on the school's website. Kakra's team is winning all sorts of games and it's obvious he is grabbing a lot of attention. There's no harm in that."

"You don't see the harm, but I do. Call the school on Monday to take down the photos. There are all sorts of child predators lurking online looking for images of children." Mensah heads to the dining room and we follow behind him. The mood is changing. He pulls a chair out to sit down.

"Don't you think that is a bit extreme? He is not the only player that was featured that day. Is this what you are going to do every time he has a game? Refuse the school or team to take photos of him?" Mensah's lips curl, but I don't back down. "What's next, a brown paper bag over his head as he plays?" Mensah bows his head and avoids my gaze. The children are silent. *For once, I think I'm winning this argument.*

"All I'm saying is we really need to limit this type of exposure. Schoolwork should be paramount."

"Yes, Daddy, I know," Kakra chimes in. Their faces look solemn and I know I have to tread gently on a compromise.

"Hey guys, why don't you watch a little TV before bedtime?" They smile and leave the dining area. I gently squeeze Kakra's hand as he passes me by. A reassurance that I will take care of it.

I bring the food from the kitchen and place it in front of Mensah. For someone who doesn't know the difference between Facebook and Twitter, he is concerned about images of his children circulating around social media. The first time I saw him lose it was nearly two years ago.

The details changed each time Mensah and the boys told it. But what was consistent was a video with over three million views on YouTube.

The scene was Van Cortlandt Park. In the beginning, there was an image of a group of kids launching their drone plane near the swimming pools. In the background I saw Kakra and MJ kicking a ball across the field. It was hard to keep my interest on the red and gold striped drone rising and falling like a bird. My attention focused on Mensah running in the background—running as though his life depended on it. Screaming, "Get out…get out of the way!" Then the cameraperson focused on MJ running and trying his hardest to kick the ball toward Kakra, but there was something else. He turned his head slightly, perhaps taking notice of a dark shadow overcoming him, and then he picked up his running pace. A white van in clear focus advanced forward on MJ's heels. The camera jolted up and down and exhausted voices yelled out, "Move, kid! Move!" A female voice was in the background. "Someone help him!" There was an image of blue Converse sneakers and blades of dull green grass and the camera panned back up. MJ looked exhausted and frozen still.

"Oh, shit...!" a voice shrieked out. More images of blue Converse sneakers and then Mensah rolled onto the ground with MJ cocooned in his arms. I heard cheers, but blades of grass filled the screen again. The video was four minutes and forty-four seconds long. It's the longest time I've ever held my breath.

Thinking of it now, my heart tries to break through my rib cage.

The video was titled, "Superman the father saves son." After thousands of hits, it was shown on Bronx Net and Mensah declined interviews several times. He also refused to press charges against the driver who lost control of the wheel because he went into diabetic shock. *What if Mensah hadn't been there?* I hate to think about it. The one thing the video didn't show until Mensah came home that evening was fear. He rarely talked about the events that Sunday. He wanted to act as though it never existed, but his behavior became more extreme and more protective.

But...Abla of course had another theory to his behavior. Theories that became embedded in my head. Over the last two years, those theories seemed tailored just like Mensah's Tom Ford suits. "Do you know why he doesn't want pictures or videos on social media? Becauz he has anotha family in California. Tell me, wat is da big deal postin' pictures of children playin' or pictures of birthday parties? Dat iz a sign of a man leadin' a double life. You see it all da time back home and, well, now here in America...hmmmm. Dat iz da reason why hez been gone so long. Yaa, I'm tellin' you, deerz anotha family out deer. You know da Ghanaian community iz small. Someone alwayz knows someone."

I shake the thought from my head. *Pick your battles, Vida.* This is not worth fighting over. I dish the stew onto the plate and place ampesi alongside it. "A meal fit for a king," I say and place it in front of him.

He examines the food and smiles. "It looks and smells good. Thank you, babe." This would be a good time to change topics.

"We have an outdooring to go to," I say.

"We do? When? Tonight?" He chuckles as I nod. "You can't expect me to go out tonight. I haven't prepared myself."

"Let's go out and have some fun. It's been a while, babe. I laid out some clothes for you on the bed."

"Whose outdooring?"

"Mike and Lizzie." He arches his eyebrows and I clarify. "…From the Apostolic Church. Remember Mike's mother goes to Daddy's church? They came for MJ's outdooring." His face shows no comprehension. I continue. "Anyway, this is their daughter's outdooring." I couldn't care less to go. It would be easier to send my donation through Abla, but I've also heard the rumors circulating about Mensah and me. They're total rubbish and being seen will put some of that gossip to rest.

"Where are they holding the outdooring?"

"Park Avenue in the Bronx." Mensah still shows no sign of interest.

"I just got back last night and I need a couple of nights of rest. Just go with Abla and I will stay home with the kids."

"I've already talked to Auntie Cece and she'll babysit." First unicorn story of the day. I haven't told her yet, but she will definitely watch the children if it means that Mensah and I can spend some time together. "I really want to go out, babe."

Mensah takes a handful of food into his mouth. I fill his glass with more water and then stroke his right thigh from his knee to his groin. He separates his legs wider in the chair. My hand cups his groin. Our eyes meet. A slight flick of the tongue and he sighs. He takes more food into his mouth but keeps his gaze on me.

"Okay, just for an hour or two and then back home."

I nearly fall out of the chair trying to kiss his kotobre stew-stained lips. "Good. We won't stay long. I promise."

"Oooh, babe, let me enjoy my food. Please." He jovially pushes me back into my chair. I sit like a child watching my favorite movie.

"So the boys said you have a new car." *Shit, not now.*

"Ummmm…yeah."

"I thought you said he repaired the Honda. So why do you have a white Range Rover in the driveway?"

"Well, it's sort of an agreement."

"An agreement?" He stops chewing. *Choose your words carefully, Vida.* I've only seen Mensah jealous once when Franklin, my ex-boyfriend, tried to disgrace him. But Mensah, always cool and collected, never stooped to his level.

"It's a down payment," I continue.

"Down payment?"

"Yes, well it turns out that I got a job. A part-time job," I clarify quickly. He doesn't say anything, but waits for further explanation. I told Mensah through various ambiguous texts that I'm working on weekends, but I never told him about the contract or the arrangement with Julius. "The gentleman that crashed the car, Julius Gallo, well, it turns out he is looking for a writer, well, you know, to transcribe some of his journals, to create a memoir, so I'll be the ghostwriter."

His eyebrows raise. "Really? What a coincidence. You got into a car accident and now he's offered you a writing job?"

"Yeah. I guess I was at the right place at the right time." Mensah listens intently as I relate the turn of events, making sure to shorten the story by not including the verbal exchanges about the car.

"And do you think you will have time between your full-time job and the children?"

"I've been doing okay for now." *Well, if I could stop crying about you or wonder who is keeping you company, then my efforts would look more obvious.*

"I don't like this arrangement. The boys say you go over there late nights and on the weekends."

I could argue that if he spent more time home, then I wouldn't have to spend my nights elsewhere, but I've argued and won two battles already. Auntie Cece comes to mind. *"Talk less and listen more, Vida. African men don't like women who talk too much. Don't be argumentative. You have to pick which evil to address. A sharp tongue will only cause cuts. Make time to relax him and then request yur demands. Make him feel in control."*

His brows furrow again. *Don't fight, Vida.* I apply firm pressure on his groin and he comes alive. "Can we talk about this later, babe?"

"Okay," he says.

*

It's ten o'clock and the boys are already asleep. Mensah enters the shower with me. "Oh babe, not now."

"Yaa…just a little quickie before we go." Mensah lifts my left leg around his waist. This is a delicate situation. Give in and he will be asleep for the night, or resist and make him mad, which will surely mean we aren't going.

"With you, there is no such thing as a quickie. Please, Mensah, just an hour or two and I promise, you won't be disappointed when we get back." My lips lock onto his. "I will show you how grateful I am later." Soap glides down his Milo colored skin and the muscle between his thighs is at the gates of Ginger. With long strokes up and down his inner thigh his breaths quicken. I have to use both hands on his *kotedenden* to make his moans cry out wildly.

He holds my hands firmly. "Alright, like you promised, when we get back. Stop stroking my dick."

*

It is standing room only and body temperatures in the hall create a Russian steam bath. Many people aggregate in the hallway to receive the cool air circulating from the front door. There are some familiar faces and many new ones. It's always interesting to see women wearing the latest fashion and hear the latest Afrobeats. Mensah looks especially handsome in his clothing. He swaggers inside the hall with his black tinted shades. I text Abla to let her know we are here.

"**Hefa, where are you? It's like a can of Titus sardines in here.**"

Her text arrives instantly: "**We are toward the back next to the bar.**" *Of course.*

"Eh, Vida, looking sweet as usual." Mike's brother stops me on my journey. I can't remember his name, so I salute him with a general friendly cheer.

"Oh, *chale*, thank you." He gives me a sweaty hug. Mensah pulls me closer to him by my waist. Mike's brother recognizes Mensah and gives him a gentleman's handshake.

"Oh, *chale*, I didn't recognize you. *Etesen?*"

"*Eye.*"

"It's been a long time. Where have you been? We are starting to believe you're a ghost."

"Just caught up in work," Mensah says coldly.

"Well, it's good to see you guys here. Please make sure we talk before you leave." Mike's brother moves toward the crowd-packed hallway.

Mensah makes few public appearances. In the beginning it added to the mystique, but now, like unsubstantiated gossip, it is something I can't stand.

"*Osamin....! Osamin!*" We stop again. Someone yells across the room. Even though the music is blaring, I know that voice. *Patricia.* She wraps her arms around Mensah's shoulders for what seems like eternity. I hate that she has a nickname for him and I hate that I still don't understand this sketchy relationship. Ex-lover? Friend? *Let's see if she forgets to acknowledge me again.* She begins a happy conversation in Twi and I pretend as though this interaction doesn't bother me.

"Hello, madam," she finally addresses me.

"Good evening, sista Pat."

"How are the children?" she asks.

"Fine, thank you. How is your husband?" *No husband as usual, but her diamond ring is a showcase on her old finger.* Patricia always attends functions by herself. *Maybe the rumors of her husband leaving her are all gossip.*

"Oh, by the grace of God, we are managing."

Her smile tones down. Mensah swears there's nothing between them. I'm not convinced. Mensah says she is lonely because her husband travels back and forth to Ghana for business. Her husband bought her the African market to keep her busy here in New York. But, according to Abla, it is just a location for her to meet and screw younger boys while her husband screws college girls in Ghana. *"She wants Mensah,"* Abla said. It made sense. *"How many women come home after a long day's work to cook for a man who is not her boyfriend?"* Abla says she has to be in her fifties, but it is hard to tell because her frame is just as petite as Nicki Minaj's. Abla reminds me constantly never to believe Ghanaians who tell you their age. Always add five more years to whatever they admit to. And if their skin looks like chewed gum, add ten.

"*Oh, Yaa, she is just an old friend,*" Mensah would say. I would agree with the old part. "*All we did was talk,*" he confessed. "*That was in the past,*" he would argue.

Talk, my ass. Any woman with that much dedication is looking to get slayed by the dragon. And I can wholeheartedly attest that Mensah is a dragon slayer.

This conversation is much too long. Patricia invades his personal space and leans in toward his ear. She says something and they both chuckle. *Keep cool, Vida. You told him to come and now he is here with you.* My cellphone is still in my hand when I get Abla's text.

"Tell dat Gold Coast AARP SSI card holding heifer to get her hands off your man!"

I chuckle and search the room for her. She is sitting next to Richard. Her curly afro wig looks fabulous. She rolls her eyes and I feel the same way. Mensah squeezes my hand, reassuring me through the awkwardness. She tries to engage him in another conversation, but he excuses himself and we take our leave.

"Sit here." Richard pulls up two seats beside them and then offers a salutary Ghanaian handshake to Mensah.

"Looking good, little sis," Abla says and then leans in to whisper. "Wow. Look at yur man. If he wasn't an ass I might like him again."

"Richard looks fine tonight," I whisper back. She bats her eyelashes without saying anything further.

A wave of hands move in similar ways, people fanning themselves with anything available, a handkerchief, an event flyer, a clutch purse, cloth from their garment or paper plates. "It's cooler by the equator than it is in here. Can't they turn on the AC or open more windows?" I say.

"Can I get you something to drink?" Mensah says and rises.

"Ummmm. Red wine."

"Richard? Abla?"

"Boss, we're okay." Richard holds his glass up to show that he has barely touched his wine.

Mensah's walk alone commands attention. He is tall and athletically built and his swag is like nothing I've ever seen. He seems to move in slow rhythmic steps to the music.

"I dought you drew all hiz clothez away," Abla says.

"Not all."

"Hello, beautiful ladies," Felix says. *Oh, shit. It's creepy how he surfaces.* Richard rises to shake Felix's hand. I haven't called him since the night at Richard's house. He sits next to me.

"Hello, Vida," Felix says.

"Hi, Felix." He looks better tonight than the last time we met. He is wearing a blue Ankara style shirt and more fitted blue jeans.

"I was worried about you since that night. I heard about the car accident. Thank goodness you're alright." I search the bar and Mensah is not there. My eyes fight to scan the room with the sea of people jamming to the music. "I called you several times."

"Yes, I know. Sorry about that. I should have returned your call. I just got caught up in so many things."

"I understand. Perhaps we can grab coffee one morning?"

I feel Abla's heel digging into my foot and I know why. *How am I going to dismiss Felix before Mensah gets back?* Mensah returns with his shades off and my wine in his hand.

"Hello, boss," Mensah says.

"Oh. Good evening. I didn't realize you—" Felix looks startled and Mensah never releases his gaze from him.

"Here you go, babe." He hands me the wine and our eyes meet for a second. Felix rises and Mensah stops him. "No. Please sit down. No need to get up…yet. I am very comfortable where I am." *Shit.* I feel his sarcasm.

WizKid's voice fills the room and Richard is jamming to the beat. He is less concerned with what is happening beside him. Abla doesn't look in my direction but her foot rests close to mine.

"Let's dance." Abla rises up and Richard gulps a swallow of wine and then stands. "No, babe, I am savin' da best for last. I can't 'member da las' time I danced wit my brotha here." She taps Mensah on the shoulder and he follows her to the already crammed dance floor. A big surge of relief floods me. I turn to Felix, who is pouring sweat over his clothing.

"I didn't realize you guys are—"

I cut Felix off. "It's complicated," I shout over the music.

"Yeah, I know. It can get like that sometimes."

"Boss, let's go outside for a while." Richard motions Felix to follow him. "Yaa, we will be back." Poor Felix. I should have never given him the impression that I would call him.

I laugh when I see Abla and Mensah on the dance floor. Abla as usual turns on her freaky dance nature and Mensah meets her toe to toe. *God, can he move.* He looks even more delicious now. I can't wait to get home, or we may just start with a little appetizer in the car. A group of women sitting alongside one wall watch him with carnal desire. They must be the Champion Ladies that Abla always talks about, a social club of middle-aged women. They are well coordinated in yellow and purple Ankara outfits. One lady with an off-the-shoulder top signals the lady beside her to note Mensah's presence, then her eyes watch me. I smile. *Yeah, they are talking about me for sure. Those heifers. Alright, enough of this.*

I get up and walk over to the donation table. A well-dressed man in a blue suit takes my check and scribbles my name and number onto a notebook. He hands me a CD. I meet Abla and Mensah on the dance floor. "Babe, you ready?" I whisper into his ear. "I am so ready for you." He grabs me by the waist. We could have fucked in the car, but I will reward him properly for coming with me and looking so damned hot tonight.

Chapter 27

The hallway lights are still on and the house is quiet. Auntie Cece must be asleep by now. I tiptoe in my F-M-Ps upstairs. Panin is neatly asleep in his bed. MJ finds shelter under Kakra's shoulder.

Lionel Richie's voice fills the house.

Tonight is not a lingerie type of night. The less the better. I put the waistbeads with the colorful tassels and bells on. I have a similar color pattern on a necklace. It hangs just above my nipples. *Okay, necklace and waistbeads…that should do.* My F-M-Ps offer a nice complement. *Yeah, I'm going to keep them on. I hope I don't wake the boys up.*

The bells alert Mensah to my presence as I descend the stairs. Just where I want him, in the single leather club chair. I stand at the bottom of the stairs. He beams with a wide salacious grin.

He gawks at my nudity. His lips part in appreciation. "Nice…very, very nice, babe."

He stretches his hand toward me. I saunter with the beat of the music. The living room is dimly lit with the only source of light from the reading lamp in the far corner. My lips cover his.

"You taste like Hennessy."

"Should I make you a drink?" he asks.

"No. I want to suck it off your lips."

"Ooooh, Yaa, what else will you suck?" he says.

I kiss him again. "Let me show you." I begin to unbuckle his pants.

"So that is Felix?" *Shit. Not now. Why did he say his name as though I talked about him before?*

"Ummmm, that's Richard's friend."

"Yes, I know. And he is a fan of yours."

"A fan?"

"Yeah, of the Sassi Strikers. I used to see him in the bleachers watching the games."

"Really? You remember him from the games?"

"Vaguely, but I now know why he came to every single game." *Jesus, where is he getting all this information? Less talking, more listening.*

"Interesting."

"What's interesting?"

"I suppose I can't blame him for admiring you. But I could never picture it. Him as my rival."

"Your rival? Why would you think that?" My voice trembles.

"I hope if you decide to move on that you will make wiser choices."

"What is that supposed to mean?" My mood is changing.

"I know we still have a lot to talk about. But I will never abandon you and the boys. I will always be there for you, Yaa."

"I know."

"I'm doing all this for us." He looks sad and I don't want to change the high feeling from a few seconds ago. I sip from his glass and our eyes are engaged. I slowly lick my lips. A slight grin appears. He relaxes himself in the chair. He maneuvers the remote control for the sound system. All I can think about is getting on my knees and sucking his dick, but I have a feeling this is going to be an all-nighter. *Tame your urges, Vida.*

"Dance for me, babe."

He raises the volume on the sound system and places the glass on the table by the sofa. Bisa Kdei's voice fills the living room. I begin a slow dance for him, but I stumble a little trying to take my stilettos off.

"No, babe. Keep them on," he says. He watches me hungrily. I continue to dance, gyrating my hips and doing slow body rolls to the beat. He changes the music. A faster beat now. Beyoncé's voice fills the room.

He grabs me and steadies me onto him. I move slowly up and down on his lap while running my fingers through my hair. I eagerly take off his shirt and I lavish soft kisses over his face and chest. He moans and pulls his pants down to his ankles. I mount him again and this time ease his dick into Ginger. I tilt my hips back and forth until I find a good comfort level and then move slowly to the fast-paced music. He moans my name. I move my hips with quicker strides while taking his lips into mine. He grabs my hips and pulls me down harder and he screams, "Yaa!" I move his hands over my breasts and suck his fingers one by one. He wails again and this time I move slower, moving my hips in wide and small circles. He shudders. "Fuck, Yaa." I stop to look at the vulnerability in his eyes and then start again, but this time much faster while he takes my left breast into his mouth. Hard breathing and the rhythmic sound of the beads and bells as I move around him add to the sultry sound in the air. I raise my arms over his head and hold the back of the chair to gain momentum. The beads create rhythmic sounds as they beat against my ass. His face is firm and his mouth opens as though he is gasping for air. "Yaa, don't stop," he finally mutters and it entices me to move in firm semicircles. He grabs me and pulls my lips to his again.

"Oh, babe, you feel so good," I say. Just looking at him will probably bring me to a climax, but tonight it is all about him. I want him to know how much I've missed him and let him know why there will be no one like me.

"Yaa, Yaa…!" he cries out. The climax comes hard and deep and he seizes my hips onto his. After a few seconds of shudders, he calms down, but he doesn't release me. "Yaa…"

"Yes, babe?"

"…That was unbelievable."

Chapter 28

I love Bed Bath and Beyond sheets. No matter where my naked body lands, they still have the same warm, silky feeling. My skin is cradled in the soft sheets as though it is creamy cocoa butter. But it isn't the sheets that make me happy. I roll onto my stomach and stretch my arms to caress his firm buttocks. *He's not here.* I open my eyes and look around the room.

"Babe," I say softly. I look at the bedside table for my phone. The room is still dark and quiet. It's 5:30. I put a T-shirt on and check the bathroom. *No sign of Mensah.* I rush downstairs. The kitchen lights are on and it calms my panic. After amazing sex, we always crave munchies.

"Boo…" I say as I push the door open. There is no one to scare. The kitchen back door is open and I walk in that direction. There are voices coming from the back yard. I flick the back porch lights on.

"Yaa…up already." He sweeps me into his arms and gives me a kiss. "You must be as hungry as I am." I lose focus in his arms and hug him tightly. "Let's go inside, it's cold out here," he says.

"Were you talking to someone outside?"

"Outside at five thirty in the morning?" He chuckles. "Maybe you heard me talking to myself. I have a lot of work to do around the house. It's my own fault for being away so long."

"Oh," I say. He looks at me oddly and then pushes his hands deeper in his pockets. "You're dressed early this morning."

"Yeah." My nagging intuition tells me something is going on. *Be optimistic, Vida. Chase away those negative feelings. Talk less and listen more.*

"Why don't we eat later? I will give you that special massage you like." I nibble his ear. His stance is stagnant and he still has an odd look on his face. "What's wrong?"

"Nothing," he says lowly.

"When I usually talk about massages, you run and get the oil, but you didn't even flinch this time. You don't feel aroused by me anymore."

"Yaa, you should never say that. Of course I do." He rests his hands on either side of his hips and tilts his head to the side. He has something to say.

"Then what's wrong?"

"Why do you think something is wrong?" he retorts grimly.

"I don't know. You are fully dressed at five thirty a.m. I don't know if you are going out or coming in. I hear you talking to someone outside or maybe on the phone and you tell me it's nothing." *Your damn mouth, Vida. Are you really going to start a fight after an incredible weekend?* The words fly out before I temper them.

"Don't start this. It's been a great weekend so far."

"Yes, as long as I don't ask any questions about your whereabouts or who you are on the phone with."

"My cellphone is upstairs and I don't understand why you assume the worst from me."

"And why shouldn't I think otherwise? We barely talk when you are in California. Maybe I need to be concerned about your fidelity."

"You're joking. You question my loyalty after all we've been through?"

I pause and try to choose my words carefully. *Say how you feel, Vida. It is now or never to confront this issue.* "Ever since those kids posted that video of you saving MJ in the park you have been more distant." I take a deep breath and forge on. "Do you have another family in California?" He looks at me as though I just insulted him, but I need to set my mind free. His eyes narrow and his mouth forms into a thin line. I continue, "I can hardly reach you when you're there. When you do call me back it's from unknown numbers and it's only briefly. When you are home, you get anxious when I reach for your phone or ask about your whereabouts. It's five thirty and this is not the first time I've heard you talking in the back yard or basement for that matter. I feel as though you are hiding something. Are you?"

"Hah. You sound like your sister with unfounded conspiracy theories."

"Well, lately Abla's conspiracy theories don't seem so crazy. It's been two years since I've been able to touch you or lay down next to you. Skype, texting will not sustain a marriage. You promised to be home by Thanksgiving and then it was by Christmas. You've been out there for two years and you've moved three times. I don't even have the new address." He stands there quietly then a slight chuckle breaks the cold air between us. He pulls out a pen from the kitchen drawer and walks toward the sink for a Bounty paper napkin.

He scribbles hastily onto the paper towel. "This is the address in California. Unfortunately, but very commonly"—he holds his hands up in defense—"my cellphone dies at the jobsite. I'm in secluded areas, which can account for the missed calls, and sometimes I use my foreman's cell to call. I don't control his settings on his phone. You know I moved to another apartment close to the jobsite so I can decrease the amount of time spent traveling. It escaped me that I didn't give you the new address. But most times, as you know, I am on the road and at times it never seems the right time to call. This is a very big contract, Yaa. And if I build a solid hardworking relationship out there, the sky's the limit. I know things are not in a good place with us, but I will do better." He rests his hands on my shoulders. "A few minutes ago I went to the back yard to take the garbage out. I was just saying to myself that I really need to fix the pavement and waterproof the walls. There is moisture in the basement."

Everything makes sense. His excuses are woven tightly like a quilt. *But I still need him to say it to believe it.* "You didn't answer my question," I say lowly.

"I'm not cheating on you, Yaa." He hugs me tightly. His voice covers my left ear and I push back to look at him. "I don't say it often, but I love you and I love my family very much. I hope one day you will see that. I'm just trying to make a better life for us. That's all." He releases me and moves a few steps back. "I know this is not a good time, but I have to leave today. So many loose ends just came up. I need to address them before things get out of hand. It's a new crew and I need to get them back on track. I won't be able to establish an operation in New York if I don't complete this contract by the deadline."

"Leave today?" I step closer to him. "After all I said? And what about what you said?"

"I need to do this, Yaa."

"When were you planning to tell me?"

"This morning."

"You son of a—"

His lips curl again and his face draws closer to me. "Yaa...watch yourself. I'm still your husband." His look is firm. One thing Mensah doesn't tolerate is insults.

Anger boils from my belly and the words that spill out are laced with wrath weighted with pain. "Oh, really? I have a husband now? When are you coming back?"

"As soon as I finish this contract."

"That tells me nothing. When will you be back?"

"I can't give you an answer now. Hopefully everything will be done in a couple of months."

"A couple of months? Do you see the state we are in?"

"I'm doing this for us. We shouldn't argue. Let me leave on a positive note."

"To hell with positive notes. It takes two wheels to make a bicycle work. So far it looks like I'm the only one worried about this marriage."

He doesn't flinch from his stance. "You have the address now. You and the kids can come anytime. I am trying, Yaa. Believe me, I am."

"I can't do this, Mensah," I say angrily. "This is not fair to me anymore. I can't do this."

He walks out of the kitchen and there is luggage by the front door. I didn't notice it earlier when I came down. "Are you going to tell the kids? You're just going to leave without saying bye?"

"Panin is up. I told him. I will call them when I land." He makes his way up the stairs. Pacing up and down just brings more furor, sadness and pain. *Is he really going to leave now? Again?*

He returns with a suit travel bag and his iPhone in hand. "I have some tailored suits for the boys' graduation. If they need any alterations, make sure you send them to the cleaners on Sanford Boulevard."

"You may not have a wife when you get back."

He stops to look at me. "Don't make any foolish mistakes, Yaa." He turns around and walks to the front door.

I feel Auntie Cece grab my arm. *When did she wake up? Did she hear my banter earlier?* "Yur husband is leaving...yur husband is leaving...give him some kinds words before he goes. You don't know wat is going to happen to him along the way. Think about the children." She embraces me tightly. "Marriage is not easy, but he is still yur husband. Please show him that respect," Auntie Cece says. I hear the words, but this isn't the time for her lecture. Anger keeps my teeth clenched together. A tear falls then several. I struggle to catch my breath. He hears me sobbing, but my tears, which used to spring him into action, have no effect on him now. He continues to assemble his luggage.

"I will call you when I land. Auntie, thank you for everything. I will try to be home soon."

"Yes…we want you home soon. We will be here waiting," she says. A quick squeeze and then she pushes me gently in his direction. He meets me half way. I can still hear Auntie Cece whispering behind me. "Hold him. Hug him." He kisses me gently on the forehead, then on the cheek. I tilt my head slightly up and kiss him on the lips. I lean into his shoulder still trying to cool the rage that wants to explode in me. So much more needs to be said. I cage my tongue again.

"I will wait for your call," I say. He hugs me tightly and tears once again blur my vision.

*

"Yur going to make yurself sick if you keep crying. The children will be up soon. Do you want them to see you like this?" *Yes. Their father once again has crushed my heart.* Auntie Cece puts the kettle on the stove. She takes out a container of Milo and canned milk. She places two slices of Thomas' bread on a plate. "Should I toast it for you?" I shake my head no while trying to control the sobbing to a little sniffle. "You guys had a nice weekend; don't spoil it with tears. He said he will be back home soon. Just have patience, Yaa. Look how far you guys have come. He knows his responsibility; just exercise patience. Marriage is hard. There is no doubt about it. But you can't run away or leave when things get rough. You took a vow and you must have faith that God will take care of you."

She continues with the breakfast preparations. I wipe my face with the back of my hand and try to concentrate on Auntie Cece's words. She pours hot water over the Milo then adds Carnation milk in the cup.

"Sugar?"

"No," I say meekly.

"He loves you. Just wait and see. One day you will look back and give yur testimony. Have patience," she says again.

"Surprised to see you up," Abla says. She enters the kitchen and Auntie Cece's mood changes. Abla moves over to me jovially and whispers, "I heard you screamin' las' night. Or was it—" She stops abruptly and rests her bag on the kitchen island. She searches my face for answers. "Eh...eh...Wat happened?"

"N-nothing," I try to force the word out.

"Bullshit...look at you..."

"It's Sunday, please Abla..." Auntie Cece says. Abla rolls her eyes and continues her scrutiny.

"Look at me, Yaa...tell me..." I look at her briefly then hang my head down so the tears can drop in my lap.

Auntie Cece chimes in. "She is fine. Just leave her alone. Why are you here so early in the morning?"

"I'm goin' to church with the boys and all my clothes are here," she snaps back.

"Church?" Auntie Cece says.

"Yes, church. Lissen, Ma, iz not about you right now," Abla retorts. "Yaa...look at me...yur one and only sista...tell me watz wrong." I inhale and exhale deeply. "...Where iz he?" She doesn't mention his name and it's better she doesn't. Her voice is alarmed. "Where iz dat son of a bitch?"

"Abla, yur mouth...please respect this house."

"Trust me, God understands me." She turns her attention to me and takes my hand into hers. "Yaa, watz goin' on? Did he leave again?" I nod my head. "Hmmm...wait until I see dat motha—"Abla stops midsentence and looks at Auntie Cece.

"You will not interfere in their marriage. He is coming back soon," Auntie Cece says. Her gaze is fixed on Abla.

"Oh, like da las' time when he said he waz comin' back in six monz and look afta two yearz, we finally lay eyez on him?"

"This is none of yur business, Abla."

"No, shez my businez. When she cries, I feel it. Don't tell me dis iz none of my businez. Itz all our businez."

"Yaa, if you want yur marriage to last, curb yur mouth," Auntie Cece says. Abla dismisses her with her hand and Auntie Cece tries to lunge at her angrily. "You still don't respect yur elders," Auntie Cece says.

"Wat you goin' to do, bend me over yur leg and beat me? We're not school gurls anymore, Auntie."

"You don't respect! You are just as stubborn as—" Auntie Cece catches herself and moves back from Abla.

"—As wat? Mommy? Yes, alwayz da counsel, but don't take yur own. If Mommy lissened to me instead, she would still be here today." Abla's remark leaves a sting in the air.

"Abla!" I shout at her. "Don't say that." I divide the women.

"How…dare…you," Auntie Cece says vehemently.

"How dare I? She waz mizerable married to Daddy. You knew it. Everyone knew it. Dat iz wat killed her…loneliness and mizery. Iz dat wat you want for yur niece? To uphold a marriage dat iz not makin' her happy?" Auntie Cece moves past us and out of the kitchen. I face Abla and she bows her head down.

"She started it. Didn't you hear her?" Abla says defensively.

"That was harsh, Abla," I say.

"She knowz how to get to me. I can't control my feelinz around her."

"Stop it. Please. Just calm down and apologize."

"Me…Rosemary Abla Frimpong, apologize?"

"Yes. Please. We all need her. She is the only family we have here. Daddy is in Ghana. Please." She rolls her eyes and I embrace her. "Yes…Rosemary Abla Frimpong, my one and only sister from one mother and one father; slept in the same bed for ten years. Taught me to wash my underpants and how to walk in heels." The air around us is lighter and she breaks into a smile. I kiss both her cheeks.

"Whenz he comin' back?"

"In a couple of months. I think."

"Again? Yaa!"

"Please, Abla. I can't cry anymore." I take a sip of the Milo. It's cold, but it soothes my dry throat.

"Come to church wit us. We're goin' to Grace Baptist today."

Abla is a church hopper; just like her male companionships, commitment to one church is hard. Last month she attended Apostolic Church on 233rd Street and three months ago she attended the Pentecostal church on Bronx Boulevard. Her explanation is another one of her Ablaisms. *"People have to miss yur presenz. Itz like da first day of school, everyone wants to make friends with da new good lookin' kids. But if dey see you every Sunday, da curiosity fades and you become a regular church memba."*

However, with all her theories, she frequents Grace Baptist Church often. The boys and Pancake were baptized there.

"Not today. I feel emotionally exhausted. Pray for me, please."

"I alwayz do. You know I worry about you, datz all. You are too good for anyone to take advantage of you. You deserve da best, Yaa." She hugs me. *Sometimes the hard part is convincing myself of that.*

CHAPTER 29

I feel confident to enter the house now. I've been rehearsing my apology to Julius for the last fifteen minutes. Vincent's strong stature walks toward me. "Mr. Gallo is by the pool." He doesn't say anything else as he breezes past me. Alice opens the doors and warmth from the backyard greets me. The fire pits are lit, creating a Caribbean resort feeling for a swim. Julius is emerging from the pool in a skimpy blue swimsuit. It barely covers the package between his legs. *Holy cow, there is no way that's all him in that swimsuit…but then again why pad your groin to swim?*

"Hi Julius, it's me, Vida."

"Yes, I know, Ms. Frimpong." I make it a habit to announce myself as though we are speaking on the phone. Max is waiting to hand him a towel. I follow them both through sliding doors behind the fire pit.

I'm amazed at how serene and beautiful it is here. I should have been more curious and toured the house, especially after discovering the secret chamber and elevator.

Another door slides open and they enter another room. *Wow, it's a bedroom.* I pivot, admiring the navy blue and gold décor. *Where did they go?* "Julius?"

"One moment, Vida," Julius says.

"Like I was saying, sir, we really need to consider Audiohead's offer. This technology will be in the forefront of music streaming," Max says. He glances at me and continues talking. I take a look at my reflection in the mirror by the door. The extra mascara hides the dopey eyes. *You can hardly tell I've been crying all morning. Damn it.* There is a thin white line pressed in my inner lips from my lip-gloss. I pull out a napkin from my purse and blot my mouth. Max smiles, noting the extra care. He disappears behind a large metal decorative screen. I squeeze my checks and square my shoulders. *Pull yourself together, Vida.*

I wonder who sleeps here. There is a king sized sleigh bed on one end of the room. Beige tiles decorate the floor. A massive blue settee in the room faces a fireplace. There is a hint of vanilla musk in the air.

"Enough. I need a few days to think about it," Julius says.

"Okay, sir."

"Is that all?"

"Um, yes sir. That's about it," Max says.

Max emerges from behind the screen. "Ms. Frimpong, he's all yours now."

His tone is peculiar. He exits through the sliding doors. There is a table and two chairs close to the door. I sit comfortably, waiting for Julius.

"Yes, Vida how can I help you?" *Shit. What the hell?* I stumble getting up. I try to turn my head, but it pivots back to confirm what my eyes are looking at. Julius…is…naked.

"You're naked."

He sighs at the obvious and walks robot-like toward the bed. His palms tap the bed until he finds what he is looking for. A towel. The movement between his legs heeds my attention. It's like three caramel colored legs walking toward me. It's in front of me now…I mean he is standing in front of me now. *Look away, Vida. Move.* Auntie Cece would be so disappointed in me. *Why am I still standing here?*

"Yes, I am. Do you have a problem with nudity?"

"Noooooo…I mean yes…I wasn't expecting it. I mean you right here in front of me like—" I'm pointing to the obvious definition that makes him a man.

"I am a hundred percent sure you have seen a cock before."

Huh. "Well, yes…but not a big white cock." He hears me. *I thought that was my inside voice talking. Of course, I've seen white cocks—I mean dicks—before, if you count inserting catheters in patients and watching porn. But never like this. Swinging with so much energy and determination. Neatly groomed with a set of balls to enhance the landscape.* Oddly, he drapes the towel around his shoulders and continues to walk around the room in all his glory. I can only imagine what it would look like when it's reached its full potential. *Stop it, Vida…turn around.* After I've burned several images into my brain, I finally turn my head. *Ooooh, wait until I tell Abla.* "So, is this something I am going to have to endure? Your nudity?"

"Endure?" He gives a big laugh. The inappropriateness of my words is evident. "I don't know. It all depends on how much you can endure." He chuckles.

"I didn't mean it that way. I meant, are you going to walk around here naked all the time?"

"As long as I live here, I am free to do whatever I please. This is my home, and you should feel comfortable in your home at all times. Don't you agree?" I ponder his words, but I don't answer. "As you are aware, I don't have staff, which allows me that liberty." He stops moving but I still feel my personal space is closing in. He squares his shoulders and rests his hands on either side of his waist. I try again to turn my head away. "The human body is a beautiful thing and I have nothing to be ashamed of."

"Clearly." *Fuck. I really need to stop talking.* He chuckles again.

"Plus, shall I remind you about the confidentiality agreement contract?" I turn to look at him. He is still pacing the room. *For goodness sake, just tie the towel around your waist.* I have no idea what he is talking about. "Remember, the contract we both edited and signed?"

"I don't recall reading anything that stated that I would be subjected to your nudity."

"Oh, it's in there. In legal jargon of course…something to the effect of said party, Julius Gallo, will be free to exercise his personal and private liberties as he chooses, etcetera, etcetera, etcetera. If you need to feel at home, Ms. Frimpong, please feel free to remove your clothing as well. We are both adults."

"Even at home, I don't walk around naked," I say.

"Well, as you choose. As much as I enjoy talking to you, I would really like to have my shower. How can I help you?"

"Oh yes, the reason why I came here." I can't help but read him like DOT signage. A well-crafted vessel. Several birthmarks grace his abdomen to his groin area and upper thigh. *Focus, Vida.* He walks past me in search of something else. "You have omitted sections from the journal. Is there any reason why?" I am within arm reach of his ass. He definitely takes good care of himself. He stops in front of me. *Shit.* He has slight freckles around his nose and some brown spots on his shoulders. No tan lines. His ass matches the rest of his suntanned caramel skin. His lips are a pale hue of pink and he has a delicate dimple in his chin. *His eyes…oh my, his eyes…they are not ordinary blue. Deep blue? No. Ocean blue? No…it's…it's…like Royal Dansk cookie tin blue.*

"What makes you think I have omitted sections from the journals?"

He breaks my trance. "Some of the sentences are cut off and you can tell when a page is torn out of a well-bound journal."

"Is that right?" He moves away. *What is he looking for?*
Lord have mercy...It's a beast...that large muscle between his legs. And swinging around with every movement.

"But back to your original question. It's been a while since I've read them. You will have to point it out to me which pages are torn out."

"So, who is Stacey Ann?"

"An old girlfriend in Jamaica," he answers quickly.

"And Diego, is that your nickname?"

He pauses. Silence. *Did I strike a nerve?* "You have a lot more work to do than I thought." His words upset me, but he is right.

"I'm going to get to it sooner or later. Just wanted to know why some of the pages are ripped out."

"I see." Here we go again. I'm beginning to detect that this expression doesn't lead to any further clarification. His face becomes constricted. The jovial smile has turned downward. He doesn't say anything, but walks in my direction. Now he is making a clicking sound. He stops. Clicks. Moves his head left and right. Clicks.

"Do you need help finding something?" I finally ask.

"No," he says. I canvas the room for what may be the reason for his search. He walks slowly to me and that Beast pulls me into another trance. My mind brings me back to Penny on those nights she screamed 'fucked me harder'. *Brave woman.*

Shit. He quickens his pace in my direction. I can't move. There it is again. Click. Click. Click. He moves his head left then right. Click again. "Excuse me." I hear the words, but I'm arrested with his gaze. It's as though he is looking right into my eyes. "Vida, pardon me." I don't understand what he wants me to do, but I rise. *Please, dear God, don't let him try to seduce me.* I take a few steps away. He reaches for the brown paper bag that I didn't notice. He removes the contents. Two plastic bottles. He opens one and smells it. He smiles. "Vida." I hear my name and I search his face for any more details that I may have overlooked. My behavior so far is quite inappropriate, but I continue taking inventory of him as though he is a rare sculpture. "Vida!" I hear my name again more loudly.

"Yes?"

"To save time, perhaps you would like to join me in the shower? That way you can touch and scrutinize everything that makes you curious." I blush. My gaze probably burnt through his skin.

"I…I…I…I just wanted some clarification on the memoir. You're making it harder if pages are ripped out."

"Stick to what's there and don't concern yourself with what isn't there. Comprende?"

"Si." *Why is he still standing next to me?* Embarrassed and a little bit warmer, I scurry toward the sliding glass door. "Okay…see you next weekend…"

I practically run through the main house and into my car without even waving goodbye to Vincent. I begin the crawl onto the Queensboro Bridge. *What the hell have you gotten yourself into, Vida?*

Chapter 30

He's sitting opposite me making corrections to the document. This is more tedious, but I succumb to his wishes.

"Stop, Alice." Alice pauses again during the reading of my document. "American grammar is something I don't think I will ever get used to," Julius says.

"That many grammatical mistakes?" I chime in after several grunts and hmmms.

Julius continues. "Alice, delete the last sentence."

"Ms. Frimpong will need to change the wording in the next sentence."

He hands me back the laptop and I rephrase the sentence. This time, I read it back to Julius instead of Alice. "Although Mama encouraged me to learn braille in several languages, I continued my penmanship every night." He gives another sigh.

"Why don't you wait until I transcribe all the journals before we edit?"

"If I make changes now, then hopefully you can follow my reasoning. We can do major edits when you are done." He communicates with Alice wirelessly and he commands her to move my last paragraph to page fourteen. "I hate waiting. Consider it one of my vices. We can work on restructuring as we go along."

Julius volunteered to come to my house on some nights to work. I don't think he fully trusts me with his journals in my possession. I still don't understand the secrecy. It's not like he is FBI's most wanted or from nobility or some big time drug lord. *Well, I guess for some, penning their life's work comes with a lot of detail and care.*

"Hmmmm. As you wish." He rises and walks fluidly toward my kitchen. I take the opportunity to inspect his tinted shades on the table. Flickering red and blue lights sparkle in the grooves of the handles. They are lighter than I thought. I place them on briefly and there is a bell chime. I quickly take them off before he reaches the table.

"Do you like?" He takes a mouthful of Guinness. *I'm surprised he found the bottles in the fridge.* "The glasses?"

"Oh, yes." *He's discovered me.* He sits beside me and places the glasses back on.

"They detect ownership. The light chime indicates to Alice that someone else is in possession of them. Sort of an antitheft mechanism."

"Wow, that's quite interesting." He opens his mouth just enough for the bottle to rest on his lips. He tilts his head slightly back and takes another mouthful of Guinness. I position myself for the question that I should have asked long ago. "Can I ask you a silly question?" He rests the bottle on the table and waits for me to continue. *Alright, Vida, you got his attention. Go for it.* "How is it possible that you are able to navigate without using a dog or cane? I mean, you get around so effortlessly and I've seen blind people—I mean people with visual disabilities—navigate using devices and I don't really see you using anything except for these glasses and sometimes you make those sounds with your mouth and I have been doing some research and I discovered that you've been echolocating, but you don't do it often and you still manage to get around better than the average blind person. I believe." He leans back in the chair and rests his forefinger on his lips. I continue. "It's quite interesting watching you. So, how much eyesight do you have? I know you can't really believe everything on the Internet, but I did Google you and found a lot of conflicting information. As a child, you were bitten by a snake in Taiwan, which resulted in your blindness, but then I read somewhere it was a tumor that started in your left eye, which was removed and then occurred again in your right eye. I tried to find concrete details in the journals, but nothing yet." Silence. "Like I said, a lot of conflicting information. I did come across a journal where you recount the last travels with your mother. I believe you said these will be the 'last days of sun and moon.'" Still no response, but I continue. "I've only gotten through three journals so far. I just wanted to hear from you, that's all." He repositions himself in the chair and opens another bottle of Guinness.

"I've been preparing for this day. And I'm wrestling with if I should tell you the whole truth. But I'm worried if you can you handle it." My interest is piqued. He stands up and walks to the window behind me. "You know, Vida, I have to be honest with you, but so much is at stake. I need to tell you everything. I thought that you might have discovered it in the journals, but I have no choice now but to tell you. I can't hide the truth any longer." He seems timid. His back is toward me. "Remember, I said this assignment needs a level of trust. Can I trust you, Vida?"

I ponder the question then reply, "Yes. Yes."

"I mean, you would be the only person on Earth that I divulge this secret to. Do you understand, you cannot tell anyone?" He hesitates.

"You can count on me."

"It's time you got to know who I really am." He sighs more deeply. "I hired you because you are probably the one person that could help me." His brows are furrowed and pinch of skin rests in between. His mood is not the same ten minutes ago. "It's very easy to put out information on the Internet. In fact, I contributed to a couple of articles in Wikipedia. These journal entries don't tell the real story. Candidly, there's so much more. What I am about to tell you is not written anywhere. Only you, Vida, will be the source of this information. You cannot tell anyone." My heart is going to tear through my chest. *What is it? What's so secretive?*

"Not even Rosemary?" I take deep breaths.

"No one, Vida. I need to trust you." My bladder automatically feels full. But I can't go and pee now. He may change his mind. *No, stay and wait to hear the secret.*

"Okay, I promise, no one. Tell me, Julius. Your secret is safe with me. Tell me." I tug on his arm like a kid wanting a bag of M&Ms. I love secrets, especially secrets entrusted just to me. If he could see my face, he would see the cracks that are going to split open.

"Vida?"

"Go ahead, Julius. You can trust me. Absolutely." I'm doing Kegels to prevent an accident. He steps back and kneels down in front of me. *Holy shit. This has to be the holy grail of secrets.* His Royal Dansk cookie tin blue eyes look up and then drop down. His lips part and I place my hands into his. He squeezes them. His hands are firm and soft.

"Please, Vida. Please listen to me." He holds my hands tighter. "This is my last journey to Earth. I need your help."

I chuckle. "Cut the BS." I try to push him away, but he secures my hands into his.

"Ms. Frimpong…Vida…I know this sounds crazy. Just listen, please." His voice drops to a deeper tone. "I need you to listen to me and I need your trust right now." He pulls my hands into his chest and his heart is racing. "Earth is not my home. I come from the planet Amet. The night we met—the night of the accident—I was trying to get back to my spacecraft. I thought my mission had failed." *I'm waiting for the 'hahaha…I got you' chuckle.* "Please don't be scared, Vida. I won't hurt you, but you have to help me…help us." *Does he need to be taken to Bellevue or Betty Ford?* I try to stand up, pushing him away. But he grips my shoulders. "Please, Vida, we need your help."

This has to be bullshit. Or is it? He looks scared. He's not laughing. *Shit…is this happening to me?* I'm scared. *I was hired by an alien?*

"Who is 'we'?"

"Penny and I. She is one of us," Julius says.

"Oh my goodness, Penny?" I'm still dumbfounded. "Shit, really? As much as she drinks?" He rubs my shoulders and his palms feel damp. He's not bullshitting me. My mind races back to when she invited me to the nightclub. *Maybe she was trying to bodysnatch me then. Fuck…All this shit is happening and I'm busy worrying about Mensah cheating?*

"Alcohol doesn't affect us. It's just her disguise on Earth. We only have a few more weeks before we report back to Alice. She is our leader. And we have to finalize the offspring or Alice will punish us." *Shit. Is that why she kept trying to get access to my phone?…She was getting information about me. Fuck…this is not happening right now.*

"Offspring? What do you mean?"

"We need to try to procreate before the end of this voyage. Penny and I have tried to mate with several women—"

"Yeah, I heard it in the *kotodenden* room."

"The what?"

Vida, you've said too much. "Yes, the room upstairs." It's all starting to make sense. Several women, multilingual, attractive, rich, out-of-the-ordinary capabilities, and then The Beast between his legs. *Not to say it can't exist, but the whole good looks, money, women, power and a big dick is a bit too cliché. So now it makes sense, Julius and Penny are aliens. Shit, Julius is an alien…Fuck…Like I don't have enough shit to contend with. No, really fuck…HE IS AN ALIEN…*I push back and lean my back against the window.

He grips my arms again with his alien Hulk strength. "Vida, you need to help me."

"Me, help you? To do what?"

"You need to give me the offspring."

My mouth hits the ground. Kegels don't help and I squeeze my thighs tighter together. "Me! Why me? I've got three kids already and I'm married." A perfect time to flaunt this.

"You are the perfect match for procreation."

"So, I have to have alien sex?"

"Yes. But I promise I won't hurt you." I feel dizzy, but this is no time to black out. The kids are upstairs; I can shout to warn them. My phone is resting on the charger in the kitchen. *What can I do to escape?*

"You know, honestly, I am not a good candidate for all this. Lately, I've been having high blood pressure and I have bad eczema in the winter time and I'm allergic to cats and I'm pretty sure aliens. My eyes run like Abla's credit card bills. I'm a hypochondriac. It's only by the grace of God that I had these children. And now you want me to procreate with you, and not even regular human procreation, but alien sex. It's just too much for me. I got enough going on. What you need to do is start going to church and look for virgins or something. They make better mating for aliens…" He grabs me again.

"Please, Vida, calm down. I'm only telling you this because I know that I can trust you. We just need a couple of hours to mate and about two weeks for the offspring to hatch."

"Huh? Hatch? What am I birthing, chickens?"

"No," he says sadly.

"For goodness sake. And how do you think it's gonna go over with my African husband that I just procreated with an alien? Do you know the amount of gossip that will plague my family? I'm not even worried about Homeland Security, but the Ghanaian community would make you wish you were never born. My children's children will be outcasts. We won't be able to show our faces at outdoorings, funerals or birthday parties ever again."

"The whole process can be done before your husband returns." He pulls me in closer and I push back. "You will be saving me if you do this for me. No one will have to know the reason. Trust me, Vida…Please, I need you. Don't be afraid of me. I won't hurt you." He staggers back. *Something is wrong.* He shakes his head vigorously and slowly raises his head. *His eyes…Shit.* His left eye has gone from Royal Dansk cookie blue tin to…to…Mountain Dew green. *Shit, Vida, what have you gotten yourself into?* He continues, "Let me show you how." He takes off his jacket.

"Don't show me shit! I don't want to see anything or hear any more." I stagger toward the stairs. *I need a plan. I'll wake up Panin and lock the kids and me in Kakra's room.* "Writing assignment, my ass…this was all a ploy to use me and my body. Why did I listen to Abla?" He moves toward the step. "Listen, don't come any closer, E.T. I will split your head open like a piñata." I pick up an umbrella next to the front door and swing it over my shoulders. He retreats back to the dining table and sits down. He bursts into thunderous laughter.

"Well, Vida…Not bad for a unicorn story. Don't you think?" His laughter roars. "Oh, Vida…Vida…I couldn't hold it in anymore…Oh my goodness…!" His excitement is voluminous. "You definitely should seek a career as a writer or an actress. You have such genuine responses. Quite entertaining." I stand guard. After a few more bursts of laughter he settles down. His face turns salmon in color and tears stream down his cheeks. "Wow. It's been quite some time since I laughed so hard."

I'm still prepared with the umbrella over my shoulder. I move toward him. "What's so funny?" He belts out more laughter. And it is apparent the joke is on me. "You're an asshole."

"Oh my. My face hurts. Oh, Vida, oh my…that was all too entertaining."

"How could you make up a story like that? That is not a unicorn story, that's a miniseries drama on FX. Unicorn stories are little white lies. What you just gave me is angina." I drop the umbrella and sit farther away from him. I rise up again feeling wetness in my panties. I rush into the bathroom to bring dignity back to myself.

When I return, Julius is still wiping the tears from his face with a monogrammed handkerchief. After an hour, when I think he has gotten all the laughter his stomach can bear, he starts again with a slight grin and then a full hearty laugh.

"You know you're going to hell, right?" I say.

"Oh Vida, lucky for me, I don't believe in those things anymore." I want to delve deeper into his statement, but his laughter is contagious and I join in on my ridicule. His phone rings and he sobers up to answer it. *Hmmm, Italian. Maybe it's Penny or Vincent.* "*Ciao,*" he finally says and hangs up quickly.

"Ms. Frimpong, as always, but especially tonight, I am very pleased to be in your presence." He grabs the empty Guinness bottles.

"Julius, I'll take care of that."

"No. Please, I can manage." He pauses and turns to face me. "These glasses are instrumental in helping me distinguish between light and dark, which also helps me walk unassisted at times. My million dollar bionic left eye allows me to see some images in silhouette. For instance, the twenty-four steps to your kitchen; the Guinness on the top shelf in the refrigerator; the thirteen stairs the children race up to the second floor; the six-chair dining set; the oversized couch in your living room; the two club chairs next to a reading lamp. And of course, some things I can only imagine, like the pictures hanging on the wall, the children's artwork on the refrigerator door and your penmanship on the thank you card you sent me."

He smiles and my heart wants to melt. I could never imagine what it must be like for him every day without seeing the simplest things such as the color of a flower or Penny's face.

He continues, "It was a tumor that caused my blindness. Stubborn fucking thing. It keeps coming back. Several surgeries and over a million dollars to successfully remove it. There's a microchip installed in the back of my eye and it sends images back and forth to my brain. I won't bore you with surgical details—that's for a rainy day. I suffered some damage to the eye during the car accident, which causes my pupil to turn lime green at times, something the brilliant scientists in Australia are remedying."

He grins as though he is recollecting an occurrence. "Many moons ago, there was an elder Ghanaian man who taught a frightened twelve-year-old boy how to travel independently..." He pauses. "Your research this week, Ms. Frimpong, can blind people drive? I look forward to your response."

He enters the kitchen and I follow close behind him. He stands over two bins. "The left one." I say. He places the bottles in the recycling bin and moves past me toward the door. He pulls out the black leather sneakers from under the entrance table and navigates his feet into them one at a time. "I have a conference next week in L.A., so if you should need me, just have Alice contact me."

"Ahhh yes, Alice."

"Are you not fond of her?"

"No, she's a real gem. She seems almost human." I recall our banter at times.

"Well, I wanted to make you feel at home, so I incorporated some euphemisms just for you."

Chapter 31

I need a break from all the reading this evening. Music coming from behind the stairs gives me a reason to see what Julius is up to. "What's that?" I ask standing in the doorway. Thin cords surround his arms like vermicelli noodles.

"It's something I invented long ago. It's supposed to be a game with physical interaction."

"That's interesting," I say. I enter the room further.

"Well, these cords are fixed into these armbands, which are supposed to track your arm movements, and these foot pads track your foot movements. So it records any activity, say jumping and swinging arms."

"Oh, it's similar to Wii."

He sulks. "Yes, it is. That's the main reason I've given up on it. The design is less complicated than these apparatuses." He holds up the bands with what looks like dental floss attached.

"I'm quite sure you can add your spin to it. You know…do something that the Wii doesn't do."

"Perhaps. Do you want to try?"

"The game? What am I supposed to do?"

"Can you dance?"

Do I like Haagen Dazs butter pecan ice cream? "Of course."

"Okay, let's have a little fun, shall we?" A large screen lights up. He places the armbands on each of my arms. Before I can stop him, he kneels down, removes my shoes and places the footpad on my right foot. He secures it with a Velcro strap. His warm hands glide over my calf muscles and down to my feet. I'm flushed. *I hope my shoes don't smell funky. I should have worn socks.* He secures the left foot the same way. "How does that feel?"

"Good. It doesn't feel like I am wearing anything." He rises.

"That's the purpose, so it doesn't hinder your movements. Take a look at the screen." A large projection lights up. "Alice, program it to dance mode."

"Yes, my Lord."

Julius instructs Alice with several commands and they appear on the screen.

"So you're Crush Stomper?" I turn to face him. "I hope you live up to your name."

He smiles, but offers no comment. Alice requests my alias. I yell into the ceiling, "Rump Shaker."

"What?" He laughs loudly.

"You know, like booty, but I want to use the word rump."

"As you wish, Rump Shaker. I certainly hope you can live up to that name."

"Talk is worth cedis. The proof is in the score."

"Agreed, Ms. Frimpong. So this is how we are going to do this. Spin the wheel by swinging any arm three hundred sixty degrees. The faster you swing, the faster the wheel will move. As you can see, there are several categories of music, so whichever the dial lands on you have to strut or rump shake for thirty seconds. The armbands and footpads track movement, so the faster the movement, the more points you accumulate. Inevitably, the contender with the most points wins. Got it?"

"Got it." I'm hopping from foot to foot like a kid in Toys "R" Us.

"What color are your bands?"

"They're glowing green."

"Good. Green is always good. Whenever they glow a different color that means the bands are not connected to the screen. Okay, with that said, lady first."

I leap into position and swing my arm. The wheel moves with the same force of my arm swing. The dial moves like the Wheel of Fortune dial. Alice announces the mark on the dial.

"Nineties R and B music."

This is a piece of cake. Blackstreet's music fills the chamber and I move my legs to the rhythm of the beat. The points increase under my pseudo name and at the end of thirty seconds, I acquire 300 points.

"Not bad," Julius says. "I was expecting Rump Shaker to bring a little more oomph, but the night hasn't aged yet."

"Yeah, yeah…your turn, Crush Stomper."

He spins his arm in a wide circle and the wheel rotates several times until finally the dial rests on a category. *This should be interesting.* He steps away from me.

Alice announces: **"Dancehall music."**

Zebra Katz's deep voice fills the room. *Shut...the...front...door.* He has moves like Chris Brown...No, wait...more like Usher. *No way.* His points increase with every movement. His arms pump with several breakdance moves. He surpasses my score. At the end of the thirty seconds, he accumulates 660 points. With his chest heaving and a big smile, this tells me he is a contender. "How's that for Crush Stomper?"

I straighten up and do a couple of stretches. *There is no way he is going to beat me in this.* I swing my arm with determined force; the wheel makes four full turns and Alice announces: **"Reggae Dance."**

Sean Paul's melodic voice propels me to gyrate my hips swiftly and then slowly. I bend over to display some booty shaking action. I turn several times and raise my arms above my head, dancing to the beat. I look at the wheel and I've only accumulated 200 points. *Hey, something is wrong.* "Alice, stop the music."

"What's wrong? Are your bands still green?" Julius asks.

"Yes. But all that booty shaking and I've only accumulated two hundred points."

"Were you dancing?" Julius asks, examining my bands.

"Of course I was. And I had about a dozen body rolls. Look. I'm shaking my rump right now and there are no points accumulating. It's still at two hundred."

"Hmm. Unfortunately, this is one of the hiccups I have to solve. The band doesn't detect subtle hip or ass movement. You've highlighted the importance of those movements. More research is needed."

"Can't you just create one for the waist? Like waist beads?" My mind recalls the bells and tassels on the set Mensah bought me and our own movements in the club chair. *Stop it, Vida. It's not the time to be thinking about him.*

"Perhaps. But too many gadgets would dissuade the average teenager. Back to the drawing board."

"I'm sure you'll figure it out in no time. You're smart. This machine. These bands and pads are as light as first aid bandages. It's amazing what you've accomplished."

"Thank you, Rump Shaker." We laugh. "Let's get you out of these bands." He moves closer to me and begins to release the armbands and, before he bends down, I startle him with the anxiousness in my voice. He moves back.

"I got it." I bend down and try to release the footpads. I tug with extra force in several directions. The pads won't come off.

"Are you okay, Vida? Do you need my help?"

I try the other leg and it yields the same results. "Umm…I think the Velcro around the pads is stuck."

He kneels down again…right in between my legs. He doesn't find anything odd about this because he continues to talk right into my pussy. "How did that happened?"

"Aaaaah…not sure." I look down and it's just two pieces of fabric, my black ruffled skirt and a fuchsia thong, that separates his mouth from the furnace between my legs.

"It's moist." *Tell me about it.* His warm breath ignites the furnace. "Oh boy, that's not good. The perspiration from your feet might have fused it together. I'm going to have to cut it off."

"My foot?"

"The pad attached to your foot." He chuckles.

"That's not necessary, is it? I hate to ruin your gizmo thing and all."

"It's a prototype. No worries. This will only take a minute." He stands up and makes the clicking sounds as he exits the room. Julius returns with what looks like Edward Scissorhands blades.

"Umm. You can give that to me. I can cut it." I reach my hands out to grab hold of the scissors.

"Oh Vida, don't you trust me?" He chuckles again.

"I'm just saying that's…a…big…pair…of scissors."

"I've handled sharp objects before. We will be fine."

"Would it be easier if I sat in the chair?"

"No, as you are." A childlike grin appears. He kneels down again in between my legs. My mind is drifting again to places it shouldn't. He slides his hand from the back of my knee down to my calf then to my ankle as he lifts my foot up. "Now how did you get fused together so quickly?" he whispers.

"What?"

"I'm thinking out loud," he admits. "Hmmm." More warm air pushing against the fabric. He tugs again, but no release.

What's taking so long? What is this thing made out of? Titanium?

"Don't move," he commands. And I stop looking down and even hold my breath. He moves to the other leg. I feel the sharp cold steel blade against my skin.

"Do you need my help?" I say anxiously.

"No. I know exactly what I'm doing." *Even if he used a butter knife this would have been cut by now.* "You have very soft skin. I would hate to cut you."

I can think of a dozen ways of getting these off and they wouldn't involve his face in between my legs. Perspiration between my breasts builds up. It's hard to tell if this is arousing or uncomfortably inappropriate. Maybe he wants to see me squirm under pressure. *He clearly doesn't know who I am.*

"Are you uncomfortable?" he says.

I raise my foot and place it on his thigh and apply my weight against the wall behind me. My right hand rests on his shoulder. My skirt brushes his face and his lips align at the right height perfectly. "Now I'm comfortable." He laughs. He uses his left hand to cut through the band and uses his right hand to balance my foot on his thigh. He removes both pads without any harm to my skin.

"There you go." He massages my calf muscle. And it feels unbelievably good. "Your calf muscles are amazingly firm. Do you still play soccer?"

"Not as much as I used to." He slowly rises up with the pads and scissors in his hand. Fine wires run through the torn pads. Quietness surrounds us. I break the silence. "You know I won."

Chapter 32

I call Abla for the second time. It's only 9:55 p.m. She couldn't have fallen asleep already. I text her and wait.

Instagram keeps me entertained until Abla's call comes in. "You got tree minutes. Bullet points unless iz wat I dink it iz and den I will call you afta eleven."

"Why after eleven?"

"You see now. Yur already wastin' time."

"Did she sleep with him yet?" a familiar soft voice echoes in the background.

"Is that Mrs. Lindsey?" I ask.

"I don't dink so…and yes," Abla says. "Wait, did you?"

"Did I sleep with Julius? Why on earth would I even think about having an affair with him? Things are rough right now between Mensah and me, but Julius would be the last person on earth. He's my boss. The guilt alone would give me a heart attack."

Disgruntled sighs in the background. "Shez not built like us, Lilly. Dat would be history," Abla says. Mrs. Lindsey's cackling laugh comes through the phone.

"Stop polluting her mind with your crazy stories," I snap at Abla.

"Pleazze, you haven't heard half da stuff she uzed to do in her dayz. Anyway, watz so important? Judge Judy iz on in two minutes."

"Is that why you said I have only three minutes? Judge Judy is more important than what I have to say?"

"Lissen, I will talk until tree a.m. if you, like, just give me one hour."

"What is she waiting for?" Mrs. Lindsey's voice is now as clear as Abla's.

"I don't know," Abla says.

"How does Mrs. Lindsey know about Julius?"

"I told her."

"I thought we were just keeping this with the family?"

"It iz. Who iz Mrs. Lindsey gonna tell? Most of her friends are dead or having affairs of deer own. Dis iz her only form of entertainment. Please. I beg. Call me back in an hour. Bye."

"Hefa!" She is always rushing to get off the phone when Judge Judy comes on even though I have shown her several times how to use the DVR.

It's probably nothing. My encounter with Julius today. Just a little flirting. Yeah, nothing. Anyway, why do Abla and Mrs. Lindsey think I would cheat on Mensah? We have our problems, but I don't think I could ever do that. That would mean destroying my family, my marriage. The guilt. Plus, I'm not attracted to him. Looks, a big dick and money is...is....so...but those eyes and those lips...the way they form a perfect heart shaped curve on the top....Stop it, Vida...go to sleep.

Chapter 33

"Where did you guys meet?" Julius asks.

"Oh, gosh. Almost eleven years ago, I was part of this women's soccer league, Sassi Strikers. Practice was every Tuesday, Thursday and Sunday at Memorial Field. He just started showing up to the games on Sundays. He sat on the bleachers at the same exact spot every game, and on Thursdays attending our practices, not really interacting with anyone. The men's soccer team practiced right before us, so I assumed he was a recruiter or something. One day during practice, I kicked the ball in his direction and he got flustered. I apologized. He wasn't friendly. His face intimidated me. I swore that he was going to curse me out, but he just threw the ball back onto the field. After one of our games, he approached us and congratulated us on a good game. We started talking and he said he was supposed to meet up with a friend there, but loved watching us play, so he came often. It was one of the worst pickup lines I'd heard. But I let him roll with it." Julius leans back in the chair and crosses his legs. He opens another bottle of Guinness and takes a sip. I continue.

"Abla usually picked me up in the evening, but that night after the game, she was running late and Mensah offered me a ride." My mind drifts back to events over a decade ago. "He always wore dark denim and polo shirts. And dear God, the way he walked…like he was walking in sync to a soundtrack. Our first date was at a local diner on Baychester Avenue." I close my eyes envisioning us in the corner booth of the diner. "I remember. I ordered a western omelet and he ordered a…a…a…lunchbreak, some sort of brunch with a T-bone steak. He sent the waiter back several times until they got the steak just right. We spent hours sitting in that diner. I thought I bored him to death. Auntie Cece always said I could talk Jesus into coming back to earth. At times, I can be a bit talkative."

"Really? I haven't noticed." I roll my eyes at his sarcasm.

"Well, I must have said something right because after that date, we dated several months and then I became pregnant with the twins and the rest is history."

"So what keeps you up at night crying, Ms. Frimpong?" He takes another sip of the bottle. *Don't open the doors of hell, Vida. I don't want to cry on his shoulder. Do you really want to resurrect every argument, every moment of espionage tracking, every doubt, every voice inside me that tells me something is not right? Take a deep breath.*

"We agreed on six months. Now it's more than two years. He heard of some contracts out in California with government housing. He said that was what we needed to get our family in a better position. More money, better opportunities, etcetera, etcetera." I feel my mood changing. Moist palms and harder breaths. "You know, I knew when we first met he wanted to leave New York and see the opportunities he could get to start his business. After we got married, he seemed lonely, miserable and became more isolated. It wasn't the job and part of me debated if he loved me." *Stop it, Vida. You've said too much.* I stop.

He leans forward in the chair, invading my space. "I'm still listening, Vida."

I've never talked to anyone besides Abla about my marital problems. Part of me still wants to keep it a secret. Auntie Cece always tells me it is not good to discuss what goes on in your marriage with anyone else. Her solution, just pray and go to bed. But I feel my shoulders come down. I continue. "When I became pregnant with the twins, I wasn't sure what I was going to do. I knew it didn't fit with his plans, but he stayed and did the honorable thing. He said I wasn't going to be alone and that he would take care of me. He did…I mean, he is. I just wish…he was here…that's all." *That's it, Vida. You said too much.* I get up and move away. "Well that's marriage, I guess. Fast forward to the present and we're still married."

"Happily? I don't mean to pry, but I wanted to hear, 'We are still happily married.'" Julius's comment stirs many feelings. Happiness is not one of them. Mensah wasn't happy here and I knew it. He had dreams. I had dreams. *A writer one day.* No one's life goes as planned. Arguing over silly things just creates distance.

"No condition is permanent. My mother used to tell me that we need to pray for our husbands because only wives have the heart to deal with them. That is why God created us second: to help them. If two captains are on board a ship, that ship won't move. The captain commands the ship, but the crew makes the voyage possible."

"Ah…religion again…so is the point of being married to have the title? It shouldn't matter whether or not you are happy? The eyes of the law is the only concern, right?" His sarcasm is biting. "A wise person told me that marriage is supposed to be enjoyed not endured. What is the sense in being committed to someone that you are not happy with? Oh, that's right, the virtuous God will console you in your pain. The same God who is capable of inflicting so much pain will rescue you from yours."

The atmosphere is heavy with his comments. He's made several such references to religion before. I need to pry. "Are you an atheist?"

He laughs. "I'm a realist."

"No, seriously, don't you believe in God? Your mother spent years building churches in Ghana, but you don't believe in God."

"Church is just a building. It's the people who attend the church that makes it a testament of the faith. I'm not turning this into a debate about religion. You have your belief and I obviously have mine. Let's just leave it at that." I've never seen him so serious except for the time he dismissed me from the hotel after the interview. But behind his words, there is sadness that I haven't seen before.

"Thank you, by the way." *Shit, Abla already warned me about mentioning how her goods arrived in Ghana so quickly.*

Once Abla investigated Julius living in Ghana, she found that Julius Gallo's name is known in small and influential circles. It turns out that Julius still secretly invests in several businesses and one of them is in the shipping industry. Last week Abla spoke to the chairpersons at the port and mentioned that she was working for Julius Gallo. Later, she was told by our family that her shipment of goods, which usually takes six weeks, arrived in three days.

"For?" he asks, rising from the table. *Shit…I need a quick unicorn story.*

"Ummm. Just for your candor." *He is convinced. Saved.*

"Well, it's getting late and tomorrow's a school day." He takes the empty Guinness bottles to the kitchen. I pack up the laptop and hand it to him.

"Don't forget your laptop and journals," I say.

"It's safe here. Good night, Vida."

Chapter 34

It's been two months since I slept next to Mensah and loneliness occupies the space again except for the occasional nights MJ sneaks in. I said some pretty harsh words the last time he was home. *Vida, are you going to throw away ten years of marriage? What about the children?* Life would be so different for all of us. It's not my fault. He put me in this situation. *Vida, you don't deserve to live like this. You deserve better...You...deserve...better.* I lay on the pillow weeping again. My cellphone alerts me to a new text and I search for it under the duvet covers in hopes it's Mensah.

"I am sure you are not asleep. And if you are awake, are you doing what I think you are doing?"

Julius's texts always warrant a response. "What do you think I am doing?"

His reply comes instantly. "Nevermind. The fact that you responded in a timely manner has given me reason to think otherwise. Good night, Ms. Frimpong."

"That's it? You just texted me to see if I was doing what you thought I was doing?"

"Yes."

"Are you implying sex?"

"No, are you?"

"No. Just answering your question."

"Which is?"

"What you thought I was doing."

This time no instant reply. Maybe he fell asleep. Sixteen minutes later his text arrives: "DON'T CRY YOURSELF TO SLEEP."

Instant tears begin to form and I close my eyes, trying not to stare at the words. But I pick up my phone again and reread it. Bold cap letters. My nights are filled with this. Even a blind man can tell that I am suffering from a broken heart. "ENOUGH!" I say and wipe my face. I look at the phone again. Nothing. My eyelids feel heavy. The phone vibrates. Another text message.

"Are you going to sleep now?"

I'm surprised by his text. As though he is sitting in the room with me.

"Yes. I am going to sleep. Why are you still up? Are you working in your study?"

"No. I just had sex."

I burst out in a loud laugh. Another text.

"I bet you're laughing."

"I am. Did you seriously have sex just now?"

"What do you think?"

"I believe you did. I never pictured you for a minute man." Shit. Did I go too far with that last text?

"Good night, Ms. Frimpong."

"Helloooo???!!!"

I hold the phone hoping for another text.

Chapter 35

It's six months since I met Julius. He's cocky at times and sometimes he can be a box of treats. He surprises me weekly.

"What time is it, Alice?"

"Ms. Frimpong, it's ten minutes to ten p.m."

"Do you have to go?" Julius asks. I detect disappointment.

"No. But we have been at this for nearly one hour."

His face is perkier. "Are you feeling defeated already, Ms. Frimpong?"

"Me? Defeat? I know no such word." No wheel this time, but an apparatus similar to a karaoke machine is keeping us entertained.

"What was the bet again?" Julius asks.

"We never actually placed a bet. I thought we were doing it for pure entertainment."

"Uh, I should have placed a bet. Your dancing may be better than your singing."

"What? What's wrong with my singing?"

"Oh, nothing. You sing all the words, but let's just say mating seals come to mind."

"You're an ass," I quip. "First of all, placing a bet with Alice's assistance is not fair at all. She's too smart to let you lose."

"Was that a compliment, Ms. Frimpong?"

I bite my lip. "Yes. But don't let that go to your gigabytes."

"Should I retrieve the next song, Ms. Frimpong?"

"Come on, one last song," Julius says.

"What difference does it make? You're already leading."

"As always, my dear." I admire his determination. He reminds me of Panin a bit—a fearless resolve at times and the same drive for independence. The huge screen lights up and the lyrics for the next song appear. Even with the words prominently displayed on the screen, I manage to mess up some of the lines. He has sung every word of the past fourteen songs from memory including some Twi songs. I feel a bit ashamed that he sings better in Twi than I do.

"Okay, one more," I say.

"Alice, another random English song." He jumps up, preparing for the next selection to play. His excitement is amusing. "Are you ready? It's your turn," he says.

The melody begins to play. "Say, Say, Say" by Paul McCartney and Michael Jackson fills the chamber.

"Ooh, I love this song," we both say in unison.

"I haven't heard it in ages," I chime in.

"Let's do a duet," Julius says.

He alerts Alice to repeat it and play it through the subwoofers. A brief hush and I hear the hum of the subwoofers as the bass begins to kick in. "Wow. This sounds amazing. It feels like a concert hall." He smiles satisfactorily.

"All right, I'll be Michael and you'll—"

"Alice, pause." The music stops and Julius looks toward me for the cause of the interruption. His face is confused and his eyebrows raise higher than usual.

"What's the matter? Why did you stop the music?"

"Oh, no…No…No, boo boo…Listen here. You can't be Michael."

"Why not?" His face looks like an upset toddler who was told to go to bed early.

"Because it's obvious you can't be Michael."

"Excuse me? It's not obvious to me. Do you mind pleading your case?" He waits for my plea. I can't help but give a little chuckle at his melancholy. I regain a serious composure.

"Because you have to be Paul and that's it."

"I have to be Paul," he states again. "Unfortunately for you, your case is over before it began. You have no grounds for this determination."

"Listen, any court will uphold my argument. You have to sing Paul's lyrics and I will sing Michael's."

"Still more reason for your case to be thrown out of court. It is inconclusive," he says.

"Okay, now for my closing."

He chuckles. "Closing? You couldn't even offer a decent opening, let alone a justifiable case."

"Excuse me, counselor. I have the floor now. As I was saying before I was jealously interrupted. My closing argument: Julius must sing the lyrics of Sir Paul McCartney because they are both British and I will sing the lyrics of Michael Jackson because we are both Virgos. Thank you to the court for their time and indulgence. Let's proceed." His composure is more relaxed. He removes his hands from either side of his waist and gives a large clap. We both burst into laughter.

"The court thanks you for wasting its time. We will have you disbarred for improper use of its judicial system, but not until the defendant thrashes you mercilessly in the last round of karaoke."

"Oh, so you think, Alice?" I yell into the air, "Rewind the selection and play." The beat fills the room once more. "I hope you know Sir Paul's—"

His voice stills me again. *It's captivating*. When Michael's part comes up, I exaggerate the lines with a little more 'he ha' than usual. Julius laughs. "I don't recall that part in the song."

"Because it is called music interpretation," I answer defensively.

"I must declare this a tie." We sink to the floor amused. I move closer to face him.

"Yeah, a tie." The sound of our breathing fills the air between us. "I haven't seen Penny in a while. Did she travel?"

"Yes. She's at another photo shoot in Hawaii."

Although I have yet to see her grace any magazine covers, she is in high demand, even popular, for someone I assume is in her late thirties. But veteran hands at Photoshop can easily turn back the years. *So who was the woman leaving the kotodenden room last week?* I shouldn't pry, but in my fashion, I do.

"Do you guys have an open relationship?" He runs his hands through his hair.

"What do you mean by open relationship?"

Surely you've gone too far, Vida. Just forget it. Mind your business. Say good night and leave. Nope. I continue. "You know. Like seeing other people or having other relationships with the understanding it's okay."

"Hmmm, Penny and I have an understanding. We've been together for several years. I don't know what to call it, but it works."

"Oh. So that means you tell her when you sleep with other women and she tells you when she sleeps with other men?"

"Penny doesn't have other men," he says. He smiles but it's a smile that begs for more questions.

"How long have you had other sexual partners? Is it because you have a sex addiction?" *I'm surprised that wasn't an inside thought.* He pivots his head around like an old puppet.

"Pardon me?" *Shit!* He adjusts his posture with both elbows relaxed on his lap. "As I stated before, Penny and I have an understanding. I enjoy sex perhaps more than some. But that doesn't qualify me as having a sex addiction. I'm not fucking anything with a pulse. Sex should be equally and fully enjoyable and not engaged in to fill a void. Does that answer your question?"

"Yes. I guess. Most people can't admit to their addictions anyways."

"Why do you assume I have an addiction? Because you just so happen to be here on nights when I have company? Or because I have multiple partners?" He chuckles again. "Or…" He pauses. "…that my cock is the length of a fufu stick?" *Fuck! Those were Abla's words. So he did hear our conversations earlier. What else has he heard? I mean, we haven't mentioned his activities lately, but I've heard the noises upstairs.* The sounds from the *kotodenden* room and his energized appetite for work and play never go unnoticed. *Shit, if I had known he understood and spoke Twi, I would have reserved the gossip for home.*

"Excuse me?" I'm trying to play naïve.

"Oh, come on, Vida, don't play coy. I've heard most of the chatter, but I should feel flattered that you and your sister think so highly of me. And to answer some of your questions: I don't take Viagra or sex enhancement drugs. I don't pick up strange women at clubs and have sex with them. I don't discriminate based on race or religion. But that doesn't mean I have a harem of women on standby…well, not anymore…when I was younger I was a bit of a bad ass. I've gotten older and gained some wisdom. Anyway, I test every year for HIV and STDs. I don't have submissives and I'm not into domination. There is only one type of shower I enjoy and that includes soap and hot water. There's a guy in Asia who gives me something to take care of my sperm count. I'm a bit selfish. Kids? Mmmmm? Maybe. But definitely not now. And yes, I enjoy having sex with Penny and her girlfriends."

"So you basically heard every conversation that I've ever had in your house? I wish you'd told me that I was being recorded. Shouldn't you have to disclose it or something?"

"Everything is written in the contract that was drafted, edited and signed. Well, to put your mind at ease, that was a while ago. I stopped." He pauses. "You and Abla are very entertaining, but one thing I could not tolerate was the crying. It makes me feel uncomfortable." Silence fills the space between us.

"I'm sorry for talking about you behind your back. I have no business gossiping about subjects that don't concern me. It is not professional or kind to speak about you in that way. Please accept my apologies."

"No need to apologize, Ms. Frimpong. I can take humor sometimes at my expense. If there is anything else you want to know, just ask me."

"Okay. So do you think you can go four months without sex?"

"I don't know, and why would I ever want to do that?"

"I'm just saying, most sex addicts don't know they have a problem until it's too late. And God forbid you start fucking a whole in the sheet because you're so far gone from reality."

"So you really think I have a problem?"

"I strongly believe you need intervention. Well, let's make a bet. Four months with no sex whatsoever," I say.

"Why four months? Is that some clinical threshold to determine if you have an addiction?"

I laugh. "No. But hopefully I will be done with your project by then."

"Hmmm. Goals. I like that you've set up that timetable for yourself, considering you've only transcribed three journals." *Mensah has preoccupied my mind long enough. No more crying. I will get this project done in four months.* He continues. "And if I were to entertain this bet, what would be my reward?"

"The reward is that you are not a sex addict."

"I don't need a bet to prove that to myself."

"Well, I can't imagine betting money. There must be something that you want."

"Oh, there's always something. So, what do you want if I should fail miserably?" Julius says.

"Hmmm…I am not sure. Definitely not another car." I laugh. Julius doesn't. *Okay, maybe that's still a touchy subject.*

"I will publish your book," Julius says.

"My book?" *How does he know that I was writing a book?*

"You are a writer, aren't you, Ms. Frimpong? Surely there's something stored away under a mattress or in a secret drawer. A story that one day will be published. Maybe it's about time you take it more seriously." He stands up. "Start writing it again, so that way we can add published author to your many talents."

"You're serious?" He nods.

It's been two years since I've written anything. A couple of chapters are saved on the computer I can't remember the passcode to. The book with no title, few paragraphs with no order and horrible grammar. A story of a woman miserable in her marriage. *Maybe it should be an autobiography. So, if I win this bet, he will publish my book. And if he loses, which I bet he will, then he's a sex addict. But my book—me a published author. After all these years. Of course, I have to be serious and write. I need this incentive.* I stand up and Julius rises to face me.

"Deal?" He extends his hand toward me.

"Deal." I grab his hand.

"I've never held a bet that involved sex. So this should be interesting."

"But you haven't told me what you want." There's no way he is going to win, but I ask anyway.

"I need time to think about it. But I am sure it's something you can handle. I promise nothing criminal or degrading."

"Okay, so the clock starts today."

"Are you joking? Give a bloke a break. The clock starts tomorrow. Tina will be here in an hour."

"Tina?"

"The masseuse." I did recall meeting her one morning in the *kotodenden* room. *Yeah, he won't survive past a week.*

"Make sure you take care of *everything* you need to take care of." I draw out my words.

"I get your meaning, Ms. Frimpong. I plan to," he says. I instantly feel sorry for Tina.

*

"It seems yur coming home later every weekend." The dining room lights cast a soft glow on Auntie Cece. A teakettle and cup sits on the table in front of her.

"Oh, Auntie, were you waiting for me?"

"Yes. Last weekend I drove past the house after midnight and yur car was not here. I've been here since ten p.m. and it is now three a.m. Are these the hours you plan to keep with this new job?"

"I don't come home this late every weekend. It's just that I'm trying to get a lot more work done now. I have a deadline." *Another unicorn story; well, actually not. Now I have a four-month deadline.*

"Yaa, sit down." *Shit. I feel a lecture.* These lectures are always laced with some moral obligation and lessons about marriage. Her mantras are not Ablaisms, they are Ceceisms:

"Don't over talk your husband."

"Always greet your husband lovingly when he comes home, even if you are upset with him."

"Don't disturb your husband if he is troubled by something."

"Make him feel happy, especially when he lies next to you in bed."

"Don't listen to yur sister—that is why she isn't married."

"Marriage is not easy and yur doing a good job, but…"

She begins and I bite my lip to keep from sighing. "I know Mensah and you are going through tough times now, but no one said marriage is easy. It takes a lot of patience and understanding. It takes the heart of a woman to turn a blind eye to some matters that weigh the heart. If you want to be happy, then you cannot focus on all the things he is doing wrong. Turn all yur frustration to God and keep God in yur marriage. The devil doesn't come looking ragged or ugly. He comes sometimes in a good suit, a beautiful face, fancy words, expensive gifts, but he is only coming to take away yur joy." She pauses to sip her tea.

"Auntie, I know what you are thinking."

She places the teacup down and shifts her eyes toward me. Her lips are turned down into a scowl. "Do you?" Her voice is stern and her face firm. *I can't answer.* "I am thinking that my daughter wants to throw away her marriage because she says she's not happy. But the only way to be happy is to turn yur troubles to God and have faith that he will turn things around. Mensah is in California making a better life for his family. What woman doesn't want that? But instead you want to be swept away with false promises and candy toffee lies. Yur too smart for that. Every relationship has its challenges and you will not find happiness if you don't appreciate what you have. Stop peeking over the fence. Water the grass in yur yard."

"Auntie, it's so hard to keep loving him when he doesn't consider my feelings." I think about the last night we spent together and the morning he left. Even with my angered tears he didn't think twice about staying.

"You were not born together, so don't expect him to think like you. Remember, he has no family but you and the kids. Just imagine a kid growing up through orphanages in Ghana and then coming to the U.S. to live on his own. You and the children are all that he has. You have to fight for yur marriage." The image of a young boy selling water by the motorway because no one was there to take care of him enters my thoughts. Mensah told me his mother died when he was a young boy and his father remarried and moved to Nigeria. I picture a young Mensah moving from orphanage to orphanage then to the status of houseboy and finally winning a prestigious award to attend school overseas. My heart softens a bit.

"Auntie, it takes two wheels for a bicycle to work." That is an Ablaism, but it doesn't impress Auntie Cece.

"And it takes a God fearing woman to keep her home." *She always has a better comeback.* "God gave women bigger hearts because of what they can endure. Go to him and let him know he means everything to you. Don't fight over the past. Yaa, you can do this. Just think about the boys. They love their father. Try to make it work, please."

She rises. The chat was a bit shorter than what I'm accustomed to, but effective. *Maybe I should take a trip to California. I've used so many excuses not to go, but if anything, I owe it to the kids to try again.* "Good night. I have a doctor's appointment this morning. I need to get some rest. Put God first and he will fight all yur battles." She leans forward and kisses my forehead.

*

I was hoping after my bath to relax underneath my new pink and purple duvet blanket from Bed Bath and Beyond. Abla occupies the edge of the bed.

"Is everyone waiting for me to come home these days?"

"I was on my way down when I heard the *abrewa*. Is there somedin' you need to tell me?"

"Like?"

"Come on...iz almost time for breakfast. Don't make me beg."

"I've been working all night." Another unicorn story, but she wouldn't believe we've been battling at karaoke all night.

"Oh, please. Dis iz big sista...tell me...tell me."

"You keep saying he likes me, but Julius probably likes every tight hole."

"No, he really likes you. I see it. All men haf a certain way dey behave around women. Eida dey play yur-one-of-a-kind-I-can't-live-witout-you foolish kind of way or dey secretly dink yur annoyin'-but-cute. Dey try to hide it by actin' uninterested, but all dey want iz an openin', a look, a kiss dat tells dem you feel da same."

"You watch too many Lifetime movies. I'm still married to Mensah and I need to try to make it work." She rolls her eyes.

"Dear sista, dis iz no marriage. Yur not happy and he could care less. Don't waste any more time on him. You won't be young foreva." Abla and Mensah's relationship may never be the same again. I poisoned my sister against him with many nights crying in her arms or over the phone. So much complaining and then silence. No family member should see a loved one in so much pain. I've allowed her to witness too much. Now her hatred toward him has surpassed mine. It's my fault she has so much anger for him. I swallow hard before I can form the words.

"Abla, I am going to California." Her eyes usually reveal exactly how she is feeling, but right now she looking at me blankly. "It's perfect timing. The kids are on spring break next week."

"Wat?"

"I need to fight for my marriage. The enemy wants to take control and I can't allow it," I say.

"Lissen to yurself. You sound just like da mizerable woman downstairs."

"Abla, I have to try one last time. If it doesn't work, then I can say that I really did my best."

Silence falls between us. I was expecting her to leave. I undress and crawl under the sheets. She moves over, allowing my legs to extend the full length of the bed. Her face is a bit relaxed. "Dat son of a bitch doesn't know how lucky he iz. If it had been me…hmmm…" She pauses and her lips turn up in disgust. "It iz always da good ones dat suffer. Yur too good for him. But God knows wat he iz doin'."

She lies beside me. My face nestles underneath her chin. "It will be well, Abla."

"It has to be." She hugs me tightly. "Don't tell him yur coming. After all, yur hiz wife and yur free to come and go as you pleaze. Dis should be a good surprise for him." I know exactly Abla's thoughts and part of me fears the worst.

Chapter 36

A week flies by and I still have so much to do on my list. Richard and Abla drive us to the airport. The kids seem anxious and I ask them again if they've heard from Daddy. A unanimous no, which also makes me feel happy that this surprise is actually going to work.

"Did you tell yur boss you will be out of town for a couple of days?" Abla turns to me in the backseat.

"Of course I gave them notice."

"No. I mean RBD."

"I tried reaching him. He must be out of town. I did inform Alice that I would be back next week. I'll try again once I get settled."

"Don't forget to call me once you land." She bear hugs the boys and me as we exit the car.

*

Thank goodness we take a late night flight. I am glad that the pediatrician prescribed Dramamine for Panin. It makes for a smooth flight. When we arrive in Sacramento, it is just a little past seven in the morning. We get our bags and make our way to the car rental unit. The boys look freshly rested. I enter the address on the GPS. "Mommy, how far is it?" MJ asks.

"Not far, baby."

"Shouldn't we call Daddy so he can pick us up from the airport?" Kakra says.

"I told you already, it's a surprise. We can't let him know we are here until he sees us. Okay, guys?"

"Okay," they say sulkily.

"Alright, it's not that far. Fifty-three minutes away."

"That's almost an hour away, Mommy," Kakra says.

"Yes, almost one hour," MJ repeats Kakra words.

"Where are we going?" Kakra asks.

"We are going to Stockton."

"Is that where Daddy lives?"

"Yes, for now."

We pass several malls. The GPS navigation alerts us we are two minutes away. I'm anxious. I catch my reflection in the rearview mirror. *Not bad at all without makeup.* My hair is still neatly pulled into a bun. We pull into a housing complex. He did write apartment 2004. The kids are sleeping. This allows me to say a little prayer and add some color to my face.

"Hey guys, we're here." They open their eyes slowly, trying to comprehend their new environment. Panin is doing well. He doesn't like change, but no outburst so far. We step out of the car still groggy from the flight and make our way through the promenade. It appears nice and clean. We walk up to the second floor landing and look for the apartment number. Nerves and anxiousness with my heart thumping like Congo drums makes the stair climb almost impossible. I grasp the railings. *Don't fear the worst, Vida. He wouldn't have given you the address if he had something to hide. Make it work. Talk less and listen more.* I knock twice on the door. MJ adds a third knock and I swiftly take hold of his hand.

"That's enough. It's still early in the morning. We don't want to wake up his neighbors."

"Who is it?" a man's voice startles me.

"Ummmm…" I step back and examine the address and the apartment number that Mensah wrote on the Bounty paper towel. "Good morning, I'm looking for Mensah Asare."

"Who is looking for him?"

"I am. His wife, Vida."

No more response from the man behind the door. "Mommy, maybe we have the wrong address. We should call Daddy," Kakra says.

I knock again. "Excuse me…" The door opens.

"Well. Well. Well and well. What do we have here?" It is a man's voice, but it doesn't look like a man. He is wearing a long pink silk robe and heavy geisha-like makeup.

"Excuse me, do you know my husband, Mensah?"

"Oh yes, dear. I know Mensah and let me say it's an honor to finally meet you."

"Finally meet me?" I swallow hard. *Think good thoughts, Vida…good thoughts.*

"Oh yes, honey, I've heard a lot about you. And there is no denying it. You look like Mensah's secretary."

"Secretary?" I ask.

"Yes, honey. Just the way I pictured you. You know, a wife of your stature." He…she…he examines me like the latest issue of *Vogue* magazine. "And look at here, are these little Junior Mensahs?…Oh gurl, that Mensah gene is strong. You all look just like your daddy." *I beg to differ, but this isn't a time for a debate.* "They are just as handsome as their father. Please come…come…come in." He opens the door widely and ushers us in like birds under a mother's wings. "Yes, honey, these handsome boys gonna have the ladies and men banging down your door in a couple of years. Too adorable. I'm gonna call you the Mensahlites." He pinches Kakra and MJ, but Panin raises his hands to block the adoration.

"No, Panin. No fighting." My mind is still trying to wrestle with who is actually addressing us. "Sorry. He doesn't like to be touched."

"Yes, you are every bit like your father," he…she…he says.

I look around and there are signs of Mensah's existence. The large African mask sculpture…the leather couch and armrest I ordered for him online. Nude wall colors and a mini bar in the corner. A large sound system and large screen television against another wall. But as I eye the apartment, not one of the family pictures is displayed. There is a large fish tank with an assortment of fishes. My eyes continue to canvass the apartment and then land back on him…or her. I examine the person in front of me like a recipe, reading every detail that makes up his…or her persona. The tree bark-like skin; a large stocking cap on the head; costume makeup; eyelashes that look like eagle wings; a feminine silk robe three sizes too big; and pink furry kitty heels. Our eyes meet.

"I betcha I know what you're thinkin'," he…or she says. The children move closer to the fish tank to observe the assortment. He…she..he laughs loud. "Yes, honey, you definitely have secretary qualities."

"I'm sorry, who are you again?"

"Ooh, where are my manners? You can call me Ms. Charles."

I stretch out my hand. "I'm Vida." The handshake confirms to me that Ms. Charles is a man.

"Yes, I see—the original secretary. Maybe we should give you a nickname also. How about 'Vida Caliente'?" He continues his examination of me.

"Okay, Ms. Charles...you obviously know my husband. Do you know where he is?"

"Nope." Ms. Charles places heavy emphasis on the letter p.

"Do you know when he will be back?"

"Nope." Again with the same pronunciation, the word pops out of his mouth. "For a secretary, you're not very good at knowing where your husband is."

"Why do you keep referring to me as a secretary?"

"Oh honey, secretary, wife...Same thing, but depending on how you play it, you should be both." He can see the bewildered look on my face and he continues. "You know, a wife organizes his clothes, prepares his food, sometimes bears his children, keeps quiet and goes along with the show. But a secretary, now that is a woman about her business. She is not only a wife, but a confidant. She keeps his secrets as well as her own. She forecasts ahead of time so she knows what the boss needs before he does. She's always prepared. A good secretary keeps dates, appointments, contacts, phone records, videos and pictures. She makes her position secure as possible, because you never know when the CEO will start downsizing and eliminate her position. She prepares herself because after all, a man is a man."

I am not sure if I follow, but I smile knowingly. "And..." he leans a bit closer and lowers his voice. "...a wife can do a blowjob, but a good secretary knows how to give good dictation...you know, short hand and sometimes long hand. Never shortchange him, always give him the long hand..." He winks and bursts into a cackling laugh. "So you see, you're his wife, but that was a secretary move coming over here without notifying him."

"Oh, okay...did he go to the jobsite already?"

He stares at me and crosses his hand over his chest. "Take a closer look. He...is...not...here. I was once like you." His face appears deep in thought as though he is recalling a specific event. His demeanor changes. "Don't go losing your job to those aspiring secretaries. Yes, honey, the world is full of aspiring secretaries. Some make it to the top and some just get used and shuffled down to the mailroom."

"Are you suggesting that Mensah has other women here?" I grit my teeth.

His tone becomes deep and snappy. "Honey, if you listen carefully you will hear everything you need to know. I digress. May I continue?" I nod. "You know what's worse than an aspiring secretary? Those bottom of the barrel temps. They don't care if there are vacancies or not, they wait for the secretary to quit, or break a leg, or go on maternity leave so that they can take the position. They sashay around in their Payless shoes just waiting to grab his attention and then BAM! All of a sudden, he is telling you to stay home more often because those dinner parties are only for employees." His eyes narrow down on me. "You gotta watch those bitches. Gurl, take care of your business and his business. You get me." My stomach is in knots. *I can't think of infidelity now. I don't have any proof.* Ms. Charles's face softens up with a little more cheer in his voice. "Don't worry, gurl. As far as I can see there is no competition here. Oh yes, honey, you are definitely a Mensah secretary." His words bring me little comfort. *I still don't know what the relationship between this man and Mensah is. Roommates? Business partners? Definitely not…not…there's no possible way Mensah could be gay.*

"Gurl!" His voice startles me. "Is that ass for real?" He circles around me. "Honey is that all you?" He lowers his voice again. "Silicone, fat transfer, cement? Gurl, this is the roundest ass I've ever seen." He looks at me and then takes two steps back to eye me again. "Give me the number to your surgeon."

"My ass? Surgeon? Like plastic surgeon?" I chuckle. "No, this is equal parts genetics from the motherland and religious squatting."

"Yes, honey, you're right…there is no denying the hands of God. Yezzz …yezzzz…honey…you are the real deal, sista."

Frustration is already taking a toll, not to mention my anxiousness just to see Mensah. *I have to ask.* "Excuse me, but do you live here?"

"Of course I live here. Didn't I let you in? Oh my goodness, where are my manners? What can I get you to drink? May I recommend…Canei wine two thousand fifteen…that's about all I have in the house. Sorry, Mensahlites, no juice or milk."

"No, thank you, we're fine. My husband gave me this address and said I could find him here. Do you know when he will be home?"

"You mean coming back here? Oh darling, didn't we just go through this drill already?" He reaches for my hand. His look like long fingered raisins. "Okay, real talk from a former secretary who doesn't want to see another secretary be sidestepped by some temp bitch who doesn't know the difference from a hard drive and a thumb drive. Listen closely…presidents, CEOs, CFOs don't get to where they are because they follow all the rules. Definitely some rules are broken and some feelings hurt. But one thing I know for sure is that they can't sustain it alone. They need someone to understand them and always have their back. You may have to blink longer sometimes, but never too long."

"What do you mean, 'blink'?"

"Just blink like this." He closes his eyes. I am fixated at the layer of lashes that cover his eyelids. About a minute passes by and he opens his eyes. "You see? Okay. Do it. Come on, gurl." His voice grows louder. "Do it. Blink, gurl, blink." I close my eyes as he commands me.

The motor from the fish tank and the boys' jovial conversation fill my thoughts. I count slowly to five. "This is stupid," I say.

"Now, what did you see when you blinked?"

"Jay Ellis…" A bit of sarcasm escapes me and he chuckles. "Nothing," I say.

"Precisely. What you don't see doesn't disrupt the beauty sleep. Now, be a good secretary: take notes, remember dates and contact information, blink from time to time, keep yourself in shape and always, always make sure you have your papers in order. You're young, but don't worry, you'll get it. But to answer your question, your husband doesn't live here."

Finally a response. Mensah lied. "Do you know where I can find him?" My voice lowers to a hard whisper.

Ms. Charles gives me a once over. "You know what? I usually don't break the guy code, but you are one fine woman, and since I can't take either side, here's what I do know. There is this sloppy Walmart shoe-wearing flatfoot bitch who comes here weekly to pick up mail. I nearly fucked her up the last time. Mensah and I have an understanding that he would call first before coming over to get his mail, but this bitch wanted to take it upon herself to come unannounced. She was trying to do a secretary move, but it nearly cost her her life. She is no secretary, honey, not even a sub temp. That bitch interrupted me while I was taking care of my wifely duties."

I am afraid of where the conversation is going, so I stop him. "I get it, Ms. Charles…the kids are within earshot."

"Oh yes, honey, I got you. Well, anyway, ever since we had the little scuffle that day, I haven't seen her. I thought she would come back for her wallet and her ninety-nine-cent handbag, but she didn't. She's a real cheap bitch. Who walks around with cheap handbags? Really. Gurl, she ain't shit. She only had that mugshot driver's license and five dollars—and I mean three one-dollar bills and coins that added to two dollars. What grown woman walks around with five bucks and no credit cards? I tell you what type of woman: a broke ugly bitch, that's who. She must have some hot pocket down there because—"

"Ms. Charles!" I interrupt him again.

"Oh yeah, the kids." He lowers his voice. "That size ten double-wide duck-foot bitch would think twice about fucking with me again. Anyway, I digress." He walks over to the open kitchen and pours a glass of wine.

"Is Mensah staying with this woman?" My stomach is in fisherman's knots. "Do you still have her driver's license?"

"Now what type of secretary do you think I am? That sort of information is valuable in the right hands." She walks over to a desk next to the front door and pulls out the handbag. "Here."

The license reads Kate Pennington. A young white woman with long blonde hair. DOB is July 1, 1989. More disappointment seeps into me.

"Us secretaries need to stick together, after all." I grip the license and tattoo her face into my thoughts. The woman in me is roaring. "Honey, because I'm in that type of mood, I think I will come with you. I can't stand these type of bitches breaking up a happy home. Look at these beautiful children. Give me ten minutes; I need to remove these lashes and put on my fuck-these-bitches-up gear. I'm dying for a reason to stomp on her ass again."

I am going to explode into a roaring fire. I can't believe this day has actually come. Me confronting the other woman. "No, Ms. Charles. I got this."

He taps my shoulder. "That's my gurrll. From the moment I laid eyes on you, I knew you were the real deal."

"Let's go guys. Mommy is going to find Daddy." I usher them out of Ms. Charles's apartment and I hear his voice trailing behind me.

"Hey gurl, do you need Vaseline?"

Chapter 37

"Don't Worry. Be Happy." God planted that bummer sticker on this blue Hyundai going fifteen miles per hour in a thirty-five zone. *I know what you are doing, God, but it's not going to work. No prayers right now can release this anger. That's right, Mensah, God himself can't save you from my wrath.* The image of my hands over Kate's neck consumes me. My fingers grip the steering wheel more firmly. Moisture fills my palms. "Move. Come on, move." I honk the horn again for God and the blue Hyundai to get out of my way. My heart drums fast and hard.

"Mommy, are you okay?" MJ says.

"Where are we going now?" Kakra says.

"That son of a bitch…Kate Pennington." I eye her driver's license on the dashboard.

"Mommy, are you talking to us?" Kakra is alarmed. *I didn't realize I was talking out loud.*

"Nothing. I'm just praying."

"Praying?" MJ says. The blue Hyundai finally pulls over and allows me to surpass normal speed limits. "Are you praying for us?" MJ continues.

"Yes, for all of us, babe." I look at him in the rearview mirror and he seems content with my response. Panin and Kakra still have a look of concern. The GPS alerts me to a quicker route and I feel satiated that in fifteen minutes I will have the answers I need.

It's a town house and the car is barely in park before I leap out of my seat. *Maybe the kids should stay in the car. This could get ugly.* "No," I say loudly. "Kids, come on. We're here."

"Is this where Daddy lives?" MJ asks.

"It better not be." I ring the bell and follow up with a hard knock. Kate opens the door. She looks younger than her driver's license photo. Her hair is wet and shorter than the picture. She must have just gotten out of the shower. Her limp hair drips down the white Hanes T-shirt she wears backward and inside out with XL branded on her chest. My stomach tightens. That's Mensah's size in Hanes.

"Hi. Can I help you?"

Please, Vida…don't lose it now. There has to be a clear explanation. Be cool. I mentally pry my mouth open so the words can come out. "Hi, I'm looking for Mensah Asare."

"Men sore who? I'm sorry. You have the wrong house." She has an accent, but I am not sure what nationality she is. She looks bewildered.

"Babe, who is it?" Babe…Babe…That word rings in my ears vividly. That voice. But I can't see the face. "Babe…" Before I can say anything else, there he is. Mensah descending the stairs with another Hanes T-shirt on and a brown towel wrapped around his waist. The kids rush past Kate and leap into his arms. *Move, Vida.* I can't. Adrenaline fuels my veins. I have enough energy to lift up this house. My breath is heavy and my heart is taking flight. Our eyes meet and he wears a look of shock. His brows creases as he says my name: "Vida. How did you…? Why didn't you tell…?" He wants to say more, but words escape him.

He sees it. *I know he sees it.* Pain in my eyes. This is different from the many fights and tantrums over the phone. This is disappointment staring back at him. Sure, I made accusations, checked his phone, read emails and verified bank statements. No confirmations. The secret conversations in the back yard when I was asleep. New clothes and late meetings. The traveling for long periods of time and then the voicemails that I always encountered on his long trips. It was never enough evidence to go by. No name or person that I could identify. Over the ten years we've been married I never ever saw him with another woman…until today.

Smash her head against the wall, Vida. Charge him, Vida. Start the beat down. The woman in me champions me on. I know I have the strength to do it. Mensah is talking, but I don't understand what he is saying. I feel like I'm in a black and white silent movie and I am the only one in color. The children's voices and Kate's voice swirl over my head. Nothing is making sense. Mensah approaches me and grabs my hand. I fling it away, still not sure why I can't understand him. Panin moves away from his father and stands beside me. He is breathing deeply, but his head hangs down. It's a sadness I have never seen before. Kakra also retreats from his father. I saw that look when he lost the championship last year. It is a look of disappointment. MJ hovers near his father, but keeps a close eye on the woman who now realizes who we are.

Panin allows me to take hold of his hand. I squeeze it just like Abla does to me; it's a reassurance that everything will be okay. The adrenaline is leaving my body. *Where is my anger?* God is here. I feel sad, but not enough to cry…It's betrayal and it sits in my belly like food poisoning. I will never forget this day. The day when all my suspicions came true.

Mensah's voice breaks through the silent movie. "Please Vida, are you hearing me? Let's step outside. It's not what you think." I need to move. My legs need to move. *I can't believe it. Today I, no, we met Mensah's mistress.* He seems so small to me now. Mensah is scribbling on a piece of paper. He pushes it into my hand, but I let it drop to the ground. "Vida, please." He tries to lower his voice. "Please. This is not what you are thinking." Kate stares at me with her arms wrapped around herself. She doesn't move or say a word. I turn around and see the quietness of my surroundings. The boys hang their heads down. They look ashamed. *No, my boys don't ever have to hang their heads down. How can I make this better for them?* "Vida, please go to this hotel." Do I want to be Kwabena's wife fighting in the parking lot with her kids witnessing the desecration of their family? *No, Vida. The boys deserve better than that. They deserve a strong and confident mother. Not a spectacle.*

"Let's go." God gives me the energy to move. The boys are more than happy to leave this awful situation and trail behind me. I hold MJ's hand and move swiftly to the car. Mensah chases after us. Kate mutters something inaudible. He yells back at her to stay.

"Funny, your wife and children should leave and your mistress should stay." I find my voice outside.

"Vida, Vida," he starts whispering in Twi to me.

"Don't you dare. You want to hide who we are from your mistress?" I turn to face him, but temper my tongue because MJ is still holding my hand. Mensah continues to talk, but I turn my back on him and continue my race to the car. The boys rush into the car first and I secure MJ's seatbelt. Kate is standing in the doorway witnessing Mensah creating his own spectacle. He drops the towel to reveal another one of my Target shopping spree items: dark green Hanes boxer shorts. She yells something to Mensah. He rolls his eyes and responds in Russian.

"Impressive, Russian. What else did she teach you? But then again, this entire morning has been a big learning lesson."

"Vida, for heaven's sake. Please, this is not what you think. I love you. You know that."

Our eyes meet. *This is not love. Coming to meet my husband living with another woman.* I try to fight the tears, but gravity is winning. Tears cascade down my cheeks. I gently pull off my wedding ring. "This is the last time I will do this." I've taken my wedding band off before after heated arguments. A couple of days would pass and I would miss the symbol it represented. No matter what, it was always in my possession. No one would know it was missing because I would quickly place it back on my finger after a day or two. Today is different. In front of our children, it takes courage, but I hand it to him.

"Vida. No, Vida. I know you hate me right now, but just go to the Folsom Hotel. It's not far from here. I will be there very soon. I promise, I'll explain everything." I stare at him blankly. "Please, Vida…the children are here. Not in front of the children." Despite being a horrible husband, he is a good father to them. I try to push the ring in his hand but he refuses it. I finalize my stance and drop the ring on the ground.

He quickly picks it up. "Vida…I'm sorry, please don't do this. Not here. Please." I buckle my seatbelt. The windows are rolled up and he bangs on it. I raise the volume on the stereo to drown him out.

"Please move." He stands in my way.

"The Folsom Hotel." The boys roll down the window and say bye to their father. "I will be with you guys shortly, okay?" he says. "Vida, I mean it. I will be there shortly."

*

I'm exhausted and the last thing I want to do is get on a plane. We are in queue at Sacramento Airport. My mind is still in a daze. All I want to do is to crawl into a ball and cry some more. *Keep it together, Vida. Not here and not in front of the boys.* I left the rental car at the airport not even sure if I completed the paperwork correctly or who I handed the keys to.

It's our turn and a tall pleasant woman greets us at the counter.

"Good morning, ma'am. How can I help you?"

"I need four one-way tickets for any available flight to New York ASAP."

"Let me check." She types a few words into her keyboard. "Four, ma'am?"

"Yes, one adult and three children."

"We don't have any flights available now. I do have a couple of seats on a six o'clock flight tonight." I look at my watch and it's only 11:30 a.m. I can't wait another minute here. I raise my voice. "Please, can you check again? I don't mind taking a connecting flight." My tone is hoarse and abrupt. The tears are forming again and I blink several times to fight them back.

"Is everything okay, ma'am?"

Her words strike me. *No. Everything just went to shit today. My husband has a mistress.* I've had a feeling all along, but now I have all the proof I need. My marriage is over. *Don't think about it now, Vida. You have to get home. Don't lose it here.* A tear escapes and rolls down my cheek. I crack an eccentric smile. "Yes…everything is okay. Just eager to get home."

"Yes, I understand. One moment, ma'am. Let me check again." Her tone reminds me of Alice. My phone rings and it's Abla. Oh shit, I forgot to call her. I answer it, masking my voice with excitement.

"Hi!"

"Hey, you guys okay?"

"Yep, we're here in sunny California."

"Good. How are dings goin'? Did you see Mensah yet? Is everytin' okay?" I knew if I answered her call, there would be a deluge of questions. *I'm not ready to tell her.*

"Ma'am? I think we can get you another flight, but it's not direct. Will that be okay?" The receptionist is kind and she tilts her head to the side in sympathy for whatever is going on with this strange black woman and three children in front of her.

"Where are you?" Abla asks.

"I'm in California."

"Yes, but it sounds like yur in da airport."

"Yes, we just landed." The beginnings of a unicorn story and I don't want to stretch it any further. I have to get her off the phone. "It's really busy here. I'll call you once we get settled. Bye." I hang up quickly and drop the phone in my bag.

"Should I book the flight, ma'am?"

"How much is it going to cost?" I fumble through my bag looking for my wallet.

"All four tickets will cost forty-eight hundred including taxes and fees."

I take out one of the credit cards and hand it to her. *How will I manage on my own paying bills? I don't even know how much is owed on each card. But I know how to spend Mensah's money.* Kakra's phone rings and I'm guessing it's Mensah. I preoccupy myself with the receptionist when Kakra hands me his cellphone. "I don't want to talk to your father now. Tell him I'm busy."

"Mommy, it's Auntie Abla." *Shit. She can smell trouble.* I push the phone away.

"Tell Auntie I will call her in five minutes." He walks slightly away and I just know she is interrogating him about what is going on.

"All set, ma'am." She hands me back the credit card and four boarding passes. Kakra returns.

"Auntie said she's worried and she can tell when you are lying. She said you and her come from one mother and one father and that we need each other. She'll be waiting for your call."

"And what did you tell her?"

"I told her that you decided we are coming home because Daddy told us to go to the hotel and we couldn't stay at his house because of the white woman." *Yeah, that would send her over the edge, alright.* The tears fall one by one. *Fuck.* I wipe my face with the back of my hand.

"Mommy?" Kakra is alarmed again. I give him a hug, comforting him. He hugs me back like a favorite blanket.

"Let's find a seat and wait for our flight to be called, okay guys? You can play with your iPad and phone until we board the plane. Okay?" My phone rings and it's Abla again. I send the call to voicemail. A succession of calls come through from Abla's and then Richard's phones. Then a series of unknown calls. No doubt it's probably Mensah calling. The children look worried, taking occasional glimpses at me. *They need reassurance.* "Hey guys, you know we are flying to another city before we land in New York? Wouldn't that be fun to see another city? Maybe we can stop and do some shopping before boarding our connecting flight?"

Kakra's cellphone rings again. "Don't answer it, sweetie," I command him.

Abla's text comes through: **"Give me the flight information."**

I reply to her text. **"No need to worry. We should be home by this evening."**

Mensah is calling again. I don't answer it. Then another succession of unknown calls come one after the other. I turn the phone off to preserve the battery.

"What about if Daddy wants to reach us?" Kakra says.

"We'll call him when we get home." I look at my watch and we have another hour to wait. "Anyone have to use the restroom before we board?" They all shake their heads no as they look around at the comings and goings of the people in the terminal.

I hope Mensah doesn't come running through the airport. I'm anxious, mad and sad again. A tall Caucasian man walks in our direction. I tap MJ. "You see that man?" I point, trying to make this an educational moment. "That's a captain."

"Wow, he flies the plane?"

"Yes, he does. They all have to wear that uniform."

The captain is standing before us. MJ gives another big "Wow." Up close his presence is striking. "Do you know the captain, Mommy?" MJ says.

I'm confused and before I can answer no, he addresses me.

"Ms. Frimpong?" the captain says.

"Yes?"

"I am Captain Barnes." *How does he know my name?* The boys are standing in complete awe. "I work for Mr. Gallo. He informed me you need a flight back to New York. I am sure I can be of some assistance to you."

"Oh, how did you know who I...? How...? Did...? I'm going to New York?" The words come out as though English is my second language. Fortunately, his wide smile reassures me that he understands.

"Please, let me contact him for you." He reaches into his coat pocket and pulls out a cellphone.

"Yes, Mr. Gallo. I've located them. Yes, of course sir...Ma'am." He hands me the phone and I shyly take it from him.

MJ says again, "Wow. Mommy knows a real captain."

"Hi."

"Hello, Vida." He exhales. "I don't have much time and I don't want to hear that you are fine. Because you are not. Just get on the plane and come home. Captain Barnes will transport you and the children on my plane. You should be home by this evening. Take care, Vida." Before I can get a word in, he ends the call.

"I guess we are flying with you."

"Very well. Let's go. Can I help you with any luggage?" I look around and the boys seem to have their backpacks snuggly on.

"I think we're good. Oh, I should cancel the tickets I just purchased."

"Don't worry, Ms. Frimpong. Mr. Gallo has already taken care of that."

We get on the plane and there are several attendants already aboard. "Where is everybody?" MJ asks.

"It'll just be us on the plane, champ," Captain Barnes says.

"Wow, the whole plane to ourselves. Isn't that cool, Mommy?" MJ says. I am glad that the events of the last two hours seem miles away from their thoughts.

"This is so awesome, Mommy," Kakra says. "Wait till I tell the guys on the team we flew on a private plane. Is this Mr. Gallo's plane?"

"Yes, this is his plane." A flight attendant takes the hand baggage and secures it.

"Ms. Frimpong, what can I get for you?"

"I'll take a glass of white wine, please."

"Pinot grigio, right?" the pleasant woman says.

"Right," I answer. The other flight attendant attends to the boys and they all yell as though they are ordering from a fast food drive thru. "There are no burgers and fries here, guys." I turn to her. "Whatever you have would be fine for them."

"Ms. Frimpong, we have burgers and fries."

"Oh," I say, dumbfounded.

"We also have fresh lobster and sirloin steak."

"Just the wine for me. Thank you."

"As soon as we are in the air, I can install the game station." The boys all jump excitedly.

THE BORROWED WIFE

The flight attendant hands me a glass of pinot grigio. "Ma'am, is there anything we can get to relax you during the flight? Mr. Gallo has an inflight masseuse." She points to a tall beautiful woman with muscular arms. Her proportions seem odd. She has a tiny waist and huge breasts, much like Tina the masseuse…Julius certainly has a preference. That encounter dissuades me from the massage.

"No, I think I'm good for now."

"The food will be out shortly for the children. There is a phone and computer on the desk behind you. The shower and restrooms are located to the right. We also have a closet full of clothes if you decide you need to feel more relaxed. If you need anything there is a bell beside your armrest that will alert us." I'm too sad to feel amazed.

"Oh Mommy, I need a massage," Kakra says.

"No, you don't. Stick to the game station."

Chapter 38

The deep red droplets on the area rug don't bother me. I pour more wine into my glass. More droplets sprinkle across the cream and gold rug. An automatic urge would usually have me rushing to wipe up the spills, but tonight the whole rug could catch on fire and I wouldn't care. I try to maintain my balance before walking toward the stereo. No more Melanie Fiona tonight. Let's try something a bit upbeat. I place the *Miseducation of Lauryn Hill* CD into the changer. I skip to my favorite track. "You might win some but you just lost one," she sings. I jack up the volume as I take in the words to the song. *Yep. I am totally getting fucked up.* I stumble onto the carpet again, creating more freckles. It's been a tumultuous twenty-four hours. The emptiness of the house is both welcoming and saddening. Chin to the rescue again. I didn't have to go into details, and even with her hands full with a newborn baby, she told me to bring the kids over for the weekend. *My mission because I choose to: drink wine, cry, eat and pass out. In no particular order.*

The doorbell rings. I ignore it. *It's much too late for Jehovah's Witnesses.* A second ring and a firm knock. I turn from the door in hopes that whoever it is will go away. A third ring. "No one's home. Go away." Now a firm knock. *Maybe it's Mensah. No, it can't be. Why would he ring the bell to his house?* The clock above the front door indicates a few minutes to midnight. *Who the hell could it be?*

"Vida, I know you are there. Please open up." *Shit...it's Julius.* I take a huge gulp of red wine and struggle to get on my feet. The swift movement up and my unsteadiness confirm that I am on the road for a bad hangover tomorrow. I face the closed door.

"Hiiii."

"Good evening, Ms. Frimpong."

"Julius, tonight's not a good night to go over any work. Can we talk next weekend?"

"That's fine. If you would please indulge my presence for a few minutes, I have something for you."

Uhhh, just go away. "Right now? Must you give it to me right now?" I'm still yelling from behind the door.

"I would really like to give it to you right now," he says. I open the door. Even though everything around me seems to be moving, staring at Julius alerts me to how handsome he is, clean-shaven and hair finger combed back. His jet-black hair matching his black tailored suit. "I was in the neighborhood and saw the lights on. So I figured this would be a good time."

"Now look who's telling unicorn stories."

"Point well taken. But I wouldn't be here if I didn't think I could help. May I?" He pushes me aside and enters the house not waiting for an answer. As usual he takes off his shoes and pushes them under the hallway table.

"What's that?" I try to refocus my gaze to what's in his hands.

"Merlot two thousand six." He raises his right hand up to show me.

"No, in your other hand."

"Oh this? This is what I wanted to give to you," Julius says. He raises his arm above his head.

"You came here in the middle of the night to give me a stick?"

"Oh, I assure you Vida, I don't walk around with a stick. It's much bigger than a stick…don't you think?" *It is bigger than a stick. But why is he giving it to me?*

"Well, yeah, maybe a club."

"Do you know you don't have trees in your back yard?" Julius says.

"I did. I cut them all down. You didn't answer my question."

He moves inside, taking the needed steps down into the sunken living room. He removes the tinted shades and places them on the sofa table. "Why did you cut the trees down? Don't you like what mother nature has to offer?"

"Why were you in my back yard?"

"How else would I have known you didn't have trees?" *Either I am totally drunk now or this conversation isn't making sense.*

"There were only two trees. It's not like I had Sherwood Forest back there. I cut them down after Hurricane Sandy. Too much damage to keep them."

"I see." He stands facing me, club in hand. "Well, we will have to improvise. Take it." He points the club in my direction.

"What for?"

"Too many questions, Vida. Trust me and take it."

I know I just finished off one bottle of red wine, but this sounds crazy. I look at the club and nothing about it is striking or unique. It is just a big damn stick.

"Vida, please." He acknowledges my closeness with a smile.

"What do—?"

"Eh, eh, eh…just take the club." He cuts me off and I reluctantly take the club from him.

"Now, is there anything that is heavy that you don't want any more inside this house?"

"Why would I keep something that I don't want? I want everything in my home."

"Correction, let me rephrase…is there something that could be replaced in case it gets destroyed? You know, something without sentiments attached."

"I don't understand. Just what is it that you need, Julius, or want me to do?"

He walks cautiously to the dining room and taps his fingers on the chair. He then glides his hands up and down the chair's back, armrests and down to the legs of the chair. He repositions himself and tosses the chair over his shoulders, dropping it in front of me.

"This will do."

"What are you going to do with this?"

"Oh no, Ms. Frimpong, not me. You," he says with a sinister grin.

"Me? What are you talking about?"

"This chair represents something. You are going to beat out all your fear, anger, frustration, everything that you need to release from your body and soul. All your anger and disappointments are going to be released onto this chair," Julius says.

"That's the silliest thing I've ever heard." I liberate the club from my grip and it makes a thunderous sound as it hits the floor.

"Trust me. It's not," he says slyly. "Vida, pick up the club and hit the chair."

"This is absurd. I'm fine. I just need to be left—"

"By yourself so you can cry yourself to sleep again tonight, tomorrow and the next night? Or better yet, maybe you will find comfort in a bottle of wine. Tonight it will be one bottle and then tomorrow two or three. Or maybe eat to fight the pain away. These are not solutions. These feeling will not go away overnight. Trust me. You take it one day at a time. You are not the first person to suffer a broken heart, and as long as people continue to procreate, you definitely won't be the last. The healing will begin tonight. Let's start with one hit." He stretches his hand to motion me to pick up the club. He appears sincere and, as skeptical as I am, I find myself with the club in my hand again. He takes a few steps back in anticipation of my move.

"Hit it anywhere?" I ask, unsure.

"No, why don't you ask the chair where it wants to be struck and then we can go from there?"

"You're such a smart ass." I cut my eyes at him. I pull the club above my head and with extra force slam the club into the chair. It cracks in half. The wood splitting sounds melodic. I raise my hand above my head and hit the chair again. It crumbles into smaller woodpiles. I hold the club with a better grip and continue to beat the wood into smaller bits. *It feels awesome.* Julius places another chair on top of the decimated one.

"I can't break all my dining chairs. Where will we sit for dinner?"

"Dining chairs can easily be replaced," he says.

"Yes, I know. But this set cost me nearly eight thousand dollars."

"Again, dining chairs can easily be replaced."

"Says the billionaire," I say.

"Let's not start this tonight." He motions me to continue.

I pound on this chair as I did the one before. The chair shatters into even smaller pieces. He stands back and closes his eyes as though he is listening to a symphony. The crackling of the wood replaces Lauryn's voice. I continue to beat on the chair until I am satisfied with the pile that accumulates on the floor. I prompt him for the next chair. He places another on the growing heap of wood. I feel the anger turn into heated rage. At times I find myself mumbling out loud. I recall all the promises Mensah made to me. The look on the children's faces this morning. Disappointment and distrust. I hit continuously until the pile covers the entire living room floor. Tears stream down my face. At times loud cries overtake the beating, but I don't release the club. My cries become louder and the thumping of the chair crueler.

"No more chairs. Let's continue with the table," he says. I raise the club above my head and with all my might, I explode onto the table.

"I hate that you lied to me! I hate that you made me see you with that other woman." Another swing. "I hate that I believed in you…in us." Another swing. "Why? Why wasn't I enough?" More hits. Finally, I discover the table's weakness. I grow wild and swing at it over and over again until the legs buckle. I cry out again and yell obscenities. This dining table has memories. I beat harder to erase those memories. The first night they delivered the table, Valentine's Day, a couple of times on Christmas Eve. Every memory will be beaten out of it. The table shares the same fate as the chairs. I finally collapse to the ground in exhaustion.

"Where do you keep your wine opener?" Julius yells from the kitchen. I hadn't noticed his absence.

"The third drawer down next to the fridge." There is a loud crash as something hits the kitchen floor tiles. I struggle to get up amongst the rubble.

"I'm fine. Stay where you are. Everything is okay," Julius shouts from the kitchen.

I sit back down on the floor and push the rubble away with my feet to stretch my legs on the area rug. The table and chairs mount high in front of me.

"I assume these are suitable wine glasses," Julius says. He stretches his hand out offering one of the children's plastic cups. I don't question the loud crash in the kitchen.

"Thanks."

"Well, I can imagine the landscape of your house has changed." I laugh. He kicks some of the wood aside and begins to sit.

"Wait," I say. There are loose screws on the floor. I move them and kick the pile of rubble farther away from us. I take his hand and motion him closer to me. He sits down in front of me Indian style and pours me a cup full of wine.

"Very nice," I say.

"Of course, on a night like this, we need something extra special." He smiles.

"Thank you."

"For?"

I give a big exhale. "For everything. Thank you."

"Feeling a bit better?"

"Yeah, much better than I did before you came. How did you know it would work?"

"When I was younger, I witnessed someone doing something similar. Crying and beating a tree with a large stick. It seemed to have a relaxing effect afterward." I want to ask more, but I am grateful for the little bit of peace I feel.

"I must say you have unique ways of dealing with situations."

"If you feel like crying some more, cry. Cry and cry until you can't cry anymore tonight. Because after tonight we won't cry over the same matter again." He clicks my cup and I take another sip.

"Do you want to know what happened?"

"No. There is no reason to bring it up. You went for the right intentions—to be with your husband. I know one thing is for sure; always trust that little voice inside of you."

"What happens now?"

"Well, I will clear the rubble if you can find some upbeat music to listen to. We can't spend the whole night in this depressed state."

"Let me help you."

"Vida, I can manage." I sense his arrogant independence creeping back. "Just play something different. Where should I put the debris?"

"There's a large bin to the right of the house. Whatever can't fit, you can put beside the bin."

He places his tinted navigators on and moves in and out of the house effortlessly carrying the rubble. When he leaves the house, I quickly pick out the loose nails and sort the rubble into little manageable piles. I thumb through the CD library and decide to listen to The Weeknd. With the last of the debris removed from the house, it's clear the rug could use some steam cleaning and vacuuming tomorrow.

We dance for a couple of hours and finish two more bottles of wine. He talks endlessly of Ama. She taught him all the dance steps. His smile is like lightning with the mention of her name. *I think he still loves her.*

"Have you ever been in love again?"

He stands up from the couch where we've settled ourselves. "No."

"What about Penny?"

He shrugs. "I care for her a lot, but I wouldn't or couldn't compare it to how I felt about Ama. I guess that type of love only happens once in a lifetime. But when you do love someone genuinely with all your heart and they betray you, that is a very hard thing to overcome. That is how love is sometimes, I guess. You take your chances. Anyway, that is another book."

Is he still talking about Ama?

"You're leaving?" He gets up and walks toward the door.

"Yes, unless you need me to stay. Do you need me, Vida?" *Who would have thought this arrogant ass had a heart?* The clock above the front door shows it's 4:30 a.m.

"I suppose we should get some sleep."

"Yes. You should."

"Do you think he will come back?" He turns to face me.

"Oh, Vida, he would be a fool not to. But—" He pauses.

"But…but what?"

"You are asking the wrong question. The question you need to answer is…whether or not will you take him back. You are a good person and you should never forget that. Always trust what your instincts dictate. Good night, Vida."

Chapter 39

I arrive at the twins' school and sit in the parking lot. I pay attention to my deep breaths. *Just behave like everything is normal.* I avoided Abla's phone calls all week. But that is not normal. I imagine crying on the phone to her and her consoling me with kind words. *Everything is going to be okay.* The pale skin color where my wedding band used to be is a clear indication that things are different. In one day my marriage came to an end. I always knew something was wrong. I had that gut feeling and I kept turning it away. *Vida, how stupid can you be? There were all these signs and I never paid attention to them.* I envisioned discovering him having an affair once, particularly with Patricia. In my vision, after I discovered it, he tried hard to win me back. I vowed that I would never take him back if we didn't go to marriage counseling. He was reluctant, but then he agreed. This picture burned through my thoughts had him moving back to New York, us having another baby, moving into a bigger house. And living happily ever after. *Silly Vida.* The woman in me chastises me.

But never in my imagination did I ever expect silence. One whole week and not even a phone call or a bouquet of forgive-me-flowers. His last message to me after he was discovered in California was, "Where are you?" That's it. No messages checking to see if the boys and I made it home. No explanation. *I mean, really, this is insulting. I'm a fool. So his relationship with Kate is more important than his family.* I search for my phone to dial him. Anger is creeping inside me again. *Wait…wait…silly woman. Put the phone down. Pull yourself together.* The meditation CD helps in time. *Breathe.* I've been sitting in the car listening to the CD for almost twenty minutes. The voice reminds me to breathe. I close my eyes and relax my face. I take air in and push air out slowly. The CD is finished. I open my eyes.

Mensah has a side chic. It's the first thought that comes to me.

*

"You know next year are big changes. It's middle school and that means a different school and new groups of friends. It gets tougher. I know your reservations about putting John in a specialized school, but these are major things to consider." Principal Pratt claps his hands on his desk. There is hardly white space left on his walls. Accolades of degrees, certificates and plaques occupy all four walls. On his desk is a family picture: a wife, two boys and one girl. They look happy. I stare longer than I should. "Ms. Asare, I know—"

"He has exceptional grades," I retort back to Principal Pratt. Panin excels in his studies, but socialization and his outbursts remain a constant problem. He struggled through English two years ago, but I hired a private tutor and it has made a positive impact.

"He has always done exceptionally well in his studies, but there are some concerns. This is the reason why I called this meeting." The frequent calls started in the first grade, but died down as Panin's grades excelled and he is now an honor roll student. It is alarming that I am being called in about his behavior.

I recount the number of times that I spent in Principal Pratt's office. There was the time he spent his lunch hour organizing the kitchen's pantry; or the time he took toilet paper and lined every seat he sat down on in class; but the constant that brought me into the school at least once a week was the jam sessions. Panin would lock himself in the music room and hold jam sessions for an hour or two. He was a rebel at times, but some teachers appreciated his love for music. Others, including the school psychologist, were worried that his behavior could cause a problem at another school. These jam sessions became so constant that the school installed a palm key lock to the room. This solved the problem until the maintenance staff found it impossible to clean the room due to a rotation of staff. But through all the ordeal, he adjusted well to the school.

"Middle school brings a lot of peer pressure just to fit in. It is the social aspect that concerns me. John is a bright kid and talented in so many ways, but if the pressure is too much for him, then I am afraid of how it would manifest itself."

Dr. Samson is seated next to me; he has been instrumental in keeping Panin in this school. Panin visits him twice a week in the office. He uncrosses his legs and turns to address me. "Ms. Asare, we spoke at length of some of the options and…" He raises his hands up defensively. "I know your concerns. The teachers and I have started to see it."

"See what?"

"We sent home several notices before the break regarding missing assignments and failing quizzes."

"No way, not John. I had no idea." If they had said Kakra, I would have the same reaction, but in my heart, I would know it is possible. But Panin has never failed a quiz or exam.

"I'm surprised he never gave you the notices. Well, in any case, it is good that we are having this meeting now."

"Why didn't anyone call me? I would have…"

"Well, Ms. Asare, that's just it, we weren't concerned until now. I know he had the flu these last couple of days."

"Flu?"

"Yes, he missed his session twice this week. His brother James told us he had the flu."

Flu? Why would the boys lie? My mind races as to why would Kakra and Panin lie. *What is going on with those two? Wait until I get home.* I'm sure I look lost. "This is the first time I am hearing this. The boys haven't been sick since they had the chickenpox."

"Ms. Asare, I apologize that you were not aware."

I release the hard tension from my face. "I will deal with the matter when I get home. Please, let's continue."

"And as you know, I don't shelter John from taking part in any activity, so I am not going to start now. But middle school will be challenging. He is going to need a lot of encouragement and one-on-one interaction. We all know how sensitive he is to change. There is a list of specialized schools and programs we can enroll him into based on his development spectrum. Every day we are finding new information in the studies done on autistic children. There is no set prescription for everyone. So we are going to work together to see how we can help him," Principal Pratt says.

"I am not prepared to put my child in an environment just to make other people around him comfortable. He deserves to excel just as any other child. I know you've suggested specialized school for him, but I don't believe that would be good for him."

"Okay, Ms. Asare. I accept your position. However, this is not the only reason why I called you into the office. We are in the third marking period and so far his GPA has significantly dropped. This is a list of the preliminary grades for the third quarter." I scan it and see several C's and

D's. "At first, the teachers weren't concerned because we knew that he could do the work. But as I stated earlier, his last few assignments have been missing or incomplete. He failed a couple of quizzes and didn't hand in a paper that was due two weeks ago. He has forgotten his tablet on numerous days to class. When he does communicate, he writes on scraps of paper 'yes' or 'no' responses. He hasn't visited the music room in the week before break or this week, which is really odd for John." Dr. Samson nods his head in agreement.

"Is there something different or something that has changed in the household?" Dr. Samson says. His question is like a ticking time bomb in my chest. I want to lay down on his Ethan-Allen-like chaise and pour my heart out. I swallow hard and provide a unicorn story to Dr. Samson.

"No. Everything is fine at home. I can't understand what could cause him to change."

"Let's continue to work together," Principal Pratt says.

"Of course."

"Can I make another suggestion?" Dr. Samson says.

"Yes," I say reluctantly.

"This summer, try something different. Give John a change in environment…maybe a mini vacation. Try staying some place new for the whole summer. I don't mean a hotel or grandparents' home. If you can, go stay with friends out of town or visit a family member that you don't see often. Let this time away be a learning experience for him. Take him out of his comfortable and familiar surroundings. Try a week or two and gradually maybe one whole month. It's important that we get him out of a routine and get him to expect the unexpected sometimes."

Dr. Samson's voice trails away as my thoughts are consumed with Panin. *Just look at what is happening under my nose.* My heart breaks for him. "Thank you, gentlemen, for your time. I will email you regularly to see the progress in school and let you know if anything out of the ordinary takes place at home."

"We truly appreciate your support as always, Ms. Asare. Like the saying goes, it takes a village." I smile gently.

"What class are the boys in now?" I ask.

"They are taking a quiz in English right now, but we can peek in the window before you go," Dr. Samson says. We exit the principal's office and I walk down the halls admiring the students' artwork and science projects. We stop at Ms. Carconia's room. I canvass the bowed heads until I recognize Kakra and Panin. They are seated in the same row. Panin stares at the door. I move swiftly out of view.

"Mrs. Asare, I know you don't want to separate the boys, but just in case, let's have a backup plan."

"There is no backup plan, Dr. Samson...my Panin...John will excel in the same school his brother will attend. I will make sure of that." He raises his hand defensively again.

"It's only a recommendation. You're his mother. You know best."

Chapter 40

I call out from work again. My mind can't keep steady with this morning's news. Maybe a round of karaoke with Julius will cheer me up. Alice announces that Julius is in the study. I grab the laptop from the library and head to his study. He is busy working on a device. His attention is so focused that he doesn't acknowledge me until I enter the room.

"Good afternoon," I say and place the laptop on an empty table.

"Good afternoon, Vida." He stops moving. "No work today? How are you? The children?"

"No, I had a meeting this morning. The kids are good. How about you?" I try to camouflage the worry in my voice.

"Feeling inspired."

"I see. Busy at work." There are several tables full of gadgets and tools. There is a screen lit up above the fireplace.

"Do you need my assistance in anything?"

"No…I'm good. I've started reading another journal."

"Okay, great." He walks over to another desk and glides his hands gently over it until he reaches what he is looking for. A pair of screwdrivers.

"Maybe I should leave you alone. You look busy."

"You are more than welcome to stay." He moves to another desk and picks up a large piece of equipment and places it on the floor.

"Still working on speech to text device?"

"Yes." He smiles brightly.

I open the journal and then sit by the desk. I stare at it, but I am not really reading the words. My thoughts are of Panin. *What is happening to him? Is it because of what is happening between his father and me? This is not the time to lose it. I need to protect the children from the chaos going on.* A deep exhale escapes me. Julius looks childishly entertained by his project. I give another big sigh, but he doesn't break a beat. He moves from his big desk to another small table to another table and back again. *Who can I talk to? I can't call Abla right now; she will surely blame it all on Mensah. So much is going on and I feel like I can't handle it all.* I lean back in the chair close my eyes and remember the practice from the meditation CD. Take slow breaths in and push out your fears. *God, are you listening to me today? I need strength and mercy, God. I don't know if I can deal with it all.* I take another deep breath in and push air out.

"Okay, say something. Or are you thinking of a career as a hot air dispenser?" Julius says.

"Sorry. It's nothing." *No, it's everything, Vida. But don't disturb his momentum.* I turn a page in the journal. It's in Italian. This has to be his mother's journal. *I can't bother him now for interpretation.* I pull out the preliminary progress report from this morning's meeting and reread it.

"He's averaging a D in math. A D in math. This is someone who can add eight-digit numbers in his head. A C in English. He was doing well, especially with that tutor I hired. A D in social studies. He loves history. What happened? A B-minus in science. Science is his other favorite subject. He memorized the entire periodic table. What fifth grader does that? Panin, that's who, but now something is wrong. I need to fix it." I turn the paper over. "He failed gym. How do you fail gym? He's not as athletic as Kakra, but gym is easy. Just show up every time, wear your uniform, and try not to get hit during dodgeball and you get a passing grade." The teacher notes lack of participation. "And music. I can't believe he got a C...God only knows how many restless nights I stayed up so that he could play on his drum set. A whole new security system was built around him, and now he doesn't even want to go into the room. This isn't the Panin I know. It probably has everything to do with what is happening between me and Mensah. It's taking a toll on him." *Shit, I'm talking out loud.* Julius, undisturbed, works eagerly from one desk to another in what looks like a triangle pattern. From his workstation to a smaller desk then to a stand where his device is propped up. He begins twisting wires and then hammering nails into this device.

I continue pouring heartbreak into the air. It feels therapeutic to hear my voice. "I don't know, maybe I am going about this whole parenting thing wrong. Maybe I should send him to see another psychologist. I should call Mensah, but I don't want him to think I am using this as an excuse for him to come back home. He knows what he has done and he should be ashamed of himself. The betrayal. A whole week and not even a phone call to me." Julius is not paying attention to the ramblings of a frustrated mother. He moves again in the same triangle pattern. I inhale and exhale deeply. "I should take a leave of absence over the summer. Maybe I need to take the kids away and also focus on my writing. That's what we need. A change of scenery. Next year is middle school and they want me to separate the boys. Hell no. Panin can do the work. I just need to find out what's wrong. Or maybe I should send him to a specialized school so he won't feel overwhelmed, pressured to fit in. But Mensah would never agree…but Mensah is not here. It's all up to me. I wish—"

"Wrong cord, Lord Gallo." Alice's voice startles me. It's creepy how she's so omnipresent.

"Fuck. Examine it again," Julius says.

"Yes, my Lord. One moment please."

He runs his fingers through his hair and waits patiently for Alice.

"Please try the circuit again."

He drops the device and moves to another table. I continue airing my thoughts.

"They should be together attending the same school. He has to try. My Panin, I know he can do it. He is a good student. I just need…need to help him." I'm getting a headache. Too much thinking. I push aside the laptop and rest my head on the desk.

The alarm from my cellphone wakes me. *Damn it. I dozed off. Shit. It's almost three o'clock. I have to pick up the kids today.* Julius strings wires from one device to another and he has a determined look on his face. I push the chair back and get up to stretch. I don't feel any better, but I know I need to talk to Panin. I gather my things and grab the laptop and journal.

"Well, I really need to go. I have aliens from Amet coming over for dinner tonight. They get anxious when dinner's not ready. They really like my peanut butter soup, you know." He is so focused. I continue the jest. "The aliens from Amet said they are going to make me their queen. I told them I would have to think about it. You know, since I'm in such high demand and all." I raise my voice a bit higher, but still no response from Julius. He continues the same triangle pattern. I admire his work ethic. Even a whiny mother yacking for an hour doesn't dissuade him. I take a few steps toward the door and his voice turns me around.

"Vida, two D's, two C's, one B-minus and one gym failure is not a cause for concern. It's only the third marking period. There's still time to change things around for the fourth marking period. My guess is that it has nothing to do with the schoolwork. He's a bright kid. This is his last year at a school he has known since Kindergarten. Like most students his age, he is probably fearful and excited of the unknown. He has a routine I bet, and he has to prepare himself for something different next year. He is dealing with a lot of issues right now. So cut him some slack. Maybe and just maybe he feels like failing will lead him to repeat the fifth grade at the same school with the same staff. This would of course give him something that he would be used to. He knows something is going on with his parents. I'm guessing you haven't had the talk with the children about what is going on because you are waiting to see what Mensah will do. Children always know, so don't pretend." He screws another bolt into the device. "Let's try it again, Alice."

"Yes, my Lord." He waits patiently and before I can form my mouth to speak, he addresses me.

"Just one second, Vida."

"Sorry, my Lord, wrong wire."

"For fucksake." He rests the device on the table and moves his hands onto his hips. "Don't send Panin to another psychologist. You said it yourself that it takes him a while to feel comfortable around someone. So many things are changing and he may want something familiar to relate to. The psychologist offered some sound advice, but the decision ultimately lies with you. Because you know what is best for him. You should tell Mensah what is happening with his son. What he chooses to do with the information is entirely up to him. But from what I can gather, he loves his children and he should know." I move closer and lean on the desk opposite him. "You're doing a great job as a parent. Don't second guess yourself. I can only surmise that parenting is not easy, but communication is the key. Panin needs his brother now more than ever to help him with the transition, so having someone familiar close by will probably ease the anxiety. Who doesn't know a kid with behavioral issues? I do believe that troubled behavior can be countered with good behavior." As though a lightning bolt hits him, he races to the desk behind me. He opens the device and takes out series of wires and works quickly tying them into several knots. Then he moves past me and screws the wires into the device. "Alice?" We wait patiently for Alice's verdict.

"Lord Gallo, the circuit is functioning."

He claps his hands and says, "Yes." I am happy for him, but I don't even know what he has done. "Pay no attention to my erratic outburst. I've been wrestling with this circuit all morning." He removes a cigar from the box on his desk.

"I'm glad that it's working. Thank you—" He interrupts me again.

"Taking a leave of absence is an excellent way to reconnect with the kids and take their minds off what is happening between you and Mensah. It will benefit you, especially if it means writing more." He leans on the desk in front of me with a satisfied grin. He indulges in his cigar and his recent accomplishment.

I can't control the trickle of tears that show up. "I thought you weren't listening."

"To you?…Sometimes." He chuckles. I rest the journal and laptop on the desk. I nearly knock him down trying to hug him.

"Stop it. No tears while working."

"Okay. I'm good. I'll leave you to your work. I'll be back Friday night."

"Oh, Vida, lest I forget. Whatever you feed will return. So, if I were you I would tell the aliens from Amet that tonight's their last supper. I don't know what type of offer is on the table, but your visitors should know taking you away is highly impossible. Here on Earth, we fight for our queens."

I haven't smiled in over a week. But his words leave me exposing a wide grin. "Thank you, Julius."

Chapter 41

A knock on the door at ten o'clock would usually have me concerned, but lately it brings a Cheshire grin. "Maybe I need to make you a key."

"I was in the neighborhood again. My nights and days are not as amusing since this silly bet." Julius removes his shoes at the door and places his jacket on the hallway table. He shifts a large black duffel bag underneath.

"Do I smell defeat?" I quip.

"No, not at all, but I do smell dinner."

"Yes, it's peanut butter soup and fufu tonight."

"It's been quite some time since I had that." He turns around and stares at the door. "Are your friends from Amet stopping by this evening?" He laughs.

"No. I relayed your subtle threat and it worked. Please stay for dinner."

"I will gladly accept your invitation. There's something else I smell."

I wait to see if he recognizes the flowers on the entry table. He walks backward to the front door. His head scans left and right. He moves his hands to the tabletop and then glides his hands slowly up the vase. He caresses the flower buds and tilts his head down to smell them.

"Tulips."

"Yes. Or in this case, P-F-M-F, please-forgive-me-flowers. Overdue, but well expected." Mensah's arrangement came this morning with a two-word card attached.

"Come and sit. I'll prepare the fufu for you." I don't know why I take his hand and navigate him to the dining room. He's been here several nights this week. He added a wall cabinet to the new table and dining chairs the day after my meltdown. I'm sure it cost a fortune, but telling Julius how to spend his money is not up for discussion. It's hard for me to accept his extravagant expenditures, but I am learning just to say thank you. He offers to help me in the kitchen. I would really like to see him maneuver, but he is a guest having dinner in my home. "Please, let me serve you. Would you like a glass of wine? I have Yellow Tail Chardonnay."

"No, thank you. I am reserving my appetite for my meal. Are the children asleep?"

"Yes, thank goodness." Kakra and Panin are still on punishment for lying to me. *I really have to talk to them about Mensah and me.* "The quietness has given me time to do some writing. I've been feeling inspired lately. It's funny how you can feel less motivated to write until you have a story to tell."

"That's very good, Vida. I would really like to hear it one day after you lose your bet."

"Confident that you will win, huh? Why? Have you severed your penis?"

"Ouch. Those words even sound painful."

I turn the stereo on and play a selection on the sound system. "I'll be back, going to start the fufu. Dinner will be ready soon." Inside the kitchen, I combine the fufu ingredients with water in a heavy steel pot and then place it on the stove. I return and Julius is sitting just as I left him. The huge duffel bag is still underneath the table.

"Are you traveling soon? What's with the duffel bag?"

He turns his head toward the place where he placed the bag and then returns his focus in my direction. "Do you like Cesaria Evora?"

"To be honest, I didn't know who she was until I read it in your diary. You said your mother sang this song often, right?" The deep raspy voice of Cesaria Evora brings a relaxing ambiance.

He smiles. "Well, Ms. Frimpong. You have been catching up on your homework."

"Well, that particular journal was very interesting."

"Oh, do tell." He sits back in the chair and crosses his legs.

"You traveled to a couple of villages in Ghana. And I recall you feeling scared, especially when she used to blindfold you." I pause remembering the words I read. *"Fear stagnated me. The world was black. Mama held me in her arms and said one day the world will be like this."* I continue. "She was preparing you…for…" My voice drops to a low whisper.

"Yes," he says, anticipating my question. His mood changes. His face becomes a bit more constricted.

"You described your favorite place. Your mother called it home." I close my eyes recalling a favorite passage in his diary. "*Solid blue cool waters covered the warm white sands like a blanket. The green foliage created a canopy of shade along the sands. I feared going deeper into the foliage that I would tangle up in the vines that look like jump ropes. When the sun fell asleep, the moon created a soft light that cooled the sands and made the foliage more mysterious than ever. There are no buildings or people to share this vision with. Mama tells me to touch the waters, kiss the sand and eat the leaves. This is love she says. This is home.*" I imagine a young Julius raising a handful of sand to his lips and face. "I can't recall many of the details, but the one sentence that stood out to me that stays with me still is—"

"*I will always remember the place that God lives on earth,*" Julius says, interrupting my thought.

"That's beautiful, Julius."

"It is a beautiful place."

"I don't suppose you will tell me where it is?"

"Absolutely not." He laughs.

I race back to the kitchen. The fufu is beginning to solidify. I provide the needed arm muscle to turn it. The starchy mass thickens to a peanut butter consistency. Still a bit lighter than I want it to be. I lower the fire and leave the pot uncovered. Air will make it a bit firmer.

Julius is sitting on the edge of the chair with another chair facing him. "Vida, I would like for you to indulge me. Please come and sit here." I move toward him and he pulls me down in front of him. He lifts his hands to my face. I'm reluctant and tilt my head back.

"Please? I won't hurt you."

"Okay." I freeze.

"I'm curious, that's all." He raises his hands to my face again. He touches my ears and then my chin with a gentle motion. His brows creases as though he is trying to make sense of something. Then he relaxes his face. He puts his hands down and gives a big sigh. "Hmmm...Fuck. Not what I expected."

"What?" I say, alarmed by his exploration.

He sighs again. "I thought you would be pretty."

"You know what? Kiss my ass." I rise up and his laughter seals the air between us.

"Promise."

I can hear him still laughing as I turn the fufu over on the stove again. A few quick stirs and it's done. I empty the contents into a bowl and mold it neatly round. I pour the peanut butter soup with a mixture of chicken breasts and legs over it. Napkins and a side plate to accompany the food on the tray. *Does he eat with his hands or does he do like most foreigners and eat with a spoon?* I place the spoon on the tray just in case. On another tray, I carry a bowl to wash his hands with, hand soap, a hand towel, a tall glass and pitcher of water. I maneuver the trays like a waitress into the dining room. His face is a bit rosier now.

"Still laughing at my expense?" He smiles. He has already rolled up his sleeves. He rinses his hands in the bowl of water I place in front of him. I move the tray away and place the food in front of him.

"Wow. Smells enticing, Vida." His hands circle the outside rim of the bowl and he slightly lifts the bowl off the tray. "All this for me?" He has a childish grin.

"All for you. I've already eaten." He places a napkin across his lap and moves the tray closer to his chest. He begins by using his right hand maneuvering chicken to one side of the bowl. Then he squeezes his fingers together as if he is holding a pencil and presses them down into the fufu. It is still hot, so he licks his fingers and presses down again, this time cutting the handful of fufu into the soup. He bends his head into the bowl and takes the first gulp down. He eats fufu like a native. I can't take my eyes off of him. Slow bites, making sure his mouth meets his hand over the bowl. He uses a napkin to dab his mouth occasionally. *Stop gawking, Vida.* I return to the kitchen to soak the fufu pot and wash the remaining dishes.

Upon my return to the dining room, I see he has devoured nearly half of the fufu and soup. Chicken bones chewed down to the exposed marrow are placed on a napkin next to his bowl. I pour water into the tall glass and place it beside him. "There is a glass of water to your left," I say.

He continues eating, exercising the same etiquette until finally he lifts the bowl to his mouth and swallows the rest of the soup in several gulps. I change the music to 103.9FM. Hall and Oates fills the room. He finishes the glass of water and a belch escapes his mouth.

"Pardon me. I enjoyed that immensely. Thank you."

"Well, I'm glad you did."

He washes his hands in the bowl of water by adding the soap. He dries his hands with the same hand towel and then walks in the direction of the bathroom. His familiarity with the floor plans of my home makes his navigation swifter. I empty all the dishes and trays into the sink. *What can I present as dessert?* Nothing in the pantry except a tin of Royal Dansk cookies. I neatly place the cookies on a plate. No cappuccino or espresso. I check my assortment of teas and can't decide which one he would prefer.

"If you had to choose, which tea would you like to drink?"

"I don't like tea," he says.

"Really? I thought all British people enjoy tea."

"Huh. Well, if Ms. Frimpong takes the time to make me a cup of tea, I will drink the cup of tea."

"Okay, then. One cup of Ms. Frimpong's finest tea coming up."

When I return to the table, he is sitting on the edge of his seat again. "Sorry, it's not much of a dessert. I have cookies and ginger peach tea."

"That's perfect, Vida," he says. I arrange the food in front of him and then grab my notebook.

"Anything you want to share tonight?" It's easier to jot down notes when he talks about growing up in different countries. I learned in the past month that he's traveled to sixty-four countries and speaks seven languages. His mother was a linguist, so learning languages came easily to him. Sometimes there is a sadness when he talks about Ama and then there are times his face is as bright as a campfire. I want him to tell me the story at his own pace, so I watch his facial expressions intently. There's a different disposition about him tonight.

"Vida. Please. Sit here." He pulls out the chair beside him and I sit down facing him. "May I touch you again?"

"Oooh no, my friend. As the saying goes…Fool me once and then twice…well you know the rest."

"Please, Vida? Just for a moment. I promise, no jokes this time." He smiles and then he relaxes into a somber countenance.

"Okay," I say reluctantly. "Make it quick, and if you try insulting me again, you're going to feel a hard sting across your face."

He laughs. "I'm sure." I exhale deeply and release my shoulders. He begins again and I close my eyes. With a gentle touch, his fingers move slowly. I open my left eye. His face is constricted and then he relaxes it again. *What's wrong?* He doesn't say anything, but he continues outlining the contours of my face. *Just relax and close your eyes, Vida. This will be over soon.* His fingers are warm and I still smell the peanut butter soup on them. He navigates toward my eyes. He takes extra care around the edges of my eyelashes and then traces the bridge of my nose to each nostril. His index fingers move back and forth across my cheeks. I feel several fingers walk across my jawline and then up to my ears. They rest there for a moment and then he glides his fingers down my neck. My skin warms to his touch and my breathing becomes harder. The tips of his fingers caress my collarbone and he moves back to my face. He stops. Then he rests his hands on my thighs. "Hmmm." His moan forces my eyes open. He quickly retreats and then relaxes in his chair.

"Is that it?" His eyes are closed and I'm anxious about his exploration. *He still hasn't said anything.* "Julius?" The alarm on his watch causes him to open his eyes. He moves hastily to shut it off. "Time flies when...well...you know the rest. I have to go, Ms. Frimpong."

"Oh." He looks anxious. He rises and I follow him to the front door.

"This duffle bag contains most of the journals." He puts on his shoes and jacket.

"Journals?" I ask.

"Yes. From the vault. There are also a few that Vincent has. He will give them to you when you are ready."

"Has something changed with our arrangement?" *Why now? Is it the stupid bet?*

"If I don't see...If you don't hear from me tomorrow, please continue with our arrangement. I would like the memoir published just the way you've started it."

"Where are you going?"

He exhales deeply and struggles to continue.

"Julius?" *Something is up.* I have never seen him so anxious. He looks down and then up and he forms his mouth to say something, but can't. He smiles but it's not a happy or 'that's-a-funny-story' smile; it's uneasiness, shyness or maybe fear.

"Tomorrow morning I am scheduled for surgery. With any surgery, there is always a possibility of...well, death." He swallows as though he has just ingested food. I've never seen him lost for words. "The nagging tumor has returned and I need to remove it or face death. Nevertheless, if things don't go as planned, Vincent is aware of what has to be done. You will be fully compensated, Vida, and as I stated before, please write the memoir how you see fit. We've gotten to know each other a lot more and I trust your judgment."

I take his hand. It's cold. "Julius, don't talk like that. Everything is going to be well."

"It will. But I also have to prepare myself for any outcome. I know the routine." He kisses my cheek. "Dinner was lovely. Good night, Vida." *That's it? Good night?* He turns to leave and I grab his arm.

"Wait. Let's—"

"No. Please. No prayers. I haven't spoken to God since I was a teenager and I am not going to start tonight." He takes my hand in his. "Good night. My regards to the children." He releases the hold and leaves quickly through the front door.

Long after Julius and Vincent drive off, I don't know if I need to sit down. *Vida, you should have said more. This is no way for him to go after the news he just shared.* "Oh my God. Julius."

Chapter 42

"*Digame.* Did you kill him yet?" Even at one in the morning, Abla has a sense of humor. After telling her about my excursion in California, it bothers her that I didn't fly back to beat up Mensah and Kate. Usually, I punish myself by thinking of Mensah lying beside Kate. Her arms wrapped around his waist and she's kissing him. *Who am I kidding? Mensah is probably fucking her as I think about it.* Two months ago, I would drink more wine and cry. *Stop it, Vida. Don't start this again.* Tonight, I want to cry for a different reason. *There's no way Julius can die. He will be fine.* I say it over and over again in my thoughts, but I can't manage to talk.

"Oh my goodness, tell me. Wat iz it?" Abla's voice is heightened. Mrs. Lindsey's anxious voice in the background also inquires. "I don't know," Abla yells back to her.

"Is she okay? Are the children okay? Is Mensah back?" Mrs. Lindsey's soft voice again. I've called Abla at all times of the day and night, but since the discovery of Mensah and his mistress, it seems as though everyone is on heightened alert.

"Vida. Yaa. Tell me. Watz goin' on?" Abla pleas with me again.

"He may die tomorrow." I say the words quickly, still fighting the tears.

"Who? Jezzus Christ, talk to me and stop cryin'."

"Julius!" And I cry into the phone.

"Calm down. Why? Wat happen to him? Did Mensah dretten him?" Mensah. Huh…It is obvious that Mensah could care less about what is going on with me. I recite the last hour of my night with Julius and his admission about the surgery and journals.

"Haf faith, notin' iz goin' to happen to him. God iz in control. I'm sure he has da best doctors."

I sober up so that I can hear Mrs. Lindsey's faint voice. "Surgery is surgery, dear. Anything can happen, no matter how skillful or knowledgeable your doctor is. We leave it up to God eighty percent of the time," she says.

"Mommy?" MJ enters my room sleepy-eyed.

"Yes, honey. Come in." Like clockwork, he still climbs into my bed in the middle of the night. I've been lazy trying to wean him out of my bed. "Abla, I'll call you later. MJ is here."

"I told you to lock da door when you go sleep. Dat iz da only way hez goin to get uze to sleepin' in hiz bed," Abla says.

I hang up the phone and rock MJ to sleep in my arms. His mouth forms an O with a big yawn. He struggles to keep his eyes open. MJ won't be young forever. He will grow into his manhood and have a successful career, hopefully as an entrepreneur just like his father. No, better than his father. I caress his hazelnut complexion and admire his long fingers. His toes look like mine. He will follow in Kakra's footsteps and play soccer I'm sure. Oh, my little MJ. He will get married and have children. He will have Sunday dinners together with his brothers and their wives. Hopefully, he will have a room set up for me in case I want to visit for the weekend. I will remember this moment, when MJ is small enough to cradle in my arms. I kiss his forehead and it brings me comfort this evening.

Chapter 43

It's 1:30 am. This is my third call to Julius. I didn't leave a message the first time, but right now I have to say something uplifting, positive, reassuring or even kind. Perhaps he's asleep. I adjust MJ on Mensah's side of the bed. *Huh. Mensah's side. What a silly thought. Stop thinking about him, Vida.* I climb back underneath the covers and stare at my phone. I'm sure the second message is only heavy breathing. The words struggle to come out. *Okay, Vida, one more time and that's it for the night.* I dial his number again, anxious just to hear his voice. Maybe for the last time. *Stop it, Vida. Good thoughts. You need to be strong.*

"Hello, Vida. Still up?" I wasn't expecting him to answer on the second ring. I sit up.

"Yes. I—"

"Oh, Vida. Please, you don't have to say anything. I appreciate the phone call."

"But you just can't tell me you are having major surgery that may leave you—" I don't say the word. "—and then leave me with a bag full of journals and tell me to keep it in case—" I stop myself again. "I mean, you can't just leave like that." I'm screaming at him, but his coolness is even more frightening to me.

"Vida, please. It's late. Get some rest."

"Wait, wait Julius." *Think of something poignant, Vida, but no prayers. What do you say to a man who doesn't believe in God anymore? My possible last words can't be good night.* My mind catches up with dry hoarseness in my voice. Efya's song, "Best of Me" is the last song I listened to this evening and the words seem fresh in my thoughts. I don't know half the words in Twi, so I hum the missing ones and close my eyes to recall the melody of the song. My voice is no Whitney Houston, especially singing a cappella into the phone; it could easily be mistaken for emergency response signals. My voice is burdened with tears, but I continue to bellow out lyrics that I have no business singing.

"It's confirmed. You can't sing at all, Ms. Frimpong," Julius says. I laugh. "I don't think Efya would take too kindly to you remaking her song the way you did." He laughs. The first laughter since he told me about his operation. "But I do love to hear your voice." Silence again.

"Julius…"

"Good night, Vida." Silence on the other end alerts me that he has left the conversation. I dial his number again and it goes to voicemail. I find the courage to leave a message.

"Julius, I hope you listen to this message. I pray in Jesus's name that he watches over you tomorrow. I mean this morning. I…I…everything is going to be okay. I know it will be. God is in control, and you are in my prayers." My thoughts scatter again. I hang up and call again. Still no answer.

*

"Haf faith, notin' iz goin' to happen to him. Da surgeons, dey know wat dey doin'." Abla's voice is reassuring at 3:17 a.m. Mrs. Lindsey's faint voice enters my thoughts again. "…*Surgery is surgery, dear. Anything can happen. It's up to God.*"

"He will be fine, Yaa. Remember all da scares you had in yur life. Wit God on our side, who shall we fear?" Abla is good for spiritual uplifting. She recites from the Bible: "Out of my distress I called on da Lord; da Lord answered me and set me free. Da Lord iz on my side. I will not fear. Wat can man do to me? Da Lord iz on my side as my helper; I shall look in triumph on doze who hate me." She continues with another verse. "Don't worry about anydin'; instead, pray about everytin'; tell God yur needs and don't forget to dank Him for Hiz answers. If you do dis you will experience God's peace, which iz far more wonderful dan da human mind can understand." She continues to give me more than a dozen examples of triumph in the face of adversity. *But would God turn his back on Julius, someone who doesn't believe in Him anymore?*

"Where iz his family?"

"His family? I don't think he has any."

"Wherez dat drunken girlfriend of his? No siblings or friends?"

"Well, both of his parents are deceased. I don't think Julius has friends. Maybe Max and Vincent, the people who work for him, but I am not sure if we can call them friends or family. Penny, well Penny is still in Hawaii for a swimsuit photo shoot. But I don't think he told her. Some people are like that, I guess. They don't want anybody to know when they are going into surgery. Just like Auntie Cece when she had one of her knees replaced. Remember?"

"Yezzz, but she really wanted someone deer wit her because she waz scared. You need to be deer for him," Abla says.

"Me?"

"Yes, you. Aaah! Why do you dink he told you about da surgery?"

"Because of the journals," I quip.

"Aaah, Yaa. Yur all book smart but *la cabeza no dey*." It is her word fusion of Spanish and Pigeon language. "He didn't haf to tell you about da surgery. He could haf left you a note or told Vincent to relay da message. He came deer dis evenin' for support. You know some men have a hard time expressin' wat dey need. Yaa, he needs you."

"Oh, I don't think so. I really don't think he would prefer me over Penny or even Vincent. Plus, I work for him. He's my boss."

"Wake up! You just said a moment ago dat he doesn't haf anyone. Don't you dink hez lookin' for you to be deer?" Several thoughts cross my mind. *It wouldn't be hard to find out where and what time the surgery is. I still have Dr. Jesup's card from the first time I met him.* Abla continues badgering me over the phone for my lack of reading men. "…And stop callin' him yur boss. I can, but not you."

"I don't get your meaning." I'm ready for her sexual innuendos. It has been a constant theme when she talks about Julius. I should have never mentioned the *kotodenden* room to her. "That is all he is—my boss. Why would I think anything otherwise?"

"Well, letz see. He bought you a brand new car. Even afta you tormented him about dat old beat up Honda. He agreed to pay yur sista-slash-manaja very well in dis *cocosae* deal. Not to mention Daniel and Chin too. Entertained yur children every time you brought dem along to dis *cocosae* work office." He did allow da boys to play with da karaoke machine and da musical instruments. "And don't forget…tracked you down wit my help and flew you and da children across da U.S. in hiz private plane. Den when you reached home, you didn't botha to call yur one and only sista, but instead he waz deer nursin' you durin' a meltdown; replaced yur furniture wit very expensive European furniture." My timeline with Julius is becoming apparent to me. It's been close to a year.

"Are you still deer?" Abla's voice brings me back to the conversation.

"Yes," I say, rolling my eyes.

"Yaa...Hez not yur boss. Hez yur friend."

I remain silent with her words suspended between us. There have been few times that Abla leaves me dumbfounded. I've never taken the time to appreciate his company and all that he has done for me. I know more than ever what I have to do.

"Abla—"

She cuts me off. "I will be deer in two hours."

Chapter 44

It's 5:00 a.m. and my head never hit the pillow.

Dr. Jesup's office in Manhattan confirms he will be in surgery this morning, but will not provide me with any more details. I contact Alice, but she is not forthcoming with any facts about the surgery. I rush downstairs and the television is on. Panin must be up already. I enter the living room and there's no sign of him. I walk into the kitchen and find him already dressed and preparing his breakfast cereal.

"Sweetie, you're up early." He sits down to eat. I prepare tea and toast for myself. A car honk in the driveway causes Panin to leap out of his seat. I peer through the kitchen window to find Abla and Mrs. Lindsey exiting the vehicle. "Shit." Why did she bring Mrs. Lindsey? I rush to the front door.

"Are you ready?" Abla says.

"You brought poor Mrs. Lindsey to New York?"

"Of course. How else would I get here so quickly? She's a good driva and my license iz still suspended."

"Vida, we couldn't sleep a wink when we heard about RBD." Mrs. Lindsey looks especially nontraditional this morning. She wears lightly tinted shades and leather gloves. Her silver blonde hair is pulled back in a high ponytail. Her lips are lightly tinted with a bright red color. She could easily be mistaken for a woman in her late forties, but the truth is Mrs. Lindsey is well over seventy.

"RBD?"

She turns to Abla showing an expression of guilt. "I...I...meant Julius." It's obvious that Abla and Mrs. Lindsey have been having their own giddy conversations about Julius.

"Just how much does she know about Julius?" I whisper to Abla as we enter the house.

"Oh, stop it. Who iz she goin' to tell? She enjoys it. Gossip makes her feel youfful."

"So you have her calling Julius RBD also?"

"Hez more famous dan you dink and we didn't want Mrs. Lindsey's staff to know who we were talkin' about most of da time. Itz easier to uze dat nickname."

"She still has staff?" I direct my question to an interrogation.

"Of course. Da housekeepa, cook and nurse."

"So what do you actually do with Mrs. Lindsey? She is certainly capable of traveling on her own," I say.

"Yaa, ah! Dis iz not da time to discuss wat I do wit Mrs. Lindsey." She is right, but I will have to bring up the discussion at a later time. "So watz da plan?"

"I was thinking that you can stay and send the children off to school while I go to the hospital."

"No, Mommy. We're coming with you," Kakra says.

"You're dressed?" I say.

"Yeah, Panin woke us up, but we were up earlier when you were singing. We heard you. Is G-Money going to be okay?" My poor boys disturbed out of their sleep by a dysfunctional voice trying to bellow out a song.

"G-Money?" I ask.

"Yeah, Mr. Gallo. He said it was alright to call him that." Everybody has a nickname for him.

"I see. Well my boss, I mean friend, Mr. Gallo, is having surgery today. And he needs someone there."

"Like to hold his hand, Mommy? So he doesn't cry?" MJ says.

"Yeah, something like that."

"Okay, Mommy. I want to come too. I can hold his hand," MJ says.

"Is he going to be okay?" Kakra asks.

"Yes. He is going to be fine." I say it with conviction.

"We should all go so we can say a prayer for him then, Mommy," Kakra says.

Not wanting to dampen the mood and let everyone know that he isn't religious, I agree. "Okay. Let's vote. Hands up for going to the hospital and hands down if you want to stay." A unanimous vote.

"You see now. Letz go. We can all fit in da Cadillac," Abla says.

*

I hate hospitals. The smell, a mixture of cleaning fluids and blood. Frosty lights. Thank goodness I decided on the administrative track of nursing. The less I visit the hospital the better. People parading in white coats and monotone scrubs make me wish I had a drink in my hand. No one ever comes here happy, unless you come to see babies. And when you do leave happy, you are one of the rare successful cases.

"Hi. Can you tell me where I can find Dr. Jesup?"

"Dr. Jesup is in surgery." An older woman in a white coat doesn't look up. The desk in the nurse's station has folders and stacks of papers surrounding her. "How can I help you?" Her eyes finally meet mine. And even when I offer a gentle smile, her face is still unreceiving.

"I'm here for Julius Gallo. He is going into surgery this morning with Dr. Jesup."

"Are you family?"

I look around at our band of faces. I am not sure if this calls for a unicorn story, but it may help our cause.

"I'm his grandmother. And I need to see my grandson before he goes into surgery," Mrs. Lindsey offers a quick response. Abla squints her eyes at me. I interpret this as to let Mrs. Lindsey take the lead.

"I'm sorry, but Mr. Gallo didn't indicate any family members would be here today."

"Well, certainly you have been misinformed. Contact Dr. Jesup and tell him Dr. Lindsey is waiting here." The woman rises from her station and picks up a phone against the wall.

Dr? Mrs. Lindsey? Wow, now that is a lie. Or is it? But nevertheless, it's working. "Mrs. Lindsey. I don't want to trouble—"

"My dear, no trouble at all. We didn't drive all this way to stare at hospital walls. Did we?"

"No, ma'am." In less than five minutes, Dr. Jesup arrives with two staff members accompanying him. He looks younger, dressed in pea green scrubs.

"Dr. Lindsey, I don't know what to say. I can't believe you're here. It's been—"

"Nearly twenty years," she replies without breaking eye contact. Dr. Jesup moves closer examining her and then takes her hands into his. He turns to the two gentlemen behind him. "Dr. Richards and Dr. Flores, this is the renowned professor at Stanford University, Dr. Lillian Lindsey." They greet her and Dr. Jesup walks farther away with Mrs. Lindsey. Abla and I take baby steps in their direction.

"You've done well, as I knew you would," Mrs. Lindsey says.

"Many thanks to the professor who encouraged me to stick it through." Dr. Jesup's hands are still clasped over Mrs. Lindsey's. She blushes. We take a few more steps closer to them.

"Did I miss something here. What is going on? Dr. Jesup knows Mrs. Lindsey?" I whisper in Abla's ear. It's like trying to make sense of a story without reading the first half of the book.

"Shhh, pleaze, I beg. Keep quiet so we can hear wat iz goin' on." Abla focuses her attention on them.

Mrs. Lindsey releases her hands from his and places them in her jacket pockets. She tilts her head to one side in a girlish way. "Dr. Jesup, we need a favor." Her tone is soft and warm against the cold white coats and monotone lights. "My dear friends here want to see Mr. Gallo before surgery."

He scans our faces and lands on mine. "Ah, yes. Ms…"

"Frimpong," I eagerly answer.

"I remember you from the night of the car accident."

"Yes. Right. How is he? Can I see him?"

"Well, I…he gave me specific instructions for no visitors."

"Yes, Dr. Jesup, we are aware of that," Mrs. Lindsey says. She takes his hands into hers. "Let him know we are here waiting. Just a minute of his time, that's all. Please."

"Lillian….Lilly." He says her name like old friends and then remains still for a minute. He scans our faces once more and then releases his hands from Mrs. Lindsey's. "I will see what I can do." He returns to the elevator with his colleagues.

"Lillian…..Lilly?" I turn to Abla. She has the cheesiest grin on her face.

"Shez still got it afta all deezs years." I feel a bit envious and frustrated. Abla apparently has read the first half of the book.

"We need to talk about you and Mrs. Lindsey after everything is said and done." She waves me away nonchalantly. The children are sitting in the lounge chairs playing on the their tablets. Mrs. Lindsey pulls Abla and me aside. "He is a bit cocky at times, but I know him. He will get it done."

"Apparently," I whisper.

"Did you see da way he looked at you, Lilly?" Abla is giddy.

"Stop it, Rosemary," she chimes. "It's been decades. He couldn't possibly—"

"Oooh, yes he could. He rushed down here wit just da mention of yur name."

The woman in the white coat offers us the good news. Mrs. Lindsey's plea worked. The nurse instructs us to go to the elevator farthest down the corridor where Dr. Jesup will meet us on the second floor.

"Mr. Gallo is not pleased you are here. Nevertheless, he will see you and only you. Briefly. Follow me," Dr. Jesup says.

I look back at Abla and the children. "Go ahead, Vida. We will be here waiting," Mrs. Lindsey says.

Dr. Jesup leads me to another long corridor and into a large room. Vincent is standing by the door.

"Good morning, Ms. Frimpong."

"Good morning, Vincent." I'm glad to see him here at least. He opens another door and directs me in. Inside the large room, different monitors and equipment hang alongside one wall. The bed is empty.

"You don't take instructions very well." His voice is low and I search the dimly lit room for his presence. A bald man in a gown standing next to the window doesn't turn to look at me.

"Julius?" The long luxurious locks are gone though the cockiness is somewhat there. I move closer and try to think before I talk so I don't say anything inappropriate.

"How do you feel?" He sighs. No words. I inch closer.

"You shouldn't have dragged the children to come here, or your sister and her patient. You don't listen, Vida."

"Why are you saying this? You didn't say not to come."

He doesn't turn to face me. He looks straight ahead at the closed blinds. "But it's not necessary. I don't need you here—or anyone else. This is my third time having this procedure…it's become routine now and I…I…don't need anyone now." I feel the fear and, despite the hospital gown, he looks completely naked to me. I touch his hand. He tries to pull back, but I firmly cup my right hand over his. He remains still. My left hand encases his hand underneath. I bring warmth to his cold, damp hands. His shoulders relax, but he still doesn't turn toward me.

I chuckle. "Did you know Mrs. Lindsey and Dr. Jesup know each other?" I release my hold and open the shades. The light shines on his face and he opens his eyes. I hold his hands again, but relax my grip. He doesn't pull away. The sun breaks through the dense clouds. The light gleams onto trees and grass. There's light inside the room.

"Mrs. Lindsey?" he questions me.

Good. He is engaging in conversation. "Yeah, that's Abla patient. She took care of Mr. Lindsey until his death, but now, God only knows what she does with Mrs. Lindsey." I chuckle again, hoping to maintain the light mood.

"Dr. Jesup told me that she was one of his professors in medical school. I have a strong feeling that there was something between those two." *Wow, I'm sure there is more to this story. Could they have been lovers? I have to talk to Abla later.* Julius smiles. *I need to engage him in talking about anything else besides the surgery.* I pepper him for a response.

"Really, why do you say that?" I ask.

"He's behaving like a teenager who just lost his virginity. When I insisted he turn you away, he pleaded with me that it would be difficult to turn Lillian away."

"Hmmm. Well, well, well. Very interesting." He smiles again. "I'm glad you didn't."

"Didn't what?"

"Turn us—me—away." *Good. Three smiles in a row.* "So you see, Mr. Gallo you are definitely unique. Your doctor happens to be a student of Abla's patient and Abla happens to be my sister and you happened to crash into my car nearly eight months ago, which also gave you a chance to meet me and offer me a job, and because you are not just my boss…"

He turns his head toward me. *I wonder what he sees? My fears or worries?* "What am I, Vida?"

"You're my friend. And that is why I am here this morning with my children in tow. Because that is what friends do for one another."

He swallows hard. "Vida, there is something I should tell you…"

"Mr. Gallo…they are ready. We must finish with preparations," the nurse interrupts.

"What is it?" He hesitates and squeezes my hand.

"Thank you for being here."

"N-T-Y-B-F," I say. He stops and a peculiar look cuts across his face. "No-thank-yous-between-friends."

"Of course."

"Julius?"

"Yes?"

"I know you are not very religious, but I really—we really—want to pray for you and the surgeons. Just a short prayer. Please."

"Vida. That is not—"

"It was actually MJ's idea. Please, as your friend, I want to do that for you." Silence again and then his shoulders slump down in surrender.

"Okay."

It takes less than a minute for more warm bodies to engulf the room. I ask Dr. Jesup and his team to join in. A few staff members stand aside. "I am not asking you to pray; just join us and hold hands. I promise it won't be long." There are sixteen of us including my entourage holding hands. Julius sits on the edge of the bed. I stand next to him and hold his hand.

Abla begins a hymn in Twi. The room is silent, but Kakra knows the words and sings along with her.

"Dear heavenly Fatha, where could we be widout yur gracious mercies? We dank you, Lord, for bringin' us dis far. For we know doze who believe in you will haf everlastin' love. Our dear brotha sits among us and we ask you, heavenly Fatha, to watch ova him."

She begins another hymn. The room feels heavy and my mouth opens.

"Dear God, thank you for this day that you have given us. We are here before you from different walks of life, and we are all gathered here to witness your everlasting love on us. We ask you to guide the hands that will operate on our dear friend, Julius Gallo. We ask that you guide and lead the medical staff in every decision they make. We pray that the tumor will be successfully removed and we pray that it will not return again. We believe in Jesus's name that you will watch over Julius for endurance and patience and you will provide him the strength to overcome any pain or obstacle. Thank you, Jesus, for providing your unconditional love to us. We pray that you continue to bestow blessings upon us. We will continue to praise your name. In the almighty name, Jesus. Amen."

A unison of amens circle the room and then we release hands. Panin beats on the table. Kakra begins to sing "Great is Thy Faithfulness."

Everyone leaves and it's Julius and me again. "Julius, you can talk to God. Just speak from your heart. No matter how you feel, He is always listening," I say.

"Mr. Gallo, we are ready," Dr. Jesup says.

"Ms. Frimpong, thank you for that. I must say, in all my years, that was a first," Julius says.

I turn to Dr. Jesup. "Please take care of him. We need him. Julius, I will be here waiting when you get out."

*

"I hate hospitals." Saying it out loud won't make me feel better, but it's the truth. Memories of Mommy in the hospital still plague me. Fear, sadness and loneliness consume my thoughts and I get up and pace the floors again. Several hours have passed and still no word from Dr. Jesup and his staff. Vincent passes by occasionally to check on me. He leaves me another cup of coffee. "Thank you," I shout when he turns to walk away. Thank goodness Mrs. Lindsey and Abla returned home with the children. I return Abla's text: **"Nothing new. Still waiting."**

Another text message comes through. It's Ms. Carconia.

This is the first time I've allowed the kids to intentionally miss school. I seek comfort in knowing that the twins will be graduating soon and moving on to middle school. I text Kakra and Panin to remind them about logging in their reading log.

Dr. Jesup stands over me and I drop my phone. "Hi, Dr. Jesup." He bends down to pick up the phone and hands it to me.

"Ms. Frimpong, I've just alerted Vincent of the status of Mr. Gallo. He gave me permission to notify you as well." He exhales and rests one hand on his waist. "He's in a lot of pain right now. Vincent is taking him home tomorrow to recuperate, against my better judgment. But the hospital staff will be by to attend to his care around the clock." Dr. Jesup shakes his head. "We weren't able to safely remove both tumors. One remains and it is a precarious place; the chances are too great and I couldn't take the risk. Ms. Frimpong, I'm hopeful…I'm glad this occurred. I have a strong feeling about something. It would require another surgery, but for now, we should allow him to heal. The tumor that Dr. Braun identified is gone."

Although I'm not clear of the extent of this surgery, the words 'another surgery' scare me. "Next time?...He has to go through this again?"

"Yes. I was explaining to Vincent, I'm ninety percent sure the malignance is gone. There is a lot of research out of Australia and I will confer with Dr. Braun before we proceed. Mr. Gallo may be disappointed, but I am hopeful. I know what I saw with my own eyes." He seems to be talking in random thoughts, but choosing words carefully toward me. "I don't mean to pry, but it would be good to have a friendly face close by as he recuperates."

"Ummmm...yes...I am generally there on the weekends. I can check on him frequently."

"Great. My team will be there for a month or so around the clock."

"Thank you, Dr. Jesup."

"Ms. Frimpong, if my theory is right, I may be thanking you."

*

The image of Julius lying there is something I don't think I will ever forget. I sit in the driveway thinking about the great deal of wealth he has acquired and no one by his side when he needed someone the most. No one but Vincent, his driver/bodyguard. *Why wasn't Penny there?*

MJ opens the door to greet me.

"Mommy!" MJ leaps in my arms. I hold him tightly and shower him with kisses.

"Yaa." Abla's voice turns my attention to her.

"Oh my goodness, is he—?" Mrs. Lindsey rises and her expression is alarming.

I put MJ down. "He is alive."

"Oh, dank God," Abla says.

"But the surgery wasn't successful. There were a few complications and they couldn't remove the second tumor."

"Dr. Jesup is a good surgeon. I am sure there was a reason why he couldn't continue," Mrs. Lindsey says.

"Vincent is preparing him to recuperate at home."

"Today?" Mrs. Lindsey says.

"Tomorrow. Vincent insists. I am sure he is just following Julius's directives. And Dr. Jesup is sending a group of his staff there to monitor him. Alice can provide updates quickly to Dr. Jesup and also monitor Julius's vitals."

"Oh yes...Alice," Mrs. Lindsey says confidently, as though we've had discussions about Julius's omnipresent Alice. "So he doesn't have any family? You have been reading those journals. No selfish siblings, kissing cousins, church going aunties or gambling uncles?" I shake my head confirming there are no such people, or none that I am aware of.

"Well, we prepared dinner. Da kids are fed and bafed. Let me warm you some food," Abla says.

"It's okay. I'm not hungry right now."

Mrs. Lindsey prepares to leave. Abla helps her with her jacket and then reaches for my hand. "Do you need me to stay?"

"No. Please take Mrs. Lindsey back home. I will be fine," I say.

"I'll check on Dr. Jesup tomorrow and let you know if I get any more details," Mrs. Lindsey says. She walks over to hug me. "He is very lucky to have a friend like you."

*

Three hours later after a hot meal and shower, the image is vivid of Julius lying there in the hospital. I can't sleep. I walk down to the boys' bedroom. MJ is fast asleep. But Panin and Kakra are up watching music videos on YouTube. "It's kind of late. Why are you guys still up?"

"We took a nap earlier in the afternoon and we don't feel sleepy," Kakra says.

"Ah, I see. Did you read and log it in your journal?" They both nod their heads confirming they did what they were instructed to. "Kakra, Ms. Carconia said she got the principal's approval to include your song selection in this year's graduation ceremony."

"That's great, Mommy." I expected more enthusiasm from Kakra, but the three words just hang between us in the air. He returns to watching the video on YouTube.

"Daddy texted me." He pulls out his phone and reads the message. "I hope everyone is OK. I've been trying to reach Mommy all day. Did she get back from the hospital?"

"Hospital?" I ask. I never saw a missed call from him.

"I told him that you had to stay with G-Money because of his eye surgery. Daddy said he is out of the country working on a major project. But if he can get away for a couple of days next month, then we will see him. I asked him if we could spend the summer with him, but he said we would be bored." *Why? Because he spends his nights—maybe even days—fucking Kate. I hope it falls off or gets cemented into her pussy like this Nigerian movie I saw once about a cheating husband.* I digress. "And he is going to plan something when he gets back to the U.S."

My sadness is turning to fury again with the mere mention of Mensah. It is now or never to tell the children about their father. "Guys, turn off the computer please. I need to have a talk with you."

"I didn't do it," Kakra admits blankly.

"Whatever you claim you didn't do will eventually come to light," I tease him.

Fuck. How do I begin this? I'm divorcing your dad. Your daddy is a liar. No, your daddy really fucked up. When exactly did he call me? Because I had my phone in my lap the whole time I was in the hospital and I never got a message. I gave him my wedding ring back and you would think he would be on the next plane back to New York trying to save his marriage. But instead, I get a bouquet of please-forgive-me-flowers. He just doesn't really care. After all we've been through...I can't...

"Mommy?" Kakra breaks my trance.

Temper your words, Vida. The woman in me calms me down. "Daddy and I are mad at each other right now."

"Is that why you don't return his calls?" Kakra says. *He doesn't call me, but I won't start that campaign.*

"Partly, yes."

"It's because of the woman we saw in California, isn't it?" It is obvious the boys know more of what is going on than I want to admit.

"Your father is a good father. He could be a better husband, but that is not your concern. He loves all of you dearly. I know that for a fact."

"Does Daddy love you?" *Maybe I'm not ready for this talk.* I honestly don't know anymore. "I'll call him and ask him," Kakra says frustrated by my silence.

"No. Please don't. Love can be complicated. Daddy and I need to figure out how not to be mad at each other and still love one another."

"I know Daddy will make it better. He has to make it better for all of us. Right, Mommy?"

"Yes, Kakra." His face is bright and full of hope. Panin sits absorbing the conversation. He shows Kakra his phone.

Kakra takes it and reads the message. "Will G-money be okay?" I am relieved to switch topics.

"Yes. He will be going home tomorrow. It's getting late, guys. Let's go to sleep." I tuck Kakra into bed and Panin follows behind me to his room. He climbs into his tidy bed and I place a kiss on his forehead.

*

Two missed calls and a voice message.

"We're home. I hope yur gettin' rest. Call me if you're still up." Abla's voice sounds upbeat. I play the second message.

"Hi, it's me. I'm not sure how long this is going to go on. At least call me back, Yaa. I spoke with the boys and I learned you had an interesting day today. We need to talk, but right now another big contract has come through. And before I can turn it down, I just need to get more information. I'm not sure if I will make it to graduation. And I really want to be there. Anyway, I will see what I can do. I hope everything was successful with your boss's surgery." He sighs...I can hear a faint voice in the background. I wonder if it's her...Kate..."Ummm...I gotta go, but I will try to reach you during the week."

I wish I hadn't listened to the message. He didn't mention anything about what has occurred. I end the message and dial his number. It goes straight to voicemail. I'm fired up, but I decide not to leave a message.

MJ rolls over to my side of the bed. *What am I doing? Vida, you can't let this man consume you. Look at you. Going from zero to a hundred. Just keep your focus on the kids.* I cuddle up next to MJ and dial Abla. She answers.

"So, is your B-F-F sleeping now?" I say.

"Yeah, she went right to bed when we came home."

"I see you and your B-F-F have been having very detailed discussions about me and my friend."

"Oh, pleazze. Wat else iz an elderly woman goin' to talk about?"

"Well, since we are on the topic, what exactly do you do for Mrs. Lindsey? Because if she has a cook, nurse and housekeeper, then why does she need you?"

"Well, Ms. Nosey Thang. Afta Dr. Lindsey died, she didn't want to be alone, so you know she kept me as staff, but den my daily chores got in da way of our shoppin' and gossippin'. So she kept me along so I can help her pick out shoes and go to dinna."

"That's an expensive friendship, don't you think?"

"Hey, you got yur rich friend and I got mine. Plus, I enjoy Lilly's company. She's like an olda sista to me." I remain silent on the phone. "But no one could eva replace my one and only sista from da same motha and same fatha."

"You're cuckoo, you know that? So, tell me about Mrs. Lindsey and Dr. Jesup…"

"Hmmm…I can't say much, but all I can say iz dat da spark iz still deer."

"Were they lovers? When she was married to Dr. Lindsey?"

"Hmmmm…datz a story for anotha night, but before I forget, Mrs. Lindsey had an idea." I can't believe she is leaving me on a cliff. It has to be one of those three-D animation stories that Abla has to tell when she sees me.

"What is it?"

"She dinks it would be a good idea dat we stay wit him." She exhales deeply into the phone. "At least for a week. You know, until he gets back on his feet and all. I mean he has dis big house and he iz goin' to be surrounded by people who only know him from wat dey read on hiz chart. I saw da look on hiz face dis mornin' when we were prayin'. He waz definitely happy you and da children were deer for him. We could—"

I cut Abla off because she's had crazy ideas before, but this…this…resonates with me. *But so much to consider.* "We?"

"Yeah. You, me and da kids. You know friendly sexy African women and happy kids alwayz brings new life into a home."

"Abla, I'm not sure about that. He should have some privacy while he recuperates."

"Datz all he haz. Deerz no one by hiz side except for us. God forbid he dies. A man so talented and wealtee like dat wit no one he can count on to stand by him durin' times of pain and struggle. Loneliness iz a silent killa. Why do you dink Mrs. Lindsey needs my company?"

Her words pierce my soul. "It's just too complicated. The kids' schools are in Westchester. I would have to drop them off in the morning and come back and—"

"And notin'. Dat iz why I am comin' wit you. You said it yourself, dat you want to take time off from work to sort out yur marriage issuez. And you said da kids need some time away wit everytin' goin' on. Dis iz a stone dat killz two birds."

I never understood why Abla didn't choose a sales career. She can sell jasmine rice back to China. *Or maybe she just knows the right words to sell me.* It's crazy, but her words still linger like burnt popcorn. *A different environment could get me more focused and take my mind off the recent stresses in my life. I wouldn't have to travel from the Bronx to Queens on the weekends to work on Julius's assignment. And with Abla around, I can definitely count on her to help.* It's crazy. Yet the woman in me champions me on. Auntie Cece will never allow it. I hear her voice clearly in my head. *"Nonsense! You...a married woman, taking yur kids and sister to another man's house while Mensah is away? What will people say?...What will Mensah say? Please don't cause trouble for yurself. No matter what you do...a good name carries well."*

It seems scandalous enough. *It's crazy, careless and cocosae. But Auntie Cece is in Ghana for two months,* the woman in me reminds me. *Perhaps this will bring Mensah back on the first flight home seething with anger. How dare I take his children away without telling him, and to a strange man's house at that? Oh yes, this will definitely get him back here with or without his new business contract.*

Abla's voice brings me back to now. "So, wat do you dink?"

"Abla, start packing."

Chapter 45

"So Mommy, how long are we going to be at G-Money's house?"

"Maybe a week or two, sweetie."

"Like a vacation?" MJ asks.

"Yes, like a mini-vacation. He has the pool, the musical instruments and karaoke machine you like. And…cheeseburgers and chocolate shakes."

"Yay!" MJ claps his hands. The only person who needs convincing is Panin, but he hasn't shown any reservations so far. "Wow, wait till I tell Daddy."

"Um…guys, let's hold off from telling Daddy for now. He has a lot going on. I will tell you when to tell Daddy. Agreed?"

"Okay, Mommy," Kakra says. I look at Panin. Usually a new environment away from home is a showdown. It took us several years before he felt comfortable staying at Chin's house. Even then, three days is the max. Anything more than that would require divine intervention. So far so good. He is calmly eating his waffles with no syrup. Yes, good, but unsettling. I call Daniel and he picks up on the first ring.

"*Etesen*," he says cheerfully.

"*Bokor*." I'm pleased it sounds linguistically correct.

"Very good. Your Twi is finally improving. Still working for the zillionaire? Have you finished the assignment? You know, we should have agreed on some royalty fees. To keep the money coming in, you know."

It isn't uncommon for Daniel to ask for more money. Every opportunity is an opportunity for a business deal for him. Like the time he slept with Maame Betty to shop for free in the African market; or the time he charged Abla gas money to take her to the airport because he said he left his wallet at home; or when he collected the tenants' money and told Auntie Cece that he had to use it to make some repairs around the house that never occurred.

"You know, I see your name everywhere I go."

"Really? Where?" he asks.

"Your surname…One Way."

"Funny, cuzo. I will have to use that."

"Listen, cuz. When Auntie Cece returns from Ghana and is looking for me, just tell her that I will be working from Mr. Gallo's house in Long Island City. Abla and the kids are coming with me."

"Oh…oh…does Mensah know?" I know he heard about what happened in California because Abla asked Daniel to pick me up from the airport before she spoke with Julius. But I also know in all my years married to Mensah, Daniel has never gotten involved in our marital problems. I'm not sure if he was scared to confront Mensah or if he idolized him as a big brother. I recall one thing he said to me when I had one blowout with Mensah. *"I don't get involved in husband and wife issues. After all, I can't comment on what goes on in one's house if my house is not up to good standards."*

"Mensah is in California," I retort. "I'm just telling you so when Auntie returns from Ghana, well, you know where I am."

"Hmmmm, Yaa…you're playing with fire."

"What is that supposed to mean?"

"Nothing. So you are going to spend God only knows how many days with the boys alone in some stranger's house?" I nearly slip up and announce that Julius is my friend. It's better that Daniel is oblivious to the friendship that Julius and I have formed.

"I just need to catch up on some work and…Anyway, it's not like we are staying there alone. Abla is coming along."

"I should have known she put you up to this. Yaa, I'm not a pastor's son, but take this counsel, Abla's advice is neither here nor there sometimes." I brush off his comments because I am surprised he is giving me a lecture. A man who doesn't even live with his family. Daniel and his wife behave like a happily married couple when seen together, but behind closed doors in separate houses, it's fair game. He used his father's passing as an excuse to move back home with Auntie Cece. Even after four years, his wife has never uttered a complaint.

"Just a few weeks and we'll be back," I say.

He sighs. "Hmmmmm. Okay, text me the address just in case we need to file a missing family report."

"That's not funny."

"Anything involving you and Abla always is."

Don't start second-guessing yourself. I haven't even checked in with Vincent this morning. I call but get no answer. I try Alice. "Ummmm…Alice, how is Mr. Gallo?"

"He is home, but that is all the information I can relay to you, Ms. Frimpong."

"Is Vincent there?"

"I cannot confirm or deny his presence."

Here we go. "Can you please tell Vincent to call me. It's urgent."

"Very well, Ms. Frimpong."

I bring the rest of the bags downstairs and double check the bedrooms to make sure I haven't left anything. The front door opens and I hear the boys welcome Abla in. I run down the stairs and find her standing in the hallway, but not in her usual good cheer.

"You're here early."

"I am?"

"Yes. You made it sound like I wasn't going to see you until much later."

"Dings changed," she says.

"Are you okay, sis?"

"Fine."

I shout to the boys. "Hey guys, use the bathroom again before we leave." This gives Abla and me a few minutes alone.

"What's wrong?"

"Notin'." She sighs again.

"C'mon Abla, this isn't like you."

She pauses. "I just had…" She looks away from me. "Men. Richard."

"Oh, no. What's wrong?"

"I don't want to talk about it. Just silly stuff. Anyway, I'm lookin' forward to our little vacation. We need dis pamperin', even dough RBD—I mean Julius—is recuperatin', but it will be fun." She forces a smile.

"Is he mad that you are coming with me? You should stay then."

"It's not dat. Plus I made up my mind and I'm comin' wit you. You can't manage all dis by yourself." She moves away from me. She's pensive. "As soon as a man knows yur always available, dey start to take advantage of you. I'm okay." She sobers up. "Have you heard from Vincent?"

"No. I tried reaching him a moment ago, but didn't get a response."

"So we're just goin' to show up deer like refugees?"

"Well, yeah."

"Okay by me."

*

We arrive at the house. And Abla communicates the same first impression I had over seven months ago. "Dis place looks like shit. Why would he want to live out here? Dis iz far from our taste."

"But it's nice inside. I promise." We usher out of the car. Kakra immediately goes to the trunk and begins unloading. "Sweetie, let's see who's home first before we unpack the car." The worst he can say is no, thank you. I take a deep breath and enter the security code. Abla and the kids follow behind me timidly.

"Wow." A different response from Abla this time. She pivots slowly admiring the details surrounding her.

"Good evening, Ms. Frimpong. And good evening, MJ and Kakra. I detect a new visitor."

"Yes, this is Abla, my sister. You can call her Abla or Rosemary, whichever is easier."

"Welcome, Abla."

"*Woana kasa?*" Abla whispers to me. She looks around for the voice and before I can say a word the omnipresent Alice responds.

"*Mepaakew. Yefre me* **Alice.**"

Abla stumbles backwards to whisper in my ear again. "You never told me she speaks Twi."

"I didn't realize it until now."

"Do you prefer to communicate in Twi?"

"No, English is fine." Abla turns to me. "We can't even gossip da way we want now. I feel like Twi is da new second language. Mommy should haf taught you Ga. We could haf so much fun."

According to Abla, Twi is probably the easiest dialect to speak in Ghana. My mother spoke several languages and the little Ga I understood consists of insults and foul language. I'm sure Alice is more versed in Twi than I will ever be.

Vincent enters the hallway. "Good evening, Ms. Frimpong."

"Good evening, Vincent. I waited for your call, but then decided to come over."

"Yes, I see. With the entire family."

"Yeah. We're all here. We want to stay at least a week or two until Julius gets back on his feet." He scans our faces. And then locks eyes on Kakra. "Where is your brother?"

Shit. Where is he? I survey my tribe again. Panic sets in and I rush out of the house. He is still sitting in the car.

"Panin, open the door and come inside." He doesn't look at me but continues staring out of the passenger's side window. *I need Kakra's help.* I rush back inside. Vincent and Abla are engaged in conversation.

"Well, dat settles it. We are stayin'," she says.

"Kakra, please help me get your brother out of the car." Kakra at times knows how to manipulate Panin to do something that he doesn't want to do. Anything musical is usually good bait. I am hoping it will work now. Kakra follows me to the car. He attempts communication through the car window.

Vincent stands witness. "How is Julius? Is he sleeping?" I ask Vincent.

"He will be soon. The nurses gave him a sedative not too long ago. You can go and see him. I will get the rest of the bags from the car."

Abla and I enter the back yard to the extension in the back.

"Wow. Dis is not wat I expected at all." Abla is taking note of the ambiance. A slight knock on the door and then we enter. There are several hospital staff in the room. It doesn't look the same. The music playing sounds gothic and depressing. Abla shares the same sentiments.

"Iz he dyin'?" Abla asks.

One of the staffers answers her, "Oh, heavens no."

"Den wat are you playin'? Because if yur tryin' to kill him, dis iz how you start."

"It's chanting music and evokes calmness and serenity," one of the medical staffers says.

"The only thing you are evoking is dead spirits to come and take him," I say. "Alice?"

"Yes, Ms. Frimpong?"

"Can we have some music with an upbeat tempo?"

"Do you have a particular preference?"

"Yes," Abla and I say in unison. "Hilife."

"Certainly. One moment please."

The staffers each look around the room at one another as the loud bass kicks in. It startles them. Daddy Lumba's voice occupies the room and I don't think death stands a chance of entering. We dance for a minute or two around Julius's bed. He smiles.

"Mommy? Mommy…?" Kakra says. "We have a problem."

"What?"

"He is not getting out of the car. I even told him I would give him my points from Candy Crush." I roll my eyes and stomp toward the car under siege. *I knew it was too good to be true. He was way too calm all day. He chooses now to be frigid.* Vincent attempts to bribe him with ice cream, but it doesn't interest him.

"Vincent, it's okay. I need to talk to him." He stands back. As graciously as I can compose myself, I talk at the closed window. "Honey, you can come out now."

He motions his fingers and re-locks the car doors. *This is going to take less polite tactics.* Vincent looks on curiously. *But this is not a scene that Vincent needs to see.* I turn and ask him respectfully to give me a moment.

"Oh, sure. There is one more bag next to him, but he won't allow me to move it," Vincent says. He walks toward the house sneaking peeks at me, but I wait until he is inside before kicking my arsenal into gear.

"Listen, don't you start. I talked about this. This is for your own good. We need to be in different environments so you can learn to adjust." He covers his ears with his hands. "Oh, so now you are completely ignoring me? I am going to count to five. You better get out of this car with your bag. Do you hear me? I know you hear me."

He's relaxed and unbothered. "One." *He's not moving.* "Two." *Unruffled.* He looks up at me and then down to his MP3 player. "Three." He places his headphones on his ears. *Oh, this little…Just as stubborn as his father.* "I am not playing. You don't want me to get to five." *I can't believe this boy is letting me count to five.* "Four," I say through gritted teeth. *He's testing me.* He begins tapping his fingers on his lap. "Oh, so the music is more important than what I'm saying? The fact that you are ignoring me right now is totally disrespectful, Panin. And I won't tolerate it. Do you hear me?" *I know you hear me.* I search for any motion that looks like he will open the door. Nothing. "Five!" I yell. He pulls the headphones off and leans back in the seat. It's hard to shake his strong resemblance in appearance and mannerisms to Mensah.

"Okay...you want to see a crazy African mommy...you gonna get crazy African mommy." I pull my hair in a high bun. He watches me carefully. I unlock the door with my car alarm. He looks quite comfortable and doesn't even look bothered by my raging disposition. I grab him by the arm and pull him out. At least that is what I envision in my head. What actually is happening is me sweating like a gambler at the races when I stumble to the ground trying to pull Panin out of the car. My hands wrap around his legs and he is a solid mass. Not like the little boy I used to carry in my arms. *When did he grow calf muscles?* He doesn't exercise even a quarter as much as Kakra, but his legs tell me otherwise. I pull and tug and pull and tug and he watches me unfretted. "Panin, stop it. Let's go," I say through panting breaths.

He grunts again and I use whatever stored up strength I have to pull him halfway out of the car. Finally, in what seems like a WWF match gone bad with twenty solid minutes of swearing, his body falls choreographed to the ground.

"What do you want from me right now? I can't force you, but I want you to come inside. We won't be here long. I told you that. Tell me what I can do to make you come inside. Please tell me. Daddy is not here. It's just me. I can't keep pulling you out of cars or houses. I can't fight you anymore." Tears fall and I fight them away while still trying to talk to him. *Is it the struggle of pulling him out of the car or the struggle I'm going to face of being a single parent?* "Please, Panin, help me. I'm very tired."

"Eh...Pan, c'mon. We're all going into the pool," Kakra yells at Panin from the doorway. "Come. Let's go, big brother." Panin rises and walks toward the front door . I follow slowly behind him hoping he doesn't change his mind and bolt back into the car. I breathe a sigh of relief as he enters the hallway. *Now I have to make him feel comfortable enough to stay.*

THE BORROWED WIFE

*

"So wherez da wine?" Abla says. *I could certainly drink a bottle right now.*

"Let's sort out the sleeping arrangements first," I say.

"We already did dat. I'm upstairs wit MJ and Kakra and yur downstairs wit Panin."

"There's only one bedroom downstairs. Me and Panin in the same room?" He is my son because I gave birth to him, but I would prefer sleeping under the Queensboro Bridge than sleeping in the same room with him. Even with no words, he can be commanding. Panin's bedroom is one less chore I have to do around the house because he keeps it immaculately clean. I'm not nearly as organized as he is and sharing a room with him turns me into an ice block. The episode outside will probably be relived shortly.

"Gurl, you snooze you lose," Abla says.

"Why don't you stay with Panin and I stay upstairs with the boys?"

"Lissen, I love my nephew to deaf, but I would share a room wit Auntie Cece before I will share a room wit him." *My sentiments exactly.*

A large clash outside startles me. The noise is coming from Julius's suite. I rush through the back yard promenade into Julius's bedroom.

"Get the fuck out! I don't need a fucking babysitter." Julius is alert and loquacious. Vincent stands in the doorway keeping watch.

"What is going on?" He recognizes my voice and turns his head in my direction.

"I don't need a fucking babysitter. Just give me the pain medicine and get the fuck out."

"I'm sorry, Mr. Gallo. It's not yet time for your next dosage." The nurse is scared but firm.

"Don't fucking stare at me like a museum exhibit. I don't need you here. Get the fuck out or I will throw you out."

"Mr. Gallo, the agreement was to monitor you closely if you are staying home to recuperate. We are making sure that you are taken care of. You've had extensive eye and brain surgery and the last thing we want is an infection. We are only here to help."

"How many of you are here?" Julius says, disgusted. Vincent says something in Italian, but it doesn't temper Julius's rage.

"Everyone get the fuck out." He throws a metal bowl at the door. I sidestep quickly and bump into Vincent.

"Maybe you should stand outside," Vincent says. I acquiesce and meet Abla outside.

"What's dat about?"

"He's in pain."

"No shit."

A surge of hospital staffers quickly enter the foyer. "Hmm…wow…you may want to take our lead," one nurse says, barely putting on her jacket as she scurries out of the house. I walk back to the suite to find two nurses and Vincent. One is checking the monitors and the other is writing information on the chart.

"What time till is his next dosage?" Vincent asks.

"He has another one in four hours," the nurse says.

"Four hours will be here before you know it, Julius." He turns his head again toward my voice. "Will there be a nurse with him tonight?"

"Yes. Dr. Jesup's orders. He wasn't very cooperative last night."

Vincent walks toward me. "I will have someone here tomorrow to furnish the other rooms for the children. Give me a list of the items you will need and I will see to it first thing in the morning. I've arranged for Pio, Julius's regular driver, to take the children to school and Kakra's soccer practice. If there is anything else you need, just let me know. I have an appointment this evening. Alice can reach me if you need me. Nurse Hastings will be here throughout the night."

"Thank you, Vincent. I really—"

"Ms. Frimpong, I should…" He hesitates. "I am sure Julius appreciates that you are here."

Chapter 46

It's nearly ten at night and I am sure the children are asleep by now. The laughter and running around has quieted. I pick up a burgundy leather-bound journal.

May 1998
My God,
I was with Ama tonight. I lied to Mama, but I had to see her again tonight. She prepared banku and okra soup for me as promised. We ate until our bellies looked like kangaroo pouches. She smells like peanut butter. Her hair is like the softest cotton. I want to eat it. I ask her and she laughs. I wish we could spend the rest of our lives like this. Happy, eating under a tree, singing and dancing. She makes me happy, God.

I wake up to find my head resting on the same page. I enter Julius's suite. He is fast asleep and Nurse Hastings has set up office in the corner of the room.

"Hi," I whisper.

"Good evening. Ms. Frimpong, right?"

"Yes. How is he doing?"

"He's finally asleep. I gave him some pain medicine about a half an hour ago. It may take him through the night. So far, vitals look good."

"Good. He can be a bit moody when the pain kicks in."

"Yes. I have witnessed that. Understandable if you are in pain. He wouldn't allow me to change the catheter bag. Vincent changed it."

"Really?" I'm shocked Vincent would do something like that. Which tells me that he really does care for Julius.

"Yeah, but by tomorrow we can remove the catheter. We're just worried about his vertigo. But that should subside as we decrease the pain medicine. Nurse Cruz said she couldn't give him a sponge bath this morning. I would hate to disturb him just to go to battle over a sponge bath."

"Let him rest. Perhaps tomorrow he will be in better spirits. Is there something I can get for you?"

"No, I have all my goodies over there." She points to a blue and grey striped cooler.

"Well, I'm in the bedroom across from the kitchen if you need me."

In the bedroom my new roommate is quietly asleep. His clothes are still neatly packed in the duffel bag. He is wearing the clothes from earlier in the evening. He hasn't showered, which is not like him at all. It's better if he's asleep than go into a tug-of-war with him. I embrace the quietness and change out of my clothes. I look for a T-shirt and slip it on and then braid my hair into three large braids and finally collapse beside Panin.

"Dear God, thank you for another day. Bless this home and the people who enter and leave. Protect us from the works of the enemy and watch over our children. I pray that you provide Julius strength to recover and bless the hospital staff that take care of him. In Jesus's name, amen. And...God, watch over my husband and if he is fucking Kate, then shrink his penis into the size of a pencil eraser. No, I didn't mean that, God. Forget that ever came to my mind. Bless all my loved ones, God...even Mensah."

*

My head hits the floor hard and I scream out. I open my eyes trying to recognize my surroundings. *That's right. I'm at Julius's house.* Panin is covered with most of the duvet. I step inside the adjoining bathroom. The time on the console says 2:43 a.m. There is warm moisture in the bathroom and water residue on the tiles. I position myself on the toilet seat and exhale.

After a quick hot shower, I change into my nightgown, which Panin neatly packed into the chest. All my clothes are neatly folded into the drawers and my shoes arranged by color sit in the closet. He didn't unpack his own bags. I pray that I don't go through another challenging episode with him tomorrow. I check upstairs on Abla and the boys. The *kotodenden* room is empty. I move to the next room and the door is closed. I knock gently and then try to open it. The doorknob turns, but there is something heavy behind the door. *Gosh, leave it to Abla to barricade herself.*

"Who is it?" she asks.

"It's me."

"Wat happened?"

"Nothing, just checking on you and the kids."

"MJ and Kakra are here wit me. Deer sleepin'. Are you okay?"

"Yes, go back to sleep." I know that Abla will always have my back. It's comforting to know that she is here. I make my way to Julius's room. The suite is quiet and a bit cold. I notice the back doors are wide open. I knock gently on the sliding door and then enter. Julius is still asleep. The sheets are changed and so are the clothes Julius is wearing.

"Hi," Nurse Hastings says brightly. "Are you still up?"

"Just woke up about twenty minutes ago. I see you've done a lot since I was here last."

"Yeah, he woke up about an hour ago and Vincent gave him a sponge bath. And then we changed the sheets and his clothes."

"I see." *Vincent gave Julius a sponge bath? Wow. I think I've underestimated him.* "Where is Vincent now?"

"He was here a moment ago. I'm not sure."

"Alright, good night."

Nurse Hastings is pleasant and I like that she doesn't have any smart remarks about Julius's behavior. Granted, he isn't the best person to be around right now, but I can tell she has good bedside care. The shower makes me feel more awake than relaxed. I step into the study and decide to write. A wave of inspiration fills me.

*

It's nearly 4:00 a.m. and I pat myself on the back for writing nearly twenty pages. As I move the mouse over the "File. Save As," I ponder. What should I call it? "First Discharge?"…No, that sound like a porno flick. I settle for "First Draft" and power down the computer.

Chapter 47

"Are you still sleepin'? Iz almost eight o'clock," Abla says.

I turn my head away from Abla and notice Panin is not lying beside me. "Where are the kids?"

"Vincent brought some bagels, donuts and juice for dem. Den I went wit da driver to drop dem off to school. Wat time does da staff show up?"

Shit, I don't have the heart to tell her there aren't any. Who would have thought that a billionaire with a disability wouldn't have staff besides Pio and Vincent? I admire his independence.

"Staff?"

"Yes, da cook, maid, butla, you know—da staff." She looks perturbed. "Honestly, you should talk to Julius once he gets betta. Deer takin' advantage of him. I'm sure hez payin' dem very well and dey can't even show up to work at a professional time. Vincent is running around like da servant, butla, cook, driva and housekeepa. Honestly, dey are lucky I don't live here."

It is now or never. I get out of bed and make sure I keep a certain distance from Abla before releasing the heartbreaking news. "Yeah, about the staff...He doesn't have any."

She scoffs at my statement. "Wat do you mean, no staff? Who does da work around da house? Cookin'?"

"Well, from what I've witnessed, Julius and Vincent do it mostly. I mean, I haven't seen him cleaning, but I have noticed how he cleans everywhere he is. I think it's his way of being self-sufficient."

"Nonsense...heh...heh...Yaa, do you mean to tell me we are in dis huge buildin' wit no staff? So wat about us? Whoz goin' to cook, clean and serve us drinks all day?" Her eyes grow large with disappointment.

"Well, it's just like living at Mrs. Lindsey's."

"Oh, no...no...no. I beg...dis iz not like dat. Mrs. Lindsey has staff, includin' staff dat serves us cocktails from noon to dinner. Why do you dink I agreed to come? I dought we were goin' to be pampered, not be da help. I need to be pampered...we deserve it." She looks even cuter when she pouts.

"Abla, it's not so bad. Anyway, you said you were coming to help me out with the kids."

"Yes, but wat iz da advantage of trekkin' all da way here—behind God's back—if we can't get pampered all day?"

"Once we get settled, I am sure it won't be so bad."

"Says da fryin' pan to da jollof pot."

"I mean, there's still so much to enjoy without staff." She is not interested.

"We may haf to cut dis little 'vacation'"—she uses air quotes—"short." I caress her shoulders.

We enter the kitchen and Vincent turns to greet us. He looks well rested and is in his usual attire: black suit and shirt. "Good morning. Ms. Frimpong, I didn't get your list of items," he says.

"Oh, right. But that isn't necessary; Abla and I will go into town and get anything we don't have."

Vincent squeezes his lips. "Please, Ms. Frimpong, don't insult me."

"No, absolutely not. I just—"

"As I stated yesterday, I will make sure your stay here is as comfortable as possible."

"Ummm…thank—" He raises his hand in protest.

"Is there anything I can get for you this morning?"

"No, I'm fine."

"Rosemary, I will be waiting for you outside." He exits the kitchen.

"Ummm-hmmmm…when will you eva get it? Real men like to take care of women. Leave yur Ms. Independence I-can-do–everytin' back home. Relax and go check on yur patient. He looks much better today. I'm goin' to make him some light soup. Text me if you need anydin'."

Abla is right; I really need to pump the brakes on I-can-do-everything-myself. I move toward Julius's suite and knock on the door before entering. "Morning…" His tone is upsetting. He rubs his hand up and down his chin. He still has bandages over his eyes. He squirms back and forth. I move closer and sit on the edge of the bed.

"How do you feel?"

"Perhaps it's normal to have bandages around your head and IVs running through your arms. Or a tube of plastic inserted into your cock so you can relieve yourself. And let's not forget the strangers poking, probing and watching you twenty-four-seven. Please excuse me if I don't feel like dancing."

"That good, huh?" I chuckle, but he doesn't appear amused. He slides his shoulders up and down on the pillow. "You keep moving around. Is there something I should do to make you comfortable? Should I adjust the bed? Do you want to sit up? Do you need another pillow?"

"No," he answers angrily.

"Has Dr. Jesup been here?" I turn toward Nurse Hastings.

"Yes, early this morning. The vitals are good. We may be able to remove the IV and the bandages this evening."

"That's good news, Julius." He doesn't say anything. "How about a movie?"

"I don't want a movie," he says. He is still wiggling in the bed.

"Can I—?"

"No. Stop asking me. If there is something I need, I will get it myself." Nurse Hastings catches his sour tone and gives me a reassuring smile.

"I'm in the library if you need me."

*

It's nearly five o'clock and Abla and the children are not back yet. I text her. "Hey, I hope all is well. Just thinking about you guys."

She immediately texts me back, "We good. We picked the kids from school and doing some light shopping. Just exercising a billionaire's line of credit. Should be home before dinner time."

"Good afternoon, Ms. Frimpong. Nurse Matilda needs your assistance."

I rush to Julius's room.

"It's quite simple. You are not needed. I will ensure that you will be paid for the two weeks."

Here we go again. "What's going on?"

"It's not yet time for his next dosage of pain medicine. He wants to get up, but I'm under strict orders for him to wait until Dr. Jesup comes," Nurse Matilda says. She is the third nurse I've seen so far. She seems intimidated by Julius. Unfortunately, she is no match for Julius and his sharp tongue.

"Julius, what do you need?"

"I need you to send the babysitter home. Tell Dr. Jesup he shouldn't send any more staff without consulting me." She starts to tear up and I rest a reassuring hand on her shoulder.

"Julius, everyone is here to help you. Please don't fight."

He turns to the nurse, who is still timid of the English patient. "I don't need anyone's help. Just leave my medication and get the hell out. Ms. Frimpong will administer the dosage. She's a nurse too. No sense in having two nurses here."

"Wait, Julius." *I have to convince him to wait for Dr. Jesup.*

"Did you hear me, or do you need to be escorted out?"

"Ms. Frimpong, I don't know what to do. Dr. Jesup gave me my orders and I don't want to lose my job."

"You are more likely to lose your job the longer you stay here," Julius blurts out. "Leave now."

Nurse Matilda gathers her belongings and turns to me. "I will contact Dr. Jesup about the situation. Okay, I guess I will be on my way." She walks out and I follow behind her. She hands me the next dosage of his pain medicine. "Dr. Jesup will have to authorize the rest," she says.

"I'm sorry for that. He's a little bit grumpier today."

"Dr. Jesup did mention you're a nurse. Well, good luck. You sure have your hands full. There are extra bandages and dressings in the room." She gives me a warm smile and walks out the front door.

This is not going to be easy. I go into the library and grab the laptop and once again make my way to Julius's room. He is restless. His head moves in my direction.

"Why are you here?"

"I just want to make sure you're okay."

"No. Why are you here with the children?"

What answer do I really have? He doesn't want to hear a soppy story about friendship or some story about a friend in need. "We just want to keep you company until Penny comes back." I still don't think he even told her about the surgery. "You shouldn't be left alone."

He gives a big huff. "I don't need a babysitter, Vida. I'm not dying. At least not today."

"I know, but I want to be here." I sit at the edge of the bed. "Would you like something to eat?"

"No." He sits up. The Bible I placed on his nightstand is still there. "Where are the children?" *Spending a great deal of your money.*

"Vincent accompanied Abla and the kids for errands. They should be back by dinner time."

"Great…it's a family affair." He sulks his head into the pillow and covers his face with his right arm. I take the Bible and try to remember one of the verses that Abla told me about strength and overcoming challenges. "Trust me, Vida, the very last thing I want to hear is Bible scriptures right now."

"Okay. What about some music?"

"No. I just…" He wiggles some more in the bed. He looks rather uncomfortable. I try to adjust his pillow, but he quickly stops me. "If you are going to stay, then listen to me. I'm fine, just…just…work on your writing or something."

There has to be something to break this grumpy mood. This isn't pain talking, this is just him being an ass. I power up the laptop. *A little distraction from the pain and discomfort should bring back his humor.* I begin reading out loud.

Kyle was not like any other nurse. She had cared for patients before, but Brett was different. She healed him through his excruciating pain. Their affection grew day by day and there was no way that she was going to leave without confessing her love for him.

"Is that it?" Brett asked.

"What do you mean?" Kyle said.

"Will I ever see you again?"

"I don't know. Our lives are complicated. We can't continue this way. Someone always gets hurt in the end."

His love was so intense for her. Even if this was the last day he was going to see her, He had to have her just this once. He pulled her within the depths of his arms and covered his mouth over hers. Her tongue was inviting. Warm, wet, delicious. She moaned in ecstasy.

"Oh, Brett…this, this…Oh my!"

I pause. Julius removes his arm from his face and sits upright again. *He's paying attention. Good.* I continue.

"Oh, Brett...this, this...Oh my!" His tongue was wickedly wild in her mouth. She felt the sensation course through her body and every nerve awaken.

"Baby, I'm going to make love to you." He stripped her of her clothing within seconds. Her body was sealed underneath him. He fed her breast into his mouth, taking his time to trail long wet slow strokes with his tongue in between her breasts. She moaned and combed her hands in his hair. "Baby, you are so sweet...too sweet..." He coursed his tongue until he reached the gates of her goddess. He exercised every skill imaginable and sucked. The sound of his lips against her goddess made—

"Hmmm, goddess...I don't know about that word for pussy. You think I should change it to vagina?"

"Mmmmm...It depends. Will he perform a gynecological examination before he fucks her?" I laugh. *A smile. The first one today.* "It's all in the tone of the story. You know their relationship and then you will figure it out. First draft?" Julius asks.

"Very first draft. I started last night."

"And you already have a sex scene. Interesting, Ms. Frimpong."

The children are here. Their laughter carries throughout the house. "Abla and the kids are here. I'll be back."

"Okay," he says.

"Mommy, you should see the stuff we got today. This is better than Christmas." Kakra's face beams with delight.

"No, nothing is better than Christmas," I counter.

"You know what I mean, Mommy. We got so much stuff." Pio brings multitudes of bags inside the house.

"Where is Auntie Abla?"

"In the kitchen."

I enter the kitchen and find Abla looking nothing like when she left. "Oh, wow. Is that a new wig?"

"Yes."

"Shoes?"

"Yes."

"Clothes?"

"Yes."

"Jewelry?"

"Yes." She extends the other arm. "...And yes. I told you, I'm on vacation and I need to feel dat way. Don't worry, lil sista, I got some stuff for you too." I calculate the value of the items draped exquisitely on her body. An easy five thousand dollars' worth of new purchases.

"Don't start lookin' like dat. Vincent said I should buy wateva I want. And I askz him, wateva? And he repeated...Wateva." She imitates Vincent's voice poorly. "But I didn't go overboard. I stayed witin a budget." I find that hard to believe eyeing the diamond bracelets dangling from her wrists.

"And what was your budget?" She mumbles something as she continues to unpack the groceries into the pantry. "What? I didn't hear you."

"Roughly...twenty thousand dollarz."

"Twenty thousand U.S. dollars or Ghana cedis?"

"Of course U.S. dollarz. Dat iz not much...for a day...dink about it. Deer five of us. So datz four thousand dollarz a piece I spent. Vincent didn't even blink. He wantz to continue tomorrow, but I said no...imagine me—Rosemary Abla Frimpong—sayin' no to shoppin' and spendin' money."

"Where is Vincent? And who are those guys outside?"

"He bought more furniture and dey are rearrangin' da rooms upstairs."

"He doesn't have to go through all that...we're just staying for a week or two."

"Lissen, don't go insultin' him again. Hez a man, let him be a man and do wat he wants. You know, I was dinkin' in da car...doesn't dis remind you of dat movie? Dat movie wif Halle Berry and da rich ol' white man. Watz it called again?" She cuts a slice of baguette and devours it greedily. I can't understand her as she continues with her mouth full of French bread.

"Bi.......ches?"

"What?"

"*Bitches!*" she says loudly.

"No, it's not called *Bitches*."

"No, not *Bitches*....Beeeeeeaches.*" I swear her accent never fails. Every repetition sounds the same.

"No, that's not the title. *Beaches* was the movie about the two friends growing up and then one friend died at the end. You're thinking about that Halle Berry movie, B*A*P*S!" *We are definitely sisters and it is interesting how I thought the same thing.*

"Yeah, datz right." She taps my hand in agreement. "I can't rememba da other black girl's name. So I'm Halle Berry and yur da otha girl."

"How come I'm not Halle Berry?"

"Really…you know I look more like Halle Berry dan you do."

"Whatever, Halle Berry. Did you bring some food?"

"Yes. We ordered pizza for delivery and I brought jollof rice and chicken for da adults. Iz too late to start makin' soup. I will cook first ding tomorrow."

*

"**Ms. Frimpong?**" Alice's voice grabs my attention. "**I cannot detect Lord Gallo's vitals.**"

I drop the silverware into the sink and race to his suite. Julius is sitting on the edge of the bed pulling the connecting wires from the monitor and his body. Loud beeps and ringing goes off in the room.

"What are you doing?" He doesn't respond. After ripping the last cord from his arm, he struggles to rise, but he falls like a bag of cement. I move forward to help.

"Stop. Don't come close." He removes one of the bandages from his head. The other one is draped around his head and neck like a scarf. His stitches peek out. I move closer, but he holds his hands up. "Stop right there," he says. "Just leave me alone." He struggles to stand, but he is weak. The same fate, a quick fall to the ground.

"Let me help you, Julius. You need help."

"I don't! And for the last time, stand back." He grabs the bed sheet and tries to pull himself up and slides off the bed with the sheet covering him like an old piece of furniture. He swears and kicks the sheet off and tries again. He manages to rise momentarily and this time I rush to catch him before he falls down again.

"You are so damn stubborn. Let me help you."

"**Lord Gallo, should I reset the monitors?**"

"No. Shut them off," he says, breathless.

I rest him on the bed and stand over him. His head is bowed down. "What now? Just tell me what you need and I will get it for you."

"I have to go to the bathroom," he says.

"Where is your catheter?"

"I ripped it out and I need to take a shower."

"Nurse Hastings will be here shortly to give you a sponge bath."

"Fuck the sponge bath. I need a shower *now*. Please move out of my way," he says angrily.

"You can't even balance yourself to stand, let alone stand in a shower. It's not a good idea." He dismisses me and tries to rise from the bed. "Okay, let me call Vincent or Dr. Jesup."

"It doesn't matter who you call." He removes his shirt over his head. *He has definitely made up his mind to do this.* The image of him trying to have a shower and bumping his head or falling down comes strikingly to mind. He rises with trembling legs that seem like they will break if he stands a minute more.

"Watz going on?" Abla enters the room. "Vida, wat are you doin'?"

"Thank goodness, Abla. Please help me." She rushes toward us and holds Julius on the right side.

"Where are you takin' him?"

"He wants to take a shower."

"Can he?"

"No. But he's doing it anyway. Okay. On three we move toward the bathroom." I wrap my other arm around his waist and hold his arm around my shoulders. We step and glide until we reach the entrance of the bathroom. There is a vanity stool next to the door inside the bathroom. We place him there.

"Julius, are you sure about this?" He doesn't respond but begins removing his pajama pants.

"Yeah, he's doin' dis," Abla says. She leaves the bathroom.

"Where are you going?"

"I'm goin' to check on da kids."

"What about the shower? He can't stand in the shower alone."

"So wat do you want me to do?"

"You have experience in this."

"Experience in wat?" she says vehemently.

We move farther away from the bathroom door. "You know…bathing patients."

"Sayz who? You expect me to go in da shower wif him and bafe him naked? No chance, sista." She crosses her hands over her chest. "Plus, datz yur rich white friend. Minez back in Connecticut. You should do it."

"Me?" She raises her eyebrows and glares at me confirming what she just stated. There is no way I can do this. I peek my head in the bathroom doorway. Julius's naked body slithers toward the shower. It's upsetting to see him this fragile.

"Listen, we both can do it. I'll hold him up and then you wash him."

"Nonsense. Now you lissen." She shakes her head wildly. "Deer are certain dings sistas shouldn't do togeda. Dis is number two on my list." *I have a feeling about number one.* "And you should know wat number one is," she says.

"You're making it sound like some freaky deaky stuff. It's not. He needs help. Look at him. He's crawling into the shower." I point in the direction of the bathroom door.

"Datz why you need to help him."

"I can't. How would that look? Me, a married woman, getting into the shower with a naked man."

"Oh, stop running dat old sing song. Only you still dink yur married. You are da one makin' it sound freaky deaky. Like you said, he needz help. Yur a nurse; a professional medical caregiva, so behave like one. If a patient iz in pain, itz yur job to help dem feel betta. Are you goin' to tell yur patients you can't help dem because yur married? Nonsense." Before I can formulate an answer, she snaps back at me. "Just look at dis as sunbafin'. Instead of rubbin' sunblock on him, yur just usin' soap and wata"

Her words penetrate my soul. *She's right. He needs my help and all he wants is a shower.* Mommy used to shower us whenever we were ill. She said water had healing properties even better than some medicines. *Maybe this will make him feel better and less dependent on the pain medicine. I'm making this bigger than what it is. I've seen him naked before. Yeah, just think about it as sunbathing, but using soap and water.* I repeat Abla's words: *"Yur a professional, so behave like one."*

Abla continues her sales pitch. "I'm sure in a little village here in America dis iz happenin' and itz normal. You are doin' God's work and you will be rewarded. Just dink, extra points in heaven. You don't even haf to take off yur clothes. Leave yur bra and underwear on." She points to Julius lying halfway in the shower. "Just look at him. Hez sufferin' and he needs you to help him, Yaa." She rests her hand on my shoulders, reassuring me. Her words propel me to action. *I am the only one who can help him now.*

"Okay, I can do this."

"Good. I'll be yur lookout." She flies out of the room.

You are a professional, Vida. A quick shower and then out we go. You are a professional. Professional, all right. I believe they have a name for those ladies that starts with another P. Don't listen to that voice. Don't think too much. *Just do it. C'mon Vida…you can do this.* My black sweater and jeans fall onto the floor tile. For once I am wearing matching bra and panties. Not that anyone would know the difference, but it makes me feel like I have my shit together.

The shower is huge. Five people could easily fit inside.

"C'mon, Julius, let's get you onto the bench." With his help, I manage to raise him onto the shower bench. *Geez, how am I going to do this?* Rustic light brown tiles grace the shower from ceiling to floor. There are a dozen jet-stream nozzles all over the walls, three large shelves and four hooks against the wall. I look around the shower for a knob to turn on the water.

"Turn on shower heads," he says. Smaller jet streams I hadn't noticed above stream a gentle water shower. "It's voice recognition. Just say a command and it will adjust accordingly," he says.

Not sure where to speak, I tilt my head back toward the ceiling and make my request as though I am praying to a demigod. "Warmer water, please." The water stream adjusts and it feels warmer. "How is that?"

"Warmer," he says. The temperature gets comfortably hot. "Is this okay for you?"

"Yes, fine. How about you?"

"It's fine," he says. On the shelf to my surprise is a dark blue *sapo*. *I thought most white men just use bar soap to bathe.* There are several bath washes and bar soaps on a tray. I pick up the bar soap and smell it. It's a combination of citrus and mint. "Do you have a preference?"

"No. Any will do." His whole body trembles on the teak bench. I make my request to the demi water god for a forceful stream of water. The god answers my request and water massages our bodies. Julius tilts his head back and embraces the downpour. I slowly remove the bandages from his head and toss them out of the shower door. He touches his face and the stitches over his eye.

"It's healing nicely," I say. There is another incision site on the side of his head. It looks painful, but I touch it gently.

"How does that look?" he says.

"Hmmm. It's also healing nicely, but Dr. Jesup needs to remove the staples." *It's too late to keep it dry; we're already here. One shower I guess won't do any damage.* I lather the soap and begin my altruistic journey. He is relaxed. I press the sponge firmly against his neck in a circular motion then onto his chest. I lift his right arm and scrub firmly and gently and then move down to his fingertips. I move to the left side and continue in the same manner. I proceed to his stomach. *Damn, it's solid.* He tries to stand and I have his arm over my shoulders. He places his palm against the wall of the shower to support himself. He spreads his legs farther apart and there it is. *The Beast.* Undisturbed and at peace. *Alright, I'll save you for last.*

Continuing in the same firm and gentle manner, I wash his inner thighs then down to his calves and end at his feet. His toenails are perfectly clipped and I take my time to scrub in between his toes. I request to the demi water god to decrease the water pressure. It satisfies my request.

The Beast hangs there asleep. "Julius, place your palms back on the wall." He is still shaking and I support him with my left arm. I wrap the sponge around my hand to create a barrier between my fingers and his dick. I take it in my hands. I don't look down but focus on his face and begin to gently scrub in between his legs. I chant the words several times. *I am a professional.* I apply quick strokes as to not to awaken it. And then I take hold of his balls and scrub gently front to back. His face tenses. "Sorry, did that hurt?"

"No. I'm fine, Vida."

I continue in this manner and then squeeze the excess soap from the sponge and concentrate on his buttocks. He relaxes his cheeks and I scrub firmly the crack of his ass. I drop the sponge on the bench and allow the water to rinse the soap away. He is still shaking and though the shower mist makes the room feel warm, his body is cold. "Warmer, please." The god responds. "Julius, sit." I lather the bar soap in my hands. "Close your eyes." I stroke his face gently so as to not to disturb the stitches. Then a request for the jet streams to open and they begin to hit us in all parts of our body. I wash the excess soap and water from the sponge and then walk to the other end of the shower to hang it to dry.

"Are you ready to come out?"

"Please, a minute more," he says.

My hair cascades over my face. I pull it up and tie a makeshift knot. He is slouched against the tiles. He breathes heavily and makes loud groans. *Yes, water is a natural healer.*

"No jet-stream," I give my command. He chuckles.

"Power down, jet-stream." And the god recognizes his command.

"Oh, that was simple enough. I'll be back; let me get your robe."

"I don't like robes. The towels are to the left of the shower." *That should be of no surprise, considering he likes to walk around in the nude.*

I step out of the shower and the air is much cooler outside. I wrap a towel around my hair and another around me. I take two towels for him and step back into the shower. "Hold onto me," I say, raising him up to wrap a towel around his waist. I wrap the second towel over his head.

We slowly inch ourselves back to the bedroom. Abla has left her mark. The bed has new linens and in the center is a jar of shea butter. "That hefa."

"Is everything okay?" Julius asks.

"Yes." I sit him down on the edge of the bed. His left hand is swollen. I gently pat it dry. I'm sure it's from ripping out the IV. He looks solemn and delicate, an image that I am not accustomed to. After towel drying him, I begin to apply the shea butter to his skin. It warms instantly in my hands and onto his shoulders.

"What is that?"

"It's Abla's shea butter, she calls it 'Whip-That-Ash Shea Butter.'" I chuckle hoping to crack a smile from him. He says nothing. "Do you like it?"

He inhales deeply. "It's fine."

THE BORROWED WIFE

I continue to massage the shea butter into his skin and admire his dedication to looking fit. His inner right thigh has an usual birthmark. It looks like the continent of Africa. I rub my hands over it. *I will have to ask him about this another day.* My hands caress The Beast. *Maybe massaging it with shea butter is a bad idea.* It's still lying dormant. I focus on the rest of his body.

"Turn over so I can rub your back." He turns over limply. He is not the same Julius who would have created jest out of any situation. I mount him and my knees press into the mattress. My thighs rest slightly under his buttocks. The towel loosens and falls to my waist. I apply firm pressure as I massage his back from top of his shoulders to his buttocks. He moans lowly. I caress his arms to his fingers and then to his back making my way down his spine. He is enjoying it and I continue with deeper pressure where his back meets his butt. He moans again and I continue with kneaded fingers into his skin. Another moan, but a bit louder than the previous one, now silence. "Julius?" *Did he fall asleep?*

The door opens. *Oh, shit.* I'm frozen in position.

Dr. Jesup steps into the room with Nurse Hastings and Vincent behind him. "Excuse me, I didn't realize…ummm…I…" Dr. Jesup says. *This is one of those times when a blackout would be convenient.* I'm still hunched over Julius semi wet in my underwear and bra. Nurse Hastings' face looks like a long O. Vincent steps forward into the room and his eyebrows are knitted together. In my mere inappropriateness, although I am wearing matching undergarments, I feel ashamed. And in this shamefulness, I try to form words. I hope for something prolific or poignant, but the words escape my mouth and spiral through the air.

"It's purely professional," I say.

Dr. Jesup tilts his head slightly as if to say, 'You're full of shit.' Nurse Hastings' mouth finally closes, but she forms a wide smile then a snicker. Vincent turns to face them.

"Why don't we give him a minute or two?" Vincent says.

"Oh, certainly," Dr. Jesup replies and they leave, perhaps still dumbfounded about what they witnessed. Vincent moves closer to me and examines Julius. He says something in Italian and walks away to a separate room. He returns with a pair of pajamas and places them on the bed beside Julius.

335

"Let me know when he is ready and I will escort Dr. Jesup back." *Fuck…what must he be thinking? You really fucked up now, Vida. Shit…Shit…Shit…*

"Okay," I reply softly. I place the pajamas on him one leg at a time. He awakes to assists me with the top. Julius relaxes himself in a comfortable position on the bed. I quickly grab the clothing from the bathroom and then grab several towels, cocooning my body like someone wearing a large a king sized sheet. I open the door and Vincent is standing guard.

"Do you need my assistance?" he asks.

"No. I'm done." *I should explain to Vincent what actually occurred.* "Vincent…"

"Ms. Frimpong…" He pauses.

"Yes?"

"The children are looking for you." I anticipate more, but whatever is going to be said will probably be said another time.

"Okay. I'm heading in that direction," I say softly.

*

At least there is Haagen Dazs butter pecan to take my mind off the events of the last hour. One thing that Abla was able to do right today was buy enough butter pecan ice cream. The quart will be done in no time. I still have the image of Nurse Hastings' face in my head. *She's probably thinking I'm just some sleazy nurse trying to take advantage of him. And Dr. Jesup…Oh my goodness.* I take another spoonful of ice cream trying to shake the image from my head. As selfish as it may seem, I believe this is the time if any Jesus should have made his appearance to the world. He could have said something like: *"My dear children, cast not your eyes on what you see, but believe that this virtuous woman—okay, maybe not virtuous—this humble woman is exercising a command to help her fellow man. Do not judge her, for she is a good woman."*

More tablespoons of ice cream fill my mouth. There is a knock on the kitchen door and I hide the container of ice cream behind a ceramic bowl.

"Hey." Abla catches my gaze and I retrieve the hidden goodie. She pulls out another stool and sits beside me. "Da kids are fast asleep." I don't respond, but eye her nightgown. She is wearing a long black silk robe. Probably one of her new buys from today. I continue satisfying my sweet tooth.

"Who knew deerz a back entrance straight to Julius's room? It makes sense dat dey would pass drew da back because itz a shorta distance, but I dought dey would ring da bell and come drew da front door." She chuckles, but I'm not amused. She continues anyway. "Da kids and I were here in da kitchen. I dought Vincent was upstairs arrangin' furniture. I didn't even know deerz an elevator in here. Did you know deerz an elevator in here? Iz so conpikuas…" She means inconspicuous, but I'm not correcting her this time. "Ummmm …anyway I had no idea dat dey would be enterin' drew da back. And dat Alice. Wat kind—"

"Do you need my assistance, Abla?"

"Oh, now you want to offa azzistance, afta my sista haz been shamed to death in front of her medical peers? Only God knows wat types of rumors are bein' spread about her as we speak." I hold my head in my hands. "No, dank you. We don't need yur azzistance…" She pauses. "And from now on, you call me Mizzes Frimpong." She rubs my shoulders to comfort me, but I've eaten all my real comfort. "I bought you one of deezs too. Itz in a light pink color." She twirls around in front of me displaying the robe.

"Ms. Frimpong, Mr. Gallo would like to see you now."

"Do you want me to come wif you?" Abla says.

"Okay," I say. I've forgiven her already. It's hard staying mad at Abla. She is all I have now, besides the children.

"Like I said, Dr. Jesup, I don't need a night nurse. Ms. Frimpong is here and is more than capable of making sure I get my medication and she can contact you if anything warrants attention. She assisted me this evening without your staff. She can administer the medication and showers if necessary." Abla squeezes my hand and I want to say there will be no repeat performance. But maybe he is just saying that to get rid of the staff. "I am in capable hands. Vincent will see to it that the nurses are paid for the full month. I need my independence. Having staff here around the clock never makes me feel comfortable."

"That is not what I am applying by having staff here, Mr. Gallo. I will be by in a couple of days to examine your progress and run more tests. But I can't say that I like the idea without at least one of my PAs here. At least for some routine checks." Dr. Jesup searches the room for some support.

"I understand your concerns and I've made up my mind. If there is anything that is a concern, I will inform you. Thank you, Dr. Jesup."

"Very well. Can we talk further about the other tests?"

"Good night, Dr. Jesup." Julius is firm.

"Okay. I will follow up with you at the end of the week. And hopefully we can continue our discussion." Vincent leads them out.

Abla and I move closer to him. "What's going on?"

"I was a fool to have trusted him. I should have consulted with Dr. Braun again," Julius says.

"Concerning?"

He breathes deeply. "Never mind. It's nothing."

"Why did you get rid of the staff?"

"They are pretty much useless. Anyone can take temperature and scribble notes. You can do that."

"Oh," I say defensively.

"I don't mean that offensively. I'm not comfortable with people examining me and making me feel useless."

"Yur not. You just had maja surgery. Itz alright to ask for help, Boss," Abla says.

"I understand, but right now I don't need help," he says.

"Oh, you don't?" I say. He remains silent. It was just an hour ago that I held his balls in my hands.

After Abla leaves the room, I draw nearer to Julius.

"Do you need anything?" He shakes his head no. "Alright, I'm going to shower and go to bed."

"You're going to shower again? I thought we showered together."

"No. I bathed you. I need to have my own shower."

"Oh, I see. Can you give me my medication before you leave?"

"Your next dose is in four hours. It's right here on the chart." I tap the chart on the bedside table. "Don't think because I'm here you are going to take advantage of me."

"I wouldn't dream of taking advantage of you."

"Good, because there is a reason why I chose the administrative track of nursing. My bedside manners suck."

CHAPTER 48

Boom! Boom! I rise up from bed. "What the hell?"

"Mommy! Mommy, come quick!" Kakra's voice sounds urgently from the hallway. I leap from the bed. The foyer is still dimly lit, but the door behind the staircase is open and lit brightly.

"Kakra?" I yell. No response. I enter the room behind the stairs.

Boom! Boom! Solid thumping of drums. I don't need to see who it is, because only one person I know can manage to find a drum set in the middle of the night and begin a concert.

"Panin. It's after midnight. What are you doing here? How did you get inside?" All the lights are on and Kakra stands beside him as he beats against the drums. Panin is anxious. I can see it in his eyes, erratically searching for something. He's in a strange house that I forced him to stay in. He can't cope. *This will comfort him. He needs to release his frustration.* Kakra and I both know it. Abla stands behind me and I can smell the cologne that Vincent wears. Kakra picks up one of the drumsticks and drums along with him. *This may take a couple of minutes.*

I turn to apologize to Vincent for the disruption, but he has settled quite comfortably in Julius's corner.

"I know he needs dis. Let him be. Hez not hurtin' anyone," Abla says. After a few minutes we find an empty space on the floor and nestle together watching brothers comfort each other.

Chapter 49

It's been over a week since I embarked on this selfless excursion. Julius's walk is a little steadier. A walker is much more suitable, but he insists on struggling with a heavy wooden cane. He still needs assistance in the shower and at times has terrible trembling fits as a result of the medication. This is our fifth shower together and I still haven't gotten used to it. I pick up a soap. I bring the bar to his nose and he inhales it. "Is the minty one finished?"

"Yes," I answer.

"I will have to remind Max to pick up more of that soap. You can't get it here in New York."

"Fancy stuff?"

"Not really…made overseas. Perhaps there is a distributor here, but Max knows where to order it. It's made in Greece."

"Hmmm…like I said, fancy stuff. I'll stick with my Shea Moisture products."

"Okay, we should use it next time." *Next time? Abla has to find someone to continue doing this.* "You know there are professionals—" *There goes that word again* "—who do this?"

"Do what?" I lather the soap on his scalp and scrub firmly. "Bathe patients? Oh really, a professional bather? Interesting." His lips part and his eyes remain closed. *He's enjoying this head massage.*

"Yes. They probably do a better job than me," I continue.

"I really find that hard to believe. Your hands feel…" *Yeah, enjoying this more than he should.* "…feel really good." *His voice sounds aroused.* I stop and continue onto his shoulders. "That felt wonderful," Julius says.

"Your hair is growing back, so your scalp is a bit more tender."

He moans. I continue washing from his shoulders to his arms and torso, thighs and feet. I save The Beast for last. "Okay, stand up." He does so shakingly. His palms press firmly against the tiles as I scrub his back. I rinse the sponge and grab the bar of soap. It slips from my hand into the pool of water by our feet. I bend down to chase the bar with my fingers and I suddenly feel pressure on my ass. *It's The Beast.* Julius grabs my butt cheek.

"Hey! What are you doing?"

He seems disoriented. "My apologies. I wasn't sure what…" I look down at the resurrection. Just as I remembered it from the first time. I drop the soap a second time. *I'm definitely not picking it up again.* "I'm sorry…I just didn't know what you were doing." *It's confirmed: never drop a bar of soap when you are in the shower with a man.* The Beast is pointing north and it doesn't look like it's heading south anytime soon. *I can't touch it now.* There is an unsettling silence between us. He sits down. "I think I can manage." He holds out his hand and I give him the sponge.

"I'll get the towel."

Heavy white terry cotton towels hang outside. I grab my robe and towel my hair into a turban. I take two towels for Julius and wait outside until he is done. He places one of the towels over his waist and I pull his arm around me as he exits the shower. He breathes a sigh of relief when his ass hits the bed.

"What color are they?" Julius asks.

"What?"

"Your waist beads? I felt three."

"Red and gold. Well, two gold and one red," I say. It's an unusual question to ask, but then I suppose it wouldn't be for Julius. *Should I have disclosed that?* Mommy used to say if another man tells your husband the color of your waist beads, then it is a confirmation you are having an affair. Waist beads should be hidden underneath your clothes and for your husband's eyes only. It's a silly idea, but with recent events, I can see how things could get distorted.

"Are you still upset with Dr. Jesup?" I say, hoping to close the distance between us.

"Yes. No. Not really."

"He seems very optimistic," I say as I apply the shea butter to his back.

"Yeah, you would if you are out to make a name for yourself."

I'm not sure what he is alluding to. He begins his gentle moan. And this time I rush through the massage in fear I may resurrect The Beast again.

"Are you going somewhere?"

"No. Why do you ask?"

"You seem hurried."

"Well, actually I promised to call Felix tonight."

"Oh, Felix, the friend."

"Yeah, it's been a while since we spoke and I feel guilty that he's called and that I never returned his call. He drives a yellow cab at night, so this would be the best time to speak with him."

"I see." He seems unimpressed. I finish the massage and wipe the excess shea butter off my hands.

"There you are. Shiny like a brand new penny." He chuckles. "Speaking of Penny—"

"No I haven't told her and I am not ready to call her. That's all I'm going to say on the matter."

"Okay." I hold my hands up in surrender. "It's getting late, so if you need anything just ring. Have a good night." As I make my way to the door, he stops me.

"Vida?"

"Yes, my Lord?" He smiles.

"Thank you."

"N-T-Y-B-F."

*

It's nearly eleven o'clock and Abla is still on the phone. *That can't be Pancake.* She is speaking in Ga, which tells me that she is definitely talking to one of her Ghanaian friends. Pancake understands Ga well, but never truly learned to speak it as fluently as Spanish. I grew up similarly, but never mastered another language the way I wanted to. Which is why it is even more important for the children to learn Twi.

"Richard says hi."

"Hmmm. I guess everything is back to normal." She never revealed what made her upset with him.

"Yes. All iz well. We were goin' to have Skype sex before you came in here." I roll my eyes.

"With the kids in the room?"

"Oooh, pleazze. Dey sleepin'."

"Why are you guys still sharing a room anyways? Didn't Vincent furnish the other room for the children?"

"Sista, I've watched enough haunted house movies to know I don't want to sleep by myself. Plus we are all comfortable here." Kakra and MJ are asleep on the opposite bed. I lie down on the edge of Abla's bed. *It does look cozy in here.* "I haf good news and den I haf really good news."

"Okay, let me have it."

"I spoke wif a professional bafer."

"You did?"

"Yep. Her name iz Greta and she will start tomorrow." *I should be happy that I don't have to do this task again, but then again who is this woman? And more frightening is how does Abla know where to locate these people?* "Didn't I tell you I would look out for you?"

"Where did you find her?"

"I called some agencies."

"Some agencies?" More skepticism.

"Yeah. A friend of a friend told me about one. And deerz a company. I'm sure dey provide otha services. So I described wat we needed done and we needed causefidenlitty."

"Confidentiality?" I correct her.

"Yep, that too." Sometimes she gets it and sometimes she doesn't.

There are dozens of questions that plague my mind, but I decide to have faith in Abla that whoever is coming tomorrow will be a professional. Plus, after the episode earlier with Julius, I would welcome a fairy godmother if it was possible.

"Iz set for tomorrow den."

"What's the next good news?"

"Felix has been burning up da lines tryin' to reach you. Richard says datz all he talks about. He's worried about you. I dink hez kinda of jealous dat yur stayin' here."

"I'll call him after my shower."

"I don't understand why you insist on double work. Why showa again afta you bafe Julius?" I turn my head and glance at the boys. They are fast asleep but I gesture for Abla to lower her voice. "You should just showa while you are deer wif him."

"And that won't be inappropriate."

"Please. He can't see and deerfore don't know wat iz goin' on."

"It doesn't feel right to me." She shakes her head.

"Anywayz, how does it feel?"

"What?"

"Washin' hiz balls?" She laughs loudly and then tries to silence her laughter by covering her mouth.

"I'm not beginning to have this conversation, Abla. There is nothing sexual about this. I'm just…" I dread the word 'professional.' "I'm just helping a friend out."

She smirks. "Mark it on da wall dat Rosemary Abla Frimpong said dis." She rises from the bed and marks a cross with her fingers on the wall.

Mark it on the wall is a usual African declaration. It represents something foreboding, an ultimatum or even a threat. When someone tells you this, it is a cautionary warning. Only God knows Abla has marked enough walls to erect the Smithsonian. I listen in anticipation of what mark this is. "Are you lissenin'?"

"All ears."

She continues. "Da woman who holds a manz ballz in her hands haz total power ova him."

"Wow, Abla. That sounds prophetic," I say sarcastically. "Is that another Ablaism?"

"Hmmm…okay…you will come back one day and tell me somedin'. For now I'm just watchin'."

"Whatever, oh great one. I'm going to have my shower."

"Lissen, after da shower wear da pretty pink robe and matchin' kitty heels I got you. It will put you in da mood when you start talkin' to Felix."

I wave at her dismissively.

Chapter 50

"Hello, Ms. Fretpon. I zink we haf big problem." Greta is standing in the kitchen. She looks anxious. She twists her fingers as though she is squeezing water from a rag.

"What is it?" I say.

"Mr. Gallo say no to shower. He say he wait for you."

I hear little chuckles. "Hmmm...Hmmm. Looks like yur baby wants hiz mommy," Abla says.

"No, Greta, that's why you here. I explain to him you come today to bathe him." I find myself speaking in the same broken English.

"Umm, Ms. Fretpon, I zink he...ummmm...scared... maybe you talk him again."

"For the love of God. Why does this have to be so difficult?" Abla's laughter is louder. "This is not funny, Abla."

"Oh, yes it iz."

I follow Greta back to the room. She is prettier than I imagined. Young, tall with long blonde locks. Her arms give the appearance that she works out. She isn't wearing a bra. Her boobs have a perky jiggle as she walks. She reminds me of a young Heidi Klum. *I wonder what his problem is? I assumed he would like this.* Greta gives a gentle knock. "Mr. Gallo, me again and Ms. Fretpon." Her German accent limits my name to whole new pronunciation.

Julius answers. "Come in." *His voice sounds peculiar.*

"Hi, Mr. Gallo. I haf Ms. Fretpon. I know you want shower so we help you. Okay?"

"I don't feel comfortable taking off my clothes to a complete stranger," Julius says.

"What? You're joking," I scoff.

"Ms. Fretpon, zat's fine. You haf much pain. No worry, we try and make you good again." Julius actually looks vulnerable.

"I am used to Ms. Fretpon"—he pronounces my name in the same German accent—"showering me. You know, once you get used to someone it's hard to just acclimate to someone new."

"I know, Mr. Gallo. Ms. Fretpon, maybe you do sponge bath in shower with Mr. Gallo."

"Well, Greta, like I told Mr. Gallo, I may not always be available to give him his showers and we already talked about hiring a professional. That is why you are here," I say.

"Oh yes, I do recall you mentioning something like that. But with the medication and all, it's so hard to remember basic conversations. I am really trying very hard to exercise a level of independence. I hate to rely on someone to do such a simple task as giving me a shower. I am sorry, Ms. Greta, that you had to come all this way. It's just a big step for me. You know...this change. I hope you can understand." He expresses enough sentiments to turn this to a Charles Dickens story.

Greta looks as though she wants to break out in tears. I smelled bullshit from the time we entered his bedroom. *He may be a contender in narrating unicorn stories.* She kneels beside him and holds his hand. "Oh, Mr. Gallo, you brave. You want to free again. Letz try zis. Me, you and Ms. Fretpon, we all shower together."

"What the hell?" *I did say that out loud. I mean, really. She must be fucking joking.* Julius raises his head and I know that Machiavellian grin.

"Really?" he says, sobering into a smile.

"Yes. All us together, zen I watch Ms. Fretpon shower you. I learn and zen I do same zing. Zis will make you strong and brave." She beats her chest.

"You know, Ms. Fretpon is very good at bathing me. Not many people take as extra care as she does. I don't want to put too much pressure on you to do an equally good job."

"No problem...no matter how long...I learn."

"That's good to know." The grin is wider. Julius takes a deep breath and exhales. "You know, Ms. Fretpon is very strong after the shower; she usually massages me with shea butter."

"Okay, we do together too." She strokes his hand and he gives another deep sigh of empathy.

"Well, let's try it today and see. I know you want to make me feel good," Julius says.

Greta removes her blouse, confirming she is not wearing a bra. She turns to me. "You take off cloze, Ms. Fretpon."

"Hold on, Heidi—I mean Greta—can you give Mr. Gallo and I a moment? I want to prep him a little bit before the shower."

"Okay. Okay. I go get coffee from kitchen. I don't have underwear, so I no take long."

"I bet." Julius hears her admission and a bright smile cuts through the room. "Wow, that Greta is…is….Where did you find her? And to think, she thought about this all by herself."

"Bullshit."

"Excuse me, Ms. Fretpon," Julius says sarcastically.

"You are some piece of work. What did you think was actually going to happen here today?"

"I don't know. Why didn't you tell me you hired a professional bather? You mentioned it, but I didn't take you seriously. I didn't even know that people like her existed. Is there a directory?"

"She came recommended."

"From who?"

"Abla found her."

"Ahhh, yes the PR-slash-manager-slash-sister."

"This is beside the point; we can't keep showering together." He looks disappointed.

"I didn't know that it was such a burden on you."

"It's not. It's just that you know that you are getting better and…" The flashback to his full erection when I bent down will forever be tattooed in my brain. "Well, it wouldn't be right."

"What are friends for?"

"How many friends do you know that would actually get in the shower with you and bathe you?" He pauses in thought.

"Just two."

"Two?"

"And you are one."

"Who is the other one?"

"That will go with me to my grave."

"I see. You know you're milking this, right?"

"How so?"

"Your reflexes are coming back and you are much steadier."

"Says who?" He is already standing and positions himself in a Superman stance. If his erection is coming in full swing, then I know his reflexes are probably picking up. I've seen him before detect something waving in front of him like the time Daniel waved his hand in his direction. Or the kids kicking a ball toward his head. I pick up the remote control by the bedside table and throw it in his direction. *Just as I expected.* He catches it.

"Huh. Says me."

He laughs. "Ms. Fretpon, it appears that you've uncovered my bluff."

"Should I send Greta home then?"

"I don't know. Are we going to try this once?"

"Not in this lifetime."

"Okay. It was worth a try. Send her on her way."

Chapter 51

The purple satin jumper with black spaghetti straps clings to my body in all the right places. It's one of Abla's picks for me from one of her shopping sprees. *I just may ignite a fire in this outfit. If this doesn't grab his attention, then he is definitely not a fan.* The house is unusually quiet. *Where is everyone?* They are not in the kitchen or in the library, but I hear giggling and short outbursts coming from Julius's study. My heels click against the travertine floors as I travel in that direction. Abla, Vincent and Kakra are sitting around a table playing Ludo. Julius stands over them appearing amused.

"Wow, Mommy, you look beautiful."

"Thank you, dear. Why are you still up when your brothers are sleeping?"

"But tomorrow is a half a day."

"It's still a school day," I say.

"Well, well, missy, now datz da lil sista I rememba. You go gurl wit yur sexy self," Abla says.

"Bellissima," Vincent says.

"Thank you, thank you. I'm stepping out this evening." *Huh, no remarks from Julius.* His lips tightened.

"So where is Felix taking you?" Abla asks.

"I'm not sure. I just told him to pick me up in an hour, so he's on his way over."

"You were serious," Julius finally says.

"What?"

"About going out tonight," he clarifies.

"Yeah. I told you I had plans this morning."

"I assumed plans meant writing or something. I didn't know…" He sighs deeply and then silences his thought.

"Kakra, itz way past yur bedtime, and like Mommy said, tomorrowz school."

"Good night, Ms. Frimpong." Vincent takes the lead out of the room.

"Good night, Vincent." I turn toward Kakra. "Okay mister, it's time for you to go to bed. Good night, dear." I give him a kiss on the cheek and he follows Abla reluctantly.

"You never mentioned Felix when you alluded to your plans this evening." *Is he still on this topic?*

"Okay, well now you know." He pushes his cane to the floor and leans against the sofa.

"Isn't it late to go out?"

"What time is it?" I pretend as though I'm concerned about the time. *Let's see where he takes this conversation.*

"Alice?"

"Yes, my Lord."

"Time please?"

"Nine forty-two p.m., my Lord."

"Thank you. It's almost ten p.m. on a Monday night. Where could he possibly take you at this hour?"

"I don't know and right now I don't care." *Where is my cellphone? Did I leave it here or the library? Oh yes, there it is on the desk by the window.* I brush past him to get to the desk and his hands caress my thigh.

"Is that silk?"

Unbelievable. He has the audacity. "No, satin."

"You should change your clothes."

"Excuse me?"

"You heard me. Wear something else. This is not suitable."

"What is wrong with my clothes?"

"There is nothing wrong with your clothes. It's the way you look in them."

"And what way would that be?"

He appears frustrated. His hands rest on his hips and his brows furrow in disapproval. "I don't think you should go out with Felix wearing those clothes and especially those shoes."

"Oh, now my shoes are included in your displeasure?"

"You know exactly what I am alluding to."

"No, I don't."

"C'mon, fuck-me-pumps at ten p.m."

"These are not F-M-Ps."

"I know fuck-me-pumps when I hear them. And those are definitely fuck-me-pumps."

"Huh. This heel is not even three inches high. And even if they are, maybe that's the point of me wearing them."

"By Felix? You're joking."

"Why would I be joking?"

He pauses. "Vida. Change your clothes."

"Now look who's telling jokes. There is nothing wrong with what I am wearing. I think I look very sexy."

"That's the problem. I can tell your clothing clings to your body like plastic wrap on pasta. Trust me, you need to change."

"Because Father Gallo says so?"

He laughs again. Now his arms are folded across his chest. His brows are more furrowed than two minutes ago. "May I?" he says. He extends his hands until he feels mine. I move closer, waiting to see what he wants to discover. He moves his hands from my neck down to my shoulders, touching pieces of fabric on my shoulders and then he lightly touches my breast and notices the deep plunging neckline.

"What the hell?" I step back.

"Enlighten me, please," he says. I sigh and allow him to continue. He slides his hand from my waist down my thigh and around the back of my knee. He stops and lips are squeezed tightly together. "You are not wearing undergarments. No panties?" His voice is a bit louder.

"How can you tell?"

"This is not my first dance."

He positions his arms in a Superman stance again. "I heard your beads dancing on your buttocks the moment you walked into this room, which concludes you're either wearing a thong or no undergarments. And since I know they haven't invented a thong that can suit you, I am sticking to my second assumption."

"Mother F-er. What the hell do you mean they don't make thongs in my size? First, let me remind you that my father is retired and living in Ghana. Did he make you his spokesperson? Even then, he would never—" Furor rises in my voice. I digress. "Second, I am not changing my clothes because Lord Julius Gallo says so. Third, they do make thongs for full-figured women. In fact, I'm wearing one. Perhaps if you were fucking some voluptuous women instead of these stick figures marching in here, you would know. Thank you for being concerned, but boo boo, I'm good."

"All right, whatever you say. You still need to change your clothes. Men look at you and especially the way you look and different thoughts cross their minds."

"What do you mean, 'especially the way I look'?"

"Big asses always attract attention and those clothes just accentuate those features. And that makes men turn and look at you in a sexual way."

"Ohhh, my God…what did you say?"

"Oh, please. This is not breaking news. I am not the first man to tell you that, I'm sure."

"Big, fat, donkey booty, apple butt, bubble butt—these are all synonyms that mean the same thing. I can't believe you just said that."

"Wait. You are taking it the wrong way. There is nothing wrong with a big ass. You said it a moment ago that you were full-figured. I am just emphasizing you have a nice shape and certain clothes just accentuate that."

"You know what? My big black ass and my fuck-me-pumps are leaving. Thank you for your critique, but I'm good just the way I am."

"Vida, don't walk away."

"Good night, Julius. I'm not entertaining you any longer." I grab my purse and stomp toward the door.

"Vida! Vida!" he calls to me, but I don't want to hear any more. "Alice, lock doors please." The doors swing closed within two steps from me.

"What did you just do?" He stands upright, shoulders still squared.

"I am not done talking to you."

"Did you just lock me in this room?"

"Vida, I told you what to do and I will not repeat myself."

"Alice, open the door please," I yell into the ceiling.

"I'm sorry, Ms. Frimpong, but Lord Gallo's directive supersedes any other directive."

He stands firmly by the table. "You will thank me one day." An angry chuckle escapes my mouth. The room seems small and he even smaller to me. *I can't believe that he is commanding me to do something as though I were his child.*

"Julius, you have three seconds to open this door before this goes to a whole other level. Trust me, this will not end pretty."

"Change or spend the night in this room," he says.

"You're out of your fucking mind." He doesn't flinch or waver in his stance. *Okay, this is how you want to play it, Lord Gallo? Well, your castle is going to crumble before you.* "I am going to count to three and this door betta be open. One…"

"You don't intimidate me, Vida." He towers over me even with my black pumps on.

"Two…"

"You are being unreasonable. I know men. One look at you and only one thing will come to mind: their cock in between your legs."

"Three…"

No movement from Julius or Alice. I slip out of my black pumps and survey the room for something heavy. I grab his cane from the floor and I move over to the French doors behind the desk.

"What are you doing?"

I tear down the curtains covering the doors and knock on the door to feel the weight. The doors are heavy pane glass. We are slightly higher than ground level and I believe I can jump out the window if I have to. *Really, Vida, jump out the window? Fuck. I can't back down now.* I push the desk back to give me enough room to make my swing, nearly running over his foot in the process.

"You are not serious. You wouldn't," he says, alarmed.

I take one good look at him and warm up my arm with his cane in my right hand. *Hmmm…this is the rush baseball players must feel.* Afternoons at Yankee Stadium with my father fill my thoughts. I believe I am holding the cane like Derek Jeter at bat. I tap the glass gently where I want the cane to land.

"Vida? Vida? This is not funny."

One more look. *Okay, suit yourself, Lord Gallo.* He swallows hard. I pull my arms as far back as I can and he yells out.

"Alice!"

Alice is prepared. My arm's still in mid-air when the door automatically opens. Julius slumps over the desk. The cane makes a loud thump when I drop it onto the travertine floor. He looks more ashamed than angry.

"Never corner a lion unless you are up for the fight," I whisper to him as I pick up my pumps and purse once again. "Thank you, Alice."

"You are welcome, Ms. Frimpong."

Chapter 52

A night out with Felix is feeling like a waste of time. I hate to admit it and prove Julius right. Of course there is no movie available at this time of night. We have been driving around for some time now. He talks beautifully about his children, but seldom inquires about mine. The few times he does ask, it feels like a competition of achievements between his daughters and my sons.

"Do your boys do karate?"

"No, not yet. I am hoping to try MJ next year. Between music lessons and soccer practice with the twins, it's hard to find time."

"Gabrielle just received another notch on her belt. She is doing very well. It requires discipline. My other two daughters are taking up soccer now, but they prefer softball. Do your boys play softball?"

"No. Kakra loves soccer. His team has won several games already this year."

"Yeah, maybe you can sign the kids up for karate and we can carpool together." I smile but don't respond. *Talk less and listen more, Vida.* "It's a lot of work raising boys. I think it's more work than girls. What do you think?"

"I believe every child, regardless of the sex or age, comes with its own blessings and challenges."

"I like that. And it's very true. So, do you want more children?"

"Ha." *That was a bit loud, Vida.* Felix takes a glance at me. "The shop is closed."

"Oh c'mon, you are still young, Vida. You are very beautiful and you definitely keep yourself in good shape. Don't give up too soon. I can see a little Vida running around with the same beautiful bouncy hair and the same beautiful eyes."

Okay, Felix, keep the compliments coming. "Thank you." Honestly, the last thing I want to think about is another child, especially with anyone else. Auntie Cece nags me enough to try for the girl. It takes two to make it happen, is my usual response. Mensah traveled so much during our marriage that I'm surprised MJ came along. "It's in God's hands. If it's meant to be, then it is meant to be."

"I bet you and I could have beautiful kids together." *Wow, hold up. Let's rewind a bit. I haven't even kissed you, and already you're moving in and turning us into a Modern Family?* I smile, not knowing how to respond politely. "What about a drink?"

"Okay. I know a spot in Harlem if you want to drive a bit farther uptown."

"Sure, why not?" He maneuvers the steering wheel skillfully with one hand. Something about the way he drives makes me feel at ease, surely the skills he gained from many years driving New York City yellow cabs. "You know, I was a bit concerned when I learned you were staying with your boss. I mean, that's unheard of. Just watch these rich folks; I don't want anything to happen to you."

"Abla and the children are with me and we are doing fine. Julius just needs a little support during this difficult time. He has his ways, but he's a good person." The incident earlier this evening says otherwise, but I'm glad I set him straight and set my boundaries. *The nerve of him telling me what I can and cannot wear.*

"Hmmm. I'm just saying watch out. That is how *they* came to Ghana. The *obrunis* holding a Bible in their hands spreading love and peace, and before you know it, they were shipping our mothers, fathers, brothers and sisters to another land."

"Point taken."

"So, does your son go to a special school?"

"For?"

"You know, his studies. I can only imagine your frustration. It must be hard not being able to talk and communicate with him."

"I communicate with him just fine. It may not be the way other people are accustomed to. But we do understand each other."

"Yeah, but that's not the real world. You're his mother, and for sure you can tolerate certain behaviors, but the world is not kind to people who are—"

"Who are what?" I adjust myself in the leather seat.

"You know—different. If this were Ghana, when he was still a baby you could have sent him to the herbalist. But this is America and they want to give special names and conditions to children. Don't get too Americanized; the way they do things here is different from back home."

"I don't know if it would be any different if he was sent back home. We are doing everything we can here to make sure he gets the proper services. He is actually doing a lot better than some of his classmates." I feel the need to defend Panin. It has always been a fight I will take up any day or time. *We need to change topics or I may say something I may regret.* "What CD are you playing?"

"Oh, I got this one from Mike and Lizzie's outdooring. You haven't played it yet?" I remember that Mensah took the CD and I imagine it blaring in his car in Sacramento with Kate sitting beside him. "I like the way you dance."

"Really?" I'm still a bit disturbed by his Americanized comment, but putting on a fake smile. Why do some Ghanaians always make it seem like being Americanized is a bad thing? After all, my mother and father came here in search of a better life. *Is it so bad to be Americanized?* But Americanized means the clothes you wear, how you speak English, the friends you associate yourself with and the schools you attend. I honestly feel blessed because I have the best of both worlds.

"Is that you ringing?" I detect the ringing in between the breaks of the bass thumping.

"Oh, yes. That's my cellphone." He presses a button on the dashboard and the call comes through the car speakers.

"Felix, where are you?"

"I'm out. What's going on?" *It must be the Mrs.* His tone changes. More firm and indifferent.

"I'm in the hospital with Jessica—come quick."

"Which hospital?"

"The Children's Hospital at Montefiore on Gun Hill Road."

"I'm on my way." His voice rises in fear. "What happened? Why?"

"Just hurry," are the last words Felix's wife utters.

"I hope everything's okay." He says nothing, but maneuvers skillfully through New York City traffic above speed limits. *Maybe I should get out and take a cab.* I can't form my lips to say it. He looks petrified. "Do you want me to drive? You're upset."

"What could have happened to my baby girl?" he says softly.

"I'm sure she is going to be fine." His face contorts with more anxiousness.

"I shouldn't have left them tonight."

"Don't think the worst. Let's get there and find out what happened." It's a miserable feeling that I know too well. Like bricks weighing you down and making it hard to breathe. You don't breathe until you see your child and you know everything is okay.

We arrive at the hospital within twenty minutes. This is a perfect time to hop into a cab and talk to him later, but he needs a friend. I accompany him through several double doors and into the ER waiting room. Felix's wife and two other daughters are seated in the back of the ER.

"Daddy!" they cry when they spot Felix.

Maybe it's me and the fact that Julius's words are still ringing in my head, but I swear these sad and sickly faces in the ER immediately animate when I appear. The sight of my bright clinging purple jumpsuit with the plunging neckline, to say the least, is a spectacle. A boy leaning over his father's lap coughing profusely immediately raises his head as though it is Christmas morning. His hacking cough quiets and his pale white skin takes on a slight tan. I walk beside Felix with my arms crossed over my chest. Mothers look at me with envy—*okay, maybe a little disgust*—while others welcome the needed distraction. The security guard who looked asleep when we first stepped in wakes up to watch as I walk across the ER. His eyes focus on me like a man focused on racetrack numbers. The click-click of my pumps bring added attention to me. The floor tiles are slippery and I take my time to walk. It seems like I've been walking toward Felix's wife for hours. Slow walking only makes my stride more noticeable and quick steps bring attention to my body's movement in the jumpsuit. *I can't control the rhythm of my ass. It's going to jiggle no matter how slow or fast I walk, more noticeable with satin clinging to the curves of my body.* Julius was right; I should have changed clothes, especially now in view of children. *I must be the greatest show on earth.*

Felix's wife is none too happy to see me. I contemplate waiting outside, but Felix grabs my hand and leads me closer to his family.

"What happened?" Felix says.

"She was crying and then she started throwing up. She had a slightly high fever. So I brought her in. She's in the restroom," Felix's wife says. That doesn't seem like a big emergency, but nevertheless I listen without saying a word. She continues, "We just got finished with the doctor. He gave her Motrin and told me to follow up with the pediatrician tomorrow."

If his wife's eyes could emit lasers, she would cut me into fun-size pieces. I move away from her eyesight and find an empty seat next to Felix's youngest daughter and a colicky baby. The colicky baby struggles for my attention. He stretches his doughy arms toward me. He must think I have food to soothe him. *Poor baby. The jugs are out, but not for baby consumption. In fact, this outfit wasn't meant for children's eyes, or even Felix's. Just something to pick up my spirits again. If I knew my night was going to end up like this, a bedsheet would have been more appropriate.* The room is filled with adults in pajamas or last minute pulled together outfits and here I am looking like I came to church wearing a bikini.

"I think she was upset that they were not staying with you tonight," Felix's wife says as Jessica emerges from the bathroom.

"I told you girls that I will pick you up this weekend. Come on, Jessica, you really had me worried. It's only a few more days and we can spend the whole weekend together," Felix says.

"I know you. You're Alba's younger sister, right?" Felix's wife moves past her daughters to stand in front of me.

"Yes. I am." I rise to shake her hand, but she leaves me hanging. *Vida, you knew that was coming.*

"Is this the reason why you don't have time to spend with your daughters?" The disdain in Felix's wife's voice and her laser-like eyes could unleash a catfight at any moment.

"Please, don't start. The children are here." Felix turns to Jessica. "How are you feeling, princess?"

"Much better now that you are here, Daddy. I want you to come home, Daddy. Come back home to us," Jessica says. It's an awkward situation and my bootyhugging-satin-no-underwear-jumpsuit-with-F-M-Ps has to leave. I rub's Felix shoulder to get his attention.

"I'm going to go. I'll call you later." I bend my knees slightly to bring myself to Jessica's level. "I'm glad you're feeling better." She cuts me with her junior laser-like eyes, no doubt inherited from her mother.

"Let's drop you home first," Felix says.

"No, please. I can manage getting home. You need to be here with your family. Have a good night." I make my way across the ER again, cursing myself for wearing this outfit.

A toddler yells out, "Barney!" *I'm done.* Felix's wife's seals my embarrassment with her loud voice. *"Ashawo Acatta!" I guess in this outfit, I could pass for an American nightwalker…No, Vida…a high-priced escort.* In any case, it is an insult.

*

Uber brings me home within thirty minutes. The lights in Julius's study are dimly lit. I make my way toward the staircase to check on Abla and the children. Julius stands by the study's door. He is the last person I want to speak to tonight.

"Good evening, Vida. You are home earlier than I expected."

"What time was my curfew?"

He laments deeply. "I'm sorry, Vida. I had no reason to treat you like a child or command you to do anything. I feel rather imprudent for my behavior earlier."

I sigh without commenting on the last hour with Felix. "All is forgiven." I continue ascending the stairs. Abla and MJ are in one bed asleep and Kakra is in the other bed spread diagonally across it.

In my room, my side of the bed is neatly tucked in. Panin has fallen into a deep sleep. I undress quickly and remove my makeup and lie next to him. A few minutes pass and I realize I'm not nearly as tired as I thought I was. *I need to do some writing.* I take the laptop from the library and head to Julius's study. Phil Collins is blaring through the speakers. The door is open, but I still knock. "Hi."

"Hello?"

"Do you want some company?"

"Yes," he says hastily. I find an empty desk to lay the laptop. He resumes typing on his braille machine. "So, how was the movie?"

"We couldn't get a show." *And that's all the information you are going to get, Mr. Gallo.*

"Not many good places to eat at this time during the week." *Still fishing, huh Julius?* "Are you hungry?"

"No. Are you?" He doesn't reply. Truth is, I am hungry, but that would only let Julius know that my date was not successful. The hunger pains scream out of me and the blank screen welcomes me to type. I send Felix an IM message letting him know that I reached home safely and wish Jessica a speedy recover. The laptop pings almost instantaneously.

"I'm glad you are home safely. I'm home with the girls but only for tonight. Sorry about this evening. I will call you in the morning."

It is clear that his wife still loves him and that his daughters are the center of his universe. Felix should try to make it work with his wife. *I need to tell him that the next time I see him.*

I can't resist the food cravings any longer. *Let's see what I can procure from the kitchen.*

"Where are you going?"

"To the kitchen. Would you like something?"

"No," he says indecisively.

I return with a bowl of Haagen Dazs ice cream and two spoons. A little reward for a rough evening. Julius stops typing at his braille machine. He recognizes the scent and paces the room. I chuck my kitty slippers and bury my feet into the loveseat. He moves closer to me.

"I have another spoon if you're interested." He smiles brightly and navigates his way onto the loveseat.

"What are you working on?"

"Two things. I am updating Alice's security system. Sometimes you get persistent hackers trying to hack into high security walls. And a prototype that came to me in a dream." He points to a black box that looks like a cable device. "It's not much yet, but I'm piecing together what I saw in my dream."

"Interesting." I want to ask him what his dreams are like. *Does he dream in color? Who does he see?* But I save my inquisition for another night. He needs to know that he can't command me like a child.

"So when will I have the extreme pleasure in officially meeting your friend?" Julius says.

"Felix?"

"Yes. Felix," he says whimsically.

"I don't know. Perhaps when we go out again." I am not sure of that future, but Julius doesn't have to know that.

"I see. You don't sound sure of a second date." *There he goes, fishing for more information.* I shove a spoonful of ice cream in my mouth, avoiding the answer. Haagen Dazs to the rescue. "So, a nice dinner late on a Monday night. He is a strategic planner." *Hmmmm. Go fish, Julius.*

"We had interesting topics of discussion." I take one last scoop and decide four scoops are just enough. Julius continues eating, taking half spoons of ice cream in. His lips are tinged pink. He sticks his tongue out just a little before the spoon enters his mouth and then he holds it in his mouth for few seconds longer than I would. He licks the corner of his lips and pauses before taking in more ice cream. The next scoop enters the same way, but this time he sucks his bottom lip and then the top lip. I'm trying to turn my attention onto something else. I grab the laptop and try to take my concentration off his lips.

"Alice?"

"Yes, my Lord."

"Please continue with the last album."

"Should I start from the beginning?"

"Yes." Phil Collins' voice fills the room. "We need some wine," he says and takes one last scoop of ice cream before navigating to the end table. He steers through the room remembering the landmarks, except for my kitty heels that I move to the other end of the loveseat. "Red or white?" he says.

"What?"

"Wine?"

"Oh, I think I would drink anything Mr. Gallo would offer me." We both laugh.

"Okay, then I will be back with anything."

*

I feel a bit chilly. Mensah rubs his hand up and down my back. I moan as his warm hand strokes my waist to my buttocks and down the back of my thigh. When did he come home? And why do I allow him to touch me in this way? I should be mad. Fuming. Throwing tantrums. Screaming. Fighting. But right now, I don't want that. His warmth makes me feel good. It doesn't matter. He's home and he wants me as much as I want him. I pretend to let the sleep overtake me, not opening my eyes to the hard-on that my feet feel. He moans as it comes alive and I rub my feet up and down more firmly. It's as hard as wood. I feel wetness between my legs. I'm gonna ride his dick. It's been so long. Yes. Fuck now and fight later. I hope the kids are still sleeping, because I'm going to make him scream. He's going to forget about Ms. HotAssEuropeanMatchstick when I get done with him. He is going to beg for my forgiveness, but not until after I let him know what good pussy feels like. I dig my feet in between his legs rubbing my left foot up and down the bat-like shaft. I need him. I can't fight anymore. I really want to fuck.

He moans longer and louder. "Vida," he says my name. *That's right, no one can make you feel this way.* "Vida," he says again, but his voice sounds different. My face is buried in my arms. I move them away. The scent hits me. Haagen Dazs. And I blink several times recalling my surroundings. I turn to face Mensah...no...it's not Mensah.

"Vida...Vida," he says lowly.

Shit. It's Julius! *Beat me in the head with a brick and then run me down with a truck. What the fuck did I do?* My clothes are still on, which is a good sign. Julius's hand is still resting on my buttocks and I peek at the tent in his pants. *Fuck, Vida...what the hell did you do that for?* There are two empty wine bottles on the side table. My foot is still resting against a massive hard-on.

Abla says there are different levels of erection just as there are different variations of pepper. There's the lukewarm-mild-comfortable-just-getting-started level and then the spicy-good-tolerable level and then the full-fledged-Jamaican-scotch-bonnet-pepper-I'm-scared-you-gonna-tear-my-ass-apart level. *This definitely qualifies as the third level.* He turns in my direction and even though he can't see me, I shut my eyes.

Okay, play it off like you're sleeping. I begin with noises like I'm ruffled in sleep. I quickly move my foot and retreat into a ball in the loveseat. "Hmm..." I bury my head. He moves his hand. I peek glances at him. He's placed his hand over his forehead and the other hand moves under his pants to dismantle the tent.

"Vida...Vida," he says lowly again. I continue with my performance, sighing and talking gibberish. His erection is decreasing. I hear the sounds of birds chirping and sunlight is coming through the room. I had no idea that we slept on the loveseat together. My last memory was singing Phil Collins and drinking from the bottle. *Wine...oh, wine...the elixir that will make you do bad things.* He rubs his face and combs his fingers through his short hair. He leans forward and touches the table. "Vida," he whispers my name again.

I moan and turn my head and then bury it again into the loveseat. *Okay, that should be enough dramatization.* "Hmmmmm," I muffle out.

He gets up slowly and looks back at me and again I shut my eyes instantly. I peek again to find him readjusting himself in his pants. He whispers, "Fuck. Fuck," and he trips over one of my kitty heels. He yells another, "Fuck."

"Julius," I murmur. He struggles to get up and looks for what caused the fall. "Are you okay?"

"I'm fine. Go back to sleep. It's still early," he murmurs and picks up one slipper and feels along the ground for the second one. He places the slippers closer to me at the foot of the couch and continues to stumble as he leaves the room.

CHAPTER 53

I've been avoiding Julius for an entire week, hiding away in the library and spending a lot of time at Bay Plaza Mall. It appears he has been avoiding me as well. The children are entertained with his music machine and instruments. *Maybe I will go shopping later. No, it's really unnecessary.* Abla and Vincent have it all covered from food to clothes. Hiding away in Panera Bread allows me to indulge in a carrot muffin. Less writing and more eating. The thought of my foot stroking his dick causes me to shove another piece of muffin into my mouth. *Dear Lord, what must he be thinking? Okay, enough, Vida. Go home.* It's nearly dinnertime.

The twins' graduation is a week away and I haven't heard from Mensah. After several debates in my head, I decide to call him. No answer, but I leave a message.

You mother f— The beep alerts me and I start again, this time talking into the phone.

"Hi, it's me. As you know, the twins' graduation is next week. They haven't heard from you in a month and you should call them. They are expecting you to be there. The ceremony starts ten a.m. sharp. Bye."

It's cold, brief and to the point. No need to talk about the state of our marriage until we are face-to-face. My mind begins the unnecessary journey of what Mensah might be doing. I shake my head. *No, Vida. Don't do this to yourself. Focus on you and the kids.*

*

The smell of fried ripe plantain perfumes the foyer. Abla must be making red-red. Julius's house not only has a distinctive smell, but it looks and feels different now. MJ's basketballs peek in hallway corners. Kakra's cleats are lined by the front door. School papers and announcements sit on the table next to the huge bouquet of tulips. *Speaking of tulips, this is a different bouquet from yesterday.* I touch the yellow petals and inhale the scent. But something else is competing with its fragrant scent. I enter the kitchen and there is a pot of black-eyed peas and smoked fish stewed in palm oil. My mouth salivates. No one is here and it looks as though no has eaten yet. Music is coming from the secret chamber. I take two pieces of fried plantain in a napkin and search for the boys. Vincent passes me as he runs to the front door.

"Is everything okay?" I say.

"Just in a hurry. Need to run an errand. Will be back shortly." His sentences are brief with no explanation. *He's always running off somewhere.*

"Okay. Drive safe."

Everyone is in the music room. Abla is seated in the corner and MJ is napping in her lap.

"Oh, just in time," Abla says.

"For?"

"Anotha battle. Dey been at it since da boys came from school."

"Battle?"

"Yes, Mommy…G-Money here has challenged me to a karaoke dance competition."

"Oh really?" I say.

"He started this. Someone is a very sore loser," Julius says.

"We'll see who's a sore loser. Yo, Money, do you need tiger balm on those joints?" Kakra says laughingly.

"You talk a lot of smack. Let's just hope you sing and dance better than your momma," Julius says.

"Oh yeah, are you talking about my momma?"

"Yeah, I'm talking about your momma." They both laugh. Julius adjusts the bands to his arms and then the footpads. "Does it feel better?"

"Good."

"This time we will have Panin play some music," Julius says. "I want to go easy on you."

"Listen G-Money, you haven't seen anything yet. Maybe you should have an ambulance close by."

"Hahaha. I think you need a serving of humble pie," Julius says.

"Big brother, give us a beat." Panin is at the drum set and begins hitting the drums. "Okay. I'm feeling this one. A little Michael," Kakra says.

"I got this one," Julius says.

"No, I got Michael," Kakra says. Neither one of them is singing or dancing. Panin stops.

"What is it with you and your mother and Michael Jackson?"

"Listen, it's obvious that I can sing and be a better Michael than you."

"It's not obvious to me…" Julius says sulkily. I don't intervene, but the exchanges between Kakra and Julius are amusing.

"Listen, G-Money…you haven't seen my moves and I don't want to hurt your feelings, but I'm about to mop the floor on you with this Michael joint. But if you want to start out the gate losing, fine by me."

"So young and so naïve," Julius says. "Let's do a duet and see who's going to cry themselves to sleep tonight."

"Ha," Kakra says. "Big brother, one more time." Panin begins drumming. This is a different beat. "You Rock My World" fills the room and Abla and I eagerly wait to see the outcome. Alice puts the words on the screen, but Kakra's back is facing it. He is confident because he knows every Michael Jackson song. I think we all know every Michael Jackson song because Panin has played them over and over again for years. "You gonna hit the first verse or should I?"

"Youth before beauty," Julius says.

"Oooh, is that how we doing it? Aight, listen and learn, Money."

Kakra sings the first verse and Julius sings the second. They both take turns dancing and imitating Michael Jackson's moves. Kakra's robot is better than mine. He looks so mature dancing. He reminds me of Mensah. Julius's movements are more coordinated than some people with sight. His voice has the right tempo and bass. It is smooth and at times deep. I could listen to him sing all day.

Abla pokes me in the hip. "Did you know he could move like dat?" I nod my head confirming. "Mmmm…mmm. Yaa…a man who could move like dat, no tellin' wat kind of moves he has in bed."

I pinch her. "Stop it." Thank goodness I didn't tell her about the occurrence the other morning.

"You not da least bit curious? You must be frusdrated az an armless nun on da deserted island."

"What?" I say, laughing.

"Dink about it, you'll get it."

Panin finishes with a loud clash on the cymbals. It is a hard call to make, but of course I cheer for Kakra.

"It's a tie," Alice announces.

"A tie my—" Kakra says.

"Watch yourself, sweetie," I catch him before he finishes.

"Okay, let's go again," Julius says. "Or do you need to take a nap first?"

"Big brother, hit us with another beat," Kakra says. They continue singing and dancing. MJ wakes up finally from all the commotion.

"Okay guys, can we break for dinner? The plantain will get cold." They reluctantly agree. "Abla, did the boys try on the suits?"

"Which suits?"

"I texted you. The suits Mensah bought for them for graduation. I packed them in the luggage."

"Da suits Mensah brought monfs ago? Doze suits are too small. I dought dat was why you went to town dis mornin'."

"No. Well, I may have to pick up two from J.C. Penny."

"I have a tailor," Julius says. I didn't realize he was listening. "I will have Vincent bring him here tomorrow evening. He's good and fast."

"You don't have to, Julius—ouch." Abla kicks me in the leg and then gives me the African stare-down.

"Are you okay?" he says.

"Yes. I stubbed my toe. I don't want to inconvenience you or your tailor."

"Stop it. He gets paid to design suits. He will measure them and bring the fabric so you can choose. Tomorrow we can get shoes and other accessories. They'll be ready for graduation," he says.

Chapter 54

This is ridiculous. I am barricaded in the library pretending to be busy writing, but all I want is someone to talk to. I grab the laptop and march myself to Julius's study. He is not there. I enter the back yard to the suite and knock on his door. No answer.

I peer inside and hear water running. "Julius?" I say. Perhaps he is having a shower. I turn to leave.

"Wait, Vida."

He emerges from the bathroom with a towel wrapped around his waist. It evokes instant memories and I turn around. "Sorry, didn't mean to intrude."

"You are not intruding. Please stay."

"I'll come back when you are decent."

"I will never be decent." He laughs. "Stay, please. It's been a while since we chatted." Okay, I definitely need to address the other morning.

I sit on a chair. He returns to the bathroom and closes the door. *What the hell are you doing here, Vida? And what are you going to say? Sorry for stroking your dick; I thought that dick was Mensah's dick and that is why I was prepping it for Ginger.*

He returns from the bathroom with pajama pants on and a long sleeve T-shirt. More clothes than I've ever seen him wear in this room.

"Nice pj's," I comment.

"Trust me, they can easily come off."

"So why wear them?" I laugh.

"If me wearing pj's makes you feel comfortable, then I will wear pj's." The distance between us is silly. I move closer to him on the bed. "Are the children asleep?"

"Yes." I rub my neck. The pain from sleeping with Panin at times. The other night he must have had a disturbing dream. He slept wildly and I woke up feeling like I boxed with Mayweather.

"Do you want to watch something on Netflix?" He retrieves the remote control from the bedside table and a large wall splits in half, revealing a television. He pulls out a pair of earbuds from the bedside table. "Your choice. Anything you want to watch, I'm game for."

"Cool." I readjust myself on his ultra king sized bed, propping the pillows one after the other underneath me. I scan through the selection. And land on *Superman*.

He lays on the bed with his head on the end where my legs extend. "Is *Superman* okay?"

"That's perfect." He places the buds in his ears and takes one pillow behind his head. *I guess there is no reason for him to look at the screen.* The movie plays and I probably watch Julius's expression more than I watch the movie. We both smile and laugh at the same scenes. His left hand rests idly on my right ankle and I feel a heated sensation course through my leg. He rubs it lazily while the movie plays.

"Why *Superman*?" he says when it ends.

"Don't you like *Superman*?" I ask with a long sigh.

"No, I've always liked *Superman*, but of all the movies on Netflix, you choose *Superman*." He sits up and faces me. *Gosh, it feels like he is opening my soul.* I shrug.

"I don't know. I suppose it's something I knew we both would enjoy." *That isn't it.* There is silence between us and he stares a little bit longer at me. *The words want to come out.*

"I remember, in second grade coming home from school in a crying fit because the kids in the class started a lyrical song about me." I close my eyes recalling the words: "...*Vida...Vida...kanka from Africa...her hair like Medusa...and her skin like charcoal...Vida...Vida...the African Medusa.* I told my mother about the chants and torments and she tried to comfort me the best way she could. Usually TV provided me an escape and that night I watched *Superman* probably for the sixth time. I believed that I could be him. I remember tying a towel around my shoulders and jumping from the window. Of course, I landed on the ground in several attempts. I convinced myself that if I could fly, then I could impress my classmates, especially Tina Williams, with this new revelation. So I tried again to harness the powers from the universe." I laugh, but Julius remains solemn. "I just wanted to fit in and I wanted friends. If I could do something that would impress them, then they would like me. And I thought if I had that kind of power maybe Daddy would stay home more. And things would be better. So, like I said, after several attempts, I failed miserably. But..." I chuckle. "...at seven years old, I discovered the reason for my failure was not that I wore a pink towel as a cape, or my hair was tightly threaded, but the failure was that I wore Alexander's cotton lace white trim panties and didn't have the red underwear Superman wore. I remember when I asked Mommy to buy me the underwear and told her the reason, she unplugged the television for my entire second grade." I laugh.

"There's nothing wrong in believing that you are special. I think we all secretly believe we are something we aren't."

"Yeah. But I really believed it was possible. If the kids could see that I had special abilities, then they would accept me in their circles."

"And there's nothing wrong in wanting to feel included. To be a part of something or someone." He pauses as though he wants to say something, but then closes his mouth. "It's good to accept your uniqueness. After all, there will never be a woman lying on my bed at one o'clock in the morning talking about her quest to be Superman."

I laugh loudly. "Sorry, I didn't want to turn this into a therapy session."

"You're not. I'm glad you shared that story. And just when I thought you were just good looks." *Hmmm…he thinks I'm good looking.*

"Mr. Gallo, is that a compliment?"

"Absolutely." My face turns strawberry red. "Alice, some music please."

"Yes, my Lord. The usual selection?"

"Oh no, not again." The words are out and he looks at me surprised. For a few weeks, it's been Phil Collins putting me to sleep. Last night "True Colors" was on repeat a dozen times.

"I thought you said you were a fan of Phil Collins."

"A fan, yes, not a stalker." A smile then he erupts into laughter.

"That mouth of yours. At times I want—" He stops himself and rises from the bed. "Alice, how about some Commodores tonight?"

"Oh, real old school. What do you know about the Commodores?"

"Listen up, old young one." He moves with a little two-step as he sings along to the music that fills the room.

*

It's almost two o'clock and I've managed to type four additional pages of "First Draft." I'm still restless. Julius collapses onto the bed with his head nearly on my lap. "So, Ms. Frimpong. What are you wearing this evening?" Clicking sounds of the keyboard fills in the pause in music. I type the word 'has' repeatedly trying to pretend as if I haven't heard him. He taps the back of the laptop and it is hard to ignore him any longer. "Ms. Frimpong…I'm waiting."

"I'm wearing…" *Think. Maybe I'll have a little fun with Julius.* "I'm wearing a robe and a nude pink teddy. The ensemble is quite lovely."

"Really? Do share, Ms. Frimpong. Garter belt?"

"Why, yes."

"Panties or thong?"

"A thong, of course." He raises his head from the bed with a sly grin.

"Silk or satin robe?"

"It's a silk robe, but it's warm in here so I took the robe off." His lips part.

"What did you do with your hair?"

"It's flowing past my shoulders in soft wavy curls." His hands graze my thigh.

"Your skin is so soft. Smooth."

"Abla's shea butter," I say. He removes his hand. His eyes stare right at me. *I wonder what he sees?*

"Is the teddy lace?"

"Why don't you find out?" His lips part again and he breaks into a smile. *I'm having too much fun.* He will soon discover the most undesirable ensemble of a sweatshirt, boy shorts and an overly worn headtie. His fingers graze my calves more than once and he glides his hands down to my feet.

"Do you know what?" *Perhaps this is going too far.* I feel sprints of sensation running through my body.

"What?" I hold my breath in anticipation of what he has to say. He pulls on my pinky toe, causing me to squeal and squirm.

"I think you are full of shit."

"Pardon me, Lord Gallo?"

"I smelled the tiger balm as soon as you entered this room. Hardly enticing." I yell out a roaring burst of laughter and my head hits the pillow.

"Well, Mr. Gallo, it appears you caught my bluff. Rough night yesterday with Panin. I might have slept on his feet."

"You are always welcome in my bed," he says. I'm searching for a response, but he fills in my doubts. "Of course, I can sleep in the *kotodenden* room." I'm relieved that the mood is becoming less tempting.

I rise from the bed and gather the laptop. "As my mother used to say, tomorrow is another day. Good night, Julius." He follows me to the door.

"My offer is always good in case you have a rough night."

"Noted, Lord Gallo."

Chapter 55

As promised, the tailor is here with a team who measures, cuts and begins designing the twins' suits. They take up shop in Julius's study. Instead of me making my way to Queens Center Mall, he insists on having Max deliver a variety of shoes, handkerchiefs, ties and shirts for the boys to choose from. Gratitude cannot be overstated for Julius's kindness.

"We're going to church this morning. You're more than welcome to come."

"Thank you, but no thank you."

"Hmmmm…Still haven't made your peace with God?" He is uninterested and unresponsive. He takes another sip of his espresso. "Well, in case you change your mind it's Grace Baptist Church. Alice has the information."

"Enjoy."

"I will pray for you, Julius."

"I suppose someone should." He turns and walks away.

Chapter 56

"Okay, Mommy. Time us," Kakra says.

The tailors are still busy in Julius's study and a dozen or more shoes, shirts and accessories for the boys are laid over the desk and ottoman. Julius is a connoisseur of fine clothing. His hands glide over several shirts and ties inquiring about their color and fabric. He's much like Kakra, who weighs every decision from suit cut, color and texture. No average ten-year-old can possibly care about so much detail, yet Kakra, like his father, can have a full discussion on cufflinks and proper neckwear. Panin makes his decisions in less than a minute and never changes his mind.

"What are you guys up to? I thought you were picking out a shirt and tie to go with your suit."

"We have a bet going on. G-Money here thinks he can tie four classic knots faster than me."

"Ooooh. We are betting with ten-year-olds now?"

"He started it." He laughs and a wide smile takes hold of me.

"Which kind of tie knots?" Mensah taught me three tie knots, but in all my years of tying neckwear for the boys, I only mastered one.

"Whoever finishes four different tie knots first, wins," says Kakra.

"Okay, how am I supposed to know if it is tied correctly?"

"Let Panin judge. I think he has a handle on this," Julius says.

"So what's the prize?" I ask.

"Well, if I win, I am getting the new Jordans," Kakra says.

"And if I win?" Julius asks. Kakra laughs. "What's so funny?"

"That you think you can beat me."

"Well, I've done it before."

"That was a tie and for real Alice just gave you extra points."

"Well, what do you expect? The house always wins." Julius stands confidently with both hands on either side of his waist. "Too much talking." Panin lays four ties in front of both of them. Julius and Kakra suspend their hands over the ties as though they are each applying a spell over them.

"You are giving me a head start, right?"

"Nooooo," Julius says.

"No? Why not? I'm a kid with kid fingers."

"If that is your only handicap, then consider us even. I won't hold it against you if you don't hold mine against me. Enough talk; let's get started."

"The first tie is the half-Windsor," Kakra says.

"Okay. On your mark, get set, go." The seconds move by rapidly and both connoisseurs race with anxious fingers grasping the tie at both ends.

"Go, Kakra." My excitement is a bit overwhelming. Kakra moves swiftly with hand over hand and Julius moves the tie in a coordinated slow effort. Who is doing it the right way? Julius's knot looks complete.

"Done!" he yells.

"Damn it," Kakra says.

"Watch your language, mister. Forty-four seconds," I say.

"I was so close," Kakra says. Panin examines the tie around Julius's neck and on his notepad under the letter J, he writes a check mark.

"Okay, next tie: the Eldredge knot," Julius says. They loosen the ties on their necks and hover their fingers over the next set of ties. The clock is already set on my cellphone.

"On your mark. Get set. Go." Hand over hand again tossing the ties over their shoulders and then bringing them back to the center. Several swift maneuvers and Kakra tucks the short end underneath the tie collar. He yells, "Done." Julius appears frustrated. He continues working the knot, but it looks nothing like Kakra's.

"The time is two minutes and fifteen seconds."

Panin rechecks the ties and on his pad, gives a check mark to Kakra. "Yes," Kakra yells out.

"Lucky shot," Julius says.

Kakra examines Julius's tie. "That's the Trinity knot," Kakra says. Julius touches it.

"That's right. After all these years, I still confuse the two. Okay, next tie?" Julius says.

"The Cape knot," Kakra says confidently.

"Well, you certainly don't hold back. Wait, give me a moment. It's been ages since I used that one," Julius says.

"Do you need to go and take your memory pills? I can wait," Kakra says. Julius signals me to set the clock.

"On your mark. Get set. Go," I say again. They both work tirelessly. This time Julius is working much faster than before.

"Done," he yells out.

"Shit," Kakra says.

My stare cowers his head, but he still continues looping one end over the other. "The time is two minutes and thirty-nine seconds." Panin examines Julius's tie and tugs on the knot. Kakra yells out done. Panin examines Kakra's tie. He takes his pad again and gives another check mark to Julius.

Julius bows his head down and gives a snickerly grin. *So that's two for Julius and one for Kakra.* "Okay, last tie and whoever wins this one is the winner. Let's begin. We are doing the L-T-K." *Acronyms are my thing, but what is LTK?*

"I got this, Mommy," Kakra says.

"Okay, on the count of three and for the official Tie Knot Championship," I say. They flex their fingers in anticipation of my final word. "One. Two. Three." They go hand over hand again, this time more swiftly than the first three times, but I can't tell who is leading. *Go Kakra. Go Kakra.* This is going to be close. Already three minutes. Kakra's got this one. He yells done, but Julius continues. "The time is three minutes and twenty-nine seconds." Panin inspects Kakra's tie and then waits for Julius. *Oh please, Panin, let Kakra win.* We all wait for the checkmark that will make the deciding factor. He places another stroke mark underneath the letter K. Kakra yells in jubilation and then inspects Julius's knot. *Well, at least it's a tie.*

"You didn't make the wings broad enough. Here, let me show you." He takes Julius's hands to readjust the tie.

"I must say, it's an honor competing with you. How does someone so young know so much about tie knots? Most grown men don't even know a complicated tie knot such as a Linwood Taurus Knot."

"My father taught me. I used to watch him all the time and he always told me it is important to look your best. He told me clothes say a lot about a man, so make sure people have good things to say about you."

"Indeed. Sounds like your father is a good guy."

Kakra proudly raises his head as though he is adjusting another tie. "My dad is a great guy."

*

"How do you pronounce your name again?" The tailor gives a satisfied grin with the suits he has created.

"Just call me Nicki," he says pleasantly. "And this is Marco and Tony." Two other gentlemen who worked all day to provide bespoke clothing for the boys nod their heads.

"Thank you all so much. The suits are beautiful. And you guys sew so fast." A bashful smile appears on Nicki's face.

"I will do anything for the Gallo family," he says. "And thank you for da wonderful meal. Rosemary's beef stew was very dalicious. I'm sure we will sleep like babies on our trip home."

"Where do you live?"

"Cortona." His Italian accent gives it a new pronunciation.

"Oh yeah, in the Bronx by Tremont Avenue." I know of the little Italian neighborhood in the Bronx from frequent visits to Artuso's.

"No...Cortona," he says. I repeat 'Cooorrrrtona' trying desperately to roll the r. Another example of a language spoken for several years yielding a trained tongue.

"Si," he says with a wide smile.

"In the Bronx, right?"

"No. No Bronx." He waves his hands. "In Tuscany, Italy," he says firmly. "Next time Mr. Gallo comes to Italy, he bring you to my home. Prepare a big feast for you and your family."

"Wait a minute. Is that where you're going now? Italy?"

"Yes. Home."

"You flew from Italy yesterday to come here and sew suits for my boys' graduation?"

"Si. I fly any place for Mr. Gallo."

"Oh. I see." Vincent helps Nicki and his team of tailors mount their equipment and luggage into the car. Julius steps out of his study to say his goodbyes. *Close your mouth, Vida, and don't mention it. Not possible. Okay, just get some clarification.*

"Oh my goodness, Julius, if I had known you were flying him from Italy just to sew the boys' suits...I mean...I could have gone to J.C. Penny or Marshall's or something for their suits. That's a bit excessive, don't you think?"

"Oh, stop it. I didn't do anything that I wouldn't have done for myself. Have you seen the boys in their suits? I can only imagine anything you bought off the rack would pale in comparison. Nicki is an old family friend. There is nothing he wouldn't do for me. Every suit I have ever worn since I was a child was sewn by this man's hands. I'm glad he took my advice and started training his nephews. Skills like that cannot be taught in any school." He rests his hand on my shoulder. "I like to treat people they way I like to be treated. It's just as simple as that."

"So he just drops everything and comes running when you call?" My voice is more elevated than usual.

"Are you upset?"

"Yes. I mean no. I just thought he lived here in New York and I didn't know you interrupted this man's life just so…so you…"

"So I can what, Vida?" There is no doubt that Julius is powerful, basically getting anything he wants from a simple command to commanding what he wants from across the country. Vincent, Mr. Hollanderman, Dr. Jesup and Nicki at his service whenever he chooses. *Why does this make me feel uncomfortable? Or maybe what is really bothering me is that I don't think I deserve this.* He is waiting for my response.

"Nothing, Julius. I really appreciate what you've done. I don't want to take advantage of you, that's all."

"I don't think that is possible. I wouldn't allow you to do anything that didn't please me."

I mean, really, what can I say after that?

*

Mensah is not here and today is graduation. The auditorium is overly crowded. Daniel sees us in the crowd and we shift our seats to give him the last available one. Vincent doesn't have a ticket, but I am not surprised that he still was able to get inside. His huge stature and deep accent can be intimidating sometimes. *If I'd known Mensah wasn't going to make it, I would have given the extra ticket to Julius to attend. No, maybe he will surprise us again and show up.*

A procession of teachers and staff speak and now the announcement for the fifth grade class commences. The students are called up one by one. Kakra leads his brother by the hand and they ascend the stairs. Tears flow down like rain drops. "Stop it. You gonna haf me cryin' any minute," Abla says.

Huge applause is heard as both boys walk onto the stage. Kakra waves to his fans and Panin tries nervously not to look at the audience. The principal shakes Kakra's hand, but Panin doesn't offer a handshake and tries to rush off the stage. People told me that Panin couldn't lead a normal life. There was no future as an independent black man with autism. This is the day I've been waiting for. The sign that everything will be fine. Vincent offers us handkerchiefs and we put them to good use.

Chapter 57

This excursion started with the premise of staying only two weeks and here I am over a month later. By request, Max set up a soccer field with an outstretched canopy. *Max should consider a career in event planning.* Grass, nets and a scoreboard are prominently displayed. Julius hired an official referee, which makes me wonder if this really is a friendly match. He is definitely a competitor like Kakra. We all have custom jerseys with light reflectors on them. Kakra, Vincent and I are wearing a soft blue while Julius, MJ and Abla are wearing a hunter green jersey.

It's past eight o'clock and the skyline begins to change from fire orange into denim blue. The lighted soccer ball looks like a moon bouncing up and down the field. The goals are highlighted with solid white lights and the roof above us lights up like stars. I've never played soccer like this before, but I am overly excited when we begin. Abla plays a couple of rounds and then settles beside Panin as they idly watch us run breathlessly across the field. Julius is like a child, amused with excitement. It's hard to believe that this man can be egotistical. He falls to the ground when MJ and Kakra try to side step him.

We finish one match and the referee automatically calls Julius's team winners. The score is four to three and I watch as Kakra argues his points of cheating. Julius is not bothered, but requests a rematch. We sit down for a barbecue that Vincent has already prepped.

"You know, for a second there, I thought you were holding back and throwing the game so that I could win. But I know that I beat you fair and square," Julius says.

"It's been a while. Four years to be exact since I've played on a soccer field." *I hate losing, especially in front of Kakra. He was counting on me to win this. I need to get back into shape and start practicing again.* MJ shows the same interest in soccer as Kakra. It will be much easier for me to practice with both of them. I make a mental note to contact the Sassi Strikers when we get back home.

"Dinner is ready," Vincent announces. We all sit down in our full soccer gear, sweaty and hot.

"Wow Vincent, you made all this?" Sausage, hotdogs, burgers, steak, ribs and chicken grace the table. I can tell Abla made the salad with the eggs decoratively displayed over the heavy salad dressing. The boys begin to dig into the food before washing their hands. I signal them, but Vincent waves my request off.

"We eat first and wash up later," Vincent announces. The kids agree and continue stuffing their faces. Julius hides a napkin under the table.

You learn a lot about someone by living with him. And one of the many things that always makes me curious is the amount of detail Julius gives to his hands. In the shower, lying in bed with him, sitting for dinner, dancing, singing, typing at his braille machine, sitting in his study and meditating, he pauses as though he is holding his breath and strokes each finger. I've seen him on numerous occasions trimming his nails and massaging each cuticle. Then he caresses his palms and with an index finger. Once satisfied, there's a noticeable exhale as his chest relaxes.

I am sure this is what he does when he secretly takes the napkin underneath the table. He laughs when Kakra promises to wipe the field with him after dinner. The napkin resurfaces, crumbled on top of the table. It is just as clean as it was before he used it. He takes another napkin and graces it over his lap and then takes a rib that Kakra offers to him.

"This is delicious, Vincent." Vincent gives a head nod.

"Thank you. An old family recipe." Everyone devours the ribs, which leaves us with barbecue sauce-stained lips. I've never seen Julius eat so ravenously. This image reminds me of Panin when he eats ice cream, the only food that he eats in a hurry because he doesn't want the ice cream to turn milky.

"Do you know Mommy iz a sore looza? She can't take it if she loozes," Abla says to Kakra.

"Yes. I am starting to recognize a bit of winning envy," Julius says.

"Give me two weeks and I will be in tip top shape," I say.

"Excuses," Kakra blurts out.

"Now I see where he gets it from," Julius says.

"Excuse me, boy…but who taught you everything you know?" I say.

"You did, oh great one," Kakra says. I fling a napkin his way.

"Pardon the interruption, but Ms. Pucilli is here. Should I instruct her to come upstairs, Lord Gallo?"

"Yes, Alice." Julius's response sparks a change in everyone's disposition. The atmosphere seems heavy and quieter than a few seconds ago. Penny enters the rooftop and her mouth falls into her chest.

"Oh sweetie, you've done all this whilst I was away? You've been very busy. And you've cut your hair…And you have company…a party?" She turns her lip up and cuts her eyes several times scanning the faces at the table.

"Hi, Penny." My voice stings with a bit of false happiness. She opens her mouth and kisses Julius. Her long blonde hair falls into his food.

"Hmmm, barbecue. Tastes good. Ms. Frimkong, well, what do we have here?" Her eyes gaze at the boys a bit too long for me.

"These are my sons." I point to Panin sitting beside me and then MJ and Kakra who sit opposite us. "And you remember my sis—I mean my manager, Rosemary. And the referee for our game." I can't remember his name. Penny offers a forced smile and then turns her attention to Julius.

"Quite interesting." Vincent pulls another chair toward the table and Penny squeezes it tightly between Vincent and Julius. "I see a lot happened since I left. You told me that you would be away for a couple of weeks. I had no idea this"—she stretches her arms to reference the transformation of the rooftop—"was happening."

"I changed my mind," Julius says.

"Oh sweetie, you should have told me. I would have come back sooner." Julius doesn't comment, but grins slightly.

"Hey G-Money, can we go to Disneyland for our birthday?" I give Kakra the African stare-down and he silences his amusement. *He knows better than to ask an adult for something, especially Julius.*

"Of course. When is it?" Julius says.

"Sweetie, I thought you guys wanted to play laser tag at New Rochelle?"

"Yeah…" he says solemnly. "Hey G-Money, we should have a swimming competition tomorrow. Like a relay race."

"Sounds good. Same teams?"

"Yeah."

"Very well. You have another chance to redeem yourself tomorrow, Ms. Frimpong," Julius says.

"Wow, Ms. Frimkong, you certainly…I didn't realize you had all this time with your writing responsibilities. Is the memoir completed?"

Completed? Not by a long shot. "No, I'm still working on it." It is clear that Julius is not going to offer any information as to why we are here…or why I haven't completed the assignment.

"When did we start adding daycare services?" she leans forwards and whispers to Julius, but I can still hear her. He brushes her aside and she purses her lips.

"How was Hawaii?" I ask. She pauses before she answers me.

"Fine. I am in so much demand that I just had to take a break and see my sweetie." Penny wraps her arms around Julius's neck and disturbs him with loud kisses. He gives her a light kiss and pulls away.

"I thought that you would have spent another two weeks in Spain," Julius says.

"No, I couldn't. I really missed you." She continues with her overtures. Her hand slips underneath the table. He says something low in Italian and she withdraws her hand. Her eyes search the table to see if anyone notices his dismissive action. Our eyes lock and I quickly focus my attention on MJ.

"Just how many hotdogs did you stuff in your mouth?" He shrugs his shoulders and devours another hotdog without the bun. I glance at Abla, who looks like any moment from now she will unleash a can of whip-that-ass. I kick her underneath the table. She leans toward me and whispers in Twi. The tension is brewing. *Oh, dear God, please don't let Penny say anything to set off Abla.*

I return my gaze to Penny. She continues her overtures and Julius tries to ignore her. Vincent addresses her in Italian and then places a plate in front of her. "No, some of us are watching our weight," Penny says. And her eyes jump over me and land on Abla. There is a brief stare-down until Kakra's voice breaks up the pupil fight.

"G-Money, can we watch a movie later?"

"Sure. What kind of movie do you have in mind?" Julius says.

"*The Incredibles,*" MJ says enthusiastically.

"Not again. Panin has been watching that all week," Kakra says.

"Movie later?" Penny's eyes search his face. "I'm home, sweetie." She leans toward Julius again and gently whispers in Italian. Julius mutters something back but his lips are turned down.

"Enough," he says firmly. His voice is louder than usual. Penny pouts and leans back into the chair. She crosses her arms over her chest.

"You know what, guys? Let's get ready to go. We can watch movies once we return home. Auntie Cece is back from Ghana and she's been asking for us."

"Tonight?" Julius says. The truth is Auntie Cece returned last week, but I have been avoiding her calls. I've offered only a combination of ambiguous texts and short messages in the middle of the night when I knew she would be fast asleep. It first started as a unicorn story, but then I finally told her that we were working on a special assignment and she didn't have to worry. We would be home before the Fourth of July. But tonight, Penny's presence will have us home sooner.

"We can watch any movie here," Julius says.

"Auntie Cece has been calling me frantically and I promised her that I will be home soon. She hates being alone. Plus this is perfect timing. Penny is back now." Julius's left eyebrow goes up in skepticism.

"You don't have to leave. The children can watch any movie tonight or tomorrow."

"Tonight? Tomorrow?" Penny says disgustedly. "Is this place a shelter now? I'm surprised they haven't moved in yet."

This is déjà vu. I dreamt this scene. In the dream, Abla leaps over the table and begins pouncing on Penny. Well, it doesn't take long before I feel the rise of the phoenix behind me.

"Exxxxxxcuuuuuuze me!" Everyone focuses on Abla when she stands. I pull on her hand to pull her down but she pulls away.

"Lissen, missy. We already moved in. My bedroom iz upstairs and iz quite comfortable, dank you very much. Tonight before I go to bed, I may take anotha swim in da pool dat I have been swimmin' in for da past month. And tomorrow, I plan to make Belgian waffles in my new Belgian waffle maka our boss bought for us. And if I feel up to it, I will buy anotha outfit wit shoes and a bag to wear just because our boss treats us very well. And we treat him very well. In fact, so well dat he iz now family. Now you are caught up wif wat has been goin' on while you were in such high demand. Don't worry, he wazn't bored. Right, Yaa?"

She turns to me for confirmation. The children snicker. *Thank God she didn't mention the showers.*

Penny's face is apple red. Her gaze waits for a response from me. I offer another false smile and clear my throat. She pushes back from the table and rises as though she is going to approach us. She begins shouting at Julius. He closes his eyes, which tells me this is something he is accustomed to. Damn, I wish I knew Italian. Julius tries to temper her in a soft voice, but she's angry and I know she is talking about me. She looks in my direction and then back again at him with the same fury in her eyes. Abla watches intently, waiting I am sure for Penny to point a finger, giving her a reason to lunge at her. "If I hear my name, huh…heh. .heh…heh…itz on and poppin'," Abla says.

Penny's voice quiets with the sound of another man's voice. The voice is low but firm. It's Mensah! We look around. Where is he?…No…No…No…it's not Mensah. I wouldn't believe it if I wasn't sitting next to him. *Panin speaks!* He doesn't lift his head from the steak he meticulously cuts through. His voice is just as controlled and firm as Mensah's. He is speaking in Italian. I drop to my knees beside him and I cannot control the tears that pour out of me.

Everyone is speechless listening intently to the voice that sounds like Mensah but belongs to Panin. He continues to talk and with equal measure cuts the steak into perfect bite-sized squares and then he places two pieces into his mouth.

"Holy shit! I told you, Ma. I knew it. I just knew it. He speaks and now he knows Italian." Kakra drops his hamburger flimsily onto his plate.

MJ squeals, "Panin can speak." Abla kisses his head as I kneel beside him trying to pull him to look at me.

"Panin. Honey. Is that you?" My voice is shaking and excited. He forks more square-shaped steaks into his mouth. He doesn't face me, but I shower him with wet kisses all over his face. I raise his face toward mine. "Let me hear you again. Honey…Mommy wants to hear your voice again. Talk to me. Please. I want to hear you again." He doesn't say anything, unbothered by the affection I pour onto him. Apparently whatever he said hushed Penny. Julius rises and apologizes on her behalf. They leave the rooftop. Vincent looks baffled and follows behind Julius and Penny.

*

"You're leaving?"

"Yeah, we should go. Today has been…anyway Penny is back. I'm sure you have a lot to tell her. Hint, hint…"

"She's gone and probably back at her apartment. I told her that I have guests staying with me and if that bothers her she can return next month when I get back."

"Next month?"

"Yes, I have a little trip of my own. I am meeting with Dr. Braun in Australia. I was hoping at least we could spend some more time together. I mean all of us."

"How long will you be gone?"

"Maybe a month or two. You are welcome to stay here whilst I am away to catch up on your reading." He laughs.

"Did you know?"

"Know?"

"Did you know that Panin knew Italian?" He pauses and enters the bedroom.

"Yes."

"And you never said anything to me?"

"I had to be sure. Certain conversations with Vincent clued me in that he understood very well. He's a smart kid. A real smart kid."

"I've been fighting hard so that he can lead a normal life. So no one would ever tell him that he couldn't do anything or for anyone to label him. He is so much more than a kid with autism."

Julius laughs. "What constitutes normal? What society tells us is normal? We all don't learn the same way or see the same things. But that doesn't make us unusual; it makes us human. The world is full of billions of people and I would really like to meet someone who wasn't like the last five people I've already met. Do I seem normal to you? Or Abla, Vincent, MJ or Kakra? We don't need to fit neatly in a box to be a gift. Everyone spends a great deal of time trying to be normal. What you want from him is to be the best Panin he can be."

"You're right again, Julius."

"Of course I am."

"So what did Penny say?"

He sighs and I know he is reluctant to tell me. "It's not worth repeating. In fact, I totally forgot about it."

"I'm giving you a bullshit stare by the way." He laughs. "At least tell me what my son said in response." He leans against the dresser. He closes his eyes and then begins.

"'My mother is beautiful and not because she is my mother, but because she makes everything and everyone around her beautiful. You may not like her, but that is okay because she cannot make you look beautiful. She has a lot of love within her. You can see it. Don't insult my mother or my family because you are not beautiful. My mother is beautiful because she makes me and everyone around her feel beautiful.'"

The room is blurry and tears continue to fall without my will to stop them. "He said all that?"

"Yes."

"That's my son. He's awesome, you know." My breathing returns to a normal pace.

"Yes, he is. Looks like Panin is turning into a man, Vida." My head sinks into his chest and my arms rest around his shoulders. "Don't leave boogers on my shirt," he says and we laugh. "Stay till next week. I promised the twins a trip to Disneyland and a party for their birthday."

"But I reserved laser tag at New Roc City."

"Yeah, well we have the whole summer for laser tag. And I don't want to hear objections because you know I've made up my mind. We leave tomorrow and will be back Saturday evening."

"But I don't have—"

"Uh-uh...'I don't have' is not something we say in this house...Everything is taken care of. Shoe size eight and a half. Dress size a four."

"Really," I snicker. "Close. A four...teen."

"Okay. I already know the children's and Abla's sizes."

"You do?"

"Let's just say that your sister is very consistent with her shopping." Laughter replaces the tears of joy.

"Julius?"

"Yes?" He turns around before leaving the room.

"Thank you."

"Vida...N-T-Y -B-F."

Chapter 58

"So mister, what is keeping you busy in Australia? Are you keeping your bet or do you have a harem of women coming and going?"

I hit send and wait for a response. His message earlier doesn't give me much to go by. He simply stated he was staying another week in Australia. It would be nice to have another challenge on the karaoke machine or another soccer match. *Focus, Vida, continue reading. No. Haagen Dazs is calling my name.*

"Alice, please lower the volume."

"As you wish, Ms. Frimpong."

No hard feat, Haagen Dazs butter pecan in one hand and Julius's journal on my lap. Page after page comes alive with imagery. A teenager running through the farms in Ghana and blades of grass caressing his face. At times a boy who is happy and most times a boy who is sad. I can picture a joyful smile with a bit of mischief. And finally, I picture a boy in love with a girl.

It wasn't long before I realized Ama was more than a friend. With great eagerness, I waited for her under the palm tree at 4:30 p.m. I made sure that my clothes were clean and my appearance was presentable. I scrubbed my hands diligently. I did it again before I approached the tree. When she finally arrived, I feel the little flutters in my stomach again. I'm worried. Did I comb my hair well? Are my hands clean? Do I smell good? I lift my arm up and pray that I don't smell as if I were wrestling with pigs.

"Well, Kofi, we meet again." That was her greeting to me. Her soft voice engraved in my mind. Her voice is beautiful. A mixture of melodic sweet sounds. Her hands give new meaning to softness and she smells like peanut butter. Her hair always smelled like jasmine.

She read for about twenty minutes and then we talked about anything that occurs to young minds. She told me stories of one day being a famous designer and living in Paris or Italy. I always chimed in, "I will take you there on my plane when we finish school." We laugh and sing songs. She dances and I listen to the movements of her feet against the grass and ground. Her arms create gentle winds in rhythmic gestures.

"Come, Kofi, let me show you," she says. She grabs my hands and I quickly stand up, eager to be close to her. She stands behind me and orchestrates my moves like a puppet. She laughs. "Don't be so stiff. Come on, you have to relax yourself or you can't enjoy the music."

I went to impress her. I study the sounds of her feet and the sounds her arms make when she dances. We start again with another movement, and with a few footsteps I performed in front of her. "That's right, Kofi, you got it. Now move your hips a little more. You see, you are a natural dancer. You are moving all right."

I was ecstatic. It made her happy and it made me happy to see her happy. Our afternoons are beautiful and I wanted to spend my entire existence under the tree with her. "Ama, show me another move," I begged her. Still anxious to learn.

"Maybe tomorrow, Kofi, it is getting late." Those words always brought sadness to me, but I didn't show her my disappointment. As usual she gathered her schoolbooks and before we departed, she nestled her head into my chest. I breathe in deeply to take as much of her inside of me before we separate.

"Ocrina," she says. I sulk when I no longer hear her footsteps. Tomorrow seems like years.

Julius filled sixty-two pages with his love for Ama. The other journal urges me to pick it up and continue reading. Perhaps there will be more images of a blossoming romance. The black leather jacket smells like an old shoe. Heavy black ink; it is written in Italian. Another one of his mother's journals. Eighty-four numbered pages of a language that I know nothing about fills the journal. *Are these pages filled with good memories? Does it finally tell the story of why a young woman with no husband decided to settle in rural Ghana with her visually impaired son? Is it filled with memories of Julius's father and her? Well, I won't find out tonight.* I move to pick up another journal. A deep purple leather journal calls to me. The pages are much lighter than the previous journals. It begins:

Dear God, I hate you. May 1995.

"Ms. Frimpong, there are visitors at the main gate. I've displayed the image on the screen." Alice's voice diverts my attention to the television screen above the fireplace.

"A visitor?" *Who the heck is coming over here at this hour?* Alice produces the image on the television screen. A tall slim man appears and someone's arm is wrapped around his neck. Julius never mentioned visitors while he was away.

"Ms. Frimpong, I have provided audio for you to communicate."

"Hello," I yell into the air, not sure what device to talk into.

"Hello. Is this Julius Gallo's residence?" The distressed voice comes through the speakers next to the television.

"Yes, it is, but he is away on business."

"Ummm, well I'm here with his girlfriend and she's pretty wasted. She told me to bring her here."

The closer I get to the screen, the more clear the image. That is Penny barely standing behind the man with her arm draped around him. *Now what the hell am I supposed to do with her?* He should just leave her like an Amazon package on the front step.

"Hello, can someone help me out here?" the anxious man says.

"Okay. One second. " Julius needs to know. His number is saved on autodial four right after Auntie Cece. Straight to voicemail. *Damn it.*

"Hi, Julius. Sorry to disturb your vacation, but call me when you get the chance."

I should just leave her out there. *No, Vida. That's not right.* She has every right to be here.

"Alice, let them in."

"Should we contact Lord Gallo first?" *Even Alice has her doubts.*

"I just left Julius a message. We can't leave them outside, so let's see what's going on."

"As you wish."

The young man stumbles in barely holding onto Penny. She collapses to the floor. "Hey, babe. Does this place look familiar to you?" he lowers his head to ask Penny. She looks around and bursts into laughter.

"I guess that is a yes. Hi, I'm Sam, the photographer. Penny and I work together every now and then."

"Hi, I'm Vida."

"Ooooh…you're Vida," he says as we shake hands. "Not exactly the way Penny described you." *I'm not surprised, given her present state.* "Well, let me say that words don't nearly describe how beautiful you are."

"Thank you." He holds Penny up as they follow me toward the library. I turn around to make sure she is still moving and I catch him staring at obvious places. My hands strategically move behind my back pulling my T-shirt further down.

He looks around the foyer. "This is some digs, huh? It just looks like an industrial building from outside, but this is some fancy setup." He admires the floors and the paintings on the walls. Penny tries to compose herself in her drunken stupor. "We had a bit of a long night and maybe just a little bit too much to drink." He holds his index finger and thumb apart demonstrating how much a little bit is. "We arrived in New York about an hour ago. Do you know when Mr. Gallo will be back? I have some business matters to discuss."

"I'm not sure, but you can leave me your name and number and I will relay your message."

"Just tell him Sam stopped by. He knows how to get in contact with me. So, I will entrust Penny under your care."

"Here?" I say.

"Yes. Well, she lives in downtown Brooklyn and with all this rain, I think it's better she stay here. I have a flight to catch first thing in the morning. It was a pleasure meeting you, Vida." He lowers himself to Penny's level. "I will call you if any more gigs come up. It's just bad timing right now. That's all. You know how this business is."

She waves him away dismissively. The photographer takes the lead to the front door with me trailing behind him. "Good night and safe trip." He smiles back at me and stares a bit longer than I think he should before closing the door.

"Let me try Julius one more time," I say.

"I already know he's out of town." She slowly rises up. "Ever since you came, he's not the same. He doesn't want to fuck me like he used to. He doesn't want to fuck any of my girlfriends like he used to. Even Tracy. What did you do to him?"

"Me?"

"Yes, you. Are you fuckin' him?"

"You're drunk."

"Maybe so. But it's the truth. How many times you fuck?"

"My relationship with Julius is purely professional." *Okay, Vida, don't use that word ever again.*

She ruptures into a big laugh. "Professional what?"

"I'm a writer."

"I know he wants you. I've seen the way he behaves around you. He doesn't act like that with my girlfriends. And even me. " She walks closer to me, leaving wet footprints on the travertine tiles. "He's greedy, you know. He doesn't want to share you."

"What? You're talking gibberish. I'm leaving. You can try Julius yourself." *Let her stay in her muttering confusion.* Work awaits me in the library.

Now where was I? The laptop is on, but no words are on the screen. *Which journal was I reading?* My mind recollects the purple journal still laying on the desk. A big clash stops me from moving. My ears perk up, straining to hear another movement. *What the hell was that?* I'm not alone, which doesn't offer me comfort. Dishes crash to the floor. *Okay, let's see what missy is doing in the kitchen.*

Two dinner plates and a wine flute broken on the floor caused the noise. Penny is sprawled on the floor eating my leftover chicken parmigiana.

"Hey, that's my dinner," I say.

"I'm so hungry. I haven't eaten in two months. Just Red Bull and cigarettes."

She eats it straight from the platter, cold. *This is such a sad scene.* She wolfs down the food like a nomad who just discovered meat. She holds the platter close to her face so no morsel of food escapes and she doesn't lift her head until the last ziti has succumbed to her ravenous mouth. Remnants of marinara sauce stain her face and fingers.

"Tat was so good." Fully satisfied, she rests her head on the kitchen cabinet. I hand her a paper towel. There is still some coffee leftover from this morning, so I heat it in the microwave.

"Here, you're going to need this." She shrugs her shoulders indifferently and takes little sips while blowing on the coffee. "Let me get you something to change into." There should be some of her clothes in the *kotodenden* room.

An "I love NY" shirt, black leggings and pair of socks should do. She is not in the kitchen when I return and the empty platter and broken dishes are still on the floor. *Great, now I'm a housekeeper. A grown woman and she can't clean up after herself.* I follow the damp footprints to the library.

"You've made yourself at home here. So, tell me what is so secretive in these journals that he has to lock them up?" I'm not sure how much information Julius discloses to Penny, but I don't think talking to her about it is a good idea.

"Here, take these. This is all that I could find upstairs." She takes the clothes and begins undressing, leaving the damp clothes in the middle of the floor.

"Do you know why I wanted you to be his writer?"

Oh, come on, lady. Just leave me alone. Go sleep or hang from the chandelier upstairs. Maybe if she sees me typing then she will get the hint. "Leave me alone, Penny" fills the Word document six times.

"Do you?" she repeats. *Maybe she needs the African stare-down.* My eyes rise from the laptop only to find Penny standing in the middle of the library naked. *What the hell?* I try not to bring attention to her nakedness, but I observe the image in front of me. Penny is much thinner than I expected. Her breasts are maybe a B cup. Her arms and legs look like matchsticks. It's like I can see through her stomach to her rear. No ass at all. The only hair on her body is on the top of her head. No curves to show off her femininity.

"I assume because you thought I was qualified," I say and she laughs wickedly.

"The French blonde writer was more qualified, but men and their weaknesses. This was supposed to work. Hiring you over her. You don't strike me as someone who he would find the least bit attractive. A married woman with three children. Hardly a threat!" She laughs and then pauses. "So I thought. You've taught me a lesson, Ms. Fretkong. No pussy is safe around a man. Do you like it?"

"Like what?" *I really wish she would put the clothes on.* She gives a sinister laugh.

"You like fucking him, don't you?"

"Will you stop it? I am not fucking him, and please put some clothes on."

"Why? Because you like what you see?" Sometimes my face shows disappointment before I utter words. It's the face I make when they serve you tuna fish when you see steak is available. *No, I don't like what I see. In fact, the woman in me wants to gouge my eyes out.*

"Penny, please."

"He is really good at fucking and other things." She laughs again. "Sometimes when he has a long day and you think he just wants a quickie, well that's when he really wears me out. He has so much energy. Oh, God…we can go all night and morning. And when my legs feel like buckling, he rubs me, massages me." She demonstrates running her hands up and down her thigh. "After a couple of minutes, we continue. It's too good and I can't stop."

I focus on the keyboard and type "Penny is insane" a dozen times. Not paying her any attention must be working because she finally puts her clothes on. If she stood there any longer, I might have needed Julius's navigators. "Penny, trust me. I am not fucking Julius."

"Trust you? Trust you? You've changed him. He is not the same. He doesn't want to fuck me. It's been nearly four months. He usually sends for me when I'm on sets. But since you've been here, he hasn't sent for me."

Maybe I should tell her about our bet. Perhaps this will cool her anger and reassure her that there is nothing going on between me and Julius.

"He wanted to get to you before I did," she says.

"What?"

"That's why he's shipped me all over the world for different modeling gigs." *That's not the reason. He didn't want to tell you about the surgery and it appears that he still hasn't.* "I'm not stupid. I haven't been this busy throughout my modeling career, but ever since you came, I've been in high demand." *Well, is that what Julius is doing? Getting gigs for her to keep her busy and out of his affairs?* "So, have you been with a woman before?"

"No, never. The only breasts I like besides my own are chicken."

"But you don't know what you like unless you try it. I could really make you happy." She moves closer to the desk.

"I will remember that when there is a shortage of men and dildos."

She laughs. "I am going to call Julius and let him know I am here." *Yes, please go.*

It's already midnight. Now would be a good time to leave, but the rain beats heavily against the windows. Hopefully, in another hour the rain will stop so I can get the heck out of here. She's probably passed out in the *kotodenden* room. *What time is it in Australia?* Julius always returns my calls and texts. Perhaps he forgot all about our bet and is making up for the months he has had to go without sex. *The poor women* in Australia. He's probably taken out all his sexual frustration on them. Why am I thinking about him? It's late now. I will try again tomorrow morning. I finish another glass of shiraz and wait for the heavy downpour to stop.

*

He kisses me. His lips are soft. He rubs his hands over my breasts. I can't believe I am laying in his arms. I moan in satisfaction. He continues soft kisses down to my navel. My hands fist through his hair. "No," *I murmur.* "We shouldn't…" *but I hardly resist. His hands move in between my legs. He pushes my dress up toward my chest. And then he pulls on either side of my panties. I shift side to side for him to remove them. I should stop.* "No, we shouldn't," *I mouth again. The tender kisses in between my thighs make my nipples hard. His breath at the apex of Ginger. And then I feel his tongue invade me. A long wet lick.* FUCK. *This feels amazing. I shouldn't…no…no…don't stop. My hands comb through his hair again and I grab a handful. His hair is much longer now. My hands caress his forehead and his cheeks. The sensation feels overwhelming. I can't close my eyes anymore.*

"PENNY!" My knees crash onto the floor as I leap from the couch. I get up and stumble onto the floor again. My underwear tangles my feet. "What the fuck?"

"What's wrong? Don't tell me you weren't enjoying this."

"Shit…shit…shit…shit…I thought you were—" *Shut up, Vida, before you commit yourself.* "I was dreaming. I thought I was dreaming it."

"So were you dreaming about me sucking your pussy? I like it a lot. It's sweet and plump." She licks her lips. She is wearing a black teddy with an opening from her vagina to her buttocks. *It's really more than I need to see of her ever.*

"You know this is not right. You forced yourself on me when I was sleeping. You took advantage of me."

"Oh, Vida. Stop it. You were on the verge of an orgasm. I could taste it. You can't force that."

"Like I said, I thought you were someone else. I was dreaming."

"Someone else, but not your husband. Well, just dream me anything you want me to be. And I will finish what I started." She moves closer to touch my face.

"I told you already, that is not my thing."

"Don't be too confident in that. I felt your body against mine. You just need to let go and try something different."

"I have to go home."

"You don't have to leave. No one has to know. It's just between me and you."

This is not a good time to feel horny, Vida. Don't get caught up in the sensation between your legs; I will find remorse and guilt in the morning. And…Abla…oh, Abla. Just thinking about my sister has me scrambling to pack and leave. "Thank you, but no thank you."

*

It's like being a teenager all over again. Sneaking in the house after curfew hoping that my mother is fast asleep. My shoes are in my hand while I tiptoe past Abla's bedroom.

"Yaa, iz dat you?" *She is the one that I'm avoiding. Fuck. Okay, Vida. Get out as fast as possible.* Abla is in the adjoining bathroom next to her bedroom. A gentle knock and then I press the door open.

"Oh my goodness. What are you doing?" I can't believe the view in front of me.

"Ahhh, Yaa, wat do you dink?" After what happened an hour ago, the last thing I need to see is another pussy staring at me.

"Are you dyeing your pubic hairs?"

"Ahhh, yeah." She looks at me as though my question sounds silly.

"Why on earth would you do that?"

"A girl haz to do wat a girl haz to do. Da otha night Richard was lyin' between my legs and you know I like to leave da lights on—" We're sisters, but there are still things that I'd rather not see or hear. *Like the fact that my sister dyes her pubic hairs.* She continues, "—it gets me all excited when I see his head movin' up and down and side to side. I was like, *tafere me twe.* He loves it when I say, 'lick my pussy' and—"

"Okay, okay…can we move this story along?"

"Well, he was into it and he looked up at me and had a strand of curly silver hair in da corner of hiz mouth. Can you imagine?" *No. Not now and not ever again.* I cover my ears in pure shyness, but Abla as always talks as though she is discussing a new recipe. "I was totally shocked and my mood changed. He kept askin' me wat waz wrong, poor thin'. He dought he waz doin' somedin' wrong. So lata I told him. And you know wat he said?" She pauses. *Is she waiting for me to answer?* Abla's eyes grow large as though she's seen a clearance sale.

"What did he say?"

"He said deerz a lot more strands down deer and it doezn't botha him." *Is that the cliffhanger? Geez, Abla can be a real drama queen.*

"Well, that's good. So why are you dyeing it?"

"Yur jokin', right? Don't believe wat men tell you haf da time. Dey respond to wat dey see. Soon he will be callin' me da *abrewa* wif da old *twe*. And den do you know wat happens? He will stop lickin' me from front to back."

Yes, too many visuals for one night. "Good night, Abla," I say, but she continues anyway.

"Den I won't be da hot sexy pussy. He will start callin' me da lady wif da AARP pussy."

"So just shave it off." *For goodness sake.*

"A sexy pussy should look matured. Not like it just came from da womb... I need a little bit of hair, so I have to dye it." Somehow her explanations always make sense to me.

"Okay. Good night." I try to escape again. Luckily she is too consumed in her own pubic affairs to notice guilt all over me.

"Yaa...look."

"What now...?" She bends down and grabs her ankles and her asshole is in full view of me. "Abla—what the hell?"

"Look. Do you see any grey hairs deer?"

"Hell. I can see your large intestines."

"Stop jokin'."

"Are you afraid he is going to find grey hair down there? What would he be doing there? It's late, Abla. I'm going to bed." She senses my uneasiness and anger.

"Wat iz da matta wif you? I just need yur help...like I helped you when you were pregnant wif MJ and yur ass waz hangin' out and you couldn't sit. Who put cream in yur ass and help you go to da toilet? Who?"

"Okay...okay...ah! I'm just tired, Abla." She relaxes herself and bends down again.

"No grey hair...no hair at all in fact."

"Good. Dank you and good night."

THE BORROWED WIFE

*

After a long hot bath, the bright pink and white floral comforter welcomes my naked skin. My legs look good. There is still muscle tone in my thighs and calves. *Okay, Vida, you need to get back to the field before everything turns to boiled potatoes.* With smooth strokes, the shea butter melts leaving a radiant sheen. Shea butter melts in between my breasts. They feel different after many years of breastfeeding. I'm comfortable with the mango shape cupped in my hands. My index fingers and thumbs bring hardness to my nipples. They point straight up. Ginger is still damp from the shower and my fingers navigate toward her. I take the handheld mirror beside the bed to have a better view. Short curly hairs start below my navel and leave a path right to Ginger. My legs spread wider on the bed and I tilt my pelvis to the ceiling, making it easier to see her. No grey hairs so far. Trimmed moist curly hairs just around the opening. The landscape is beautiful. She is beautiful. I use my index and middle finger to rub her back and forth gently. The same fingers find their way inside. My breathing is hard and fast. My nipples perk up and with my right hand I thumb one back and forth. Oh my goodness, it's been so long since I've been able to bring myself to a climax. I hear the cellphone vibrating on the bed. I'm already experiencing the heightened sensitivity to my skin. I feel a small fire burning underneath my flesh. My hips move up and down then side to side. The cellphone keeps vibrating. *Fuck, not now.* It is distracting. My fingers are frozen in place. *Just a few more seconds and it will stop.* Another incoming call. I extend my other hand and reach for my phone.

"Good evening, Vida. Are you asleep?" His voice is deep and low. *This may work to my advantage.* My fingers are still resting inside me. "Sorry I'm now just getting back to you. I got your message."

"No, it's fine." *Shit. I sound like a sex hotline.* I temper my breathing.

"How are the children and Abla?"

"They are all good."

"I just got off the phone with Penny." *Shit.* A dozen thoughts whirl around in my head. *What did she tell him?*

"She said she was feeling under the weather, but you made her feel better." The thought about what happened earlier this evening brings coldness to my skin. I remove my fingers.

"Oh, it's nothing. Glad she is feeling better. She arrived just when I was leaving. Just thought you should know."

"Yes. Thank you. Alice also contacted me." The brief silence between us allows me to gather more information of his whereabouts.

"Very noisy. Where are you?" No response. "Well, I won't keep you. Sounds like you're busy."

"All right, Vida. Sorry. The reception here is very poor. See you when I get back."

The phone rests beside me again and sexual images of Julius invade me. I move my legs up so that my knees point to the ceiling. The soles of my feet press into the mattress. Again, my fingers slowly invade Ginger. The sensation is still there. My lips part and I can taste the air. I close my eyes. *Julius is kissing me and his lips are pressed on my neck. He sucks hard.* I rub my fingers back and forth in the folds of my flesh. The heat underneath my flesh is ripping through my body. I feel sweat under my arms and moisture running down my thighs. My fingers are delicately bringing my body where it needs to go. In and out in slow long strokes. Ginger's wetness smears around the short curly hairs. My clitoris grows larger and harder. My breathing quickens. It's been so long. Just a few more strokes and all the anxiety will leave my body.

"Mommy? Mommy…" *No, not now. Just a minute more.* "Mommy, the door is locked." It's one in the morning and like clockwork, MJ is at my door.

My right hand rests on Ginger. Maybe he will give up and go back to bed. I don't move or say a word. He knocks frantically. It's an unusual knock. *Fuck. This is not going to happen tonight. And I was so close.* I couldn't finish now if I wanted to. MJ's presence puts my mood off. I get up and wash my hands and put on my nightshirt before I open the door.

"Mommy, I heard something outside."

"Like what, baby?"

"I don't know." He clenches my T-shirt. I walk with him back into the room. Kakra is fast asleep and nothing out of the ordinary is noticeable.

"Honey, there is nothing or no one here. Go back to sleep, okay? It's late."

"Can I sleep in your room just for tonight?" He hugs me and of course I give in.

"Just for tonight." He leaps excitedly and trails behind me toward my bedroom.

Chapter 59

"Well, well. Look who's here." Julius is standing on the rooftop balcony.

"Hello, Ms. Frimpong." We stand apart. He looks amazing. He is wearing a dark blue suit with a dark blue shirt and brown shoes. His hair looks longer and he pulls back a couple of strands behind his ear. "That isn't a very warm welcome. How long are you going to stand there?" I rush to hug him and he meets me halfway and scoops me into his arms.

"Welcome back, Boss."

"It's great to be back." We both giggle.

"I see you've gained your strength back." He lowers me down but still holds me in his arms. "Nice suit, as always. Wow, your hair is longer. A new look?"

"Something of the sorts. You like?" I comb my hands through his hair. "That's not the only place where my hair has grown back in case you want to rub your hands through there as well."

"T-M-I." We both laugh again. "I was on my way home from work when I got an alert from Alice that you're home. You know I had to come and see for myself."

"Do you have Alice tracking my whereabouts?" he asks.

"No, not really...I simply asked her to notify me when you arrived. I know you still hold the strings and you wouldn't have allowed her to send me a text if you didn't approve it."

"My intention was to formally see you and the kids tomorrow. But candidly, I'm glad you are here now." He squeezes me again.

"You know I'm ticklish."

"Well, I need to do this more often. It feels good holding you." The air between us is different. He gives me a kiss on the check before releasing me from his embrace.

"Well, tell me, how was Australia? How was the visit with Dr. Braun? Tell me everything." I hold his hand and we sit together on crates that serve as makeshift stools. In Julius's absence he has commissioned the rest of the rooftop to be tiled and canopied.

"We have plenty of time to catch up." He unloosens his tie and unbuttons the jacket. "It's been over a month since I've been up here. The tiles give it a sophisticated feel."

"These are nice." I tap my foot onto the tiles.

"I had them flown in last week. You haven't been up here then?"

"It's been a while. Just that weekend when Penny was dropped off." I promised myself I wouldn't be back here until Julius arrived. And so far there is no sign of her. "It's been easier for me to work from home," I say.

"Oh, have you been writing?"

I look at him sheepishly. "No…" I say. "I've been reading your journals."

"That's good news. Anything you want to ask me?"

"Yes, plenty. But not tonight." He looks stunningly attractive this evening. I am blushing from the amount of attention I'm giving him. "Just a week more to go until the end of the bet."

"What bet?"

I rest my hands on my hips. "You know exactly what I am talking about."

"I thought that was null and void, considering—"

"So, just admit that I am the winner and that you have a sex addiction."

"Pardon me. I will do no such thing. I have a week to go."

"What about your time away? Do you mean to tell me you weren't being entertained by some young chicken?"

"Not even by a pigeon!" He laughs. His looks are striking under the moonlight. "You look beautiful, Vida."

"What?" I say, blushing.

"Something about you seems different."

"You don't even know what I am wearing."

"I don't have to see you or know what you are wearing to know you are beautiful." *Ginger warrants attention. She's preparing the grounds.*

"Thank you."

"Did I make you uncomfortable?"

"No. I was just thinking about how much you've been missed. I guess there is something to that old adage. Distance puts a lot in perspective."

He extends his hands behind his head as though he is giving my question some thought. "Does oral sex count?"

"Really? Oral sex is still sex."

"What about phone sex? Sexting?" he asks.

"It depends."

"On?"

"Whether or not you got aroused and, you know, if fluids came out."

"We are mature adults, Vida. We don't need euphemisms."

"If you ejaculated." *There, I said it.* He laughs. "It doesn't matter, Julius. It was a silly bet. Let's call it quits. So much has happened. Who am I to put sanctions on your sex life? You are a grown man. I was trying to make a point, but it doesn't matter." I get up and walk over to the balcony's edge.

"I didn't fuck anyone, nor have I had any of the aforementioned exchanges with anyone around the world. I agreed willingly, Vida. I wasn't forced or coerced. I always keep my word. And I intend to see this bet till the end. Just one more week to go to prove to Vida Frimpong that I, Julius Gallo, do not have a sex addiction."

"You don't have to prove anything to me."

"Yes, I know. But maybe I need to prove it to myself."

My phone rings and it breaks the brief silence between us. Saved by the bell. I search through my bag for the phone and he walks back inside. It's an unknown caller. The second call today. I let it ring longer. I finally pick it up on the fifth ring. "Hello? Hellooo?" No answer and the caller hangs up.

With the phone still in my hand, I call Auntie Cece and the boys. *They are probably wondering where I am.* I tell her my whereabouts and I sense the displeasure on the other end of the phone. I talk to each of the boys and let them know that I will be home shortly.

Julius returns to the balcony. His attire is different. Dark blue jeans and an army green top. He is carrying two huge bags. "A man bearing gifts."

"What is this?" He hands me one of the bags.

"For you, my lovely lady…"

"Oh, Julius, you didn't—"

"Ummmmm…" He places his finger over my lips to silence me. "Please." He motions me to open the bag. I sit across from him again. I place the bag on my lap and begin to unravel it. A big black shoebox with the words Monika Chiang written on top. Inside is the sexiest pair of red shoes I've ever laid my eyes on. Julius rises and leaves the balcony again. The smell of leather and the details of the shoe pull me into a trance. I slip the shoes on. *Ohhhh, it feels orgasmic.* I strut across the newly laid tiles. Julius reappears with a bottle of wine. "Do you like?"

"Oh, I'm in love with them. They fit just right." I strut for him and the heels clap against the tile. "Play some music. Let me break them in tonight." I start tapping my foot.

"Alice, some dancing music for Ms. Frimpong."

"Yes, my Lord."

Reggae music fills the air on the balcony. I dance, still trying to detect who is singing. It's Mavado. I wind my hips around, up and down, side to side. He sits on the crate and moves his head in the direction of the sound of my heels. "Your walk is different," he says.

"It is?"

"Yes. Whenever you wear F-M-Ps, your walk is more confident and a bit sexier."

"Really? You can hear that?"

"Yes and you should wear them more often."

"Agreed."

Chapter 60

An hour has turned to three hours. We finish the bottle of wine and start another. I call Auntie Cece and promise her that I will be home in another thirty minutes. She assures me that the boys are already asleep. Her simple answers and heavy breathing tell me she wants me to ask her something so she can unleash her prepared response. "A large package arrived this morning," she says. It's probably Mensah delivering some things for the boys.

"Thank you, Auntie. I will see you when I get home." I quickly hang up before she can ask why am I still here. My eyes rest back on the lighted landscape of the Queensboro Bridge.

"How many stars do you see out tonight?" Julius asks.

The night sky seems clear. I tilt my head back. I pivot around in my new heels and try to count as far as my eyes can see. "Maybe a few dozen are out tonight." I take the last gulp of the wine in my glass. "I should get going."

"You've been saying that for the past hour."

"I know, but I'm going for real now."

"How about if I don't want you to go?"

I feel the pressure of his words on me, which attract me to him even more. His lips look soft. The wine gives them a pinkish hue. He smiles and drinks the last of his wine and sets his glass farther away on the balcony ledge. His hand is outstretched toward me. I hand him my glass and he rests it beside his empty glass.

"I will take you home…" He pauses. "…when you're ready."

"I drove." I move closer to him. Our breath, the smell of shiraz, encircles us.

"We just finished two bottles of wine. I should take you home." He pauses. "But when you're ready."

"I'm ready now." *This is definitely flirting, but I can't help myself.* It's been so long since I've felt this giddy.

"Are you really ready?" The tip of his nose is on mine. My heartbeat is competing with the drumming music in the background. His right hand moves from my shoulder and rests on my waist. He pulls me tight in his arms. "Vida," he says my name with the right inflection and it gives me a sinful smile. A subtle smell of vanilla escapes his mouth.

"Julius," I whisper his name.

"Vida," he whispers back. I'm not sure what to do, but his lips scream for me to take them into mine. "I really missed you." The words I needed to hear. I lose all inhibitions and offer my lips to him. Our warm tongues devour each other. The softness of his lips doesn't allow me to let go. I suck on his bottom lip until the sensation consumes him and his hands slide down my buttocks and he squeezes me tightly. I separate my lips again and his tongue finds a sweet spot. His arms wrap around me; it feels like a wool blanket. It's been so long since I've been in someone's arms, holding me and reassuring me with kisses. For a brief moment, it is everything I pictured in my dreams. Soft but hungry kisses.

He stops abruptly, releasing me from the secure embrace. I move back, realizing what I've done and I feel ashamed.

"Sorry." The word escapes the same lips that were so appreciative. "So sorry. That shouldn't have happened." *Ginger disagrees.* She's prepared a moist inviting landscape for The Beast. I'm dumbfounded.

"Vida, don't apologize. I want..." He pauses again and rests his hands on either side of his waist. "Let me take you home."

I scramble around looking for things I need to leave with: bag, shoes and dignity.

"Alice."

"Yes, my Lord."

"Tell Pio to bring the car around to the front. We are taking Ms. Frimpong home."

"No...No...I drove. I can drive back home."

"We agreed. I will take you home, Vida."

"No, you said that. I'm fine."

"I'm taking you home," he says firmly. My argument is futile. In about ten minutes I'm sitting beside him in the Maybach pretending to be asleep to avoid conversation.

"How are you feeling? Try to take something warm before you go to sleep. Otherwise, you will feel the effects of the bottles of wine in the morning. I will have Vincent bring your car later this evening."

"Thank you," I say. We get home and my usual banter is nonexistent. "Julius, thank you for the shoes. See you Friday."

"I will call you later," he says.

Chapter 61

"Are you asleep?"

"Not anymore. Watz wrong?"

"Nothing."

"Datz why you call me at two a.m.? C'mon wat iz it?" I take a deep breath and begin to whisper into my phone.

"He kissed me," I say, closing the phone over my mouth, afraid maybe MJ will wake up and hear me.

"Wat?"

I clear my throat and draw out the words, this time talking slowly. "He…kissed…me." Total silence and I wait for Abla to say something. "Did you hear me?"

"Well?"

"Well, what? You don't have anything to say? Well, actually I think I kissed him…I'm not sure. I think I had too much to drink."

"Iz dat it?"

"Yeah, what else did you want to hear?"

"Where exactly?"

"On the lips. That's it."

"Datz it? You didn't give him a little blowie or somedin'?"

"You mean blowjob? No. He's my boss…well, we're friends." I'm surprised she would even suggest that. *No, I'm not. I'm talking to my sister, after all.*

"But he kissed you. You didn't do or say anydin' else?"

"I apologized."

"For wat?"

"I think I said sorry. Yeah, I said sorry." Abla sucks her teeth at me.

"You called me at two a.m. to tell me he kissed you and den you said sorry. Ahhh, Yaaa…paaa…" She mutters something quickly in Twi. She speaks so fast that I can't translate it quickly enough to get the full meaning, except one word that is clearly audible.

"What are you saying about my *etwe*?"

She repeats herself, this time drawing her words out in English.

"I…said…call…me…when…he…is…done…wipin'…da…cɔbwebs…off…yur…pussy. Good night."

She ends the call immediately. *That hefa!*

Chapter 62

I follow my usual weekday routine. But today I can't get Julius's kiss out of my head. I wake the children up and make my way downstairs to prepare breakfast.

Smack in the middle of the living and dining room are several huge boxes. *Was this here when I came in last night?*

"Good morning, Yaa."

"Good morning, Auntie."

"What time did you make it home?" she asks sternly. I know she wants to inquire further, but I want to divert my attention away from what happened last night.

"Auntie, what are all these boxes?"

"They came for you yesterday. I am sure they are from yur boss. Just like the video games he sent for the children." I step further into the living room and find the Xbox already connected. I open the large box with the sharp end of a pen. Inside are dozens of shoeboxes: Louboutin, Monika Chiang, Prada, Brian Atwoods, Fendi and countless other names. I open up one shoebox: a deep purple pair of F-M-Ps. *Are all these boxes shoes?* I walk over to the dining room and open that box. Inside several dozen more shoes. *Oh my goodness.* "Just how many shoes did he send you?" Auntie Cece's voice is alarmed.

Chanel, Sergio, Escada, all size eight and a half. There's another box in the living room, but this one is slightly shorter than the other three large boxes. I cut through the tape on the top of this box as well. A card placed neatly on top. It's Julius's handwriting.

There are NTYBF. But please accept this as a small token of my appreciation for being a part of my life. May every day of the year be a day where FMPs are needed!

With loving regards, Julius

Auntie Cece's gaze penetrates my skin. Our eyes finally meet. "What will yur husband think? Gifts from other men raises unnecessary suspicion. All deese shoes. Why do you need all deese shoes? Just for you. It's ridiculous."

"Yeah, all these, just for me." She gives me a unsatisfied look and motions as though she wants to say something, but reconsiders. She retreats back into the kitchen. *I couldn't care less what Mensah thinks. He should be trying to win my affection back.* What am I saying? Do I want to take him back? Even if I did, so much has to change. Mensah and I need to have a long talk; texting and voice messages aren't going to cut it. The events uncovered in California are still fresh in my mind. *Maybe I need to write him a letter. I can say everything on paper. Yes, write him a letter and tell him how you feel.*

I take another shoe out of the box. High black Chanel F-M-Ps. I am distracted by their simplicity and sexiness. I try them on and strut up and down the hallway. *Very nice indeed.* I walk past the boxes trying to count how many are in each package. And then a thought occurs to me. *Holy Shit! Where am I going to store all these shoes?*

Chapter 63

I enter the house and the light from his study is the only light inside. The clicks of my red F-M-Ps on the tile meet the slight echoes of the hallway. Julius is standing with his back to me. I stand in the doorway for a minute hoping he will detect my presence before I enter. He doesn't turn around. I knock lightly on the door.

"Good evening, Julius." He turns his head and then his entire body to face me.

"Well, good evening, Vida." He smiles briefly.

"How's your evening so far?"

"Better now," he says. I take a few steps closer to him. His arms are crossed against his chest and his buttocks lean against his worktable.

"Thank you again for the shoes. It was a very, very kind token. They are all beautiful. I've occupied all the closets in the bedroom and the downstairs hallway to house them." I don't mention the fact that I packed Mensah's clothes up again and moved them to Panin's room.

"You are most welcome, but you don't have to thank me again. I got your message yesterday and your thank you card." *Maybe this would be a good time to mention the kiss.* I move closer and stand within breathing distance from him. The faint smell of licorice surrounds his mouth. His posture is still the same. I wonder if he is feeling the same way: scared, happy, anxious. My heart sprints with each deep breath. I rehearsed the speech on my way over here.

Julius, I really like you. But we have to be friends. It was very careless of me to do what I did. I hope this doesn't affect our relationship. I just want you to know you mean a lot to me.

A short and simple speech, but as I stand before him, I can't utter the words. I stare at the same inviting lips. And I want to chew them again. *Slowly.*

"Do you need me?" he says. *Hell yes!* The words scream in my head. *Or is that Ginger screaming?* In any case, I silence the roaring woman in me.

"Need you?" The words sound foreign to me. "Do I need you?" I repeat it again, trying to formulate a G-rated response.

"Yes. Do you want to go over my mother's journals? I have a couple of minutes before I begin my work," he says.

"Oooh...Oooh." Scattered around the room on several work desks are instruments, braille papers, wires and wall-to-wall screens. It is more disheveled than usual. "Yes. Right. No. Anything I need. You. Busy." I am not sure if I speak in coherent sentences. His brows crinkle as though he is trying his best to understand me. I take a step back, wishing I could just vanish without looking sillier than I am. "Well, if you...me...get back your...work...let...I will...holla...if...you...need help." I am finally aware of what my brain is trying to tell me about my mouth. *Vida, you sound stupid.*

"Okay," he says. *Well, at least he understands buffoonery.* I turn around to leave and take long strides to exit his study.

*

I turn the computer on and open another journal in my lap. The words on the pages seem blurry to me. I turn the pages one by one, not really focusing. I am thinking about him and our kiss. His soft wet lips and his tongue exploring every bit of my mouth. *Vida, stop this. Why are you daydreaming about a man who is just within walking distance from you? He didn't mention the kiss. Maybe he isn't feeling the same way you are. You are worrying yourself over nothing. Okay, pull yourself together. Don't bring it up. Pretend like it never happened. We both drank too much. That was all it was. A mistake. Focus on work.*

My eyes stumble on a page in the journal. Written in all caps at the bottom.

NANA IS HERE. I KNOW IT.

It is odd the way it stands out in the journal. I flip the journal a couple pages back. No mention again about Nana. *Who is Nana?* I continue reading.

Did I miss something? I read the entire journal and comb through line by line. No more mention about Nana. Just more description of his mother building churches in the villages of Ghana. He goes on to describe the lengthy process of walking back and forth delivering sand and water to the church site. Nothing else about Nana except these six words. *But there are pages torn from the journal. Is Nana the reason pages are ripped from the journal? Another woman? This would be a good time to ask for his assistance. I mean, this is a legitimate reason. Not like I want to bring up the kiss. Maybe it's not Ama that broke his heart. This Nana may be the one.*

"Busy?" Julius is standing in the doorway. He is dressed in black pants and a black fitted polo shirt. He looks freshly showered.

"Ummm, yes…" I pause. "No, not really." He smiles vibrantly.

"Let's go."

"Go?"

"Yes. You are not going to parade all night within these four walls wearing sexy stilettos. And I'm guessing new shoes also means a new cute outfit to match."

"It's nothing new. Just a plain skirt and a simple blouse."

"I'm certain nothing looks plain or simple on you. We should go have some fun." He holds out his hand. "Shall we?"

I spring from the desk and grab my purse. "Where are we going?" He holds my hand as we walk toward the elevator.

"Anywhere you choose."

"Really?"

"Yes…anywhere." We arrive in the garage and there are twenty cars neatly arranged in each of their own parking spots.

"Wow. Did you purchase more cars?"

"Just a few more."

"Here." He gestures to a gunmetal color Mercedes Benz. The interior has far more gadgets than the Range Rover.

"Well, it's almost ten o'clock and there's this concert running all week. Old school R and B at this spot in Mount Vernon. At times they have special guests, so getting in may be hard. But we can give it a try."

"Yes, we should. I am in your capable hands this evening." Julius motions me toward the car. He gives the command, "Open doors." Both passenger and driver side doors swing open toward the ceiling. "Ms. Frimpong, please." He gestures me into the passenger's side.

"Oh, so you're driving again." He laughs.

"Something of the sort."

Really Vida, are you going to sit in the passenger side and let Julius drive?

"Trust me, Vida."

He must sense my hesitation. *Famous last words?* I slide into the passenger seat. The charcoal grey leather seating is plush and warm. The electronic dashboard is just as large as my desktop computer. Julius enters the car and the doors close.

"Good evening, Lord Gallo and Ms. Frimpong."

Alice. I've become accustomed to her soft sultry voice. Several icons light up on the dashboard.

"Should I continue your album selection, Lord Gallo?"

"No, Ms. Frimpong will choose some driving music." The dashboard lights up with several selections and I recognize some from my iPhone.

"Seatbelts," Julius says. And the belts emerge from the seats and cross over my shoulder and waist.

"Seatbelts secure."

I touch the dashboard and select one of my albums. "**Ms. Frimpong, unfortunately Lord Gallo's fingerprints are the only ones authorized in this vehicle. Please state your request.**"

"Sorry, I'm a bit sensitive about my music," Julius says.

"No kidding. Is Becca okay to play?"

"Perfect." Becca's voice erupts from the surround speakers. "Where to?"

I give Alice the address and the vehicle begins to move without any indication that Julius is driving.

"So, is this how you get around when you are not with Vincent?"

"At times."

The car navigates onto Van Dam Street and obeys all traffic signals. A bicyclist crosses in front of us and the car stops. "Idiot. That was close. He nearly got knocked down."

"**Unfortunately, this is very common in New York.**"

"Oh yes, I know, Alice."

The dashboard reveals eight cameras around the vehicle. Another car inches closer to us. He probably wants to see inside. He slows down, but I doubt if the smoke tinted windows reveal the passengers inside.

Julius slides his hand onto my lap. "So, are you pressing on the gas?" I ask.

"No. Everything is computerized, from speed limits to braking distance. I hope you are comfortable." He squeezes my hand.

"So the night we met, that fancy Lamborghini was designed the same way?"

"Yes, pretty much. But it was a newer test model and I didn't install all the functions as this one."

"I see."

"Do you?" We laugh.

We arrive at the club and the usual security check delays the flow of traffic. The bouncer tells us that they have reached their cap, but Julius grabs the bouncer's hand and slips a couple of hundreds into his palm. He moves aside so quickly that he stumbles and falls.

"Just how much did you give him?" I whisper.

"Apparently enough." We enter the doors and step aside for the arduous security check.

"Read the signs, folks. Absolutely no recording devices, cameras or cellphones…we have a check-in for all electronics. You will get it once you leave." A large black man takes inventory of the crowd assembled at the gate.

I walk through the metal detectors for the second time. This time I remove my chain and earrings. All the metal is in a plastic tray off to the side. It buzzes again. "Do you have anything else on you, sweetie? Something is setting off the detector." A large woman with dreads pats me down again.

"I've given you my purse already and I've taken off all my jewelry. Nothing else."

"Do you have any piercings…you know, down there, or nipple rings?"

"No, absolutely not."

She sighs and tosses her dreads over her shoulder. "Okay, take off your shoes and go through."

"Don't you think this is extreme? What can I possibly hide in four-inch Louboutins?" I hate that this is taking so long, but Julius waits patiently.

"Sorry, momma. Just doing my job." I walk through and no buzzing.

"It's the shoes. Are these knockoff red bottoms made in China?"

"These are Louboutins," I snicker back, but I'm too intimidated by her size to lash out at her.

"Well honey, I'm just saying, a lot of red bottoms come through here and none of them sets off the metal detectors." I roll my eyes and wait for Julius on the other side of the metal detector.

Julius removes his watch, the only piece of jewelry on him. The detectors go off again. The second time they ask him to remove his shoes and then the third time his glasses.

The line grows longer and the people more anxious. Another bouncer comes to see what the holdup is.

"Sorry, Bruce, taking a bit longer with this couple." Bruce gives a head nod to the woman with the dreads, satisfied that things are still under control. She focuses back on Julius. "I'm sorry, I can't let you in with these."

"He needs them," I say.

"Vida," Julius quiets me.

"Is this some kinda of recording device? I haven't seen anything like this before. Our policy...no recording devices."

"I wanna know, is Obama performing here tonight? Maybe I would feel these extreme measures are worth this aggravation."

"You're funny and cute," the woman with the dreads says. I turn my attention to Julius.

"Julius, we can go somewhere else instead."

"No." His voice is adamant. "We are staying. I will follow your lead." The woman with the dreads takes the glasses and I snatch the ticket away from her.

"They better be here when we are ready to leave. Those are custom-made glasses."

"Just doing my job, momma," she replies.

It is crowded and on stage is a live band. A young woman on the microphone assures the crowd of a memorable night. I whisper in Julius's ear to go to the bar. He nods. He wraps his arm around my waist from behind and we inch ourselves toward an empty space at the end of the bar. I lean into his ear again. "Guinness?"

"Yes, and what will you have?"

"Pinot grigio perhaps." I signal the bar attendant.

"What can I get you, beautiful?" Before I can speak, Julius speaks.

"A chilled pinot grigio and a bottle of Guinness."

He reaches in his pocket for his wallet and I want to offer to pay, but I know it will lead to him paying anyway. He hands the bar attendant his black Amex card.

"Should I run you up a tab?" Julius answers yes before the bar attendant can say anything else.

"Okay, two drinks coming up."

The young woman on the mic is singing an unfamiliar song, but the crowd is digging her. Julius looks handsome tonight and he smells like his minty body wash. I use the crowd as an excuse to press my body into his and it gives me another reason to whisper in his ear again. I slowly mouth the words, "Sorry if I make you feel uncomfortable. It's very crowded in here."

He whispers back into my ear. I can't help but tighten my shoulders because his voice courses through my spine. "I'm very comfortable. It's rather ideal, don't you think?" He moves his arm across my abdomen and pulls me in closer. Thank goodness I haven't eaten anything. *My stomach feels like I'm in shape.*

The drinks arrive and I pick up my glass and take a tiny sip. He picks up the Guinness bottle with his other hand and tilts his head back. He doesn't let go of me. I can feel The Beast move slightly, reminding me that he is very much there. *What are you doing, Vida?* My actions will just lead to another 'sorry' before the end of the night.

A drummer appears on stage and is harnessing his power over the drums. This gives me a reason to pull away and focus my attention on the stage. At first, Julius doesn't let me go, but I reassure him that I'm right by his side. The crowd gives the drummer a roaring applause. The woman appears on the mic enticing the crowd with her sultry voice.

There's an anxious scream in the crowd. I look around to see where the voice is coming from. It's alarming and I move closer to Julius. I can't make out what is happening or where the voice is coming from, but it grows louder. Heads turn around in search of the same noise everyone hears. I take a firm hold of Julius's hand.

"DJ! DJ!" Finally an image. A tall white woman appears in front of us. "DJ!" she shouts again and lunges for Julius.

"Hey. Excuse me," I say. She nearly knocks me down to embrace him.

"It's me. Rebecca." She's breathless. She's clawed her way through the tightly packed crowd. He grips my hand tighter and I am sure this is a sign that he doesn't want me to go anywhere. I stand at his side while this stranger perhaps has him confused with someone else.

"Oh my fucking goodness. I can't believe it's you and you're here." She takes hold of his other hand.

"Rebecca…it's been a long time." *He knows her.*

"Hell fuckin' yeah. Where have you been? What have you been doing? I've tried a hundred times to reach you, but I couldn't track you down. I went to the house for nearly ten years hoping I would run into you or get information about where you had gone. It was like you disappeared from the face of the earth. And now—oh my goodness, my prayers are answered. You're here." She thrusts her arms over his neck again and Julius doesn't move his arms to embrace her. It's uncomfortable, but he doesn't let go of my hand.

"Excuse me, Rebecca. This is Vida, my girlfriend." He pushes her back to a reasonable distance.

"Girlfriend?" she says. *Yes, heifer*…She acts like Julius having a girlfriend is a miracle.

Julius squeezes my hand and I squeeze back, confirming that I will follow his lead in this unicorn story. She examines me and I offer a small smile with no teeth. Her eyes are hard on me and I can tell that she is beginning the comparison showdown. She stares at my natural hair loosely cascading around my shoulders. Then she flings back her bone straight Kool-Aid cherry-like hair over her shoulders. She is wearing a burgundy minidress and unflattering heels. She is tall, lean and straight. The only curve I can see is on her nose. Nothing that stands out but the Bloody Mary on top of her head. She continues the showdown. *Well, in that case let me give her something to think about.* I move to the music with all intention of using every curve God blessed me with to my advantage.

"Hi," she says faintly. I extend my hand and she shakes it as though it is something foreign to her. *Now that Julius has introduced me as his girlfriend, I should act like one.*

I pretend that my focus is on the stage and I clap as soon as the woman on the stage finishes her solo performance. Julius looks for my hand and then pulls me into his embrace again. Rebecca's face hardens and I take liberty to rest the back of my head onto Julius's chest. *This heifer is still holding his hand.* He listens as she continues to reveal several years of her life. *This is so unnecessary.* I feel sorry for her. *Runway model turned to runaway train: fast and off track. I need to cut this show.*

"Babe, do you want another Guinness?"

"Yes, babe," he responds accordingly. I move slightly to signal the bartender, making sure Julius can feel my presence behind him. *I can't believe she is still reminiscing.* Now she is talking about the weekends she used to spend with him when she was studying for her accounting license. *Wait, this is interesting. What else can she reveal about Julius? Why did she call him DJ? Listen more, Vida, and talk less.*

"I never stopped thinking about you. Oh my goodness. I really fucked us up. I was so young and so stupid back then. I can't believe after all these years, you're finally here." She moves in closer and I am wondering when is he going to tell her to back the fuck down.

"Remember when we spent the weekend together when my parents went to Florida? Oh my goodness, I still remember it like it was yesterday. You've cut your hair. You look very handsome, as I imagined you would."

Okay, this is getting boring and stalkerous. "Babe, that's our song playing. I want to dance." There is no one on stage yet. The band is playing a couple of tunes, but I don't care; I have to find an excuse to pull this train into a station. I grab him by his left hand and Rebecca struggles not to let go of his right. I give her the African stare-down, but she doesn't back down. Julius must sense the heaviness in the air.

"Ummm, Rebecca, give me a moment."

She releases her grip and I guide him onto the dance floor. The woman appears on the stage again and she alludes to a special guest. She entices the crowd to make their way onto the dance floor. The band plays a familiar beat and Billy Ocean glides onto the stage.

"Wow, Billy Ocean is here?" Julius says.

"Yes, I love his music." We dance as Billy sings "Love Zone."

"So, what exactly did you do to her? I think she may want to take you home and lock you up in her bed, like, forever."

He laughs. "That was a long time ago."

"Whatever you say, DJ. A man with aliases. I haven't come across that name yet in the journals."

"Some things I don't need to remember. That was many moons ago."

"Not for her. What she really wanted to say was: 'Remember the time my parents were away and you came over and practically screwed my brains out so that I would never forget you? Well, guess what? I haven't forgotten you. And I'm not going anywhere.'"

"You're funny."

"Am I?" I look over my shoulder and, just as I expect, her statuesque presence remains. "She is staring you down like markdowns on Black Friday."

"Is she really still standing there?"

"Ahhhh, yeah."

"I did tell her you were my girlfriend. Maybe she doesn't believe it."

"To some women, that doesn't mean anything."

"Clearly."

"I may have to make it very clear that she is not needed."

"How so?" he asks.

Billy is crooning on stage and I should be excited to see this live performance, but at this moment, I just want to do one thing.

I extend my arms over Julius's shoulders and move my body into his embrace. My hands circle curls in his hair and he leans into me. His nose touches mine and I feel the tips of his eyelashes. I close my eyes and offer my mouth to his. A soft kiss at first, but then he pries my mouth open with his tongue. We kiss with his tongue chasing mine. He moves his hand close to my buttocks and my lips tug on his bottom lip. I pull back gently and look over my shoulder. It's still not enough; she is still posted at her station. I lick his bottom lip and he hungrily covers his lips over mine. His mouth is so warm and the Guinness taste fills my mouth repeatedly. Applause surrounds us and I realize that we've been kissing for a while. I turn my head again and Rebecca is gone. Excited that I was able to chase her away, I turn to inform Julius, but before I can utter a word, he grabs me tightly and kisses me tenderly on my lips and neck.

"She's finally gone."

"Well, I guess it's clear who I am interested in," he says.

Emotions tangle and my body tingles. He says we should go home but I wonder how we will make it. The kiss leaves my skin scorching hot and my desire for him even more obvious.

We are waiting for the valet to bring the car around. Our hands land everywhere we can reach one another. He kisses me again and cups his hands on my hips as though they always belonged there. He gives me gentle squeezes on my buttocks and maps out the contour of my thong.

"DJ…! DJ…!" *This heifer again.* The petulant disaster. "I want to give you my card. I'm a photographer and my studio is not far from here, on Third Avenue. It's the last building on the cul-de-sac. Give me your email. I still have some old photos that I want to give you."

What the hell? This damned cock-blocker. She clearly doesn't give a flying fuck. My sexual desire is turning into anger. Julius squeezes my hand tightly and then he addresses her.

"Rebecca, it was great running into you after all these years. I would be lying if I said I would call you or we will reconnect. I am happy you are doing well. I always knew that you would pursue your passion. It's good that you followed your heart. Speaking of which, I really must go. Take care."

He pulls me in closer. I am sure by now she wishes the floor would just swallow her up. I should look away, but I am savoring every moment. She has the look of a child who was told there is no Santa Claus. The valet pulls the car up, or rather Alice comes around the block.

The attendant steps out and the same enthusiasm is there from earlier in the evening. "Yo, this ride is hot, bro…I need to get one of these joints."

"I'll drive," I say. Julius is still distracted by the beet-colored hair model. I slip the attendant ten bucks.

She says, "Oh, of course…it was great seeing you. You look great. Well, here's my card anyways, in case you need some professional headshots or anything." She puts it in Julius's hand and begins to retreat behind the car. *Maybe I can accidentally back into her. Accidents happen all the time on this busy street.*

"Good night," Julius says.

She chuckles. "How is mother hen doing? Do give Nana my regards," she says cattily.

"Good night, Rebecca." This time his voice is sterner. He sits down quickly and commands Alice to set off.

Rebecca knows Nana. How does she know Nana?

As we speed up the highway, Julius rolls down the window and throws her card out. He moves his hand onto my lap and begins massaging my leg. My mood is definitely different from a few minutes ago and even Ginger is having trouble staying interested.

"You're quiet. Is everything okay?"

I nod my head and then say yes. "Just feeling a little buzz from the drink, that's all. I should have eaten something before drinking the wine." A unicorn story. I can't help but think about what transpired. *There is still so much about Julius I don't know. Why do I think I know it all because I read some journals?* Nana, Rebecca, Ama are still people who are intricate parts of his life.

"Vida?"

"No, really. I'm fine. Alcohol has other effects on me…"

He leans back. "…Oooh…do tell…"

"Maybe I will have to show you."

"Even better," he says. The moisture between my legs becomes more intense by the time we reach the garage. We start again, our hands like tentacles extending everywhere. His kisses are wild, warm and wet, from my lips to my neck and shoulders. We get off the elevator and I kick my F-M-Ps off and head to the kitchen. Alice begins to relay Julius's messages.

"Alice, later. Not now." He follows me into the kitchen. I take the remaining Haagen Dazs vanilla ice cream from the freezer and use my fingers to eat from the container.

"Hungry?" I ask him.

"Yes. But not for food." He takes the container from me and sets it down on the marble countertop. We begin again and this time he is moaning and calling out my name. It makes my nipples hard.

"Vida, babe." He kisses me again and again. His body is pressed against me and The Beast lets me know he is ready. He sucks my neck and the warmth of his tongue right below my earlobe makes me giddy.

"Julius, should we do this? What about Penny and Mens—"

"We shouldn't concern ourselves with people who are not here. We're adults and I think we both know what we want. Right now it's just"—he kisses me again—"me and you." He sucks on my lips. "…That's all that matters right now." He lifts me onto the countertop and moves his hands inside my thighs.

"Julius…"

"Talk to me, babe…" He begins to pull my blouse from my skirt. His hands find my breasts. And although I should be filled with rawness to be feeling this way, I can't help but wonder why Rebecca knows so much about him. *Julius never mentioned living in New York. But then again, he has the hotel. And why did she call him DJ? And how does she know Nana? Who is Nana?* Julius finds a sweet spot and breaks me from my worries. I moan into his ear.

"Julius." He trails wet kisses in between my breasts and moves his hand in between my legs. It's been so long since I've felt this good.

"Lord Gallo, urgent call."

Alice freezes us mid-ecstasy. My hands have a fistful of his hair and his teeth are sealed into my bra.

"Lord Gallo, urgent call."

He stands upright. His erection is clearly begging to come out. "Alice, not now."

He continues to kiss me, but this sudden break gives me more time to think. *You can't do this, Vida. You barely know this man. What about Mensah and Penny?* The guilt begins.

"Lord Gallo, pardon the intrusion, but I was told to put the call through."

Maybe it's Vincent. I haven't seen him at all this evening. Julius stands back again, a little more bothered than before. "Alice, I will deal with it later. No more calls." His temper is rising.

"Yes, my Lord."

I move off the countertop consumed with my guilty actions so far. He holds me again and gives me light kisses. I'm not as responsive as I was a few seconds ago. His hands pull my skirt up again and he follows the outline of my thong. And he pierces my mouth repeatedly with his tongue.

"Oh fuck, Julius."

"Yes, babe?" He unhooks my bra. His hands move to my waist. "Where…are…your…beads?" He nibbles on my lip with each word.

"I took them off because of this skirt."

"Let's go to the bedroom," he says. I'm not focused. *Vida, are you really going to do this? Ginger already has her answer. What about all these aliases: Diego, DJ? What about Rebecca and Nana and the journals? There is still so much to discover.* He tries to lead me out of the kitchen, but I am solid in my stance. He kisses me again. "Talk to me, babe…tell me what you want." Ginger is ready and so is The Beast. *No, not now. Maybe if I didn't have so many unanswered questions, I wouldn't feel so anxious and bothered. Okay, Vida, out with it.*

"Who is Nana and how does Rebecca know about Nana?" He pauses, his lips still pressed against my neck and his hands on my ass. He smiles, but not a smile encouraged by happiness. I've seen it before, the 'what-the-fuck' smile. *You pick a great time to start this inquisition.* "Did you live in New York before? I mean, I know you have the hotel, but it just seemed like it was a serious relationship between you two. I'm just curious, that's all."

"What?"

"I can't help it. My thoughts are drawing their own conclusions. You know there was an entry in your journal and it said 'Nana is here.' And this evening a woman you dated mentioned Nana. I just find that odd that there is still so much I don't know. And I'm just curious, since I am writing your memoir and all. Is Nana the reason why you've been ripping the pages from the journal?" He removes his hands and steps away. And it looks like he has three legs. The massive bulge makes me blush, knowing that I caused it. I continue despite the obvious pointing at me. "Is Nana a friend or was she your girlfriend? Were you dating her and dating Rebecca? Is Nana the person you were referring to when you said that you loved someone very deeply but the betrayal was too great? And—"

"—And is that what you're thinking about at this very moment?"

"I'm just trying to get to know more about you. I'm sure not everything will be discovered reading your journals. And we met someone from your past tonight and I'm…just curious. So when was the last time you were in New York? Did you live here before? I mean, that's all I want to know."

"That's all, huh? Nana is—was—just a friend."

"Yeah, I got that part. So did she break your heart? Did you want to marry her? Is she the reason why you ripped the pages out of the journals?" He doesn't say anything and I persist. "Say something. Aren't you going to share any information with me?"

"No. Nothing else," he says firmly. "Are we done, or are you going to persist with this as my libido shrinks to a nil?" He provides information like small appetizers instead of what I am looking for—a full course meal. *I have to address this again, but maybe not right now.* I move closer to him and try to get the fire burning again. He bends his head forward and gives me a little peck on the lips. *Oh my goodness, no tongue this time.* He raises his head and then kisses my forehead gently. *Shit. I fucked up. His mood is changing.* I apply soft caresses to his chest and neck hoping to warm him up again.

"Let's go to the bedroom," I whisper in his ear.

"Vida," he says lowly, "let me take you home. It's late."

"Home?" I jump back. "Why do you want to take me home?"

He kisses my hand. "It's late and we are both tired." The sexual atmosphere is dissipating.

"I want to spend the night." I nestle my head in his chest and wrap my arms around his neck. I begin again nibbling on his lower lip. He doesn't pull away, but offers me his full lips. We kiss again. His lips and tongue begin to search mine. He pulls me deeper in his embrace and my tongue makes its way up to his ear. I nibble and let my tongue explore the contours. I say softly, "Fuck me, Julius…" His hands move away from my ass and he pulls back.

That laugh is back, laced with skepticism. "Is that what you want, Vida?" *I'm confused. Okay, what is the right way to say you want to get laid? Maybe I should say it a bit louder with more conviction.*

"Fuck me, Julius." His face doesn't look receptive. "Don't you want to fuck me?"

He leans back against the kitchen island for a few seconds and responds. "Let me take you home, Vida." *Here we go again. In our land of make-believe. I know he wants to. His body shows it.*

"I drove here. Remember?" He hangs his head down and then lifts it up to run his hand through his hair. An awkward silence prevails.

"Do you want me to leave?" His nonverbal actions tell me it's time for me to go. "Okay, I should have gotten the message the first time." I pull down my skirt to look more presentable before leaving the kitchen. He calls out to me, but I don't turn to look at him. I move swiftly out of the kitchen into the foyer. I grab my F-M-Ps by the door and continue to make my way out of the building.

"Vida, Vida," he calls out, but I'm too embarrassed to even respond to him. His footsteps quicken behind me. In all my haste I forget my purse inside. He is standing in front of me. "Vida…Vida…" he says again.

"What?" I say, not looking at him. He moves a bit closer to me.

"Will I see you tomorrow?" I give a sinister chuckle. *Yeah, right. I played myself right in front of you.*

"Yes," I say. He cocks his head.

"Don't give me a unicorn story. Will I see you tomorrow?"

"I said yes!" I look slightly in his direction and then my head falls down. He takes my hand to place my purse in it.

"I look forward to seeing you tomorrow."

I put the car in reverse and make a U-turn away from the house. He is still standing in the same place I left my ego.

I replay the scene in my head. From the club into the car and then the kitchen. Maybe bringing up his ex wasn't good timing, but I thought I could save the night by saying I wanted to have sex with him. The more I think about it, the more embarrassed I become. *Shit, Vida. Was I really going to go through with it? Where did you get the courage?* Guilt consumes me. *No, I couldn't have gone through with it. You know damn well you wanted to see how far it would go. That's why you brought up Nana.* Maybe I wanted it, but for the wrong reasons. *To get back at Mensah? Fill a sexual void? Or maybe just plain curiosity?*

I arrive home at three and I can't bear to face another inquisition from Abla right now. She will definitely have words for me. *I'll fill her in on the details tomorrow.* I check on the children and they are sound asleep. MJ as usual has managed to crawl into my bed. I undress quickly and put on my old soccer T-shirt, wash the makeup from my face and slide in next to him. My cellphone pings and I am sure it's Julius. A text.

"Are you in bed?"

"Yes."

"Thank you for a wonderful evening. I'm still thinking about you. You made tonight memorable."

I pause and recollect my thoughts. *Just keep it nice and short, Vida.*

"I had a great time too. Thank you. We should do this again."

I hit send and regret the last couple of words. *"…do this again?" Which part, the part where his third leg basically turned to a third finger?* I send another text quickly.

"**Have a GDN.**"

That should be it for the night. I hold the cellphone a bit longer to see if another text comes through. Nothing. My earlier sleepiness is gone and I sit up thinking of what I can possibly say to Mensah. *Is my marriage truly over? Or maybe I just want revenge?* Several thoughts run through my mind and at five a.m. what started as random thoughts has become a four-page Dear Mensah letter.

Chapter 64

"*Shut...up!* Can you do dat, sista? Damn, Vida. Haf you loz all yur skillz?" Abla stands over my bed with an authoritative motherly tone. "I mean, damn it. Dis was very simple. All signals a go. All you had to do waz shut up. Da nez time a billionaire, no lez me say it again, nez time a hot, young, big-dick billionaire wants to haf sex wif you, *just shut da hell up.* We need somedin' juicy to tell our grandkids when we get olda." I hush her down because MJ is still asleep next to me. But she is more excited for me than I am right now.

It definitely was a mood breaker to inquire about the journal and his past relationship. I thought about Rebecca and how she wrapped her arms around Julius hoping he would be the answer to all her prayers. *Was the sex that good that she still thinks about him?* Her persistence was troubling and also relatable. *I remember feeling that way about Mensah once. Now, I am not sure what I feel for him. Recent events have given me a heart that doesn't long for his presence.*

"He wants you. And you want him, right?" Abla's tone brings me back.

"Huh?"

"Are you daydreamin' again, or don't you know?" I shrug my shoulders. "Lissen, nez time all you haf to do iz lie deer, stand up, bend over, kneel down and get it." She takes time to illustrate every position. "*Wo casa doodoo.* Ahhhhh, Vida, you still talk too much. The only talkin' you should be doin' iz sexy talk and just a little at a time." She begins another illustration, rubbing her hands through her wig and mouthing words Abla knows too well. "*Wo di mi...*Yeah, I can't wait for dat *kotedenden* to slide inside my wet—" I cover her mouth when I see MJ turn over in bed.

"Please, I beg. MJ will wake up." She peeks to see if MJ is ruffled by her talk. He exhales deeply and a light snoring begins again.

I know a few obscenities in Twi that Mensah used often, like *tafere me twe*. It drove him wild when I said it. That seems so long ago. It usually stirs a feeling in between my legs, but now...nothing. "That doesn't sound sexy."

"C'mon, who are you foolin'? I heard it myself."

"When?"

"We are g'ttin' off da subject," Abla says. "You don't want me to open yur report card. Don't even try to get all holy on me. I uzed to hear you and Mensah on da phone at night."

My mind replays those nights. It was early in our marriage when he first started looking for contracts outside of New York. We would stay on the phone for hours, usually ending with some hot sex talk and then occasionally an orgasm so that we could both fall asleep and—

Abla snaps her fingers. "Dis iz not da time to go down memory lane. You should have slapped dat cock-blocka. Watz her name Becky…Rebook? Wif all dat information she gave him, he could file her taxes."

"Rebecca," I clarify. My thoughts are about Julius. *What's he up to?* I promised that I would come tonight, but I won't. I'm sure he knows that. *How could I face him, especially after last night? That damn kiss. Why, Vida? What are you doing?*

Chapter 65

A few things bring me delight these days, but to have the house to myself for one whole week is one of them. Pancake and the boys are preparing for their annual camping trip with Jesus and his family. As finicky as Panin can be, he enjoys these camping trips more than the camping trips with his Boy Scouts Troop. I know Pancake's presence has a lot to do with it. She's always been protective of him. She knows how to soothe his anxiousness with words of affirmation or sing songs like Kakra does. This is the first time that I have decided not to go. I've changed my mind a dozen times. But I feel confident that this will also be a great experience not to have my overly maternal eye on them. I pack a bag and hide it in the closet in case I change my mind.

"Auntie, for heaven's sake. We will be fine. It's the same campground," Pancake says.

"I know. But I won't be there and I just want to make sure you have enough of everything." The living room is cramped with an additional cooler that I purchased last week. I packed it with extra sandwiches, water, chips. Another bag for first aid kits, batteries, ponchos, extra packages of socks, underwear, insect repellant, flare guns and an analog radio. "Here's an extra cellphone battery. It runs on solar power."

"Please Auntie, don't drive me crazy this week." Pancake laughs and places the extra cellphone battery inside the backpack.

"Oh, Yaa, dey will be fine." Abla peers through the sidelights waiting for Jesus. This is no ordinary look for Abla. Her face is painted with meticulous detail to her eyes. The bright fuchsia two-sizes-too-small dress coordinates with her pink F-M-Ps and bubblegum glossy lips. Her cleavage leaves nothing to the imagination and purposely stands at attention. "Wat time did yur fatha say he iz gettin' here?" Abla says. She paces from the front door to the living room window and then back again to the sidelights.

"By ten. It's only nine thirty, Mommy," Pancake says. Abla releases a deep exhale and clicks her heels toward the kitchen. We can't help but laugh when she is out of sight.

"Do you think it's still possible?"

"What?"

"That Mommy is still in love with Daddy." It is obvious to anyone in the presence of Abla and Jesus that there is still a low flame burning. He guards himself from her by never entering the house and making sure his visits to Pancake are accompanied with his wife.

Jesus's wife, Milly, bears little resemblance to Abla. Jesus created a domesticated life that she worships: three daughters, two dogs, and a pet pig named Andy. Milly never worked and I don't believe Jesus wanted a career woman. Abla nicknamed her "Two-piece" because every time she sees her, she wears a shell with a cardigan or a gown with a cardigan or a dress with a blazer or a pantsuit or a tracksuit. Although they only exchange simple pleasantries with one another, Abla respects Milly. She frequently drives Pancake back and forth to college and has always treated Pancake just like one of her daughters. Jesus says he is happy, but I've known him since I was in middle school and I can tell he still loves Abla.

I try to dismiss Pancake's observation. "It's been over twenty years. I think they are both happy where they are."

"But Auntie, I see the way they look at each other. And—"

"And what?" I snap back.

She hesitates before she answers me. "When I am with Daddy, he always asks about Mommy, and when I come home, Mommy always asks about Daddy. Just look how she behaved when I told her that Daddy had the chickenpox last summer. She made all this food and ordered all these herbs from Ghana to bring to him. In her Bible, I found a prayer she wrote especially for him."

"Well, she should be concerned. That is your father."

"Oh Auntie, you know but you don't want to say it." *Yes, I do*. But it is something that Abla never wants to discuss. Her behavior toward Jesus is evident to her daughter now. "That's love, no matter how long ago it was."

"So you've become an expert on love now?"

"No, not at all. But I would marry a man that looked at me the way my father looks at my mother." She is serious and I wonder if she is referring to her new boyfriend. I keep a mental note to have a talk with her before she goes back to school. "Do you still love Uncle Mensah?"

I turn in her direction. "Boy, you're full of matters of the heart today."

"I know you're mad with Uncle. That's why you don't wear your wedding ring anymore."

"Pancake…I…" The tan lines are gone and the color of my ring finger looks like the rest.

"I know this is probably not the right time, but you've never kept anything from me. It's not how it was before I went away to school. It feels different, something has changed. Auntie, you are not happy. I've heard you crying some nights."

I can't hide my feelings from Pancake. We are more like sisters than auntie and niece. "Yes, a lot has happened. But you don't need to worry about us. It's just a complicated situation right now."

"But you do still love him, right?" I have to consider my answer. *Do I still love Mensah?* It is something I never thought needed time to weigh. *I should…I want to…but I feel…no, I do.* Pancake's eyes search my face for a response. So innocent and open to the possibilities of love. I never told her what transpired in California and neither did the boys. No one should have to relive that misery. I've done it already in the past, tainted my sister against Mensah. Pancake needs to believe her uncle is a good guy. "I do love him; we are just going through a rough patch right now."

"But it can be fixed. Right, Auntie? You said it to me so many times that love can overcome everything." *Yeah, but only if you are in love.*

"Right, Pancake," I finally answer. She hugs me tightly.

"It's going to be okay, Auntie. I know it is. Uncle loves you; he won't do anything to hurt you."

"Right," I say again. "How did you get so smart? You're definitely smarter than your mother and I." The doorbell rings and Pancake opens it.

"Papa!"

"Buenos dias, Hija." He gives her a big bear hug and then kisses me on either side of the cheek. "Wow, Vida. You are looking very good. I must have a talk with Mensah and find out what's his secret in keeping such a hot wife."

"Well, I think I have a say in the upkeep." He laughs and then steps back suddenly, making sure he stays within the confines of where he feels safe. His focus is unflinching. Pancake and I notice his changed demeanor. Abla's Opium perfume approaches us before she does.

"I'm going to get the boys and load up the van," Pancake says. She squeezes my hand for me to take notice of her father's gaze at her mother.

"Buenos dias, Jesus," Abla says. Jesus's eyes are locked on her and he swallows hard. I want to excuse myself, but I can't help but watch the beginnings of smoke rising into the air.

"Buenos dias, mi amore," Jesus says. Abla extends her hand and instead of shaking it he pulls it to his lips. "Still as beautiful as your name." She gushes. I've heard this line a dozen times, but it never gets old when Jesus says it.

"How iz it dat yur growin' younger?" Abla says.

"Not at all. The grey hairs are poking out." He references the grey streaks by his earlobe. "I should be asking you, how did you make time stop while the rest of us grow older?" Abla smiles brightly and his stare is unwavering. He leans in the doorway to stabilize himself. The kids rush past us, causing us to sidestep out of their way. We hear a voice outside. Milly steps out of the car and waves in our direction. As predicted, jeans and a blue sweater set.

Abla steps outside and stands beside Jesus. "Buenos dias, Milly." Jesus tries to maintain his composure, pretending that being this close to Abla doesn't have an effect on him. Milly and Abla share a few exchanges in Spanish and she hops back into the van. Abla then brushes past Jesus as she reenters the house. I watch the kids load the van, but I am really fighting hard to hear the conversation behind me.

"I heard Milly iz pregnant again. Congratulations," Abla says. "You have everytin' now—a decorated pilot, beautiful children and a good wife."

"Yes, she is a good woman…just like a woman who broke my heart over twenty years ago."

"How could you bring dat up now?"

"It never leaves my thoughts."

Abla's voice drops to a whisper. I take a step back hoping this will amplify the audio. Abla says good-bye softly and kisses the boys. I repeat my dos and don'ts for the hundredth time.

"Tell Mommy we are going to jump off the cliffs and scuba dive off the waterfalls," Jesus says jovially.

"Not funny at all, Jesus." He waves his goodbye and enters the van.

I yell from the steps. "Call me if you need anything—anything at all." Abla is motionless in the doorway and I have to push her aside to get in. "Are you panties wet?"

"Oh, pleazze. I've moved on. Hez moved on. We have a daughta dat we are raisin'. Notin' strange to see two parents who still care for one anotha."

"That sounds rehearsed. You're talking to yur one and only sista. One motha and one fatha." I mimic her words with the same inflection she repeatedly drills me with.

"Deerz notin' deer. I have Richard and he has Milly. Case cloze."

"Are you kidding me? I don't think you guys can be in the same room together for five minutes. There's enough spark to start the Independence Day fireworks."

She becomes quiet and melancholy. "I can't change wat happened. Itz betta dat he iz wit Milly. Shez a good woman. Richard makes me happy, really."

"Are you trying to convince yourself?" She doesn't reply.

*

It's eight p.m. and seven months since I had sex with Mensah. And eight days since I've had the urge to do it myself. I pour another glass of shiraz, something that Julius has gotten me accustomed to. After a long bath, I take extra care to moisturize my skin. I lay on the bed fully naked. The Ben Wa balls I purchased over a year ago are still wrapped and I take them out of the jewel case. Two brass balls the size of marbles. The wine begins to have its effect on me. The wetness from Ginger makes it easy to glide them in. I lay there a few minutes longer to feel their placement. I rub my hand on my breasts. They feel tender. I cup them a little longer. The slow rumbling in my stomach reminds me that I haven't eaten since breakfast. I slip on a long T-shirt, which on some nights doubles as my pajamas. No underwear. I feel the weight of the balls pulling downward and their gentle bumping. Ginger immediately clenches to hold them in place.

I dial for Chinese delivery. "Hi, Ms. Pong." I have gotten used to Mrs. Kim referring to me by that name.

"Mrs. Kim, I need a delivery please."

"Go ahead, ready—" Rumblings of stir-fry and searing fill the background.

"Small General Tso's chicken. Small Singapore noodles and a small wonton soup."

"Dat all?"

"Yes. Don't forget the hot oil too, please."

"Yez, okay. Same address, right?"

"Yes, but please tell your nephew to just ring the bell." Mrs. Kim's nephew always makes it a habit to call a block away from my address so that I am standing at the door when he arrives. He lays his beat up makeshift bike with seats worn down to the metal and metal bars without protective handle bars on the front step, then watches around as though someone is ready to jump out and take the bike at any given moment. *Who the hell wants an old beat up delivery bike?* He is rude at times and pretends like he doesn't understand English. He never says thank you, even though I always give him a generous tip.

"Okay. Forty-fie minute," she finally says and hangs up.

That's about how long I will keep these balls in. I pour another glass of shiraz. I am becoming well accustomed to the effects it has on me. After the third glass, I will feel the heightened sensitivity between my legs—vibration is more like it. A few massages in the right places will probably release seven months of frustration. I play V. Bozeman to set the mood and check my phone again. A new message; it has to be from Mensah, but I decide not to play it to dampen my spirits. My reflection in the hallway mirror is not flattering at all. I rush upstairs and change into one of those nighties I used to wear for Mensah. A black and red lace teddy fits the bill. A little more snug than before. *Clothes do shrink the less you wear them.* My cleavage overflows from the top. The bottom strap practically strangles Ginger. I unbutton it and feel an instant release. I finger my hair over my shoulders and then look for shoes. I still have four closets full of shoes to break into. I've only managed to wear thirty pairs so far and this took extra effort to change in the afternoon and evening. Over three hundred more to go. My favorite ones so far are the Brian Atwood lace-up black strappy stilettos. A fine complement to a short skirt or a cocktail dress. I lace them up and examine myself again. *Not bad at all, Vida. Well, let's not stop there.* I saunter to the bathroom and apply a bright red lip stain and then my Tarte mascara. Again another twirl in the mirror. *Yeah, Vida, you're ready for the fourth glass of wine.* Before leaving the bedroom, I remember my delivery. *No sense in giving Mrs. Kim's nephew a show.* I find the matching robe in the closet and tie the belt loosely around my waist. Still a bit revealing. I decide to put on the heavy terry cloth robe on instead. *After my food arrives, I can get rid of the camouflage.*

Downstairs seems more like a club scene. My sultry music has changed to bootyshaking rompromp music. I search through Mensah's CDs and play roulette until my ears settle on Asha. I gulp the last mouthful of wine and top it off with the last swallow in the bottle. The doorbell. *Food is here!*

"Good evening, Vida." *No, this isn't food that can be digested.* "You've been a hard lady to reach lately." It's been a week since our incident at the club. I've given him every unicorn story I could for not coming over. And he knows it's bullshit, but he hasn't made an attempt to come over until now. "I spoke to Abla earlier and she said the boys went camping, but you decided to stay behind."

"I needed to catch up on some work." The beginning of another unicorn story.

"May I come in?"

"Ummmm…" I thank God I still have the robe cinched at my waist. He is dressed in all black and wearing hiking boots. My body is yearning. The effects of the wine and balls are taking advantage of me. "Julius, this is really not a good time."

"Why haven't you returned my calls today?"

"There were several unknown calls today and I assumed they were all Mensah. You didn't leave a message."

"I called from the plane and then decided to come back—"

"Come back?"

I stand a distance away from him in the doorway. He removes his shoes as he always does. *Shit. This is not going to be a short visit.*

"Yeah, I came back for you."

I step farther away. His presence compounds the effects that I'm starting to feel. High, hot and horny.

"Can we talk tomorrow? I'm—"

"Are you expecting someone?"

"Yes...No...Why do you ask?"

"You're wearing F-M-Ps." Cautiously aware of my attire, I move a few steps away from him and the front door.

"I'm just really tired and just need time to rest."

"In F-M-Ps?"

"Yeah." I unlace the straps and kick the heels off toward the door. He moves closer and I'm pinned to the wall.

"I really like you, Vida, perhaps more than I want to admit." He slides his hand over my waist. "A robe...?"

"Yeah...I just got out of the shower." That's all the information I can relay. He begins again. His nose against mine. "You smell like shiraz."

"I had a couple of glasses this evening," I mouth slowly.

"All alone...?"

"Yes," I say, breathless. He grabs me in his arms. "You should go."

"Why?" Both hands pull my waist closer to his body. Ginger feels like a wet sponge. Wetness slowly runs down my thighs. I close my legs tighter together.

"Julius, you do remember our bet?" I'm hoping this will be enough to back him off.

"Vida," he whispers as he seals his lips over mine. He moves his hands up and down my back and I feel the sensation build again. The feeling that I have been waiting for...I try to push him away...it's there and the balls...fuck, the balls are dancing around causing an unusual sensation to build.

"Only three more hours till the end of this annoying bet. Oh, but I have plenty to keep me busy." The doorbell grabs our attention. "Were you really expecting someone?"

I can barely catch my breath. My thoughts are focused on the sensation in between my legs. He waits for me to move, but I can't move...I think I'm in the midst of a slow orgasm. Any movement just may cause me to yell out in ecstasy. I have to control myself, but I don't want this feeling to stop. *I never knew I could feel so high without intercourse.*

"Are you okay, Vida?" *What the hell? Why do I feel like a dam about to break?* The doorbell again. "Vida, your breathing seems erratic."

"Ummm, just...the wine...it was only two glasses...no, it was four...the balls..."

"Balls? What balls?" he asks. I can't close my legs tight enough. His arms are still around my waist. I push him away and back myself to the wall. The doorbell again.

"Should I answer it?"

"Yes, for heaven's sake," I say anxiously. I slowly move with my back against the wall and the tingling sets my nerves on fire. I don't want this feeling to go away, but I don't want to make a fool of myself either. *If I can just make it to the bathroom without exploding onto the floor.* The more I resist the more intense the feeling becomes. *Why now? God is punishing me. I promise, if I can get away with my dignity, I won't do this again. Don't lie to yourself, Vida...Okay, maybe not for a long time.*

Julius opens the door.

"Hi, delivery. Eighteen dolla and sevteen-five cents." Mrs. Kim's nephew stands at the door and Julius ushers him in. He is wearing those damn DJ headphones.

"Vida, did you call for delivery?"

I nod violently.

"Vida?"

He can't see me. "Yes." My wallet is by the table. Julius pulls out a hundred-dollar bill from his money clip and gives it to Mrs. Kim's nephew. He of course doesn't hear Julius when he says to keep the change. *Take the damn headphones off.* He is still standing there searching his pocket for change. Oh no, the feeling is going away. *Don't go away. I need this.* Julius rests the food on the entrance table. And immediately turns his attention to me.

"You're breathing hard. What's wrong?"

"Nothing. I'm just tired that's all." I slide against the wall in hopes of making it to the hallway bathroom. He pulls me again into his arms.

"Vida, talk to me. What's happening...are you in pain? Are you having a heart attack?" *An attack all right, but it has nothing to do with my heart.* He rests his head on my chest and his cheek brushes against the lace teddy. He touches my forehead and my neck. Beads of sweat form in my cleavage and I can feel heat in my pores. He feels it. "You're warm, very warm," he says. "Do you want to take off the robe?"

"No, not now." His hands brush against the teddy. *Shit.* I push his hands away, but he's on me with a Bruce Lee kung fu grip and his wet lips brush against my face. *Oh my goodness. This must be the most climatic high that I've ever felt.* His body heat adds more warmth to my flesh. His left hand pins my waist and the other is on my neck. *Oh, dear Lord, he has to stop.* He presses against me and I can feel The Beast rising. The image of me stroking it at his house that morning and the kiss at the club, his scent like musk and juniper arouses me.

"Julius, please."

"Please what?" *He knows.* He licks his lips. I taste the air as it carries the vanilla espresso into my mouth. His lips are soft and wet and I picture those same lips resting between my legs and my knees fail me. The orgasm rips through my body, defying any insecurities that I may feel. My legs separate and the dam is broken. A big sigh of feeling pleasantly released.

"Yesssss!" I rest his head in my chest. It's not my scream of completion that embarrasses me, but the two brass balls bouncing off each other as they roll in different directions across the red oak floor.

Julius doesn't move.

"Ooooooooh…Ms. Pong—" *Fuck me! Mrs. Kim's nephew was standing there the whole time. He witnessed EVERYTHING! Orgasm, dams broken, balls falling from Ginger. Where is that blackout when you need one?* His eyes are more alert and his mouth looks like something wired open. "Ooh, Ms. Pong," he says with a sinister and devilish grin. It will be forever tattooed in my brain. *Needless to say, I can never order from Mrs. Kim again. And I really liked their Singapore noodles.*

Julius touches the ground where the dam broke. He rubs the residue in between his fingers.

"Vida…Vida…naughty Vida. All this fun all by yourself? Not fair at all." He removes a handkerchief from his pocket and wipes my legs.

"No. No…don't do that, it's not necessary." I move away. He is smiling. He picks up one of the balls not far from where he stands.

Mrs. Kim's nephew is still smiling. "I haf ball." He holds one of the brass balls in his hand. Julius walks in his direction.

"May I?" Julius says.

Mrs. Kim's nephew places it in his handkerchief. Julius is speaking Chinese to him. And then he slips him another hundred-dollar bill. The devilish grin has turned to a deadly serious composure now.

"Good night, Ms. Pong. Hope you feel betta." *I knew it. This mother f-er does speak English. I can't even look at him now.*

I go into the kitchen and grab paper towels and clean the slippery spill. Julius is standing outside speaking with Vincent. *Dear God, what could they be discussing now? That Vida holds brass balls in her pussy?* Of all my years of using them, I've never had an orgasm, and today of all days I have the most exhilarating one, but with an audience. I run upstairs for a quick shower. *Maybe he will leave so I won't have to explain myself.*

*

After the shower, I wear the most unattractive attire: ragged, old cut up jeans and an old sweatshirt top that sometimes doubles as a nightgown. When I return downstairs, Julius is dishing out food from the takeout. *Fuck, he's still here.* "Do you want a little of everything?" I'm a bit hesitant in responding. He sits at the dining table and I notice his socks are off.

"Yes," I say, waiting to see if he will comment about my one-woman show. He scoops some noodles and General Tso's chicken onto the plate.

"Are you going to sit down here?" He realizes that I am distant. I move closer and pull out the chair beside him. He has two forks in his hand and he gives me one. He still doesn't make any comment on what just happened. *Embarrassed is not the feeling. More…satisfied. I can sleep for days. Don't think about it, Vida. Focus on something else.*

"You are certainly getting around well in my house," I say.

"You keep your dishes closer to the sink and your eating utensils"—he holds up his fork—"are farther away from sink. I am not sure why, because one would think you would have them close to the dishwasher. But there are two things I've discovered." I rest the fork on the plate and give him my undivided attention. He continues, "This has to be the best tasting Singapore noodles that I've ever eaten." I nod my head agreeing and put another forkful into my mouth.

"Yes, it's very good. You need to try it with the hot oil." I open the little container and dribble a little onto the food. He takes some into his mouth.

"You're right. Very tasty." The food is not hot, but room temperature, which makes it more enjoyable.

"What's the second thing?"

"You don't like undergarments much."

"What?"

"Panties, briefs, thongs, undergarments. If you wore undergarments, then that could have saved the balls from dancing across your hardwood floor." He starts with a subtle smile and then a high uproarious laugh.

"I knew you weren't going to let that go."

"Are…you…kidding…me? Do you know how much energy it is taking me to hold myself together? I laughed for fifteen minutes while you were in the shower. Oh, Vida…" He holds his cheeks. "…you always make me forget about my woes." He pulls from his pocket the handkerchief with my Ben Wa balls wrapped inside. "I never knew you were into that sort of thing."

"Do you recall when I said my vagina is off limits?"

"Really? After all we've been through tonight, I can't comment on your pussy?" He laughs again. "You know, I would have thought your pussy was a pistol. Did you hear how those balls bounced off each other? I'm surprised they didn't shoot through the wood floors. Impressive." His face is turning salmon pink.

"Enough…You got your laughs at my expense again."

"Okay, okay…I'm done. I swear." He sobers up and caresses my knee. I playfully slap his hand off. He shifts in his chair and places the fork on the plate. He leans forward and closes his eyes.

"The ground was a bit moist. But I didn't care. It was the first time she ever kissed me like that. I didn't want her to stop." *He's telling a story.* I scrutinize him as he relives the events. "She liked reggae. I remember I made a CD for her; Junior Kelly was playing. Once we started kissing, I couldn't stop. I wanted to devour her. I was excited and she reached into my pants and began stroking me. All sorts of sensations coursed through my body. The rain began to fall again and she wanted to leave, but I held her in my arms under the tree. 'I will protect you from the rain,' I said.

She was worried that if she didn't go home soon, her parents would discover she was with me again. But that night was different from other nights. She held my head in her bosom and I took her breast into my mouth. She grinded onto me until a voice startled her. She rose quickly, but by that time, I had the most uncontrollable orgasm. I trembled into convulsions and soiled my pants while her father I'm sure looked on in fury. He nearly busted my head against the tree until Vincent came to my aid."

"Oh my goodness. Vincent was there?"

"Vincent always seems to be at the right place at the right time. Well, anyway, the moral to this story is, we all have our stories. Don't be ashamed of yours." *I feel relieved.* My shoulders, once tensed up to my neck, slump down in comfort.

"I still think mine tops yours, though."

"Vida, without a doubt." He covers his head anticipating my playful attack. Our breaths calm down and we take fork loads of Singapore noodles into our mouths.

"Come with me, Vida?"

"Where to?"

"Home. Just six nights. You'll be home before the children get back."

"When?"

"Now," he says. I scoff at the idea.

"You're serious." His demeanor doesn't change. "I haven't packed. I don't have—"

"Just come with me. You don't need to take anything." I believe him when he says it.

Chapter 66

"So, where iz he takin' you?" I can barely hear Abla and I actually find myself yelling my response.

"I don't know. I will know when we land."

"Yur on a plane? Shit. You could be goin' anywhere in da world." And suddenly Abla's words are unnerving. *What if the boys need me? How will anyone reach me?* "Dis iz some very rich shit." She is giddy with laughter. "Wat did you pack?"

"Nothing," I whisper into the phone.

"Get out!" She yells and I am sure Julius and the entire crew hears her. "Now lissen to me. Are you lissenin'?" I say yes and add an eye roll. "Haf I eva gave you bad advice?" *Hmmm. Yes.* I pause for a moment and mentally pull out the scorecard of Abla's fuckups. "Okay, forget about da past. Lissen to me, itz now or neva. Yur gonna be alone wit him for X amount of days. Itz time to dust da shelves and wipe da cobwebs off." I purposely didn't mention the episode earlier with my Ben Wa balls. *It's a good thing because that will be an ongoing lecture.* "Do I need to school you on what to do?"

"Noooo." I lower my voice.

"Don't ova think, let yur *etwe* do all da work. Lead wit her. Act real slutty and freaky." The silence in the cabin worries me. Julius is sitting within an arm's distance from me. I press the volume low button again. *I swear Abla's voice sounds as though she is talking into a microphone.* "—And den switch it back up and act like a lady who can grind him like peppa."

"Okay…okay…I gotta go. I don't need bulleted notes."

"I'm jus' sayin', itz been a while. You might haf gotten compenisdated wit dat one *kote*."

"You mean complacent."

"Right. Don't be dat. Be a lady wit good moves, good *etwe*, datz all I'm sayin'." Julius is grinning. *Shit, he probably hears her.*

"Okay, bye. I will call you when we land. Love ya."

Julius puts down the bottle of Guinness and rises with an extended hand. He takes my hand into his. "Is Rosemary okay?"

"Mentally? No." I laugh slightly. "She's fine. I don't have much details to give her as to where we are going though. Are you going to tell me where we're headed?"

"Nope."

Chapter 67

The plane sits amongst the hills. Cool breeze hits my face and the air smells of peace and tranquility. The clay sands and turquoise water glimmer with the coming sunset. I turn several times to take in the vastness of the ocean and lush greens surrounding us. This has to be it. The way she saw it and the way he wrote it. *This is where God lives.*

"It's beautiful here, Julius."

He smiles. I recall every detail from his journal. I lift the sand in my hands and it gently falls in between my fingers.

"There is so much to see. We should head to the house before nightfall." I notice a few houses resting in a semicircular pattern away from the plane. There is a crowd gathering outside the homes.

"*O meu,* Gio! Gio! Gio!" An older woman with skin color like copper runs to embrace Julius. She bestows endless kisses on him.

"Mai, you look, feel"—he brings her hands to his nose—"and smell just as I remember."

She's speaking in a dialect that I've never heard before. He laughs. "Mai, this is Vida."

"Oooooh, Vida." She responds as though she has heard my name before with a radiant smile. "Bonita." She places my face in her hands, then tilts her head up as though she is trying to recollect something. "Beeeaaautiful." Now she takes hold of my hand. "Beeeaaautiful." She gestures her hands in reference to my body, pointing to my hips and behind. She says again, "Beeeaaautiful."

"Thank you." A large gathering runs toward us. I'm not scared but intrigued by the copper-colored faces with dark hair and perfect white smiles. I've never seen Julius's face more lively. Julius leans in to me.

"I will explain later, but be prepared for a feast."

I squeeze his hand as we move with the mass more inland. After some time they haul Julius into the air like a chief. The older woman that Julius refers to as Mai takes my hand and escorts me inside the castle. There are few furnishings. It smells of antiquity and sad goodbyes. An old-fashioned lamp, tapestries along the walls and wood floors reveal many years of history. The castle is a bit reformed and modern, but it hasn't lost its character. The floor-to-ceiling windows are hidden under heavy drapery.

She escorts me up the long staircase and then into a white plastered room. She removes matches from her apron and lights the lamp by the bedside. The illuminated room reveals a queen sized wood poster bed. The carving on the wood looks like it was done by a skilled craftsman. Arches and symbols emboss the bed. "It's beautiful," I say. She grins with comprehension. A wood corner table and chair grace one side of the room. She pulls back the drapes covering the French doors, which brings the sea breeze into the room.

"Dis for you." She taps my chest. I decode it as this is where I will be sleeping. I admire the room, but then a sudden fear enters my thoughts. *Could this castle be haunted? What will reveal itself when I am here all alone at night? I need to know where Julius sleeps.*

I pick up the lamp and follow Mai outside the room. Julius is at the bottom of the stairs.

"Is everything all right?"

"Yes." I take hold of his hand. "So, this is home?" I imagine a young truant Julius Gallo running up and down these stairs. "I thought you spent most of your youth in Europe?"

"Well, for school. But every summer holiday I spent at least a week here. It's my mother's home. She spent her adolescent years here. It has always felt like home to me more than any other place."

"And who is Mai?" She walks past us and offers another white smile. He corrects my pronunciation.

"It means mama in Portuguese. She's taken care of me since I was a baby. She has been the caretaker of the land and castle ever since my mother left Cabo Verde. Most of the people left the countryside because of the droughts several years ago, but the young children here don't have any activity besides the local channels when there is electricity. I promised them a park and that is exactly what I plan to build this week."

Night falls. Music, food and drink keep us entertained and satisfied. There is no Wi-Fi, electricity or indoor plumbing. It is remarkable that this small island sustains itself without those amenities. The bonfire lights the sky, which makes it easy for me to watch the children run around laughing and dancing in the fields. *What are my boys doing now? MJ is probably asleep under the shoulders of Pancake or Kakra.*

THE BORROWED WIFE

"We can check on the boys first thing in the morning." Julius reads my thoughts. I squeeze his hand to acknowledge what he says.

"Gio! Gio! Gio! Sing for us," the young children shout. I can't help but admire their copper complexions and inky hair. *I wonder if Julius's mother shared the same appearance?* Julius finally feels the pressure and rises to join the children in their circle. Every detail of this new experience is entertaining. Vincent looks pleasantly happy. Women congregate around him giving him ample amounts of attention. The older men assemble in a circle smoking cigars with one hand and holding bottles in the other. An older gentleman with silver strands of hair in a ponytail hands me his bottle. Pushing my inhibitions aside, I take a little sip. *This tastes like palm wine.* He says something in Portuguese to a young girl and within seconds I have a bottle in my hand.

Everyone quiets. Julius's voice, strong and angelic, hypnotizes us. His voice carries to the roadside. The chatter ceases and all attention is focused on him. The breeze is welcoming. I am not sure how much of the palm wine I've consumed, but my skin feels warm and I feel like I can soar in the breeze. His voice serenades me and I feel…I feel…nice.

*

The smell of lavender awakens me. First my eyes shift around to find my bearings. I lift my head up. *Where am I?* The meticulously carved poster bed. *Ah, yes. I'm in Cabo Verde.* I don't remember coming to bed or undressing. *Who took off my clothes? Unmatched bra and underwear are still on.* My last memory is sitting listening to Julius sing. I walk toward the bathroom. There are dresses and undergarments resting on the chair and they are my size. Abla's shea butter as well as other toiletries are assembled on the vanity by the sink. Two buckets filled with hot water sit inside the tub and there is a large storage vessel for water. I recall a similar setup in Grandma's village in Dabala. I pump the vessel to add cold water to the bucket and begin my bath.

After dressing, I step out onto the balcony. *What time is it?* There are a lot of cars parked by the roadside. I'm sure the town has heard about Julius's arrival. Elevated voices pique my curiosity. It sounds like a marketplace. A large crowd is assembled in front of the castle and I feel anxious. My eyes search through the crowd trying to understand the gathering. Loud cheers ring out. I pull my hair into a bun and slip on sandals.

Mai's voice screeches out. "Gio! Gio! Stop! Stop! Gio, stop!" I rush to the balcony again and search the mass for Julius. There is a break in the crowd and Julius falls to the ground.

"Julius!" I scream and race out of the room. "What is happening? What's going on?" I shout through the castle, hoping someone will give me answers. "Vincent! Vincent!" He is not inside. I search the crowd for a familiar face from last night, but there are too many copper-skinned people and I can't recall anyone's name.

"Vincent!" I yell anxiously. He rises from an intimate setting away from the crowd. I make my way through and see a huge man towering over Julius. He is yelling something in the native dialect while kicking sand into Julius's face.

"Stop it!" I shout. Vincent enters the circle where the fight is occurring. He stares at the man, but says nothing. Julius is lying on the ground. Mai covers her face with her hands and her back faces the crowd. "I can't believe you're not doing something to stop this. This is barbaric. For heaven's sake, how could someone fight a blind man? Aren't you going to help him?" Vincent grabs my arm and pulls me away like a disobedient child. I pull away from his firm grip. "For heaven's sake. He's blind!" I shout at everyone.

"And he's a man," Vincent says. He yells something in Italian at Julius. But no response. "C'mon…you are frightening Vida," Vincent says.

"Frightening me?" I say, flabbergasted. "He is going to get killed if you don't stop this." He pulls me farther away and the fight continues.

The large man moves back and Julius rises and charges him. He stumbles back and Julius blows sand into his face. The man screams and Julius takes the opportunity to land several blows to his body and face. Vincent claps his hands. "Stop showing off and finish this already." The large man is kneeling down still trying to reorient himself after the blows. Julius puts him in a chokehold. And the man continues to scream.

"Are…we…done…here?" Julius asks him. The man, barely breathing, mutters something under struggling breath and Julius releases him.

THE BORROWED WIFE

"Sergio, that was a long time ago. Let it go. I don't want to hurt you," Julius says. Julius stands back, waiting for perhaps the next assault. Sergio catches his breath and rises. I fear another attack and Vincent stands guard waiting for the outcome.

"I am not your enemy, but we are not friends either," Sergio says. He turns to a group of men and starts a conversation. Two men follow behind Sergio as he walks away.

My heart is racing and I watch as the crowd cheers on Julius. "That is Sergio, the police lieutenant," Vincent says.

"Why is the lieutenant fighting a blind man?" *It's a ridiculous question to ask, but surely there has to be a good reason why everyone stood aside and watched.*

"Your boss—" He laughs. "Julius was supposed to marry one of Sergio's sisters. There she is over there." A group of women cluster in one corner consoling Sergio. They are just as tall as Sergio with golden French fry complexions and dark curly hair. I'm not sure which one of the sisters Julius was supposed to marry, but they are all equally beautiful.

"Jesus, just because it doesn't work out it doesn't mean there has to be a fight. What was he expecting, a shotgun wedding?"

Vincent looks indifferent. "Yes, but—"

"But what?" I ask. Vincent shrugs his shoulders.

"He couldn't marry the younger one because Julius already slept with Sergio's six older sisters." The words register sadly in my head.

"Oh. I see."

Chapter 68

The crowd becomes pairs sprinkled across the castle grounds and roadside. Lieutenant Sergio and his entourage are gone. Vincent resumes his intimate conversation with two female denizens who are pampering him with food. Julius's face is the color of a bad tan. He has paper cut-like scratches on his cheek and forehead. His bare chest is a new shade of golden pink. His hair, the color of black lacquer, is pulled behind his ears. A coppertoned little boy hands him a dampened handkerchief. Julius takes his time to bring original color back to his face. As I expect, he then cleans his hands meticulously one finger at a time. The little boy hands Julius a cigar from a brown wooden box. I want to move closer, but a long bronze arm graciously extends over his shoulders. *Who is she? Perhaps someone from his journals that I haven't read about yet.* She looks more richly polished than the denizens of the community. Her leopard color pumps give her the same height as Julius. Her clothes appeared tailored and suit her voluptuous silhouette. Julius tilts his head back in laughter and then says something to the little boy. He takes flight. *No sense in me standing here looking jealous.*

"I should omit this fight from the book, right?" I approach them and break up their cajoling intimacy.

"Absolutely—not! Did you see how I laid him out?" His devilish grin is back. "I don't mind if you embellish some details." The unidentified woman tosses her hair over her shoulders and leans into Julius. Her smile seems friendly.

"You're kinda proud of yourself, huh?" I say.

"Not really. I've fought bigger bullies."

"Is it true?"

He draws another puff from his cigar. "What are you referring to?" I scrutinize the woman with no introduction. She whispers something in Italian, but doesn't break eye contact with me. She smiles warmly again.

"Please excuse my manners, Vida. Meet Mrs. Samantha Bello." He places the napkin in his trouser pocket. "Samantha, this is Vida Frimpong." She removes her arm from Julius's shoulder and greets me. She smells like jasmine and myrrh, scents I recognize from Abla's shea butters.

"I've heard a great deal about you. All wonderful, I must add." She has an Italian accent. *Family?* So far, he has never mentioned any family to me besides his mother. Interesting discovery. *Vida, listen more, talk less.*

"Did you sleep—I mean deflower—all of Sergio's sisters?" I want to speak politely in front of Mrs. Bello. *Deflower? Really? Maybe that is why she is giggling.*

He smiles more sincerely this time. "Do you mean sex? No need to curb your tongue in front of Sammie. We are all adults." He laughs again. "Now…" He drags another puff from his cigar. "Who have you been speaking to?"

I press on. "Is it true?"

"No." *That's a relief.* He puts out the cigar on the heel of his boot. "Just six of them." He smiles widely. "I wasn't aware that he had seven sisters. I should have known after the fifth. They all had the same—Ouch!" Samantha pinches him.

"Be good, Gio," she says.

"Needless to say they kept showing up, and to be fair, two of them still insist that Sergio is not their brother."

I shake my head. "Wow." Samantha frowns and smacks him on his butt.

"Gio, what are we going to do with you? It's obvious it still runs in the blood."

"Ooh, Sammie. That was a long time ago. Young with uncontrollable hormones. Anyway, hopefully Sergio and I can put this behind us. There is no need for us to recant what is irreversible."

Samantha steps aside from Julius. She takes me by the arm. "Men, they are predictable. They get so sensitive when it comes to honor, power, respect. Now, we shouldn't waste valuable time—" She sweeps strands of hair into my bun. "Ms. Frimpong, we have to go shopping."

"Vida is fine."

"Okay, Vida. Vincent says I should spoil you and Gio agrees." She pinches Julius's cheeks and he laughs affectionately. *Gio; there goes that name again.* Maybe a nickname that the family here calls him. *A man with so many aliases.* The little boy returns with a brown satchel. Julius opens it and it looks like currency. *Cabo Verde money?*

"Some cash in case you need it. Sammie is well acquainted with shopping. She makes Abla's spending budget look like bus fare."

"Oh stop it, Gio. I've actually scaled back a bit."

"I find that very hard to believe, especially when you're adorned with Les Larmes Sacrees de Thebes."

"Well, I only buy a bottle once every year. We should enjoy life. When we die, we leave all this behind. Don't you agree, Vida?"

"I see your point, Samantha," I say. She smiles brightly.

Julius hands the satchel to Samantha. "Vida, listen to me carefully…" He has my attention. He stands in his Superman stance again. "Buy whatever you want, not what you need."

Samantha claps her hands together in a single applause. "And that is why we love these men." She gives Julius a firm kiss on the lips. *That's odd. Maybe it's customary.* "Too bad I'm already married or I would have married you myself."

"Thank goodness for that." He chuckles.

"Let's go, Vida. I promise to bring her back by nightfall."

I feel naked. No passport, ID, or even a phone to carry. A million thoughts race through my head and before I can describe my lacking, Julius speaks.

"Don't worry, you are in capable hands. I trust Samantha—sometimes with my life." She mouths something to him in Italian. "Oh, now really, after all these years?" He laughs and pulls her into his arms. *I am at a disadvantage.*

"Especially after all these years," she says. They both chuckle again and now he turns his attention toward me.

"Once you get to the capital, you can call the children." He leans in and kisses me on my cheek. "If you need anything, just contact Alice; she will get in touch with me or Vincent."

"Alice is here?" I say. "But you have no power."

"And why do you think we have no power?"

"Because—" He stops me midsentence.

"Now I know you are way behind in your reading, Ms. Frimpong." I sigh and leave it at that.

*

"So, I'm going to give you a little tour of our beautiful islands. Where shall we start? Santiago, Sal or Boa Vista first?"

"Anything you advise. I am in your capable hands."

"And so you are. Give me a moment to change my clothes before we set off to the market." She tosses her long jet-black hair over her shoulders.

We sit in the backseat of a large black SUV. I steal glimpses of her new attire. Faded blue jeans, Puma sneakers, and a floral crop top. She blends in with the denizens of Cabo Verde.

"This is Sucupira Market. We can get some fresh fruit and find some hidden treasures." She smiles, revealing perfect white teeth. We eat passionfruit and watermelon, making our way through the crowds.

"Did you grow up here?" I ask.

"I've spent many holidays here." She takes my hand and we step off the main path. "Here, let's take a shortcut." The market reminds me of the marketplace in Tema. Even though I'm sure we have enough money to buy everything in the market, it feels culturally native to haggle with the women in the marketplace. A large woman with a bronze complexion addresses us firmly. The woman shakes her head no and Samantha says a few words in the dialect. Samantha doesn't look pleased with the conversation and she takes my arm to leave. The woman pulls on Samantha's arm to come back. Within a few seconds, the large woman wraps a carved wooden bowl in a bag and places it in my hands. Samantha counts the money and places it in the woman's hand. She seems happy. She takes a bracelet and wraps it on my wrist.

"She says she wants you to remember her," Samantha says.

"How do you say thank you in the dialect?"

"You just did. She understands English." We laugh.

*

It is another one of Julius's private planes and I sit across from Samantha. She has replaced her marketplace attire with European sophistication. Her hourglass figure is striking. She pulls her cellphone from her purse.

"Pardon me," she says. *Are they cousins? What sort of family relation is Julius to Samantha?* As far as I know, his mother was an only child, but he hardly speaks about his father. *Maybe on his father's side?* She laughs heartily and throws her hair back. "Un momento." She hands me the phone. "It's for you," she says smiling with a porcelain gleam.

"Julius?"

"The only one. Samantha tells me she has a full itinerary planned for you. Enjoy. I will see you when you get back." His voice sounds reassuring. I end the call and hand Samantha her cellphone.

She forms her mouth as though she wants to ask me something, but she reconsiders and looks out the window.

"May I make a phone call?" I ask.

"Oh, certainly." She reaches for her phone and instructs me in which sequence to dial outside the country. I check my voicemail. The only message is from Kakra saying they arrived safely and are going fishing early in the morning. I dial his cellphone, but no answer. *Should I call Mensah? What would I tell him if he asks where I am? But then again it's none of his business.* I call Pancake's line. No answer and I leave a message.

"Hi, just checking on you guys. I got Kakra's message that you guys arrived safely. I hope the boys are having fun. I'm shopping with a friend, so I will try you guys later tonight."

A little unicorn story. No need to mention the shopping is in Africa. Satisfied with my message, I hand the phone back to Samantha.

"We will be in Fogo in about fifteen minutes."

"Great. That wasn't a long flight at all."

"Not when you own a G six-fifty," she adds.

"Well, I guess he can afford it."

She laughs and it's contagious. I chuckle along with her. "To say the very least." Her eyes search my face. *There's that look again. The look that she wants to say something, but she is thinking about it.* I smile and then turn my attention over the skyline.

"He trusts you."

"What?" I heard her, but I don't know how to respond. I never thought about it in that way, but I do feel Julius and I are getting closer. *Yes, don't fuck up the friendship, Vida.*

"Vincent must trust you to bring you here. He's always been a good judge of character." *Vincent? I thought she was talking about Julius. Why would Vincent have a say if I come or not? I'm confused. Talk less, Vida, and listen more.*

"It means a lot to me that he can trust me." *Maybe she can give me more insight.*

"Consider that one of those rare wonders of the world. Gaining Vincent's trust is like asking a pig to wear a corset. It is impossible of course, but some may make the attempt." She laughs. Silence fills the cabin. A volcano is in plain view.

"Wow," I say softly.

"Indeed. We should go hiking."

"Today?"

"Why not? I have plenty of gear. I think we are about the same size. A thirty-nine, right?" I'm not sure of the conversion but I eye her feet and I do think we are the same size.

I say, "Yes."

"Great, we will start with a hike on Pico do Fogo."

I shyly agree, not sure what I'm getting myself into. We pass by a huge turquoise building and it stands out amongst the neutrals and oranges of the countryside.

"That is a Catholic church," she points out.

"It's beautiful."

"Hmmm…Indeed."

As we approach the volcano, fears sit in my stomach. I convince Samantha to give me a raincheck.

"How about a selfie?" I ask.

She agrees. We pose in front of a sign that reads, **"Bem Vindo Ao Parque Natural Do Fogo."**

"Let's go to Sal for clothing."

"Are we going to a mall?"

"For clothes? Oh, no. We rarely buy clothes off the rack. Dear, we must always look like we are crafted from a rare piece of stone. I have a dozen tailors in my flat from Milan and Paris waiting for us. Gio would be highly disappointed if I didn't spend his money well." She pats my knee. She reminds me so much of Abla. *Shoot. I should try to call her today.*

*

When Samantha said flat, I envisioned an elegant apartment by the water. We are sitting on the balcony of Samantha's flat sipping Boerl and Kroff from long stemmed crystal champagne glasses and snacking on roasted turkey sandwiches on French baguettes. *This is not a flat. This is a midsized hotel situated in a villa.* "How many bedrooms are here?"

"Ummm, eighteen," she says. *Wow.*

She continues to command seamstresses and tailors like a captain of a ship. Her fluent Portuguese, French, English and Italian present definitive demands. Her team of workers oscillates in and out of the flat like an army of ants; one after the other showing us fabrics.

"This one just arrived, madam, from India. Pure silk," the gentleman with fancy wingtips says.

She examines the cloth more closely and then pulls it up to her cheek. "Hmmmm…" She looks at me for approval.

"It's beautiful," I say.

"Long gown and make sure you put more emphasis on her waist," Samantha says.

"Certainly, madam." The wingtip man disappears. They come one at a time to hear my responses. I agree to everything except for one fabric.

"Tweed," she sighs. "I don't care for it myself. The word itself makes my skin itch." She laughs. "While they sew, let's go see a dear friend of mine. She has the most interesting collection of lingerie." I agree.

We fly to Sao Vicente. She doesn't reveal too much about Vincent's and Julius's relationship, but we talk endlessly about our children. She has a boy named Ronaldo and a girl named Elizabeth. And a busy husband who travels the world in search of new oil enterprises. She has several houses in Europe and in the U.S. But home is a small villa in Sicily. I make a promise to come back and visit with the children.

Our time in Sao Vicente flies by and we are back in Samantha's flat. I'm not sure how much she arranged in advance, but it feels surreal. Bespoke clothing made while we sip expensive wine. Shoes, jewelry and perfume await us when we return. "Choose anything or everything." She laughs and opens up a jewelry box that reveals a huge diamond bracelet. "This will look lovely on you." Over the course of six hours, eight tailor-made suits and dresses are produced to revamp my wardrobe. When I mention my recent collection of shoes, she scoffs and says that is not nearly enough shoes for someone of my caliber. I instantly feel a bit of regality. "A lady can never have enough shoes, jewelry, clothes or handbags."

On the flight back to Santiago, she sits farther away while talking on the phone. She is speaking in French and I can't make out what she is saying, but she looks upset. Her voice rises and falls repeatedly. She ends the call and takes the seat opposite me again. The handkerchief in her hand dots the corner of her eyes. Her eyes are slightly red. She pulls out her makeup compact to reapply a red lipstick. I offer her a warm smile. "These allergies, I must remember to carry some tablets with me. I always forget," she says.

"Yes, I suffer from them too." *Looks like I'm not the only one with a database of excuses.* Quietness sets in and I finally find the courage to ask her. "How do you manage it? Having a husband always traveling and hardly home? Don't you feel lonely?"

She tilts her head to one side as though she was anticipating my question. "You must keep busy with your own life so that it doesn't bother you anymore." The word 'anymore.' A hint that perhaps she faced the same loneliness at times.

"But is that the way to live? Isn't marriage supposed to be a partnership? How about your feelings or your needs?"

"My dear Vida, you must find happiness wherever you can find it. You must not leave your happiness in the hands of someone else. Follow your heart and your dreams." She smiles, but it isn't one of those pearly white smiles I've become accustomed to. It is rather a smile loaded with melancholy. *Another familiar exercise that I've mastered.* She breaks my gaze and focuses on the night skyline again.

*

We arrive a little after ten. I phone Abla again. No answer, but I leave her another message to expect my call tomorrow. Samantha insisted I wear a royal blue silk dress with a black Chanel stiletto on our way back home. She also changed to a well-tailored grey dress emphasizing the curves of her body. There is a small bonfire by the playground construction. Some of the play elements are coming together. Julius is sitting next to Vincent. He turns in my direction. *How does he do that? Know when I am close by without me saying a word?*

Vincent rises. "Bellissima," Vincent says at the sight of us. Julius rises. He's sweaty still. Mud and sand are stained across his clothing. He holds a damp towel in his hands, and I am sure this is why his hands are immaculately clean. He looks happy.

Vincent approaches us. He kisses my hand. "You're a vision, Ms. Frimpong." I can't contain the cheesy grin. He has Italian exchanges with Samantha and then whisks her away.

I move closer to Julius and he meets me half way. "You look beautiful, Vida," Julius says. I laugh.

"You don't even know what I'm wearing."

"What color?" he asks.

"Blue...royal blue." He extends his hands and starts from my shoulders to the scoop neckline and then caresses his hands against my chest. He continues this sight with his hands until he reaches my waist.

"I don't need to see you to know that you are beautiful." *This could never get old.* His words are like bath oil to my skin. I'm left feeling sexy and radiant. "Mai was worried that you haven't eaten. She didn't want to go to sleep until she knew for sure." There is a slight perfume in the air of roasted chicken.

"That is kind of her. Samantha and I feasted all day long while trying on clothing."

"Were you able to speak to the children?"

"No. I couldn't reach them, but I left a message. I'll try again in the morning."

Samantha reappears. "Well, primo, buenos noches. Please stop by before you return to the U.S." She kisses Julius on the lips again. "Yaa, you have my number; don't be a stranger." She hugs me tightly and I am not sure how to respond to her when she kisses me on my lips. "I consider you family now. We always kiss our loved ones on the lips." *Who am I to judge?*

I smile warmly and kiss her back. "Thank you. It was a beautiful day."

"Yaa? Well, well, well. Take ladies shopping and they become B-F-Fs," Julius says.

My big yawn gives me away. "Perhaps we should retire for the night." He echolocates in the darkness until we reach the castle. He is familiar with the layout. He takes my hand and leads me up the stairs. We stand in front of the bedroom door.

"Good night, Ms. Frimpong." He turns to walk back to his bedroom. I stop him before he leaves.

"Do you want company?"

"You should know better than to ask." My cheeks feel warm from another cheesy grin.

"Give me a few minutes and I will be right over."

"The first door on the left. Should I wait for you to scrub my back?" he says.

"Those bath sessions are over."

"I'm still excited. See you in a few." *He's excited?* I am giddy with so many feelings. Mainly feelings that Ginger is stirring.

As usual, Mai has already arranged for hot water in the bathroom for me. After my bath, I unravel two large braids and finger my hair gently as it falls to my shoulders. I open the box and examine the nude pink lingerie again. As soon as I saw it the lingerie shop, I knew I had to have it. *Fuck, why am I so nervous?* My palms are moist again. *Am I really going to have sex with Julius? I need to think this through.* Abla's voice rings through my head. *Don't think, let Ginger do all the thinking. Ginger wants it because I want to.* The tiny matching panties are as I expected way too small. They barely cover one ass cheek. Not that he would notice, but they are also uncomfortable to wear. I take them off and go all birthday suit from the waist down. The ruffles on the teddy are long enough to cover my ass. I'm sure Julius will be fully naked anyway. *Fuck, this really seals my fate if I show up like this. C'mon, Vida, stop thinking. Just go.*

"Are you decent?" I knock on the door and then open it slightly.

"No, but come in anyway," he says. He's wearing pajamas. I focus on the room and it is decorated quite simply compared to his home in Long Island City.

"What's this—a twin sized bed? You of all people. Lord Gallo, sleeping on a twin sized bed. Where are the servants? Off with their heads!" We both laugh.

"I didn't always have extravagant taste," he says amusedly.

"I know." I caress his shoulders playfully. We share the air between us. "You turned out to be a lot more than what I thought."

"That sounds like a compliment, Ms. Frimpong."

"It is."

"Here is the real funny part. I've been sleeping on this settee since we got here." He takes my hand and leads me to it.

We sit. "Oh, this is really comfortable. You take the bed and I'll sleep on the settee," I say.

"Now what kind of gentleman would I be if I allowed you to sleep here? You are welcome to the bed."

"Come, there is enough room for both of us." I take his hand to show him the unoccupied space on the settee. The room is quiet again and there is a nervous silence between us. "Hmmm. I guess we both want the same thing."

"Do we?" He moves closer and the tip of his nose is on my cheek.

"So, what do you usually do before you go to sleep?" I ask.

"Read and take a glass of shiraz."

"Do you have some?"

He stands up and before taking a step, pauses. There is no other furniture in the room besides the bed, settee and a small round wooden table placed in front of the settee. He moves freely in the room and opens a door. Inside are several shelves full of linen and towels. He takes a bottle from the shelf and hands it to me. It's nearly empty. "Let's start with this. I have more hiding in the kitchen," he says. He motions to leave.

"No. Don't go. This is perfectly fine for both of us." I recall the episode last night by the bonfire. I don't want to end up like a lush on the bed. Suddenly, I hear the sweet voice of Maxwell coming from the balcony. "You have music," I say.

"Yes. I have this solar powered CD player that I made years ago. After all these years it still works. It's been sitting on this balcony for a long time," he says.

"So is Samantha like a cousin?"

"She is Vincent's niece. And that makes her family." I recall from the journals Vincent escorting Julius to school when he was a child in London. I suppose Julius considers Vincent family.

"Oh...but she...he...never mentioned it. Is it a secret?"

"Not really. There is a lot of stuff Vincent doesn't disclose. He's just a private man. He's been through a lot—the war and what happened in Europe."

"What happened in Europe?"

"Oh, Ms. Frimpong," Julius says, disappointed. Yet again, I'm discovered.

"Okay, okay...you made your case." I make a mental note to research Vincent's past. Julius walks over to the balcony to pick up the player.

"So the sunlight energizes it every day?" I examine the device in his hand. "Wow, that's amazing. I mean, how your mind works. Just taking a design or idea and recreating and making it more efficient and practical. You're very talented, Mr. Gallo. I'm sure your mother would be proud of you."

"Thank you." He blushes and looks away.

"Here have some." I hand him the bottle of shiraz.

"You smell different today," he says.

"Different how?"

"You smell like lavender."

"And you are correct. One of the many items I purchased today. Do you like it?" I hold my wrist to his nose. He takes hold of it.

"Yes. And the body lotion too." He smiles.

"What happened to your hand?" There are clear signs of bruising on at least three fingers.

"Oh—this." He smooths his left hand over his right. "Just manual labor. I twisted my fingers carrying a bag of sand." I touch it lightly.

"It looks painful. I wish I brought some shea butter to put on it."

"I have some in the closet," he says. He rises to get up.

"No, stay. I'll get it." I return and sit on the wooden table opposite him with a tube of Abla's shea butter. The music stops and there is silence again.

"It's the CD. It's a bit choppy after sitting out there." I rub the shea butter over his hand gently, moving up and down each finger. I rest his hand on my thigh as I rub more shea butter into my hand. A devilish smile appears.

"What? You have the biggest grin on your face."

"I'm just enjoying the little T-L-C." He sinks deeper into the settee. His legs spread open on either side of me. His right arm is spread across the top of the settee like a wing. And his left hand still warms my thigh. His fingers slowly caress my skin as I attempt to squeeze the last bit of shea butter out of the tube. I rub again. D'Angelo's voice fills the room and then it stops again.

"I suppose it will do this all night if I don't take the CD out."

"That's fine," I say. It gives us a little music at a time. I smear the excess shea butter on his forearm.

"Thank you. That felt wonderful. But my other arm is totally jealous." He extends his right hand to me.

"Well, what's good for the left should be good for the right." He rests his other hand on my thigh. It is as warm as his left hand. *This is definitely flirting 101.* I begin with his fingers, massaging them one by one. He rests his left hand against my thigh and strokes my skin with his thumb. Ginger feels hot, but my nerves are running cold.

How Does It Feel is barely audible, but it denotes the mood. Julius sings along. "Mr. Gallo, you can add singer to your infinite list of talents."

"Thank you," he says. He rubs his hand up my thigh. And I hold my breathe. *I'm all nerves.* "You're cold." There are tiny bumps on my legs. "Let me close the doors on the balcony."

"No. I'm fine." The breeze feels good.

"Are you sure?" he strokes both hands up and down my thighs. The goose bumps immediately disappear. His strokes move farther up and I remember that I am not wearing underwear. I grab hold of his hand.

"What's this?" He releases his hands from mine and touches the fabric. "May I?"

"Yes," I say softly. He begins slowly touching the lace and moves up my stomach, then around my waist with both hands. *Temper your excitement, Vida.* His hands rest on top of my shoulders.

"What color?" he asks.

"Guess?"

A smile of remembrance and he asks, "Nude pink?"

"Yes." He offers a gold-medal smile and then continues. His hands gently touch the lingerie, moving along the pattern of the lace. I close my eyes and feel his warm fingers outlining my cleavage. He stops.

"Vida, you're beautiful. Very lovely," he says. *Ginger is preparing the entrance.* I barely mouth the words 'thank you.' He moves again, slowly with one hand over my breast. His breathing becomes heavy.

The music stops again. He cups my breast. I exhale loudly. He moves his right hand up my thigh. But he stops again. "I heard your beads when you entered the room." His nose is resting on mine. "Vida," he says softly, "...no panties to match the nude pink teddy."

"No. I feel more comfortable this way." He moves his hands toward Ginger. I'm frozen and I want him to touch her, but I've never felt this nervous.

"Vida..." He says my name like the word *yes*. Confident, reassuring and sexy. He guides his hand again over the teddy. He brings my hands to his mouth and gives them wet kisses. There is music again...this time it's Phil Collins' voice that fills the balcony.

"Are you happy?"

I ponder his question. At this moment..."Yes. I am."

He releases my hand and then grabs me by my hips and pulls me on top of him. My knees dig deep in the settee as I straddle him. He kisses me passionately. Our mouths move wildly from lips to neck to cheeks to fingers to ears and back again and again. I build momentum and slowly grind on his lap. The Beast wakes up and Julius holds my face in his hands. "Vida, I want you so much." His words cause shock waves through Ginger, instantly causing her to roll the carpet out for The Beast's arrival. I create moisture on his pajamas and I feel The Beast's need to break free. My hands caress his curly hair and I tug it back a bit trying to contain the ecstasy I am feeling.

"Julius," I whisper.

"Yes, babe," he says.

He slips the lingerie from my shoulders and it falls around my waist. He moves his hands over my nipples. They're hard and he gently squeezes them. I shy away from the sensation. He continues his passionate kisses. He brushes my hair away from my face and kisses me on my nose, forehead, eyes, ears, cheek and then back to my lips.

"Vida..." he whispers my name again. The sound of wet kisses adds to the music on the balcony. He cups my breasts and wets my nipples with his tongue. His warm mouth and tongue are a delightful presence. He gyrates his hips into mine. Mariah Carey's voice is loud and it startles me. He smiles and strokes his hand on my back to soothe me. *Not this song...not now.* Julius maneuvers me from his lap and lays me down on the settee. His head nestles in my bosom. He stamps long wet kisses from my breasts to my navel. His right hand moves in between my legs. I'm wet and he feels the moisture in between my thighs. The song *We Belong Together* is distracting me. Mensah loves this song. *Why now? Shit.* The music seems even louder than before. It should cut off any second.

"Are you all right, babe?" The goose bumps reappear, but this time on my arms. He holds me tightly and kisses me.

I kiss him back deeper, trying to get Mariah's voice out of my head. But it feels forced. He tries to remove the lingerie tangled around my hips, but I stop him. *What are you doing, Vida? This song is fucking up my mojo.*

"Fuck," I say out loud.

One of the first dishes Mensah cooked for me was okra soup and banku. He knew it was my favorite. I recall sitting in the kitchen while he cooked and his boom box on the counter played *We Belong Together* on repeat. That was the first time he told me he loved me. He sang the entire song to me in the kitchen.

Oh, no...why am I thinking about him now? I wish the music would cut off. It usually does after a few seconds. I close my eyes and focus on the present. *Mariah, shut up already.* I squeeze my eyelids shut to block out the memory. Julius kisses me on the lips again and then on the cheek.

"Vida," he says, this time alarmed. "What's wrong? Are you okay?"

"Yes. Yes," I say frantically.

"You're crying." He says it, but I don't believe it. I touch my cheeks and feel the wetness on either side of my face.

"Fuck."

"Vida." He scoops me up and places me on his lap again. The Beast begins to retreat.

The song finally stops, but the mood is not the same. *Really, Vida? Is this what we are doing? Crying during foreplay?* I try to kiss through the emotion, but he doesn't accept my kisses. He picks up the lace teddy entangled around my waist and slips it back on me one arm at a time.

"It's just the cold air," I say.

"Vida, don't tell me a unicorn story. We don't have to rush into anything. It's probably much too soon."

"No, Julius. I want to be with you. I'm just a bit nervous. That's all."

"You, nervous? I find that hard to believe." He takes my hand and gently kisses it. "You mean a lot to me, Vida. I want to be with you when you are ready." I rest my head on his chest. He holds me and we sit in silence until my legs begin to fall asleep. I lay down and he nestles beside me.

"Am I foolish?"

"Foolish?" he asks. "You are far from foolish, Vida. I don't want you to feel like I am taking advantage of you. I like you a lot and I don't want to jeopardize what we have. I know things are complicated now. We should take it slow. You still love Mensah. Nothing wrong to love somebody with all your heart. Love is tricky and at times painful and at times…unexplainable. Never feel bad for giving love one more chance." He kisses my forehead.

"I don't want to ruin our friendship." I turn to face him.

"You won't and I can't allow you to do that. I can't explain what's happening between us, but I really enjoy being with you. Those feelings will never change. No matter what decision you make. Meeting you is one of the best things that has happened to me. And I cannot dismiss that." More tears fall and land on his nose.

"I'm sorry."

"Enough. Stop apologizing."

I snuggle underneath his neck. We hold each other for a few minutes longer. *Is The Beast asleep? My poor Ginger has given up all hopes of feeling anything tonight.*

"I should go to my room," I finally say.

"No. Please. Stay. Lay here with me." His words hit my neck and course through my body. "We can sleep here." He squeezes his body into the contours of the settee.

"Are you sure it's okay? Do you need to consult with your friend before I sleep here?" I never disclosed the nickname I gave to his *kote*. Considering the way things are going, it's a conversation for another time.

"My friend?"

"Yeah, the one that made his appearance a few minutes ago." He laughs.

"No. I run the show, not him. He will eventually go to sleep when he realizes that his play date is gone." His words are not convincing. I feel movement against my ass.

"I'm proud of you. You've made it four months with no sex and you don't have an addiction."

"Perhaps my only addiction is to a writer named Vida Frimpong who lives in the Bronx, who drives a smoke grey Honda CRV and a white Range Rover, who has three great sons and a hefty entourage."

We laugh. "So you won. What do I have to do or say—what's your prize?" I turn around to face him and my lips touch the bridge of his nose. He squeezes me gently and crosses his left leg over my body.

"Nothing, Vida. You don't owe me anything. I already have my prize." The CD finally stops. The sounds of nighttime creatures fill the bedroom. "I'm sure you know that I will publish your book?"

"Well, I had a feeling."

"Good. So keep writing." His head rests in my bosom and I feel protected in his arms.

"Why do they call you Gio?" He grins but offers no response. "I know you are going to tell me I should know by now, but please tell me."

"Giovanni Diego Julius Gallo was born in this castle, but you know him as—"

"Julus Gallo," I interrupt.

"Only close family call me Gio and I will only respond to maybe three people in the world who use that name."

"It's beautiful. So you're Giovanni and Diego and Julius and DJ and Kofi. Oh, I see now. DJ's short for Diego and Julius."

"There's no fooling you." I pinch him. His sarcasm is back. He laughs.

"Why don't you use Giovanni?"

"When I was first diagnosed with the tumor, my mother was told by some of the elders in the town to change my name so that the evil curse could leave my body. My mother never changed it, but she did shorten it to Julius Gallo. It didn't change anything. God wanted me to have this tumor and nobody could do anything to change that." His sentiments about God sadden me.

"Do you blame God?" He bellows a sinister laugh.

"And who else would inflict a rare tumor on a ten-year-old boy that eventually caused his blindness?" I prop my head on my arm because the conversation is taking a serious tone.

"I don't think we can question God for his reasons. But I do believe everything happens for a reason, Julius."

"I don't understand how the same merciful God who creates life, beautiful oceans, solid oak trees, would inflict pain on innocent children." His face tenses and he raises his head to meet mine. I comb my hands through his hair. He takes my hand and kisses it. "Sorry if I seem obtuse. Some things I will never understand."

"Don't be sorry, I can't imagine what your childhood must have been like or some of the obstacles you face now." I shift my hips deeper into his and there's a tent being erected in his pants. "It reminds me, MJ's full name is Mawuli Yaw Asare. We just call him MJ because his mannerisms resemble Mensah so much. Kakra was born James Kakra Asare and Panin's full name is John Panin Asare. I only use the their Christian names in school and at home we go by their Ghanaian names."

A long silence again. "James and John are nice Christian names. Did you pick them out?"

"No, Mensah named all his children and he was adamant that Panin was named John. You know it's traditional that Ghanaian fathers name their children." He places one arm over his head and the other on his thigh creating a slight distance between us.

"You have three amazing children, Vida. You should be proud."

Chapter 69

This is our final day on this beautiful island. I spent the night on Julius's settee again. I don't recall what time he came to bed, but in the midst of the cool night, his body wrapped around mine and gave me warmth. Standing on the balcony, I watch as a group of men work tirelessly to complete the park for the children. Slides, swings, monkey bars, tunnels, ladders, trampolines and sprinklers adorn the park. Julius is standing under a tree away from the park grounds. I get dressed and make my way toward the kitchen. Mai rises to greet me with a carb-filled breakfast. It is consistent with my carb-loaded Ghanaian dishes.

"Beautiful," she says. I reexamine my choice of dress and shoes.

"Thank you. All this for me?" *I guess one more day of fresh baked bread won't hurt.* The plate of food consists of several bread rolls, a vegetable omelet, fried potatoes and large pitcher of juice. "I will wait for Julius to come back. This is much too much for me."

"Gio no," she says and points out the window. It's hard to decode her meaning. "No Gio food. He wif mama." She points again toward the window. I'm not sure what she means, but I move closer to the window and observe Julius pacing back and forth under the same tree. It's hard to see if anyone else is with him.

"Mama?" I say. "Who is mama?"

"Si, mama jere," she says in her limited English. Mai motions me to eat. After several mouthfuls of eggs and sweet rolls, I beg her to stop filling my plate. I get up and carry the dishes to the sink but she chastises me and motions me to sit down. I comply and watch her dance around the kitchen preparing another feast for lunch.

An hour or two pass. Fragrant fried fish fills the kitchen and I help Mai blot the excess oil off the fish. Now, Julius is sitting under the tree. *What is he doing? Perhaps I should go to him.*

"Come now," Mai says as she pounds on the dough. Children's voices force my attention toward them. The children amuse themselves on their new playground. *I wonder how the boys are doing?* I spoke to them briefly last night but I still miss the laughter, the banter and inquisitive questions. In a few hours, I will have them in my arms again. It is a little after noon and finally Julius enters the kitchen.

"Good afternoon, Vida. Excuse my appearance." He is covered with sand and sweat. "I didn't expect to be there long, but once I start talking, time escapes me."

"No apologies. You must have a lot to say."

"Would you like to see something?" he asks.

"Sure." He leads me up a small hill to a big tree. Underneath the tree is a lovely garden of flowers and tall plants. A plaque is embedded at the base of the tree. The words are written in Portuguese, but my eyes settle on a name: Ermelinda Alice Ribero Gallo.

"This is where my mother is laid to rest," Julius says. The meticulous detail is breathtaking. The huge tree resembles a tall mushroom with broad green foliage at the crown. Lush grass and beautiful flowers landscape the hill. Flowers overflow the edge of the plaque.

"It's beautiful, Julius."

"It's called dragoeiro or the dragon tree." He kneels down and picks some of the bark off. A red salve comes out. He shows me.

"Wow, that's amazing."

"It's known to have healing properties. Mama used to take the sap and rub it over my face. I always lose track of time whenever I'm here." This is such surprising behavior. It makes me appreciate him even more. Julius begins to sing. I don't know what he is saying, but he bends and feels his way down to the plaque and kisses it. I bend down and arrange cut flowers around the plaque. He closes his eyes and continues singing.

"That's lovely, Julius." He smiles.

"It's her favorite."

We make our way back to the kitchen. Mai greets us again with more food. *I think I've discover something new.* "Is Alice in Queens named after your mother?"

"And here I thought you were just a pretty face." I swat a towel across his chest. It's good to see the sarcasm still there. Julius is more than I expected. He is a puzzle that is taking shape. So now I've discovered some of the names in the journals. *Oh, but Nana. Who is Nana?*

"I'm glad I came. I feel like it's all coming together somehow. Really. Yes, I know, I haven't read nearly half of the journals in the vault, but I'm impressed with what I know so far. Now all I need to know is, who is Nana?" There is this look on Julius's face with the mention of her name. She must have hurt him badly. He bows his head down and rests his palms in his face.

"We don't need to talk about Nana. That is in the past and I don't need that memory in the book." He rises. *I struck a nerve. What kind of woman would break a man's heart like that? What could she possibly have done to make him still feel so bitter?* "I'm going to take a bath. I will be back down shortly." He leaves the kitchen and the atmosphere feels heavy. Mai has a look as though she wants to say something. Our eye meet and she turns away, kneading at her dough. *She knows something.*

I wash my hands and take a handful of the dough resting in the bowl. She tries to motion me to sit, but I firmly tell her I want to learn. Her strong hands pound into the dough. She rolls it over and over again. I follow her lead. My fingers are not as strong as hers. She laughs and motions her hands over mine. "Who is Nana?" She stops and turns her eyes toward the dough. *She knows.* I take her hands into mine. "I know you know. Is it Julius's girlfriend? A wife?" She turns her head away from me like MJ does when he does something naughty.

"No. Nana…No…" She snatches her hands away from mine and moves back. "Eeeee….aaaaa…" She pauses and then tilts her head upwards as though the words are hanging from the ceiling. "Nana e Gio no…break—friend…" She uses her hands as though she is breaking French bread in half. "…break…no…long time…Nana e Gio e mama." She points to the hill where Julius's mother is buried. She shakes her head wildly. "Nana e Gio…no…no." She moves closer to her mound of dough and continues its preparation. It's not nearly enough information to decipher the relationship, but she knows Nana and whatever happened is not a secret.

Chapter 70

Just as I expect, Abla is home and no doubt waiting for every juicy detail that will fall from my lips. Vincent brings in my baggage and Julius follows behind him.

"Rosemary, *maadwo*," Julius says.

"*Yaa anua. Wofiri he?*" I'm sure Julius won't disclose where we've been, but she searches our faces for an answer. Instead, Julius offers a gentle smile and kisses Abla on the cheek.

"*Maadwo. Daa yie.*" He turns his attention from Abla and takes a hold of my hand. "I will call you later."

"*Ma jo. De yeah.*" My words 'good night and sleep well' in Twi don't sound as polished as Julius's, but a wide smile tells me he understands. I close the door behind him and Abla's eyes pierce my skin. *Fuck. Let the drama begin.*

"Wait, before you begin, let me turn down da fire on da soup so I can focus. I will meet you upstairs." *Damn it. She's not even going to wait until tomorrow.* I'm exhausted from the plane ride. All I want to do is hop into the shower and go to bed. I kick off my heels and collapse on the bed thinking of various stories to entertain Abla. *The truth? Or a really elaborate unicorn story? Or play coy and don't give out too much information?* She probes like a pimple on the tip of the nose. *Who am I fooling? Lying to Abla is like telling a toddler to sit still during family photos.* It's a hard and unnecessary struggle. Abla always finds a way to get to the truth.

Oh goodness, she's here already. She jumps on the bed beside me.

"Lez start and don't leave anydin' out. So did you give him a—" Abla sticks her thumb in her mouth to indicate her sign language for blowjob.

I recall her ranting about how she didn't like the term blowjob. "Girls who use da word blowjob are lazy. Itz work, but very good work if you do it right."

Then she argued against her own case.

"But den again some people haf made careers out of it. Yeah, blowjob fits da bill."

"Yes, then you would be classified as a prostitute, which is illegal in many states," I retorted.

"Just dink, if itz legal so many people won't be so depressed. We would haf world peace all because men are gettin' blowjobs. I should start one of doze dings, *'yefren en sen'* ...ummm...wat you call it...protest? You know, like stickers all ova da place. If you want to fight crime; give a blowjob."

"Oh, you mean slogans," I said, trying to make sense of her argument.

"Yeah...*'Tafre kotodenden* and da world will be peaceful.' Men create wars because dey are mizerable. Yur da writa, dink of somedin'."

"Really, world peace because of blowjobs?" I said, not surprised at all if she really started this campaign.

"Hey, are you lissenin'?" Abla brings me back to the present.

"Oh, Abla. It's been so long since I actually gave a blowjob, I don't think I would know what to do."

"Oooooh pleazze, hefa. Iz like eatin' fufu; nobody has to tell you how to eat it to enjoy it. Put da *kotedenden* in yur mouth and yur tongue will do wat it can."

"That's it?"

"Oh, yeah. Do you swallow?"

"No...!" I say violently. "Do you?" Even though we are sisters, she always leaves me stunned with some of the things she partakes in. She shrugs noncommittally.

"Itz not about me tonight. Start from da beginning. I'm waitin'."

Okay, I'm gonna attempt a unicorn story. "Okay, okay." I readjust myself on the bed and try not to maintain eye contact. "It was really good." I smirk a little bit remembering Julius sitting by the bonfire singing with the children. "He was gentle and took his time and everything."

"Ahhhh-jaaa," Abla says. Her eyes grow larger. "Wait, back up. Did he take yur clothes off or did you do it?"

"Ummm. He took them off..."

"Datz good. Tell me about da first time."

"The first time?"

"Yeah, you were deer for a week. Like, how many times did you have sex?" Her eyes are ready to pop out of her head.

"Ummmmm...twelve..." *Really, Vida? Twelve? Damn, I overshot. Even Ginger wants to call bullshit.* Abla's face looks like she just swallowed a bone. She gasps for air.

"Ooooh...oh my goodness. I can tell; you waz walkin' funny."

"I was?"

"You see. You didn't even notice. We'll get to da Olympic sex soon. Lez get back to da first time."

"Right. Not much to tell. It was kinda of fast then slow."

"You did use condoms, right?"

"Oh yeah, for sure."

"Did you carry some?" Abla asks. *Fuck...I know where this is going.*

"No. He had some."

"Da special onez you uze. You told him about yur latex allergiez?"

My story is unraveling. Abla knows so much about me that it should be criminal. But then it's my big mouth that tells her everything. When I lost my virginity to Kenneth, I developed a huge rash on Ginger. I swore that I caught some disease and was too ashamed to tell anyone. I finally confessed to Abla when she saw me walking funny around the house. She went with me to the doctor where I was finally diagnosed with a latex allergy.

"Well, it turns out he has a latex allergy and he uses sensitive condoms too."

"Hmmmm. Da amount of fuckin' he doez, I find it hard dat hez sensitive to anydin'."

"Yeah." I chuckle nervously.

"So, doez he have skills or doez he work like a jumbo pencil?"

"Jumbo pencil?"

"Hmmm. You know, doze big pencils dat look nice but you can't do notin' wit it. Da regular size pencils are common, uzeful and easy to manage."

"No. The jumbo pencil works just fine."

"Betta dan you-know-who?" *Mensah.* As mad as I am with him, I don't know if anyone could ever compare to Mensah. But Julius certainly knows how to kiss. I can still feel his lips on me. The taste of vanilla, espresso and Guinness on his tongue.

"Oh, no. I don't think anyone could compare to Mensah."

"So, twelve times, huh?" *Damn it. I should have said five. She is already detecting a unicorn story.*

"Yeah…can't you tell I'm exhausted?" I collapse onto the pillow.

"Wat I can tell iz dis story iz full of shit." *Fuck. And there it is. I'm caught like a refugee scaling a wall.* "I know you. Afta da first time you would cry like a baby. You…you can't do it. Guilt…you can't take it. Twelve…my ass. And dat latex allergiez; you are da only African woman I know who needs a special instrument to screw. You lied right to my face. Yur one and only sista. One motha and one fatha." She pouts as though her feelings are hurt, but it's an act to draw sympathy. "So, wat did you do besides hide from da *kotodenden* all week?"

Without exact specificity, I list my activities during the week to end the conversation quickly. "Island hopping, shopping, playing, drinking and dancing."

"Well, you know when da time is ready. I won't mention you and yur rich friend's behavior again." Her deposition is not as firm as it should be. It's like witnessing someone who swears off carbs, but the next day you see them eating jollof rice. *She will ask again.*

Chapter 71

Auntie Cece says she will be over in a few minutes. I know Mensah has contacted her by now. I refused all his calls and deleted his late night text messages. The children know something is wrong. They don't know about my four-page Dear Mensah letter. I haven't told anyone. But I am sure Mensah has told Auntie Cece. She is the only one cheering for him. She is the only one now trying to save my marriage. *Why are things so complicated now? Everything has changed.* My feelings have turned from anger to sorrow to hate back to love and now I'm somewhere in between. I don't hate him, but I don't know if I'm still in love with him either. His last voice message was the longest message he has ever left me since he relocated to California.

"Yaa, how long is this going to last? I don't know what else to tell you. You won't return my calls or my text messages. Is this how it is going to be? Silence? It's been several months. And now you send me this letter stating that you want a divorce. Oh, like it's that simple. At least hear me out before you make any decisions. I know I fucked up, but Kate is not here anymore. We need to talk and as soon as I get an opportunity, I will be back to New York. Why can't you give me a chance to explain myself? I bought you a ticket to join me in the Bahamas this weekend. I'm leaving Dubai tomorrow and I will meet you at the hotel. Just you and me, Yaa. I've already spoken to Auntie Cece to watch the children. All you have to do is show up. I've taken care of everything. Give me a chance, Yaa…please. Let me hear from you. Please."

The noise of footsteps approaches and then a gentle knock at the door.

"Hello, Auntie." She pushes the door through. Ghana suits her well. She has a tan and her hair is braided past her shoulders. She looks youthful. Her skin is the color of fried ripe plantain.

"Good evening, Yaa. Where are the children?"

"They are across the street at Chin's house."

She sits beside me on the bed and takes my hands into hers. *Oh, no…this is one of those long marriage-is-not-easy talks.* "I don't know the whole story, but what I know is marriage is never easy. There is someone who has to play the fool. Be the smart one, but don't show that you are smart. One has to see, but don't see. Nowhere is easy. You can't run away from yur problems and expect not to face them again around the corner. At times the rope is long but every rope has an end. You will cry at times and laugh another time. Marriage is sweet and sometimes it's sour. I don't know much. But I do know Mensah loves you and the children." She pauses and, for the first time in a long time, tears fall down her cheeks. "You have to forgive him. At least for the children's sake. The decision you make will not only affect you, but them as well." Now I'm crying. The boys love their father and I would never do anything to change that.

"Auntie, I understand."

"No, you don't understand." She sobers up to a firm stance. "Don't be fooled by shining things and think it's gold. Men are funny. They can want you so desperately at one time and then throw you to the side another time. You must stay wif yur husband. He stood in front of our family to promise to take care of you and love you. He hasn't moved away from that promise."

"So love includes a mistress?"

"Solomon was a wise man, but he had many wives. I am not saying that it is not a painful thing to discover, but a man who can push that aside and say he still wants his wife deserves another chance. Don't make a mistake that you will regret."

I want to respond to her. To tell her that my feelings for Mensah have changed. But it would be a series of repeated exchanges that would not result in anything. *Talk less and listen more, Vida.* She reminds me of all the wonderful things Mensah is. And that his indiscretion should be pardoned. My heart remains hardened by the image of Kate in the T-shirt I bought him greeting me at the door. *For how long was this going on? Does he think she is more beautiful than me? Is he happy with me?*

"Are you listening to me?"

"Yes, Auntie."

"It is a woman that turns the roof over her head into a home. Don't let anyone destroy that. I will look after the children. Please meet him in the Bahamas." She kisses my forehead and I nod in agreement. "Do you need help packing?"

"No. I can manage."

After dinner, I tell the children of my plans this weekend with their father. It turns out they are aware of Mensah's plan. Kakra wholeheartedly admits to the destination.

"I heard you and Auntie Abla talking about an all girls' trip to the Bahamas. You said Daddy promised you on your tenth anniversary," Kakra says. He beams with hope and I'm convinced even more that I have to go. *I owe it to the children.*

Later that night. I text Julius.

"Hi. I won't be able to come by tomorrow. Going away for the weekend. I will call you when I get back into town."

This seems ambiguous enough. The shorter the better. Julius's call is coming through.

"Good evening. How are the children?" Julius says.

"Fine," I say softly.

"Rosemary? And Auntie Cece?"

"Abla's in Connecticut. Mrs. Lindsey is back. Auntie was here earlier, but she left after dinner." *He's never asked about Auntie Cece before.*

"Hmmm. What's for dinner tonight?"

"Jollof rice and fried chicken."

"Sounds delicious." I know he wants to know more about this weekend, but is waiting for me to say something.

"I should have brought you some."

"It's late. Perhaps you can make me some over the weekend, depending on what time you get back." *And there it is, a subtle probe.*

"I'll be gone for the whole weekend. Maybe next weekend?"

"Just you and the children?" he asks.

"No, Auntie Cece will be here to watch the children." I can't tell him a unicorn story. Especially now that I have gotten to know him a little more this past week. *Vida, just say it and get it over with.* "I'mmeetingMensahintheBahamas," I rush through the sentence and wait for his reply. *Maybe I should repeat it. It didn't sound coherent.* Silence.

"...There's a really good restaurant in Nassau. They have live music; steel drums and the food is excellent. If I recall the name, I will text it to you."

"Okay. Thank you," I say. *I owe him more.* I start to apologize, but he doesn't allow me to continue.

"You must have a lot to sort out and it's getting late." I check the clock by the bed. It's 9:51 p.m.

"Julius…"

"I will see you when you get back. Safe journey." My phone flashes that the call has ended.

Chapter 72

There will probably come a time when I will look back on this day and say either I really fucked up or made the right decision. I instruct the cab driver to take me to Long Island City instead. He isn't thrilled, less than ten minutes away from the airport, to turn around and go in the opposite direction. I soothe his mild irritation by adding an extra hundred dollars to the fee for his time.

Surprisingly, he pulls in front of Julius's building within twenty minutes. I enter with my luggage and drop it at the door. Alice greets me upon my arrival. As I walk through the house, flurries of noises are coming from the backyard. The masseuse and the tall black woman I bumped into once are topless in the pool.

"Woo hoo! You're here, Vida. Now it's a real party."

She knows my name and I'm focused on her micro bikini bottom as she emerges from the water.

"Party?"

"Julius called us this morning to come over for a little get-together. I'm glad he called you too." She motions toward me and I stumble back on the wet ground.

"Where's Julius?"

"Oh. He's being such a party pooper. We asked for more champagne, but he's been on the phone for over an hour." I make my way to the kitchen. The masseuse sidesteps me.

"You're leaving?"

"I'll be back."

"Yay...Vida is staying!"

It is hard to look at them in any other way but double Ds. Their frames are tiny compared to the bags of flour sitting on their chests. *Definitely not my kind of party. Damn it. Why did I come here? I'm the furthest thing from his mind right now.*

Julius has a champagne bottle in each hand. He is dressed in shorts and a white T-shirt. He looks dry. *He hasn't been in the pool yet.*

"Vida? I thought you were on your way to the Bahamas."

"Sorry, didn't mean to crash your party. I should have called before coming. I see you are back to your unique form of entertainment. Well, you've won the bet and you should have a party. A very exclusive, entertaining and arousing party." He moves closer to me and I take wide steps back.

"Vida...why are you here?" His hoarse breath carries the smell of champagne in my direction.

"Despite what the women by the pool think, I am not here for the party. I forgot some work on the laptop that I want to take with me. That's all." It doesn't sound convincing, but I have already committed myself to this unicorn story. I move quickly and enter the library. The laptop is powered on and I search for unicorn files to make my story more convincing. Julius enters the study with one bottle of champagne in his right hand and large knife in the other. He asks me again about my presence. His brows are creased causing a v indentation in the middle. I ignore him. *Yes, it's starting to look like a stupid decision I made after all. What the hell were you thinking, Vida? Like something magical was going to happen? I should be on my way to the Bahamas trying to patch up my marriage. Why am I standing in Julius's study?* Shrill voices and swishing sounds come from the pool area. *This life. His life is not for me. Silly Vida. You need to leave.* I shove more random papers from the desk into my bag and shut down the laptop.

"Answer me, Vida."

"I told you, I needed to finish up some work, but it can wait. I'll be back next weekend." I move away from the desk.

With a swift motion of the knife, he uncorks the champagne. I stop to see where the cork lands before proceeding in his direction. He takes a large gulp and rests the bottle and knife on the floor. He charges me against the wall. For a second, my chest tightens and my heart feels arrested.

"Why didn't you go with him? You said you were going to meet him. Why didn't you go?"

Frantic heartbeats like a Congo drum cause my breaths to quicken. "Julius, what are you doing?"

"Tell me. Please. I just need to hear you. Tell me something." I break from his grip and move backwards until the desk shortens the distance between us.

"Vida..." *Why does his voice set me on fire?* "Vida," he says again. He picks me up and places me on the desk. He stands in between my legs. "Vida, what are you doing to me?"

"Julius, stop it. I have to go." *But I really don't want to go.* Our breaths race back and forth and his lips touch mine. I kiss him and he hauls me into his arms and kisses me more deeply. I cry out to stop again, but he keeps penetrating my mouth with his warm tongue. My skin burns and his lips cause wet hotspots on my pores. "Julius, please, we should—"

"Vida..." He says it with a hunger that I know well. With swift force he lifts me slightly up and pull downs my leggings to my knees. I don't have a chance to move his hands. His weight pushes me farther on the desk and my ass cheeks feel the cool wood. He kisses me feverishly.

"Vida," he says my name again, "I tried. I tried to stay away, but I can't."

"Please, Julius." His mouth trails firm kisses on my neck and then my shoulders. He caresses my ass and squeezes it like a stress ball. He finds the outline of my thong and I maneuver so he can pull them down to my thighs.

"Julius..." a gentle voice calls with knocks on the door and then she says his name again. "Julius, babe..." It's the masseuse with a conflicted facial expression.

"Julius," I try to talk through wet kisses. "She's...at...the...door." But he doesn't stop and I glance at her again, Her expression turns to giddiness. He moves his hands up my thighs. I try to pull away because she is still standing there. I struggle to pull up my thong. It cuts through my skin at the kneecaps because of Julius's weight on me. He releases my ass from his grip and with two swift motions pulls my leggings off one leg at a time. He then tears the lace thong and tosses it onto the floor like a wet plastic bag.

His tongue continues to pierce my mouth vigorously. Then he marks wet kisses from my mouth to my neck and then to my shoulders without breaking the trilogy no matter who calls from behind him. I look at the door and the masseuse is gone.

He rubs the pad of his thumb over Ginger and I moan, "Julius." It excites him and he does it again and again and again and again. The masseuse returns with the black woman. They are watching us.

"Julius..." the black woman says. But he doesn't respond to her.

"Julius." I say again after he gives my mouth rest. He finally speaks.

"Yes, babe," He finally speaks and then he slides one finger and then another inside me. His thumb continues mapping my sex. I scream lightly, and he moves systematically. I grab his hand and he pauses. "I want you to be happy. Vida. I want to make you happy. Trust me." I'm in total ecstasy. He mouths slowly, "Where… are…you…babe?" He spreads the wetness from Ginger all around her with gentle motions in and out of me. He moves his fingers like a skilled surgeon.

"Julius should we go—" I peer over his shoulder. *Those heifers are still standing in the doorway.* Now they are pouting.

"Vida," he whispers firmly. "Look…at…me." My eyes move away from the audience at the door.

"No. Please stop."

"You don't want me to stop. Look…at…me…babe," he says. My breath is heavy, deep with each thrust. His words are low and demanding. "I want to make you happy. Where…are…you?"

I try to hold back. Ginger tightens around his fingers and he doesn't stop. He goes deeper and slower, then faster. I peer over his shoulder and 'Double Dutch' is gone. My breaths quicken and my chest rises and falls sharply. I am on fire. And I feel the surge from Ginger to my toes through my back to the beads of sweat on my forehead. He smiles because he knows what's happening, but I'm holding back. Holding back a scream of ecstasy.

"I feel you. Don't hold it." His voice is deep and warm. His breathing arcane and slow. He sucks on my bottom lip. I hold his hand firm against me.

"I'm coming," I whisper. He seals my fate. One, two, three in and out thrusts and the gates are open. "Julius," I moan and he kisses me like it's a lifeline. All my anxieties leave my body and I explode on his hand.

"There you are, babe." A smile breaks from his face. He caresses Ginger with her wetness over and over again. He moans, "Oh, Vida." I wrap my left arm around his neck and the other around his waist. I feel my nipples harden and my heavy breath. He pulls from me and I feel the cool air enter where he left. He slowly sucks the same fingers that were enthralled in me.

I want him now.

"We are going to take our time, Vida." He senses my hunger. I'm satisfied and happy. Alice's voice breaks the intimacy.

"Lord Gallo."

"Not now, Alice." He kisses me again.

"I should get a towel," I say. The wetness under my ass makes it uncomfortable sitting on the desk. He takes off his shirt and lifts me from the desk and wipes it clean and then the puddle on the floor.

"My apologizes, Lord Gallo. But you have an urgent call."

He steps back. "Not now, Alice." I pick up my thong and leggings from the floor and I can tell his disposition has changed due to Alice's message. He grabs me. "I have something important to attend to. Are you still going to the Bahamas?"

"No. Is everything okay? Do you need me to do anything?"

"I'm sorry. I just need to handle this matter and I will be right over."

"Okay," I say solemnly. *Damn it. Nothing again.*

Chapter 73

Today is the day God has blessed me with. I get up and check my phone. *Christ. It's 8:15!* Six messages and one text. I read Julius's text: "Sorry, my meeting was longer than expected. I hope you had a restful sleep. I really enjoyed your company this afternoon. Call me if you're still up."

Four unknown numbers, but no messages. The last message is from Mensah.

"Vida, where are you? I got your message. I hope you're feeling better. Call me back."

I left a short message for Mensah telling him that I wasn't feeling well so I came back home. *Not convincing enough, but it will have to do.* Auntie Cece didn't comment, but left as soon as I got back. I think she knew that I wouldn't go. I crawled into bed after a hot bath and fell asleep like a baby last night.

"Happy birthday, Mommy." MJ enters the bedroom. He suffocates me with a wild hug.

"Thank you, sweetie."

"We made breakfast for you."

"We?" I ask, knowing well that the only cooking the boys do is pour milk into a bowl.

"Yes. Auntie is here and G-Money." I leap from the bed.

"Julius is here?"

"Yep. He's downstairs and you got more fancy tulips." MJ continues about the big plans he has for my birthday. "Since you are home, I'm going to take you to Rye Playland this afternoon and I'm going to get you a cake and treat you nice. All because you are my mommy and it's your birthday. What kind of cake you want?"

"Anything that my darling, caring little man gets me, I will eat." He gives me a quick kiss and sets off. My mind is focused on Julius downstairs. "Shit." *Be cool, Vida. Pretend like nothing happened.*

It's useless during the shower. I feel his presence between my legs. I shake my head violently. *What happens now? Be cool, Vida. It's nothing...No, it was something...This never...Oh, shit...Take control of yourself.*

Don't think too much. It's your birthday. Enjoy yourself. This mantra is on auto repeat as I descend the stairs.

"Oh Mommy, MJ ruined the surprise. We were coming to serve you breakfast in bed. Happy birthday," Kakra says.

"Thank you, sweetie. I appreciate all your efforts, but I want to see your beautiful faces when I sit down to eat my breakfast."

I hear Abla's laughter in the kitchen. No sign of Julius in the living room. Huge assortments of red, pink, yellow and white tulips embellish the house. I stand at the entrance to the kitchen door, but my feet feel solid like I should move. *Oh, for heaven's sake, play it cool, Vida.* Before I can make my attempt into the kitchen, Abla steps out.

"Oh, deer goes my darlin' sista. *Mema wo awoda pa.* You don't look a day ova twenty-one."

"*Medaase.*"

"You look especially shinin' dis mornin'," Abla says.

"I do?" *I doubt if Julius told her anything.* It's my paranoia setting in. *Keep cool, Vida.* "What's so funny? I can hear you laughing out here."

"Oh, Da Boss iz tellin' some nautee jokes." I become alarmed. *Did he say anything?*

She pinches me. "Rich, handsome, funny and, well, you know"—she squints her eyes—"blessed in otha areas. Penny iz very lucky."

"Yes, she is," I say coldly.

"So, do you want to tell me wat happened to yur trip to da Bahamas? Da boys said you weren't feelin' well and had to come back home." Julius steps out of the kitchen with a tall stack of pancakes. He is casually dressed and wearing his navigators. I want to move, but I find myself cemented to the ground. Abla whispers, "We'll talk about dat lata."

"Happy birthday, Vida." He sets the pancakes on the table and embraces me. His arms securely cover me and the scent of his juniper cologne surrounds me. He kisses my forehead and leads me to a chair. "Please sit." Panin places a tall pitcher of juice on the table.

"Good morning, sweetie." He pulls out a card and hands it to me. "Oh, thank you." I struggle as usual to shower him with affection. I'm hoping he will grant me another surprise and say something. I watch him intently for just a word, but he moves away from my odd goggling.

Vincent enters the room. "Many more blessed birthdays." He kisses me on either side of the cheek. *This is a first.* He sits beside Julius. This is a lovely breakfast celebration. A huge spread of bacon, sausage, pancakes, Belgian waffles, fried chicken and steak, tossed salad, fruit salad, porridge, bagels and croissants. Vincent urges me to open the bottle of wine he brought for my birthday.

"What is a celebration without wine?" Vincent says. We spend the next two hours talking, laughing and overeating.

"Okay guys, let's get ready," Abla shouts out.

"Where to?" I ask.

"MJ has a whole itinerary planned for you. Didn't he tell you?" I recollect his rantings.

"Yes, Mommy. We're going to Rye Playland for your birthday," MJ says.

I am secretly excited; if there's one thing my children know about me, it's that I'm still a big kid when it comes to amusement parks. "We have a rematch on the bumper cars, Mommy," Kakra says.

"Yur comin' too, aren't you, Boss?" Abla says.

"I don't want to impose," Julius says.

"You're not imposing. It'll be fun," I say.

"In that case, I'm coming…too."

"Good." Abla stares a bit too long in my direction. *She definitely has her eye on me. I don't think I've revealed anything so far.*

Chapter 74

How could a wonderful day end so horribly? "Mommy, we searched the bathrooms again. There's no sign of Panin."

"I will check da loz children station again," Abla says. Several security guards surround MJ and me.

"What was he wearing?" a young security officer says to me. I describe Panin's clothing. I dial his cellphone again and it goes straight to voicemail. His phone must be dead. I am constantly reminding him to charge it. "Have a couple of your guys check by the waterfront," the officer commands the other patrolmen.

"Mommy, here comes Vincent," Kakra says. I am anxious; *maybe he has news.*

"I circled the parking lot several times. No sign of him. Where is Julius?" Vincent asks.

"I thought he was with you," I say.

"He told me he was coming back here," Vincent says.

"Shit." This is turning into a nightmare. Vincent looks alarmed. The Rye police officers approach us again.

"Do you have a picture of your son?" a tall reddish-haired officer says. Kakra pulls out his phone to show the officers. "So it's been about an hour now."

"Yes," I say anxiously. *Don't break down now, Vida. Keep it together.* My worst nightmare come to life on my birthday. Tears break free and MJ cuddles me. The loudspeaker announces for Panin to meet security at the gate. *Oh my goodness, what if he doesn't return?* My legs are weak. I feel faint. *I can't stand here answering any more questions.*

I grab Kakra and MJ firmly and begin shouting for Panin. Abla runs in my direction. "Any sign?"

"No," I say wearily.

"Let's hope Julius and Vincent find him."

"Julius is missing also." I search for Vincent and he is not standing with the team of officers. "Vincent can't find him," I say.

"Ehhhh, eeehhh wat iz goin' on? Panin iz missin' and can't talk. Julius iz missin' and can't see. Oh, dear God, dis iz too much for one day." *Yes, I agree. Too much for one day.*

"Abla, stay with the boys. I'm going to check the bumper car rides again." I take heavy steps, searching the crowd of people. I mistakenly grab several boys thinking they are Panin. *How the mind plays tricks on you when you really want to believe in something.* "Panin!" I yell frantically. I feel the tears catching in the back of my throat, but I fight it. *There is no way I am leaving here today without my son.*

"Vida. Vida," a familiar voice calls from behind me. *Julius!* Panin is walking beside him. I run as fast as I can to embrace them. I hold Panin in my arms until I feel the crowd of security and police officers surround us.

I hear a series of questions and Julius responding. "He's safe. He wandered off by the waterfront." Vincent embraces Julius. This is the second time that I've seen him worried for Julius's well-being. Abla makes her way toward us with MJ and Kakra.

"Where did you go? You scared the shit out of all of us," Kakra says. Usually, I scold him for using bad words, but in this case he is right. I hug Panin more tightly.

"I think we haf enough for today. I need a drink. Lez go home," Abla says

On the ride home, I can't let Panin go. I hold him in my arms as though he is an infant but he never pushes away.

"Okay guys, wash up for ice cream and cake," Abla says as we enter the house.

Vincent and Julius talk off to the side. It is charming how much affection Vincent shows toward Julius. He probably was just as alarmed as me when I realized Panin was missing. Within a minute he was standing next to me on the line for the bumper cars and then he was gone. He has wandered off before, but never so far that I had to search for him for one hour. I downloaded an app with a GPS, which allows me to track his movements, but only if his phone is charged. My mind feeds into my fear. *What if Julius never found him? What if he really was missing, kidnapped or harmed?* I can't contain my emotions anymore. Julius embraces me from behind.

"Stop it, Vida. He is safe. There is no need to entertain fears." I cry in his arms until the children's footsteps cause me to sober up and break free. "It's your birthday; no one should cry on their birthday." I offer a smile. "Are you smiling? Or should I bring Mrs. Kim's nephew to stand in your presence?" I burst into laughter.

"I can't believe you brought that up."

"Oh, Vida, that will never get old." I punch him lightly in the chest and he recoils laughingly.

The children surround me and Abla brings out a pink and purple frosted cake. Just four candles decorate the top. I remember what Abla told me about the number of candles we put on cakes. At a certain age, we light one candle for the life God gave us and the other candles represent the life you gave to others. "If I should put a candle for every life dat you have touched, I'm sure I could light a stadium," Abla says. "Happy Birthday to da best sista anyone could have. Hip-hip, hooray!" The children help me blow out the candles.

*

"Good night, Ms. Frimpong." Vincent hugs me. I wave him a good night again.

"Yes, it is a very nice birthday. And if you come over tonight, I can make sure it ends on a high note," Julius says. I feel a wave of hot flashes.

"It's been memorable in more ways than one so far."

"Trust me. I think I can supersede that. I really want you to go to sleep tonight with very happy thoughts." *I bet.* Yesterday afternoon comes vividly to mind. Me sitting on the desk with his fingers pressed inside me. Ginger feels a rush of sensation.

"I'll see—if I'm not too tired." Ginger is screaming. *I want him like Kanye West wants a microphone.*

Chapter 75

I decide on a black mini dress with a low cut back and red Chanel stilettos. The diamond teardrop earrings look amazing with my hair pulled up. As expected, Pio is outside waiting for me. "Very lovely," he says. I don't think he has ever spoken to me before. His English is better than I expected.

I can't believe I am nervous again. We arrive at Julius's house. Alice informs me that Julius is on the rooftop. *Okay, calm down, Vida. Just take it in. It's just Julius. Ooooh my.* Julius is dressed in a dark navy suit and he looks freshly shaven. The cool minty lavender scent adds to his attractiveness.

"What are you doing here on the rooftop?"

"Admiring the moon," he says. He has two champagne flutes on a table underneath the canopy.

"Wow. The rooftop looks amazing." Half of the rooftop is tiled with decorative stones and a large fire pit is surrounded by plush seating and canopies. Royal blue, cream and cognac colors decorate the space, making it feel sophisticated and warm.

"Max finished it yesterday."

"You must be paying him a fortune. How did he come up with all this at the eleventh hour?"

"He is very resourceful and that I don't mind paying a fortune for. You look beautiful, Vida."

"Thank you." I mentally pat myself for just saying thank you when Julius gives me the compliment.

"Champagne?"

"Yes, please." He moves to the table and pours champagne into the two flutes.

"A toast," he says.

"To?"

"Vida. A remarkable writer, woman, mother and devoted friend. Happy birthday, my dear. May you live with peace, happiness, good health and abundance of F-M-Ps."

"Thank you, I will drink to that." We clink glasses. "This tastes good." I lift up the bottle to see the name.

"It's a Perrier-Jouet Rose. You like?"

"Ummm-hummmm." I nod.

"Noted. I have something for you."

"Oh?" I say anxiously. He retrieves a small blue box from his trousers. He places the box in my hand. The blue color looks familiar…it's not Tiffany blue and it's not Royal Dansk cookie tin blue. I delicately unfold the wrapping, still trying to decode what's inside. It's light and I don't hear any telltale signs of the contents. I open it. "Gift cards?"

"Yes. I know how much you like Bed and Bath and Beyond bed sheets. The max I could put on any card is five hundred dollars, so I bought several."

I burst out in laughter. "Julius, thank you." I leap into his arms. "That was so thoughtful. Thank you and thank you again. Don't tell me N-T-Y -B-F, because I really appreciate you being so attentive."

"You are welcome. But surely, you know there's more."

"Really, more?" He walks over to the canopy and pulls out a large box. I am guessing shoes.

"Happy birthday, Vida."

I open the box and sift through the gold color paper wrappings. I hold up the bright red lycra underwear with the symbol 'V' inscribed on them. A card is inside. It's Julius's penmanship.

My dear friend Vida, who brings new life to everything and everyone around her.

"Oh, Julius." I want to tear up, but I tilt my head up fighting back the tears.

"I hope it's a suitable upgrade from the Alexander's cotton lace white trim panties. I thought about having an 'S' inscribed on them, but you're way more powerful than Superman."

"This is wonderful. I love it. Thank you. This means a lot to me. Thank you so much. I can't believe how much thought you put into this." I hug him again. Julius seems indifferent and he steps back. "What? What's the matter?"

"You always surprise me, that's all."

"I surprise you? I'm speechless when it comes to all that you do."

"You make me feel like a giant sometimes. Come with me." He takes my hand and he navigates me into the center of the rooftop.

"Look up. How many stars are out tonight?" At first, it seems like a few dozen, but then my eyes adjust to the sky and I see more. And then a few more start to appear. Julius moves away from the table.

"There are too many to count."

"Really? Well, just stand here."

"Why? What's going on? Where are you going?" I ask. He walks backward counting his footsteps.

"Alice?"

"Yes, my Lord."

"Is Ms. Frimpong's gift ready?"

"Yes, my Lord."

"Alice, please help Ms. Frimpong open her gift."

"With esteemed pleasure. Happy birthday, Ms. Frimpong."

"Thank you, Alice," I say. The rooftop lights turn off. The stars and taller buildings in LIC provide illumination. Julius is standing in a corner. "Julius, what's going on?" He places his finger over his lips to gesture me to be quiet.

Case and Joe's voices fill the rooftop. Air carries the music into the streets. I am sure it can be heard as far as the Queensboro Bridge. The stars seem brighter. Suddenly, more appear. There are hundreds or thousands all at once. No, it has to be a million now that light up the dark denim sky. The stars spread across creating images…silhouette images of me kicking the ball and then images of me sitting on the grass, images of me sitting behind the computer and images of me writing in my journal. It's all me in silhouette. Images of me playing with the Sassi Strikers, images of me with the children at the park, images of me standing at the bus stop, images of me dancing, images of me and MJ walking to school, and images of me and Panin on the soccer field. Images of me flying…soaring…fill the LIC skyline. Voices from Queens Blvd rises to the rooftop. Yellow cab drivers stop and look up. Crowds of people congregate on the wide streets to view the skyline spectacle.

The music stops and more chants and applauses from the crowd. Julius is still standing by the French doors. I weep uncontrollably with my shoulders heaving up and down. Music fills the air again. This time, it is Prince's voice that commands attention. *This is better than any fireworks show that I have ever seen!*

"How? How?" I can't even think of the words to form my question. After I sober up, I find my voice. "That was beautiful, Julius."

"Did you like it?"

"Did I like it?" I hug him and shower him with endless kisses. "I loved it. Do you think I can store that in my cloud?" He laughs.

*

It's been an hour just lying in Julius's arms singing along to old R and Bs. It is warm under the canopy. "I may just sleep here tonight."

"We could do that," he says. He sits up and removes his jacket. He doesn't make any advances toward me. I wonder if the events from earlier changed his mood. I stroke his chest and slowly move down to his belt buckle.

"I don't have condoms, Vida."

"Oh," I say.

"I purposely didn't get any because I don't want to rush this. I value our friendship. And I don't want us to do something we will regret."

"Okay." *The pressure is off.* I didn't bring any myself. The last time I used condoms was eleven years ago. He kisses me. "So can I just lay here on your chest?" He smiles and draws me near.

"Absolutely."

"You know, tomorrow is another day." He pinches me.

"And so it is, Ms. Frimpong."

Chapter 76

My cellphone breaks the quietness of the rooftop. Julius is snuggled underneath the various throws on the settee. He looks completely blissful in my arms. Sunrays are beginning to emerge from the horizon. My cellphone is vibrating again. I wiggle away from Julius and try to retrieve the phone. Several text messages from Abla.

"The Landlord is HERE!!!!! Should I open the door? Then what should I tell him!!!!!"

Shit. I call her back. She is fully awake.

"Did you see my text?"

"Yeah…where is he?"

"I'm not sure. I left him inside da house. He still haz da old keys, so I opened da door for him."

"I'm on my way."

"Okay…should I take da boys to deer swim practice?"

"Yes," I say eagerly. It will be better if meeting Mensah turns into a fight that the children are not there for it. Julius is still fast asleep. I text him a note:

"**Thank you for everything yesterday. I haven't had this much fun on my birthday ever.**"

My heart feels heavy and the more I think about facing Mensah, the angrier I become.

Chapter 77

I open the door and there are rumblings in the kitchen. No sign of children or Abla. But I know he is here. The faint smell of Armani Code is lingering in the air. I walk toward the kitchen. He is searching through the fridge with his back toward me. He is dressed in a white shirt and brown pants with suspenders.

"I used to open this fridge and have my choice of food to eat. Now I'm like a stray dog looking for scraps. There also used to be a time when I came home and smelled food being cooked. I guess that's changed also." He straightens up and closes the fridge. "And how are you feeling? Well, you look radiant. It must have been a twenty-four-hour bug.

That must be my cue to answer him. But he is right. Things have changed. I remember crying for the day when I would see him in this house again. My heart used to stand still every time I saw him and my feet became cemented to the ground. *Now, I have wings.* I could care less if he chewed on ice water to fill his belly.

"Good morning." He moves more closely to examine me. He looks different, mature, well groomed. Speckles of grey peek through his beard.

"Morning."

He takes a few more steps closer and I stand at attention. *Not that I'm scared, but I wish he would try to hold me. He will feel my wrath on his cheek.* "You look great, Vida, as always." His eyes canvas me from head to toe. His lips feel warm as they land on my cheek and I push away. "Happy birthday. I arrived late yesterday and called you several times but no answer. You've changed the locks. Good thing Abla was here this morning to let me in. You are a very hard woman to reach these days. In case you are wondering, your sister took the children to swim practice. I'm sure there is a good reason why you are coming home this morning dressed in a mini black dress and red pumps. Is that why you couldn't take your children to practice—because you've been out all night? And I wonder with whom?" *The audacity of him.* I take a seat on the barstool by the kitchen island. *Oh, yes, this is going to be an interesting morning.* "Where were you last night?"

"Maybe we should compare notes. You first. Where were you last night? Better yet, where were you last week, last month…seven months ago? How's Kate? Is she boring you these days?"

He snickers. "And there goes that mouth of yours." He raises his palms to his hips. "Answer my question." He moves toward the pantry and pulls out the cornflakes. "I'm not playing games with you, Vida."

"Did you fly all the way from the Bahamas to ask me where I was last night?" He opens the fridge again.

"No milk," he says and closes it again. He opens the pantry and takes out the Carnation milk from the shelf. "Huh, I flew back because it was my wife's birthday yesterday and I wanted to surprise her with the trip to the Bahamas. I didn't get your message until late in the evening that you were not coming. So I flew back to California to get some more belongings and then to New York to check up on you. Excuse me for being kindhearted and a concerned husband."

"Kindhearted, concerned husband? Mensah, don't use words that you don't understand. I know you received my letter, so there is nothing more to say."

"Very wrong. As long as you are in custody of my children, there is plenty more to say. I need to know your comings and goings." He mixes the evaporated milk into a cup of hot water and pours it onto the corn flakes. He moves to where I am seated. "Again, where were you last night?"

"Out," I say.

"That's obvious. Where and with whom?"

"None of your business."

He laughs. He searches my face too long. *He thinks he knows me so well.* He gives a gentle smile then a furrowed look. I turn away from his harnessed stare. "I know you. You wouldn't do anything foolish." He brushes his hands toward my inner thigh. I quickly slap it away.

"What do you mean, 'anything foolish?' You mean do the things you've been doing in California? Oh, that's not being foolish. Interesting…just how much you think I should tolerate."

"Vida, I apologized over and over again. Why do we keep going back to this?"

THE BORROWED WIFE

"'This?'" I scream. "'This' was our marriage. Now this"—I spread my arms out in between us—"is the result of infidelity, lies, disrespect, pain and hate."

"Vida, I never meant to hurt you. But what you saw in California was nothing. Meant nothing. In time, you will see that you and the children mean more to me than my own life."

"Stop! Stop! I don't even care anymore." *I say it, but I do care.* I want to sob incessantly, but I keep my composure. *I won't give him the satisfaction anymore of seeing me broken.*

"I read your letter." He flings the letter onto the table. "Until death do us part. This is my family and I am not going anywhere."

"You're joking! Your family? What were you thinking back in California when you were fucking Kate? Did your family cross your mind?"

He draws closer with his bowl of soggy cereal. "Let's move on. This is getting old."

"Move on. Just like that?"

"What else you want me to do? It's not productive bringing this back up over and over again."

"Your level of arrogance and disregard is off the charts. Do you hear the words coming out of your mouth? You made this marriage unhealthy. Correction: we both did. Because I allowed it to continue. I didn't speak up when I should have. All in fear of what will happen to me and the children. This"—I spread my arms again—"has drained me and I am not going to do it anymore."

He slaps the bowl down. "What are you saying? You make it sound like our marriage was all bad, a mistake. Are our children a mistake?"

"No, our children are the best thing that came out of this marriage. But everything evolved around you and what made you happy and what you wanted. I lost myself and what I wanted to do with my life."

"I did all of this for us. You knew the situation when we met. I wasn't ready to settle down; wife, children. But I agreed to it because I wanted to make you happy and now you want to punish me for it."

"Agreed?" I scream again. "...Is that why you married me? Because you were in agreement with me?"

He continues, not realizing that his words stab me repeatedly. *What about love?* "We made a deal for six months."

"But it's going on three years. I didn't agree to that. I thought it would make you happy and in turn make our marriage better. But look where our agreement has taken us. A mistress, infidelity, dishonesty. It is not the same, Mensah."

"I'm here now. You and the children are important to me. I got a new contract in New Jersey. We start next week. I bought you a house in Westchester. Here are the approved plans." He takes a scroll from on top of the refrigerator and drops it in front of me. "If you want to add anything else, just make notations and I will make sure it's taken care of."

"You've lost your mind. How do you go from one extreme to another? You bought a house and didn't even tell me? You expect me to pick up where we left off two, three years ago and become a family now? Don't you see what you have done?"

"The past is the past. Let's move forward. What matters is that I am here now. So whatever is occupying your time, you better end it today. Vida, I know Felix has been coming around." *Felix? Is that who he thinks I've been with?* He gives a deep sigh. "Are you dropping your standards? Huh. You are not serious. Felix. He's not the type of man that would make you happy. I know you, you would get bored easily. Do you think he could ever replace me?" He brushes his hand across my breast.

"Stop it."

"All this fighting has put you in the mood I bet."

"You're joking. You see, that's the way it's been—fighting and fucking and then you go back to your same bullshit. No more. I am not playing that game. I've mastered the powerful skills of my right hand."

"Oooh, Vida…it's not the same." He laughs and takes spoonsful more of the cereal. "So, do you think there is a huge supply of men that will take on the responsibility of a woman and three children?"

"Is that what you think? So I should tolerate your infidelity because no one will want me with my three children? Oh, Mensah, you are sadly mistaken. That is the least of my worries. My boys deserve to see a man who loves his wife. They deserve to see a healthy, committed, strong relationship between two people. Not three or four. If I should ever remarry, then at least I know that I married for all the right reasons."

I can't help it, but tears fill my eyes and I turn away so he doesn't see me. He pauses and continues.

"Like I said, I will be back next week. Tell Mr. Felix the landlord is back and there are no vacancies."

I sigh. "You are delusional."

He laughs. "Oh, God. At the same time I miss that mouth of yours. Always quick with the comeback." He holds out the four-page letter that I neatly wrote and tears it up in front of my face. "I am doing all this for you." He taps his fingers repeatedly on the architectural drawings of the new house. "I am not about to let Felix or any asshole come between that. If you don't address him, I will. I am staying at the Westchester Marriott. I can't tolerate Abla today. I will be back this evening to see the boys. When your temper subsides, you know where to find me." He kisses me gently on the cheek.

"Goodbye, Mensah."

"By the way, a thank you would be nice for paying off the mortgage."

"What are you talking about?"

"I paid off the mortgage. I told you that I would do that in ten years, didn't I? Tell Abla we are debt free." I got the alerts, but I thought it was Julius. It was the same day that I got the shipment of shoes. I mailed him a thank you card with a generic thank you, but I had no idea that it was really Mensah.

"You did?" I am dumbfounded and he sees the look on my face.

"What did you think? Your new friend Felix paid it off?" His laughter subsides. My cellphone rings and I pull it out of my purse. It's Julius. Mensah grabs my phone before I can turn off the ringer.

"Give me my phone." He raises his hands higher above his head as I struggle to get it.

"Shhh…" He motions with his fingers and answers it. He keeps me at an arm's distance. Julius repeatedly says hello. Mensah puts the phone to his ear to listen.

I talk through gritted teeth for Mensah to give me the phone. He finally hands it to me and I walk away from him.

"Are you okay?" Julius says.

"Yes."

"I've been trying to reach you. You left abruptly this morning. Are you sure you're okay?"

"Yes. I'm in the middle of something." Mensah watches me intently. "Can I call you back in an hour?"

"Okay," Julius says. I hang up and Mensah continues his tyranny.

"So that's the part-time boss? The kids tell me good things about him." He moves closer. "I know I fucked up, but I will make it up to you. That is a promise, Yaa."

"You hurt me. How do you fix that?"

"By building you a home."

Chapter 78

The boys tell me on several occasions that they can't wait until they move into their new house. They rave about the pool, the game room and the popcorn dispenser that Mensah promises to install for them. I kick myself for throwing away the drawings that morning. The only thing I recall is the house is located in a Westchester cul-de-sac.

The boys look happy as they get ready for church. *What am I doing? Can they imagine a life without Mensah and me together? Things are so complicated now. Where is all that anger and hate that I had? Why do I feel like the bad guy?*

I kneel down beside my bed and pray.

Dear God,

Please help me…I want to make this right for me and my sons. Direct my path and choose my words. Help me, God, to make wise decisions, not only for me but my family.

It's been a week since I've spoken to Julius. I told him Mensah is in town. He didn't ask the status of our marriage, which relieved me because I don't know what I'm going to do. Julius wants to talk and I agreed to meet with him after church today.

Pastor Duncan announces the anniversary barbeque tomorrow. The pastor usually goes over community events and programs before he begins his sermon. It is also customary that every Sunday one of the members gives a testimony. I recall Auntie Cece's words, *"The fighting and crying will all stop and you will give yur testimony one day in front of yur peers. They will see how good God has been to you."* I look to my left and smile at my sons' faces. They look happy and they are healthy. God has blessed me with so much already.

I witness sister Dorothy rise and ascend to the pulpit. Her testimony is heartfelt. She survived breast cancer and underwent a double mastectomy. Today, she is cancer free and back to her Zumba classes. "God is good. You hear me? I have life today because of my steadfast faith. I know through Christ all this is possible." She raises her hands up in praise.

We all say, "Amen."

She continues on. "And, church folks, I am proud to say that is my testimony." She leaves the stage to thunderous applause. Pastor Duncan again mounts the pulpit.

"Dear family, let us not forget to encourage the women in our lives to get their mammograms annually. We are pressed for time." He eyes the boys sitting next to me. "But I feel the spirit is leading us in another direction and we just gotta follow. Amen." We all say amen in agreement.

"I've been married thirty-two years." The church applauds this rare accomplishment. "And if anyone tells you that marriage is easy, you betta get up and run as fast as you can. Because it ain't." We laugh. "But marriage is a blessing. Amen."

"Amen," we say again.

"I don't know where I would be if it wasn't for this woman who sits in this front row every Sunday to hear me speak and then when I get home cooks and cleans for me. I'm blessed, church." Thunderous applause again. "...And I know that there are some struggles in the home, but I am here to tell you weeping may endure in the evening..." He pauses. Mr. Trees hits a couple of notes on the organ.

"C'mon Pastor, tell it." A woman from behind me stands.

"But..." He pauses again. Another set of bodies rises instantaneously. "Y'all don't hear me. I said weeping may endure for the evening..." Pastor Duncan says.

"Yes, Pastor," a man a few rows in front of us rises and says. "Yes...yes...yes...yes..."

"But..." Pastor Duncan laughs. Mr. Trees hits a few more notes on the organ. "But joy...I said joy..." With each time he says joy, his voice grows louder. One by one, like an attendance roll call in class, people rise to their feet. "J-O-Y ...Joy...Let me hear you say it. Joy...Joy...Joy cometh in the morning...Weeping may endure for the night, but joy do cometh in the morning."

"Amen. Amen. Amen..." Voices rise in unison all around me. *Maybe this is God talking to me.*

"Now usually, this is the time I break into my sermon, but like I said the spirit is with us today and a young man called me this morning and said, could he give his testimony? He is not a member of our church and I didn't even ask him what his testimony was until he arrived. So I'm gonna let this man speak. Is that alright, church?"

"Yes, Pastor, let him go ahead." Everyone is still standing as a body moves through the crowd and ascends the stairs.

"Look MJ, it's Daddy," Kakra says. *Mensah!* It's a good thing Abla squeezes my hand or I would think I am dreaming. In all the years we've been married, I've seen Mensah in church on two occasions, for the children's baptisms. He is impeccably dressed in a dark brown suit, a cream tie knotted perfectly at his throat. He looks astoundingly handsome. He draws eyes up and down as many smile adoringly.

"Good morning, Grace Church…" he says. For the first time, he looks nervous. He says it again clearing his throat.

"Good morning. I know many of you don't know who I am. I am not a member and I guess you can say that I am not a churchgoer. In fact, today will be my third time stepping inside this church."

"Hi, Daddy," MJ says out loud. The parishioners turn and point conspicuously and comment. He continues.

"I cannot give you a sufficient reason why I haven't been to church, but I can say that I am a sinner. In fact I am not sure if what I have to say is a testimony. It's more of a plea of forgiveness." I swallow hard. I can't believe Mensah is standing there. "I am not an easy man to live with, let alone be married to. I've made mistakes and I have paid for it dearly. Why is it so hard to love someone who loves you unconditionally? Well, it shouldn't be hard, but I have made it unbearable at times. I stand here because I am not a perfect man, nor am I a perfect father, but one thing I want to tell my sons is that when you f—when you mess up—own your mistake." He takes a handkerchief from his suit jacket and wipes his forehead. "Don't be cocky with it and don't pretend that silence will dismiss it. I made a mistake. In fact, I've made several." He searches for our faces.

"Dear sons, when you find someone who loves you, flawed and all, kneel down and thank God that he has blessed you with a wonderful gift. You see, life will never be easy. You will always face obstacles, people will test you, people will always try to tell you what to do and people will misjudge you. But hold steadfast in your belief. Know who you are and don't seek validation from anyone. I can't take responsibility for the young men that you are becoming. Your mother has done an outstanding job of filling my void. And instead of holding her with high esteem, I've done things to shatter that.

"I'm not a perfect husband, nor a perfect father. I'm a man and I've made mistakes. I don't pretend that I can make up for a lot of it, but I have to start somehow. So, I say in front of this congregation, I need your help. I know my sons will continue to love me unconditionally, but the anchor to my ship, the engine to my V8, the fufu to my peanut butter soup, my left hand and my right hand; I can't imagine a life without her. She makes the waters still, the world turn on its axis, makes the sun rise in the east. And sorry is not enough, but church I need your help to get her back. You don't know what you have until you don't have it anymore. My selfishness has brought me here. And, as someone once told me, anything that brings you closer to God, you need to keep in your life."

He leaves the pulpit and kneels in front of me. "I love her and I will do anything to keep her." Thunderous clapping fills the auditorium. Overwhelming eyes stare at us. Abla squeezes my hand and I release it. Mensah grips me in a powerful hug and the children embrace us. I've never heard him speak that way about me. *Ever.*

"Alright, now church folks, if that ain't a man who loves his wife, then I don't know what is. Let's give him another round of applause. Keep God first in your marriage and he will give you the strength to endure everything," Pastor Duncan says.

*

The parishioners flow through the exits of the church. The children gather around Mensah with good cheer and bright smiles. "How about lunch?" he says. The boys ecstatically agree.

There is still so much to say, but today everyone looks happy. Abla leaves to give us a little time together. I'm full of thoughts. I don't recognize the man in front of me—the man who could get up in front of the church and apologize and confess his love to me.

"What do you say, Yaa? Lunch? Anywhere you want to go."

"Okay. I'll follow behind you." This will give me time to contact Julius. *I feel guilty.*

"Where should we go? BBQs?" he asks. I nod my head in agreement.

As we make our way to Co-op City, I leave two messages for Julius, but he doesn't answer. I will have to find a way to see him and explain. *And explain...what exactly? Vida, what are you going to say?* I find myself parking farther away next to a medical building out of sight from Mensah. It looks awkward, considering the number of available parking spots in front of the restaurant and next to the movie theatre, but this spot will give me the privacy I need to call Julius again. *Damn...still no answer.*

"Yaa, do you want to sit outside or in?" I shrug indifferently and Mensah tells the waitress we will sit outside. "There's plenty of parking here...why all the way around the bush?" Mensah asks.

"I'm trying to rack up my steps for the day. You see, I'm already over eight thousand." He leans closer to look at my progress on my Fitbit. *That was a quick comeback.* At lunch we say little to one another, but occasionally I see Mensah stealing glimpses at me. We relish in the children's stories, a mixture of chastisement and amusement.

Mensah clears the bill and we make our way back to the parking lot. "I'll meet you at home. I want to pick up a few things in J.C. Penny."

"No problem. We'll wait for you." Mensah never ever wants to go shopping with me. He says he will give me as much money as I want to shop. I'm not as bad as Abla, but I have been known to return a pair of shoes if I find it cheaper somewhere else.

"Oh no, that's not necessary. I'll meet you guys at home." I kiss the boys. Mensah doesn't look convinced. He holds my hand a bit longer. I give him a light kiss on the cheek.

"Okay, buckle up guys. See you at home soon." They drive away and I walk to the other end of the parking lot. There is a blue van blocking me. *I mean, really, look at all this available parking and this fool decides to park here?* There is a U-Haul parked beside my car and then the shrubs on the other side. There is no way I can move until this idiot moves. I stomp my feet the closer I get to the car.

"Excuse me, ma'am...what time does the mall close on Sundays?" A tall blonde man emerges from the vehicle. He startles me. "Sorry—didn't mean to scare you. I'm looking for a friend and he told me to meet him here."

"No problem. Stores usually start closing at six," I say. My phone is ringing; maybe it's Julius calling me. I search through my bag.

"Oh, that's a shame. I don't think he'll make it." I offer a gentle smile.

"Hello…? Hello…?" It's a private number again. No response and I hang up. I walk over to the driver's side of the car to enter.

"Where is he?" the blonde man says.

"What?"

The man is standing behind me with a gun pressed against my back. "Your time is very limited." He shifts his weight on me and shoves the gun deeper into my spine. "Tell me where he is and I won't hurt you."

"I don't know who you're talking about." He pushes me against the car. I can't believe no one can see him. There is a couple not too far from us, but it looks like they are having a quarrel of their own in their car.

"If you make a sound, yur children will be motherless. Be smart. Don't make me kill you today." He has a thick accent. Italian? Spanish? I'm not sure.

"I swear, I don't know who you are talking about…Please, I have three young children. You must have mistaken me for someone else." He pushes me toward the van and then knocks my head against the car. I instantly feel dizzy. The blue van makes it hard for anyone to see me now. Someone might mistake us for a couple feeling each other up in a parking lot. His body is pressed against me and his breath covers my ear. A mixture of liquor and cigarettes.

"Oooh, no. I know exactly who you are. We're going to take a ride. Get in. Any sudden movement…like I said your children will have to bury you."

"Ride? Please…" I am hoping someone will pass by and notice this man pressed against me. If he takes me into the van, there's no telling what will happen. *Don't get into the van, Vida.* "Please…" I say again.

"Shut up." He knocks my head against the van doors and I feel the side of my face for the source of the blood. He cocks the gun and more terror quivers down my spine. "Any more noise out of you and those will be your last words. Get in the van." I try to move, but I'm frozen from fear. "GET IN!" *Maybe I should faint.* Someone would surely see that. "GET—"

He falls on top of me and then his body collapses on the pavement. The gun clashes to the ground. I turn to see him lying face down. *Shit! What happened to him?* I look for the couple in the car. They're gone. *I need help.*

"Someone…"

Chapter 79

I love Bed Bath and Beyond sheets. I roll around again trying to recognize the scent of the fabric softener. It doesn't smell like Suavitel. Maybe Abla changed softeners. I'm wearing a long silk nightgown and panties. *I never wear panties to sleep unless Ginger has a cold.* I roll to the other side of the bed before recalling my last memory. *Where am I? Nothing looks familiar.*

I remember blood streaming down my face. The blonde man. A gun. The blonde man falling to the ground.

"Where am I?"

This is not my bedroom. I immediately spring from the bed. Maybe too quickly. Pain reoccurs with harsh memory. My forehead is bandaged. There is a huge diamond ring on my left hand. I rub my eyes and look twice. *Damn. This is hot. How many carats is this?*

The room is painted a greyish purple and elaborate furnishings decorate it. Every bit my taste, only I wasn't the one to decorate it. Panin is kneeling in the corner.

"Sweetie…" He rises and walks to me at the edge of the bed. *I'm alive, thank God.* He pushes his head into my chest. Mensah appears in the doorway and I've never been so happy to see him. *I have life.* Panin looks into my eyes and I can't help but shower him with kisses. He abruptly fights off the affection and leaves the room. "Thank God, I'm alive." Mensah takes me into his arms. The security that I long for embraces me.

"I was so worried about you." He holds me tightly before placing me on the bed. "How do you feel?"

"Fine, considering." I touch the bandage.

"Maybe too many pina coladas? What happened? Did you trip on your way to the car?" *Trip? No…No…I don't even know where to begin.* I find myself on my feet describing the events I remember. The whole thing sounds like a movie and Mensah listens skeptically.

"They found you in the parking lot on the ground by yourself. No one else. There was no sign of forced entry into your car or burglary. Perhaps you tripped on something. Your heel was broken," he says.

"They?"

"Yes, the security guards from the mall. They believe you fell, maybe from your broken heel."

"No. Stop saying that. I didn't trip. I told you. There was a man. He thought I knew him…He…was looking for someone…or he wanted me to tell him where he was…" I comb through my hair trying to jog my memory. I leap toward Mensah. "Something happened to him."

"Oh my goodness, babe. Calm down. Are you sure?" I look like a lunatic grabbing onto his shirt. He takes hold of my hands and sits me beside him. "The security guards from the mall found you. I called you to say the boys were stopping for ice cream. One of them picked up the phone and said you were lying on the ground. We drove right back. When I came back, you were whispering something. I didn't understand. Don't you remember?"

"No. I can't remember anything after the man fell on the ground." *Did I dream the whole thing? No, something happened. I can't piece together exactly what, but I feel it.*

"Maybe we should call the police then."

"No…" My story sounds ludicrous. I did have a couple of cocktails at the restaurant, but I wasn't intoxicated. *I don't think so.* Mensah looks alarmed. He holds my hands in his. "Maybe I'm just tired that's all." He seems reassured.

"Perhaps I can go to the mall and see if they have anything on their security cameras from yesterday."

"Yesterday?"

"Yes, you've been asleep since then. You kept making reference to copper-colored faces being after you. Don't you remember? I told myself if you didn't wake up today, then I would take you to the hospital." He wraps his arms around me again. "No worries, Yaa. I'm home and I'll look after you." He runs his fingers over the huge diamond ring. "Do you like it?"

It looks like something that should be guarded in a museum. "It's very beautiful."

"This doesn't make up for what I've done. But I want it to be a start."

"Where are we?"

"Your new home."

"Is this the house in Westchester? I didn't realize that it was complete."

"I wanted it to be a surprise for you when I moved back to New York."

"Move back?"

"Yes. I'm closing the operation on the West Coast. I've made a lot of contacts and I think I will do very well here in New York. Especially with this new contract in New Jersey."

"Oh." I've never seen Mensah so humbled.

"What should I get for you to eat?"

"Anything."

"Okay. When you're dressed, I will give you a tour. Are you sure that you're okay? Should we go to the hospital?"

"No…I'm fine."

"Call me if you need anything." He points to an intercom. "No more yelling for children. Just press here and you can be heard anywhere in the house."

"That's cool." I have an instant memory of Alice. "I'll go have a bath." I rise up from the bed slowly.

"Do you need help?"

"I can manage," I say shyly. He leaves me with my thoughts. I am not sure what transpired over the last day, but I know I have to reach Julius.

After the shower, I admire the meticulous detail of the house, from the wooden floors, ceramic, glass and stone tiles in the bathrooms, to the expansive kitchen with Viking appliances and a granite kitchen island that can double as a conference table.

I eat in silence while the boys discuss the soccer match they watched yesterday. I search the house for my purse, the one I carried to church yesterday morning. "Have you seen my cellphone, guys?"

No response from anyone. I repeat myself until I get a unanimous no from the boys. I walk toward the back yard where I find Mensah in an adjacent room. "What is this room?" I ask.

Mensah kneels down to paint the trim of the base molding. "It's your writing room or she-cave…whatever you want it to be. It's yours."

"Mine?" I take a step down to the sunken room. It's huge. The ice blue walls are warmed up by the wooden floors. "It's beautiful."

"I kept these outlets on the wall in case you decide to have a television." I pivot in circles. My eyes follow every detail. There is a chandelier with artistic stems of lights. The floor-to-ceiling windows overlook the pool. I walk toward it. "Here, just push this button and the doors will slide on their own."

I do just that and the large doors gracefully slide to the right. The setup is similar to Julius's study. I take a step out and look at the gated pool. Mensah is standing behind me.

I step back into the room. He presses the same button to close the door. I walk around the room again. Mensah is watching me. On the opposite wall, speakers are seamlessly built in. They are also hooked up to the intercom. I'm amazed by the amount of detail he put into constructing this house for us.

"Thank you, Mensah."

"Do you really like it?"

"I love it."

"All of it... for you."

"Mensah..."

"I know, baby steps. I love you, Yaa...I know I haven't been a very good husband. But I don't want you to remember me that way." He pauses and then continues, "I mean, I just want you to know that my thoughts are always with you and the children."

"I haven't agreed to stay here," I say, bowing my head.

"It's not a home without you, Yaa. There is a little cabana by the pool. I will stay there for the time being until—"

"Until...?"

"I want us to work on our marriage. I will do anything."

"So much has happened, Mensah." I am still thinking about Julius. *This would be a good time to tell him what happened. How do I tell him?* My thoughts bother me.

"You're right," he says coldly. "But I don't want to know." The memory of Julius and me comes vividly to mind. Mensah places his hands over my shoulders, bringing me back to the present. "We will make it work." I swallow hard. I've never seen this side of Mensah before. This less-than-arrogant appreciative man.

"We need counseling."

"Okay. I'll go."

"You will?" I kick myself mentally for doubting my words. *If he wants me, then he has to prove it.*

"Yes. Whatever it takes," he says again.

"What happened to the Mensah I married?"

"He is trying to be a better man."

Chapter 80

"Fingerin' iz not sex. Just dink of it like a O-B-G-Y-N exam."

"But I don't have breathless orgasms during my gynecological exams," I whisper to Abla.

"You don't, even wit Dr. Gobin?" she asks.

"Of course not. Do you?" She shrugs indifferently. "Lissen, I didn't come here to talk about me." She takes off her shoes to get more comfortable on the bed. "Dat doesn't count as sex. If it did, every woman would be accused of cheatin'. If you can't get pregnant or an STD, den it doesn't count as sex. Iz like kissin'. Iz intimate, but it depends how you feel about da person for it to count as cheatin'."

"Really? I've never heard that rule." She rolls her eyes.

"Just keep yur mouth shut. Men like Mensah don't want to hear dat anotha man can make hiz woman breaflez. Lez focus on important dings. Bossman called me five times and came by da house ten times. I didn't know wat to tell him. All I knew from da boys waz dat you had fallen and dat Mensah waz lookin' after you." Abla tells me she tried several times to reach me and the boys. Mensah was tight-lipped about our whereabouts and when she could come to visit me. "Well, at least itz a pretty prison. You haf enough room to walk around."

"I need to see Julius, Abla."

"How? Mensah won't let you out of hiz sight."

"I know, but I need to see him. I can tell Mensah that you are taking me to the house to pick up some things."

"Mensah has done well." She glances over the room again. "Wat are you goin' to tell Julius?"

"I don't know."

"Ehhhh, da devil you know or da angel you don't," she says.

*

Mensah says he is picking the boys up from swim practice. They will probably stop for ice cream afterward. I only have half an hour before he knows I am not home. Not nearly enough to go and come back from Long Island City, but I need to see Julius at least to tell him face-to-face. *What exactly are you going to tell him?*

*

The sight of Julius warms my heart. He embraces me without words. *Damn, it feels good to be in his arms again.*

"I've been so worried about you. I heard about your fall. Are you all right? Are you sure?" He doesn't let go of my hands and I'm even more conflicted. *Why do I feel this way?*

"Yes. I'm fine." I spare him my version of what I think happened. It seems crazy now, and Mensah said there was no video surveillance of any encounter.

Rough facial hairs look attractive on him. "Are you growing your beard?"

"Sort of. Partly laziness and partly too worried about you to think of anything else. I'm glad you are here. I heard that you moved and Mensah's back."

He releases my hands and moves toward his desk. I'm not confident in what I have to say, but I begin.

"Julius, you mean a lot to me. And—" He stands in his superman pose. "Fuck. I wish I didn't feel this way. I wish things weren't so complicated now. I never…" *It feels wrong and then it feels good being here.* He is listening, but I don't know what to say. My heart feels betrayed by the words coming out of my mouth. I hang my head down not sure what to say anymore. "You must think I'm crazy."

He moves closer to me and holds my face in his hands. He raises my chin up. "Vida, I think you are amazing. You will always be a part of my life. I can't negate the way you make me feel." He brings my hands to his lips. "I know it's not an easy decision, but only you can make it. I told you he would be back. He would be a fool not to. And I know Vida Frimpongs from the Bronx don't marry fools."

"I'm…I'm….so sorry, Julius."

"Stop it. N-S-B-F." I'm dumbfounded and he clarifies before I can ask. "No sorries between friends."

"Are we still friends?"

"Always." He smiles. "I'm traveling to Ghana next week. They are celebrating the twentieth anniversary of my mother's church. I will be there for a couple of weeks."

"What about the book?"

"I promise I will publish it."

"No, I mean your memoir."

"Aaaahh…yes. Let's take a break. I still have a lot more life to live. Therefore, I will have to write more journals." He hugs me. And we hold each other for several minutes. He pulls away. "Goodbye, Vida." Those words seem cruel and they weigh me down. He kisses my forehead gently.

"Have a safe trip, Julius."

Part I: Julius

Chapter 1

We are sitting in a leather booth and I can feel the heaviness between us. The smell of Armani Code is ever present. A subtle hint of musk from Vincent's cigar lets me know he is close by. *Voices.* A family of three to my left.

"Oh my, aren't you two the most good looking men that ever walked into this place? Maybe it's my lucky day...I gotta remember to play my lotto numbers tonight. Don't mind me—just making a little jokesy. Hey y'all, my name is Paula, and what can I get you, tall dark and handsome?" Her laugh is alarming.

"Do you have espresso?" Nana asks.

"Umm, no. The machine's broken. We have coffee, that's about it."

"Three black coffees then."

"Three?" she repeats.

"Yes. Vincent, no espresso. Coffee fine?"

"Water, please," Vincent says. Vincent chooses to sit away from our table and for good reason. Nana's behavior has always been unpredictable.

"Okay, make that two black coffees and a tall glass of room temperature water," Nana says.

"Oh, you know I can pull another chair to the booth if you want your friend to sit with you," Paula says.

"No. That's not necessary. I'm safer here," Vincent says. Nana is amused.

Paula's footsteps trail away. "I promised Vincent this would be a gentlemen's conversation. Should I start?" Nana asks. A balmy combination of bacon and coffee suffuses the diner. *Just like I remember it.* I have a few words to say to him, but I let him continue. "*Maakye. Etesen?*"

"Please." I hold my hand to stop the pleasantries. *This visit needs to be over as quickly as possible.*

"Well, let me start by saying thank you. I know that you had your reservations, and considering our history, I understand. The boys talk a lot about what you did. I really appreciate that, bro."

"So we are clear, I didn't do it for you." *He hasn't changed and his arrogance is overbearing.* "If it wasn't for Vincent, you probably would never see me again."

"I see you still feel the same way about me. I can sit here and go over the last twelve years, but it wouldn't change your mind about me or what you think I did. So I'll take it for what it is. If this is just you returning a favor for me, then so be it. But I'm grateful that they were safe with you watching over them." *Paula is approaching.* She is wearing soft shoes, but they squeak when she walks.

"The next time you try to hack into Alice, I am going to display every single image of you since birth all over the Internet."

"Come now, don't be so sensitive. Alice is quite a sophisticated security system. You don't know how many hackers I had to go through. You blocked my security on her phone. I needed to know what was happening at Lord Gallo's mansion." He snickers.

"I told you, as long as she is in my presence, she is safe. It's none of your business what happens in my home. You asked me to protect your family. And that is exactly what I did."

"Okay, enough small talk. Let me address the real reason why I needed to see you. Face-to-face. Man-to-man." *Paula's hairspray. Squeaky shoes.* She is close by.

"Go on. I'm listening."

"Did you fuck my wife?"

Shit. Bad timing. Paula's breath stops short. "Oh, oh, oh…" Her voice quivers with trepidation. She splatters coffee onto the table. A deluge of apologies as she nervously tries to clean up the spill. "Umm, umm. I'll give you'all a little more time to ummm, umm, look at the menu." Nana's question has left her incoherent.

"Thank you, yes, please give us a few extra minutes," Nana says smoothly.

"I still find you amusing. The CIA and London's Intel, as well the Pietro family, are looking for you. And all you can think about is whether or not I've fucked your wife."

"I'm already a dead man. So excuse me if that's on my mind right now. I don't care what happens to me, but I do care about my family."

"If you care for your family, then you should care what happens."

"Are you going to answer my question?"

"Fuck off."

"Come on, be a man and tell me the truth. I know you're not afraid of me…or are you? Vincent knows that I am still a gentleman."

"Leave me out of your boyish tantrums," Vincent says.

"Is that why you blocked the surveillance in your home? So I wouldn't see what kind of moves you were putting on my wife?"

"You selfish son of a bitch. Why did you have to marry her? Of all the women in the world? In New York, in the Bronx. You just so happened to fall in love with her?" *Calm yourself, Gio.* But I don't care who hears me now. *Why, why did he have to marry her? Did he want to get back at me for leaving? Punish me? He hasn't changed.*

"Ahhh…I think I'm getting closer to my answer. Don't tell me; she was off limits? Does the guy code include a woman you had a crush on over twelve years ago? If I had to include every woman from here to the Atlantic Ocean that should be off limits per Giovanni Diego Julius Gallo, I would have to live a monk's life."

"I'm done. You have your family back safe and sound. I think we are even.' I rise from the table and he grabs my arm. I pull back fiercely.

"*Mepa wo kyew*," he says.

Fuck. Why am I letting him get to me?

"*Gio, mepa wo kyew*. Please. Sit. It's not what you think. I didn't set out to marry her. You know that was the last thing on my mind. Things just fell together that way. She's a beautiful woman and I'm sure I've caused her a lot of heartache. But I love her. I thought I could leave everything behind and start new. Well, it was stupid of me to think it would be possible."

"She deserves to know the truth. The truth is better than the assumptions you continually feed her."

He laughs contentedly. "Vida can be resilient. It is easier for me to be looked at as a cheating husband than—"

"A British spy," I finish his sentence. Vincent clears his throat as a sign to silence us. "You're fucking mad. Do you know that?"

"Why didn't you tell me about the surgery when I came to see you in London?"

"What for? It's none of your fucking business."

"If I knew, I could have been there for you and…and…I would never have gotten you involved."

"Lest you forget, you don't care about anyone's feelings. That's not how you are built. Like I said a million times before, I don't need you in my life." An elderly man and woman sit to our immediate right. *She speaks Italian.* I'm distracted by their conversation. She tells the man don't order the coffee. Nana's voice brings me back to our discussion.

"Are you going to answer my question, old friend?" His voice drips with false sincerity.

"Old perhaps, but friends no more." The sound of Paula's shoes grows louder.

"Okay, gentlemen, is everything okay here?" she says softly.

"Yes. We'll take two Lunch Breaks," Nana says.

"Okay. That's the brunch combination. How do you want your steak?"

"Make mine well done. And he will have his medium well. My friend at the other table will take soft scrambled eggs, home fries well done and bacon extra crispy."

"Egg whites, wheat toast, no butter and no bacon. Vincent has to watch his cholesterol," I counter.

"Sorry, Padrino. Mommy dearest says no bacon," Nana says.

"Okay, coming right up then." Paula leaves.

"I'm going to need your help again. Very soon," Nana says.

"*Wa bo dam.* You're really fucking delusional if you think I'm going to be a part of this madness."

"When are you returning from Ghana?"

"How did you know that I was going to Ghana?" I turn my face toward Vincent. There are many things that Vincent chooses not to disclose to me. He believes it is for my own protection. And I know that Nana speaks to him frequently. It's no surprise that he has left out more pertinent information. I've gone down this path with him before. *Nana and Vincent—spies who pretend to lead normal lives.*

"Will you be back before winter?"

"Why?"

"I have to travel overseas and I need you to watch over Vida and the kids again." I take a sip of the coffee. *Fuck, it's horrible. This is not how I remember it.* "Are you listening to me?"

"Let me clarify. I'm done being your errand boy. If you need protection, Vincent can supply you with that, but I no longer want to be involved." His annoying laugh reappears. "Your family needs you. Stop this vendetta you started." Another sneering laugh.

"Vincent didn't tell you?"

"Tell me what?"

"The mole was one of the Pietro brothers. On Sunday after we left the restaurant, I took the boys for ice cream. I remembered the blue van from the church's parking lot and there was a blue van parked by Vida's car. I left the boys in Haagen Dazs and came back to check on her. My gut was right. That asshole had a gun shoved in Vida's back. I shot him. Vincent arrived just in time. Those tracking devices you put in her heels really came in handy. He got rid of the body and I had to make it look, well, like Vida had an accident. I put her to sleep and broke the heel on her shoe."

Anger fills in my belly and I unleash my dissatisfaction in being lied to again. Vincent doesn't offer any sign of guilt. I continue bantering with him, mindful of the Italian woman to my right.

Vincent's authoritative voice interjects, "Did you forget we are in a public setting?" *No. I didn't.*

"You lied to me. You told me she tripped and fell." The anger is still bubbling in my throat. *I refuse to go down this road with him.* "As always, I'm out of the loop." My thoughts are scattered. *What if something happened to Vida and the children?* It sickens me. I push the coffee away. "Why are they after you? Do you owe him money?" My attention is back on Nana.

"Yes and no. I paid him the twenty-three million dollars he claims I stole."

"If it's more that he wants, I can give it to you."

"I don't need your money. It's never been about money. I broke his trust. That he can never let go."

"What does he want?"

"To teach me a lesson." I never thought I would be sitting across from Nana after all these years. I never could have imagined having an odious feeling toward him. *Time doesn't heal the pain.* He continues. "My cover is blown. I know that for sure. I just need to get to them before they try to get to Vida and the kids." Paula is approaching again. Nana begins small talk about the weather. "I think the whole weekend is going to be sunny. I wish you would consider playing this weekend. We could use an extra goalie."

I interrupt his theatrics, or as Vida would say, his unicorn story. "Excuse me, could we have two glasses of water?"

"Oh, I'm sorry, sugar. I should have brought you some earlier." She places food in front of us. "Do you want me to freshen up your cup of coffee?" *The only thing that could freshen this up is a shot of penicillin.*

"No. Thank you," I say. "The water will be just fine." She places food on Vincent's table.

"Okay, enjoy." *I smell bacon.*

"Vincent, no bacon." I the stretch a napkin in his direction. He grunts but indulges me.

"C'mon just one slice of bacon won't hurt," Nana says.

"Maybe he should share his blood pressure readings with you when you guys are having your pillow talk." Nana rises to take the bacon from my napkin.

"Sorry, mi padre, I will have to eat it for you." Vincent is grumbling.

"How is it possible that your cover was blown? You of all people, so meticulous in your disguise? How is it that the great Nana, who could fool anyone—including me—could have his cover blown?" *Why did I bring it up? I shouldn't have, but I'm reminiscing in his presence.*

"*Gio, mepa wo kyew.*" He pauses. "I never—"

"Please don't. It is not worth the discussion now." He pauses and takes a sip of the coffee.

"Shit, this tastes horrible. Not like how I remember it." He pushes it away. "Before I came to see you in London, I took the kids to the park. A truck driver went into diabetic shock and lost control of the wheel and ramped through the field. It started to pick up speed as it rolled downhill. MJ was playing at the base of the park with two other children. There was a group of teenagers filming their droid plane. They saw the truck heading toward MJ. They yelled for him to get out of the way. Every reflex in me came alive. I ran as fast as I could to save him. If I wasn't there, my son...I just don't know what I would do. I will never bury any of my children." His voice is elevated and he seems anxious. He pauses again before he continues. "A few days later, the video was on YouTube and it generated millions of views. They showed it on local news channels and I knew then that things would change. I was being treated like some kind of hero. I am trying to maintain my anonymity, especially because of Vida and the children, but it seems my ways are catching up to me. I reached out to Vincent and he has been helping me ever since."

"Really? So you've been in contact with Vincent ever since? Is there anything else I should know before I leave this diner?" That question is meant primarily for Vincent.

"No," Vincent says boldly.

"Speaking of which, is there anything *I* should know before I leave this diner?" Nana says.

I shift in my seat. *What could I possibly tell him that won't enrage him? I tried to hold back from her. Even now, I can feel her lips on mine and feel her bosom against my cheek.*

"You never answered my question."

"Vida loves you. That is what you should know before you leave this diner." He gives a deep exhale.

"Gio, I didn't go looking for her. It never occurred to me that I could fall in love with her." He stabs at the steak and then drops the utensils onto the plate. "I went looking for you to explain everything, but you disappeared. You talked about going to see her play. I knew that you really liked her." He chuckles. "You changed your clothes several times and washed your hands a dozen times. You always do that when you like someone. The way you talked about her; her laughter, the way she smelled…I just knew for sure one day I would find you at the park. I went there sometimes three times a week just to look for you. I watched her play every week. She was….is…really good. She must have thought that I was some stalker." He chuckles again but I am not amused. "One afternoon, her sister couldn't pick her up from practice, so I offered her a lift home and…then again the next night…and then it started turning into a weekly thing…and…" He pauses again, trying to find the right words. "We dated a while, but I told her that I traveled a lot for work and wasn't looking for anything serious. When I returned from London, she was already four months pregnant. She was terrified of what her father would do or say. I had to do the honorable thing." Sounds of the leather creaking as he shifts in his seat breaks Nana's monologue. "When Vincent told me about your mother's death, I tried harder to track you down. But I knew where you would bury her so I flew back to Cabo Verde. I—"

"It was you. You dug up the grave?"

"I did. I saw you, but it wasn't the time to come clean about everything. There's still so much you don't know."

He was there at the gravesite. I felt his presence close by. I don't want to reminisce about this any longer. "And I don't need to know. The past is the past."

"You're still a stubborn goat." He sighs deeply. "Vincent said you were studying in Australia with Dr. Braun. I passed through a couple of times, just to check on you. Your security systems are very impressive. You've done well. I always knew you would accomplish anything you put your mind to. Gio—your father's death—"

"Silencio!" Vincent's voice is stern and hard. "This is not the place for this discussion."

"Perhaps, when you return, you will allow me to explain myself?" Nana says.

"I told you already. What is in the past should stay in the past. There is no need to take this conversation any further. I think my work here is done."

"I need your help, Gio. I will find you again." I rise to get up and pull the money clip out.

"Please don't insult me. I'll take care of the bill," Nana says.

I pull a bill from the money clip and toss it on the table. I move away from the table, but I don't feel Vincent's presence behind me. I'm sure Nana and Vincent are having one of their nonverbal conversations. Vincent has a habit of clearing his throat when he doesn't want to use words to communicate. It's something I have noted since I was a child.

*

"Why do you do this to me?" I shout above the roaring airplane engine.

"Do what?" Vincent says. His voice always seems louder than a shout.

"You constantly keep me in the dark. Literally. How do you think it makes me feel when I have to hear from someone else—Nana in fact—what is going on right underneath my nose? You told me that Vida fell. Don't play games with me, Padrino. I am no longer a helpless boy."

"I have never treated you as a helpless boy. You don't need to know everything. It's for your own good."

"I can't go to Ghana now. I have to be here for Vida and the kids."

"We are handling it. My guys will arrive this evening. We still have the GPS tracking in the shoes, surveillance on the children, and Nana has the house cameras. I have another car stationed at the house. It will be very hard for anyone to get past me."

"Yet it happened?"

"There is nothing you can do here. Go to Ghana. You need time away from her."

"Is that why my presence is so coincidentally needed there?"

"It's the anniversary of the church Mama built. You should be there for the festivities."

"Vida needs me."

"Don't force my hand, Gio. I don't want to transport you there like the last time."

"You wouldn't."

"*Si dovrebbe sapere ormai mi.*"

Yes, I do know what you are capable of.

COMING SOON

…..And of course there are a dozen of questions going through your head but stick with me. You will soon get your answers.

Julius Gallo's story continues in the next book,

Husbands On Hold Part I. Coming out Spring 2018.

Vida will return in *The Borrowed Wife Part II* in 2018.

Thank you for your support and please hit me up on social media; Facebook, Instagram, and Pinterest under Stilettosncrayons if you enjoyed reading the book.

Acknowledgements

Ahhhhhh, and here we are. You weren't just gonna turn the page without reading this were you? Of course not. Now you will see the genesis of all my pearls of wisdom and madness. Hopefully you will continue to stay with me on this journey.

First, thank you God for giving me life and the strength to triumph over my obstacles and basks in my accomplishments. Without a doubt you were the guiding hand that has brought me here.

There is a host of women that need to be acknowledged, not because they are fabulous and I know them personally, but because they were the muses that propelled this book forward.

So without further ado, and no particular order, let me start with the formidable women in my life. Not only was I blessed to have an awesome and candid mother, but God placed a funny and at times eccentric sister to mold me and guide me. Needless to say, I had to pick my battles wisely. I didn't stand a chance against these two powerhouses. If I were to remix **Lady J** and **Lola** into one body then I would I have to affectionately rename them "*Abla.*"

Also to my aunties, **Naa, Awo, Vida, Marcia and Sista Abla,** thank you for your wise counsel.

To all my English teachers who decorated my papers with red ink, I might have hissed and thrown tantrums, but I finally found my love for the English language. To my creative writing professor **Eleana Georgiou**, thank you for citing Biggie Smalls as a poet. I will never forgot that rap lyric that you broke down so eloquently during one of our creative writing sessions.

Do you have a girlfriend where no one understands your tumultuous relationship? Okay, I'm not the only one. But when I least expect it, she shows up in all the right ways. Thank you **Beverly** for your support and shade.

Next up, the **Sassi Ladies**. Each of you ladies has given me so much inspiration by just being beautiful, hardworking and fabulous women. I took a bit of each of you and sprinkled your characteristics in this novel. Especially my gurl, **Nazat,** who has become like a dear sister; cheering me on days when everything seemed so overwhelming. Thank you for your friendship and WhatsApp videos.

They say we spend a great deal of our lives with our coworkers. And over the years a select group of women I've called my friends. To the **Eat Pray and Verify ladies**, thank you for taking the time to give me your input and direction and also for making our workweeks so entertaining.

There's a lady who probably pulled her hair out more times than she combed it while reading my novel. I believe it was God ordained, our collaboration, because I literally didn't know if I could find someone who shared the same vision as me. But as the saying goes, "If there is a will, then there's gotta be a good editor." (Okay, I made that one up.) Not only did she read the entire novel a dozen times, dissecting and cursing my grammar teachers, but also at the end of our journey, I was left with a novel that I can proudly showcase to the world. Thank you **Ingrid Bevz** from Green Ink Proofreading. Your counsel and assistance was priceless to this novel.

Now I want to focus on the "mens" in my life. (You see why I need Ingrid.)

First and foremost, thank you **Kwaku**.

Thank you to **my dad and my brother, Melvin; my stepdad, Sonny , Uncle Pat and Uncle Eben** for providing me "good guys" with humor and charisma to write in my novel.

When I first starting working at my present job, I was introduced to a man who conducted travel training for people with disabilities in New York City. I was in awe with his ability to not only manage such a dynamic program, but with his ability to move from his home in Long Island to New York City and then to Queens independently. **Michael** gave me new insight into what it means to have a visual impairment because, in many cases, his independence was the muse I needed for this book. He reminds me that the only disability is the limits I place on myself.

I love being a mother and each of my sons has unique qualities. Some qualities like humility, funniness, and other qualities like autism. They were my cheerleaders when I needed to work quietly, and then there were times when they forced me to hide in my car and write. But overall, they inspire me with their unique comments like, *"When you gonna finish this book already, so we can go to Rye Playland?"* Thank you boys for reminding me to always have fun.

I'm sure when you walked by a bookstore and saw my book on the shelf or canvassed through Amazon Kindle, the first thing you thought about was, *"What a fabulous cover. I mean, the colors and the woman on the front with that huge ass....what a work of art."* I have to credit Advance Frequency for making you take a second look. Thank you **Vance** for your patience and artistic direction.

Lastly…

I know this beautiful woman and when I listen to her speak, I laugh and cry, but mostly I'm encouraged by her resilience and strength. She encouraged me to write this story not because it was entertaining, but because of the dream she had when she was fourteen.

While walking along a beach in Senegal, Auntie Naa asked her what she wanted to be when she grew up. Over the years she moved away from that desire, but every now and then that dream tugged at her like the need for hot french fries. She believed one day she would be a writer.

Only after challenges do we really see that we were growing into our true potential. I believe everything that I overcame has brought me to exactly where I needed to be.

Thank you **Eunice** for never giving up on **Yoyo** and reminding me that dreams do come true.

Thank you **Maya Angelou, Terry McMillian, E.L. James, J.K. Rowling, Alice Walker, Zane, Aksousa Busia, Chimamanda Ngozi Adichie, James Baldwin, George Eliot, Langston Hughes**, for taking me on a journey in each of your novels.

And lastly (for real…I know, stay with me…)

Thank you **New York City**—your cultural influences, restaurants, bars, parks and people make it a great place to live.

Made in the USA
Middletown, DE
15 March 2018